MEOW-ZA!

HERE'S WHAT PEOPLE ARE SAYING ABOUT MAX MEOW!

"Max Meow is a riot!"

—Jimmy Gownley, creator of the Amelia Rules! series

"I liked the part where he ate the giant meatball."

—Kevin, 1st grade

"Celebrates friendship, fun, and the fantastic, wrapped up in a ball of adventure readers of any age will pounce on!"

—Jamar Nicholas, creator of the Leon series

"My favorite character was Mindy because she kind of guides Max Meow."

—Santiago, 6th grade

"I give it 5★."

—Cole, 5th grade

"Super laughs on every page!"

—Norm Feuti, creator of the Hello, Hedgehog! series

"A super-fun romp for kids of all ages."

—Meryl Jaffe, PhD, author of *Raising a Reader! How Comics & Graphic Novels Can Help Your Kids Love to Read!*

"It's funny and amazing so you should read the book."

—Sorel, 6th grade

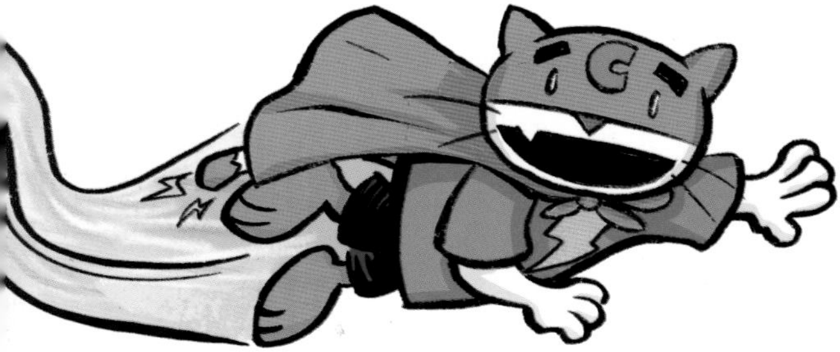

READ ALL OF MAX MEOW'S ADVENTURES!

Max Meow: Cat Crusader

Max Meow: Donuts and Danger

Max Meow: Pugs from Planet X

Max Meow: Taco Time Machine

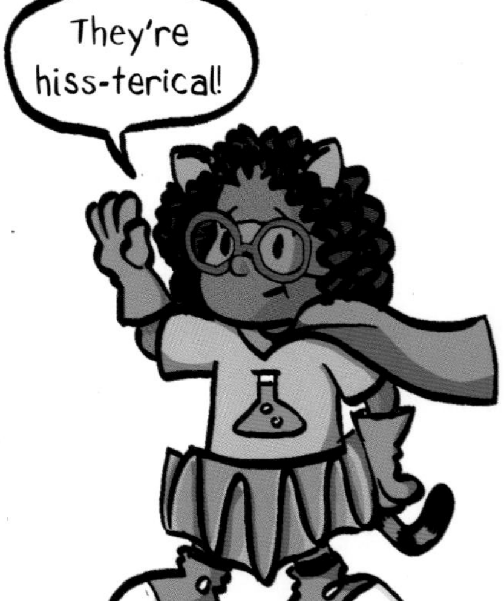
They're hiss-terical!

MAX MEOW!
TACO TIME MACHINE

JOHN GALLAGHER

RANDOM HOUSE · NEW YORK

Visit us on the Web! rhcbooks.com

Educators and librarians, for a variety of teaching tools,
visit us at RHTeachersLibrarians.com

Library of Congress Cataloging-in-Publication Data
Names: Gallagher, John, author, illustrator.
Title: Max Meow : taco time machine / John Gallagher.
Other titles: Taco time machine
Description: First edition. | New York : Random House Children's Books,
[2022] | Series: Max Meow ; 4 | Audience: Ages 7–10. | Summary: "Max
Meow and Mindy the Scientist go back in time in a time machine shaped
like a taco" —Provided by publisher.
Identifiers: LCCN 2021030149 | ISBN 978-0-593-47966-7 (hardcover) |
ISBN 978-0-593-47968-1 (lib. bdg.) | ISBN 978-0-593-47967-4 (ebook)
Subjects: CYAC: Graphic novels. | Time travel—Fiction. |
Superheroes—Fiction. | Cats—Fiction. | LCGFT: Graphic novels.
Classification: LCC PZ7.7.G325 Mp 2022 | DDC 741.5/973—dc23

Book design by John Gallagher and April Ward

MANUFACTURED IN CHINA
10 9 8 7 6 5 4 3 2
First Edition

Random House Children's Books supports the
First Amendment and celebrates the right to read.

To my fellow Jedi masters,
Vicky and Nate—
and their young Padawans,
Brooke, Chase, and Alec

PROLOGUE*

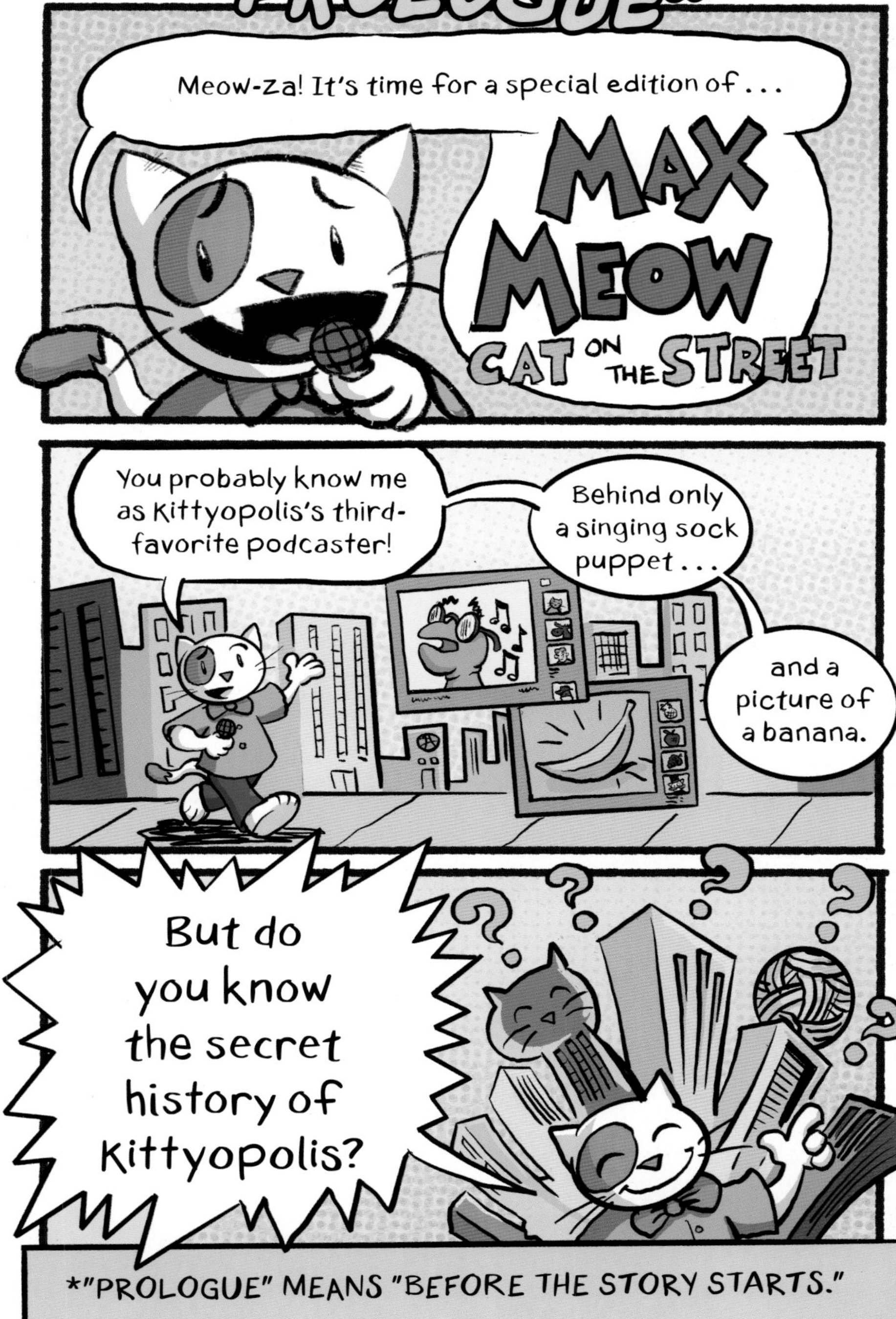
Meow-za! It's time for a special edition of . . .
MAX MEOW
CAT ON THE STREET
You probably know me as Kittyopolis's third-favorite podcaster!
Behind only a singing sock puppet . . .
and a picture of a banana.
But do you know the secret history of Kittyopolis?

*"PROLOGUE" MEANS "BEFORE THE STORY STARTS."

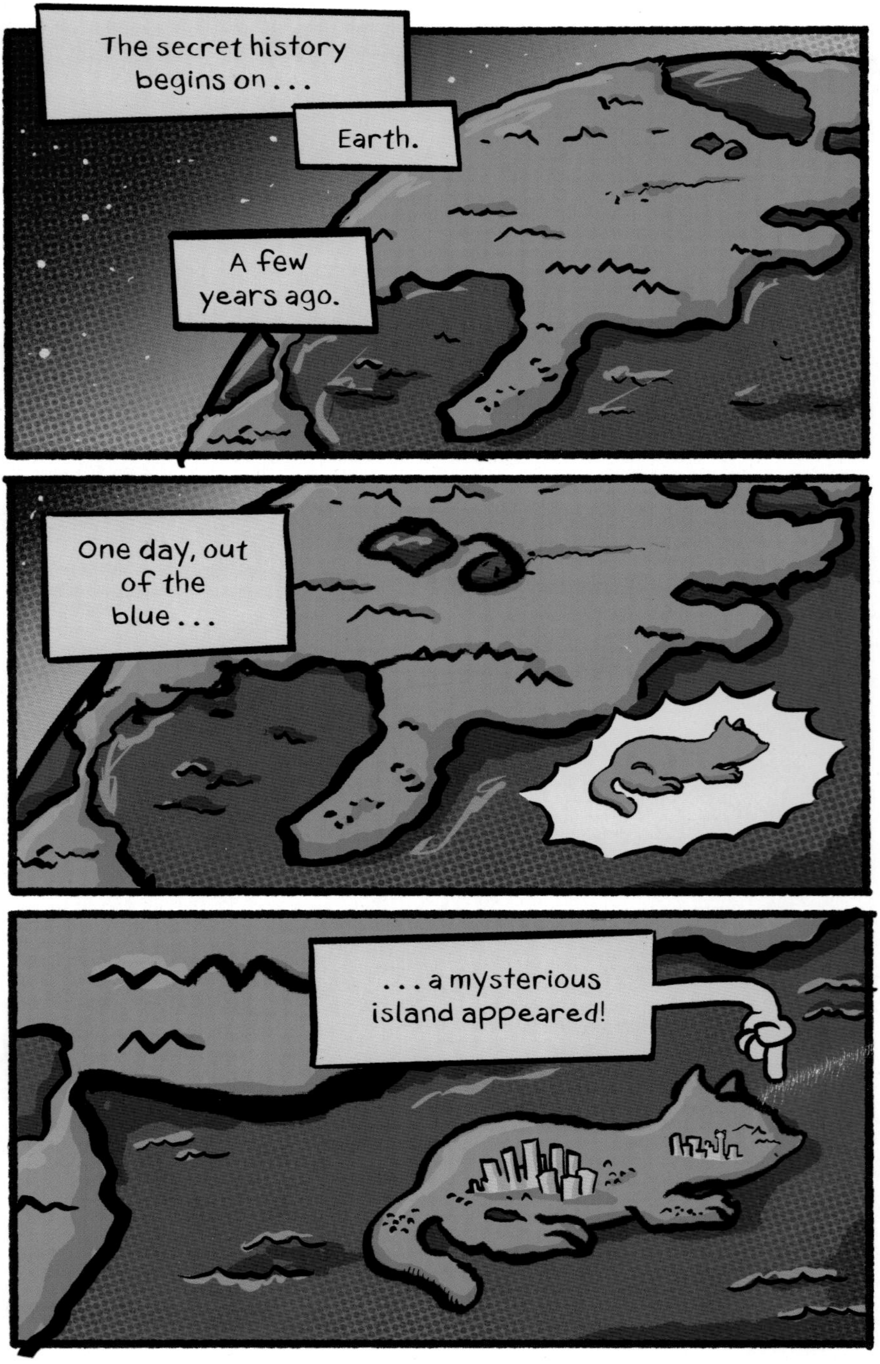
The secret history begins on . . .
Earth.
A few years ago.
One day, out of the blue . . .
. . . a mysterious island appeared!

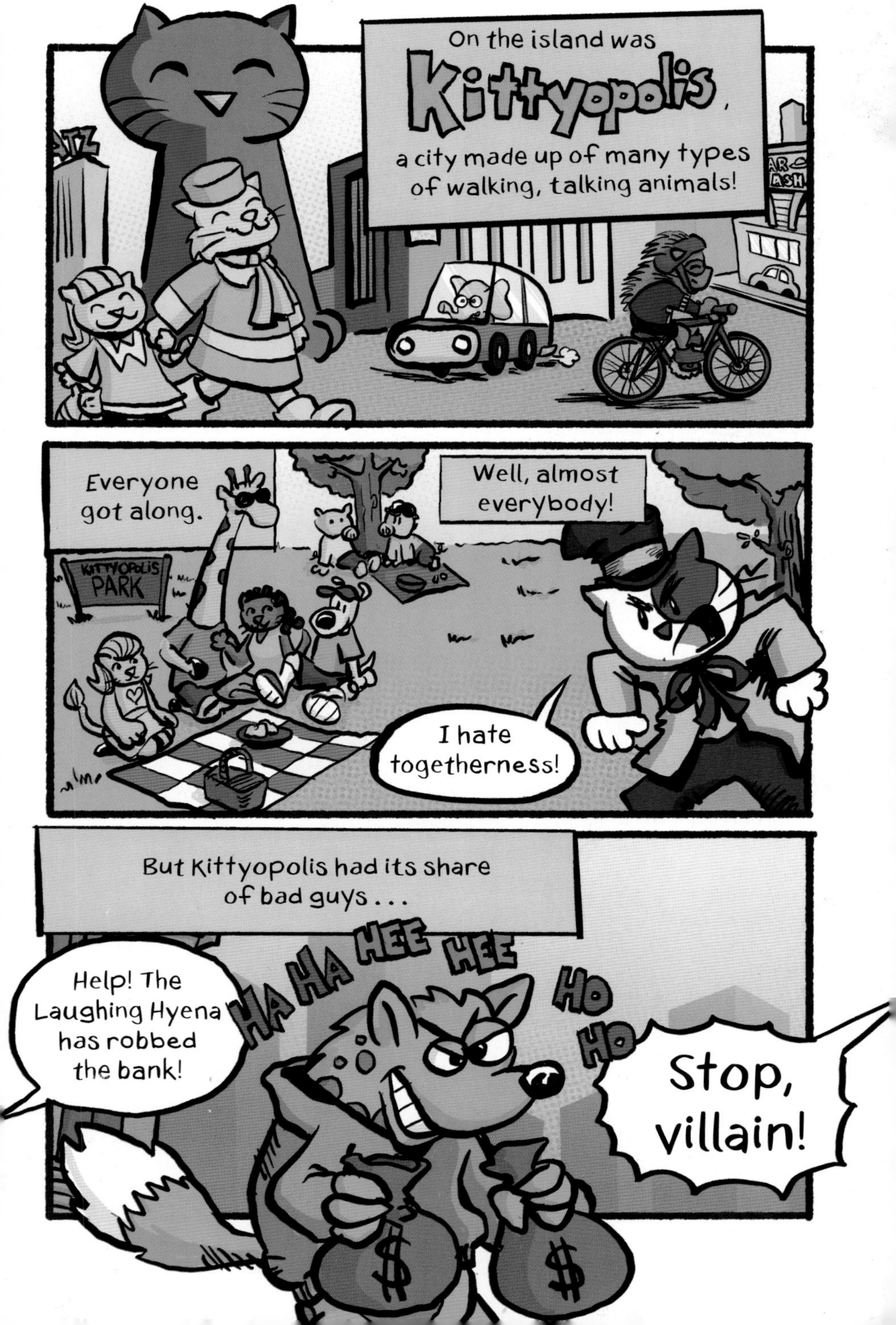

On the island was
Kittyopolis,
a city made up of many types of walking, talking animals!
Everyone got along.
Well, almost everybody!
KITTYOPOLIS PARK
I hate togetherness!
But Kittyopolis had its share of bad guys . . .
HA HA HEE HEE HO HO
Help! The Laughing Hyena has robbed the bank!
Stop, villain!

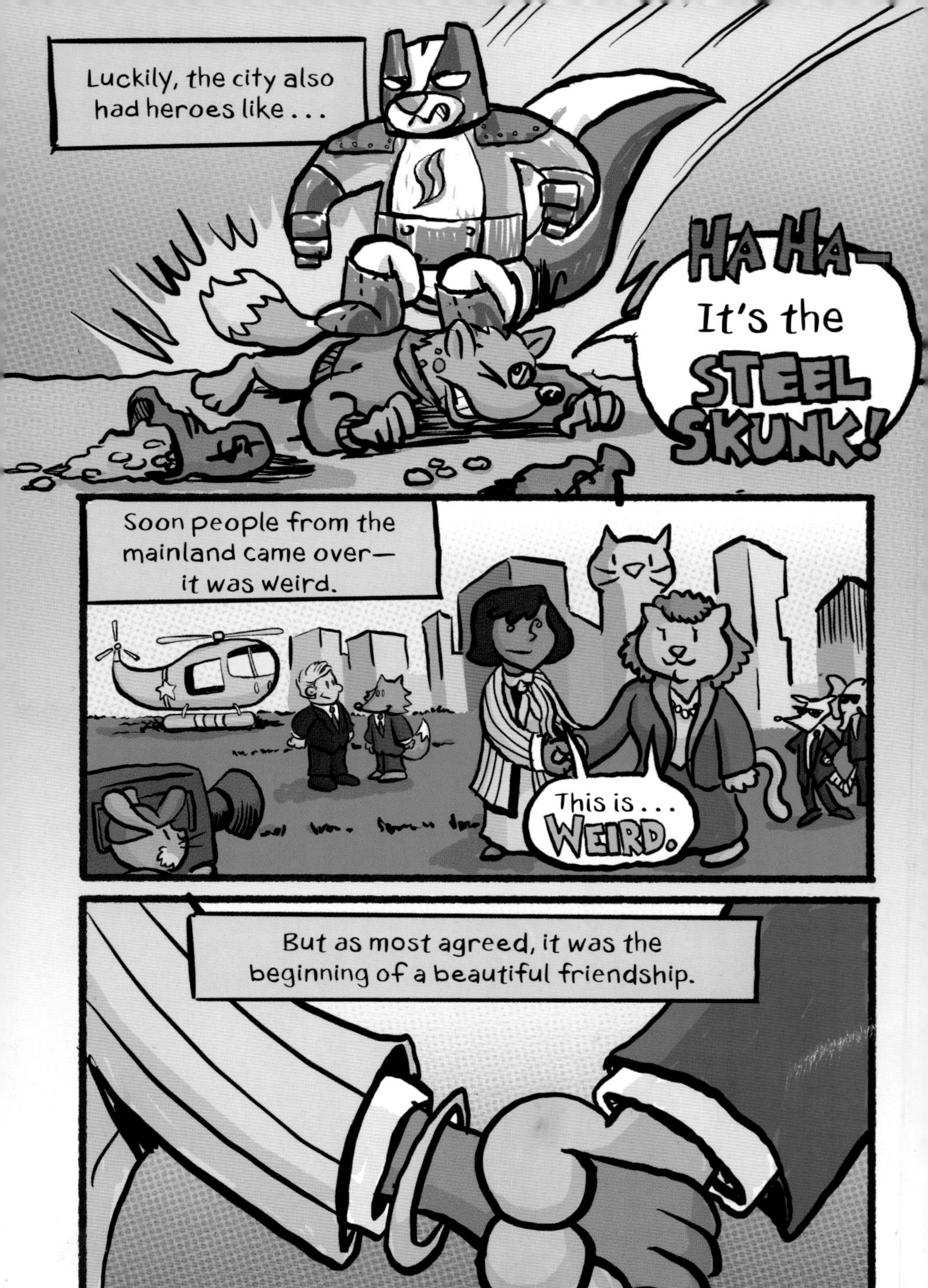
Luckily, the city also had heroes like . . .
HA HA—
It's the STEEL SKUNK!
Soon people from the mainland came over— it was weird.
This is . . . WEIRD.
But as most agreed, it was the beginning of a beautiful friendship.

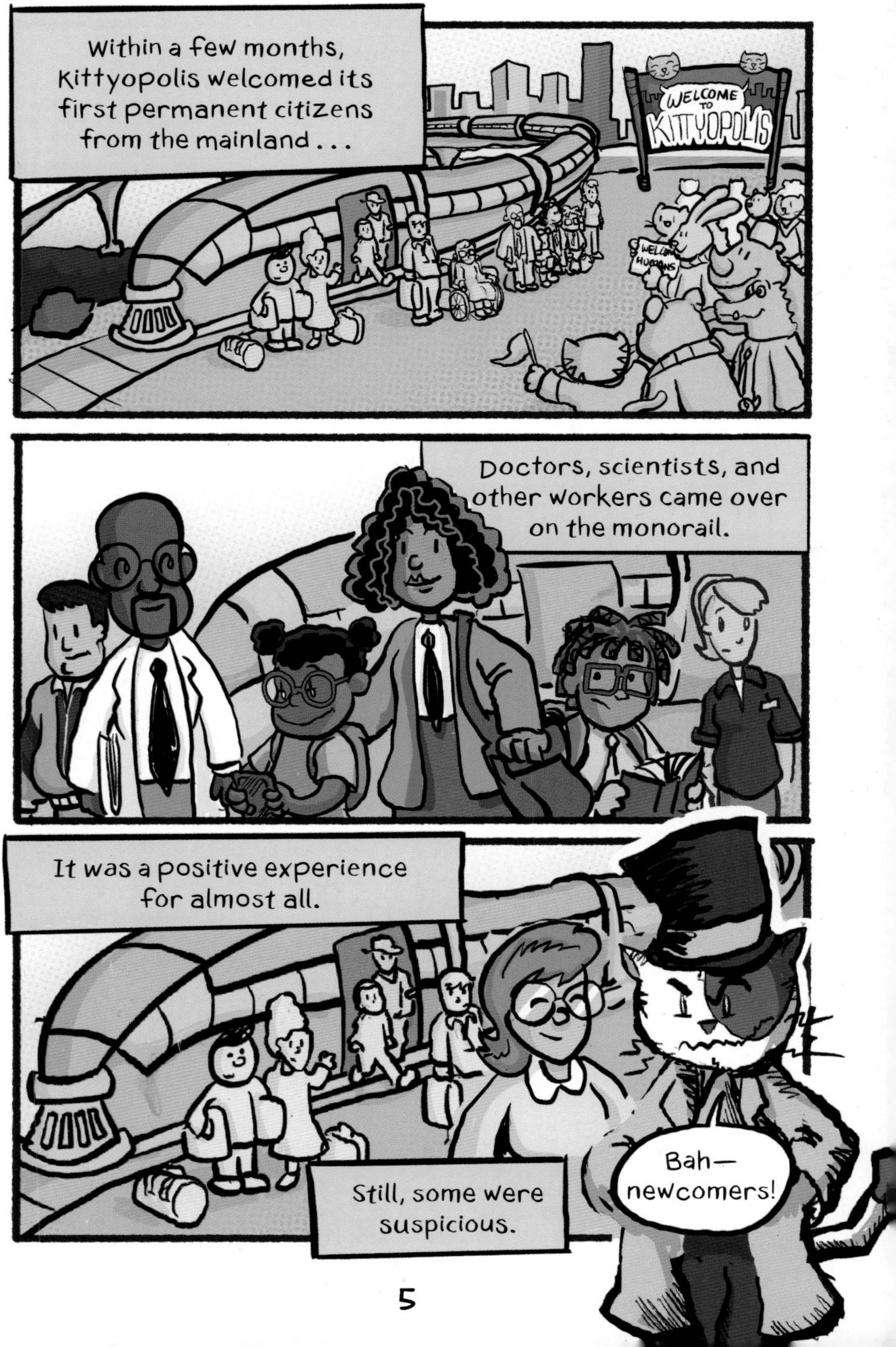
Within a few months, Kittyopolis welcomed its first permanent citizens from the mainland . . .
WELCOME TO KITTYOPOLIS
Doctors, scientists, and other workers came over on the monorail.
It was a positive experience for almost all.
Still, some were suspicious.
Bah—newcomers!

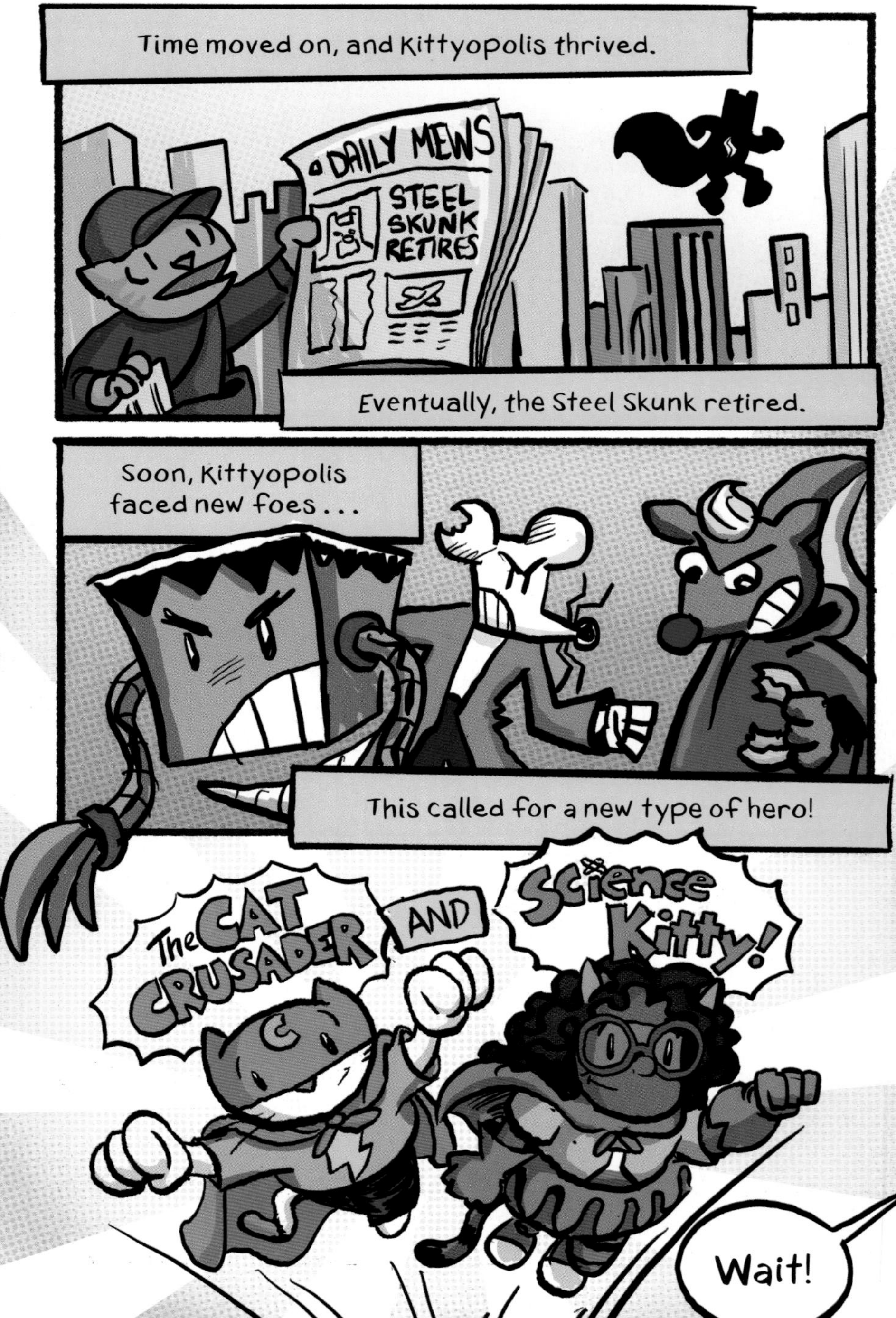
Time moved on, and Kittyopolis thrived.
DAILY MEWS
STEEL SKUNK RETIRES
Eventually, the Steel Skunk retired.
Soon, Kittyopolis faced new foes . . .
This called for a new type of hero!
The CAT CRUSADER
AND
Science Kitty!
Wait!

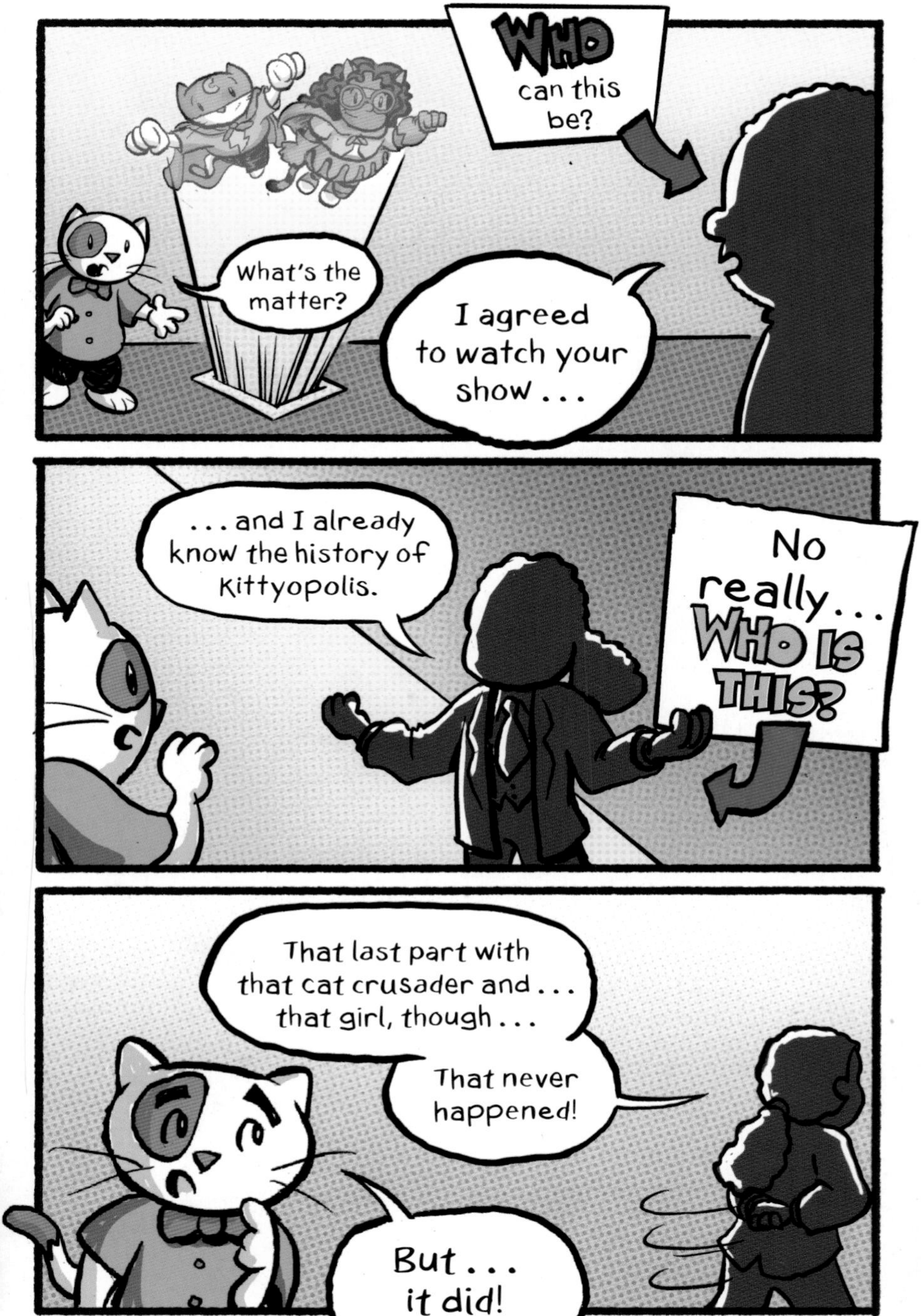
WHO can this be?
What's the matter?
I agreed to watch your show . . .
. . . and I already know the history of Kittyopolis.
No really . . . WHO IS THIS?
That last part with that cat crusader and . . . that girl, though . . .
That never happened!
But . . . it did!

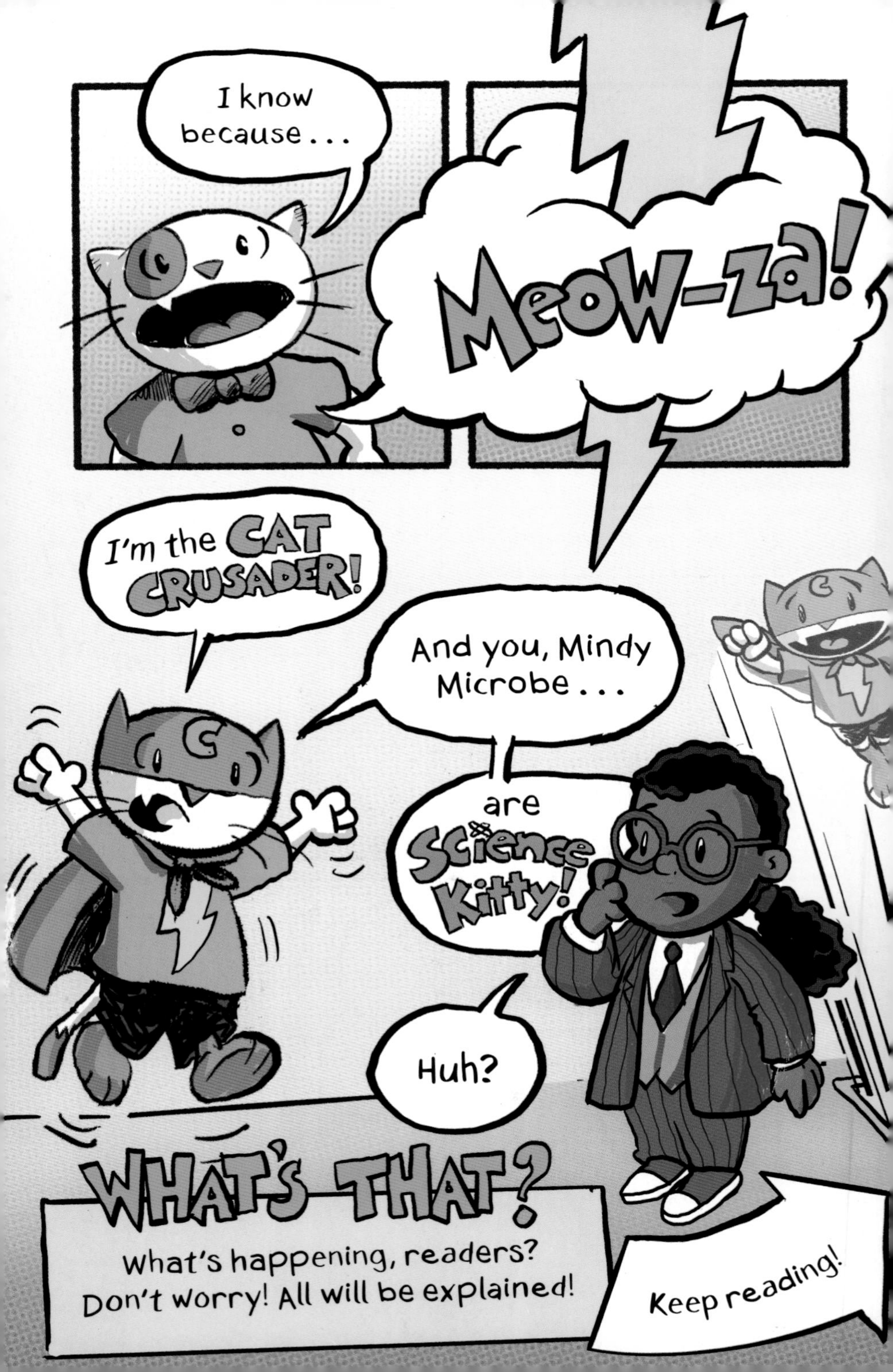
I know because . . .
Meow-za!
I'm the CAT CRUSADER!
And you, Mindy Microbe . . .
are Science Kitty!
Huh?
WHAT'S THAT?
What's happening, readers? Don't worry! All will be explained!
Keep reading!

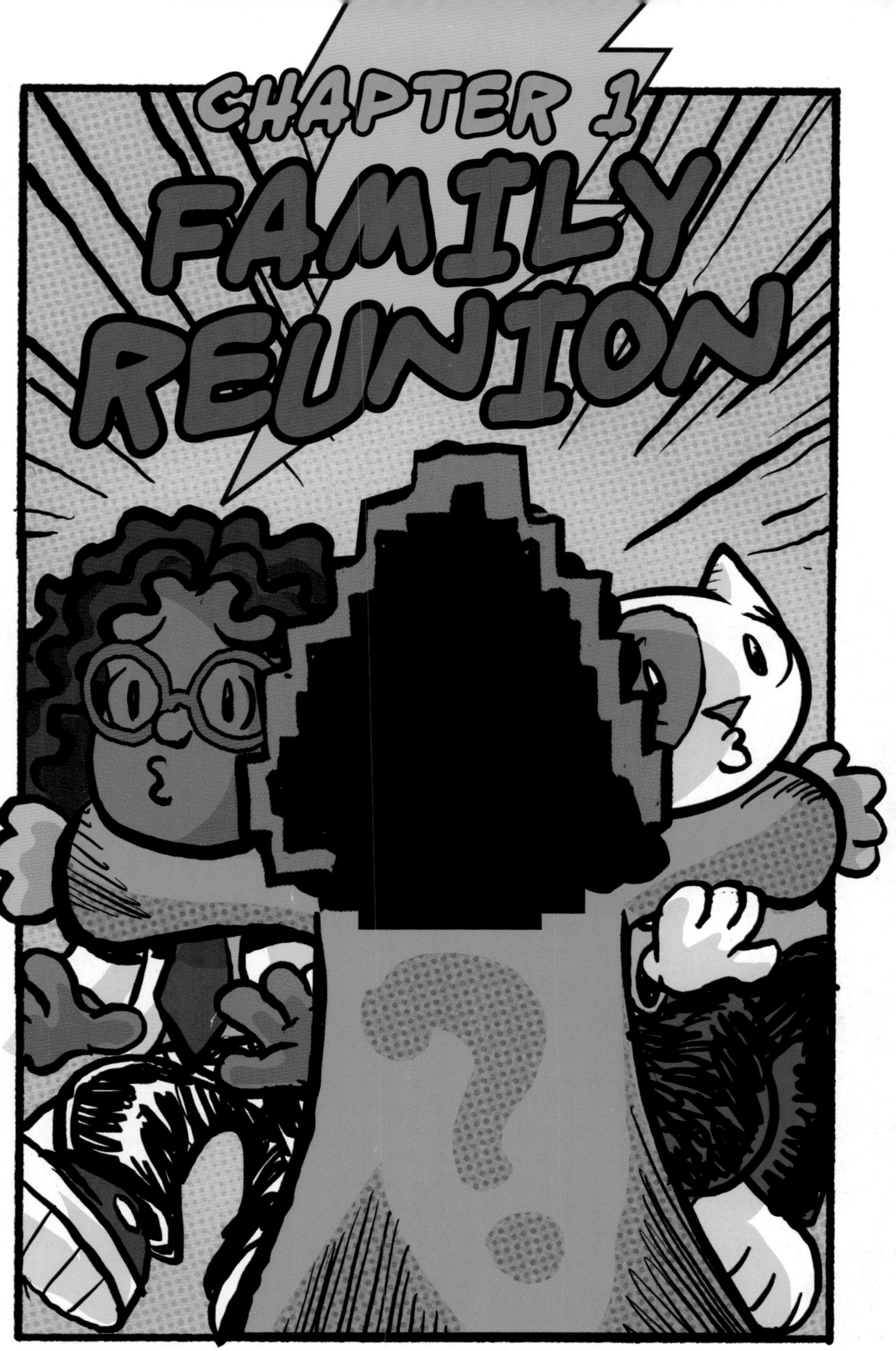
CHAPTER 1
FAMILY REUNION

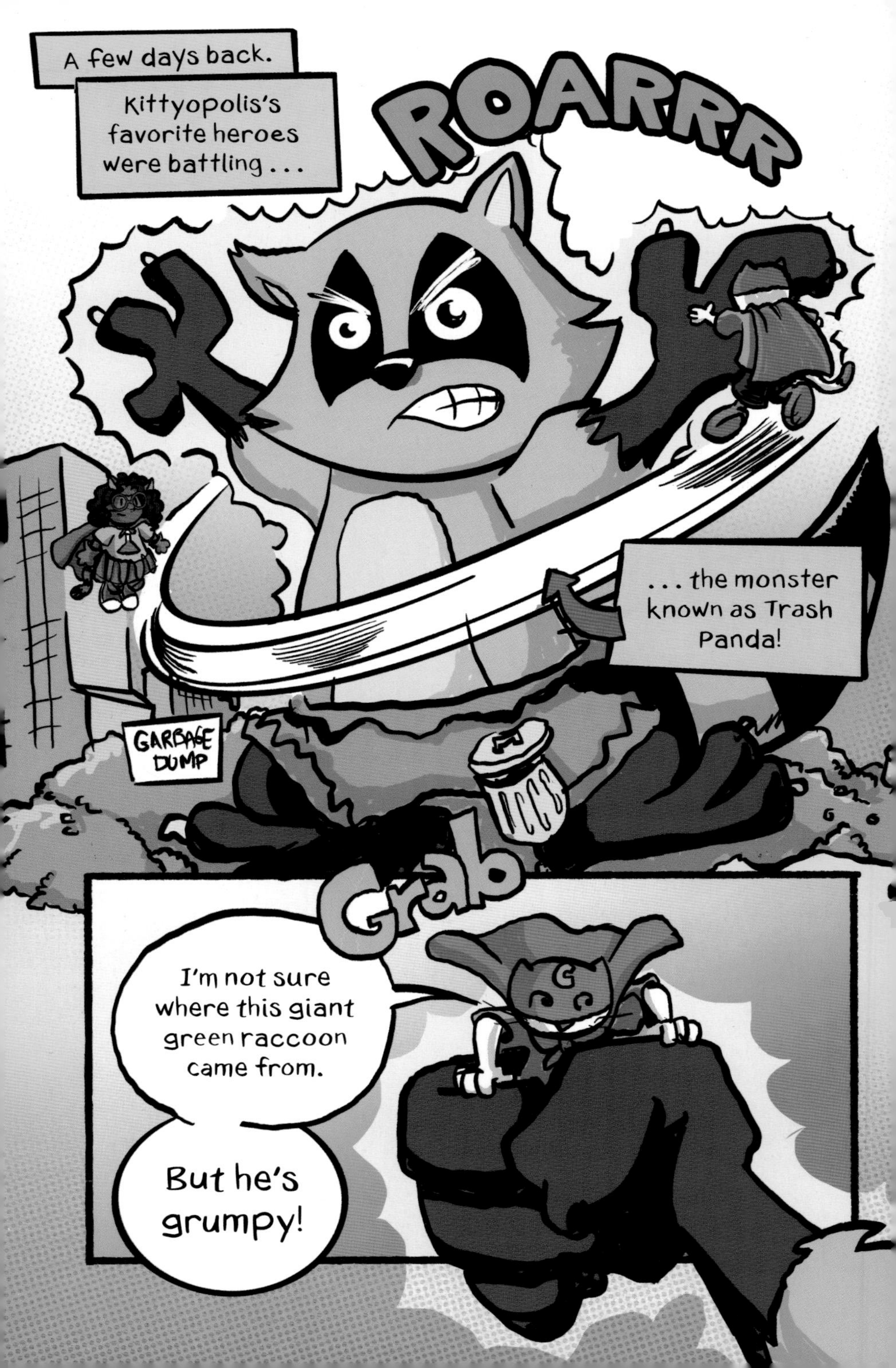
A few days back.
Kittyopolis's favorite heroes were battling . . .
ROARRR
. . . the monster known as Trash Panda!
GARBAGE DUMP
Grab
I'm not sure where this giant green raccoon came from.
But he's grumpy!

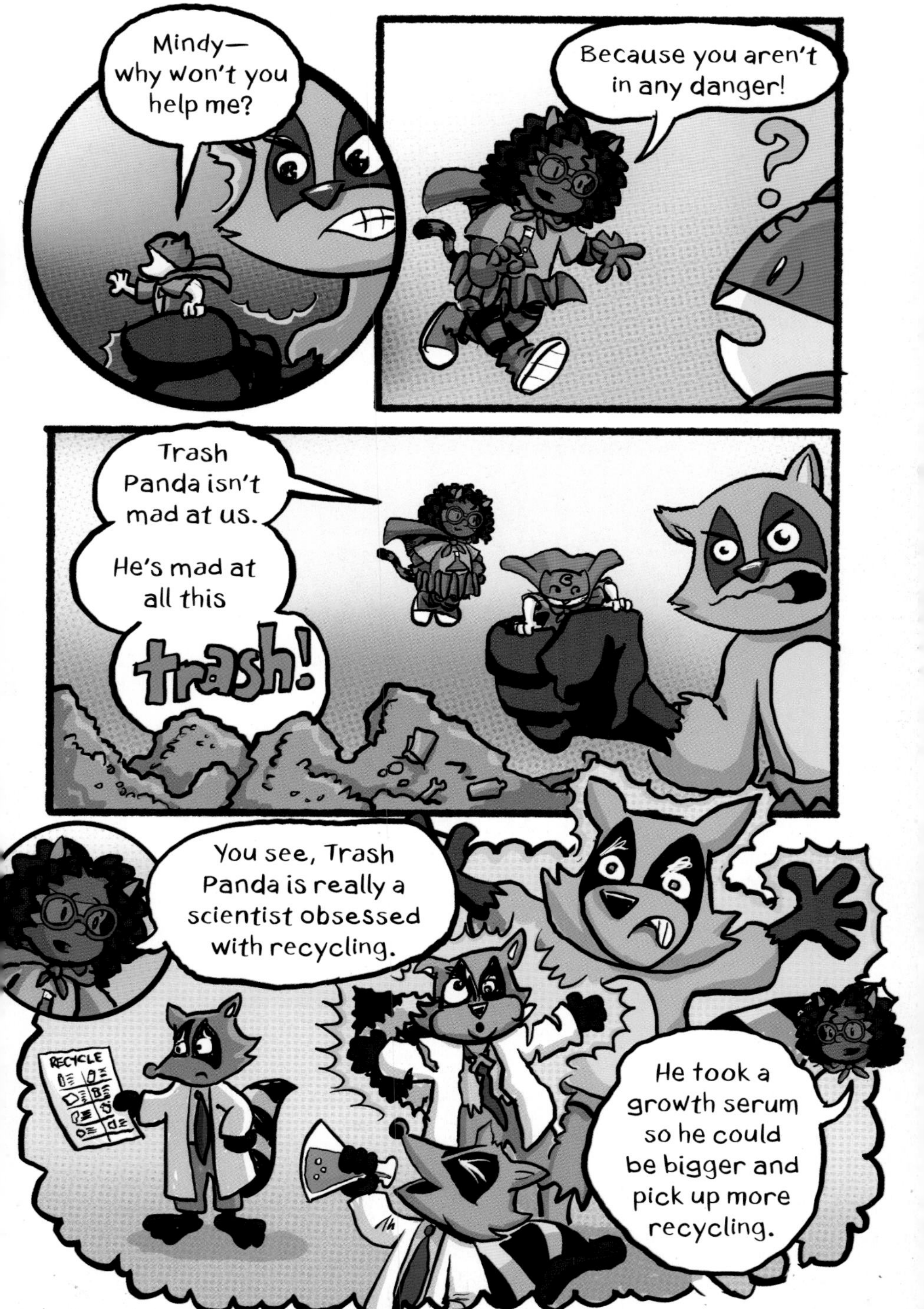
Mindy—
why won't you help me?
Because you aren't in any danger!
?
Trash Panda isn't mad at us.
He's mad at all this
trash!
You see, Trash Panda is really a scientist obsessed with recycling.
RECYCLE
He took a growth serum so he could be bigger and pick up more recycling.

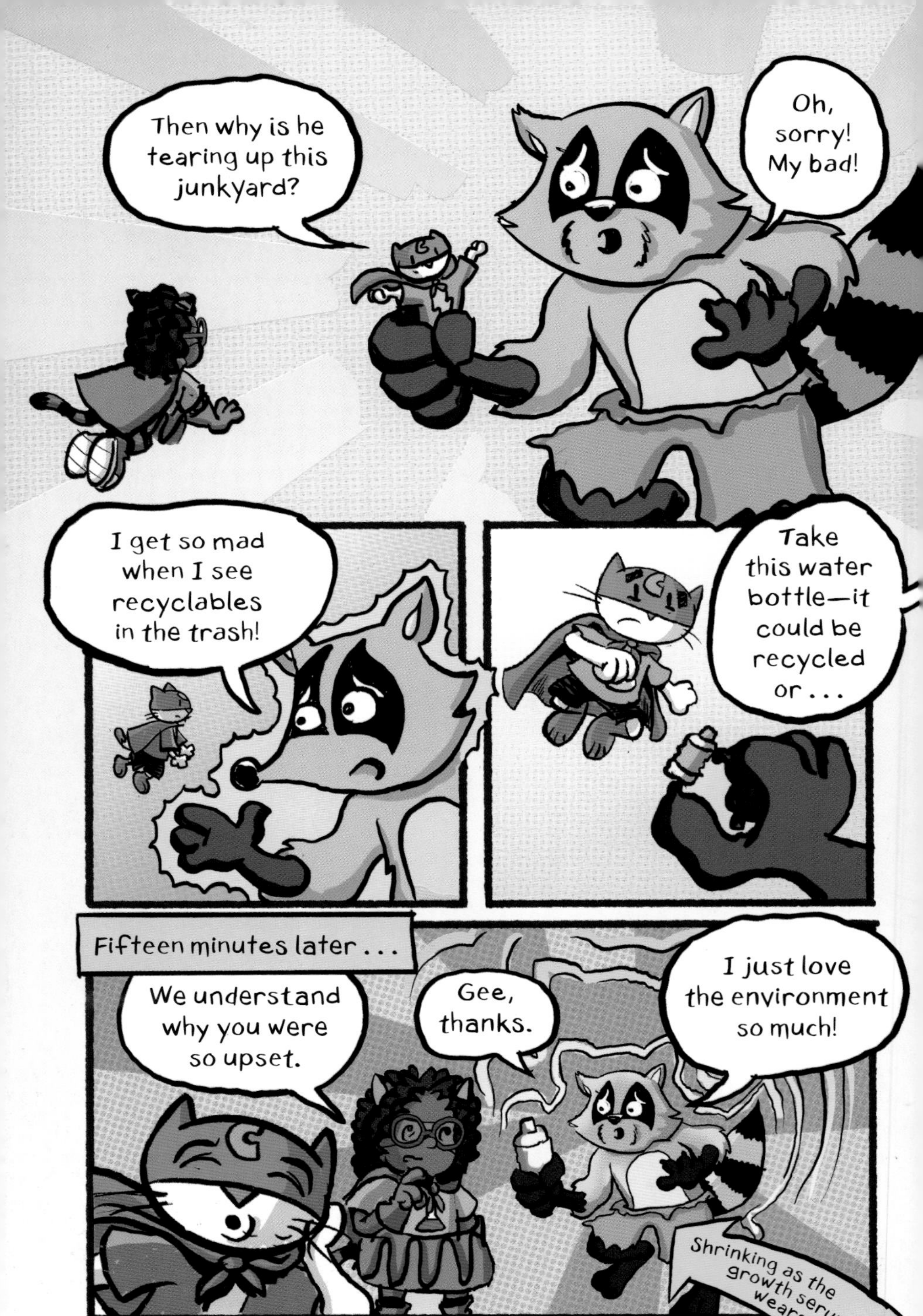
Then why is he tearing up this junkyard?
Oh, sorry! My bad!
I get so mad when I see recyclables in the trash!
Take this water bottle—it could be recycled or . . .
Fifteen minutes later . . .
We understand why you were so upset.
Gee, thanks.
I just love the environment so much!
Shrinking as the growth serum wears off.

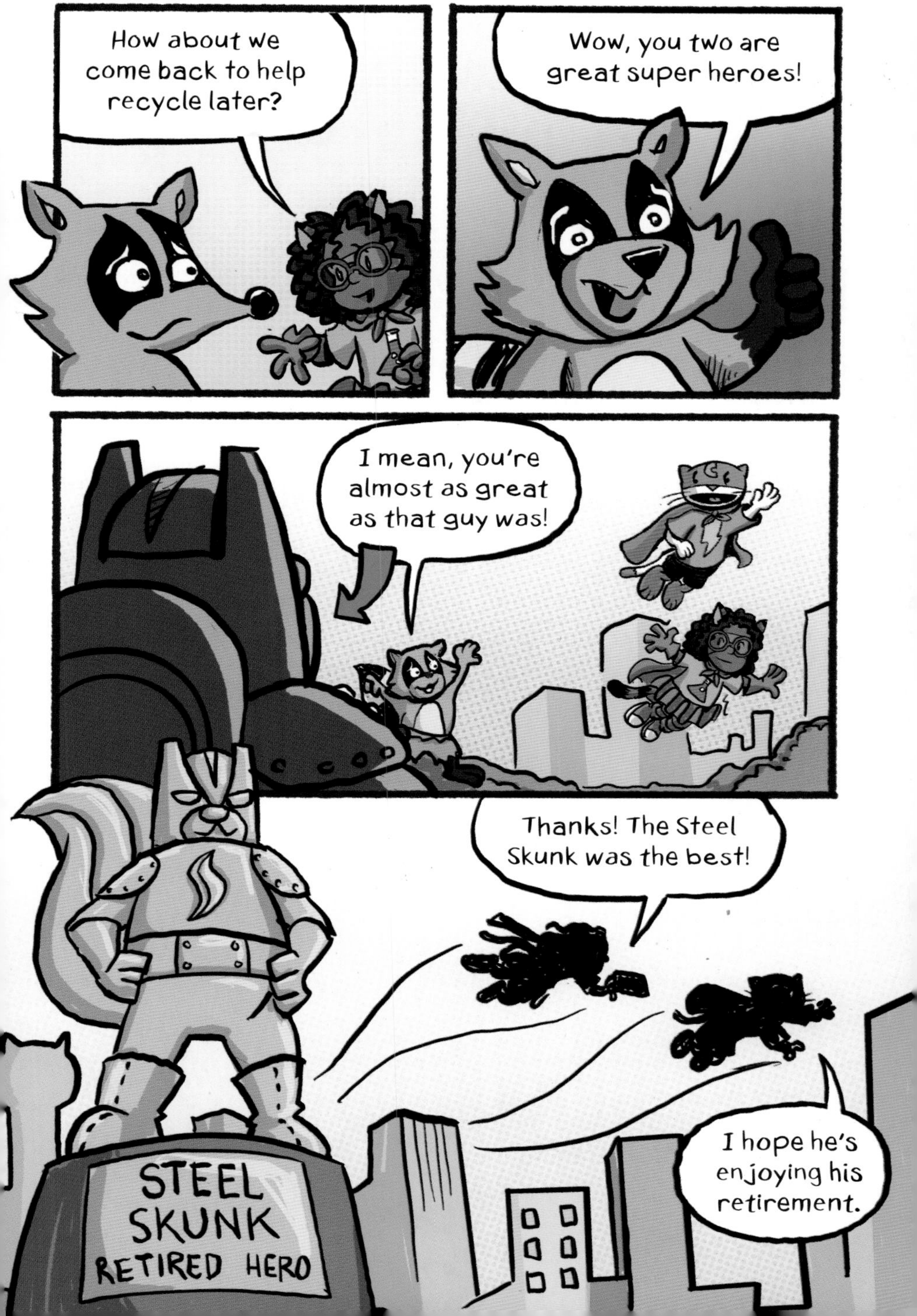
How about we come back to help recycle later?
Wow, you two are great super heroes!
I mean, you're almost as great as that guy was!
Thanks! The Steel Skunk was the best!
I hope he's enjoying his retirement.
STEEL SKUNK RETIRED HERO

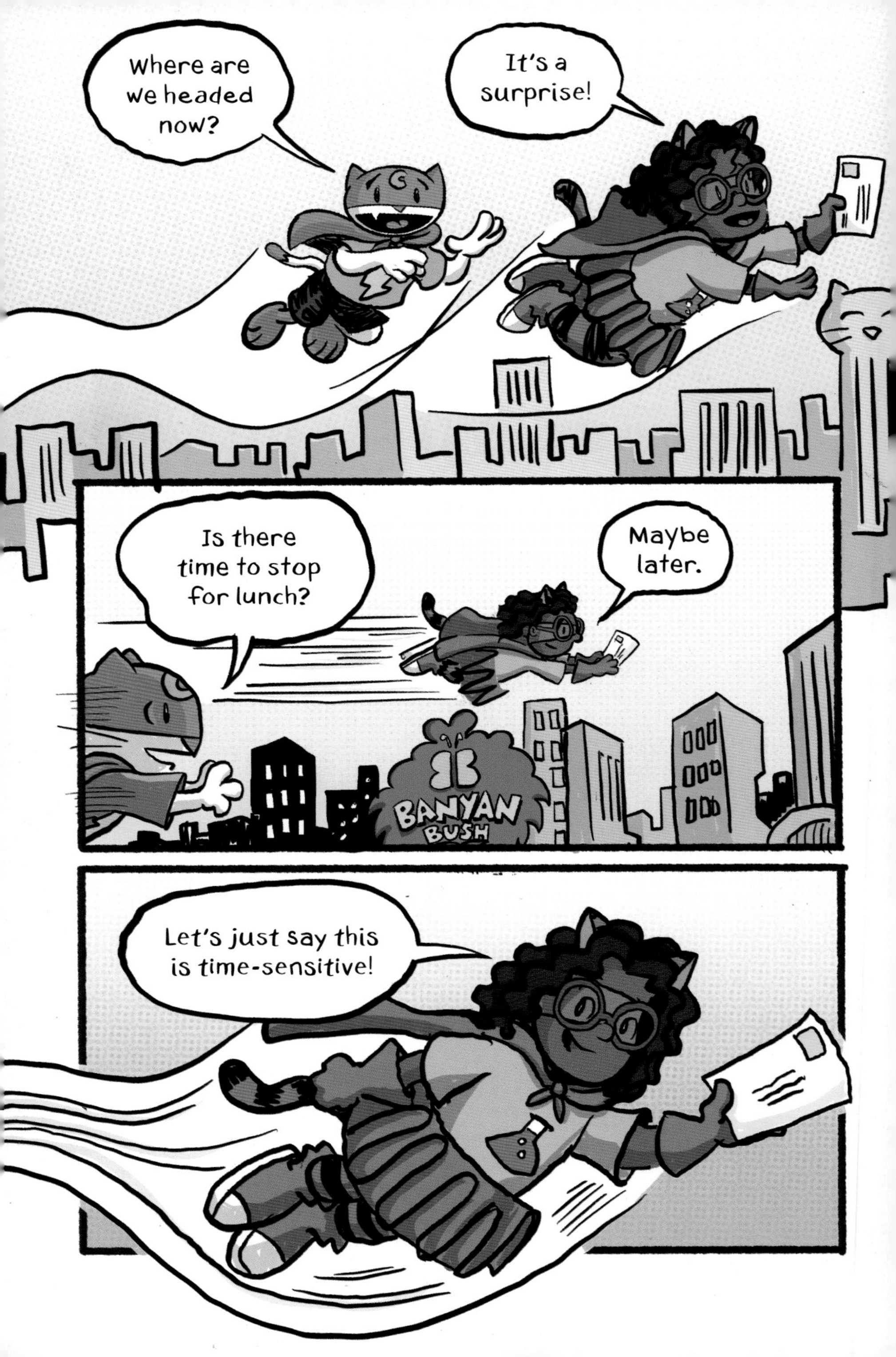
Where are we headed now?
It's a surprise!
Is there time to stop for lunch?
Maybe later.
BANYAN BUSH
Let's just say this is time-sensitive!

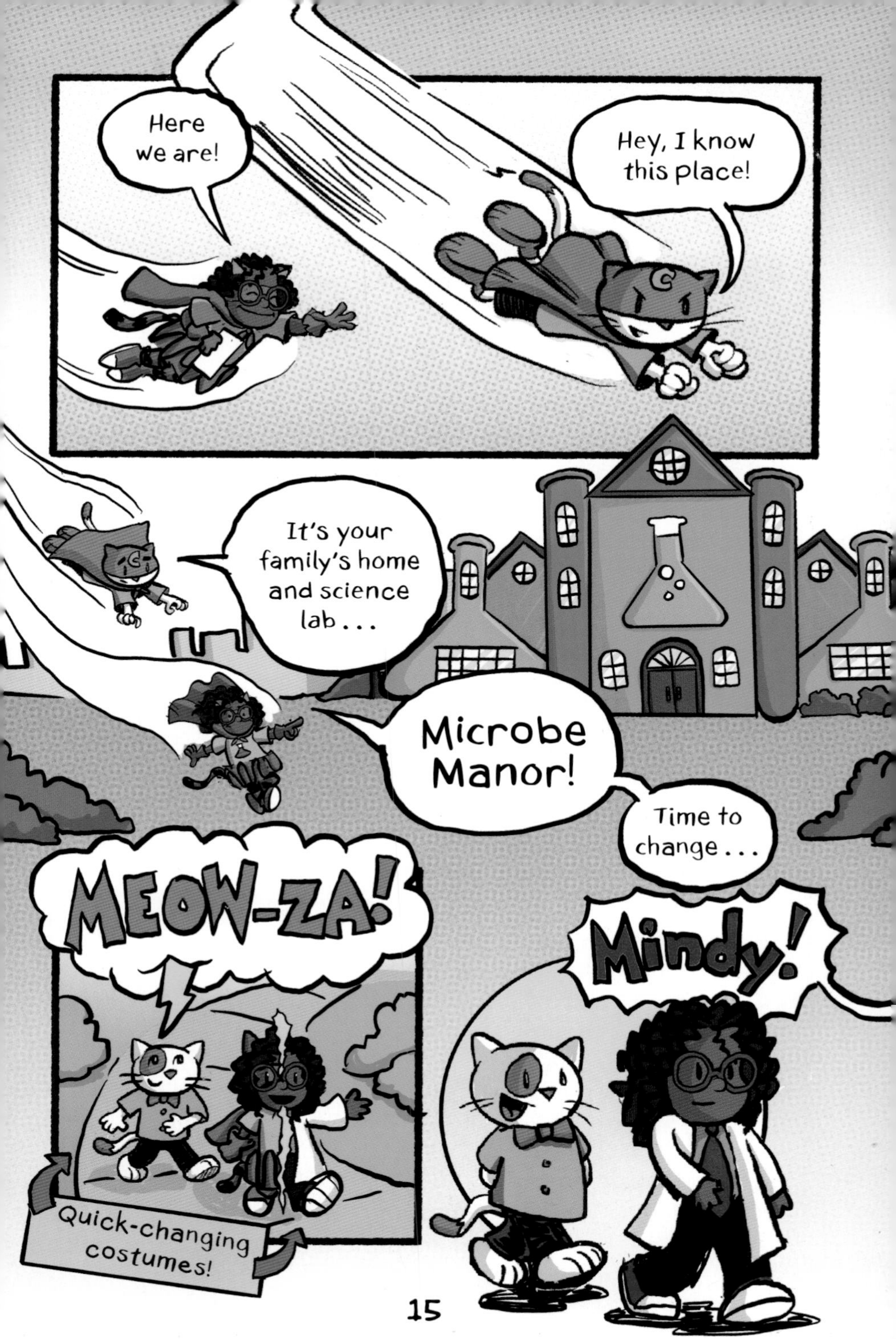
Here we are!
Hey, I know this place!
It's your family's home and science lab . . .
Microbe Manor!
Time to change . . .
MEOW-ZA!
Mindy!
Quick-changing costumes!

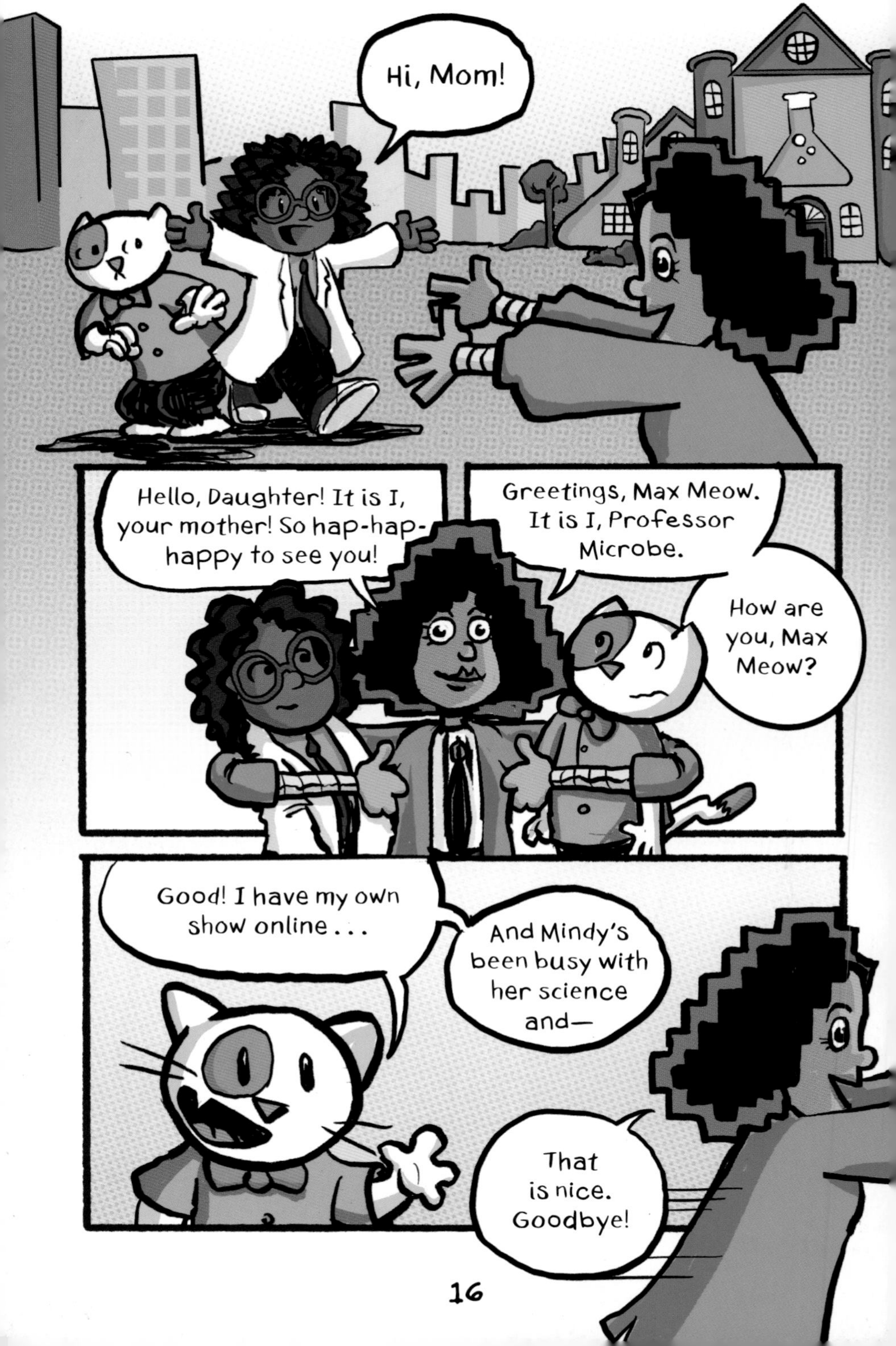
Hi, Mom!
Hello, Daughter! It is I, your mother! So hap-hap-happy to see you!
Greetings, Max Meow. It is I, Professor Microbe.
How are you, Max Meow?
Good! I have my own show online . . .
And Mindy's been busy with her science and—
That is nice. Goodbye!

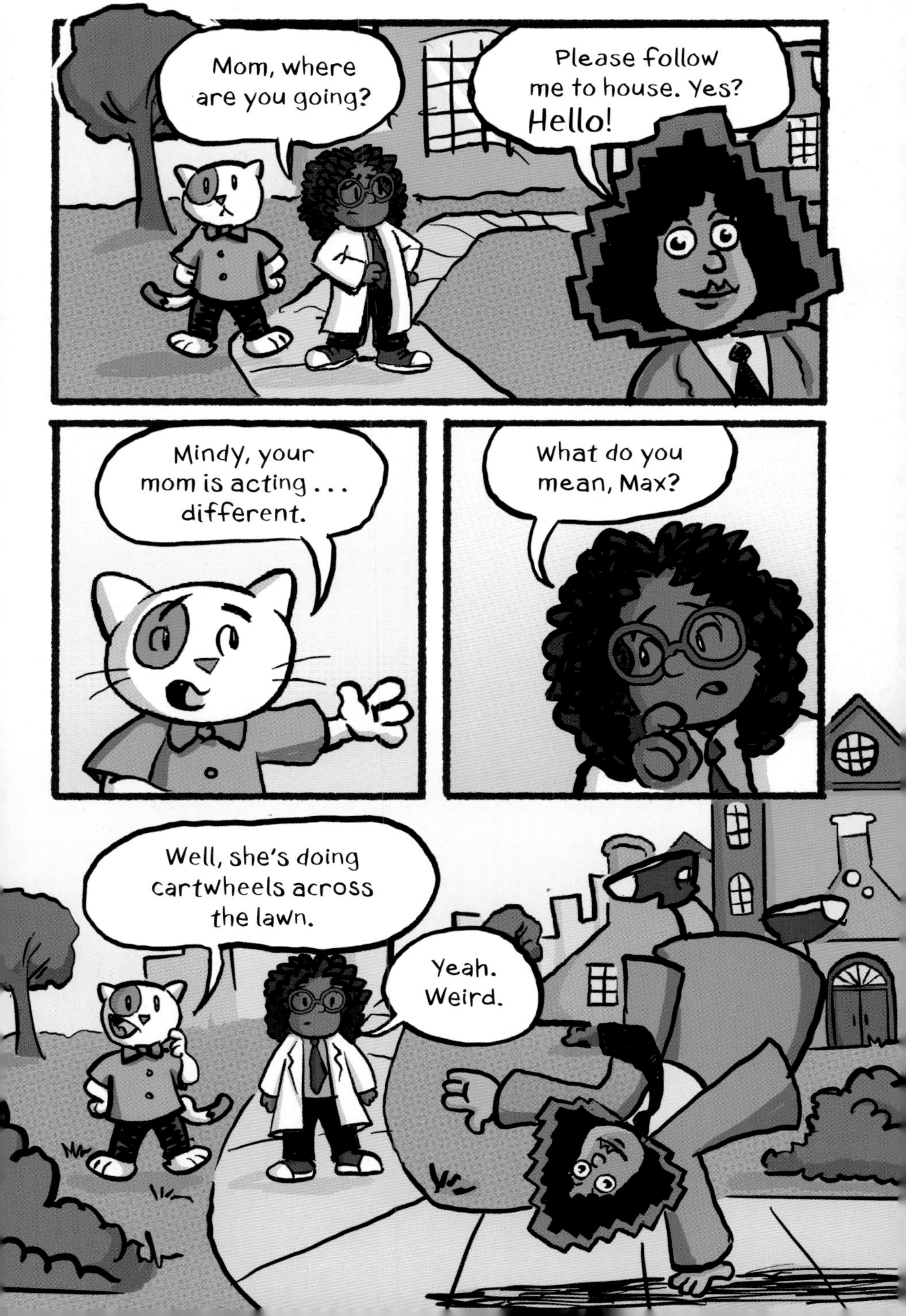
Mom, where are you going?
Please follow me to house. Yes? Hello!
Mindy, your mom is acting . . . different.
What do you mean, Max?
Well, she's doing cartwheels across the lawn.
Yeah. Weird.

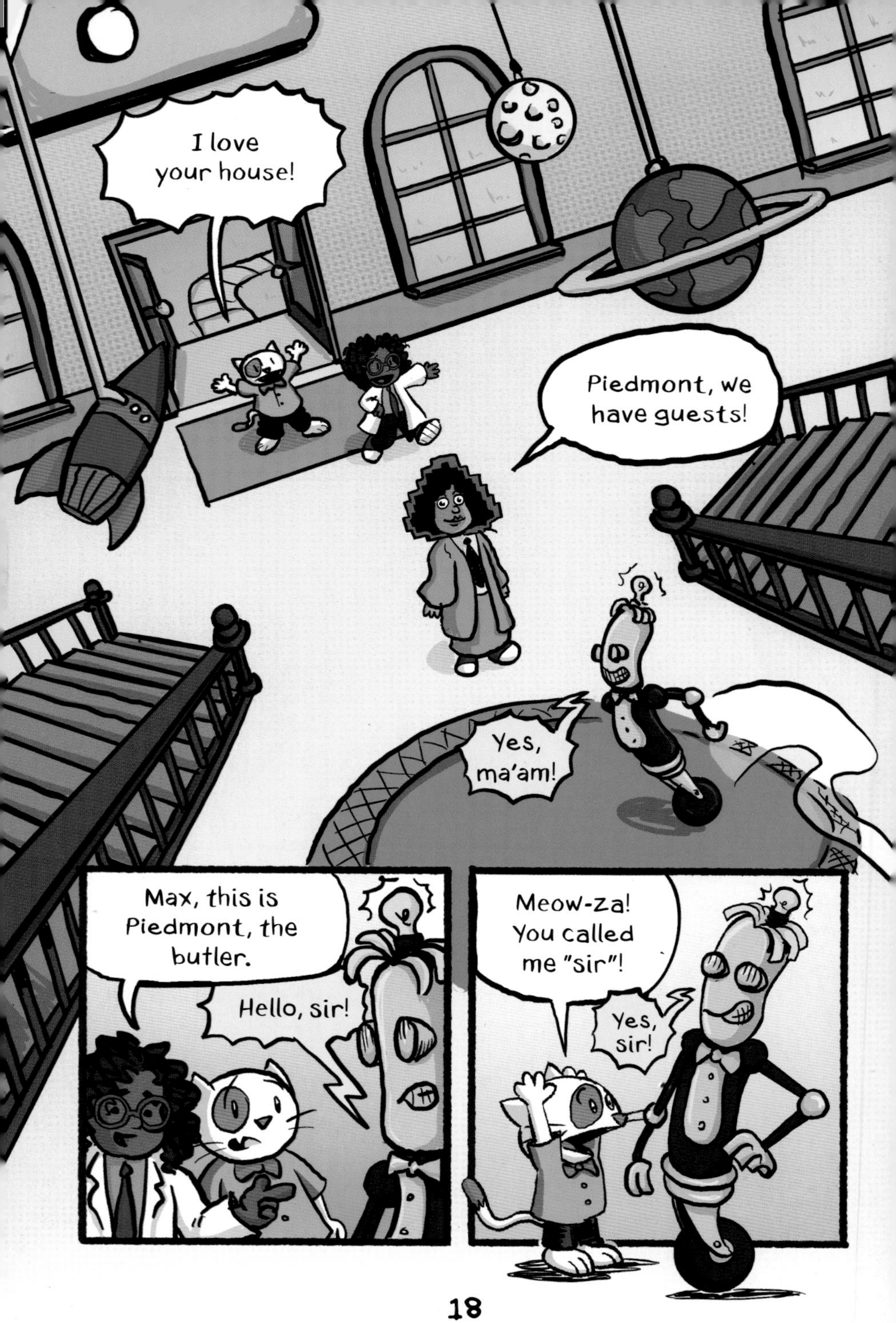
I love your house!
Piedmont, we have guests!
Yes, ma'am!
Max, this is Piedmont, the butler.
Hello, sir!
Meow-za! You called me "sir"!
Yes, sir!

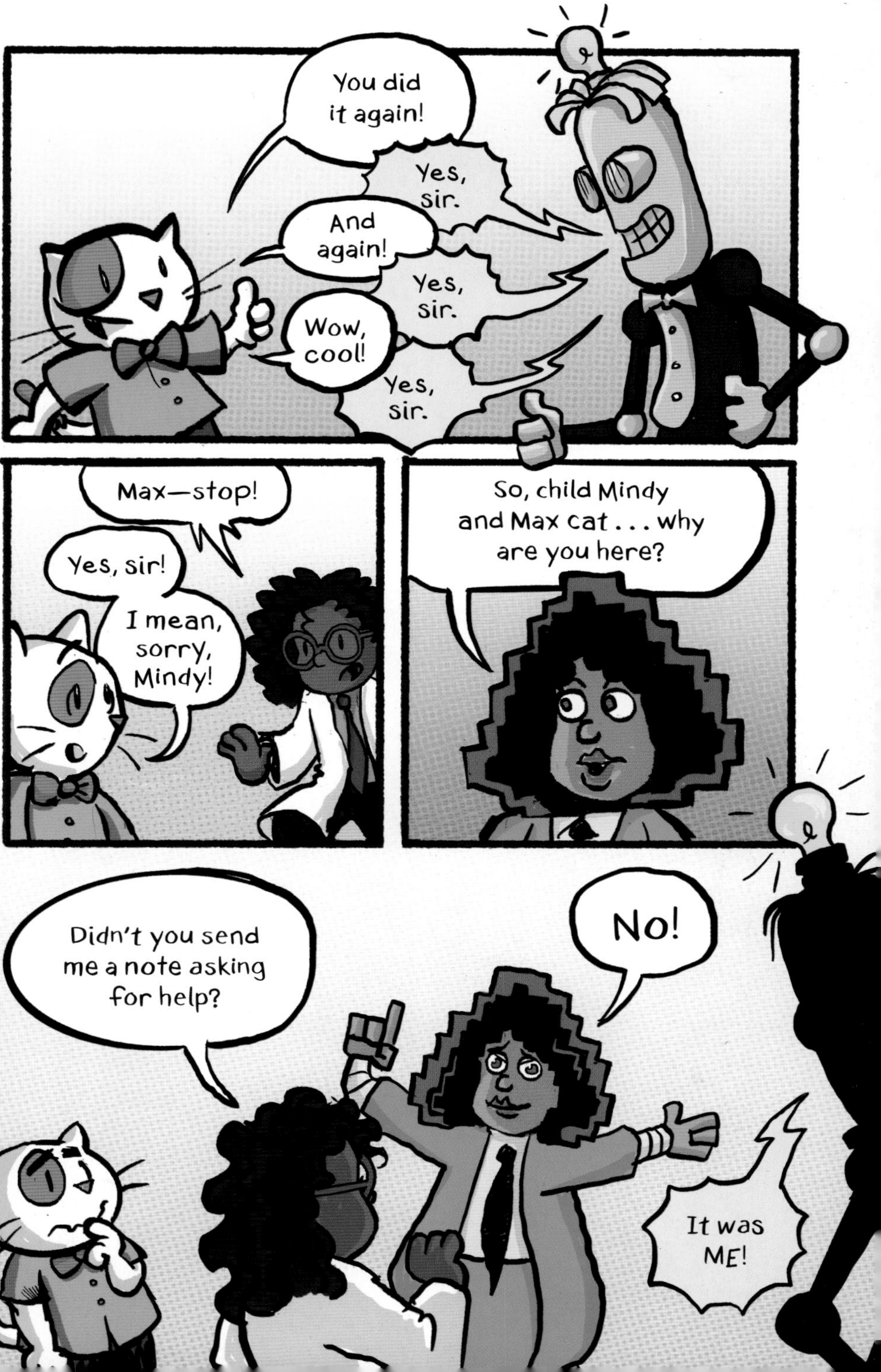
You did it again!
Yes, sir.
And again!
Yes, sir.
Wow, cool!
Yes, sir.
Max—stop!
Yes, sir!
I mean, sorry, Mindy!
So, child Mindy and Max cat . . . why are you here?
Didn't you send me a note asking for help?
No!
It was ME!

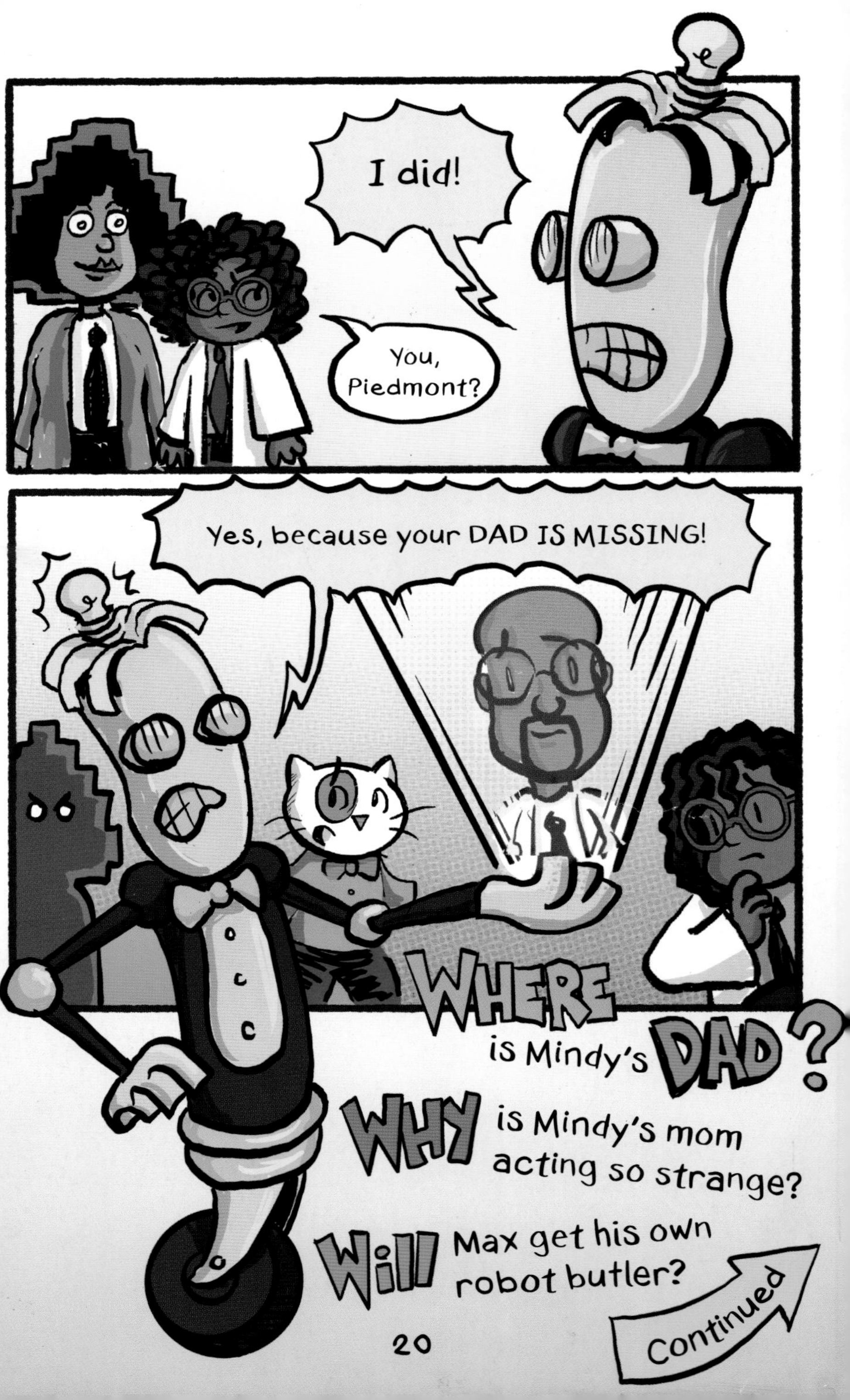

You, Piedmont?
I did!
Yes, because your DAD IS MISSING!
WHERE is Mindy's DAD?
WHY is Mindy's mom acting so strange?
Will Max get his own robot butler?
Continued

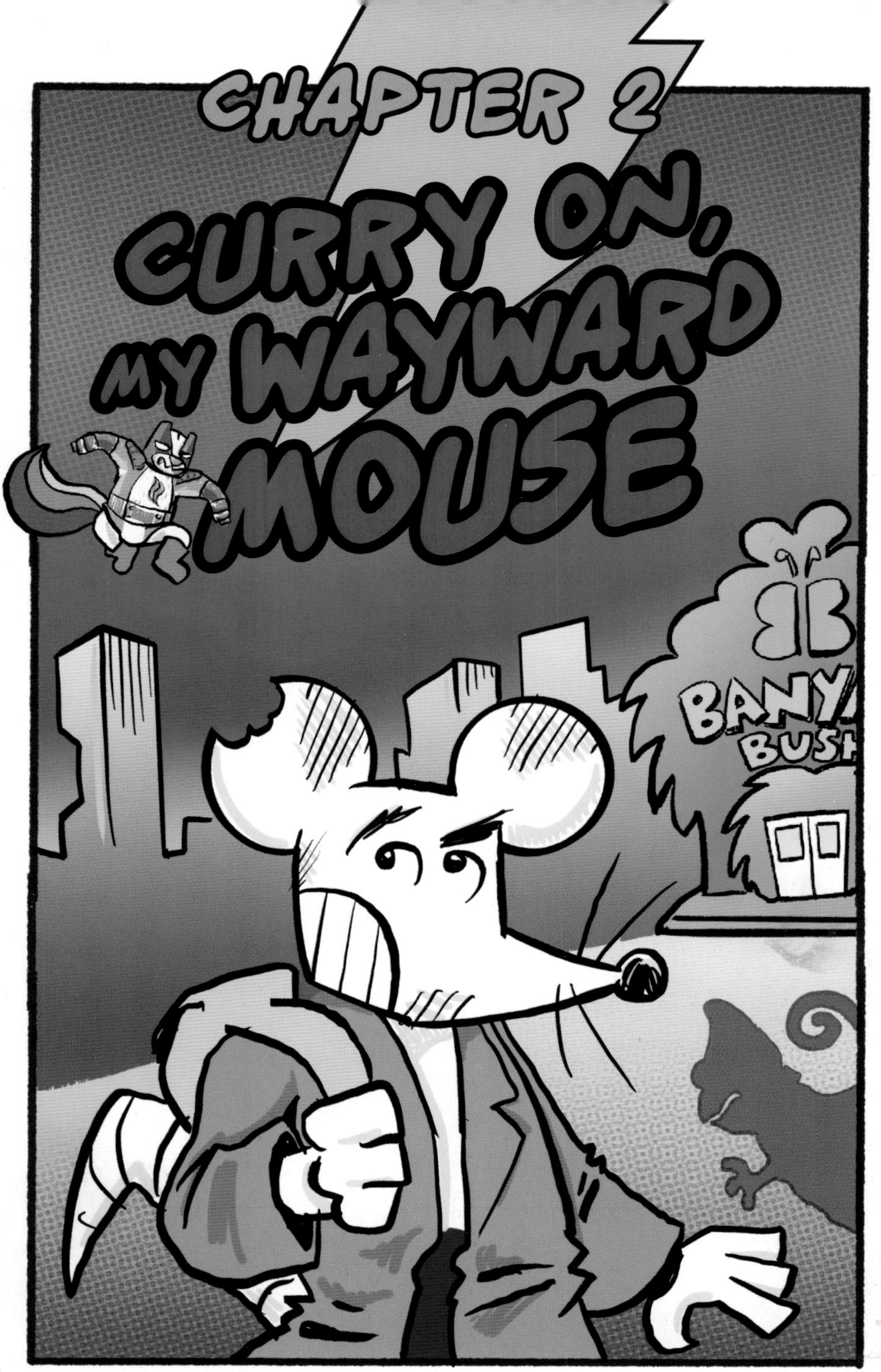
CHAPTER 2
CURRY ON, MY WAYWARD MOUSE

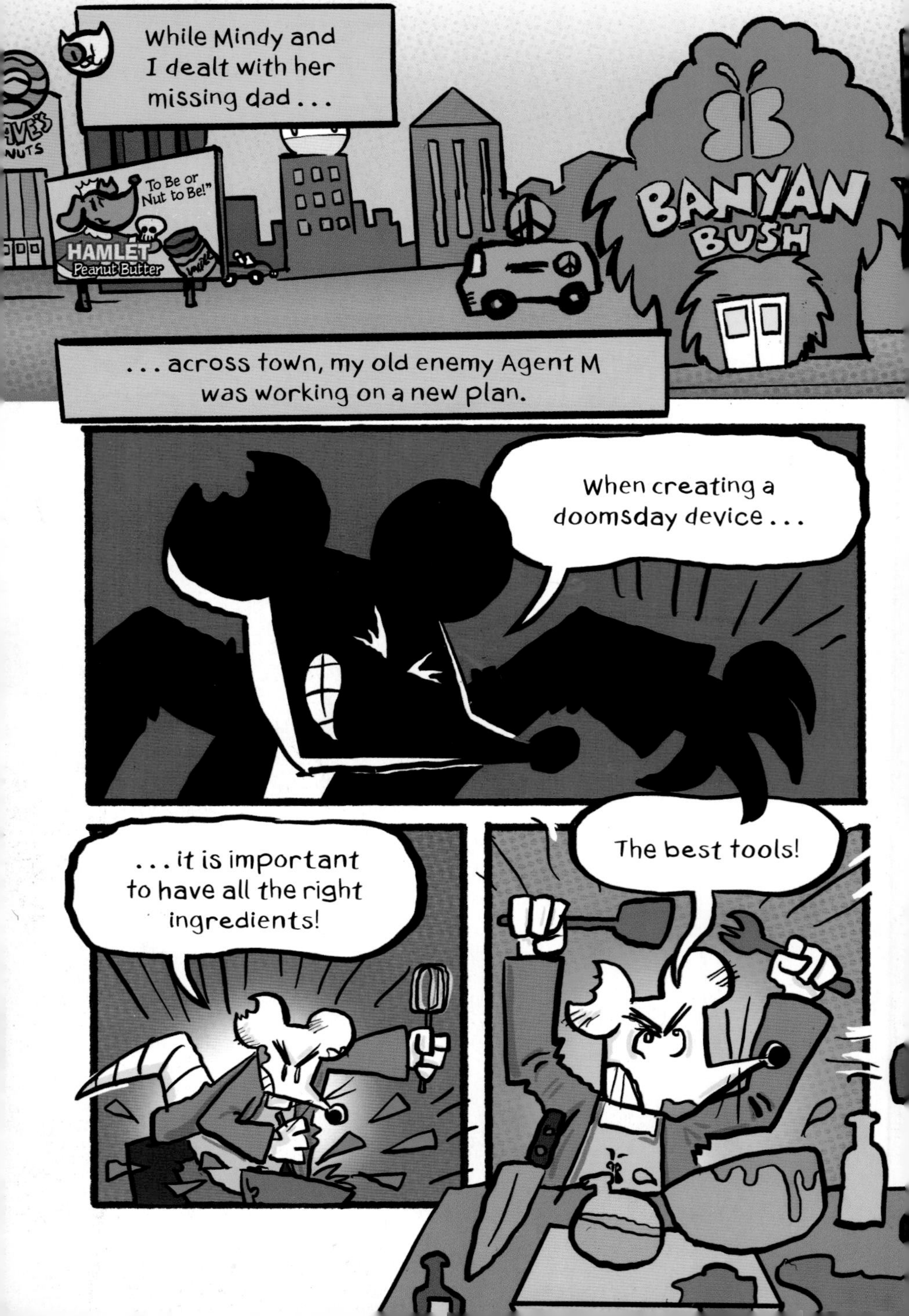
While Mindy and I dealt with her missing dad . . .
NUTS
"To Be or Nut to Be!"
HAMLET
Peanut Butter
BANYAN BUSH
. . . across town, my old enemy Agent M was working on a new plan.
When creating a doomsday device . . .
. . . it is important to have all the right ingredients!
The best tools!

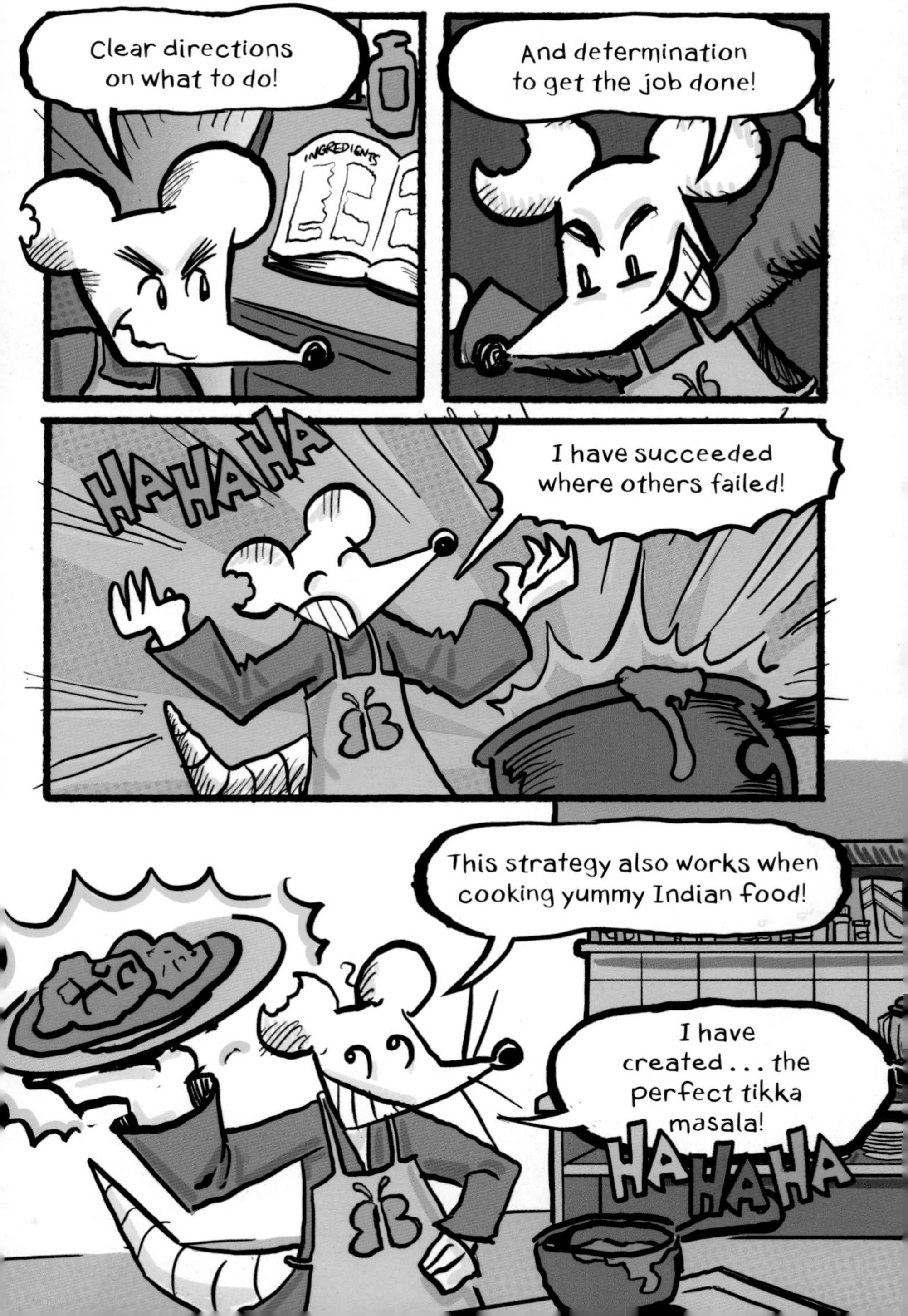

Clear directions on what to do!
INGREDIENTS
And determination to get the job done!
HAHAHA
I have succeeded where others failed!
This strategy also works when cooking yummy Indian food!
I have created . . . the perfect tikka masala!
HAHAHA

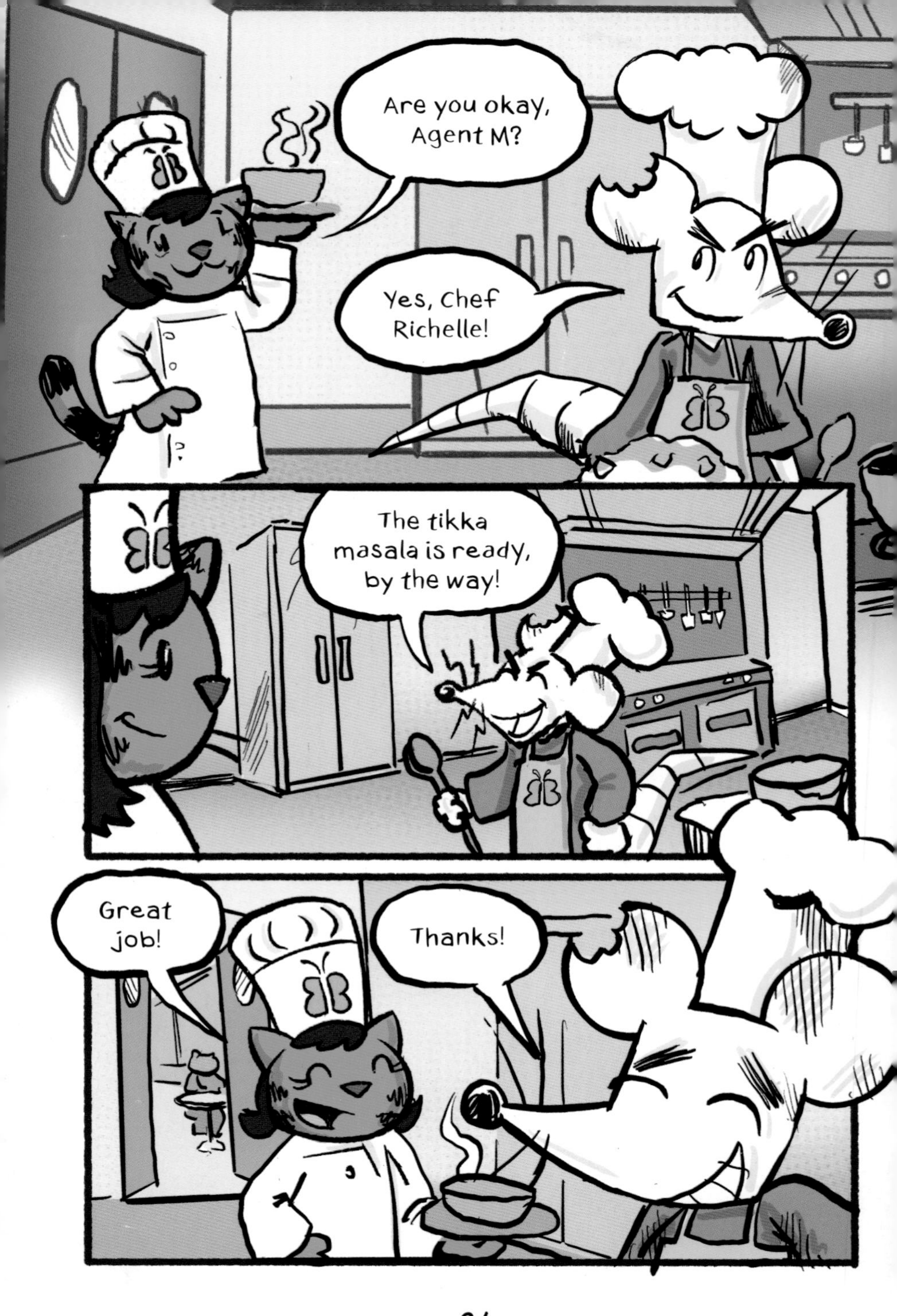
Are you okay, Agent M?
Yes, Chef Richelle!
The tikka masala is ready, by the way!
Great job!
Thanks!

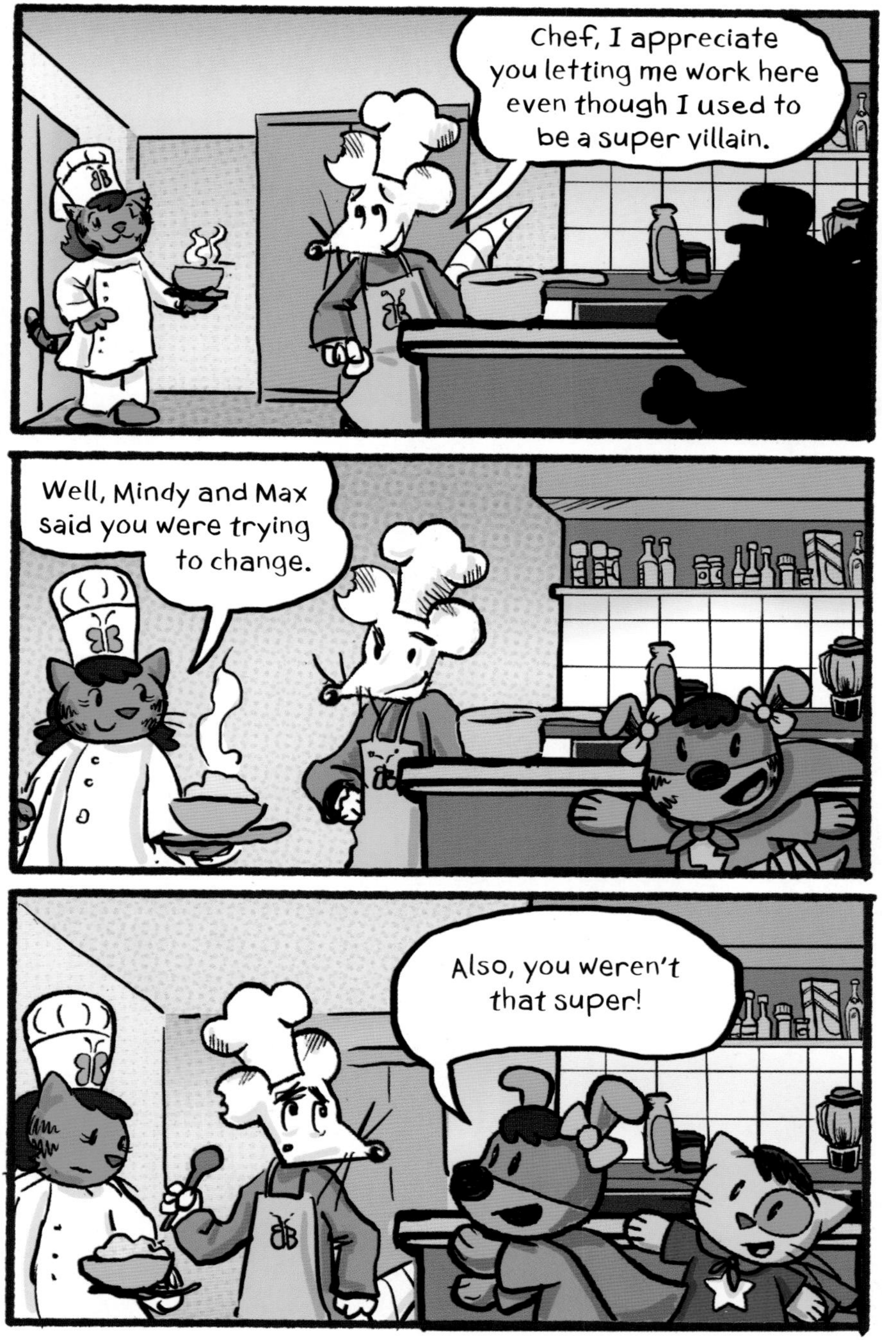
Chef, I appreciate you letting me work here even though I used to be a super villain.
Well, Mindy and Max said you were trying to change.
Also, you weren't that super!

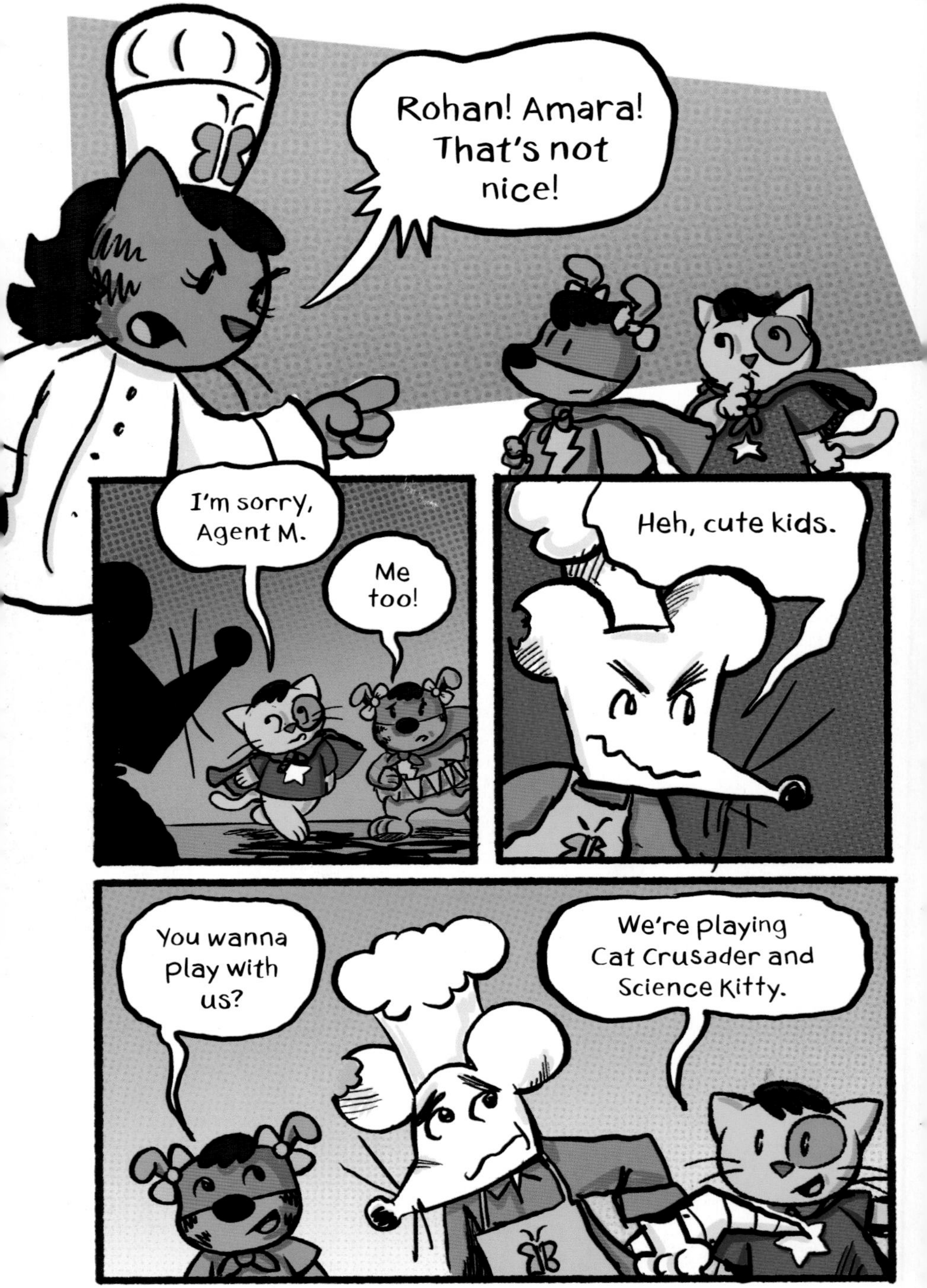
Rohan! Amara! That's not nice!
I'm sorry, Agent M.
Me too!
Heh, cute kids.
You wanna play with us?
We're playing Cat Crusader and Science Kitty.

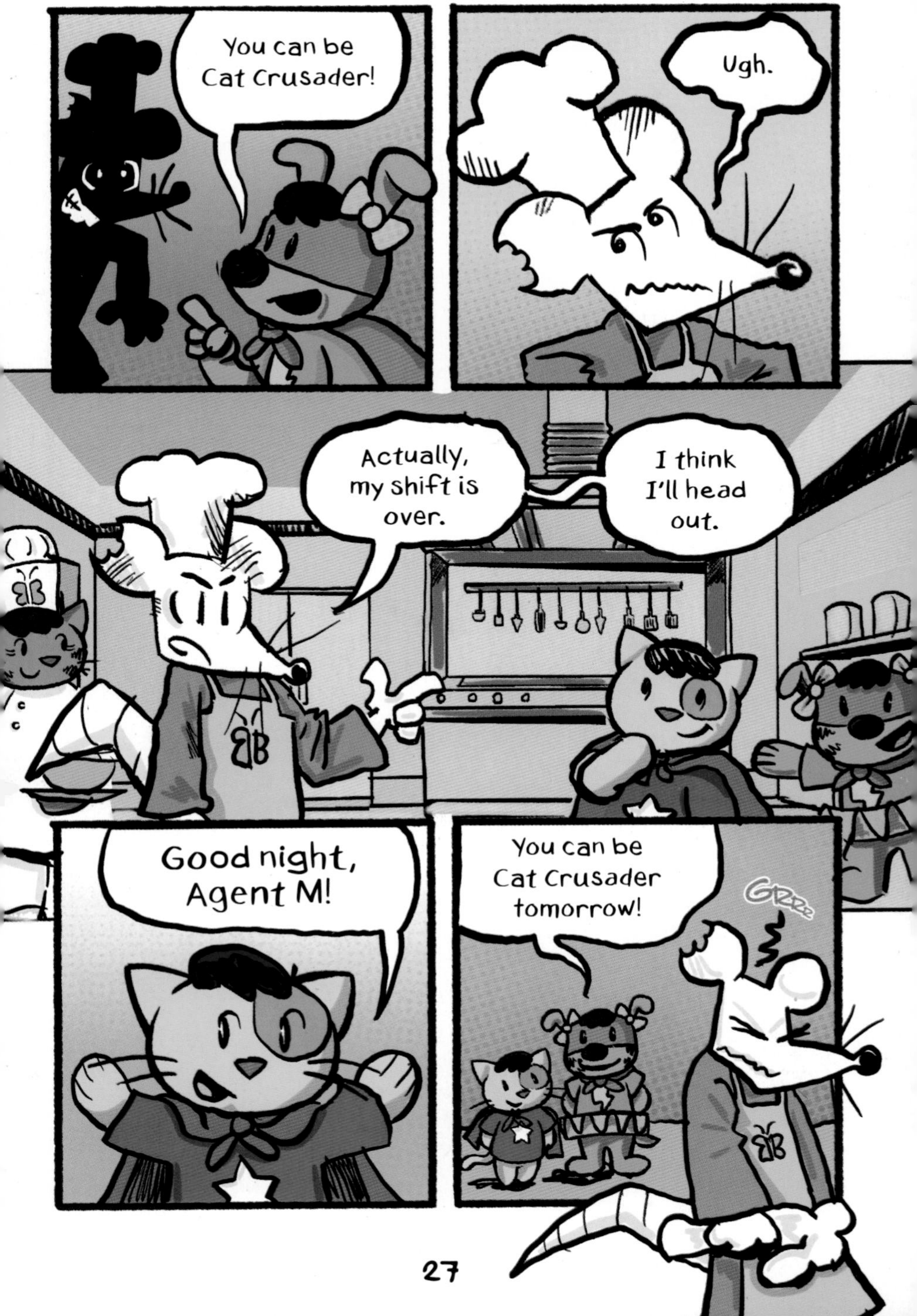
You can be Cat Crusader!
Ugh.
Actually, my shift is over.
I think I'll head out.
Good night, Agent M!
You can be Cat Crusader tomorrow!
GRRR

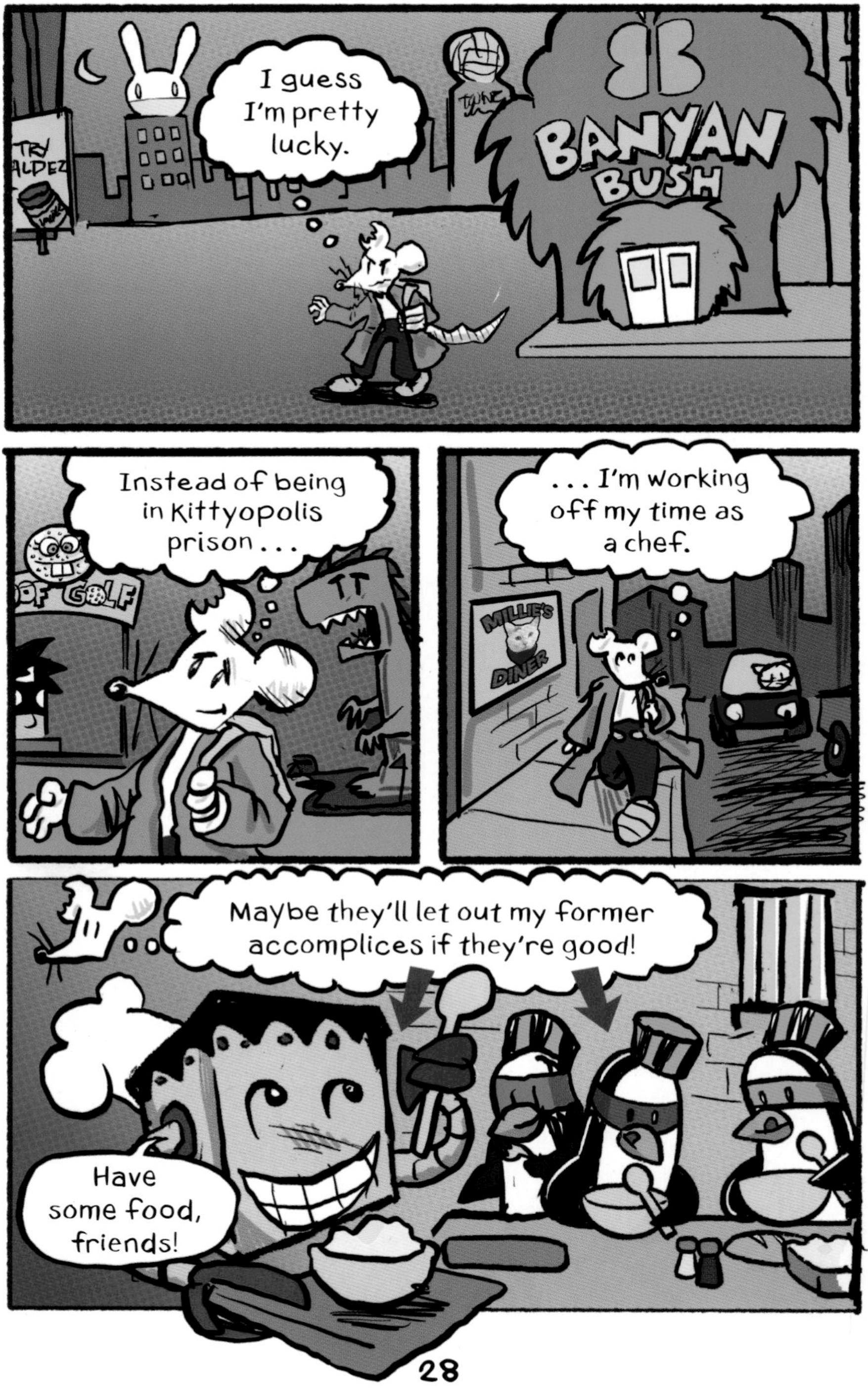

TRY
ALDEZ
I guess I'm pretty lucky.
BANYAN BUSH
Instead of being in Kittyopolis prison . . .
GOLF
. . . I'm working off my time as a chef.
MILLIE'S DINER
Maybe they'll let out my former accomplices if they're good!
Have some food, friends!

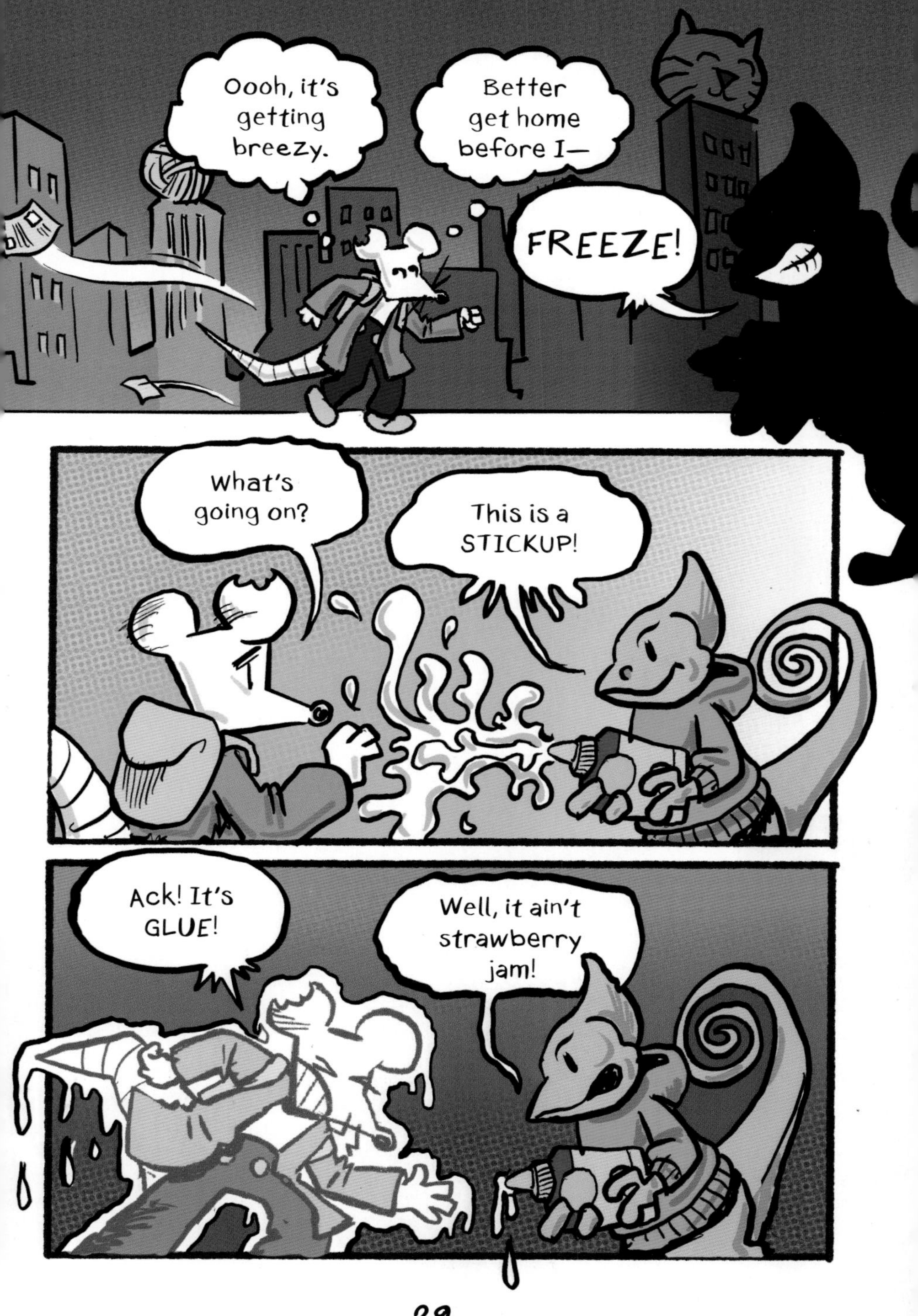

Oooh, it's getting breezy.
Better get home before I—
FREEZE!
What's going on?
This is a STICKUP!
Ack! It's GLUE!
Well, it ain't strawberry jam!

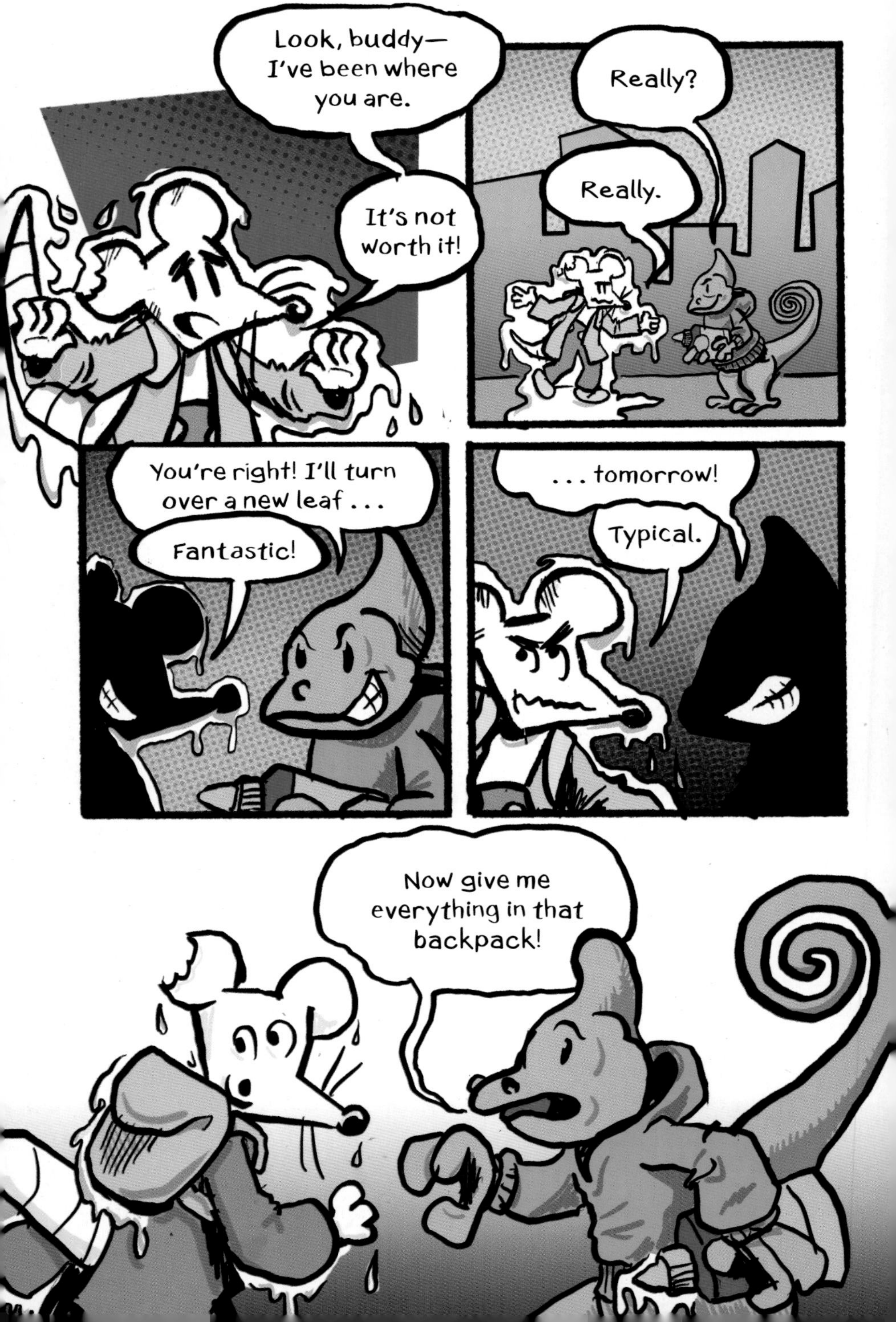
Look, buddy— I've been where you are.
It's not worth it!
Really?
Really.
You're right! I'll turn over a new leaf . . .
Fantastic!
. . . tomorrow!
Typical.
Now give me everything in that backpack!

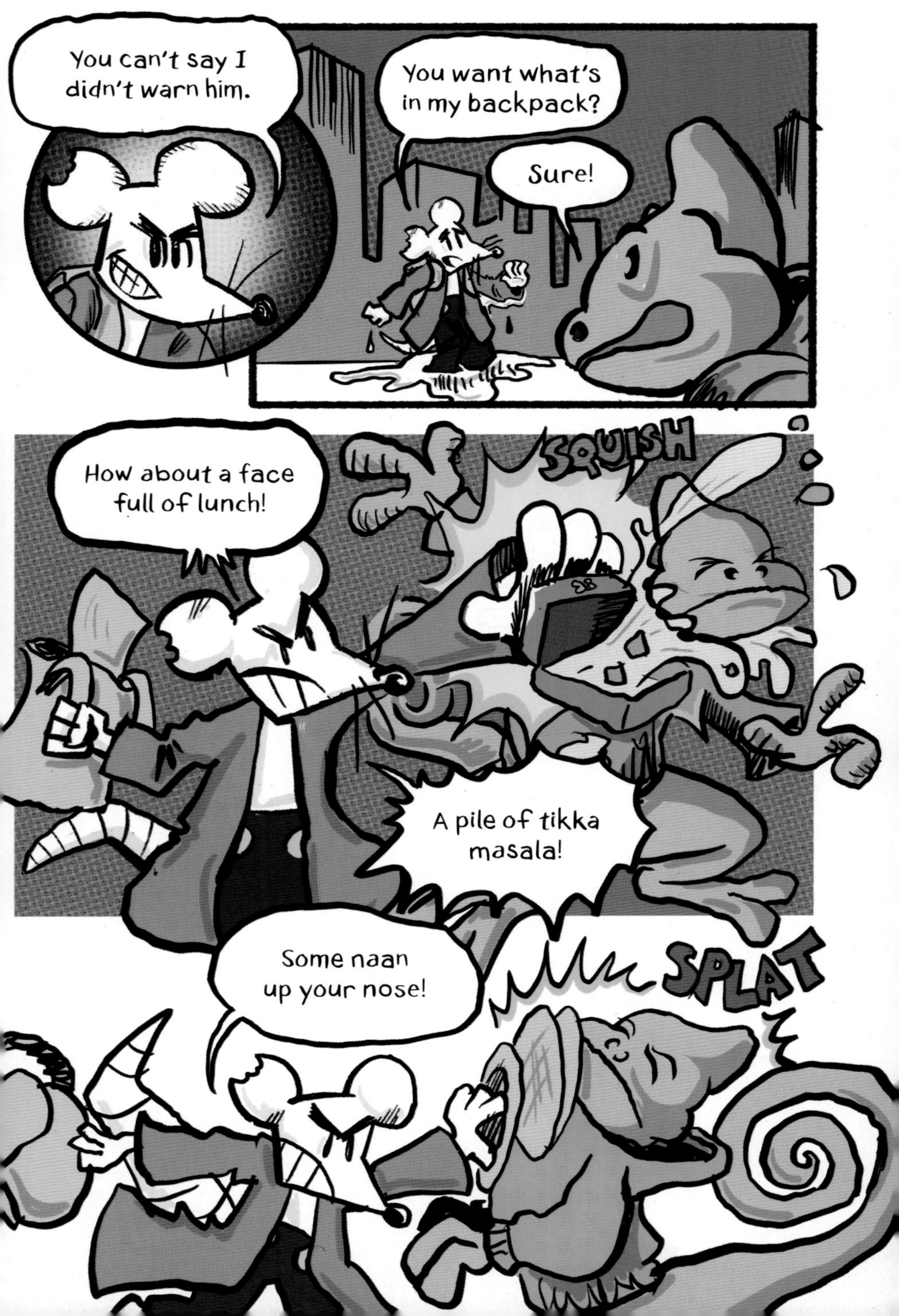
You can't say I didn't warn him.
You want what's in my backpack?
Sure!
How about a face full of lunch!
SQUISH
A pile of tikka masala!
Some naan up your nose!
SPLAT

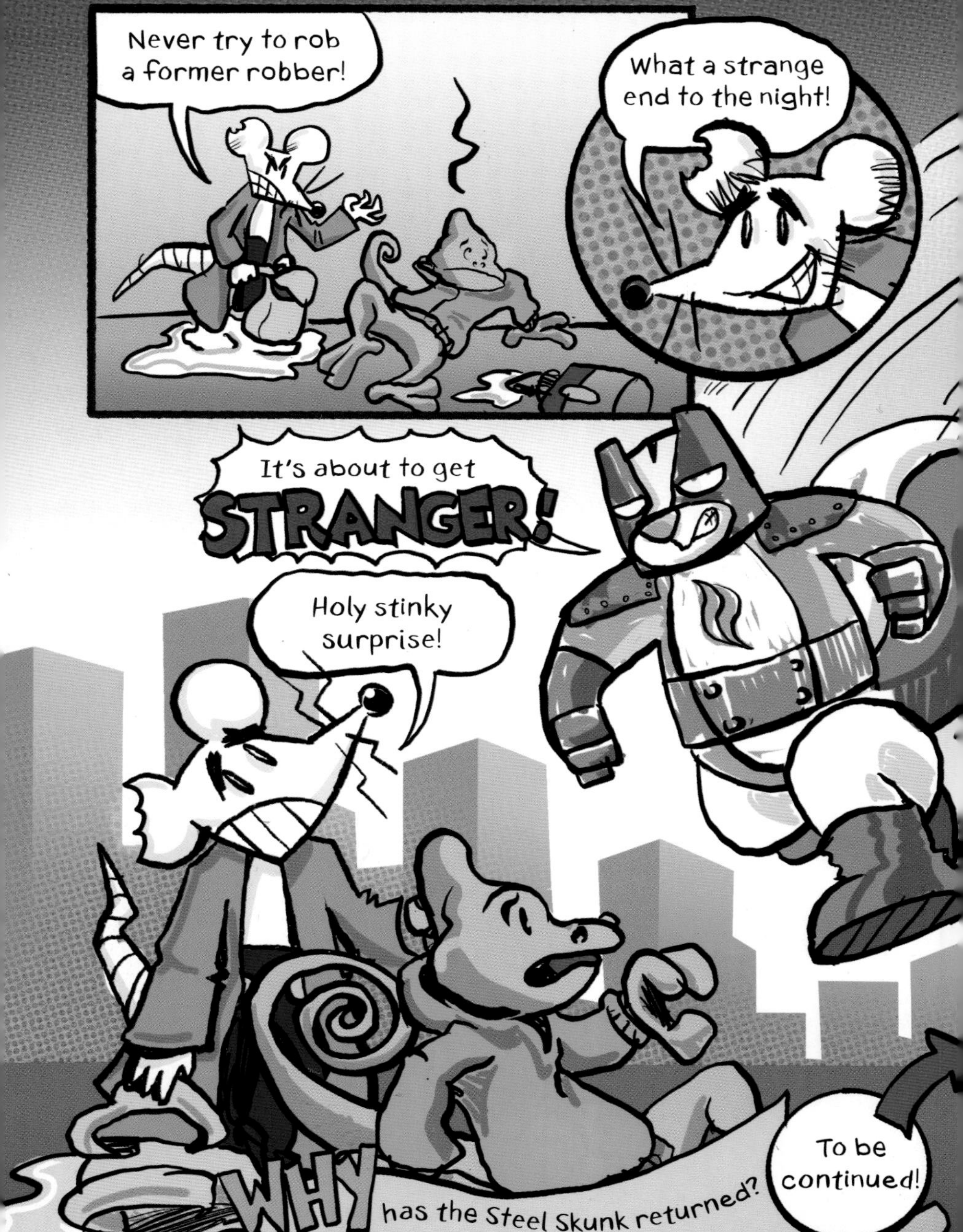
Never try to rob a former robber!
What a strange end to the night!
It's about to get STRANGER!
Holy stinky surprise!
WHY has the Steel Skunk returned?
WILL Agent M escape the glue?
To be continued!

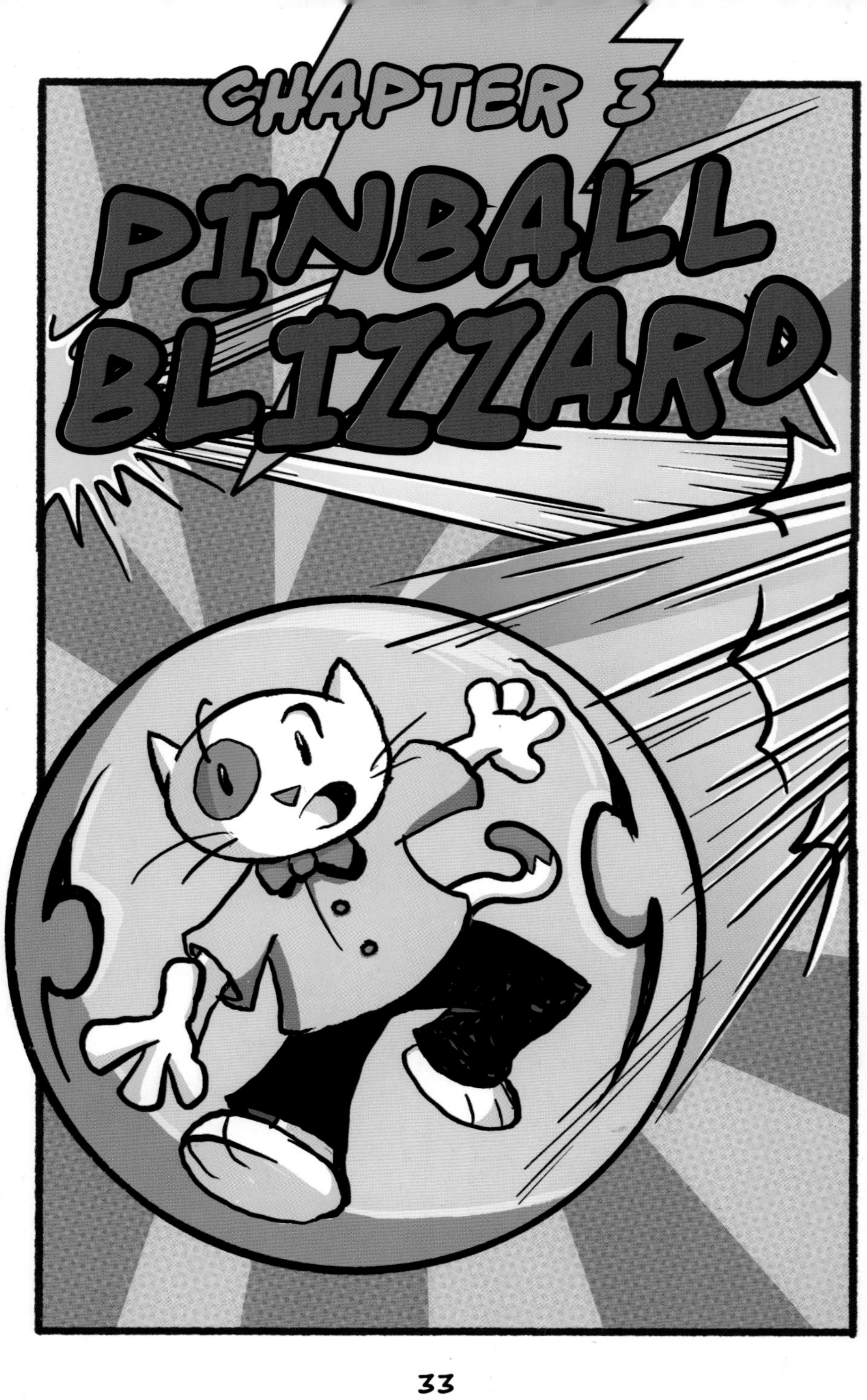
CHAPTER 3
PINBALL BLIZZARD

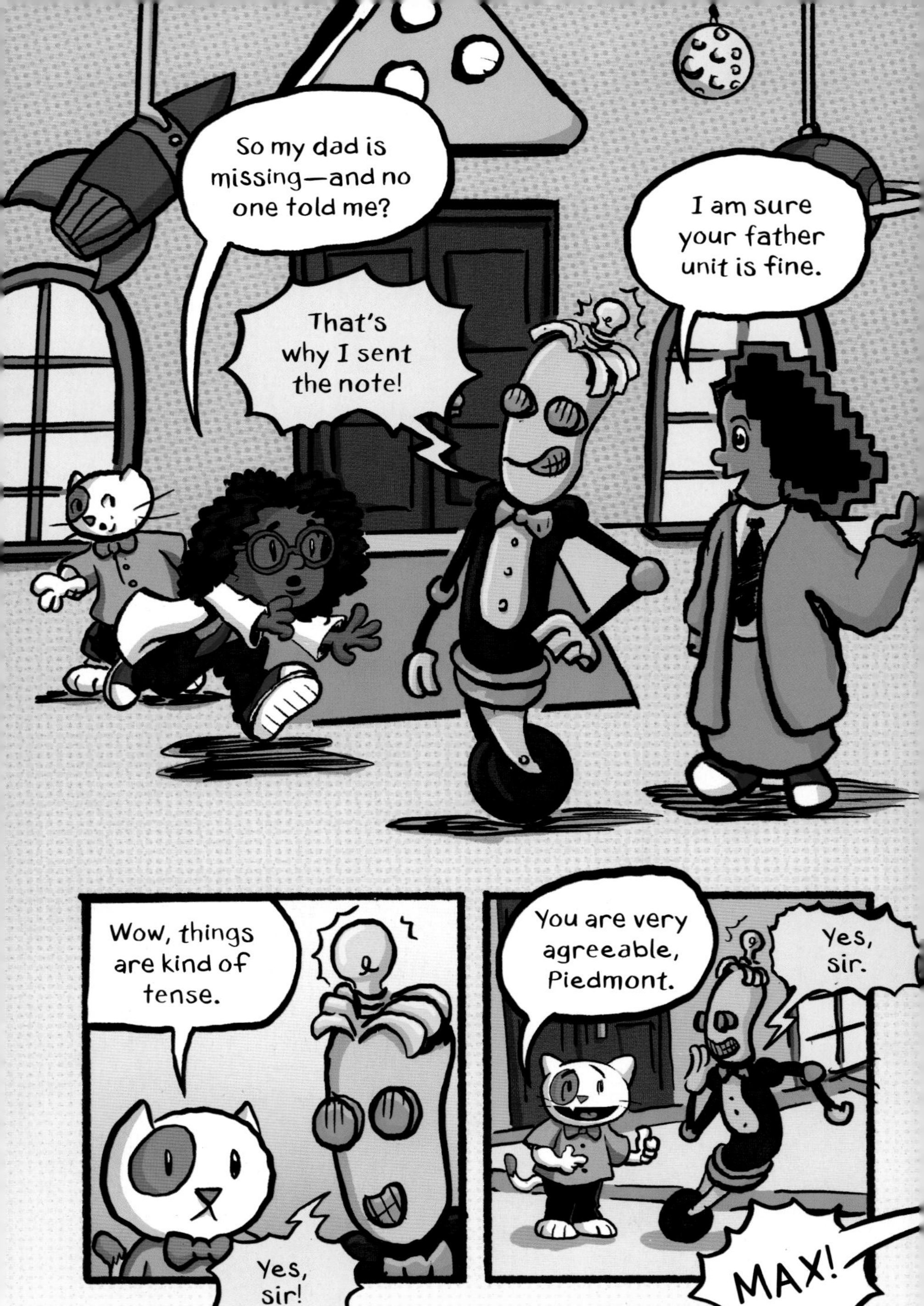
So my dad is missing—and no one told me?
That's why I sent the note!
I am sure your father unit is fine.
Wow, things are kind of tense.
Yes, sir!
You are very agreeable, Piedmont.
Yes, sir.
MAX!

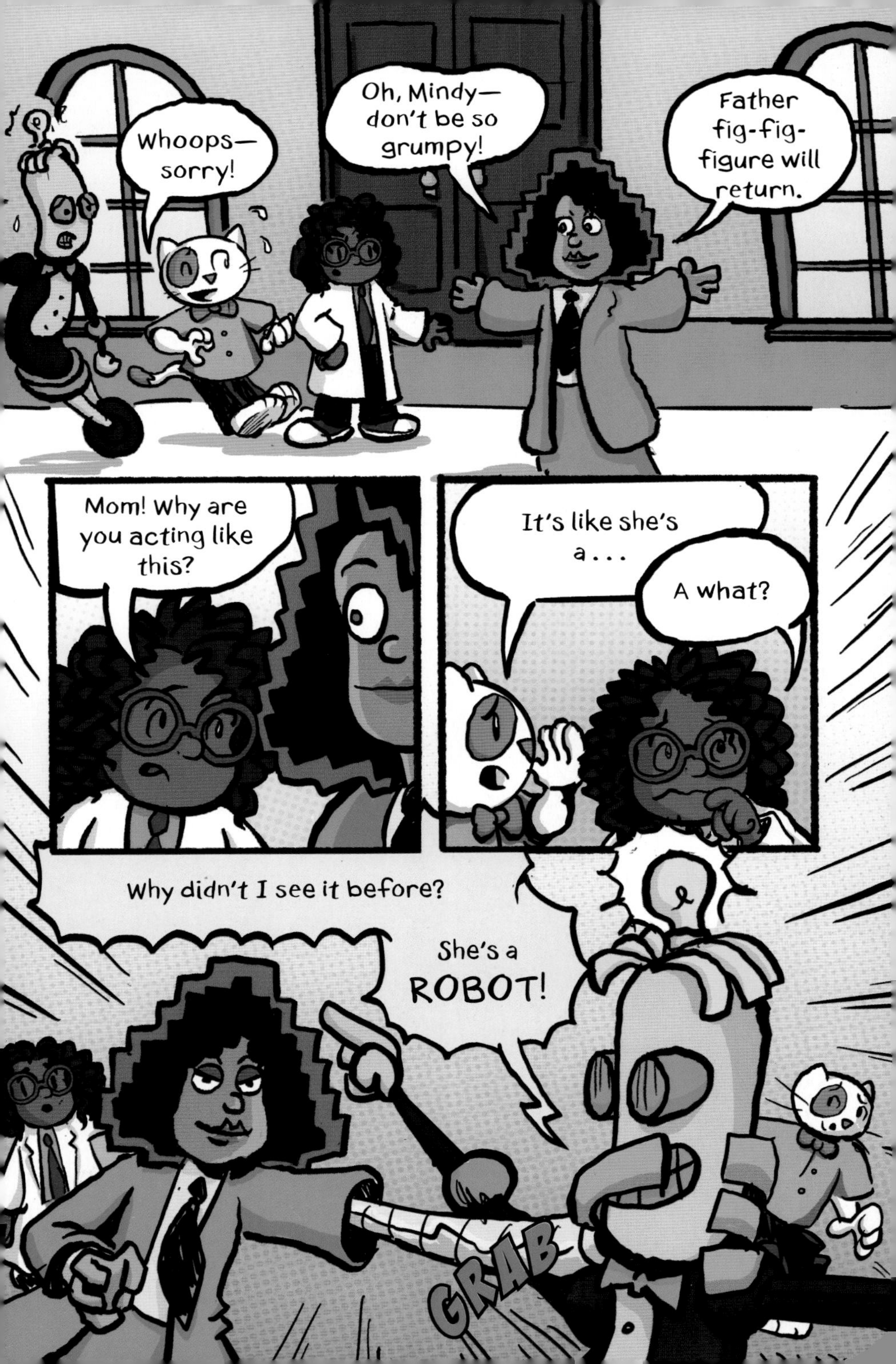
Whoops—sorry!
Oh, Mindy—don't be so grumpy!
Father fig-fig-figure will return.
Mom! Why are you acting like this?
It's like she's a . . .
A what?
Why didn't I see it before?
She's a ROBOT!
GRAB

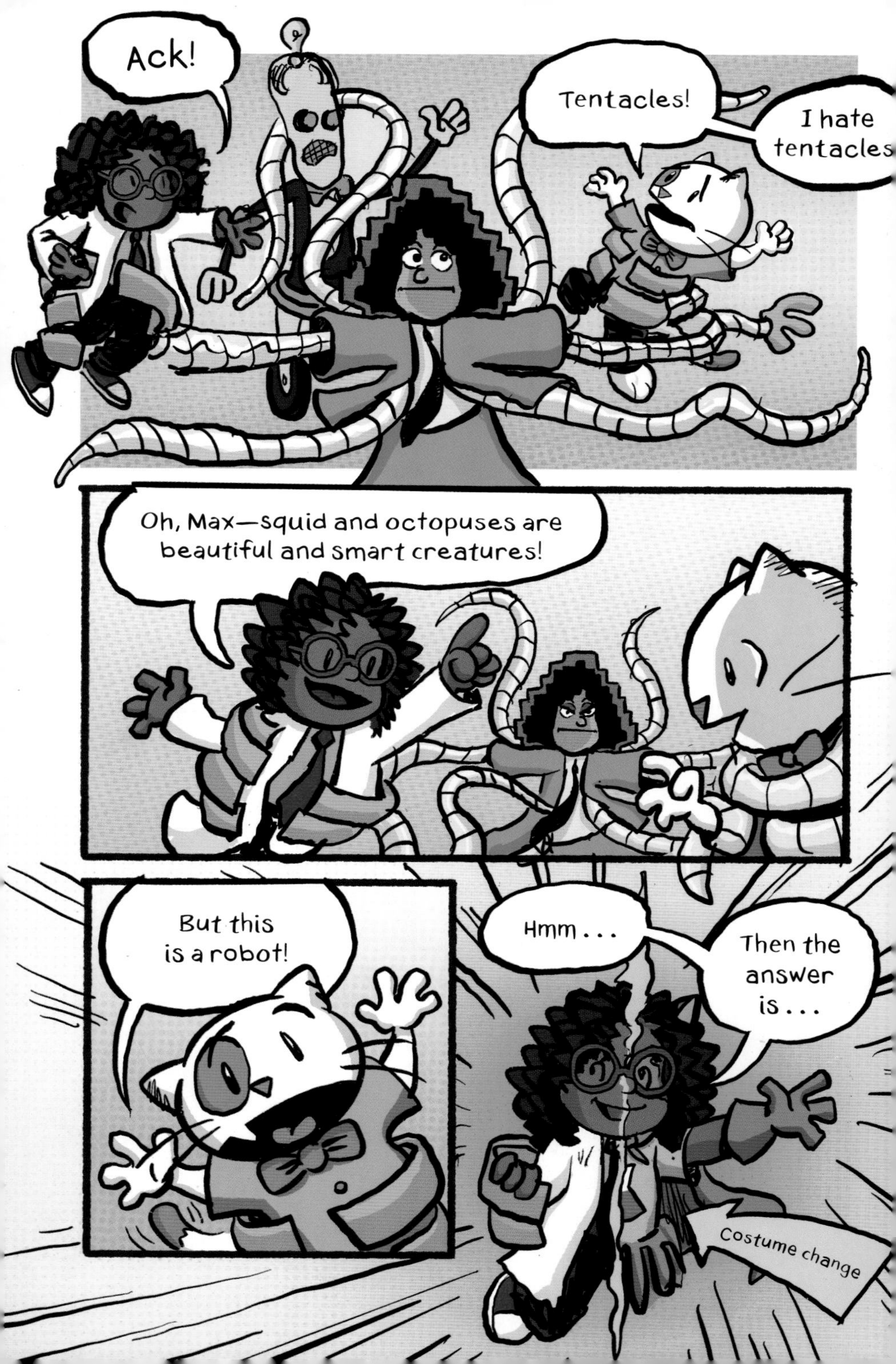
Ack!
Tentacles!
I hate tentacles
Oh, Max—squid and octopuses are beautiful and smart creatures!
But this is a robot!
Hmm . . .
Then the answer is . . .
Costume change

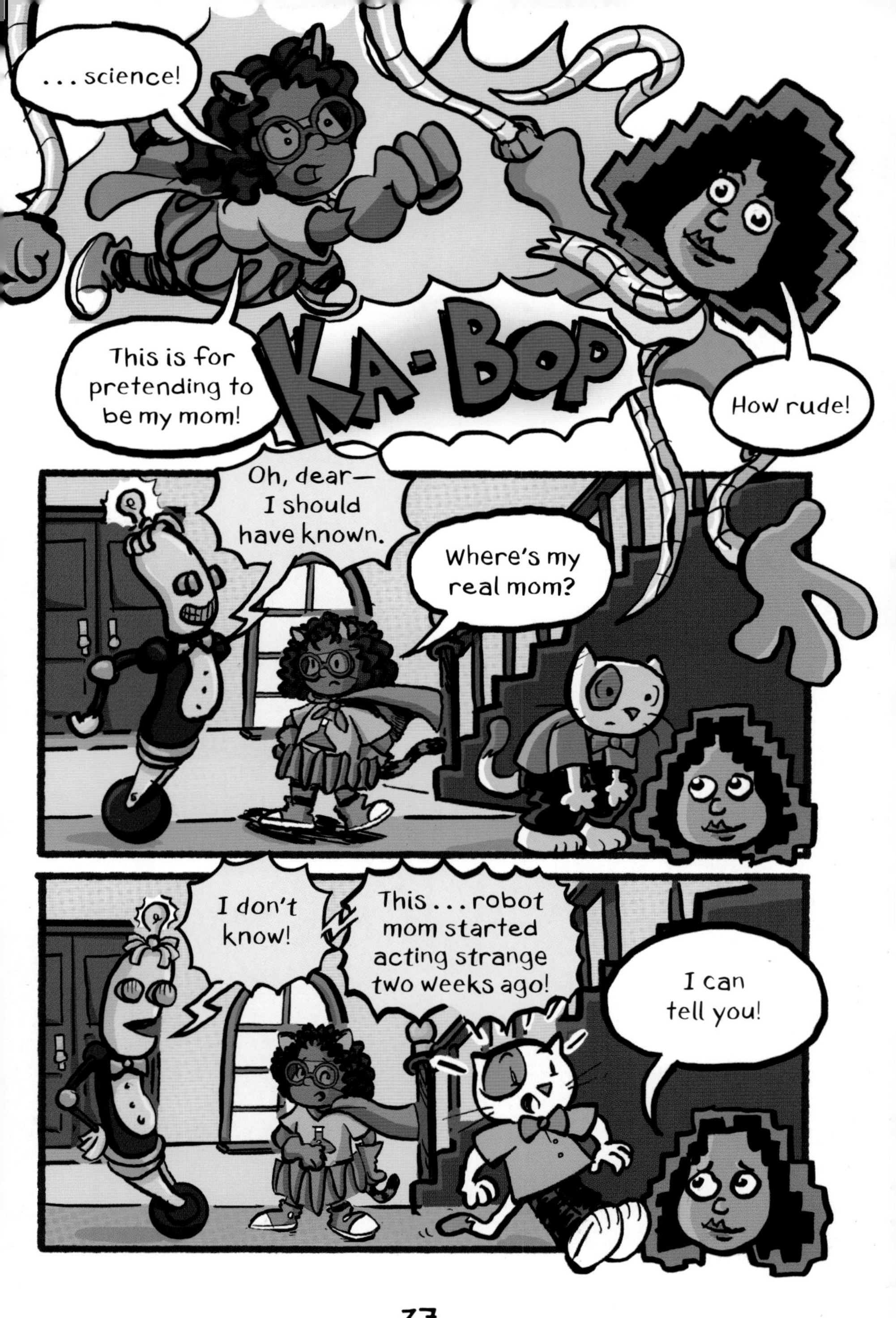

. . . science!
This is for pretending to be my mom!
KA-BOP
How rude!
Oh, dear— I should have known.
Where's my real mom?
I don't know!
This . . . robot mom started acting strange two weeks ago!
I can tell you!

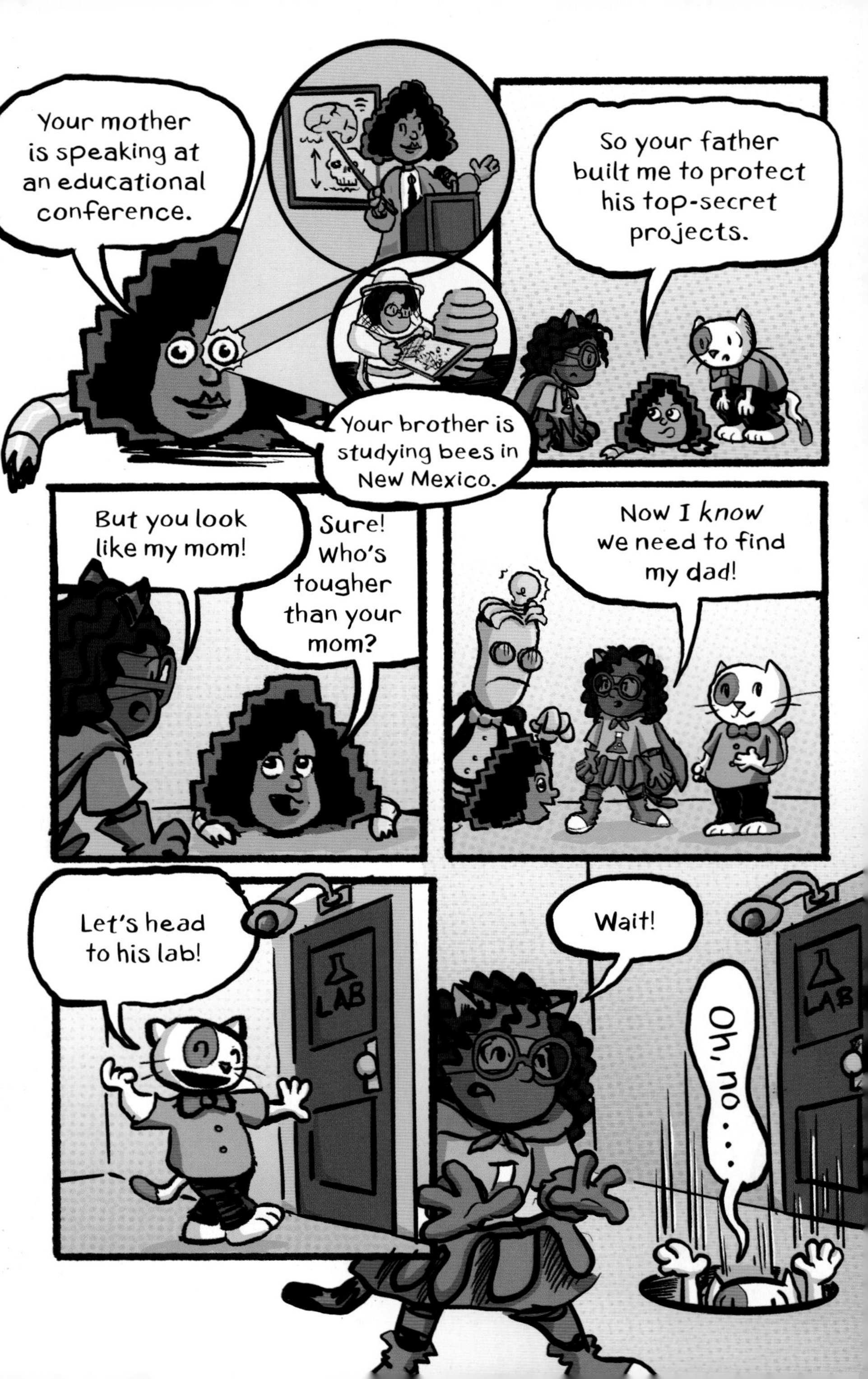
Your mother is speaking at an educational conference.
Your brother is studying bees in New Mexico.
So your father built me to protect his top-secret projects.
But you look like my mom!
Sure! Who's tougher than your mom?
Now I *know* we need to find my dad!
Let's head to his lab!
LAB
Wait!
LAB
Oh, no . . .

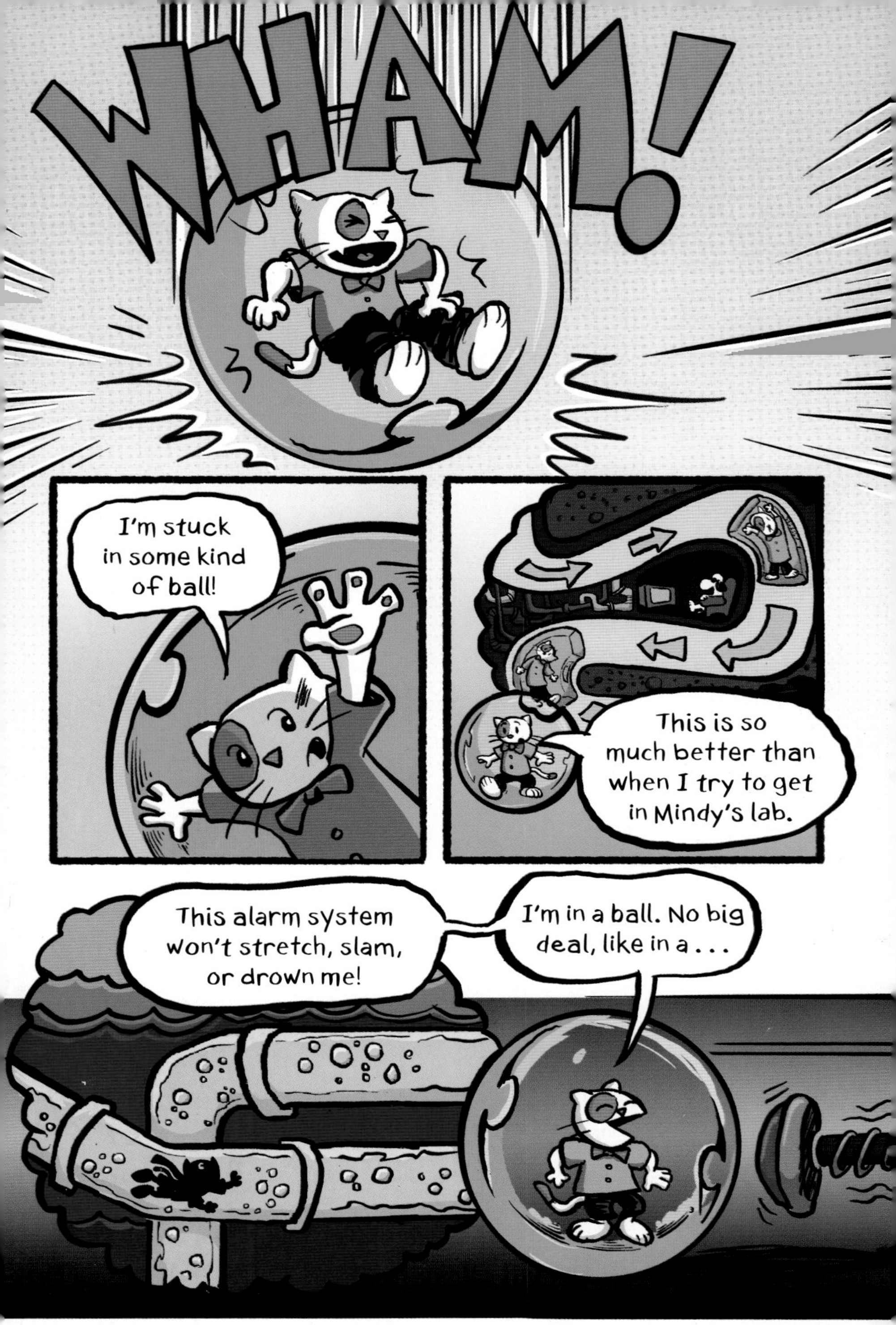
WHAM!
I'm stuck in some kind of ball!
This is so much better than when I try to get in Mindy's lab.
This alarm system won't stretch, slam, or drown me!
I'm in a ball. No big deal, like in a . . .

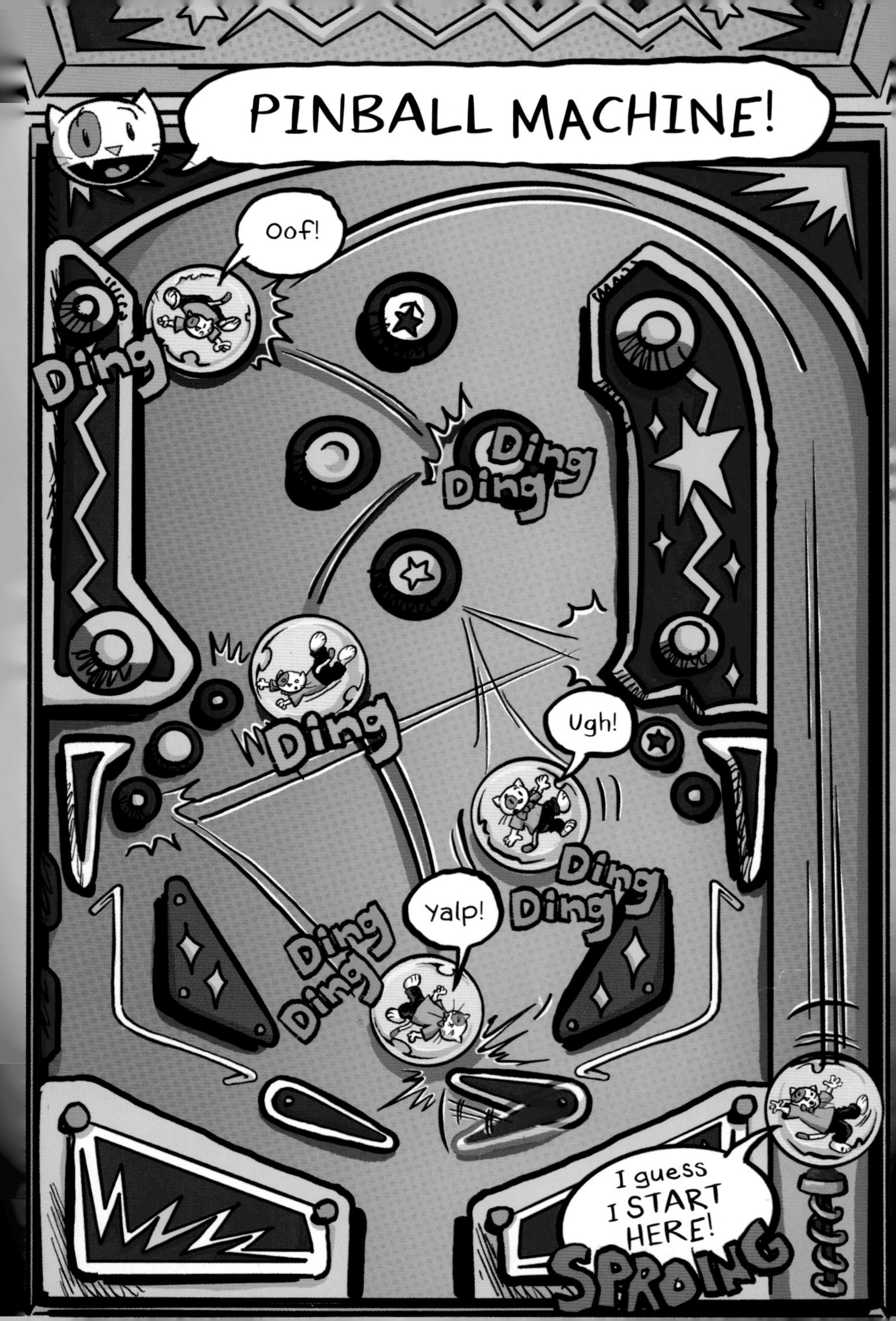
PINBALL MACHINE!
Oof!
Ding
Ding
Ding
Ding
Ugh!
Ding
Ding
Yalp!
Ding
Ding
I guess I START HERE!
SPROING

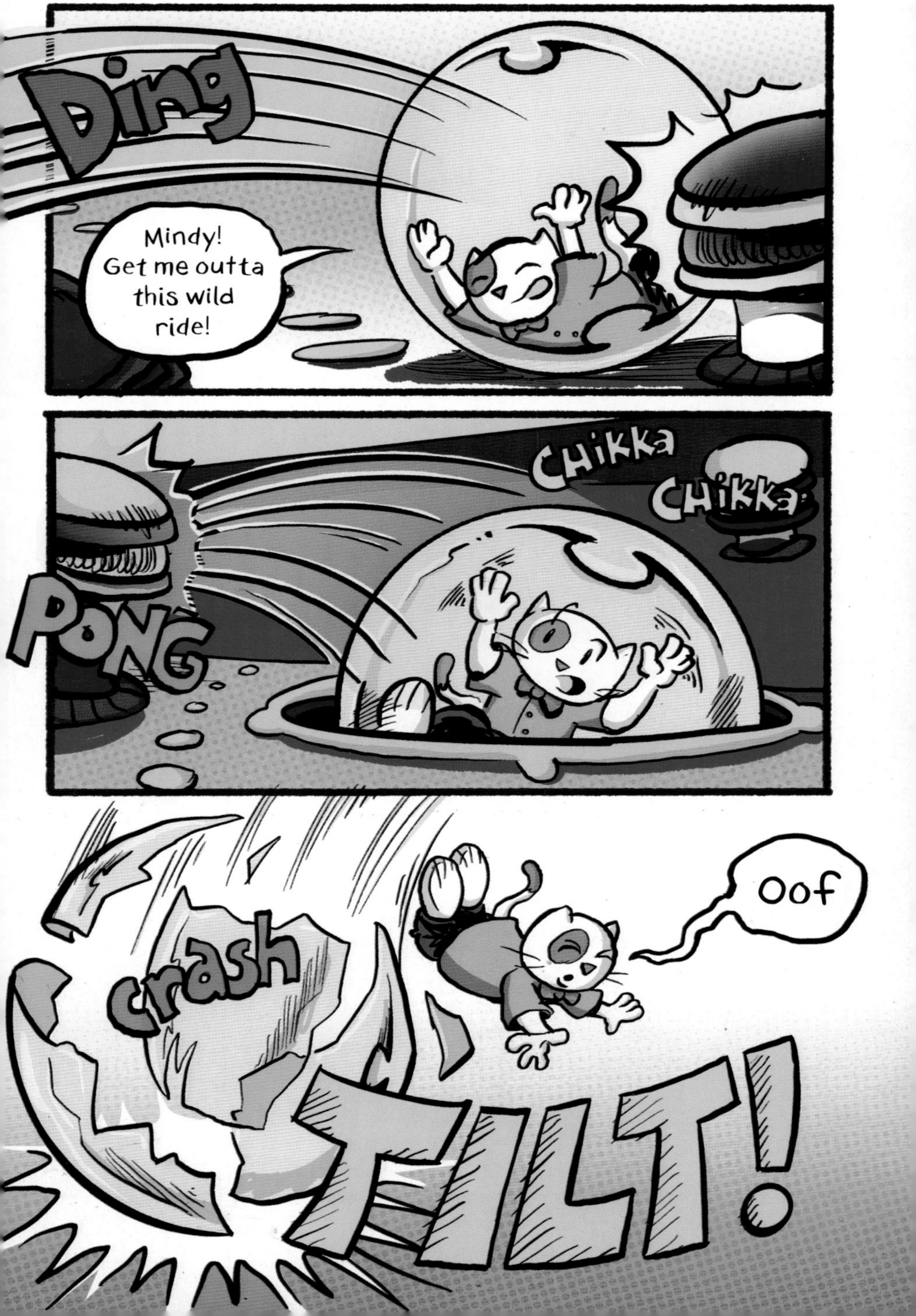

Ding
Mindy! Get me outta this wild ride!
CHIKKA
CHIKKA
PONG
crash
Oof
TILT!

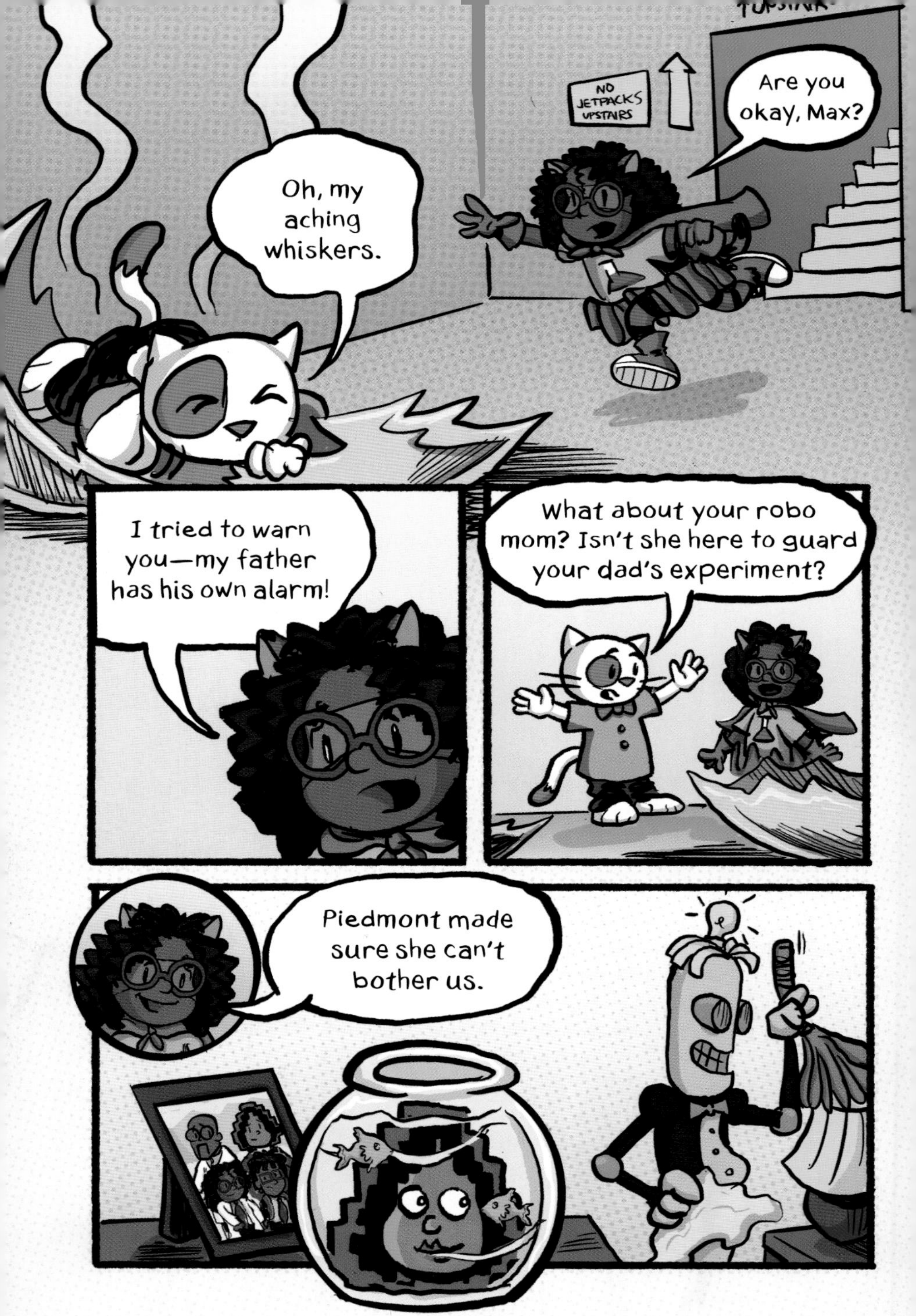
UPSTAIR
NO JETPACKS UPSTAIRS
Oh, my aching whiskers.
Are you okay, Max?
I tried to warn you—my father has his own alarm!
What about your robo mom? Isn't she here to guard your dad's experiment?
Piedmont made sure she can't bother us.

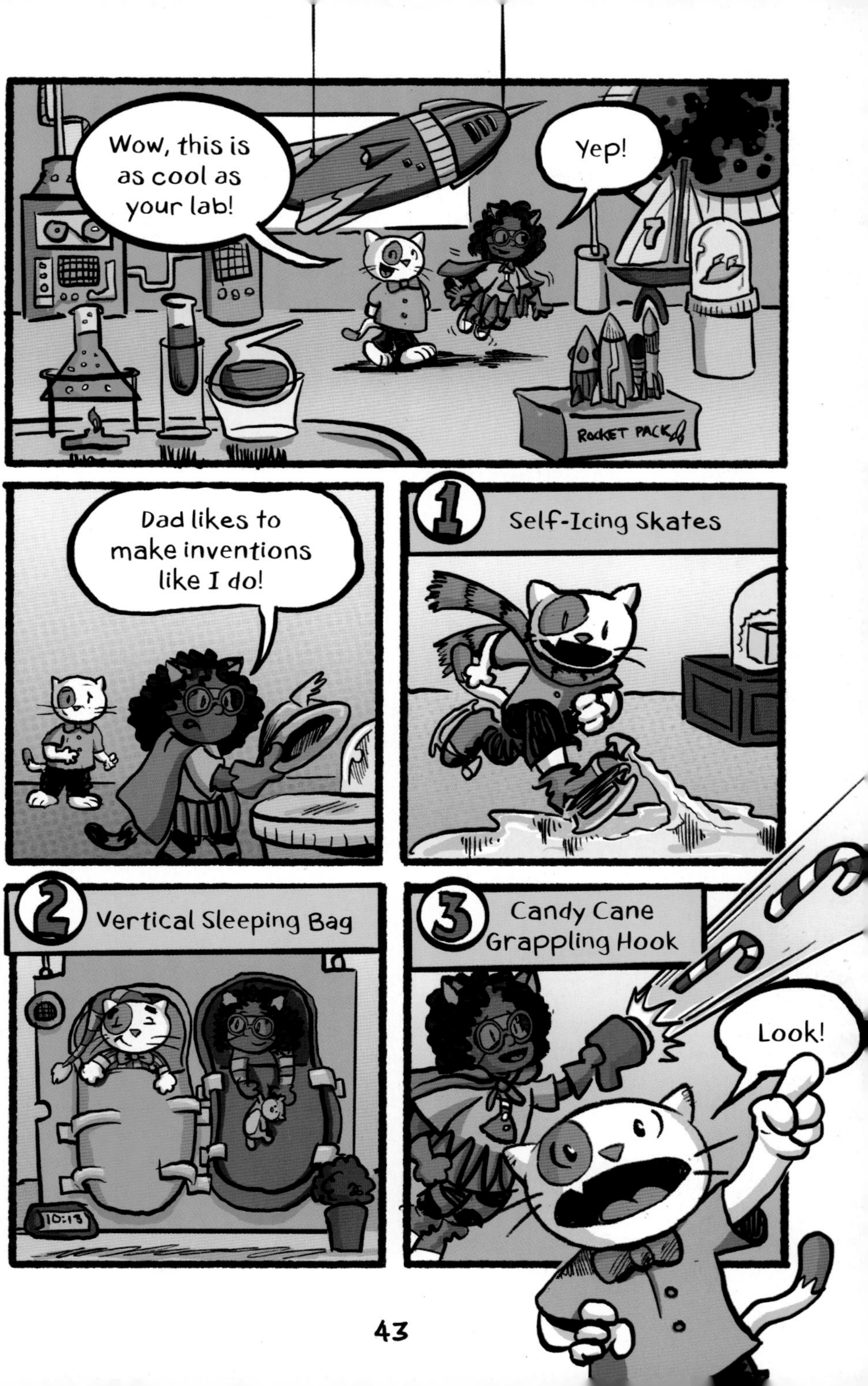
Wow, this is as cool as your lab!
Yep!
ROCKET PACK
Dad likes to make inventions like I do!
1 Self-Icing Skates
2 Vertical Sleeping Bag
10:13
3 Candy Cane Grappling Hook
Look!

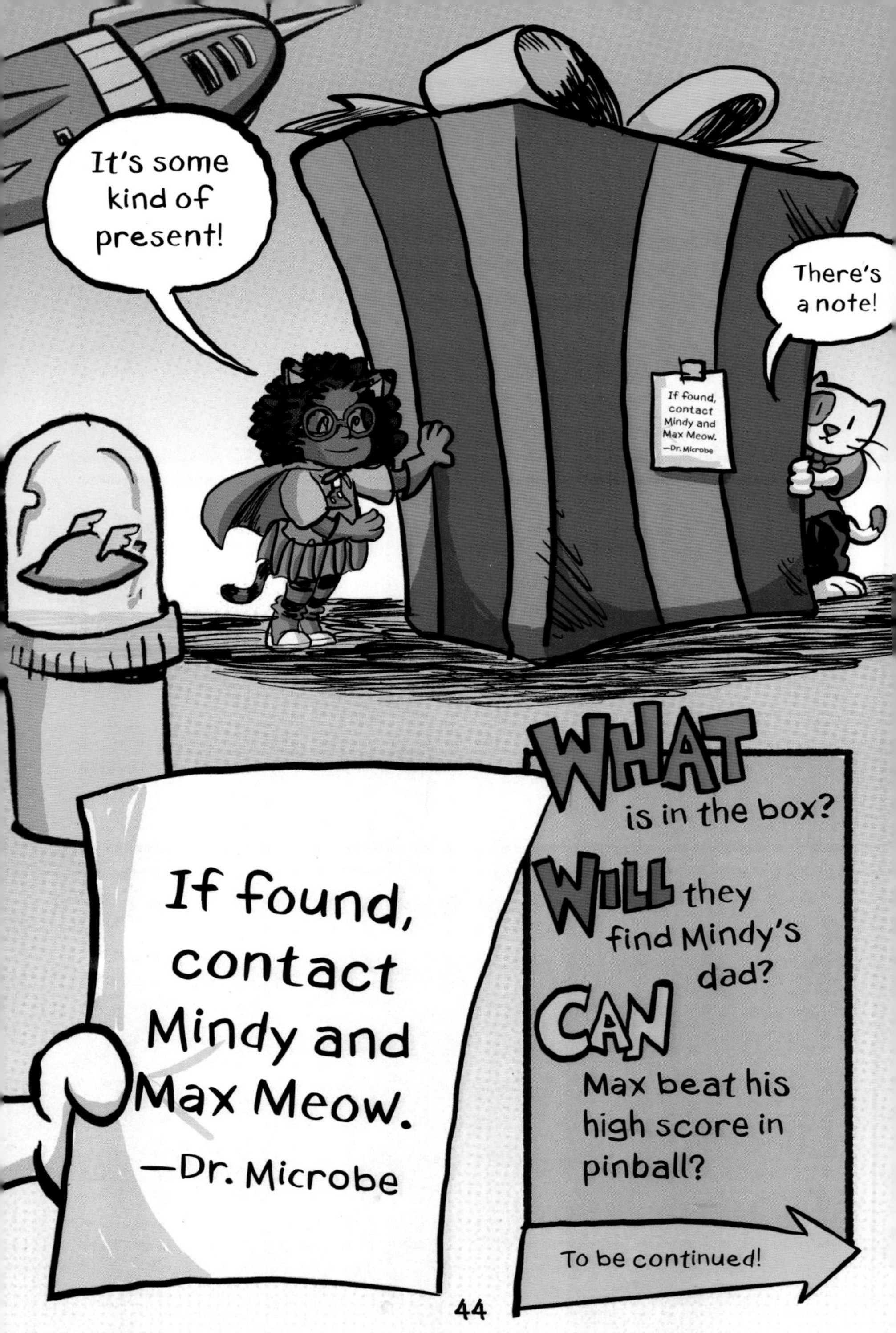
It's some kind of present!
There's a note!
If found, contact Mindy and Max Meow. —Dr. Microbe
If found, contact Mindy and Max Meow.
—Dr. Microbe
WHAT is in the box?
WILL they find Mindy's dad?
CAN Max beat his high score in pinball?
To be continued!

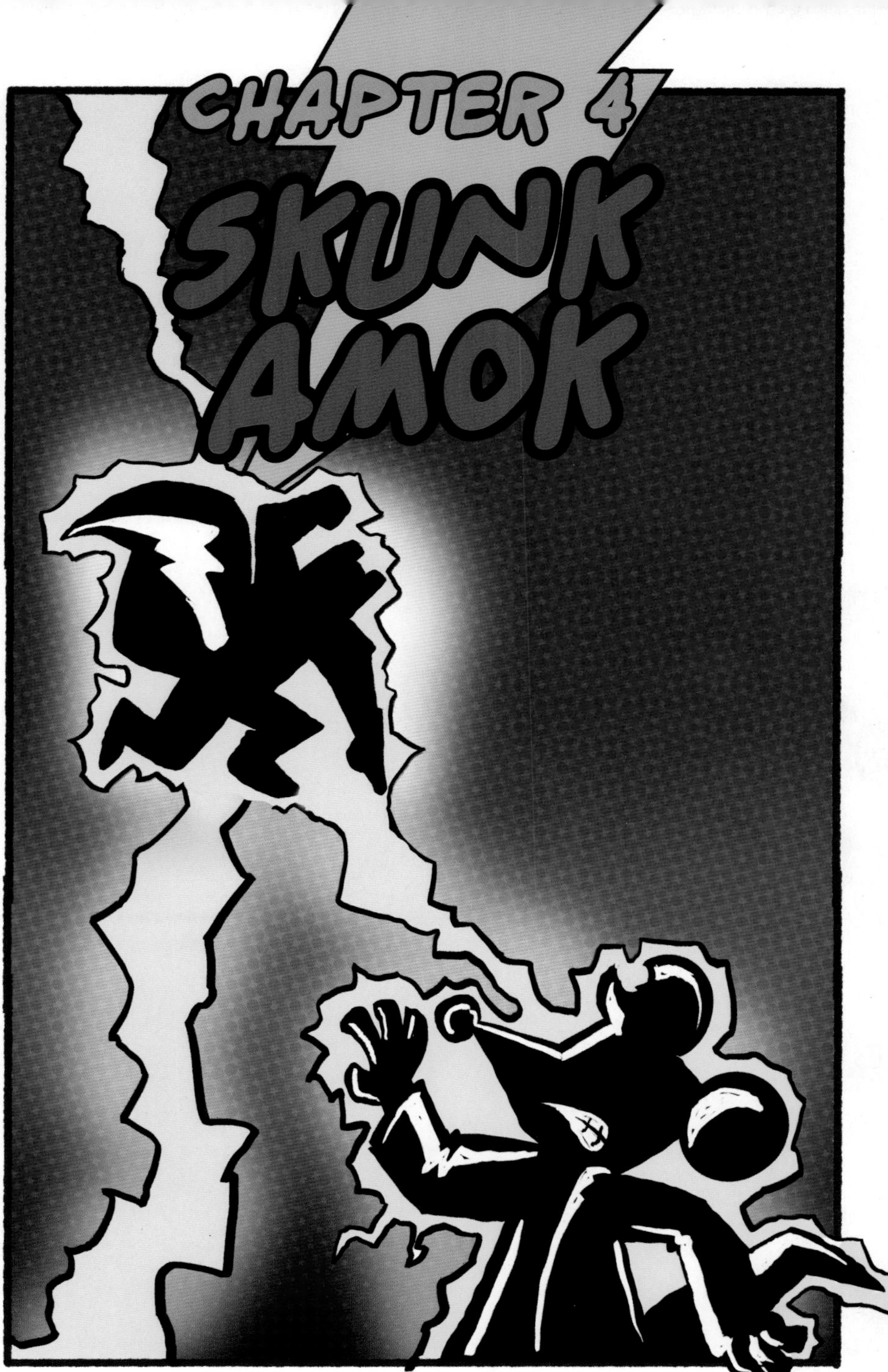
CHAPTER 4
SKUNK AMOK

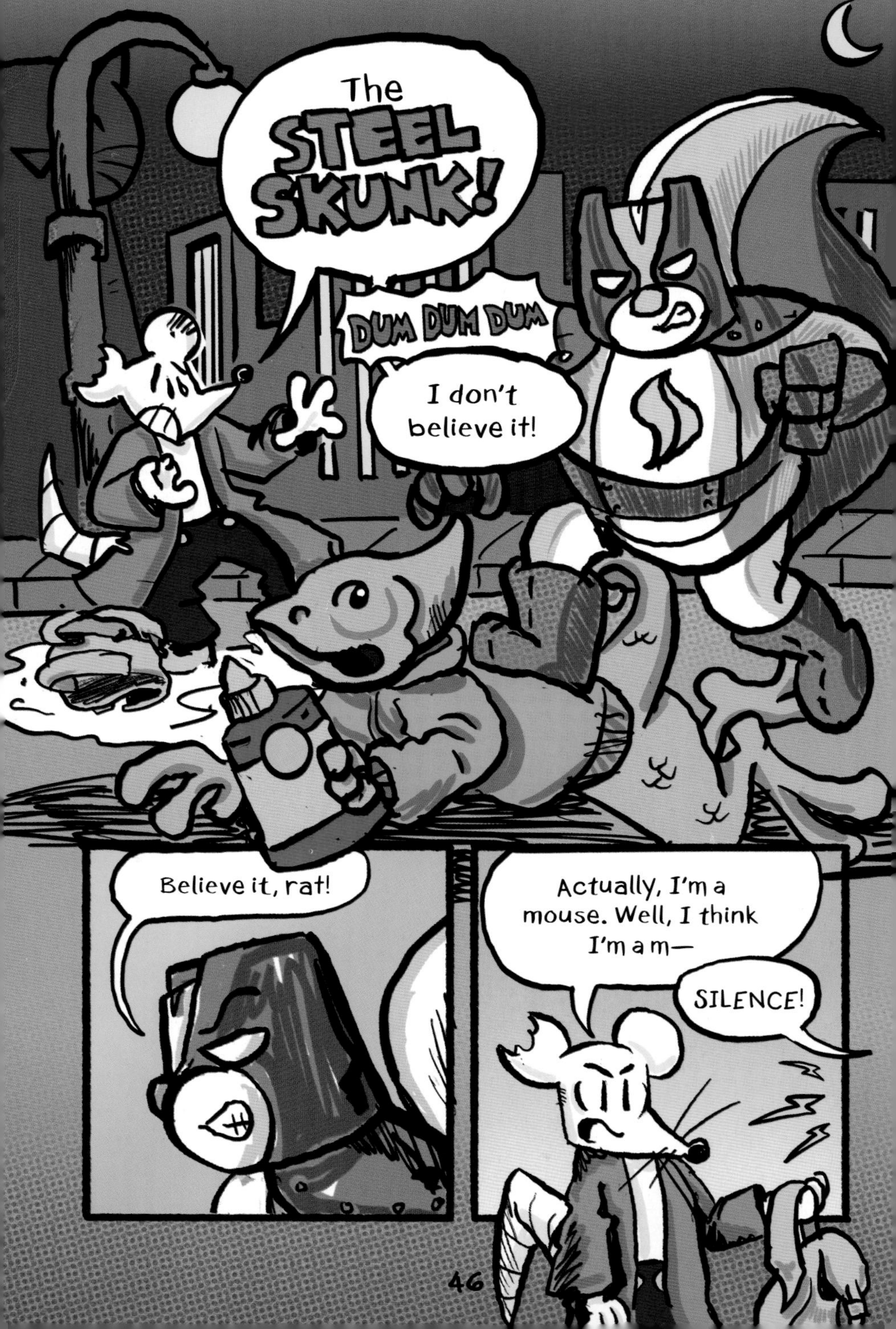
The
STEEL
SKUNK!
DUM DUM DUM
I don't believe it!
Believe it, rat!
Actually, I'm a mouse. Well, I think I'm a m—
SILENCE!

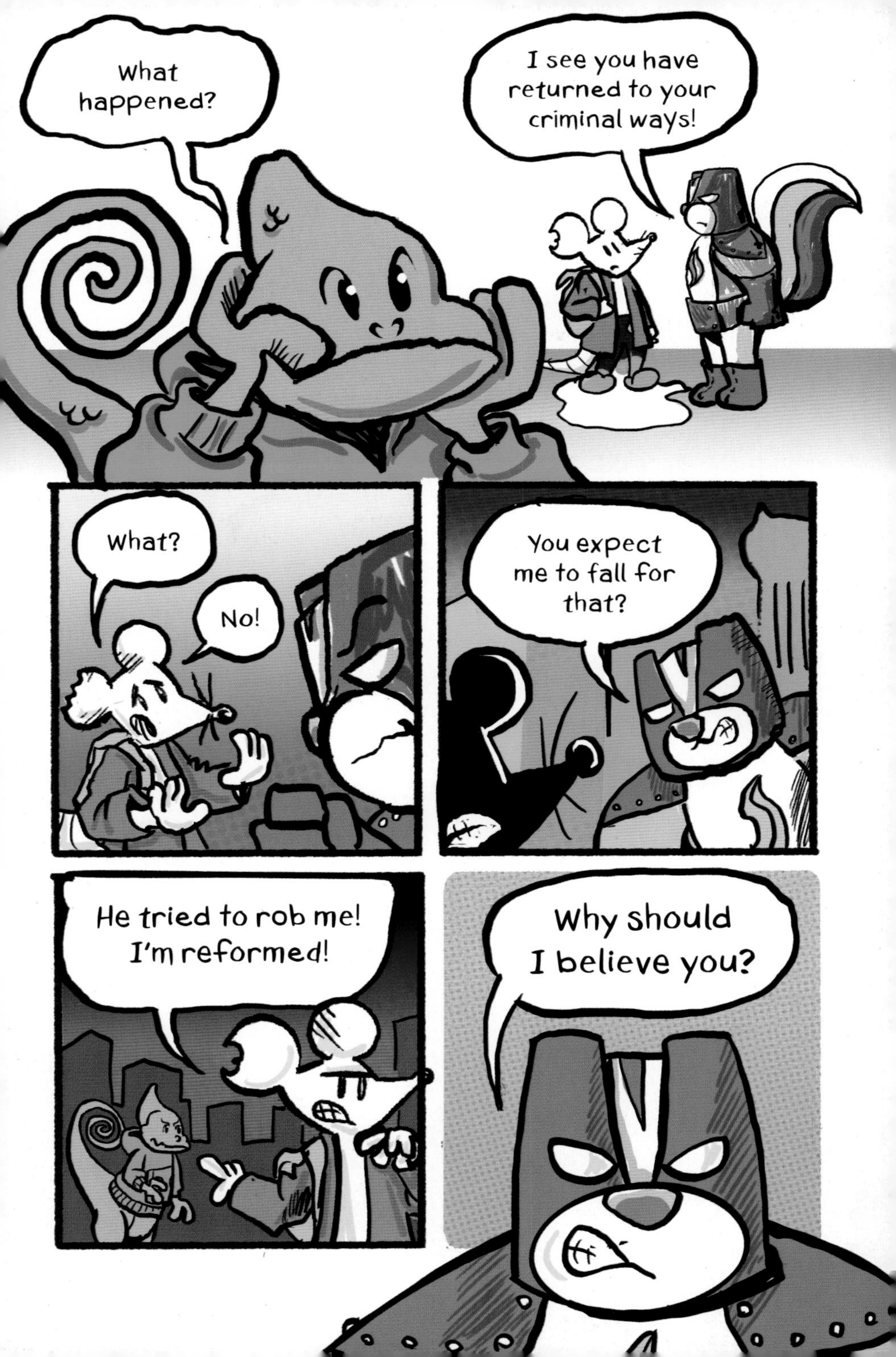
What happened?
I see you have returned to your criminal ways!
What?
No!
You expect me to fall for that?
He tried to rob me! I'm reformed!
Why should I believe you?

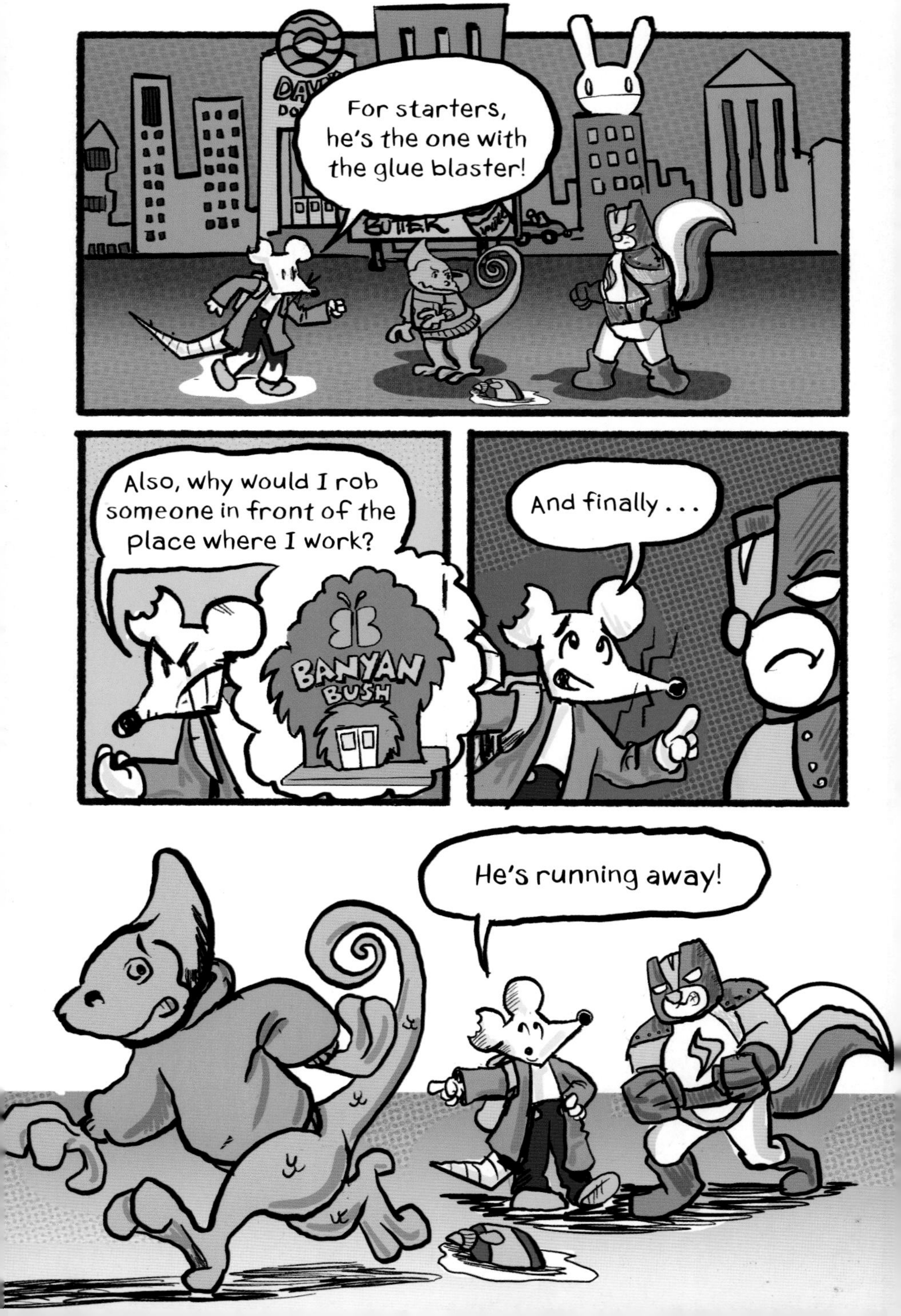
For starters, he's the one with the glue blaster!
Also, why would I rob someone in front of the place where I work?
BANYAN BUSH
And finally . . .
He's running away!

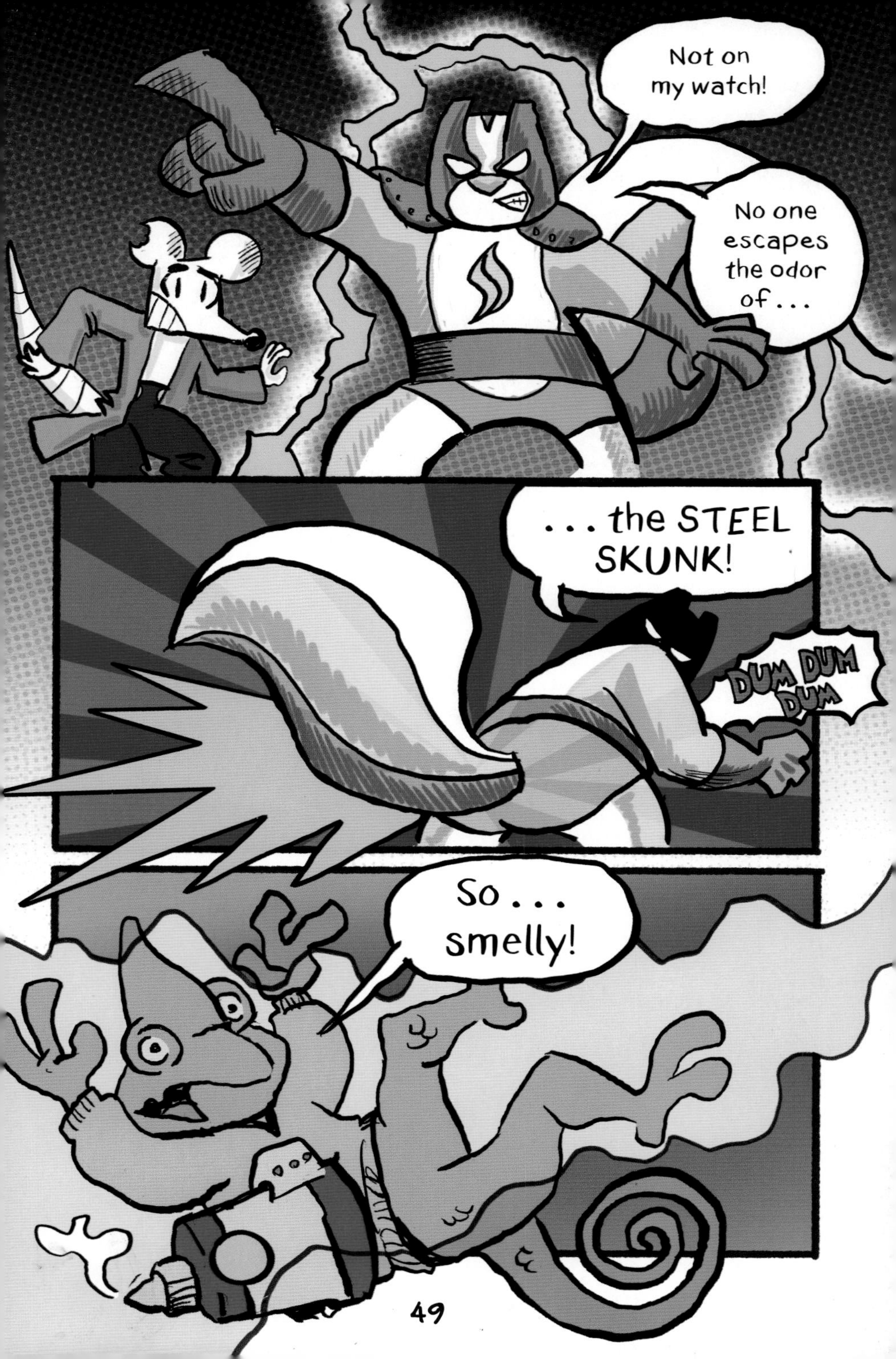
Not on my watch!
No one escapes the odor of . . .
. . . the STEEL SKUNK!
DUM DUM DUM
So . . . smelly!

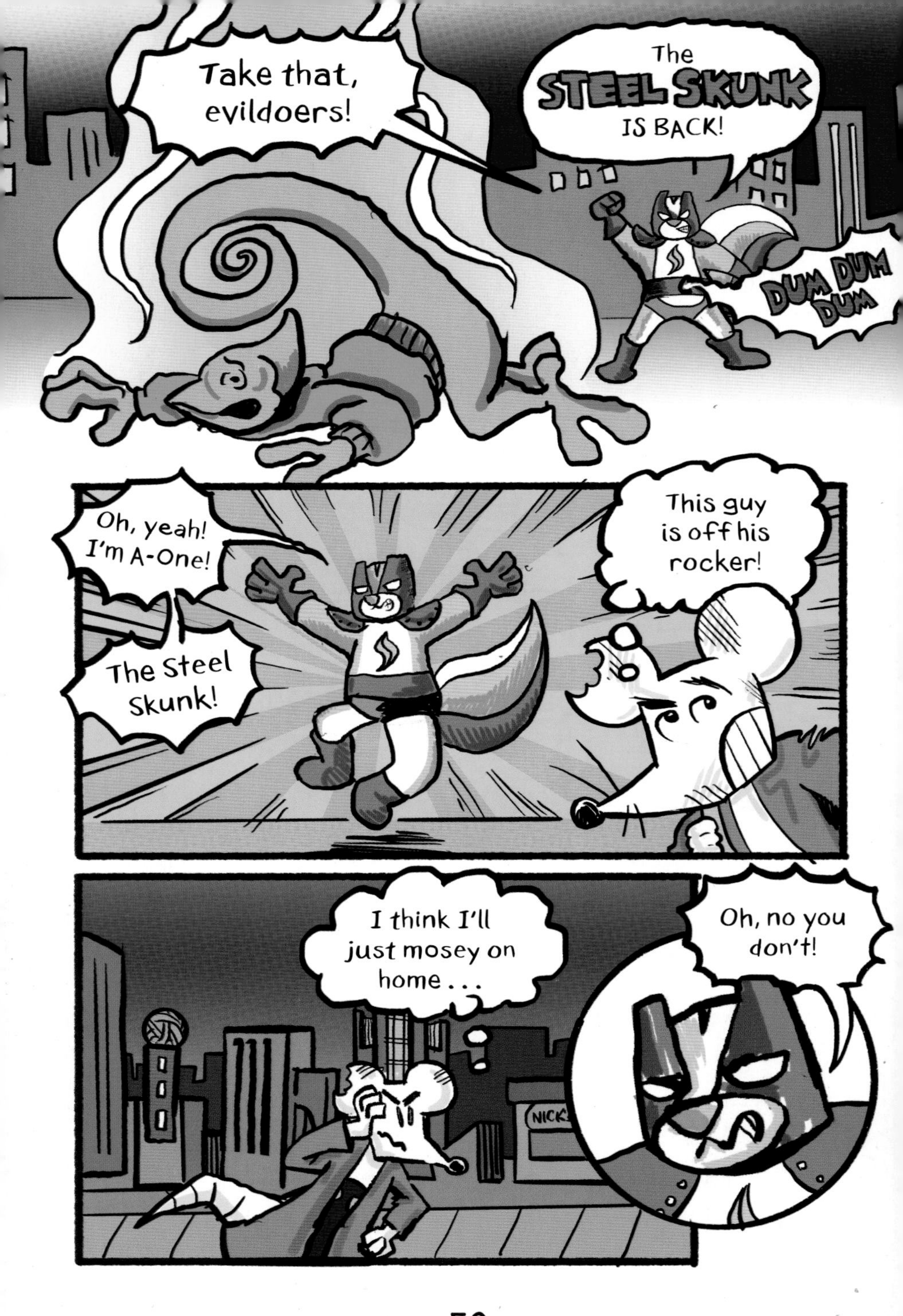
Take that, evildoers!
The STEEL SKUNK IS BACK!
DUM DUM DUM
Oh, yeah! I'm A-One!
The Steel Skunk!
This guy is off his rocker!
I think I'll just mosey on home . . .
Oh, no you don't!
NICK'S

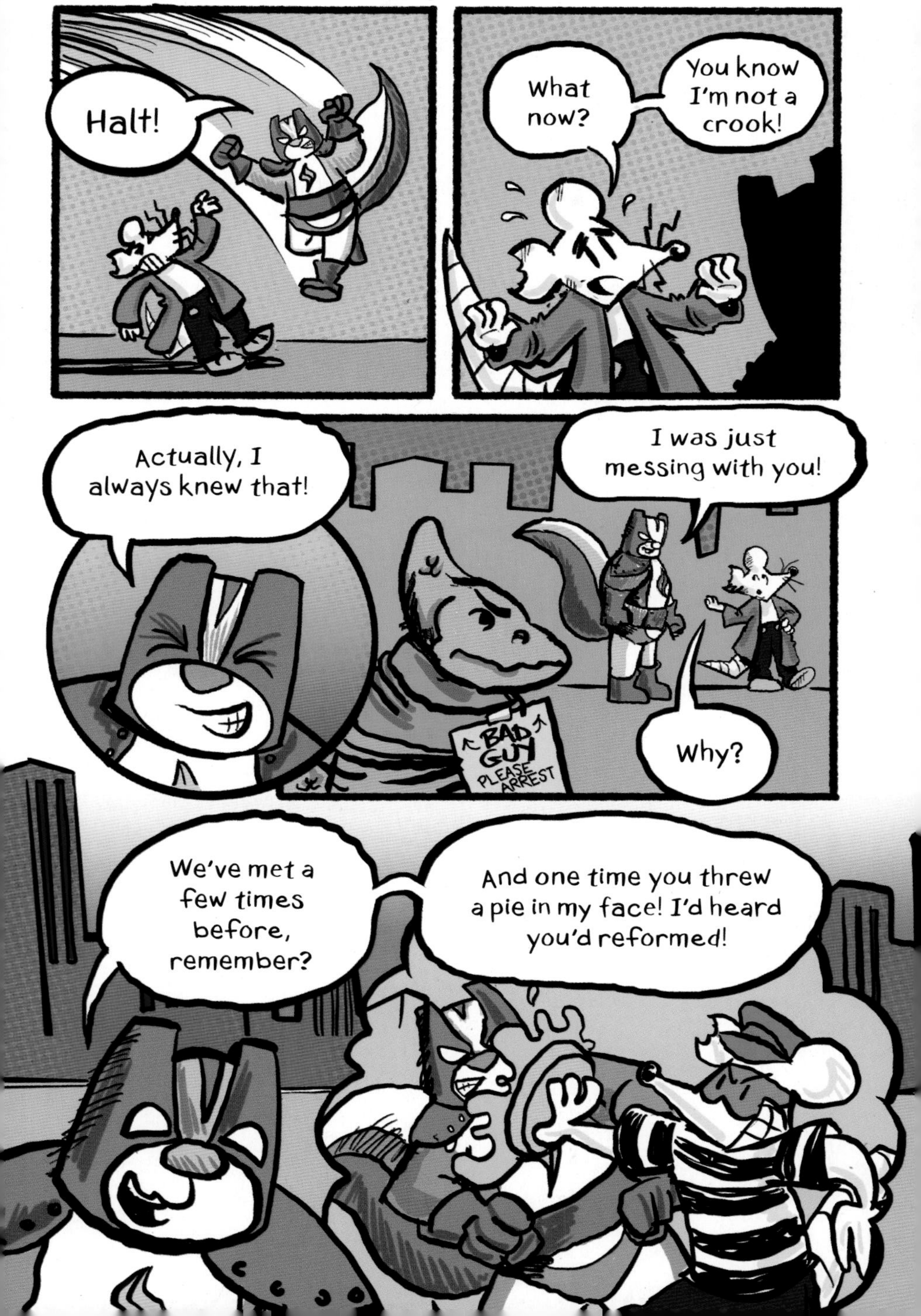
Halt!
What now?
You know I'm not a crook!
Actually, I always knew that!
I was just messing with you!
BAD GUY PLEASE ARREST
Why?
We've met a few times before, remember?
And one time you threw a pie in my face! I'd heard you'd reformed!

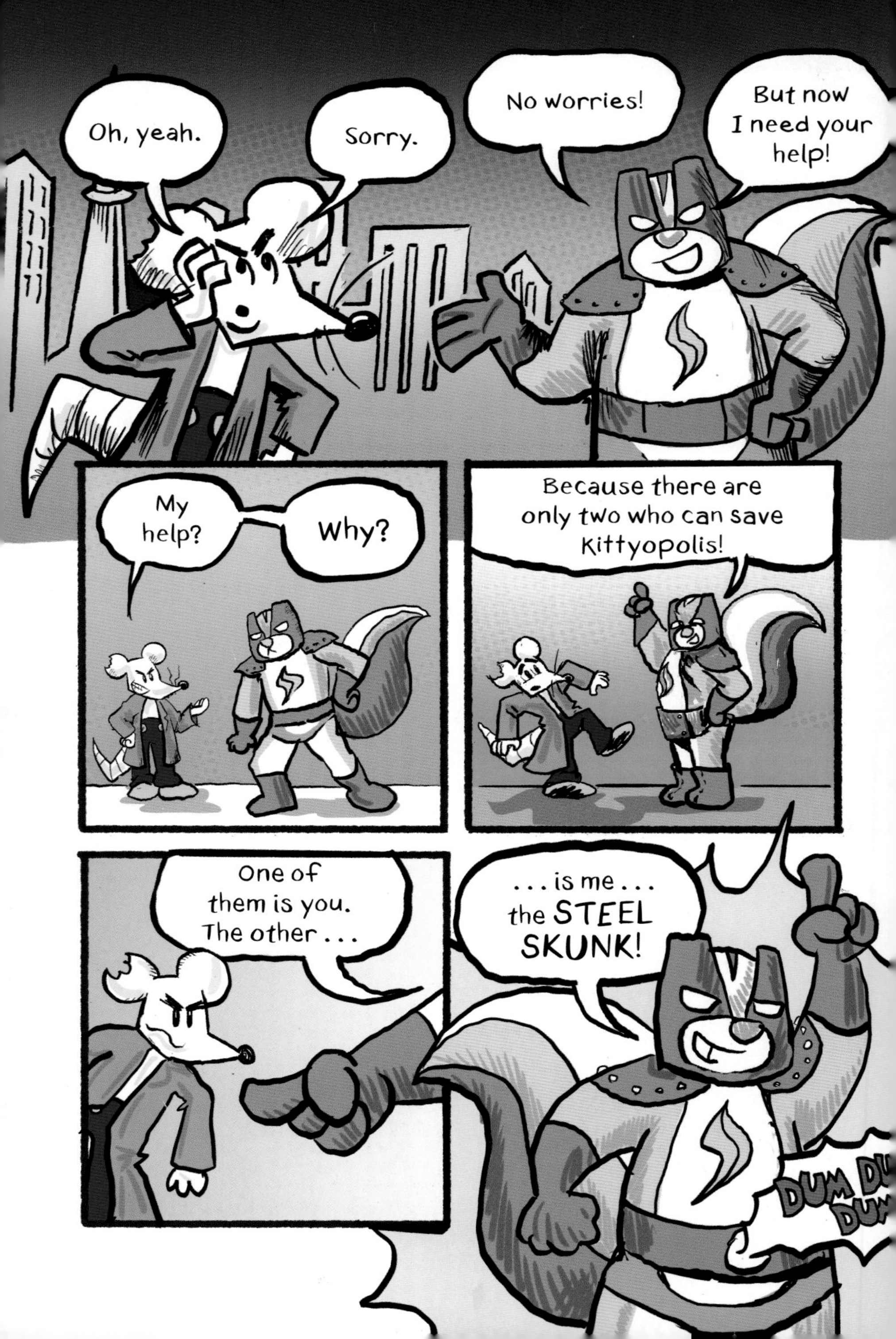
Oh, yeah.
Sorry.
No worries!
But now I need your help!
My help?
Why?
Because there are only two who can save Kittyopolis!
One of them is you. The other . . .
. . . is me . . . the STEEL SKUNK!
DUM

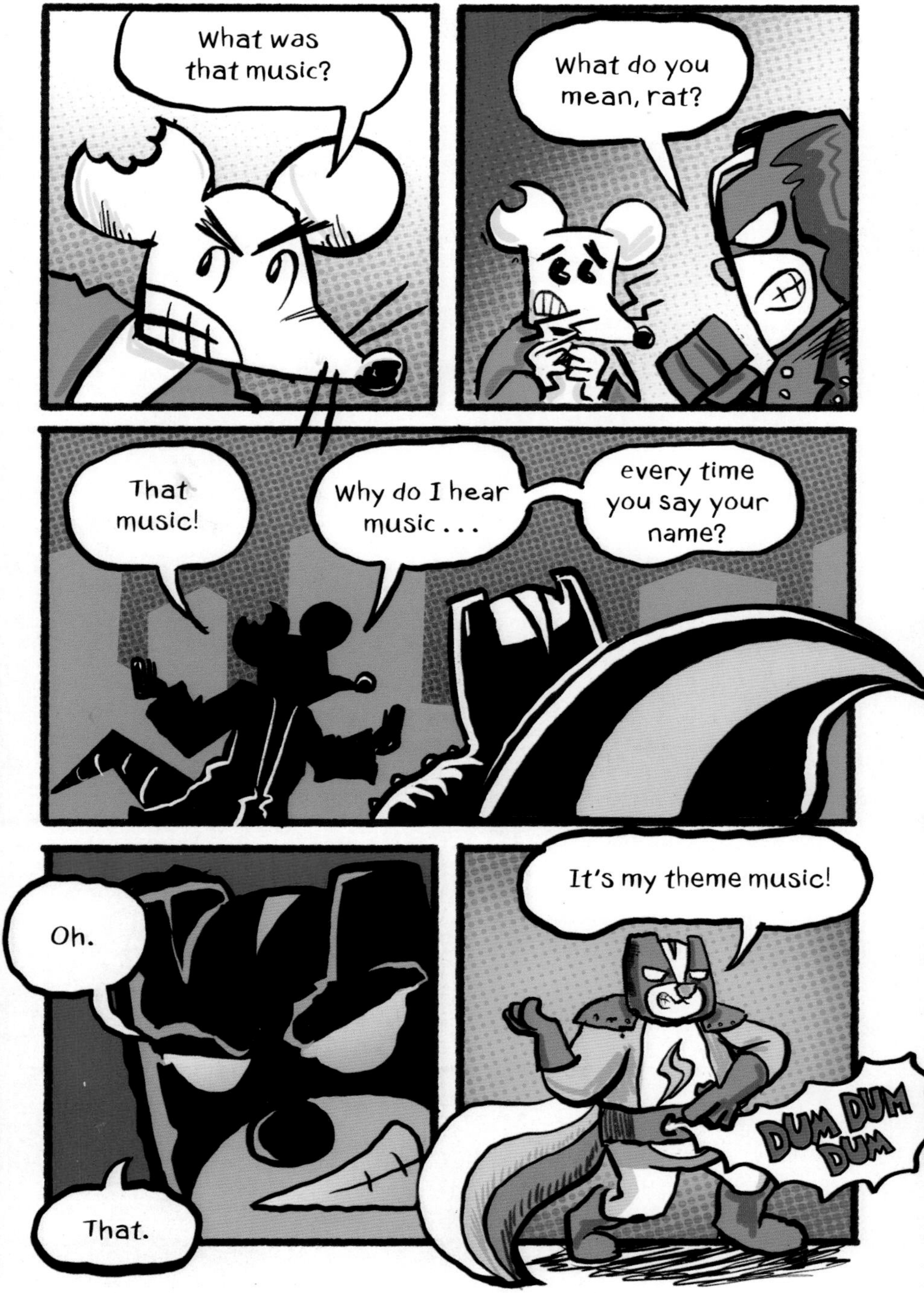
What was that music?
What do you mean, rat?
That music!
Why do I hear music . . .
every time you say your name?
Oh.
That.
It's my theme music!
DUM DUM DUM

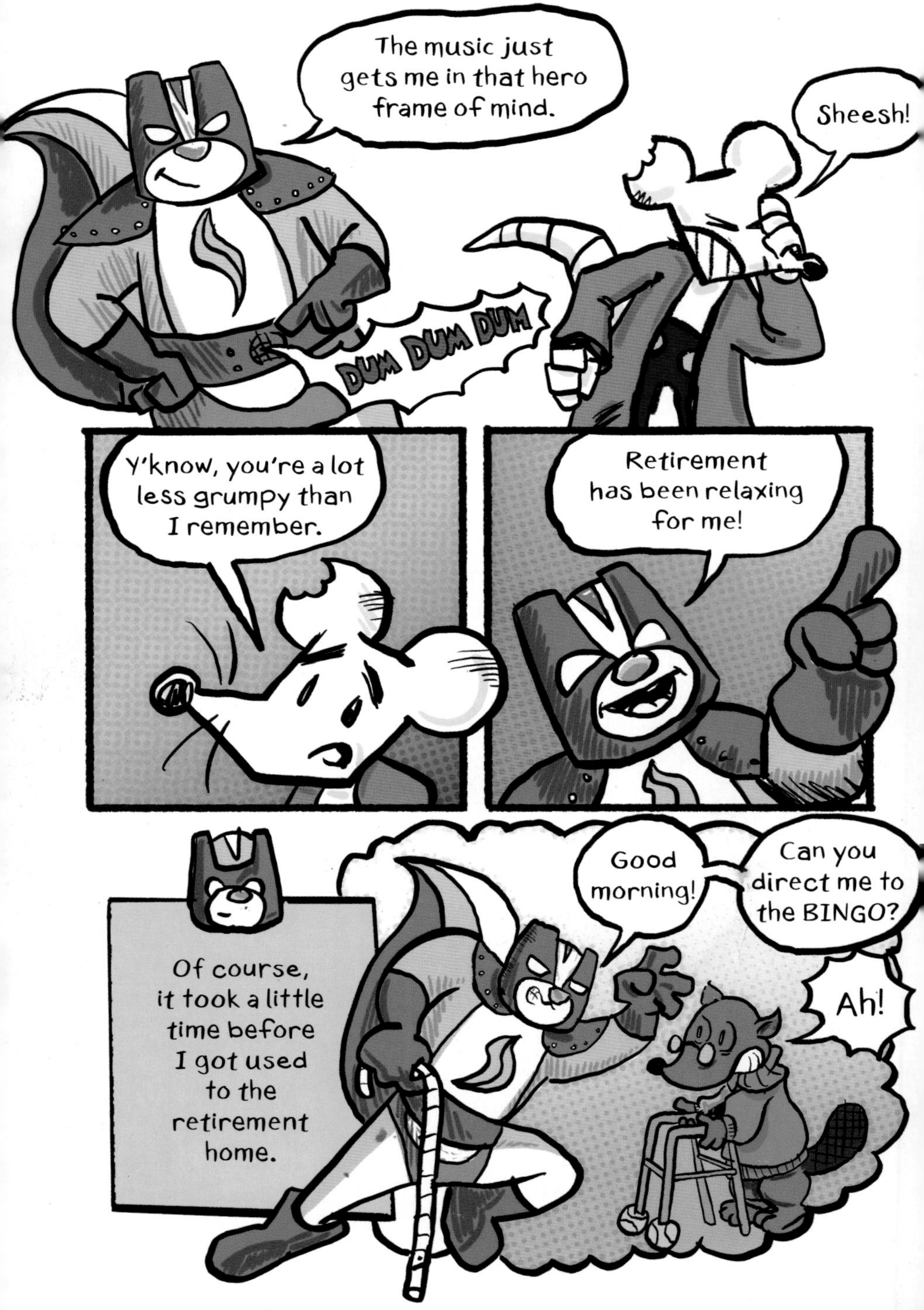
The music just gets me in that hero frame of mind.
Sheesh!
DUM DUM DUM
Y'know, you're a lot less grumpy than I remember.
Retirement has been relaxing for me!
Of course, it took a little time before I got used to the retirement home.
Good morning!
Can you direct me to the BINGO?
Ah!

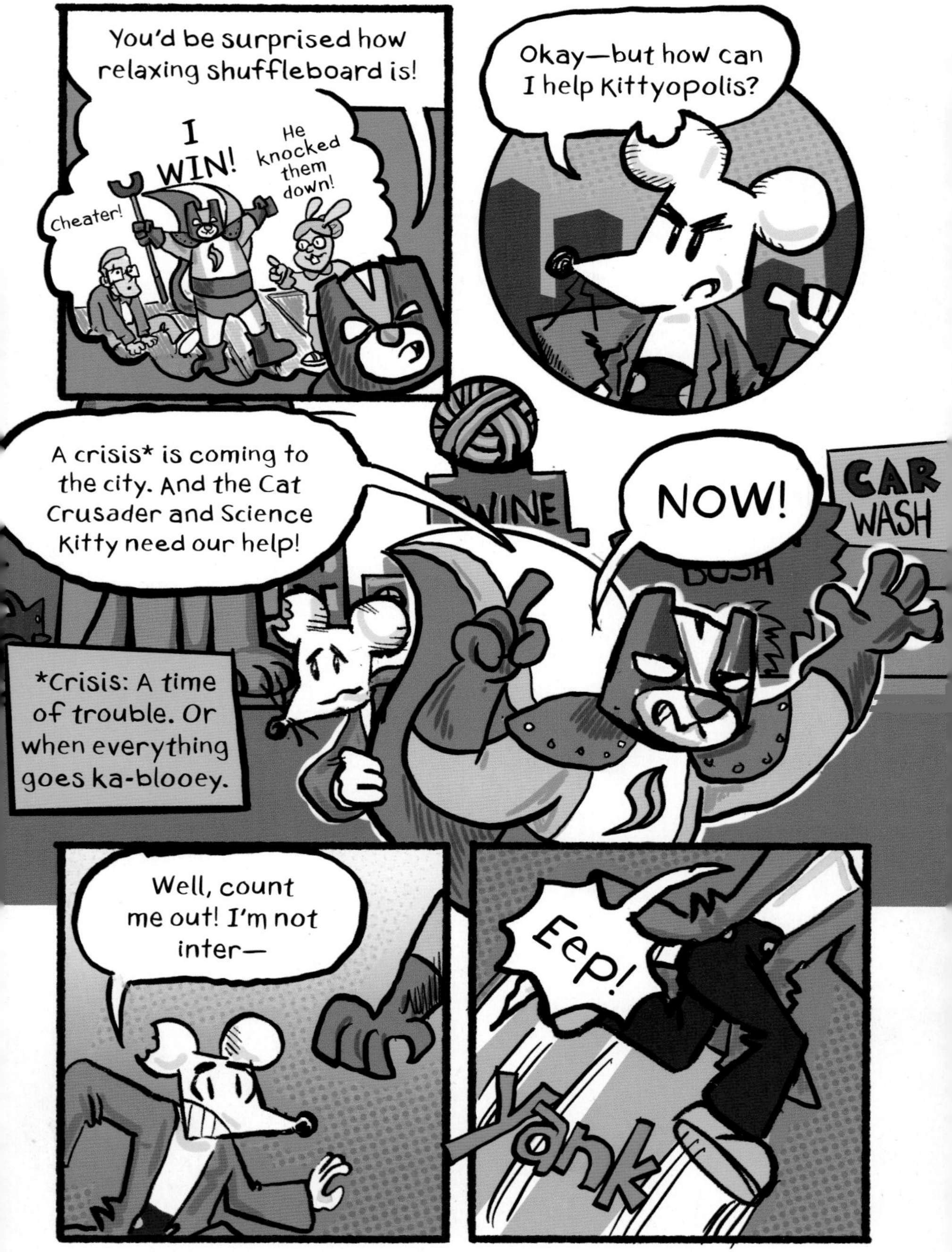
You'd be surprised how relaxing shuffleboard is!
I WIN!
He knocked them down!
Cheater!
Okay—but how can I help Kittyopolis?
A crisis* is coming to the city. And the Cat Crusader and Science Kitty need our help!
TWINE
NOW!
CAR WASH
*Crisis: A time of trouble. Or when everything goes ka-blooey.
Well, count me out! I'm not inter—
Eep!
Yank

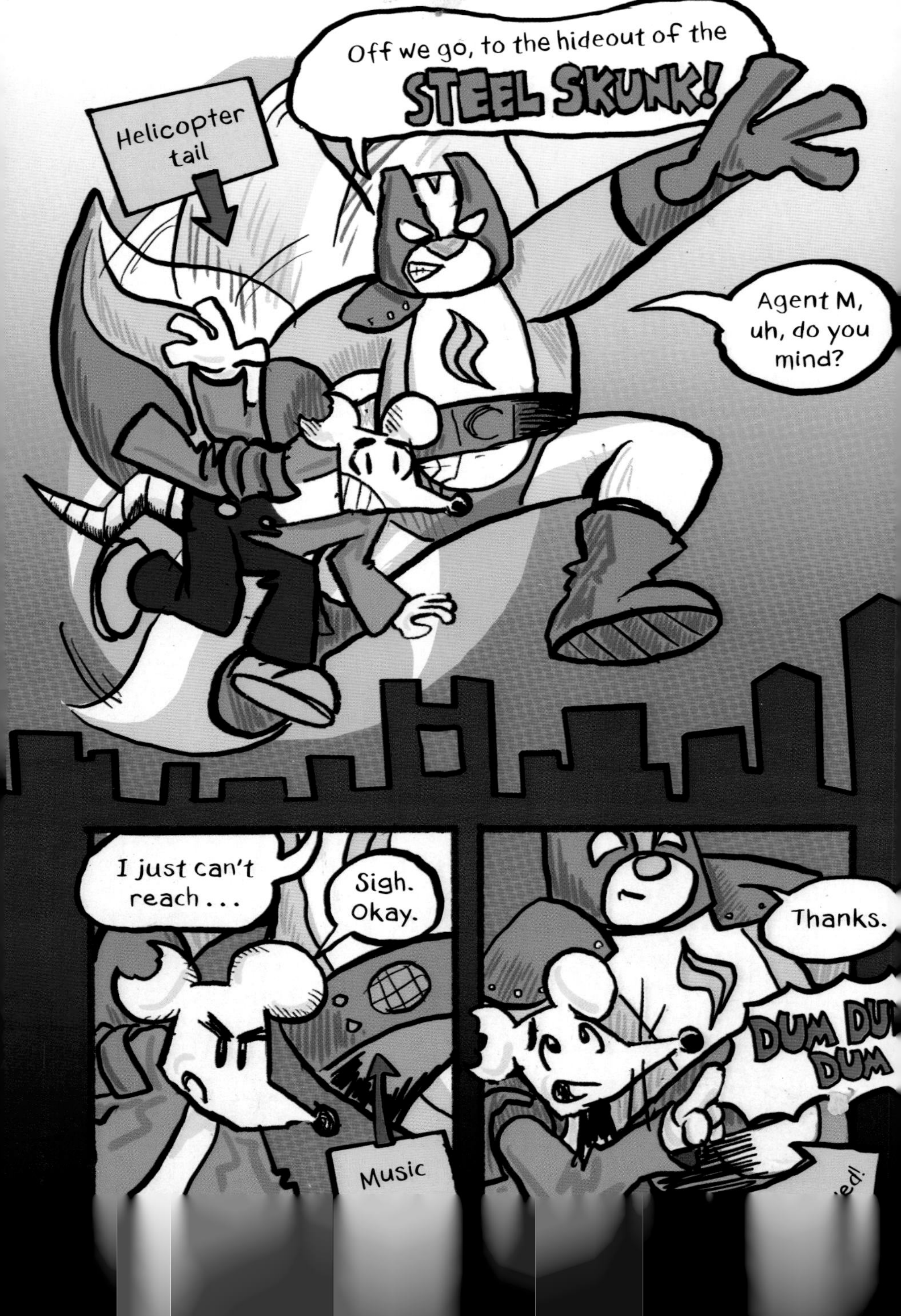
Off we go, to the hideout of the
STEEL SKUNK!
Helicopter tail
Agent M, uh, do you mind?
I just can't reach . . .
Sigh. Okay.
Music
Thanks.
DUM
DUM

CHAPTER 5

IS THAT THE KITTYOPOLIS CHOO CHOO?

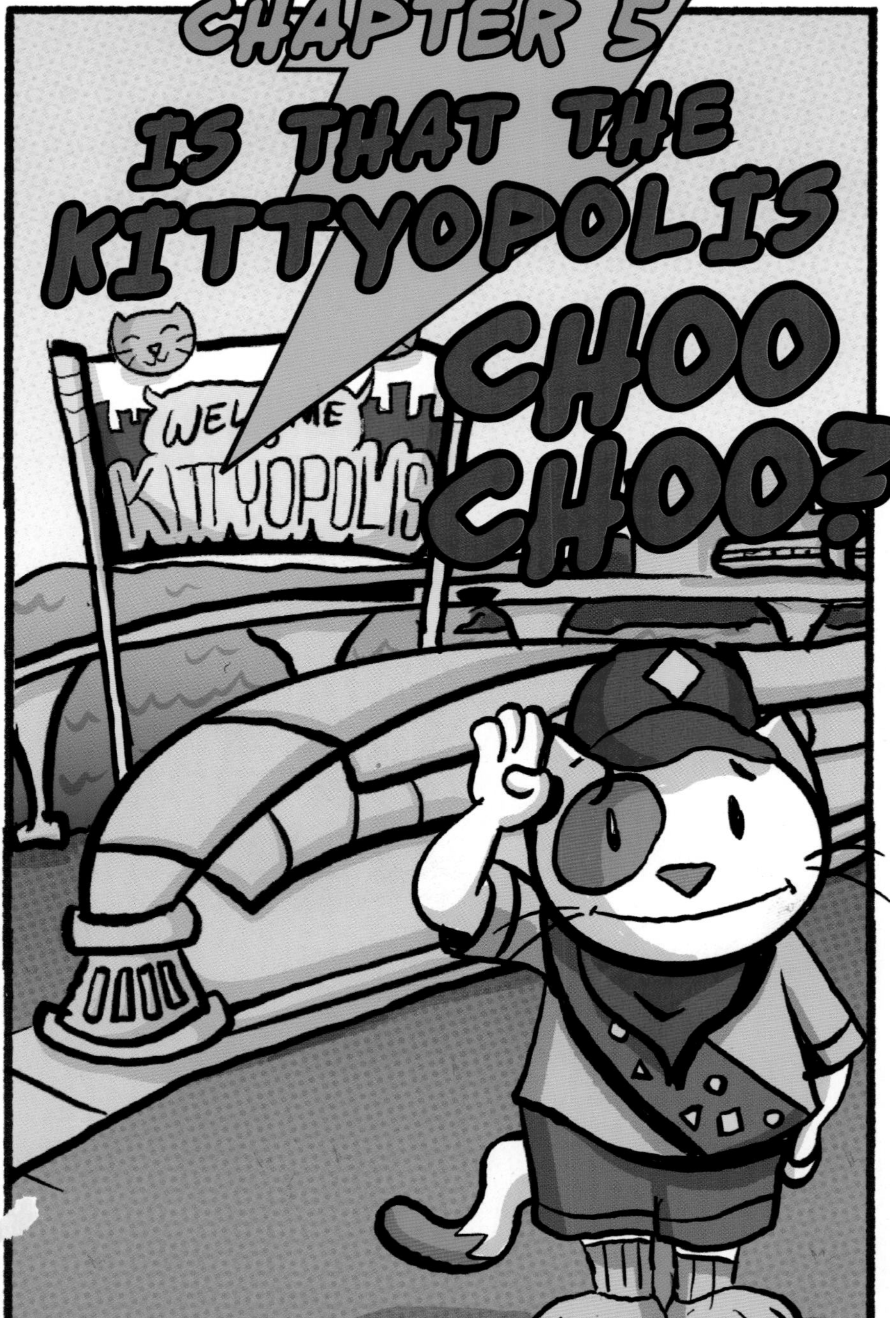
WEL ME
KITTYOPOLIS

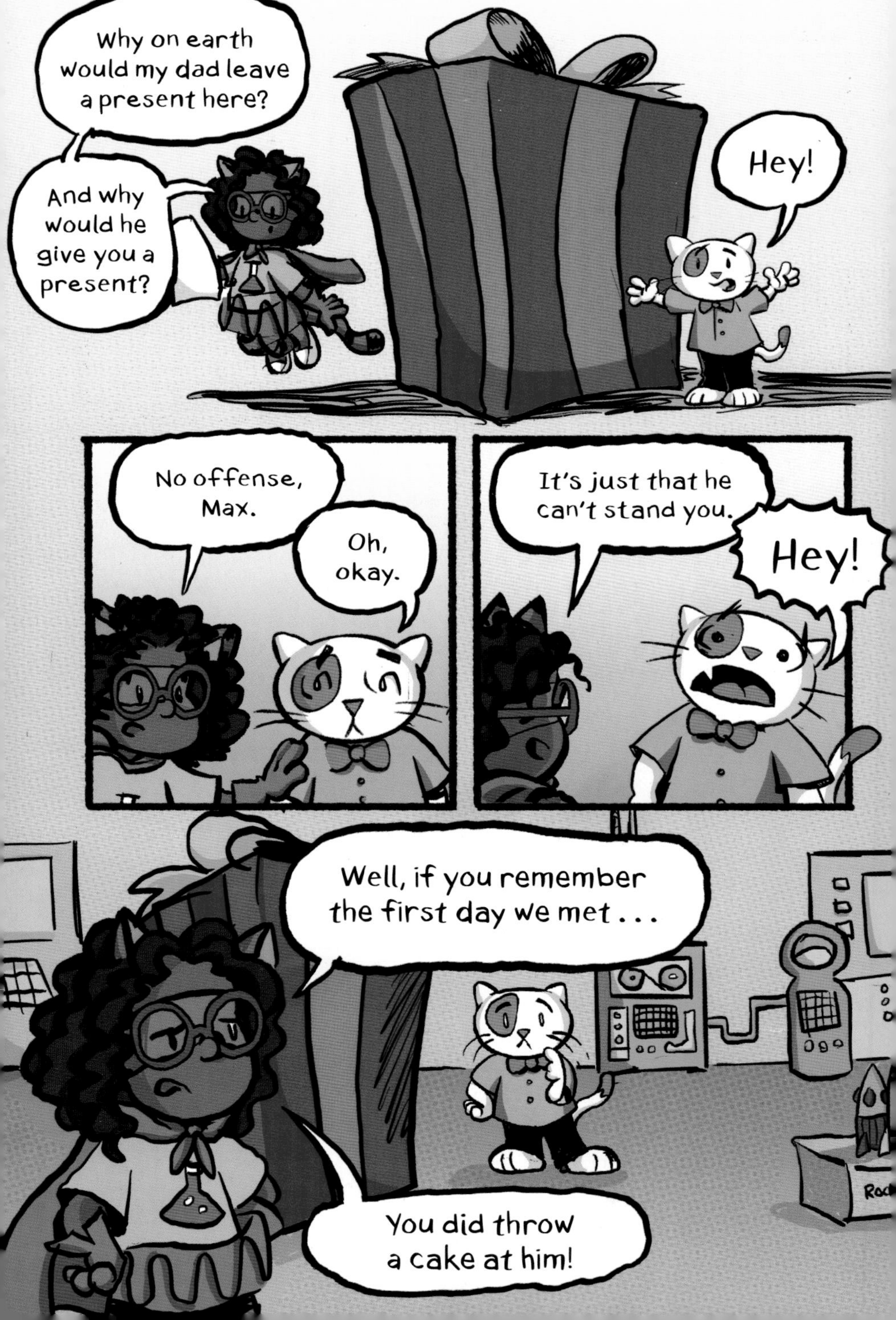
Why on earth would my dad leave a present here?
And why would he give you a present?
Hey!
No offense, Max.
Oh, okay.
It's just that he can't stand you.
Hey!
Well, if you remember the first day we met . . .
You did throw a cake at him!

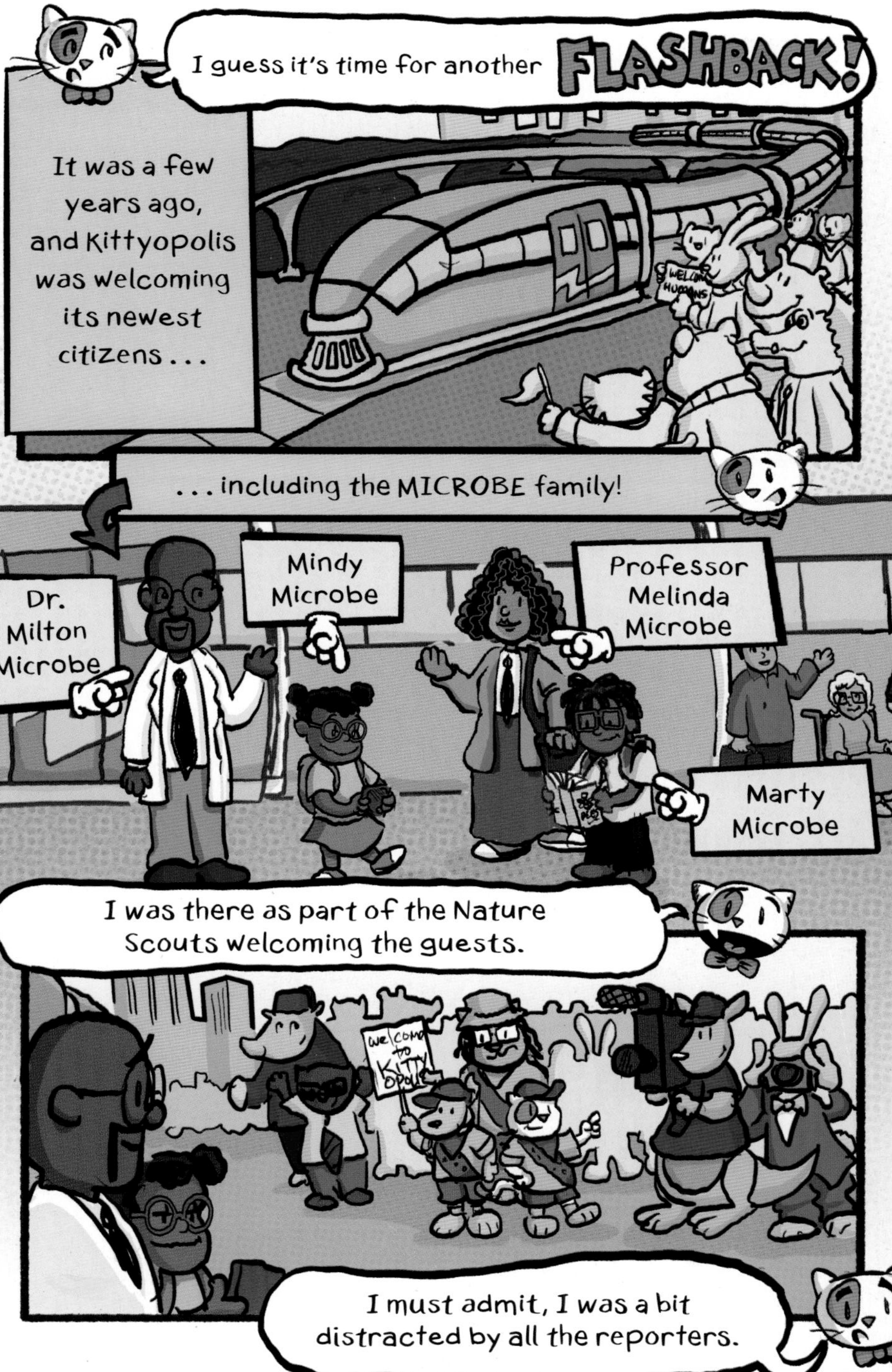

I guess it's time for another FLASHBACK!
It was a few years ago, and Kittyopolis was welcoming its newest citizens . . .
. . . including the MICROBE family!
Dr. Milton Microbe
Mindy Microbe
Professor Melinda Microbe
Marty Microbe
I was there as part of the Nature Scouts welcoming the guests.
I must admit, I was a bit distracted by all the reporters.

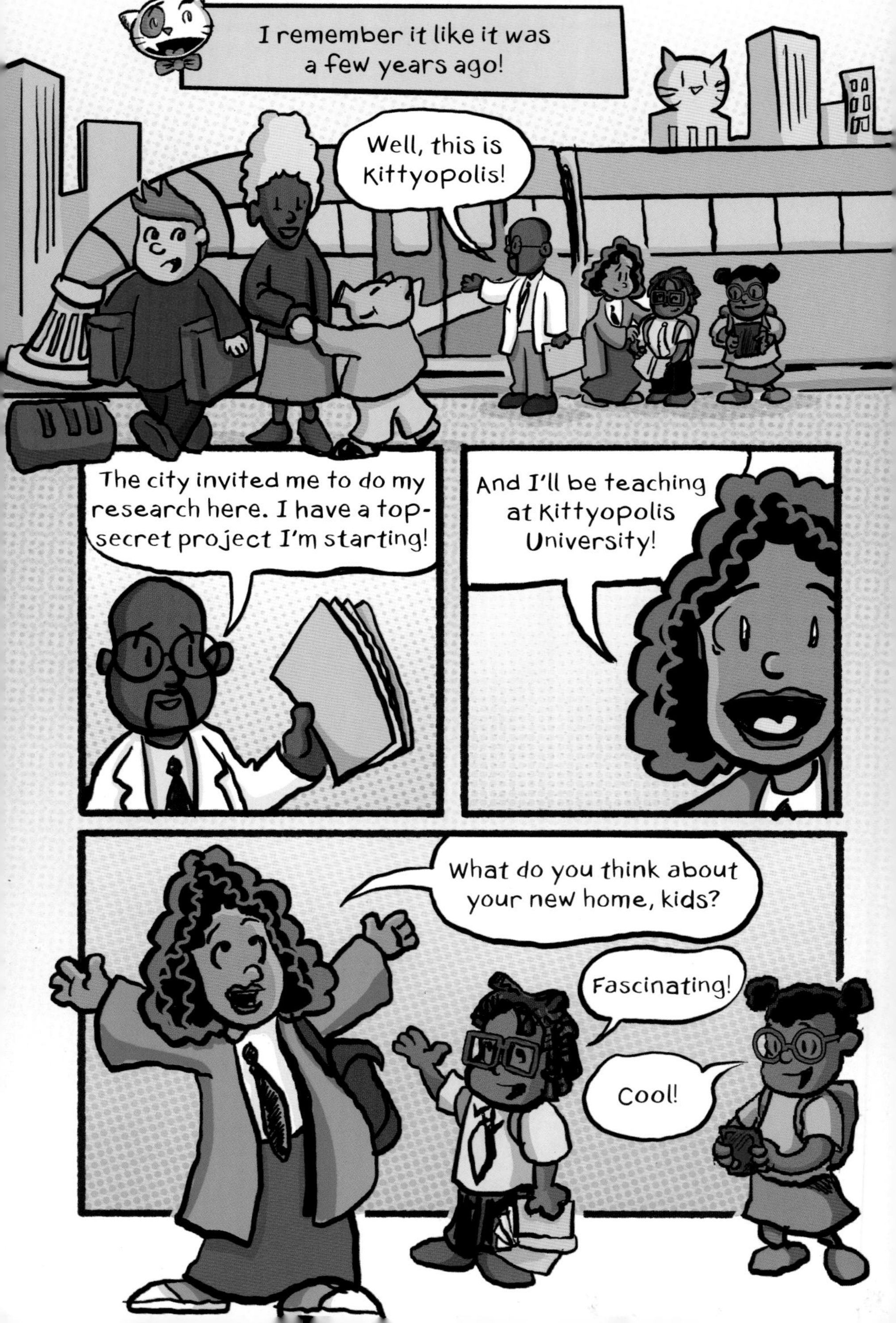
I remember it like it was a few years ago!
Well, this is Kittyopolis!
The city invited me to do my research here. I have a top-secret project I'm starting!
And I'll be teaching at Kittyopolis University!
What do you think about your new home, kids?
Fascinating!
Cool!

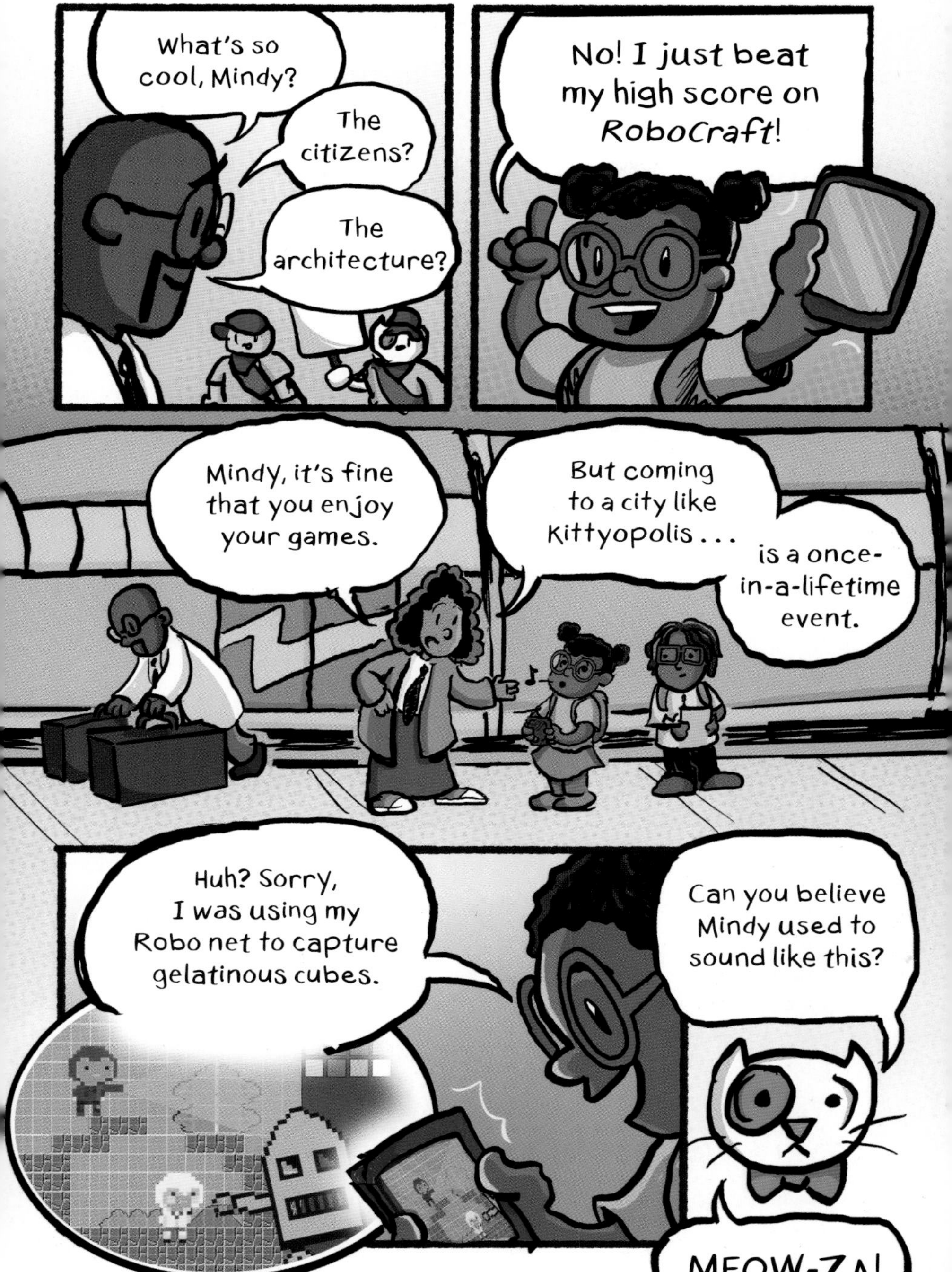
What's so cool, Mindy?
The citizens?
The architecture?
No! I just beat my high score on *RoboCraft*!
Mindy, it's fine that you enjoy your games.
But coming to a city like Kittyopolis . . .
is a once-in-a-lifetime event.
Huh? Sorry, I was using my Robo net to capture gelatinous cubes.
Can you believe Mindy used to sound like this?
MEOW-ZA!

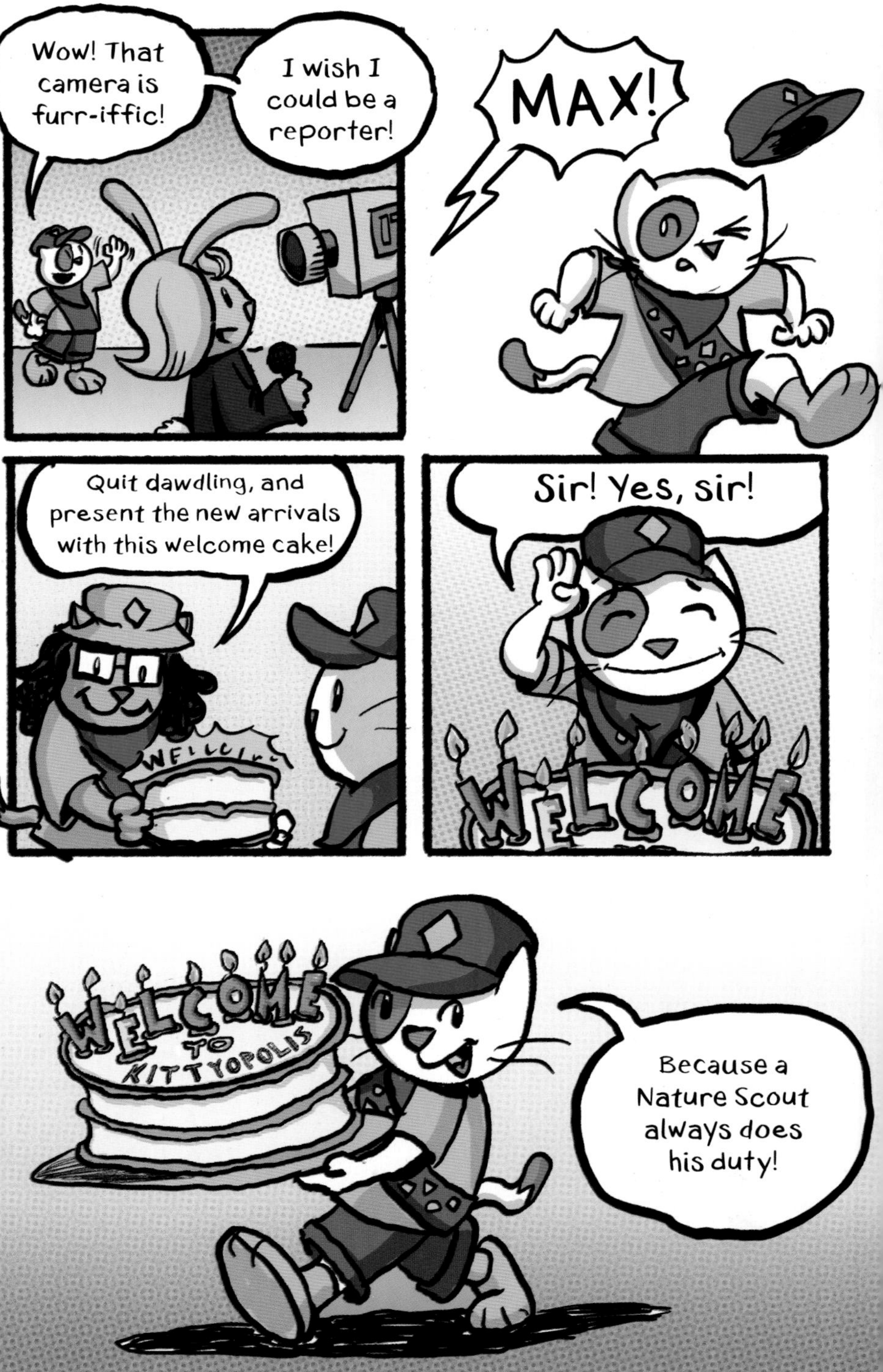
Wow! That camera is furr-iffic!
I wish I could be a reporter!
MAX!
Quit dawdling, and present the new arrivals with this welcome cake!
Sir! Yes, sir!
WELCOME
WELCOME TO KITTYOPOLIS
Because a Nature Scout always does his duty!

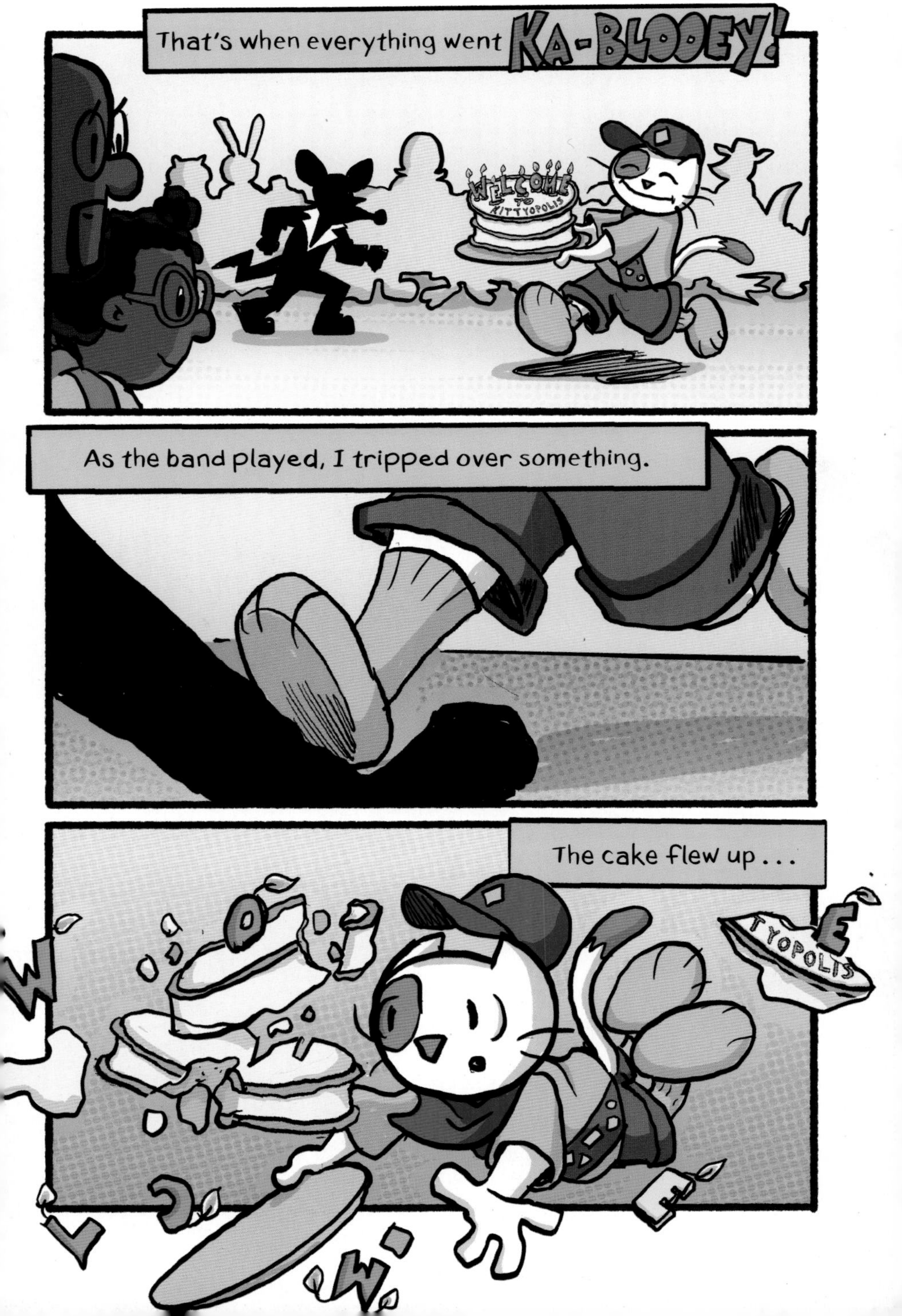
That's when everything went KA-BLOOEY!
WELCOME TO KITTYOPOLIS
As the band played, I tripped over something.
The cake flew up . . .
TYOPOLIS

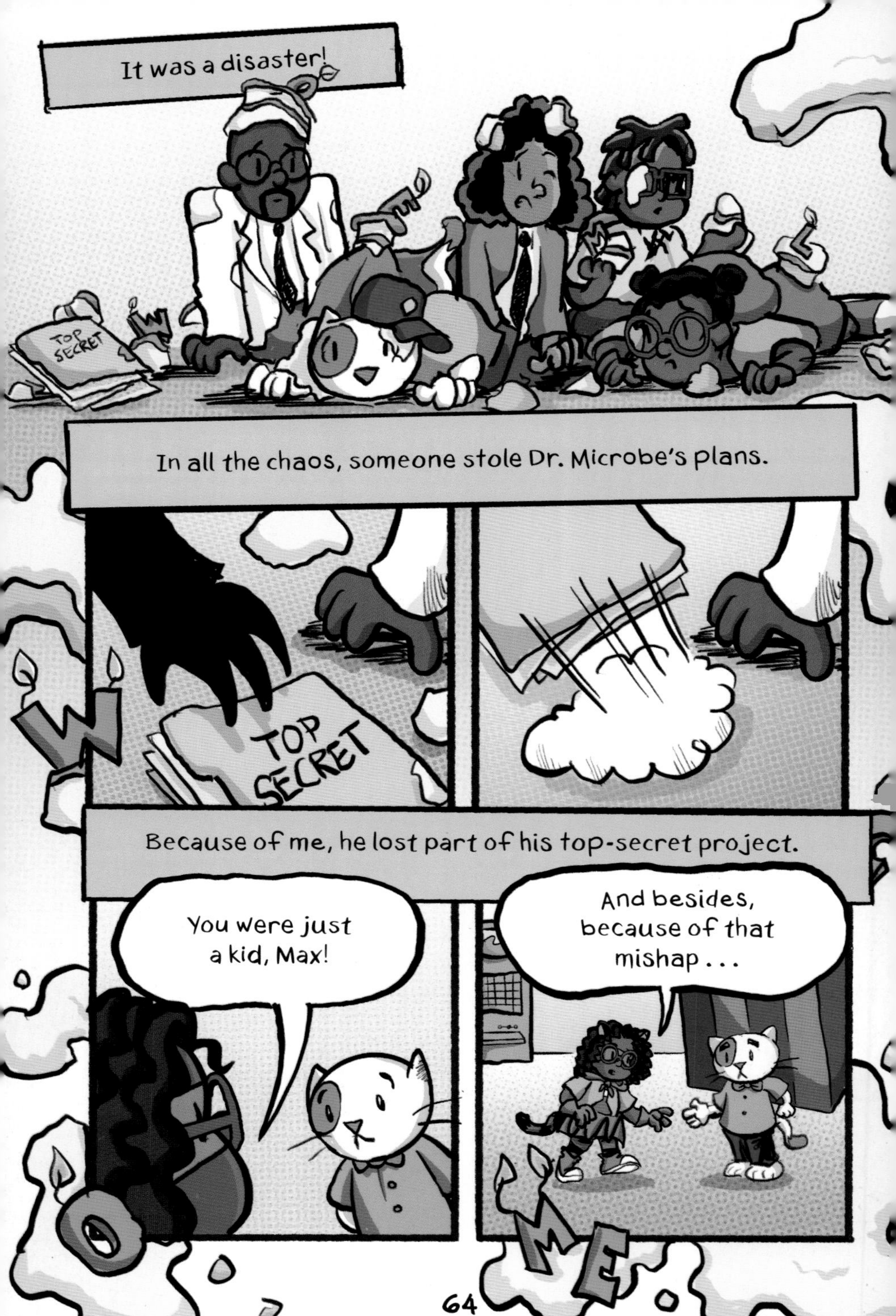
It was a disaster!
TOP SECRET
In all the chaos, someone stole Dr. Microbe's plans.
TOP SECRET
Because of me, he lost part of his top-secret project.
You were just a kid, Max!
And besides, because of that mishap . . .

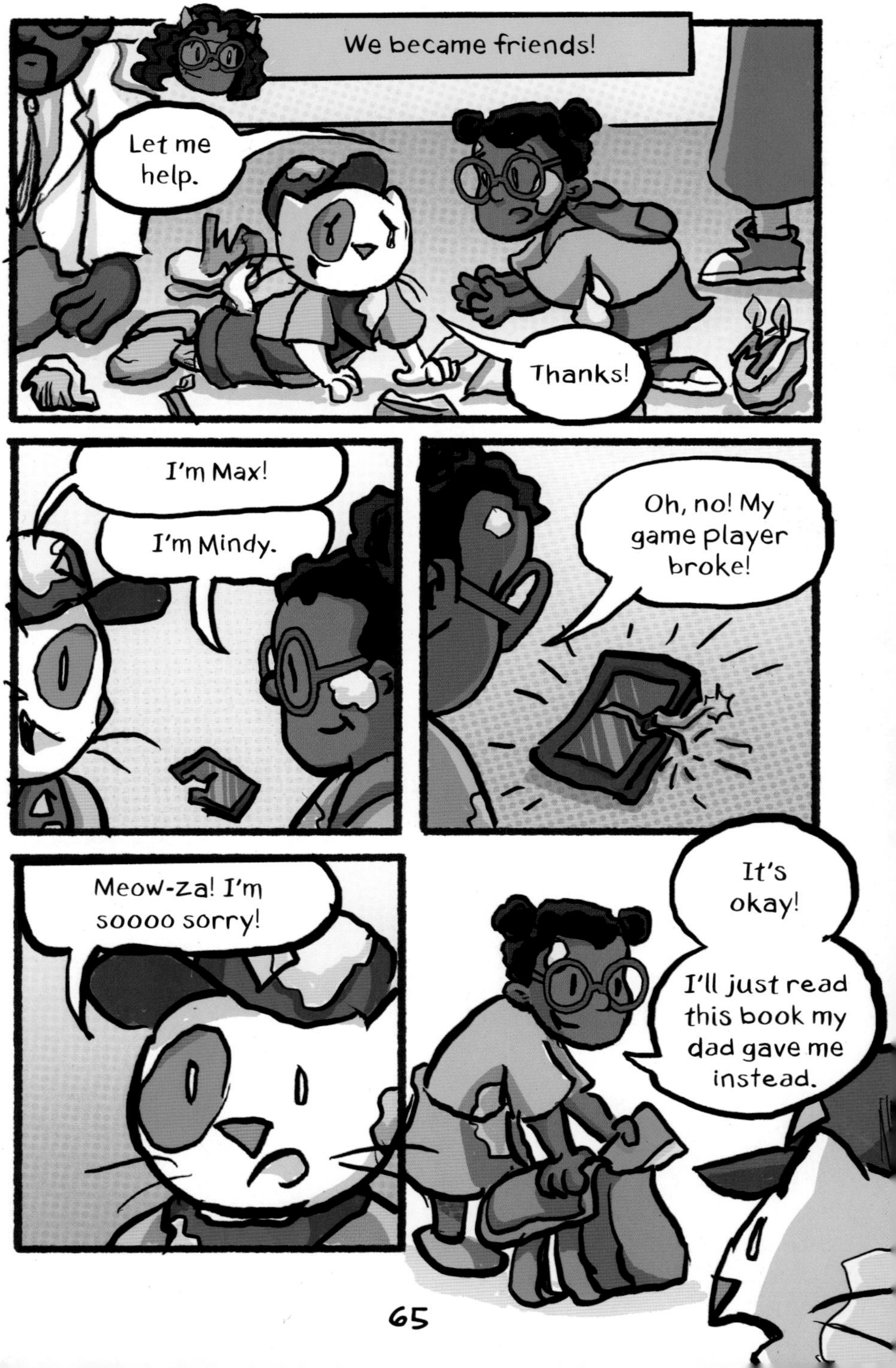
We became friends!
Let me help.
Thanks!
I'm Max!
I'm Mindy.
Oh, no! My game player broke!
Meow-za! I'm soooo sorry!
It's okay!
I'll just read this book my dad gave me instead.

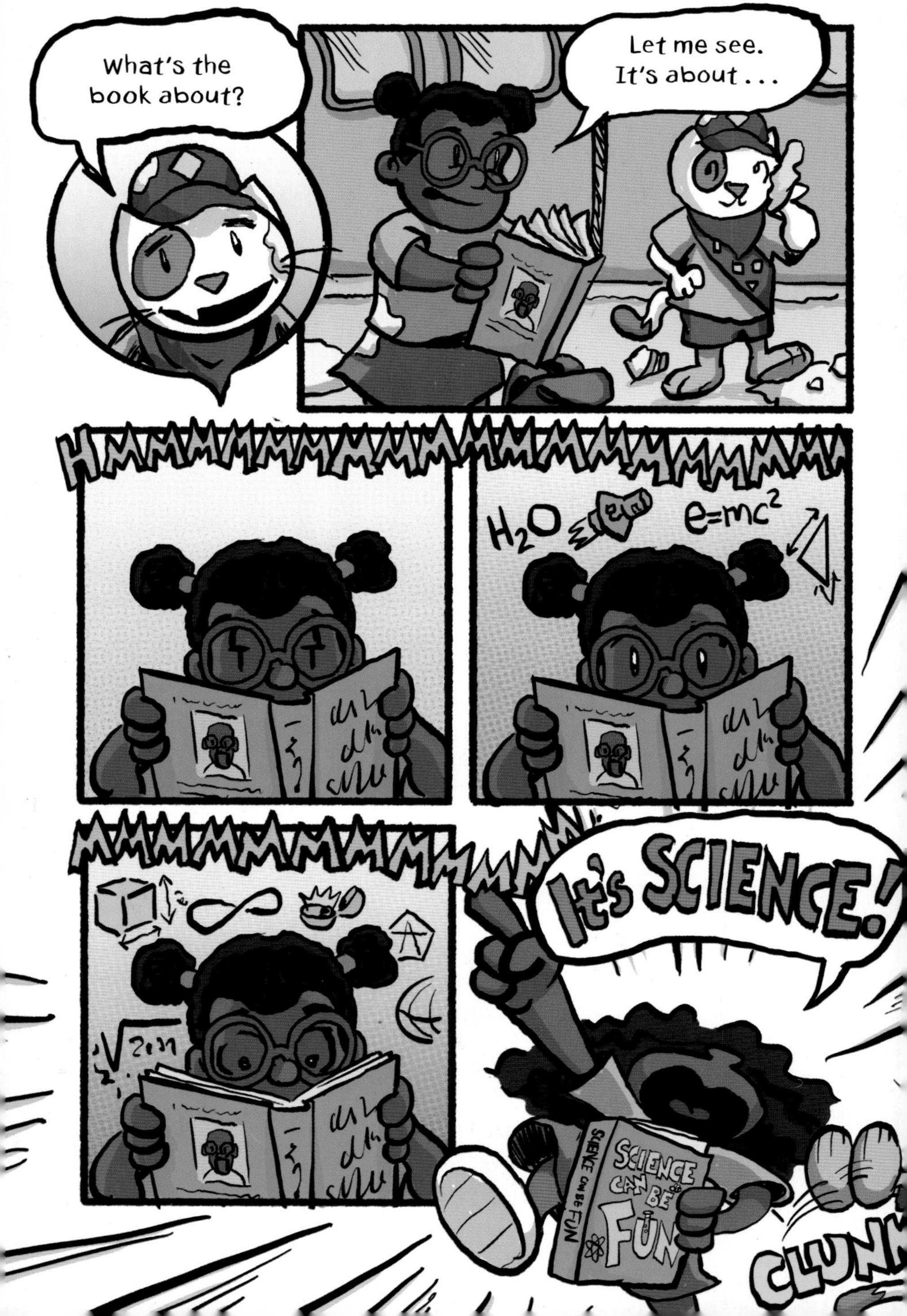
What's the book about?
Let me see. It's about . . .
HMMMMMMMMMMMMMMMMMMMM
H_2O
$e=mc^2$
MMMMMMMMMMMMMMMM
It's SCIENCE!
SCIENCE CAN BE FUN
SCIENCE CAN BE FUN
CLUNK

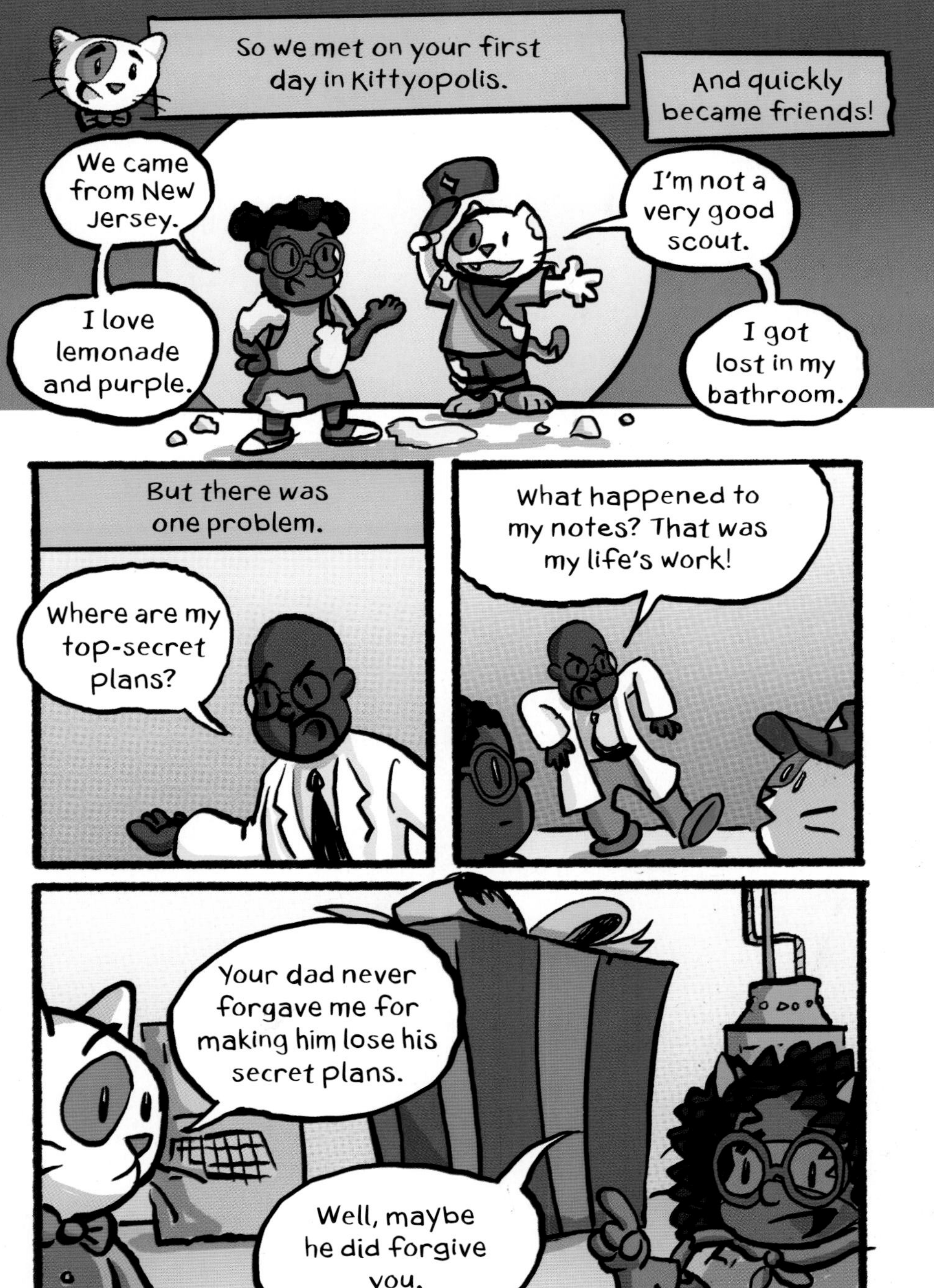
So we met on your first day in Kittyopolis.
And quickly became friends!
We came from New Jersey.
I love lemonade and purple.
I'm not a very good scout.
I got lost in my bathroom.
But there was one problem.
Where are my top-secret plans?
What happened to my notes? That was my life's work!
Your dad never forgave me for making him lose his secret plans.
Well, maybe he did forgive you.

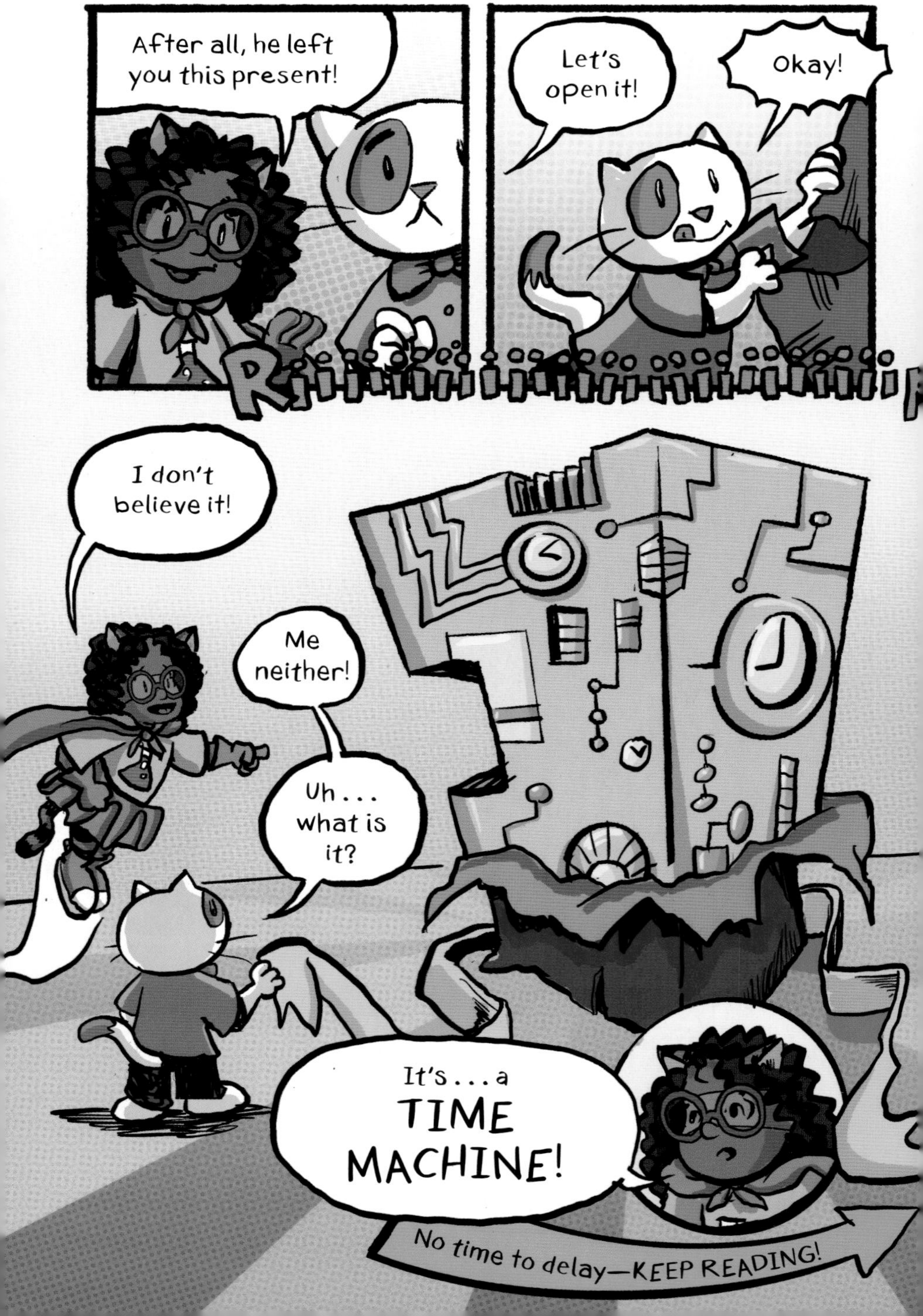
After all, he left you this present!
Let's open it!
Okay!
Riiiiiiiiiiiiiiiiiiiiiiiiiiiiiiip
I don't believe it!
Me neither!
Uh . . . what is it?
It's . . . a TIME MACHINE!
No time to delay—KEEP READING!

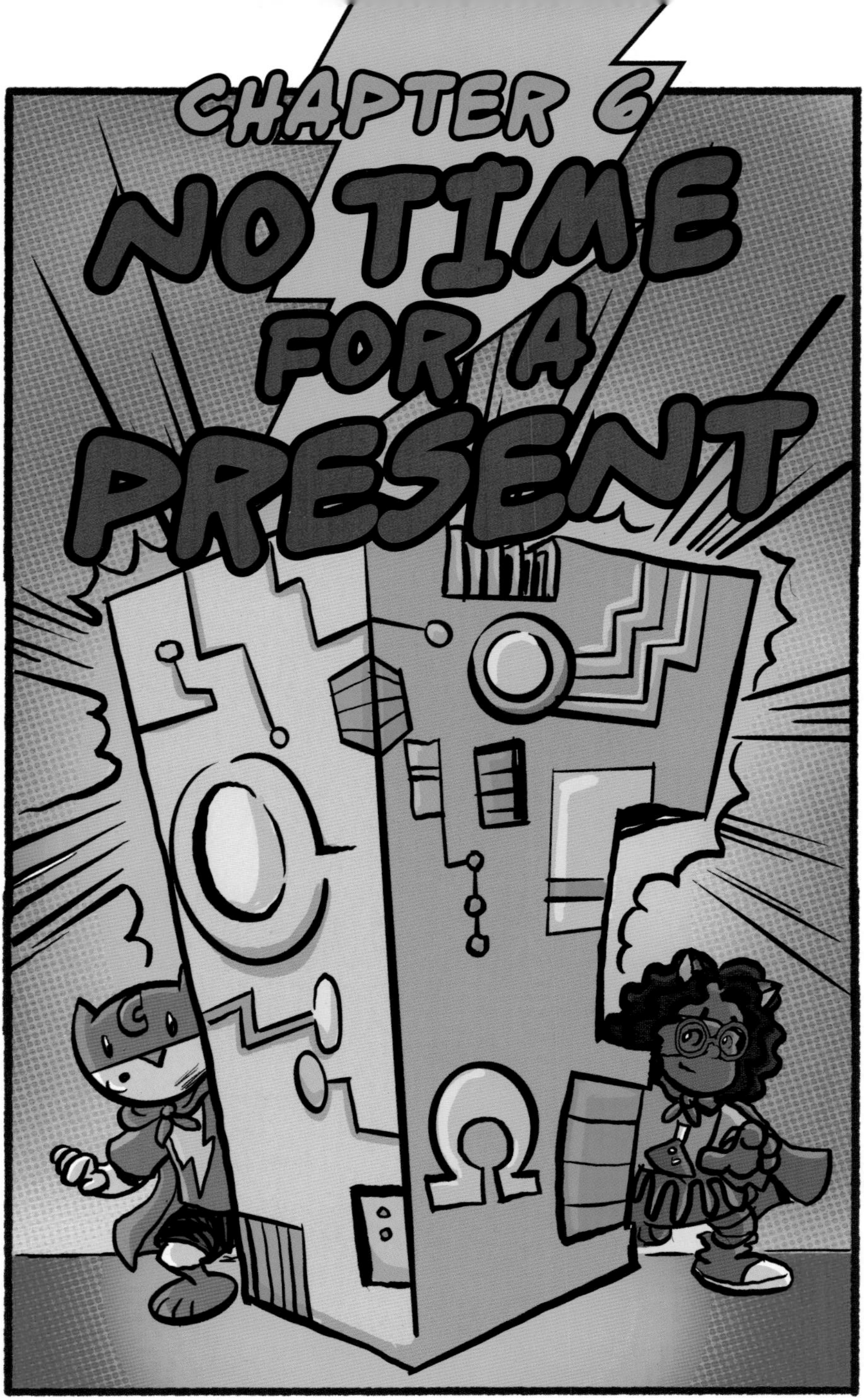
CHAPTER 6
NO TIME FOR A PRESENT

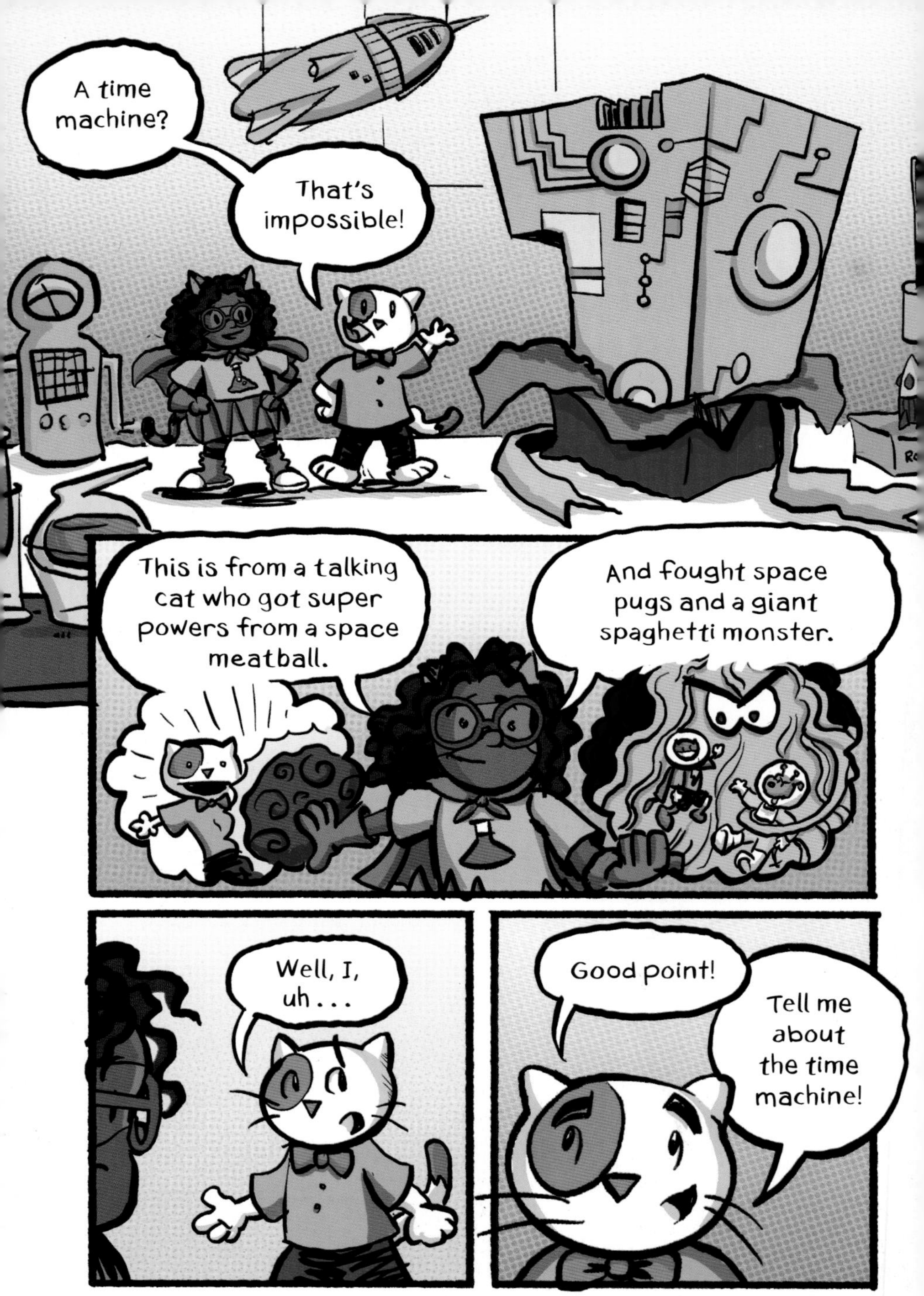
A time machine?
That's impossible!
This is from a talking cat who got super powers from a space meatball.
And fought space pugs and a giant spaghetti monster.
Well, I, uh . . .
Good point!
Tell me about the time machine!

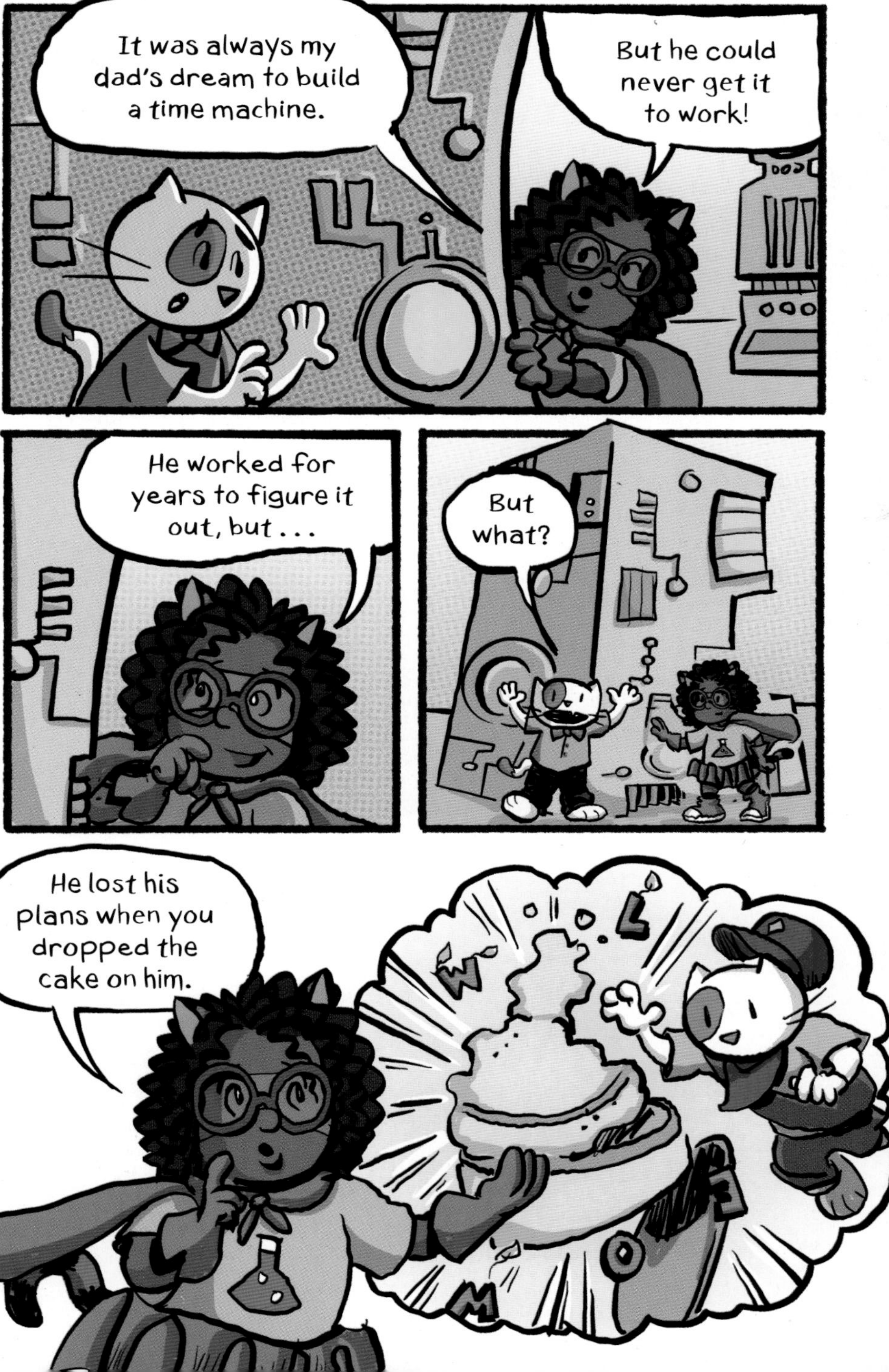

It was always my dad's dream to build a time machine.
But he could never get it to work!
He worked for years to figure it out, but . . .
But what?
He lost his plans when you dropped the cake on him.

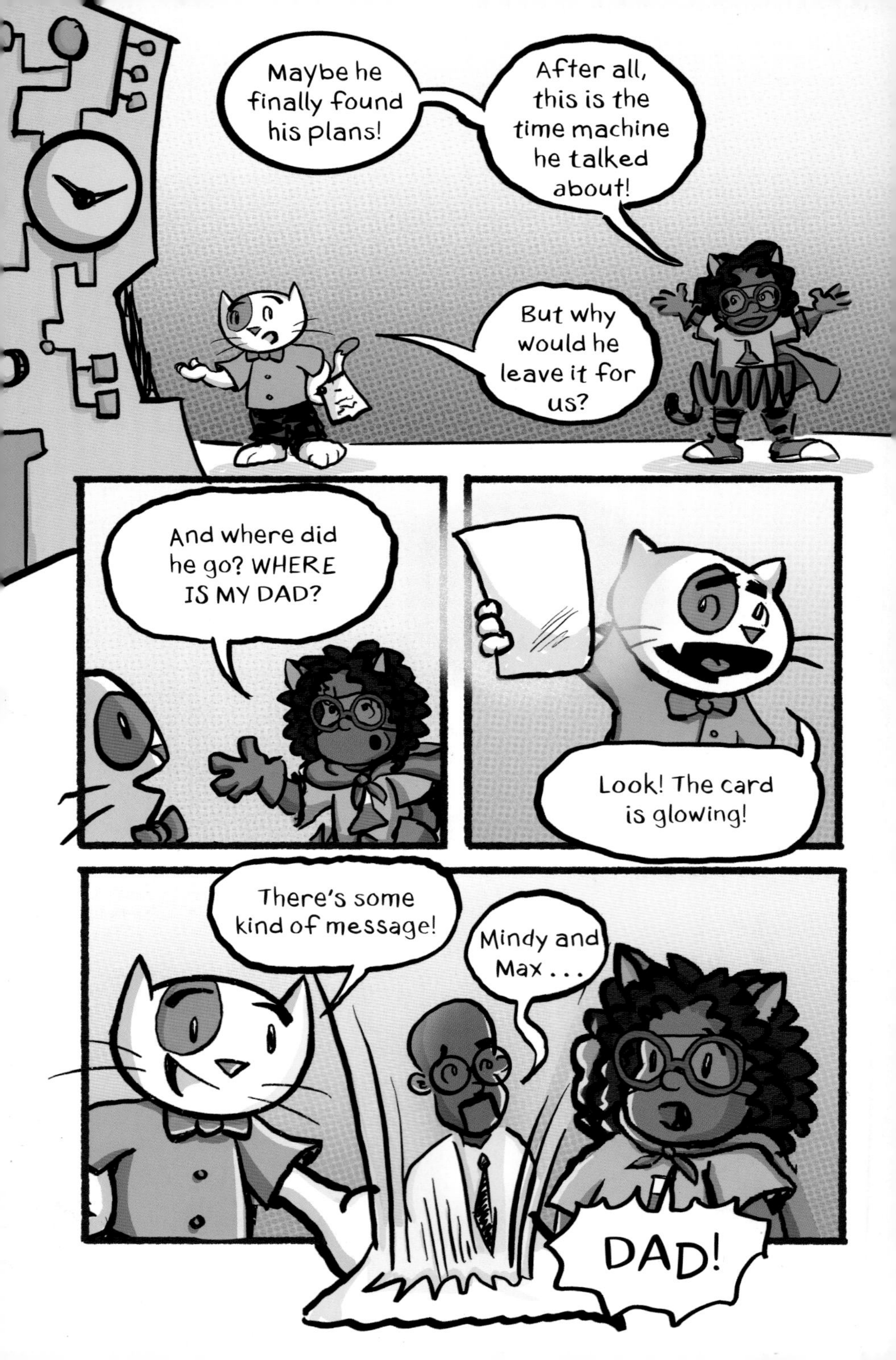
Maybe he finally found his plans!
After all, this is the time machine he talked about!
But why would he leave it for us?
And where did he go? WHERE IS MY DAD?
Look! The card is glowing!
There's some kind of message!
Mindy and Max . . .
DAD!

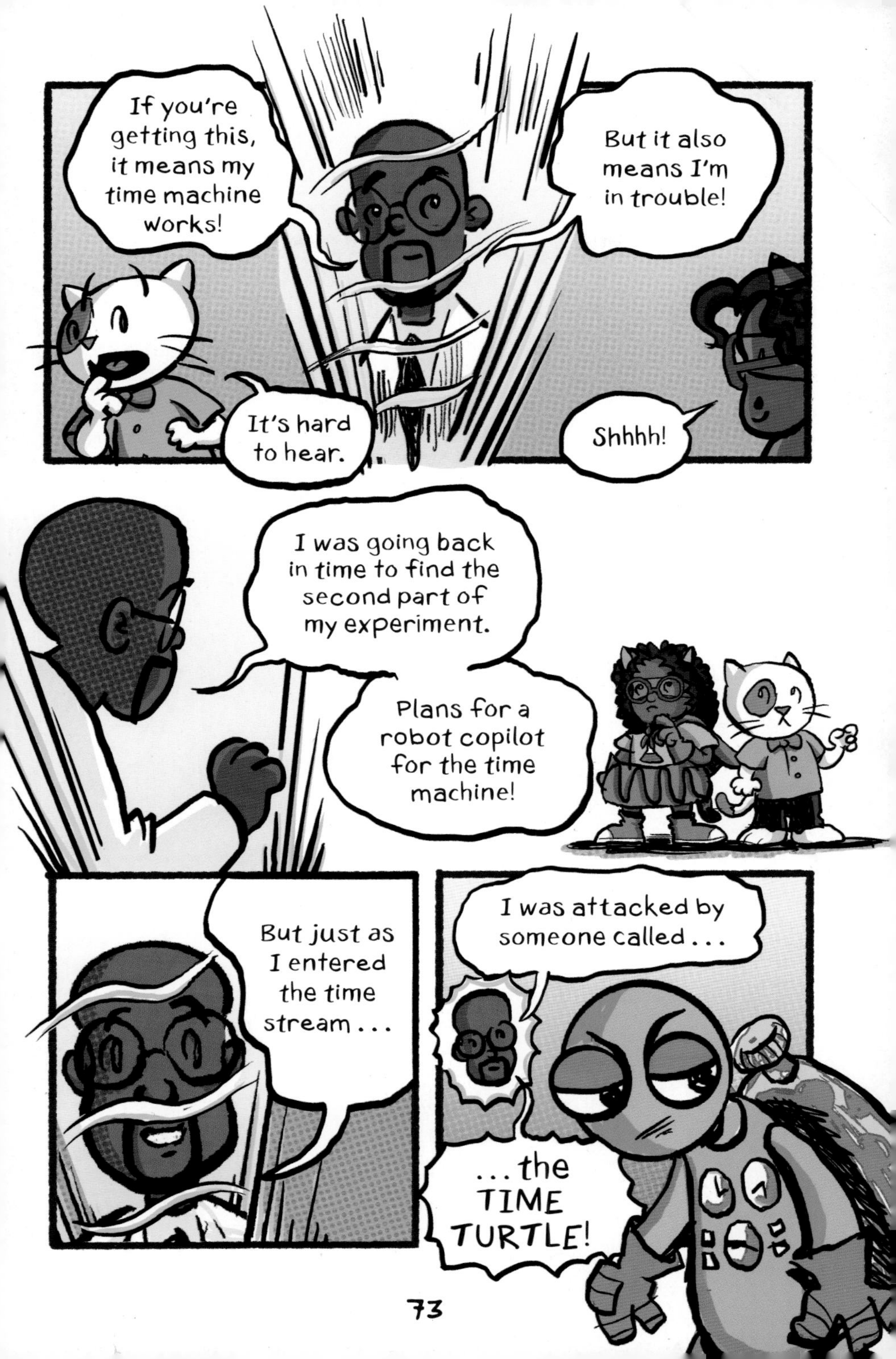
If you're getting this, it means my time machine works!
But it also means I'm in trouble!
It's hard to hear.
Shhhh!
I was going back in time to find the second part of my experiment.
Plans for a robot copilot for the time machine!
But just as I entered the time stream . . .
I was attacked by someone called . . .
. . . the TIME TURTLE!

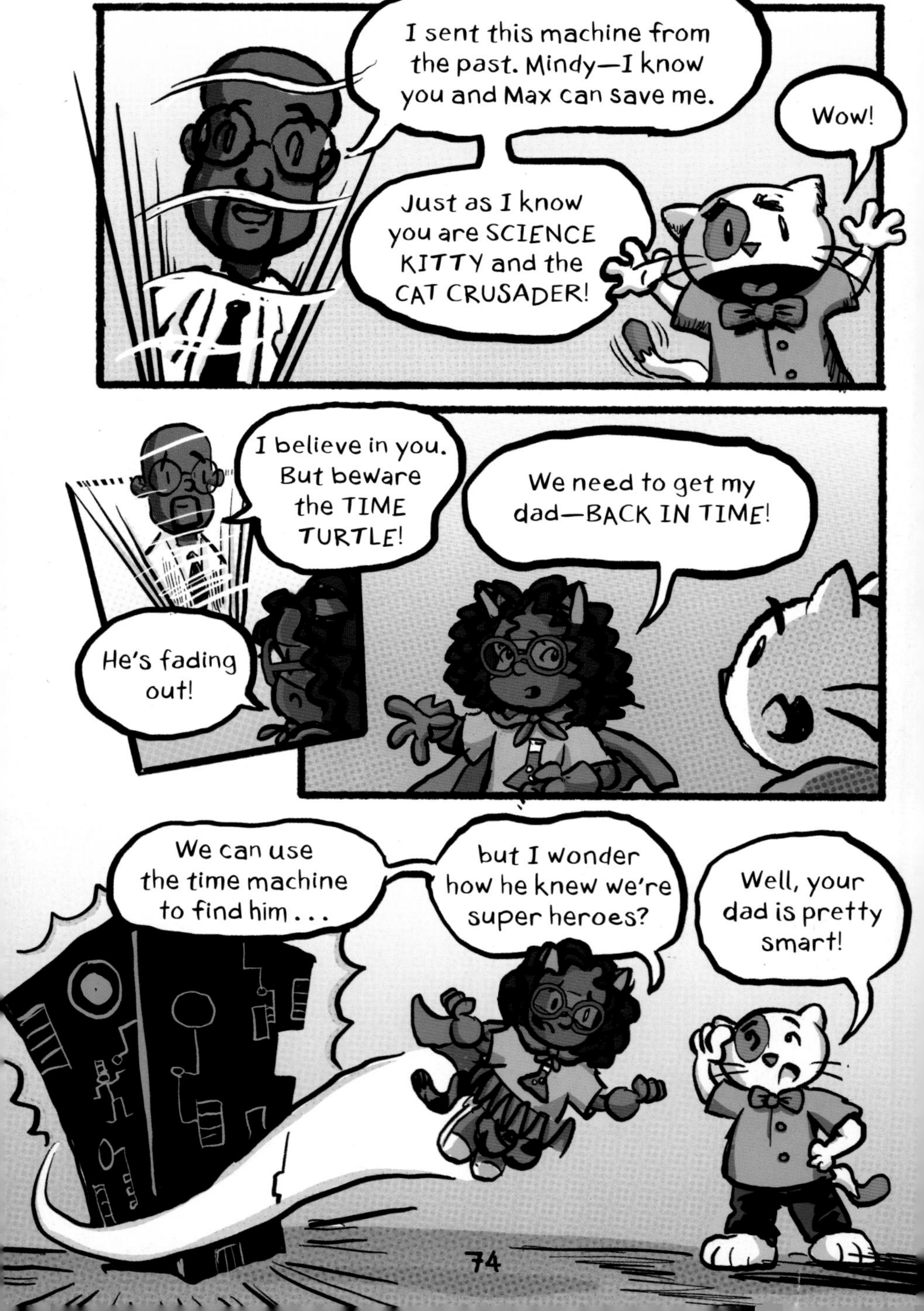
I sent this machine from the past. Mindy—I know you and Max can save me.
Just as I know you are SCIENCE KITTY and the CAT CRUSADER!
Wow!
I believe in you. But beware the TIME TURTLE!
He's fading out!
We need to get my dad—BACK IN TIME!
We can use the time machine to find him . . .
but I wonder how he knew we're super heroes?
Well, your dad is pretty smart!

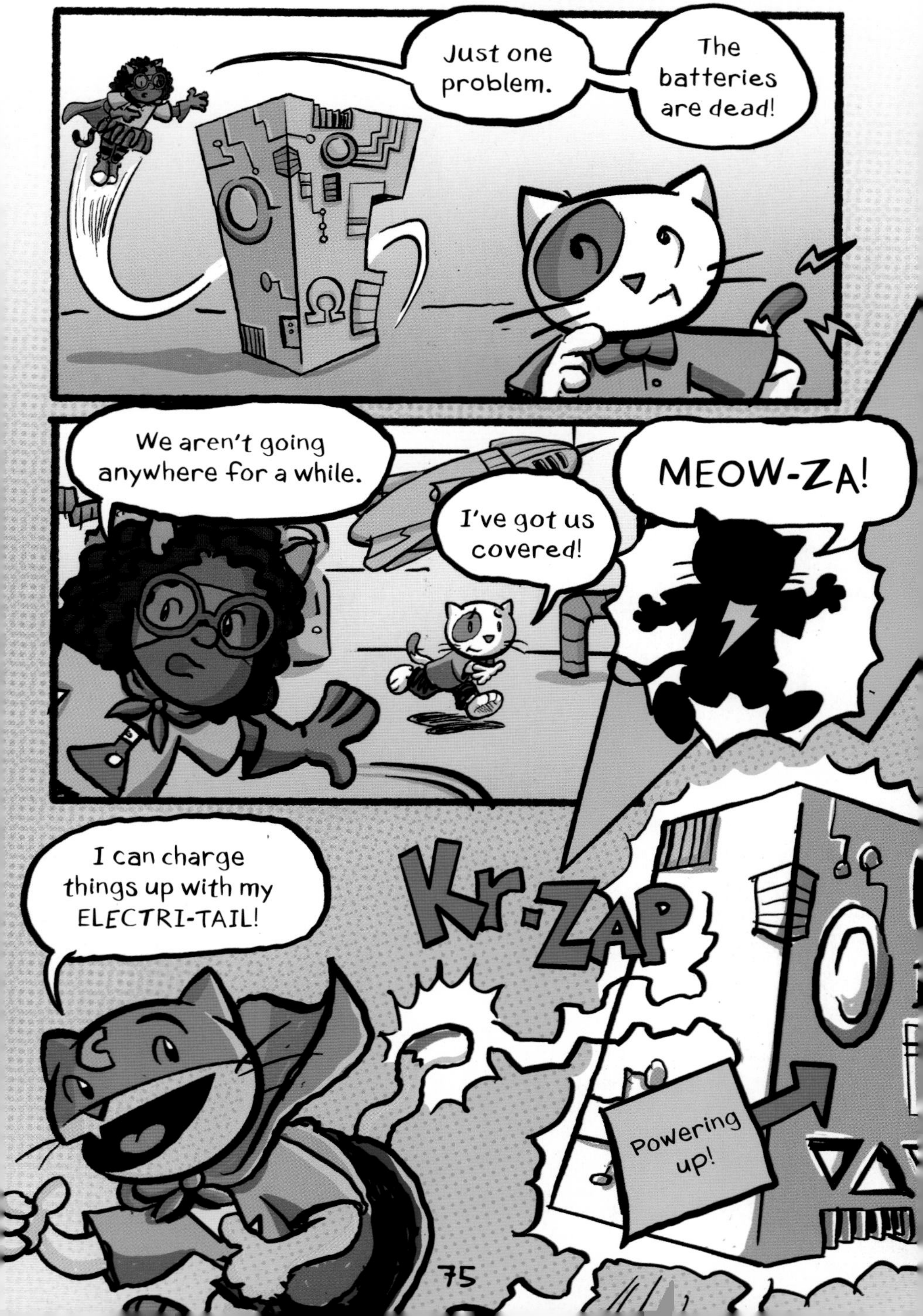
Just one problem.
The batteries are dead!
We aren't going anywhere for a while.
I've got us covered!
MEOW-ZA!
I can charge things up with my ELECTRI-TAIL!
Kr-ZAP
Powering up!

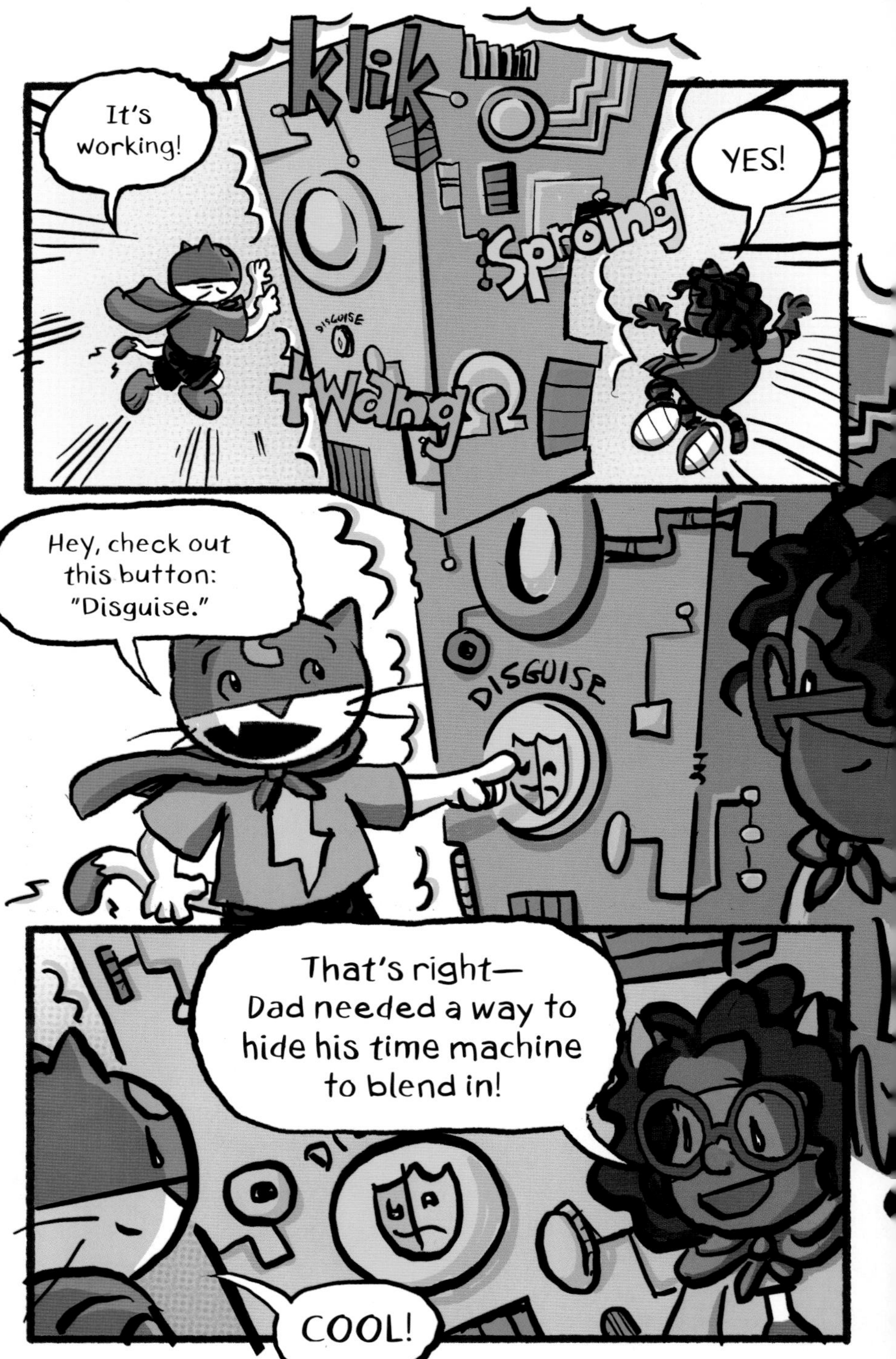
klik
It's working!
YES!
Sproing
DISGUISE
twang
Hey, check out this button: "Disguise."
DISGUISE
That's right— Dad needed a way to hide his time machine to blend in!
COOL!

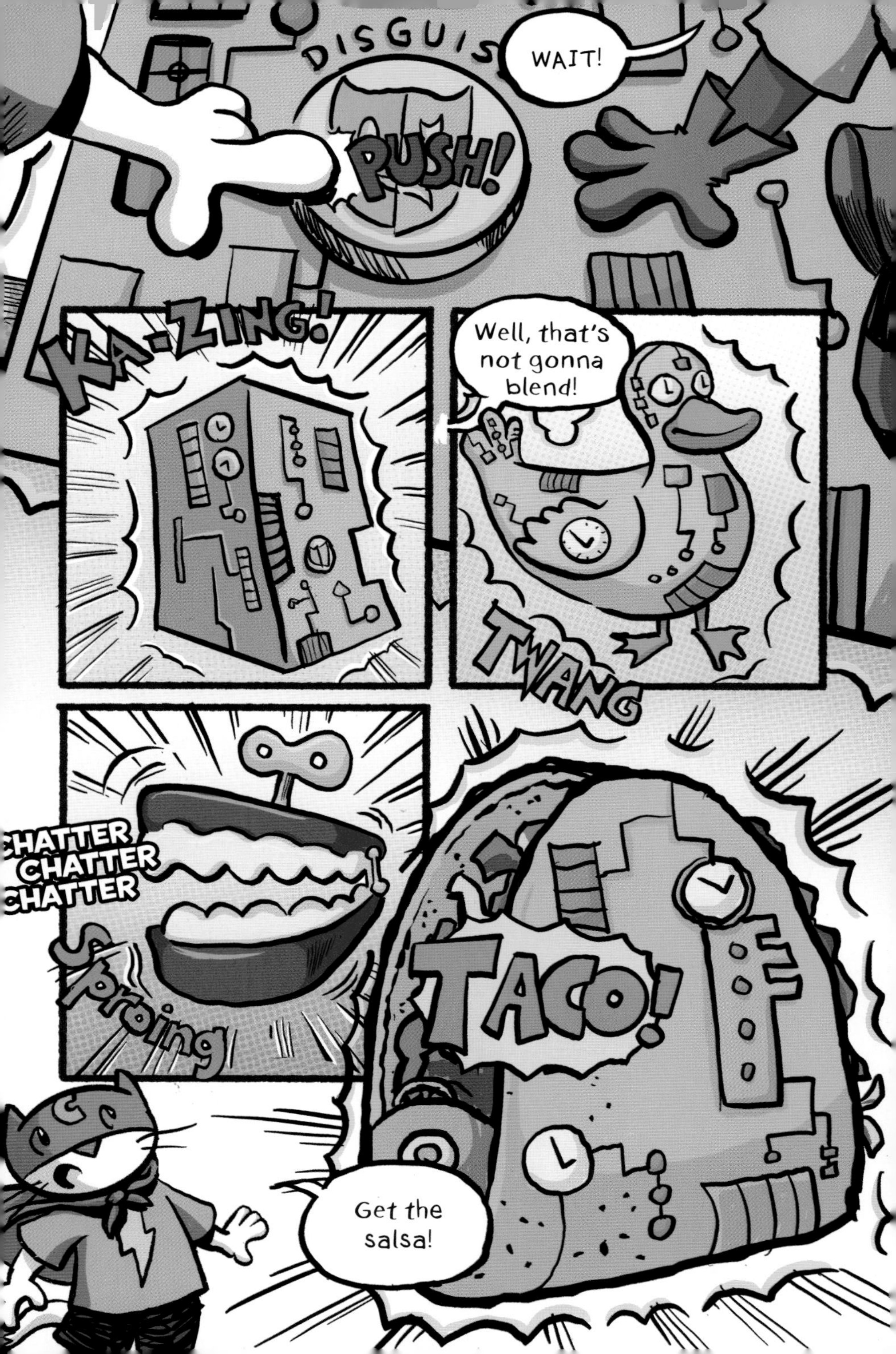
DISGUIS
WAIT!
PUSH!
KA-ZING!
Well, that's not gonna blend!
TWANG
CHATTER
CHATTER
CHATTER
Sproing!
TACO!
Get the salsa!

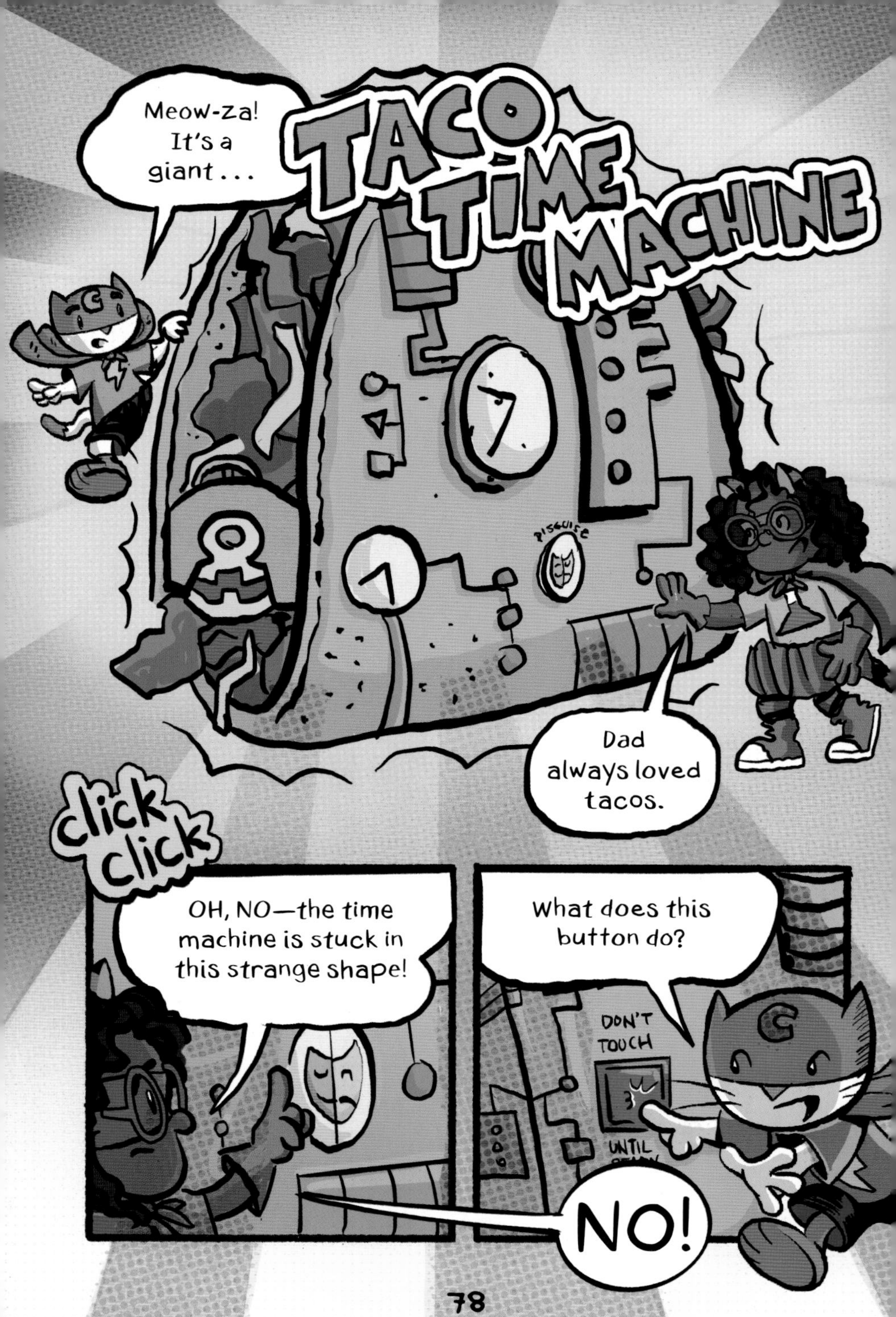
Meow-za!
It's a
giant . . .
TACO TIME MACHINE
DISGUISE
Dad
always loved
tacos.
click
click
OH, NO—the time
machine is stuck in
this strange shape!
What does this
button do?
DON'T
TOUCH
UNTIL
NO!

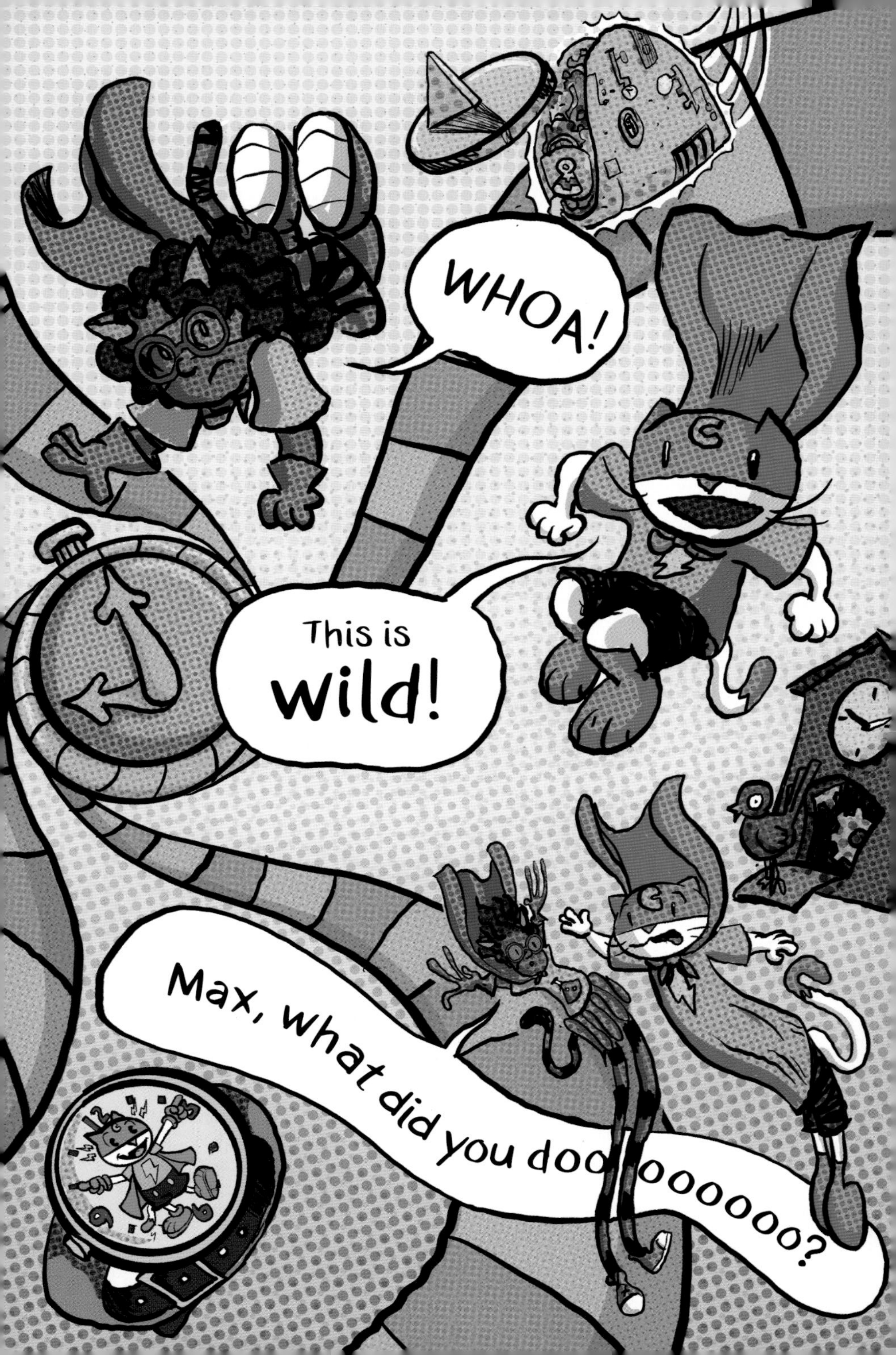
WHOA!
This is wild!
Max, what did you doooooooooo?

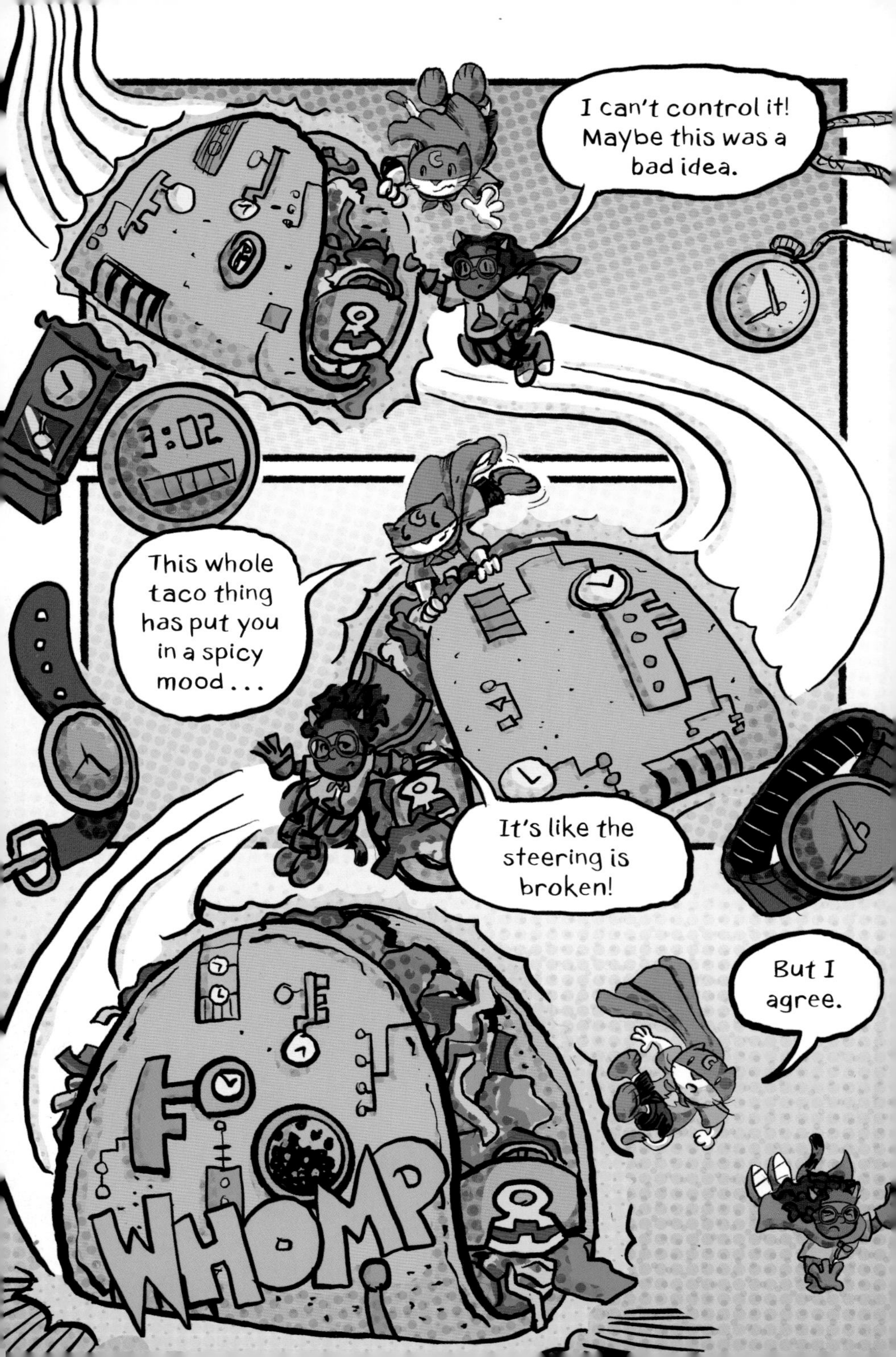
I can't control it! Maybe this was a bad idea.
This whole taco thing has put you in a spicy mood . . .
It's like the steering is broken!
But I agree.
WHOMP

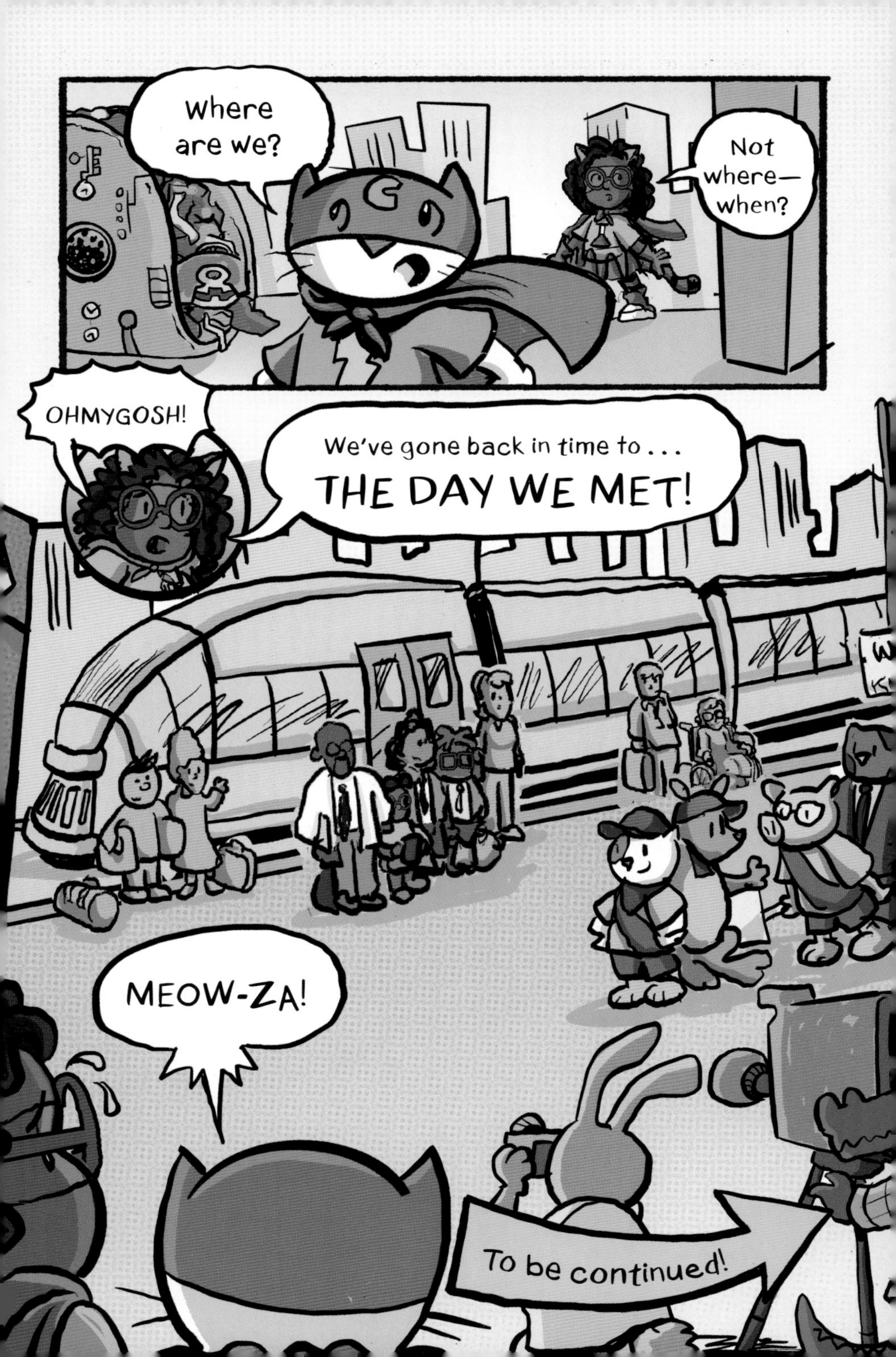
Where are we?
Not where—when?
OHMYGOSH!
We've gone back in time to . . . THE DAY WE MET!
MEOW-ZA!
To be continued!

CHAPTER 7 FORTRESS OF SMELL-ITUDE

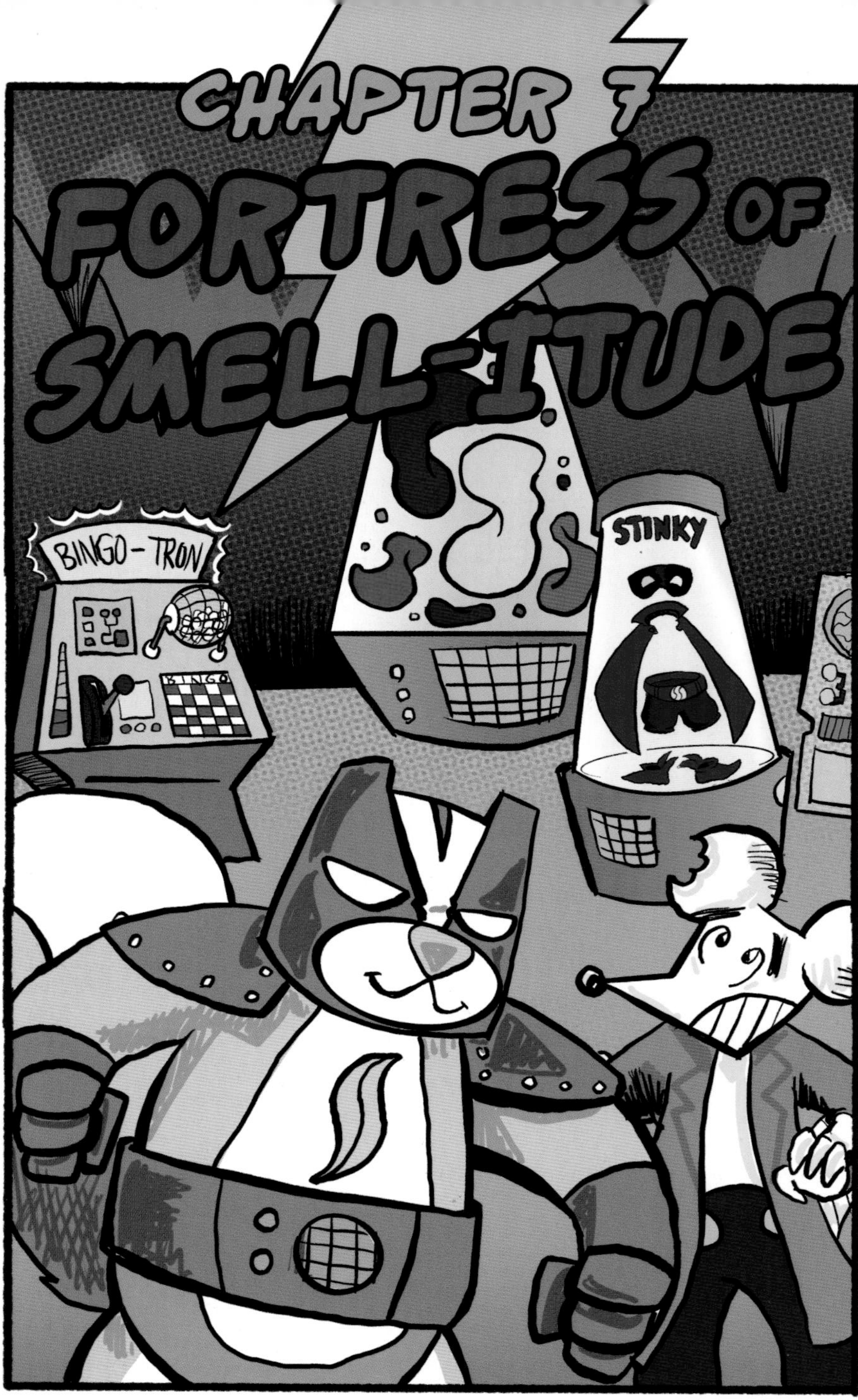
BINGO-TRON
BINGO
STINKY

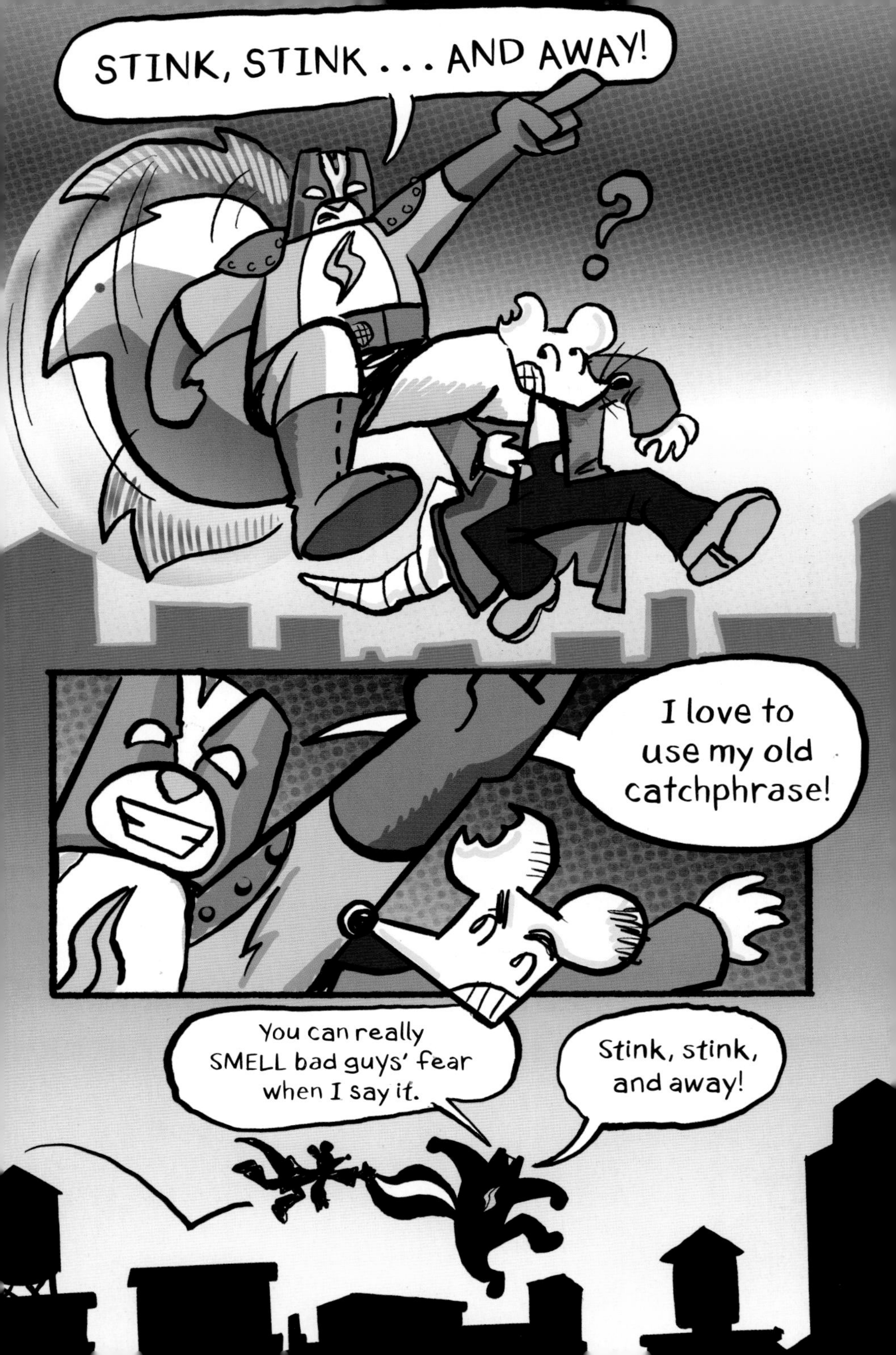
STINK, STINK . . . AND AWAY!
?
I love to use my old catchphrase!
You can really SMELL bad guys' fear when I say it.
Stink, stink, and away!

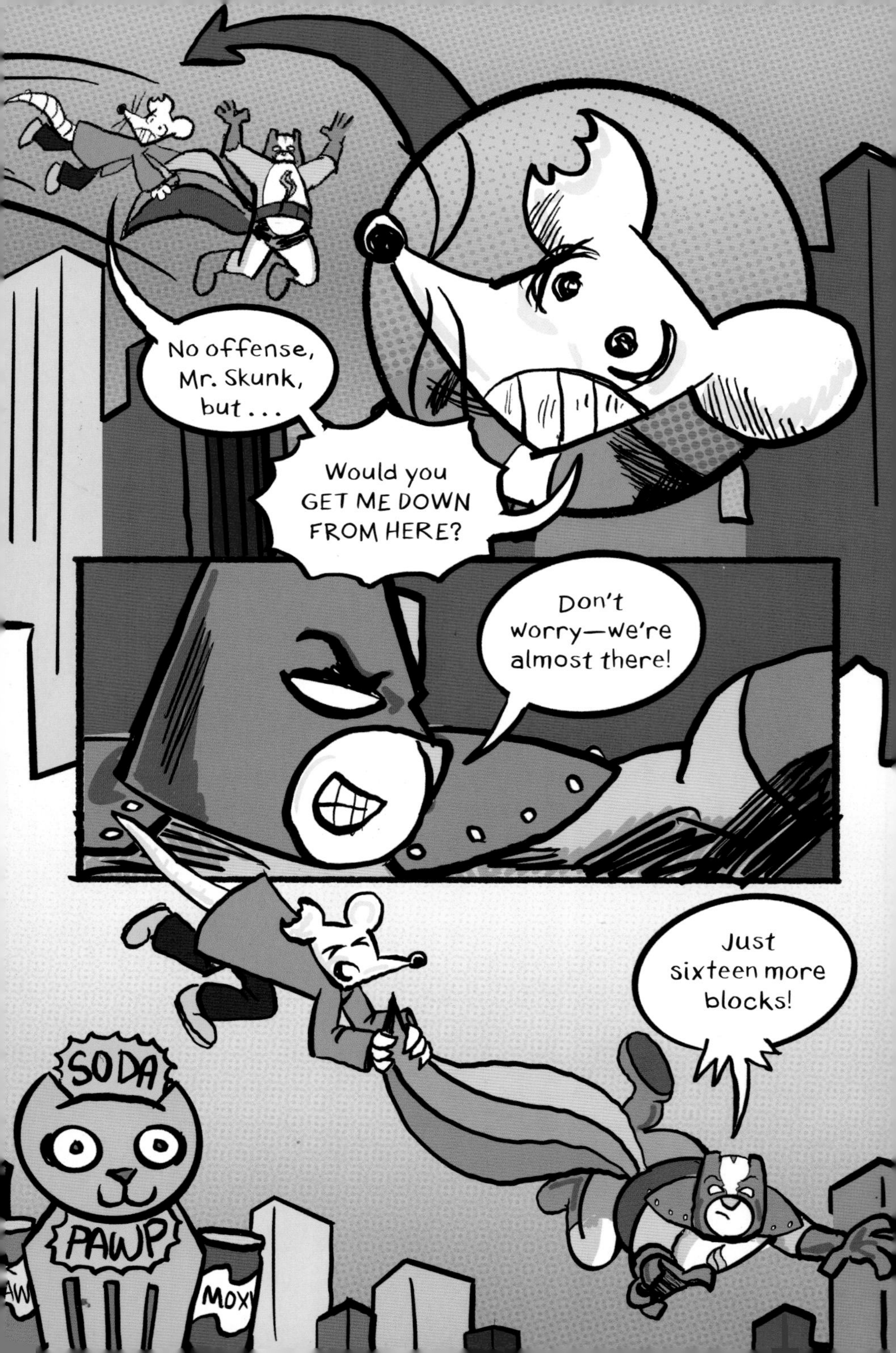
No offense,
Mr. Skunk,
but . . .
Would you
GET ME DOWN
FROM HERE?
Don't
worry—we're
almost there!
Just
sixteen more
blocks!
SODA
PAWP
MOXY

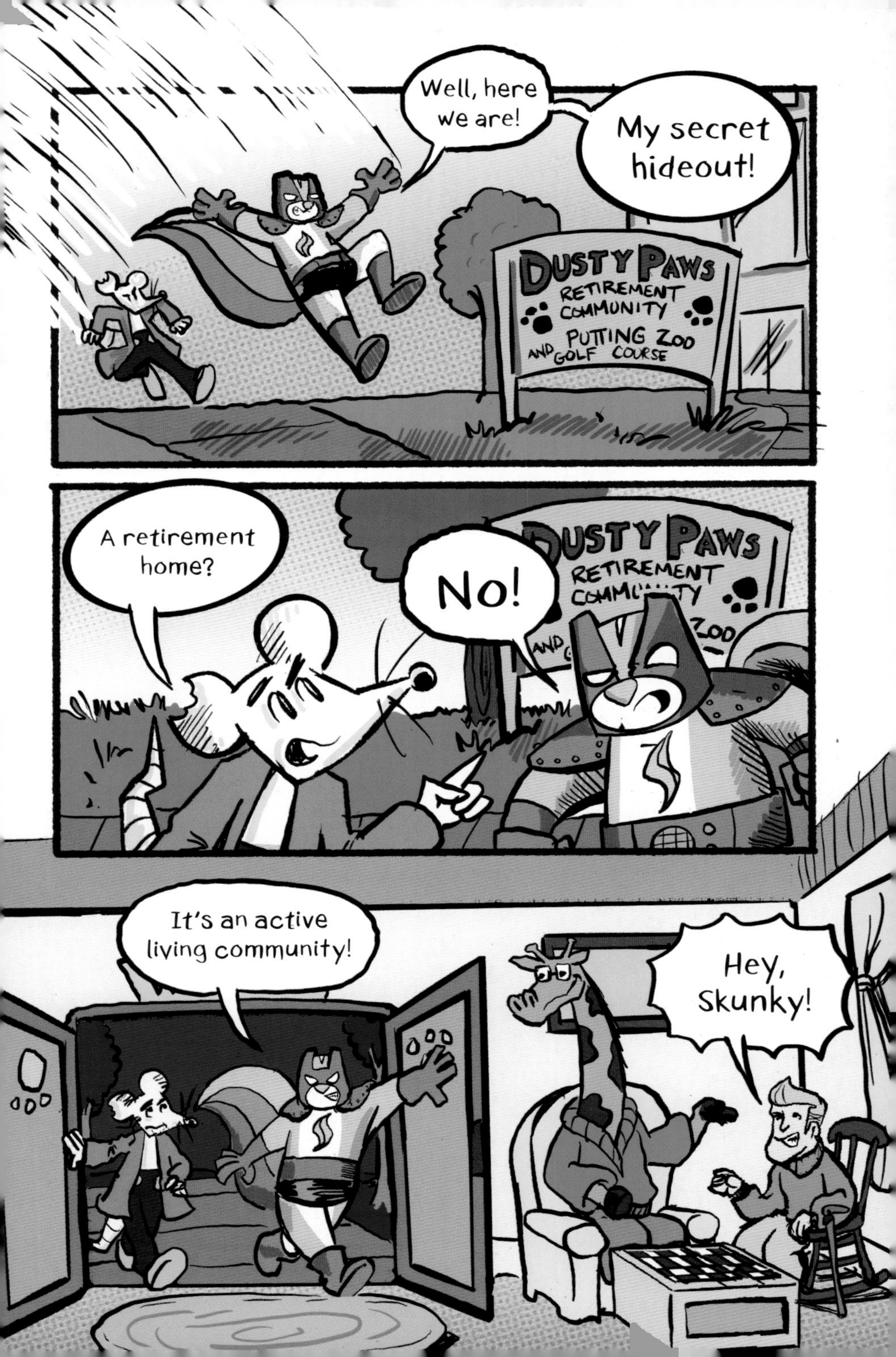
Well, here we are!
My secret hideout!
DUSTY PAWS RETIREMENT COMMUNITY AND PUTTING ZOO GOLF COURSE
A retirement home?
No!
It's an active living community!
Hey, Skunky!

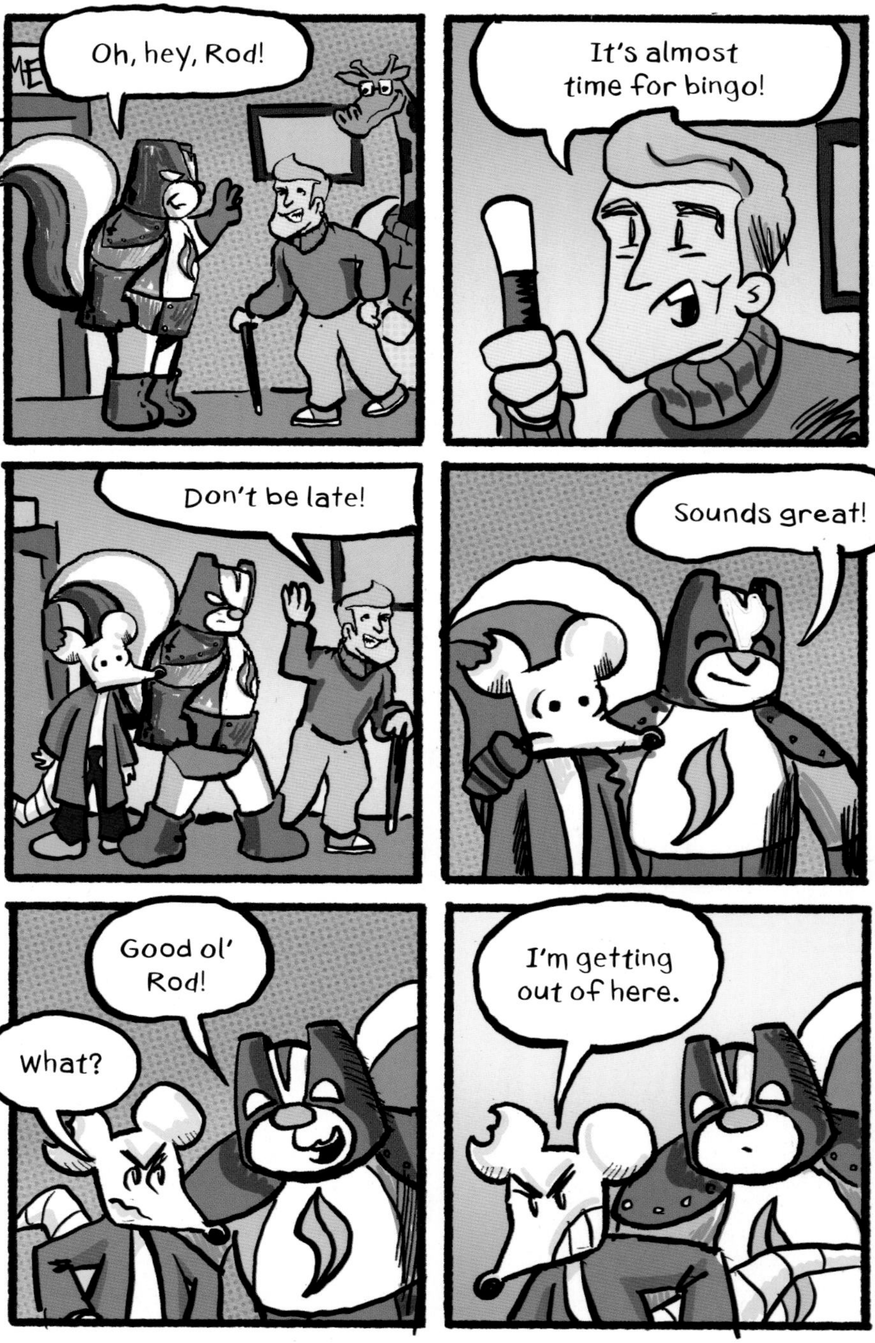
Oh, hey, Rod!
ME
It's almost time for bingo!
Don't be late!
Sounds great!
Good ol' Rod!
What?
I'm getting out of here.

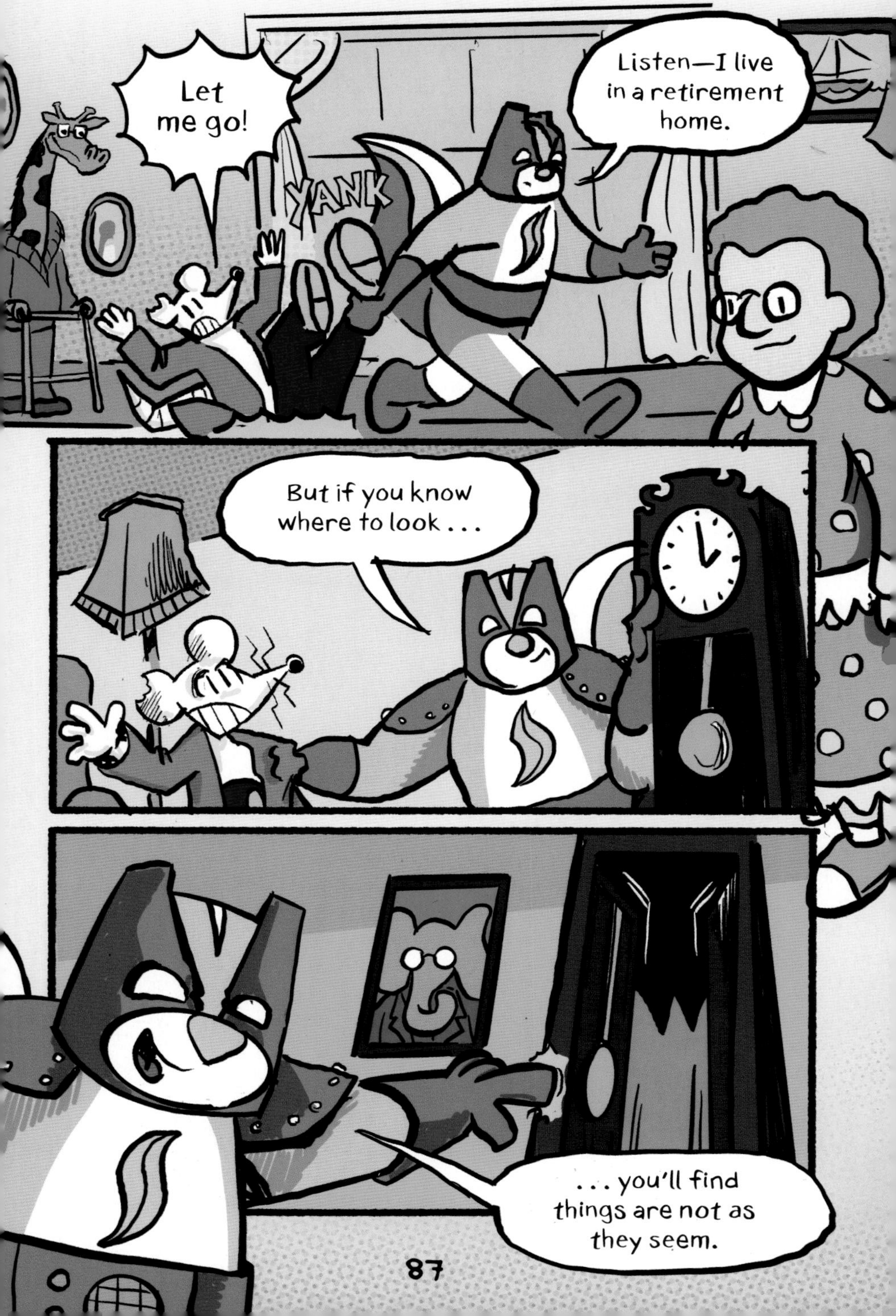
Let me go!
YANK
Listen—I live in a retirement home.
But if you know where to look . . .
. . . you'll find things are not as they seem.

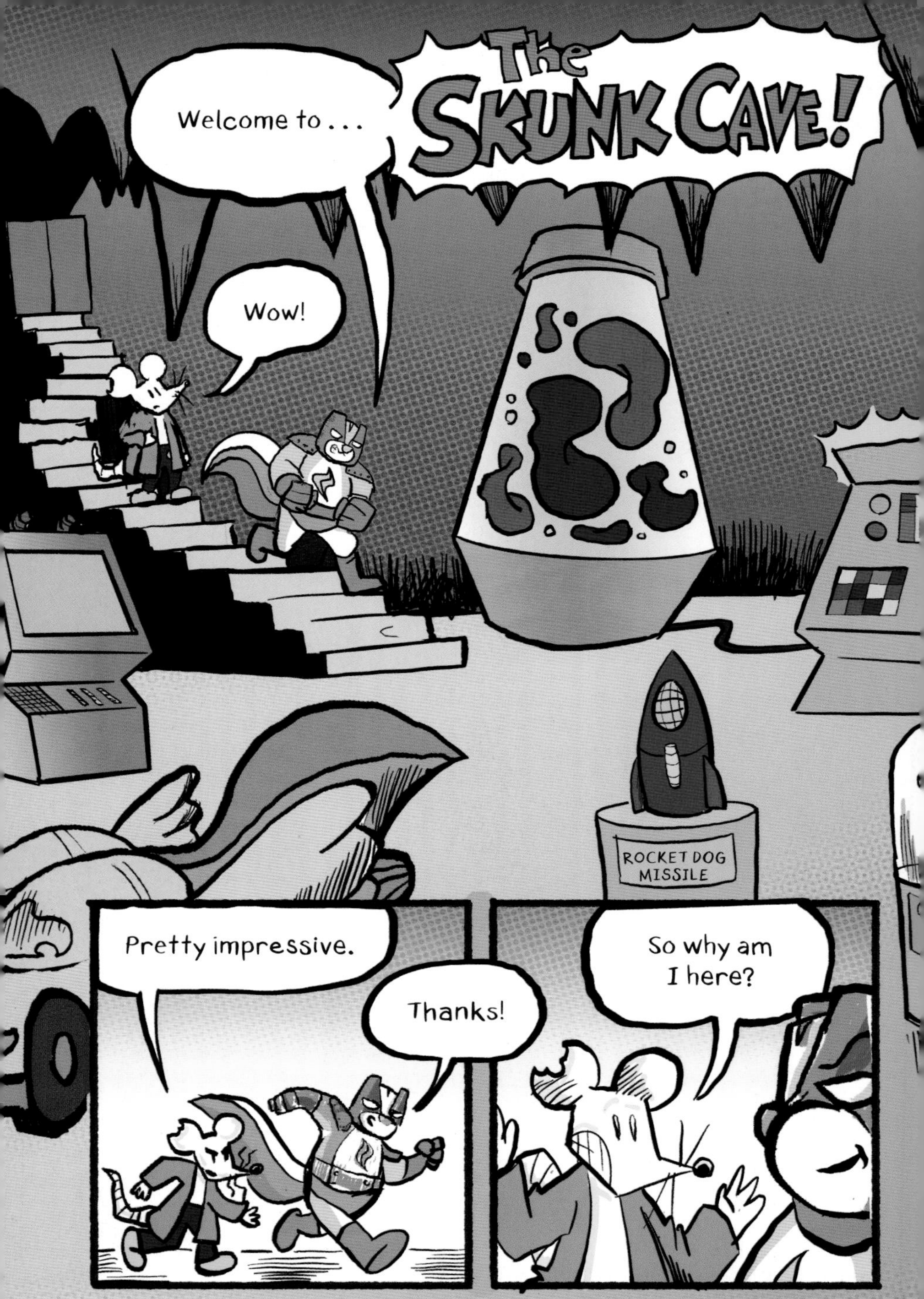
Welcome to . . .
The SKUNK CAVE!
Wow!
ROCKET DOG MISSILE
Pretty impressive.
Thanks!
So why am I here?

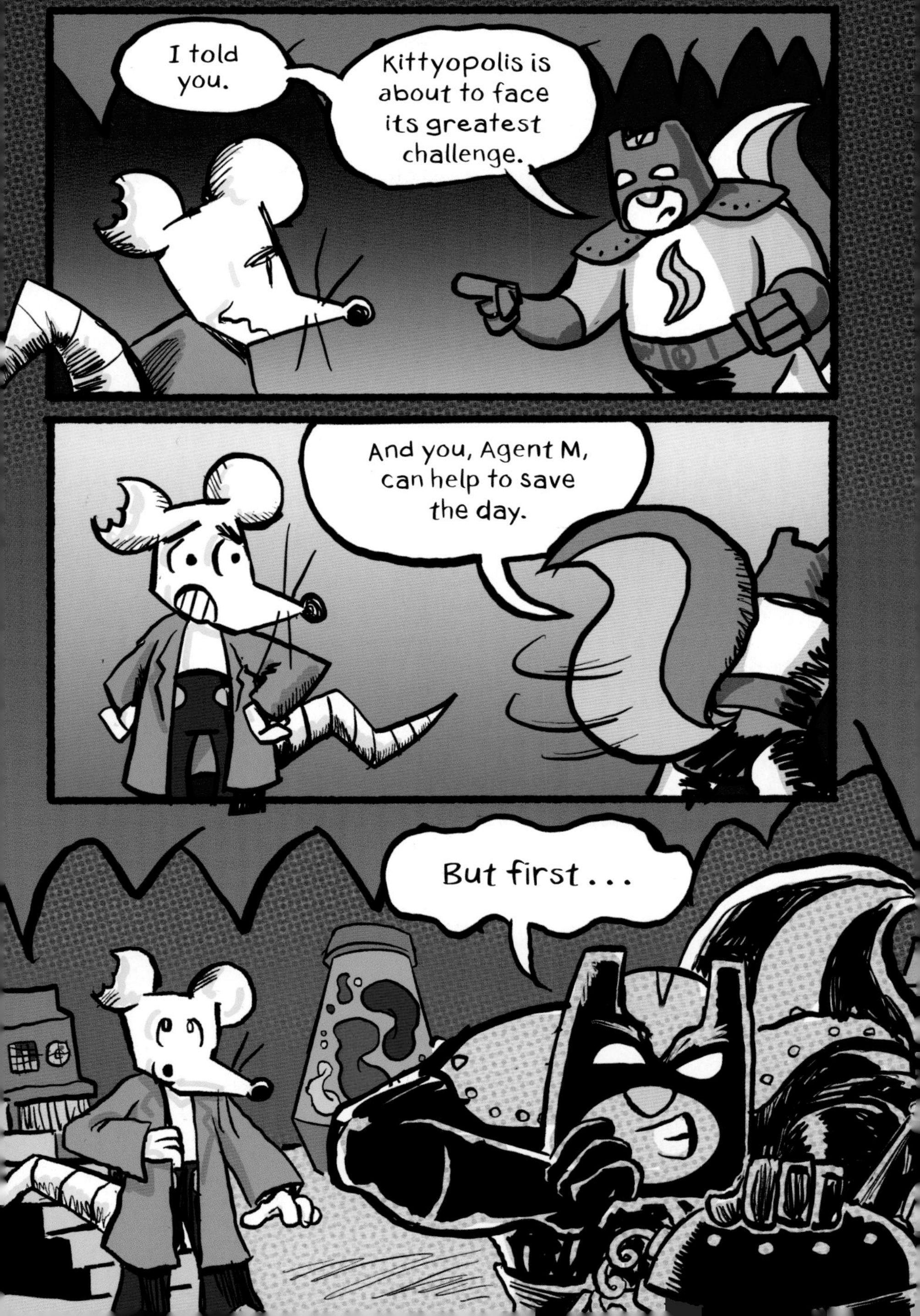
I told you.
Kittyopolis is about to face its greatest challenge.
And you, Agent M, can help to save the day.
But first . . .

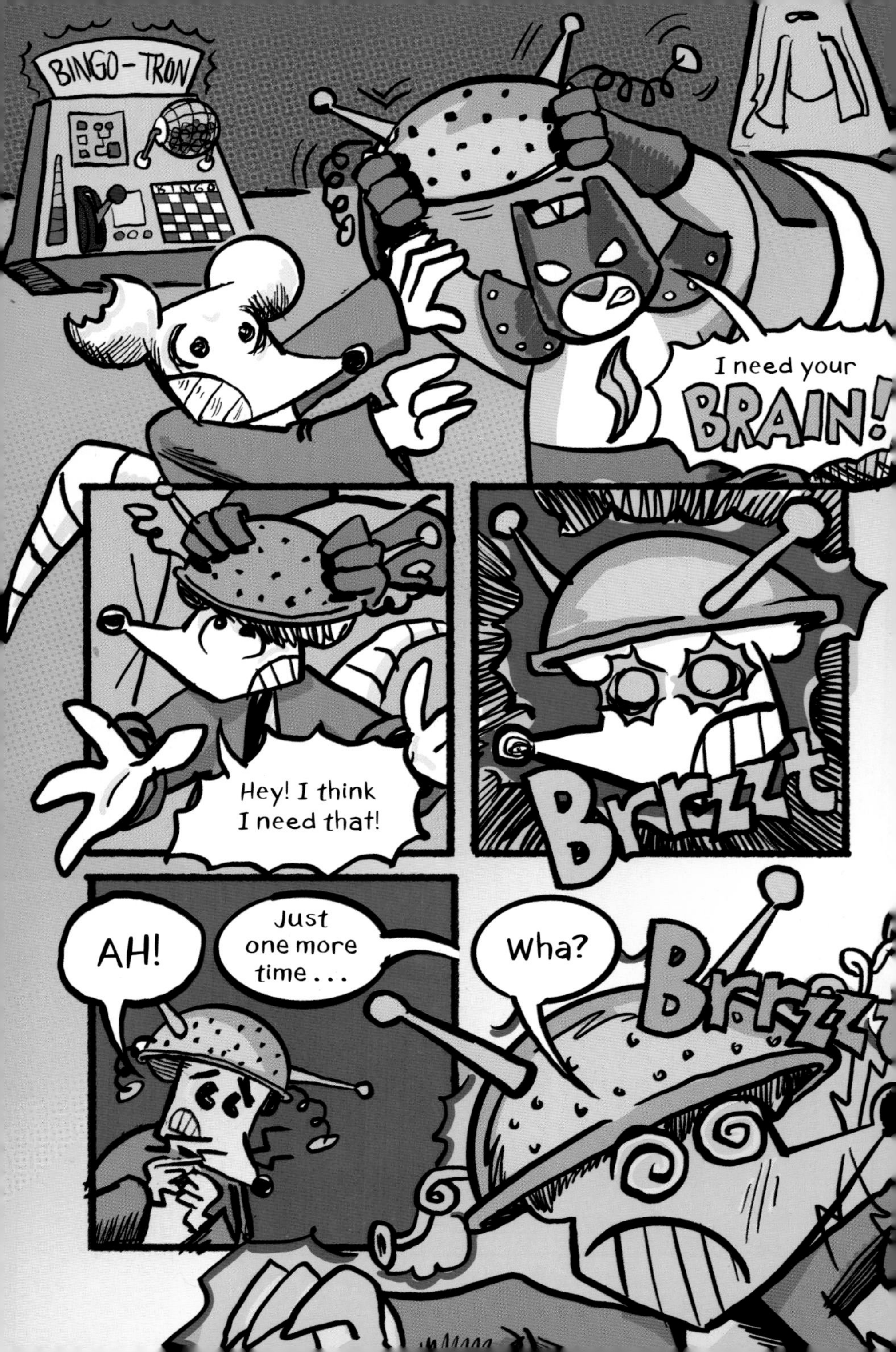
BINGO-TRON
BINGO
I need your BRAIN!
Hey! I think I need that!
Brrzzt
AH!
Just one more time . . .
Wha?
Brrzz

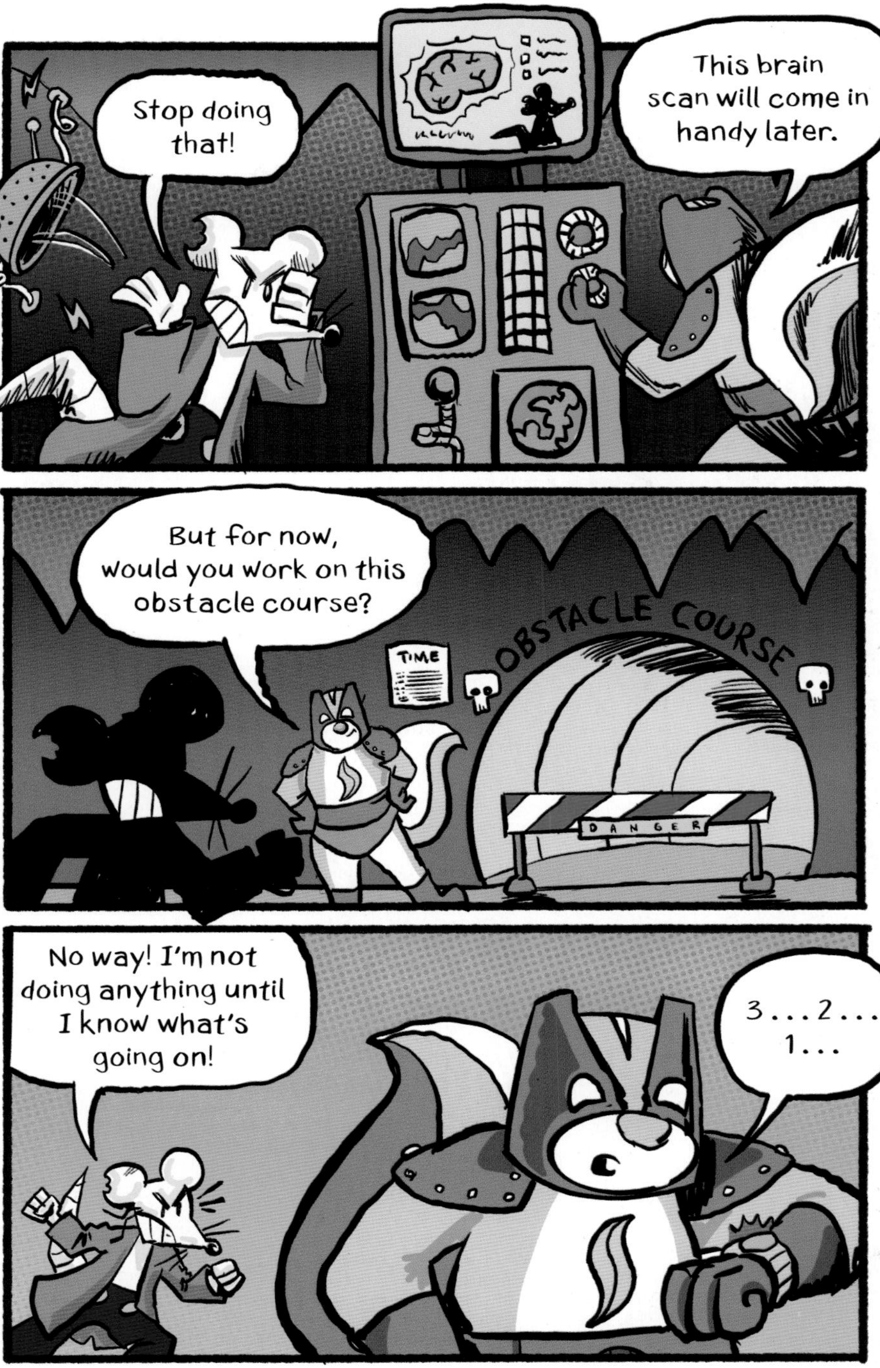
Stop doing that!
This brain scan will come in handy later.
But for now, would you work on this obstacle course?
TIME
OBSTACLE COURSE
DANGER
No way! I'm not doing anything until I know what's going on!
3 . . . 2 . . . 1 . . .

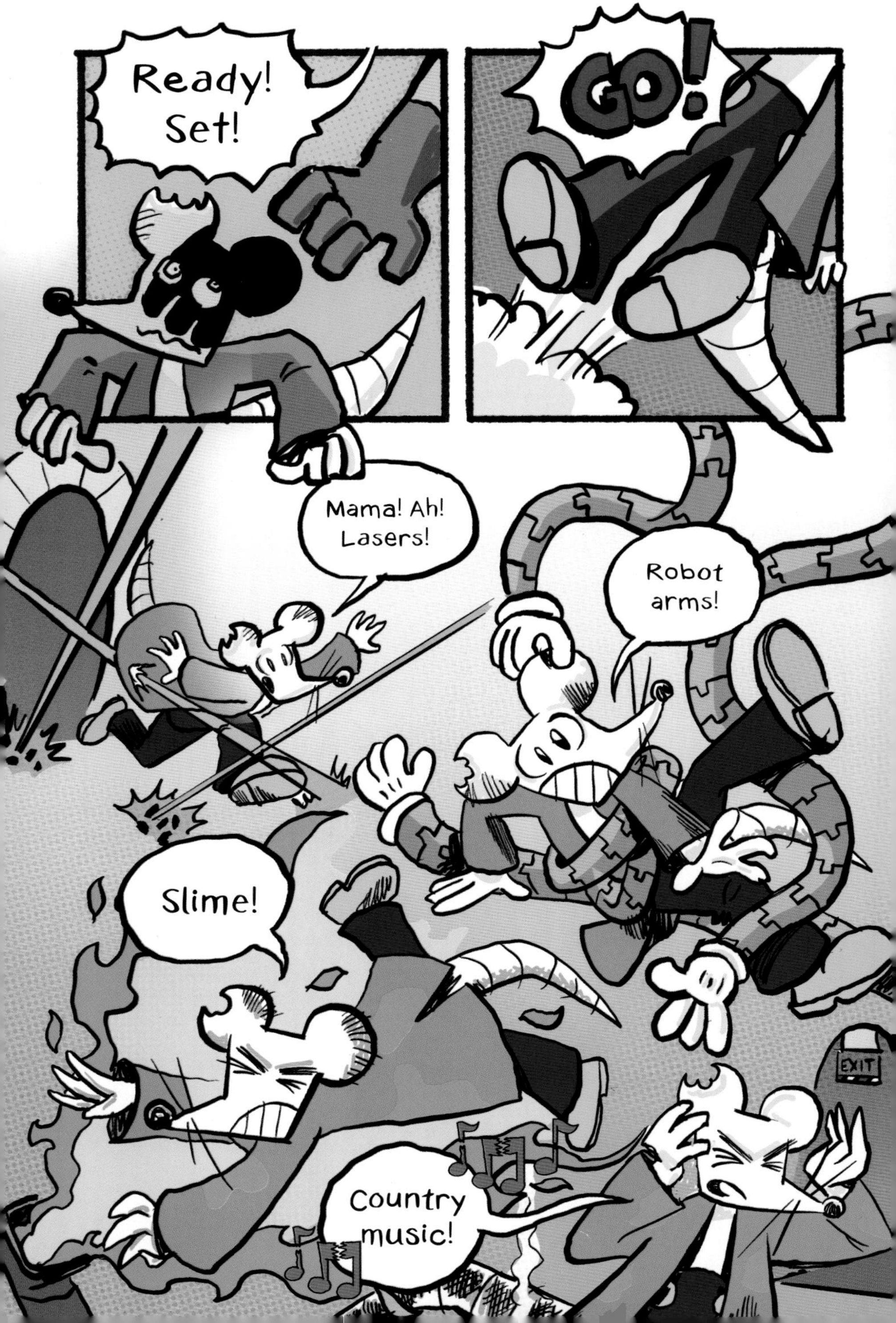
Ready! Set!
GO!
Mama! Ah! Lasers!
Robot arms!
Slime!
Country music!
EXIT

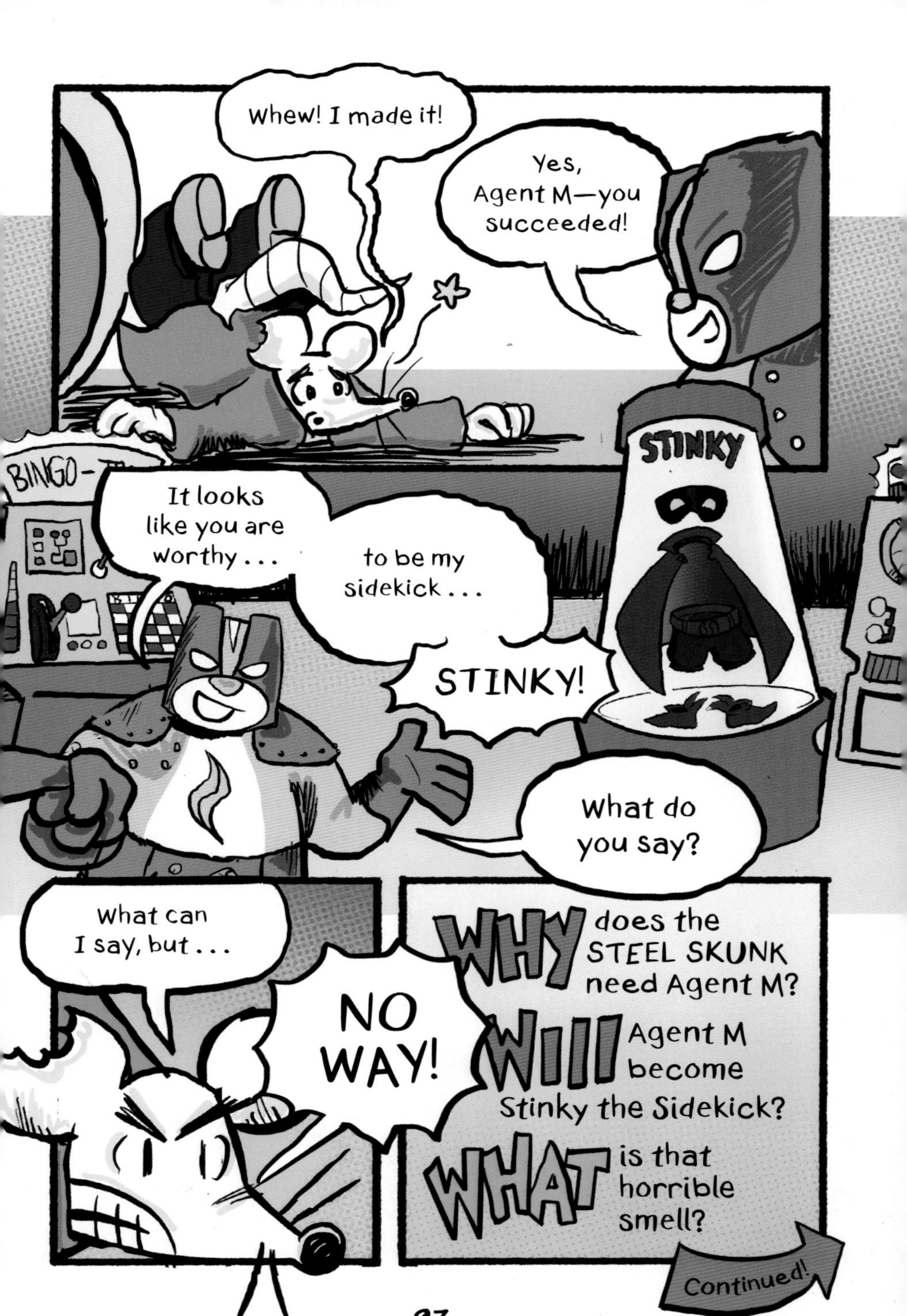

Whew! I made it!
Yes, Agent M—you succeeded!
BINGO-
STINKY
It looks like you are worthy . . .
to be my sidekick . . .
STINKY!
What do you say?
What can I say, but . . .
NO WAY!
WHY does the STEEL SKUNK need Agent M?
Will Agent M become Stinky the Sidekick?
WHAT is that horrible smell?
Continued!

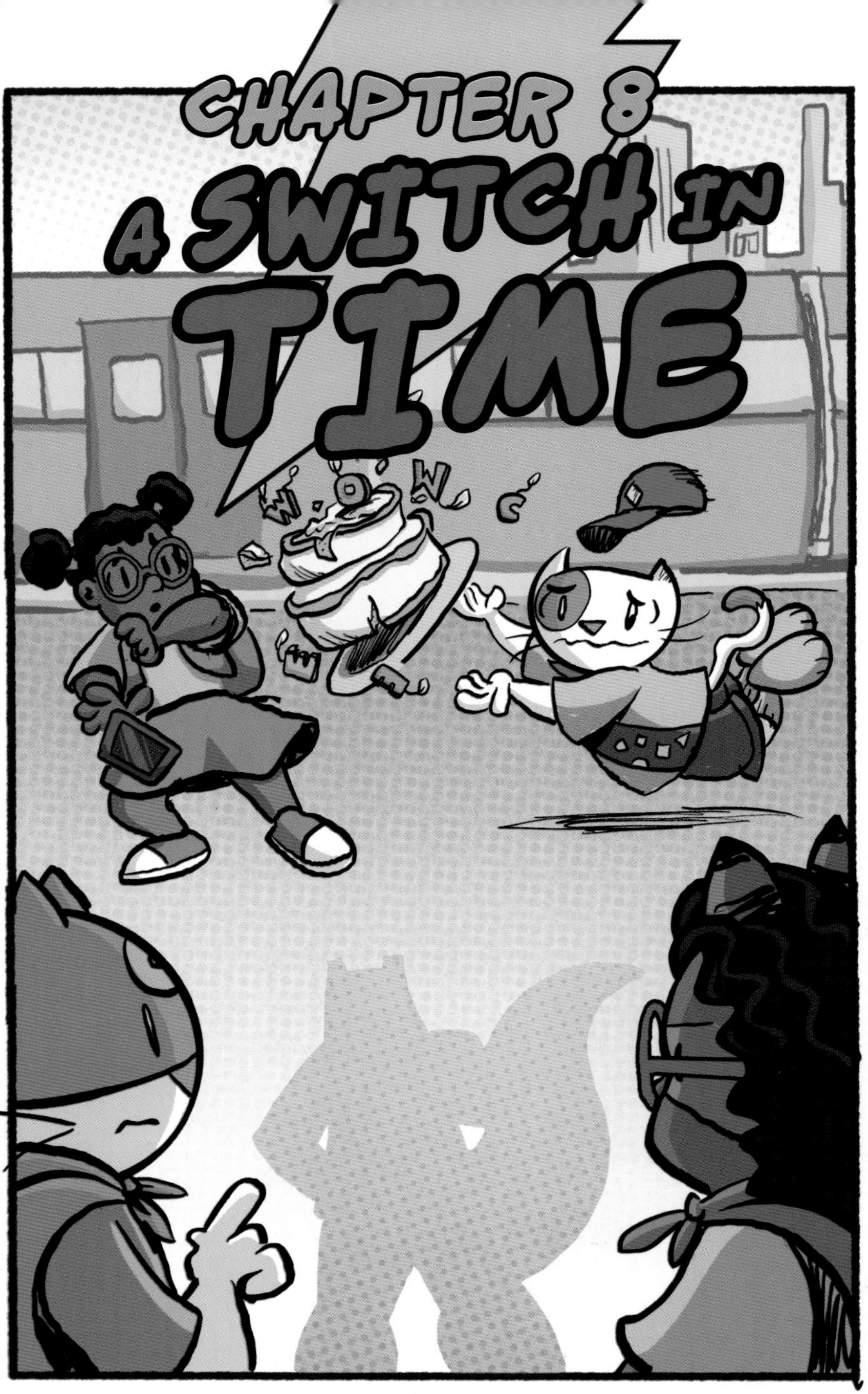
CHAPTER 8
A SWITCH IN TIME

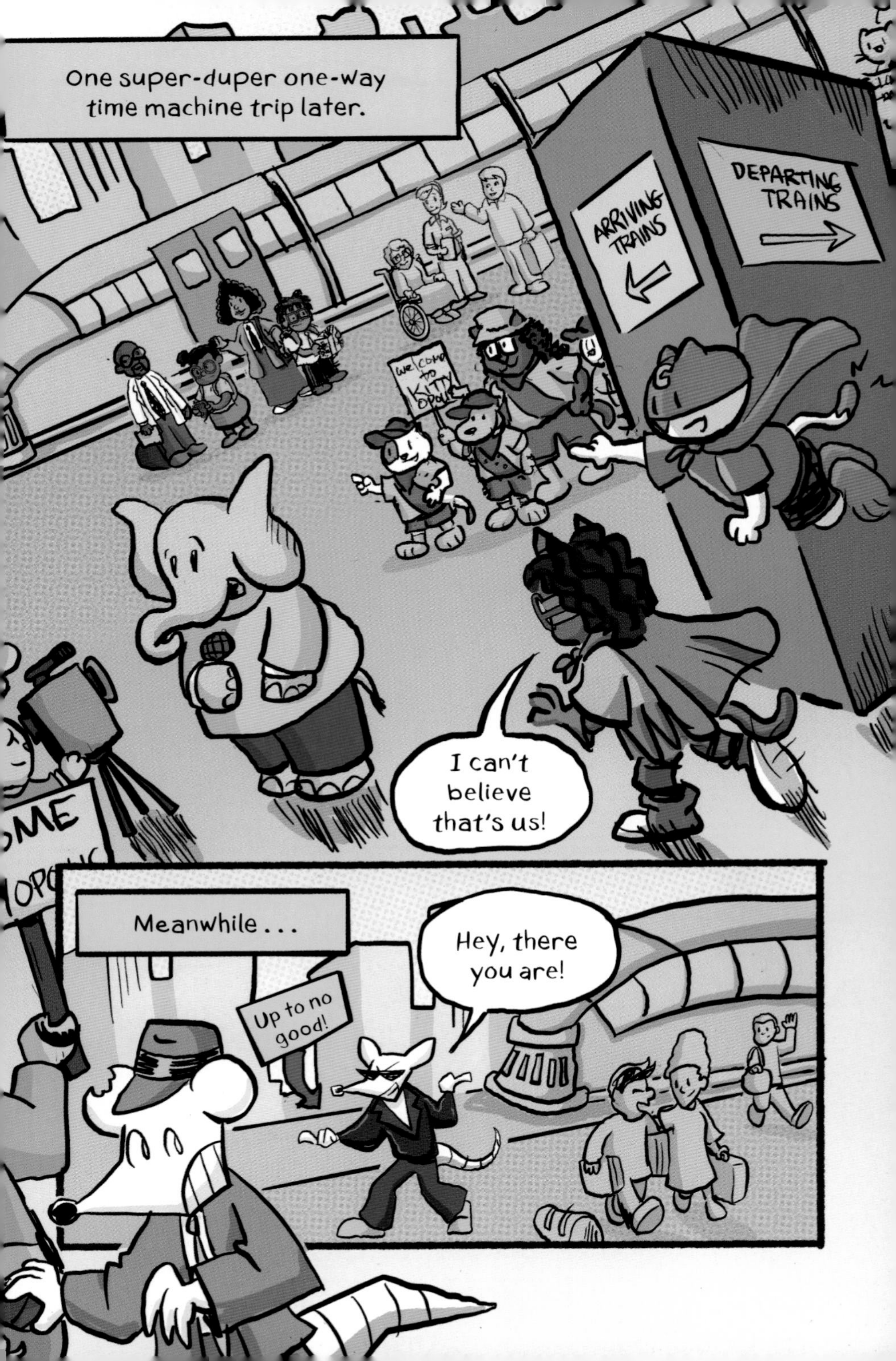
One super-duper one-way time machine trip later.
ARRIVING TRAINS
DEPARTING TRAINS
I can't believe that's us!
Meanwhile . . .
Up to no good!
Hey, there you are!

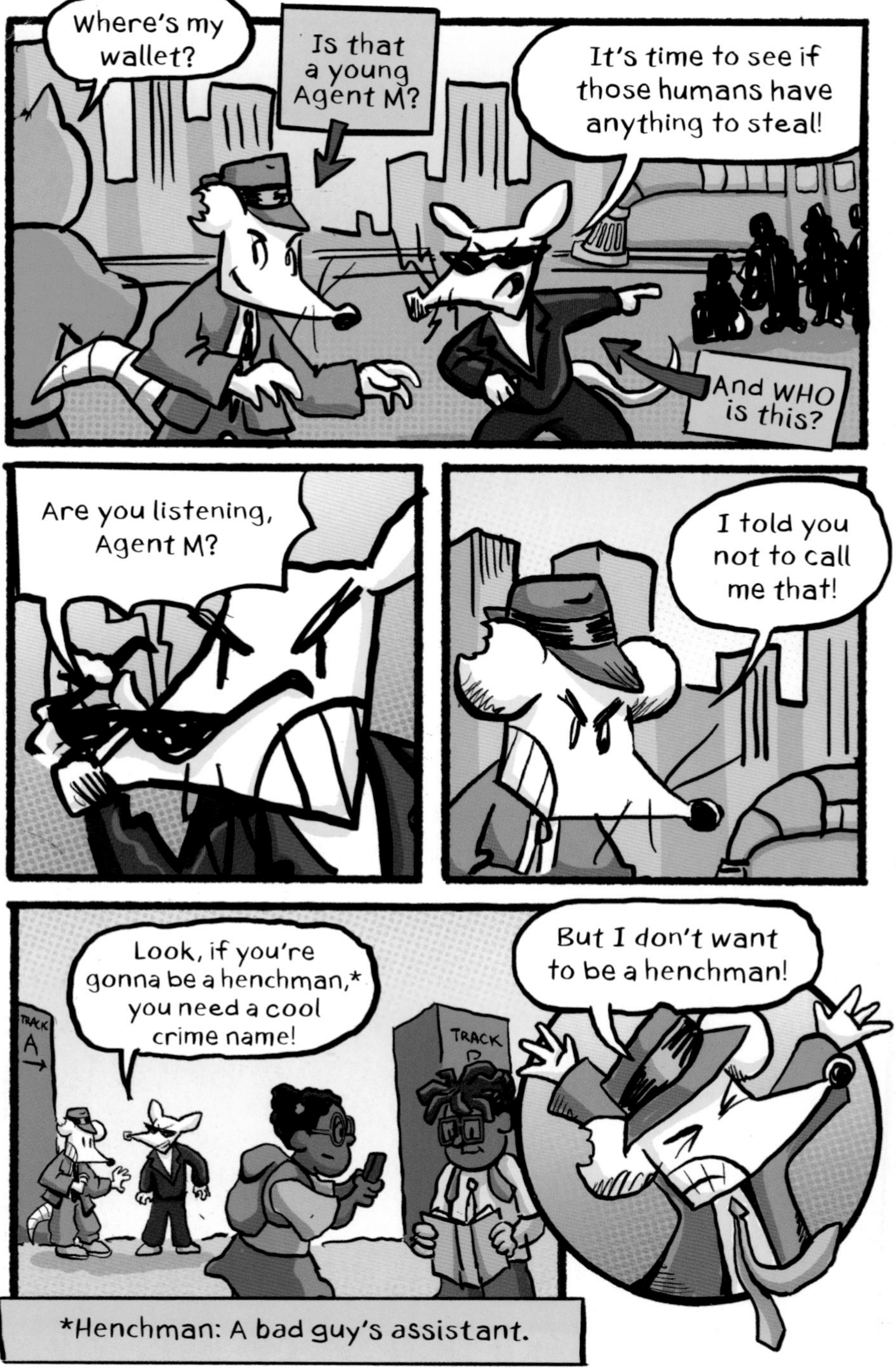
Where's my wallet?
Is that a young Agent M?
It's time to see if those humans have anything to steal!
And WHO is this?
Are you listening, Agent M?
I told you not to call me that!
Look, if you're gonna be a henchman,* you need a cool crime name!
But I don't want to be a henchman!
TRACK A
TRACK
*Henchman: A bad guy's assistant.

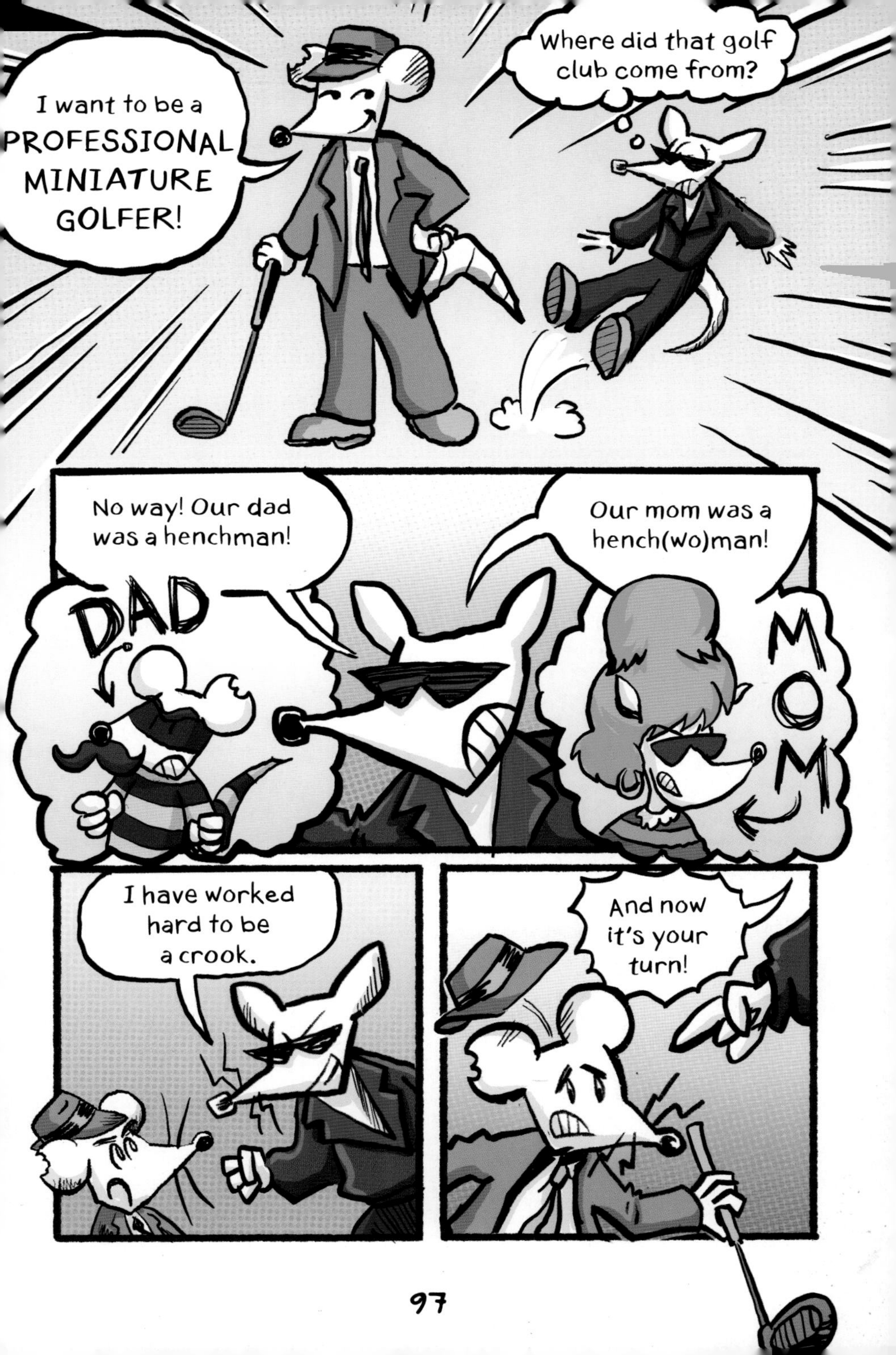
I want to be a PROFESSIONAL MINIATURE GOLFER!
Where did that golf club come from?
No way! Our dad was a henchman!
Our mom was a hench(wo)man!
DAD
MOM
I have worked hard to be a crook.
And now it's your turn!

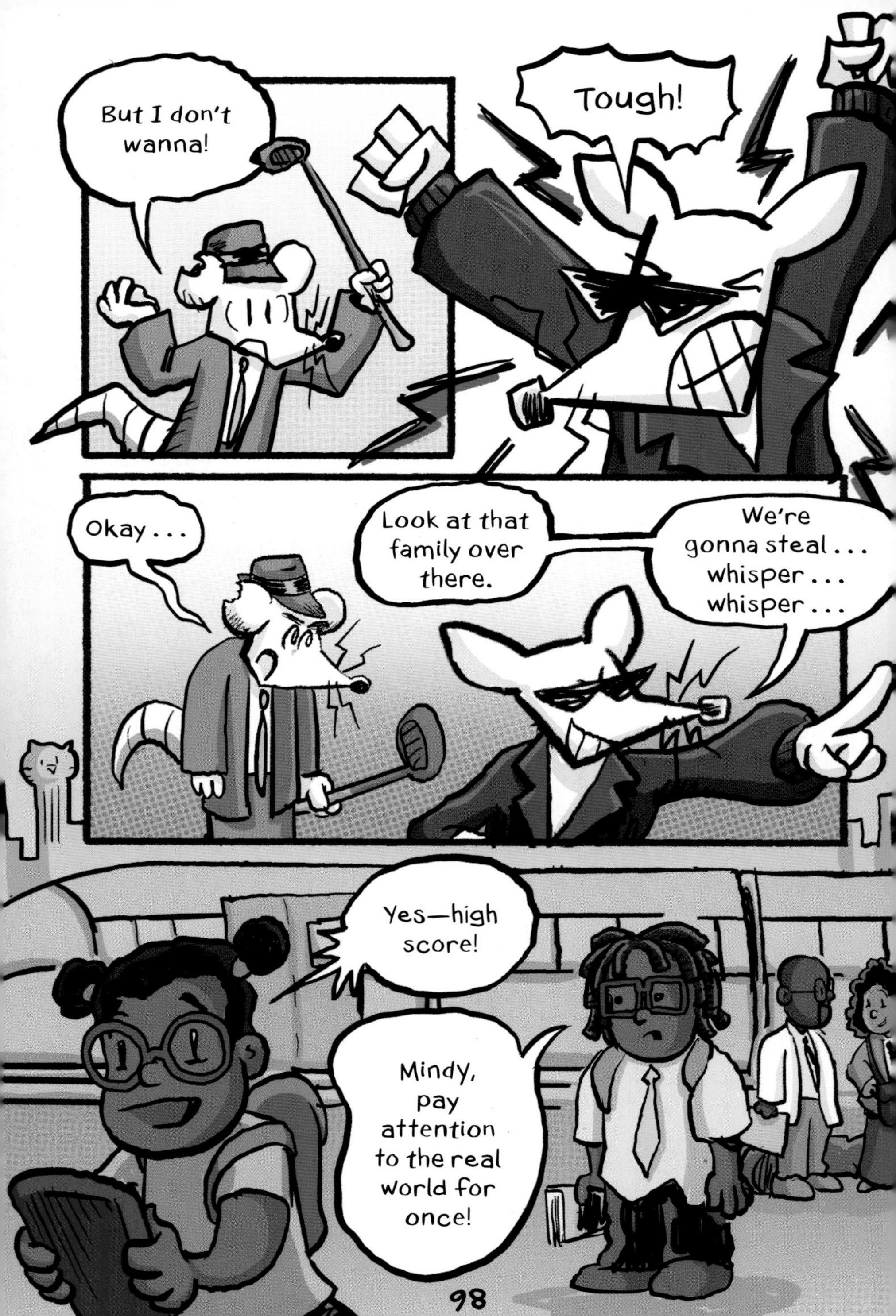
But I don't wanna!
Tough!
Okay . . .
Look at that family over there.
We're gonna steal . . . whisper . . . whisper . . .
Yes—high score!
Mindy, pay attention to the real world for once!

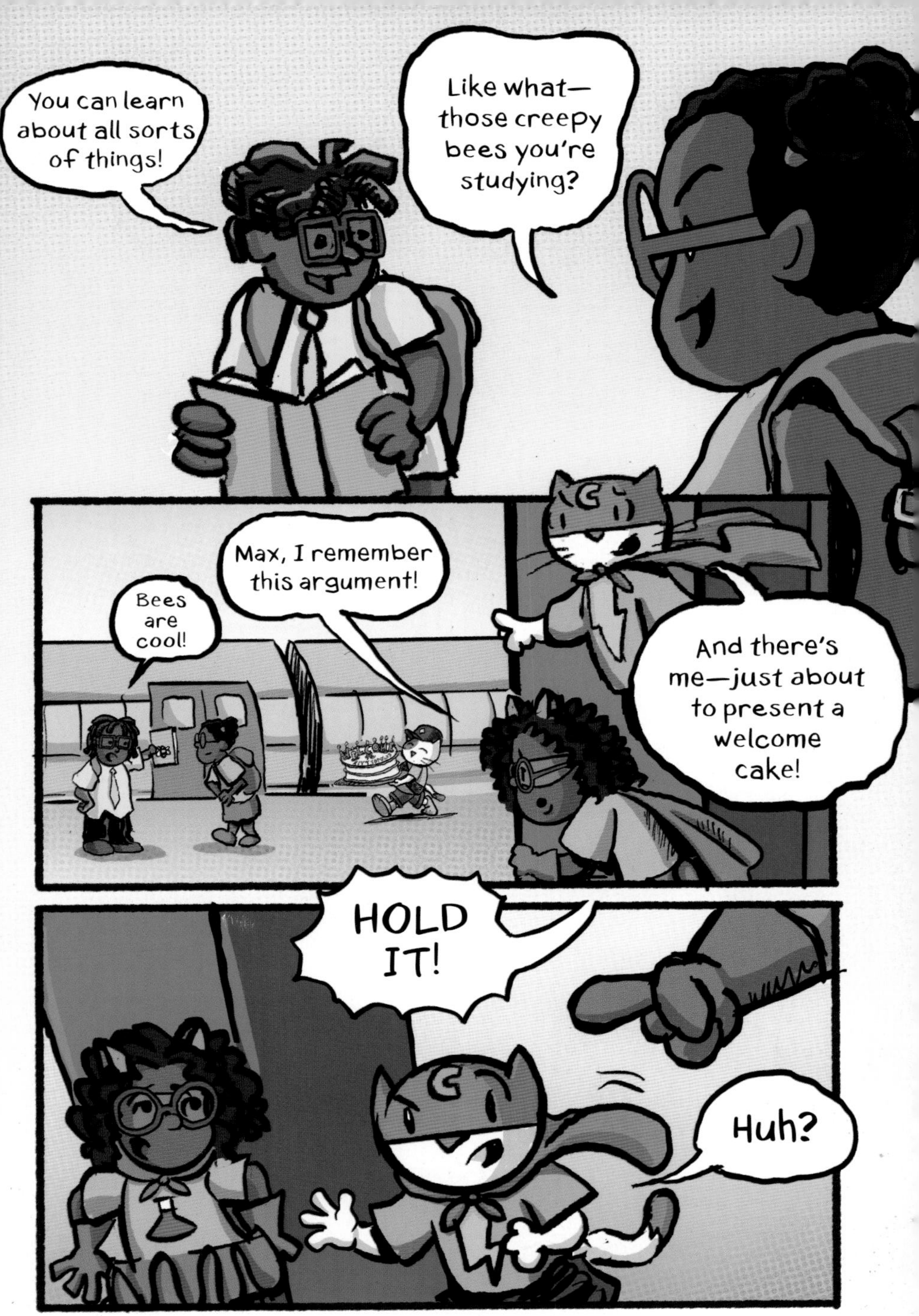
You can learn about all sorts of things!
Like what—those creepy bees you're studying?
Max, I remember this argument!
Bees are cool!
And there's me—just about to present a welcome cake!
HOLD IT!
Huh?

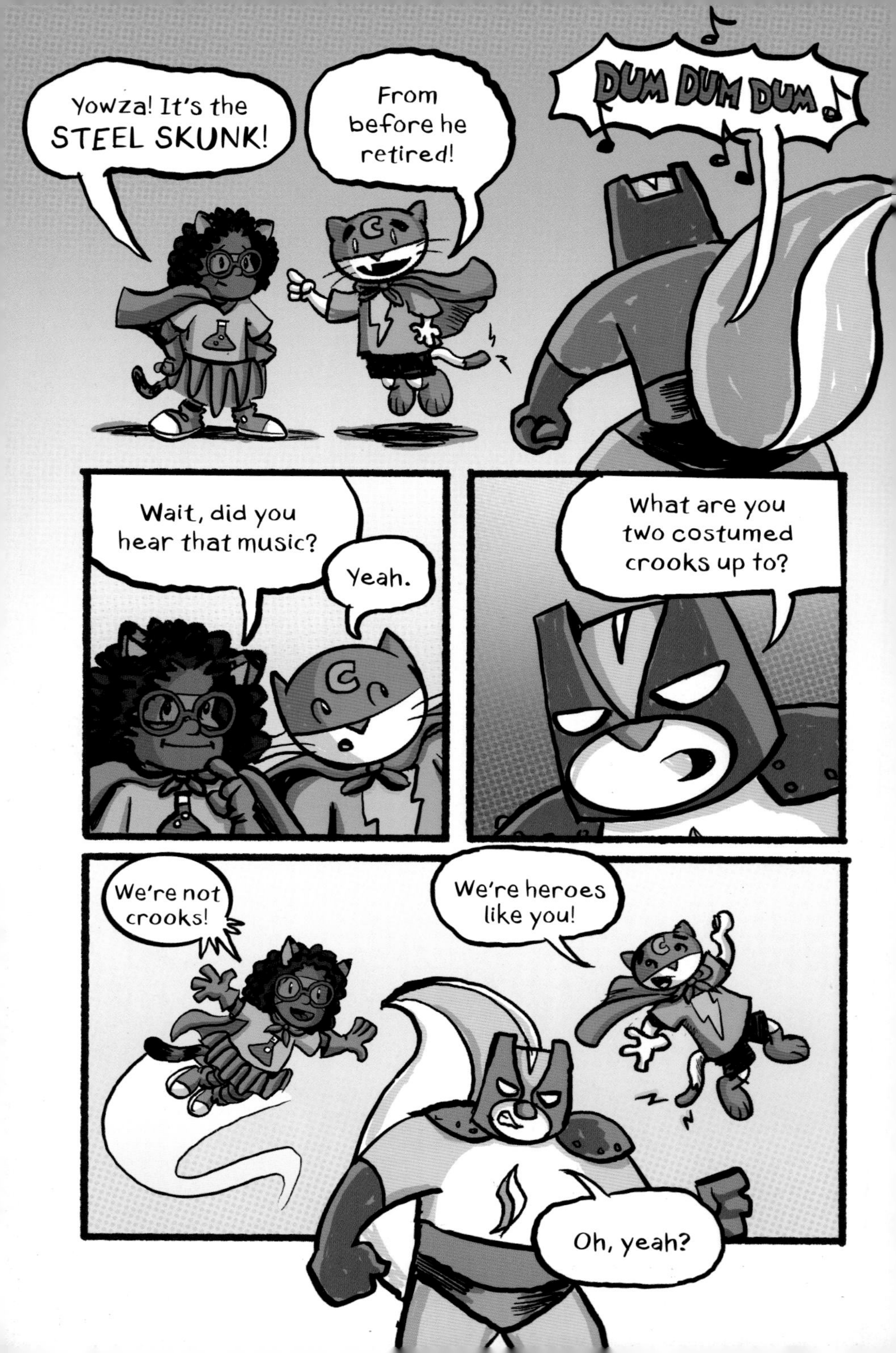
Yowza! It's the STEEL SKUNK!
From before he retired!
DUM DUM DUM
Wait, did you hear that music?
Yeah.
What are you two costumed crooks up to?
We're not crooks!
We're heroes like you!
Oh, yeah?

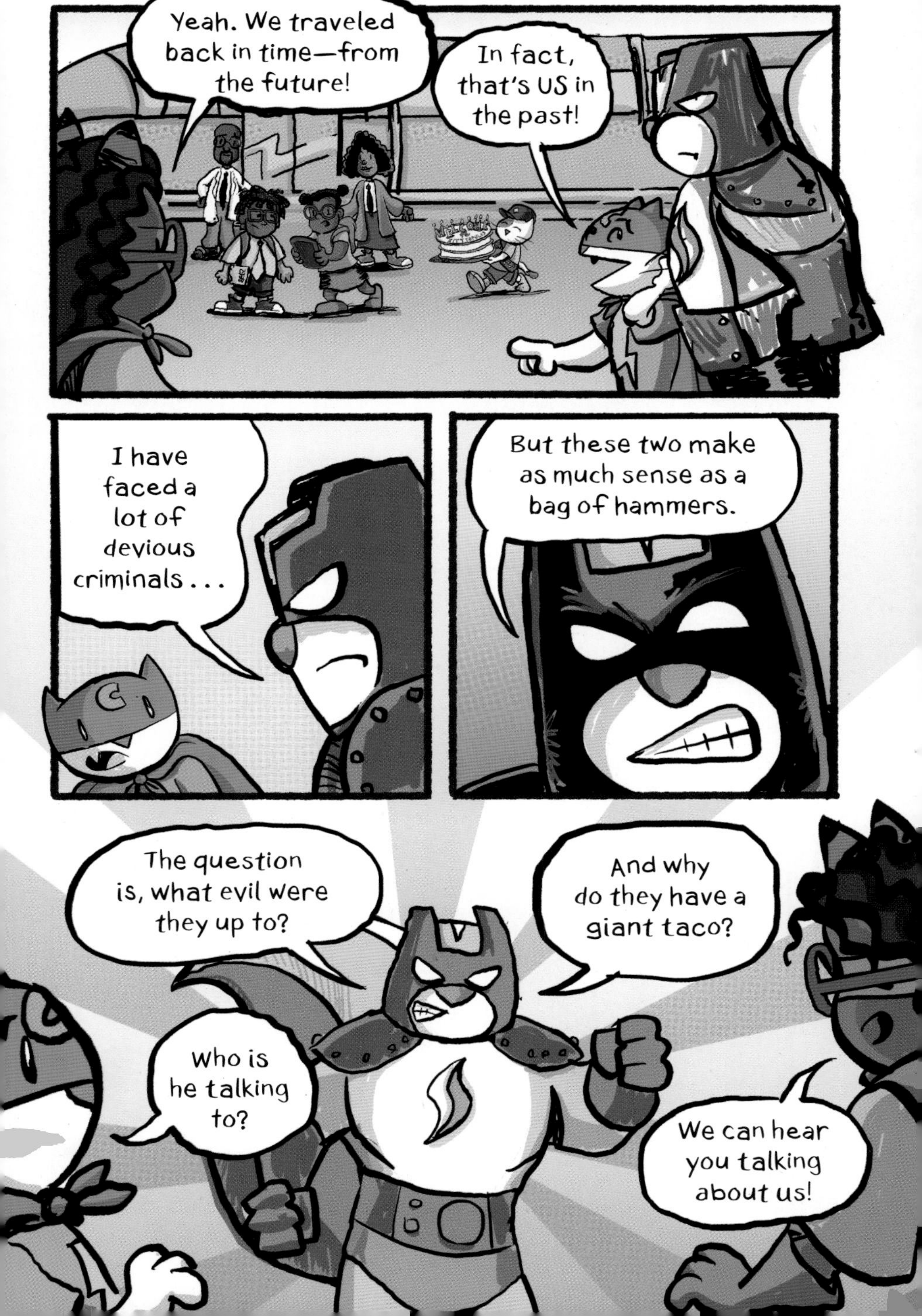
Yeah. We traveled back in time—from the future!
In fact, that's US in the past!
I have faced a lot of devious criminals . . .
But these two make as much sense as a bag of hammers.
The question is, what evil were they up to?
And why do they have a giant taco?
Who is he talking to?
We can hear you talking about us!

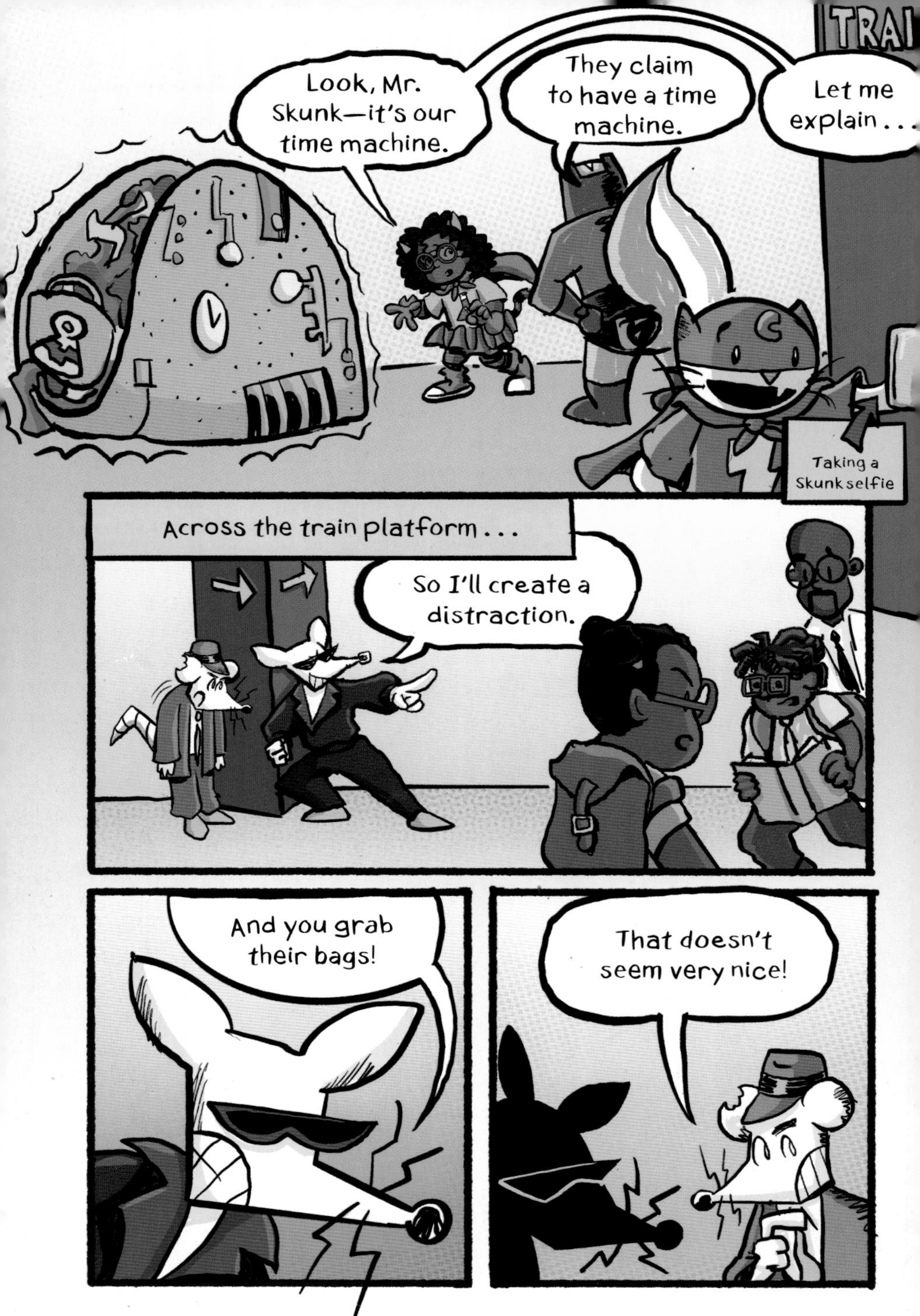

TRAI
Look, Mr. Skunk—it's our time machine.
They claim to have a time machine.
Let me explain . . .
Taking a Skunk selfie
Across the train platform . . .
So I'll create a distraction.
And you grab their bags!
That doesn't seem very nice!

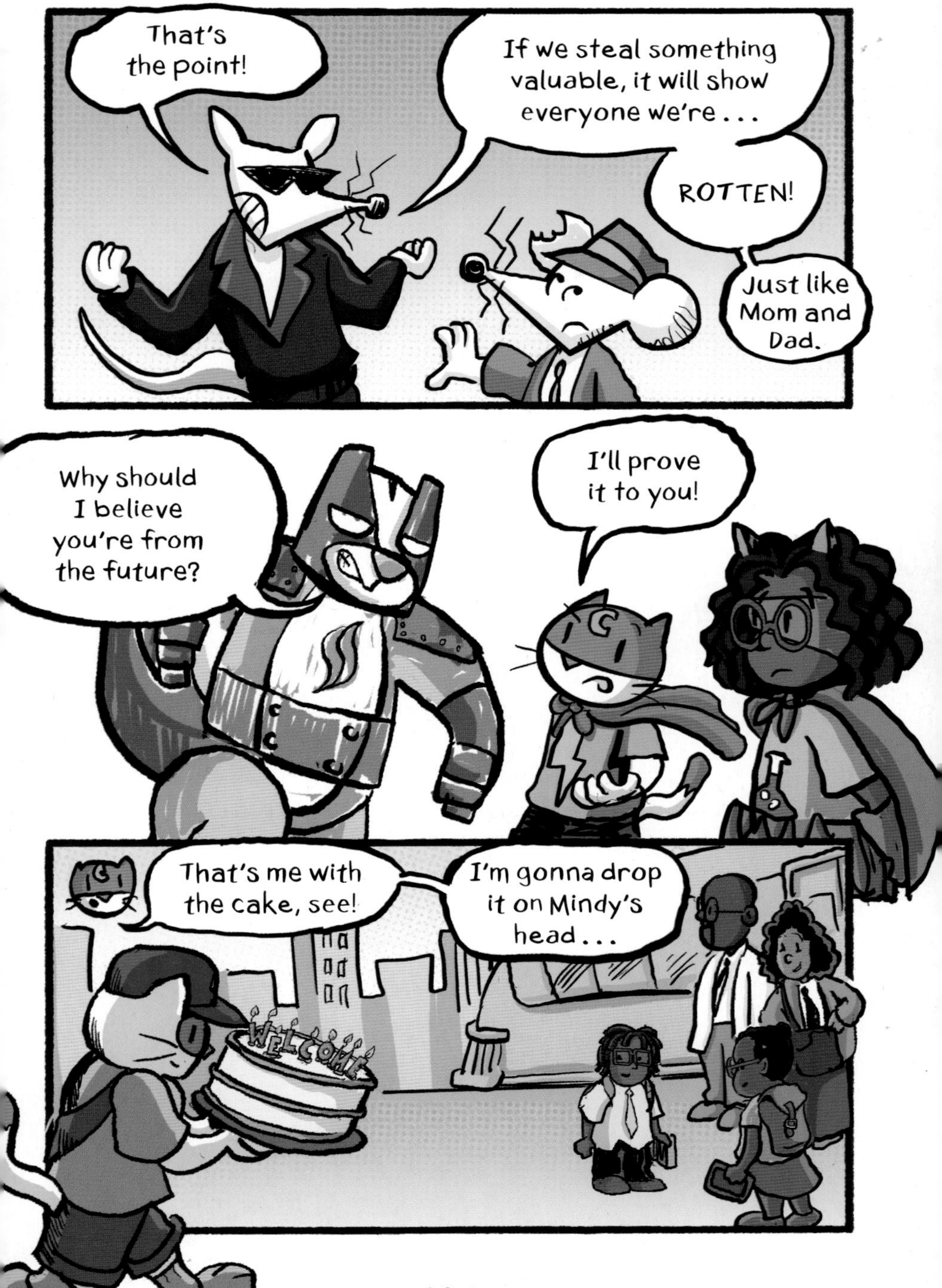
That's the point!
If we steal something valuable, it will show everyone we're . . .
ROTTEN!
Just like Mom and Dad.
Why should I believe you're from the future?
I'll prove it to you!
That's me with the cake, see!
I'm gonna drop it on Mindy's head . . .
WELCOME

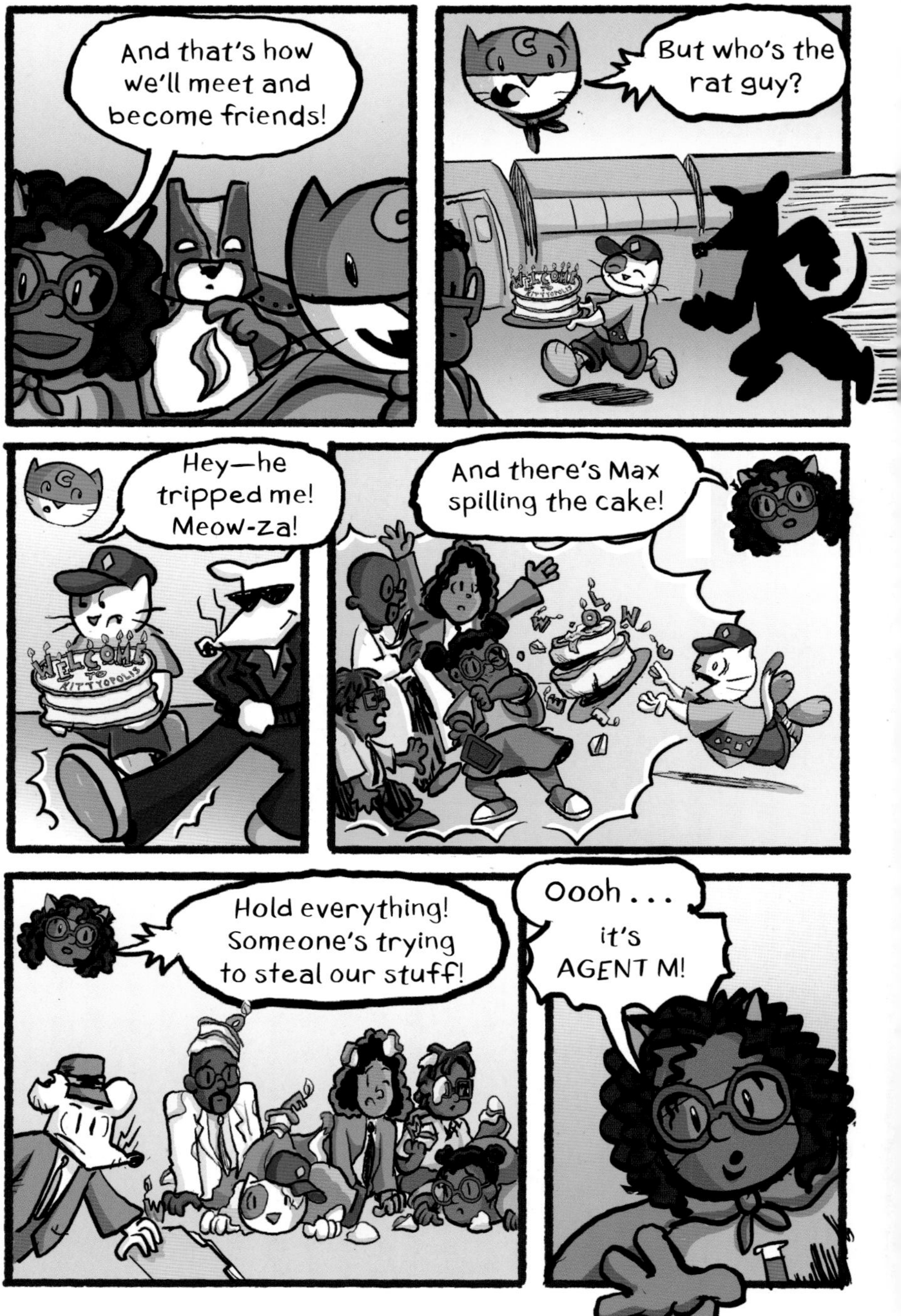
And that's how we'll meet and become friends!
But who's the rat guy?
WELCOME TO KITTYOPOLIS
Hey—he tripped me! Meow-za!
WELCOME TO KITTYOPOLIS
And there's Max spilling the cake!
Hold everything! Someone's trying to steal our stuff!
Oooh . . .
it's AGENT M!

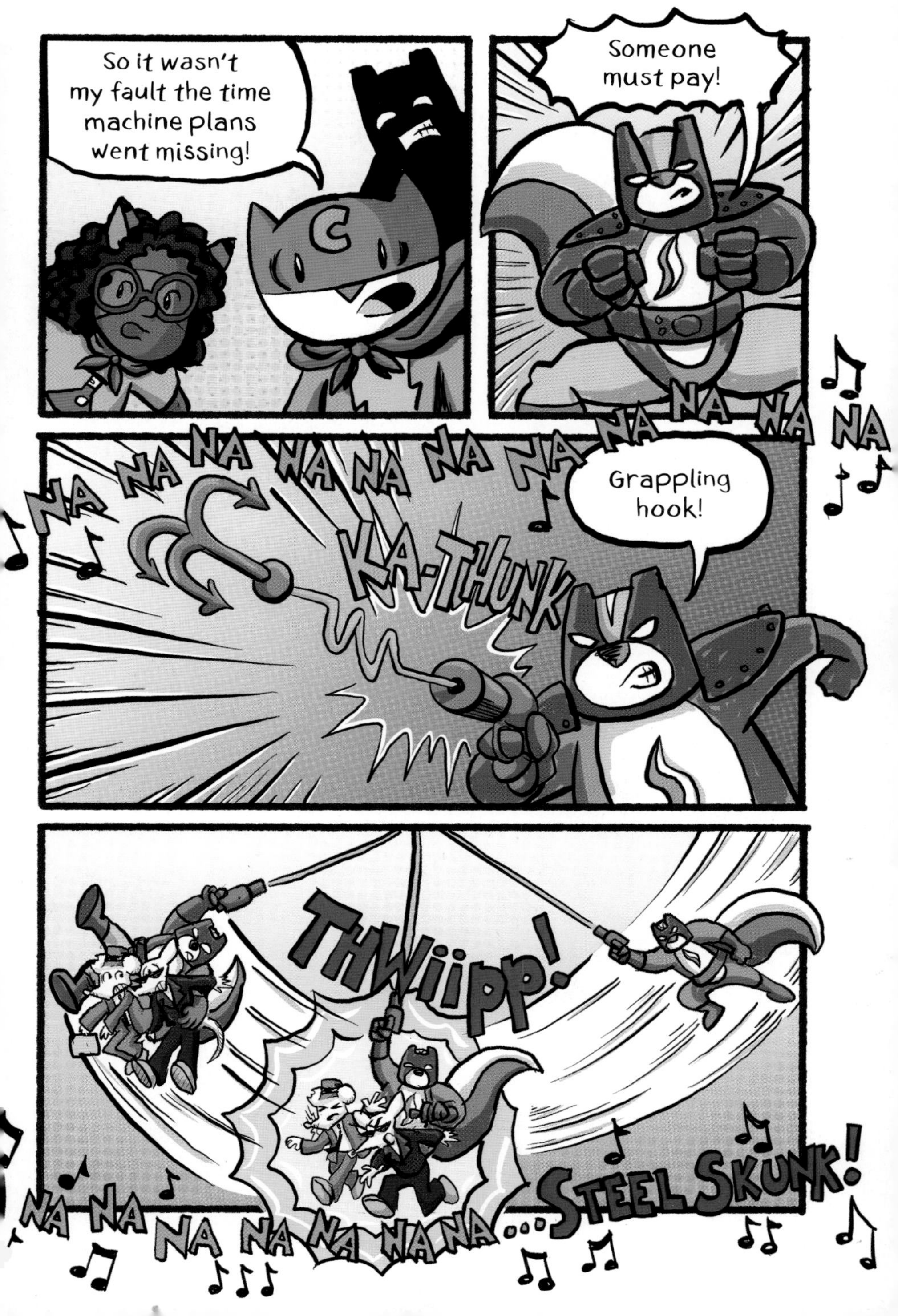
So it wasn't my fault the time machine plans went missing!
Someone must pay!
NA NA NA NA NA NA NA NA NA NA NA NA
Grappling hook!
KLA-THUNK
THWiiPP!
NA NA NA NA NA NA NA NA... STEEL SKUNK!

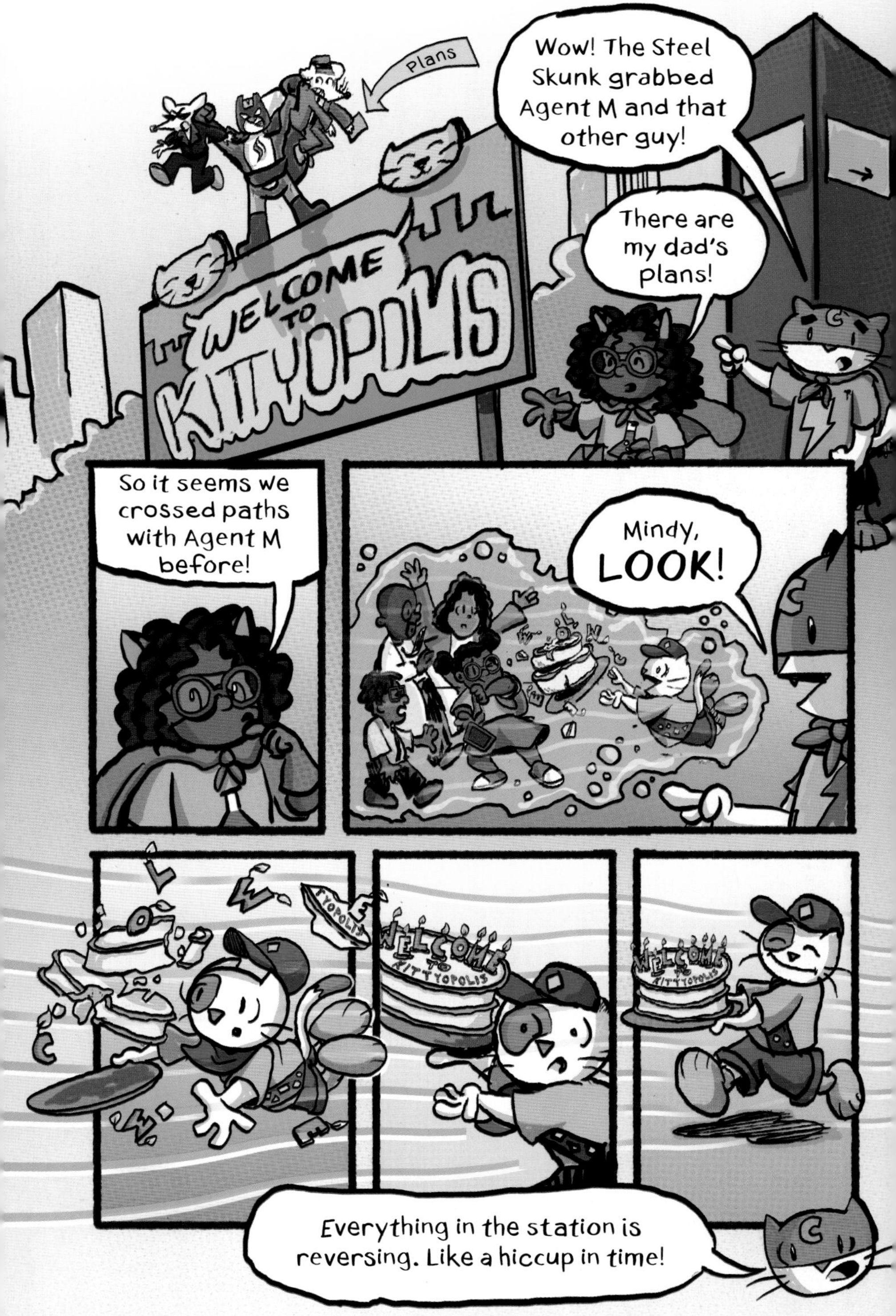

Plans
WELCOME TO KITTYOPOLIS
Wow! The Steel Skunk grabbed Agent M and that other guy!
There are my dad's plans!
So it seems we crossed paths with Agent M before!
Mindy, LOOK!
WELCOME TO KITTYOPOLIS
WELCOME TO KITTYOPOLIS
Everything in the station is reversing. Like a hiccup in time!

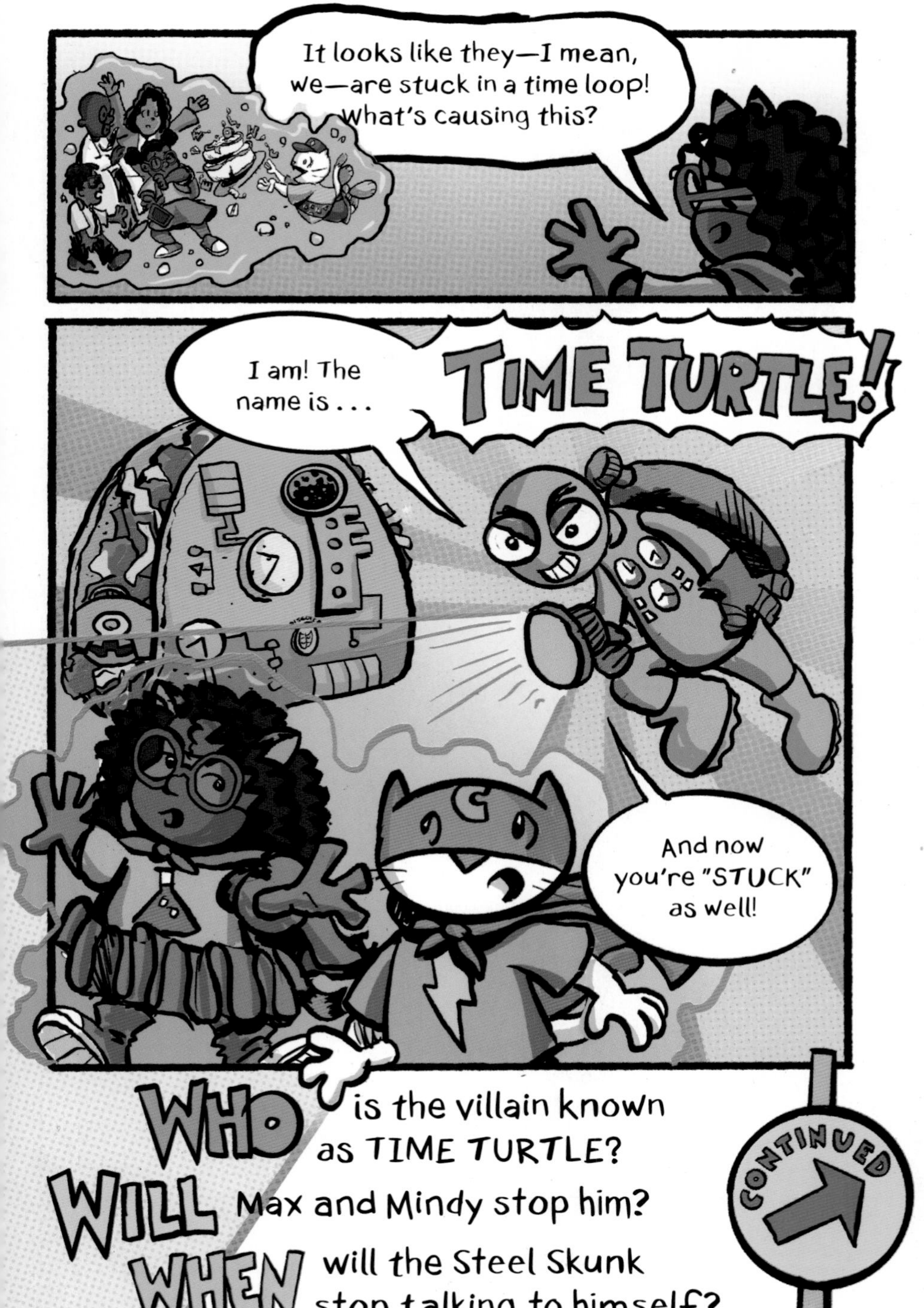
It looks like they—I mean, we—are stuck in a time loop! What's causing this?
I am! The name is . . .
TIME TURTLE!
And now you're "STUCK" as well!
WHO is the villain known as TIME TURTLE?
WILL Max and Mindy stop him?
WHEN will the Steel Skunk stop talking to himself?
CONTINUED

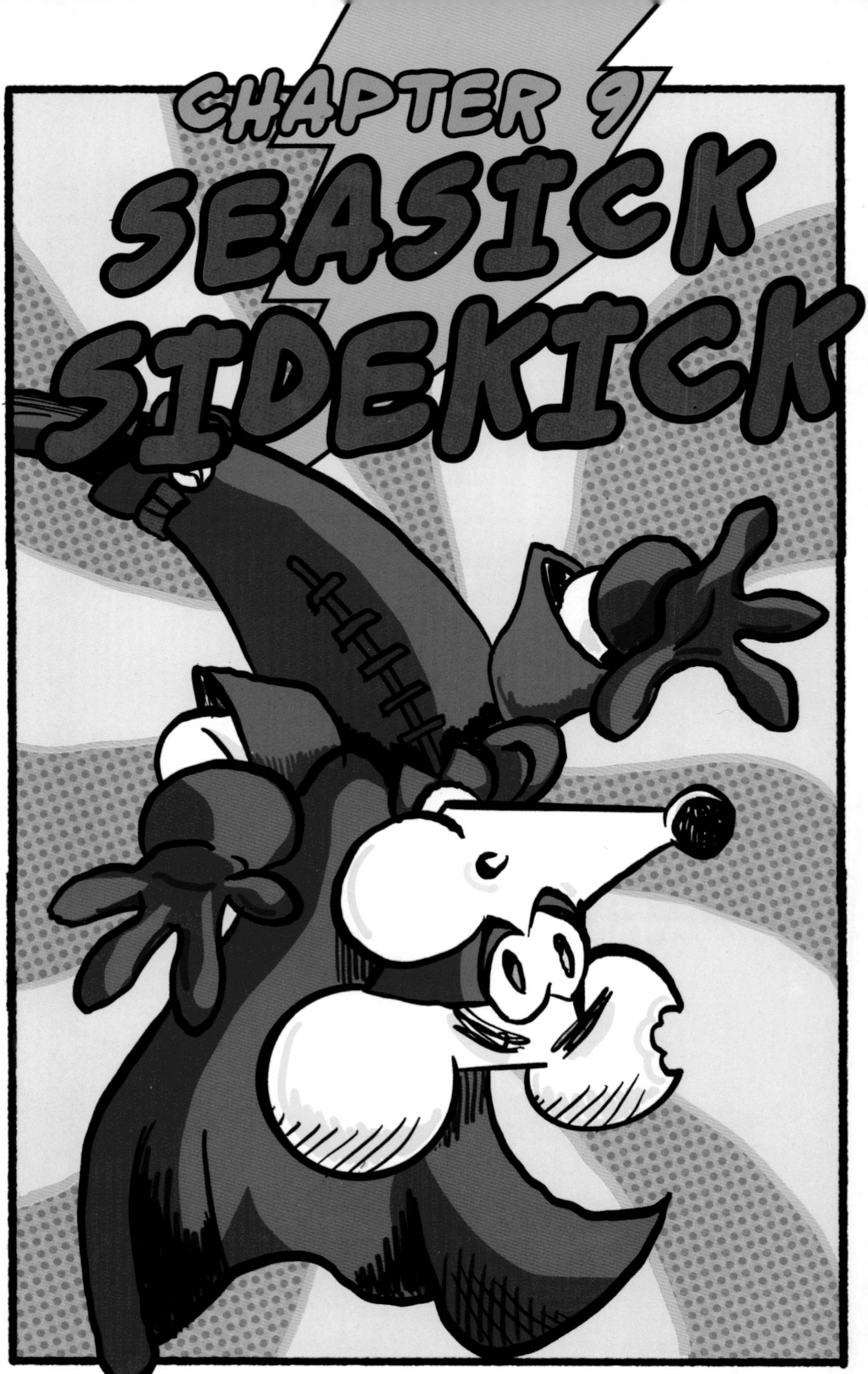
CHAPTER 9
SEASICK SIDEKICK

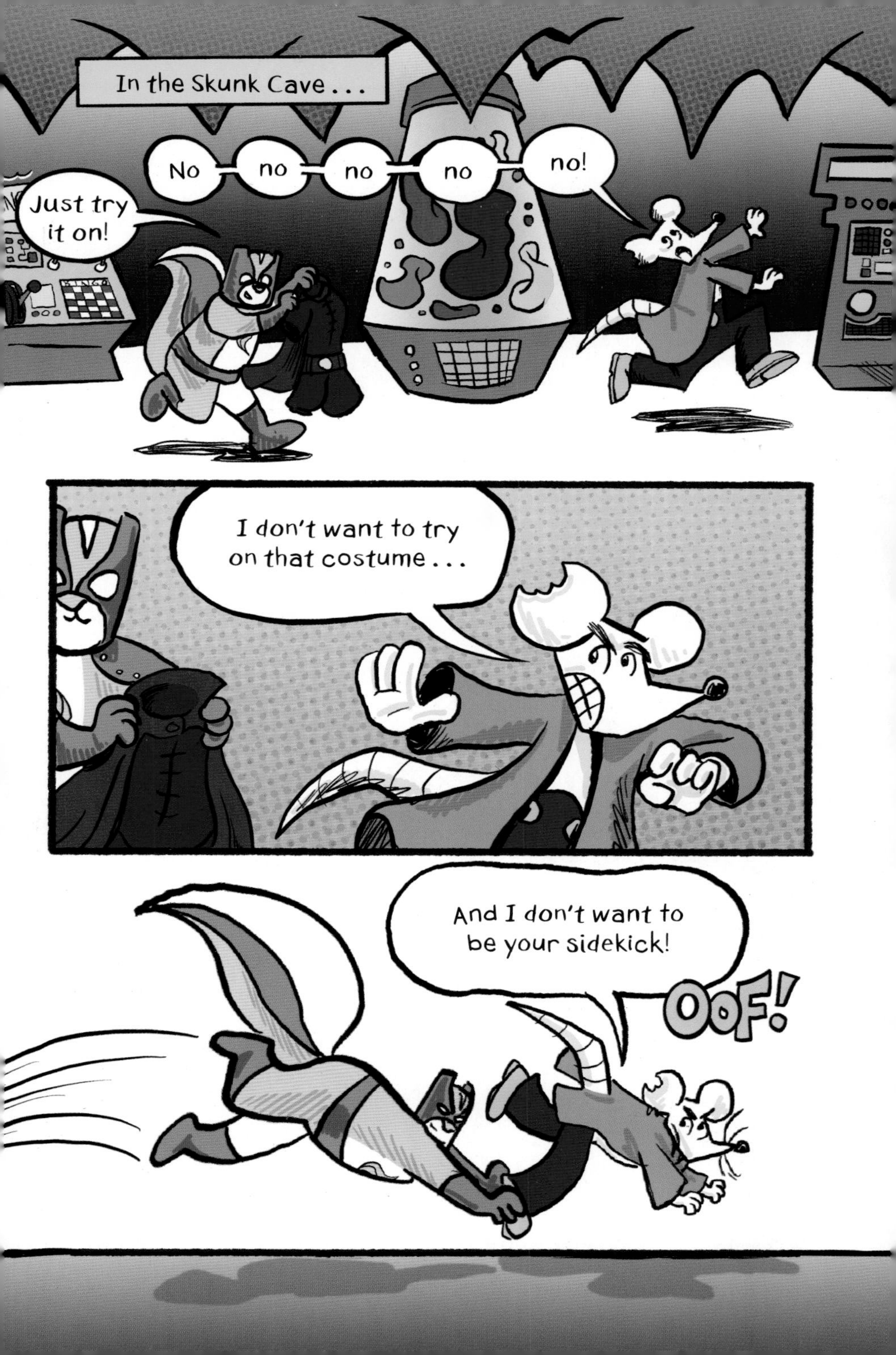
In the Skunk Cave . . .
Just try it on!
No no no no no!
I don't want to try on that costume . . .
And I don't want to be your sidekick!
OOF!

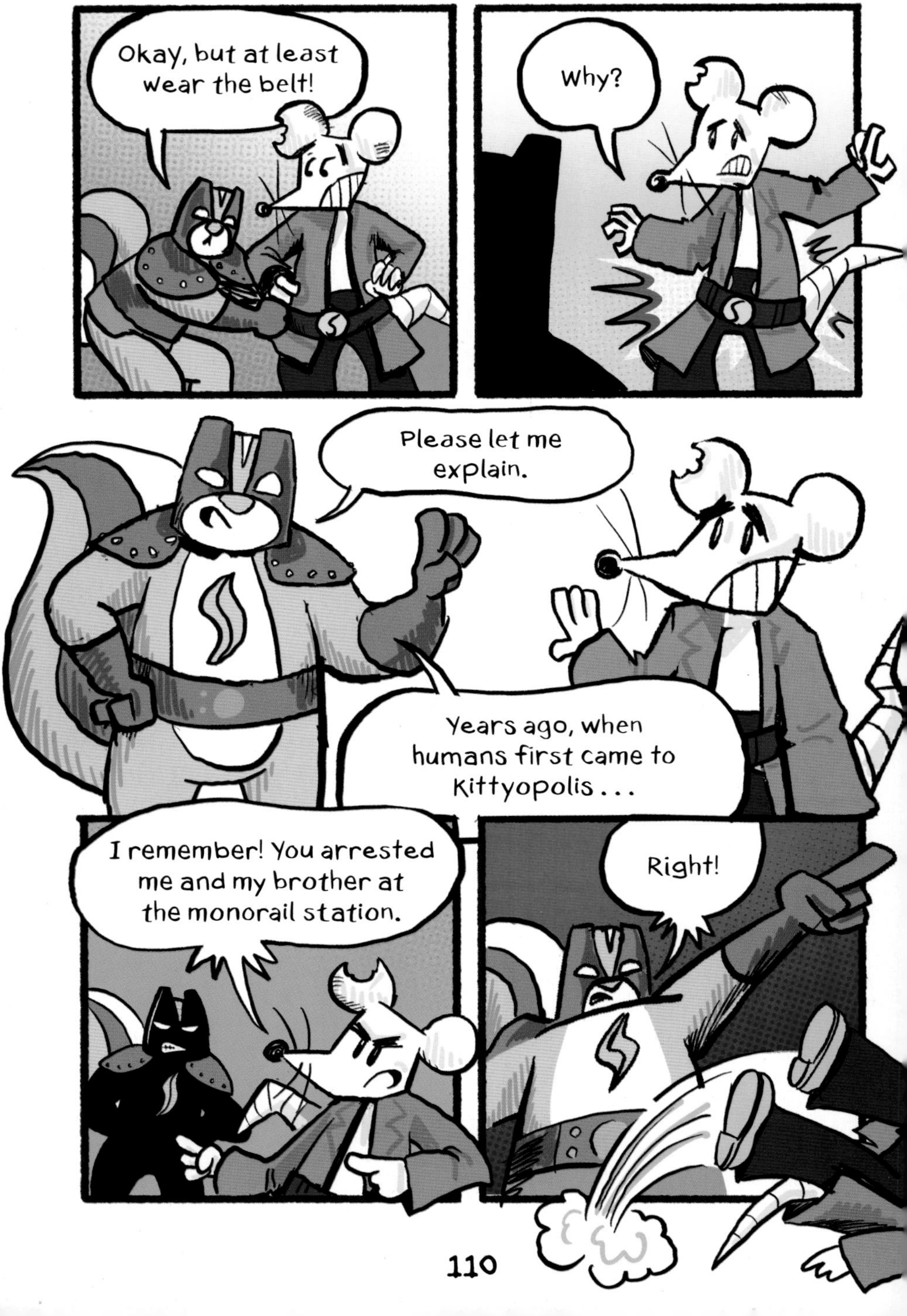
Okay, but at least wear the belt!
Why?
Please let me explain.
Years ago, when humans first came to Kittyopolis . . .
I remember! You arrested me and my brother at the monorail station.
Right!

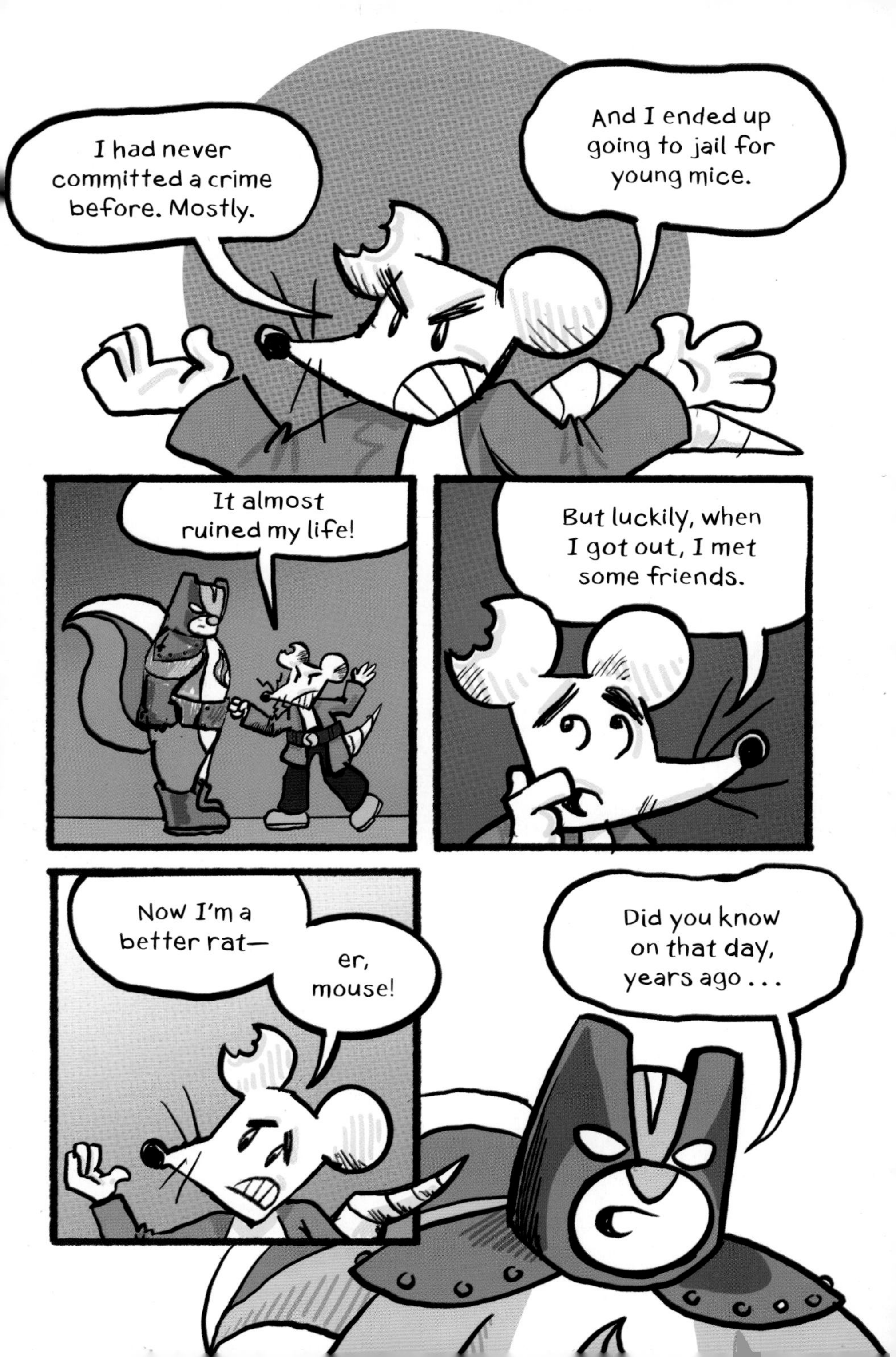
I had never committed a crime before. Mostly.
And I ended up going to jail for young mice.
It almost ruined my life!
But luckily, when I got out, I met some friends.
Now I'm a better rat—
er, mouse!
Did you know on that day, years ago . . .

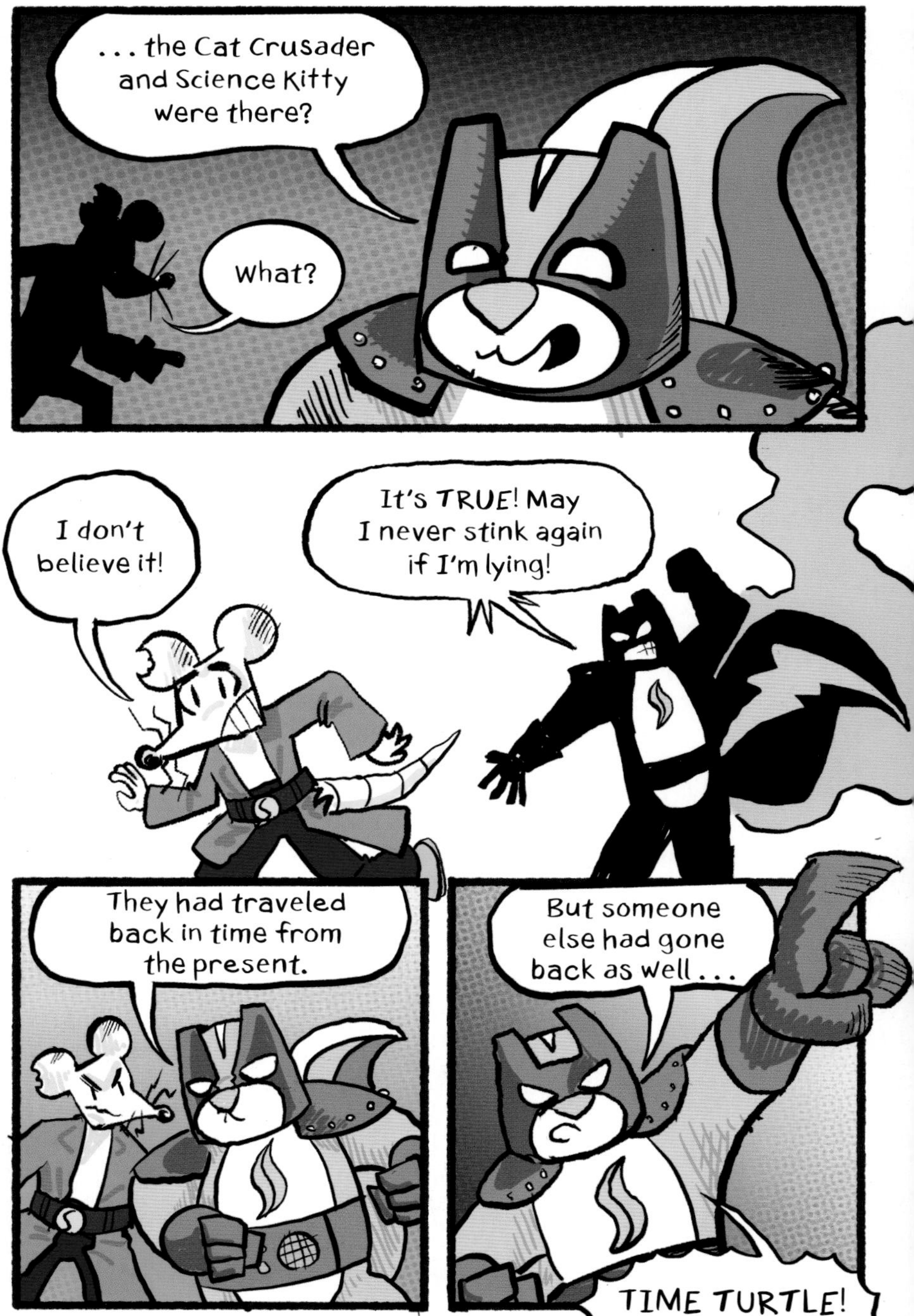
. . . the Cat Crusader and Science Kitty were there?
What?
I don't believe it!
It's TRUE! May I never stink again if I'm lying!
They had traveled back in time from the present.
But someone else had gone back as well . . .
TIME TURTLE!

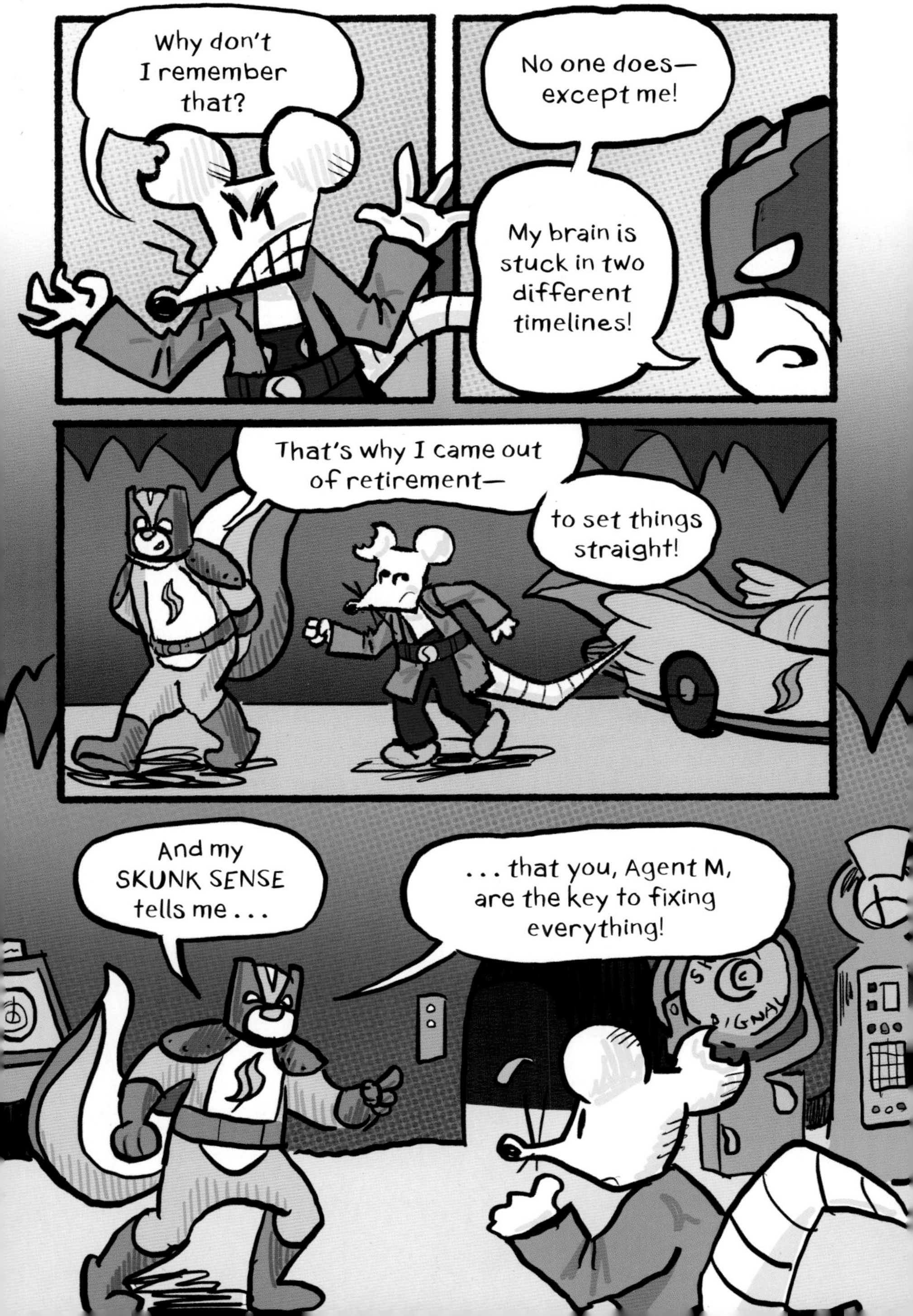
Why don't I remember that?
No one does— except me!
My brain is stuck in two different timelines!
That's why I came out of retirement—
to set things straight!
And my SKUNK SENSE tells me . . .
. . . that you, Agent M, are the key to fixing everything!
SIGNAL

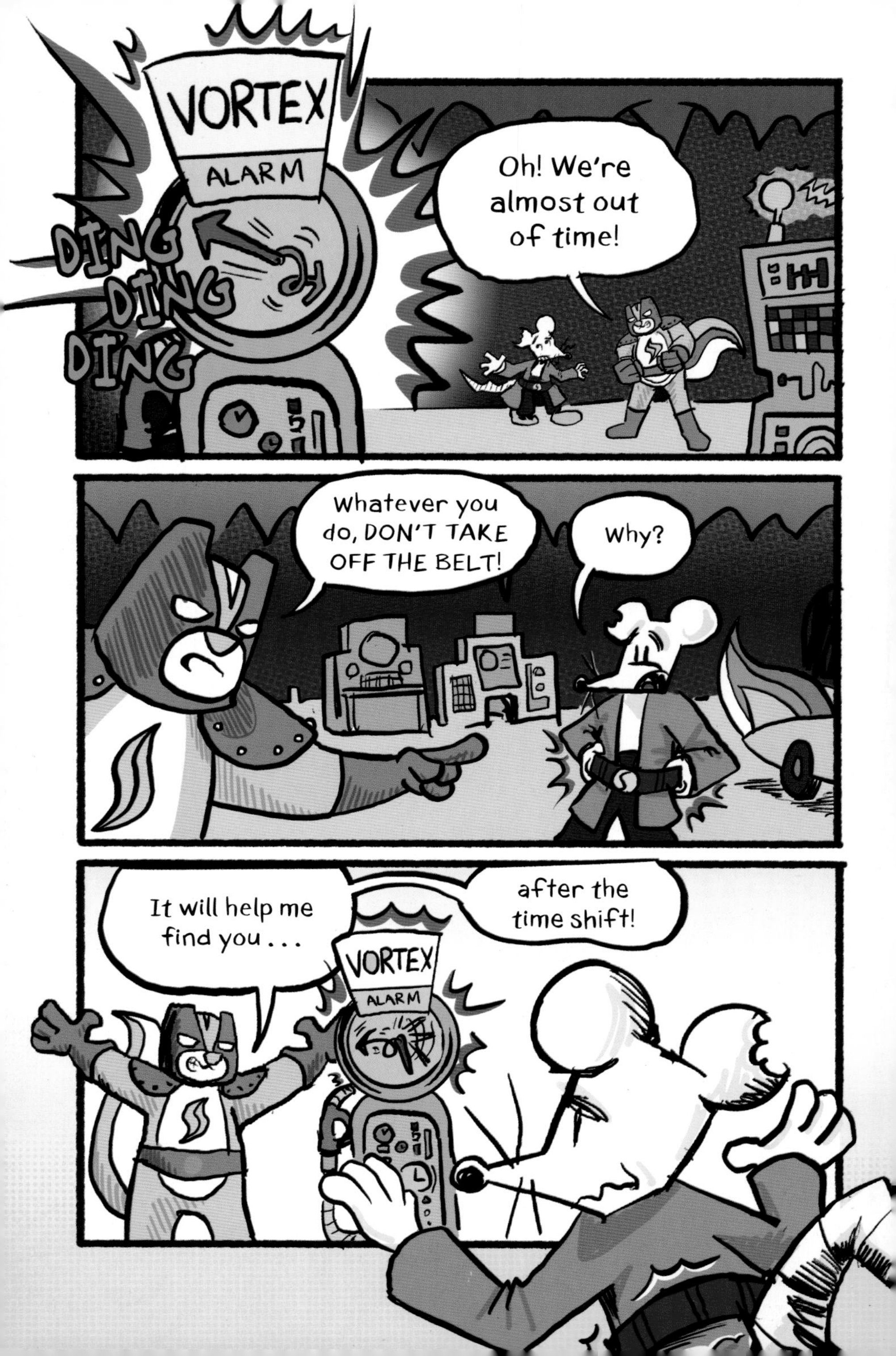
VORTEX
ALARM
DING
DING
DING
Oh! We're almost out of time!
Whatever you do, DON'T TAKE OFF THE BELT!
Why?
It will help me find you . . .
after the time shift!
VORTEX
ALARM

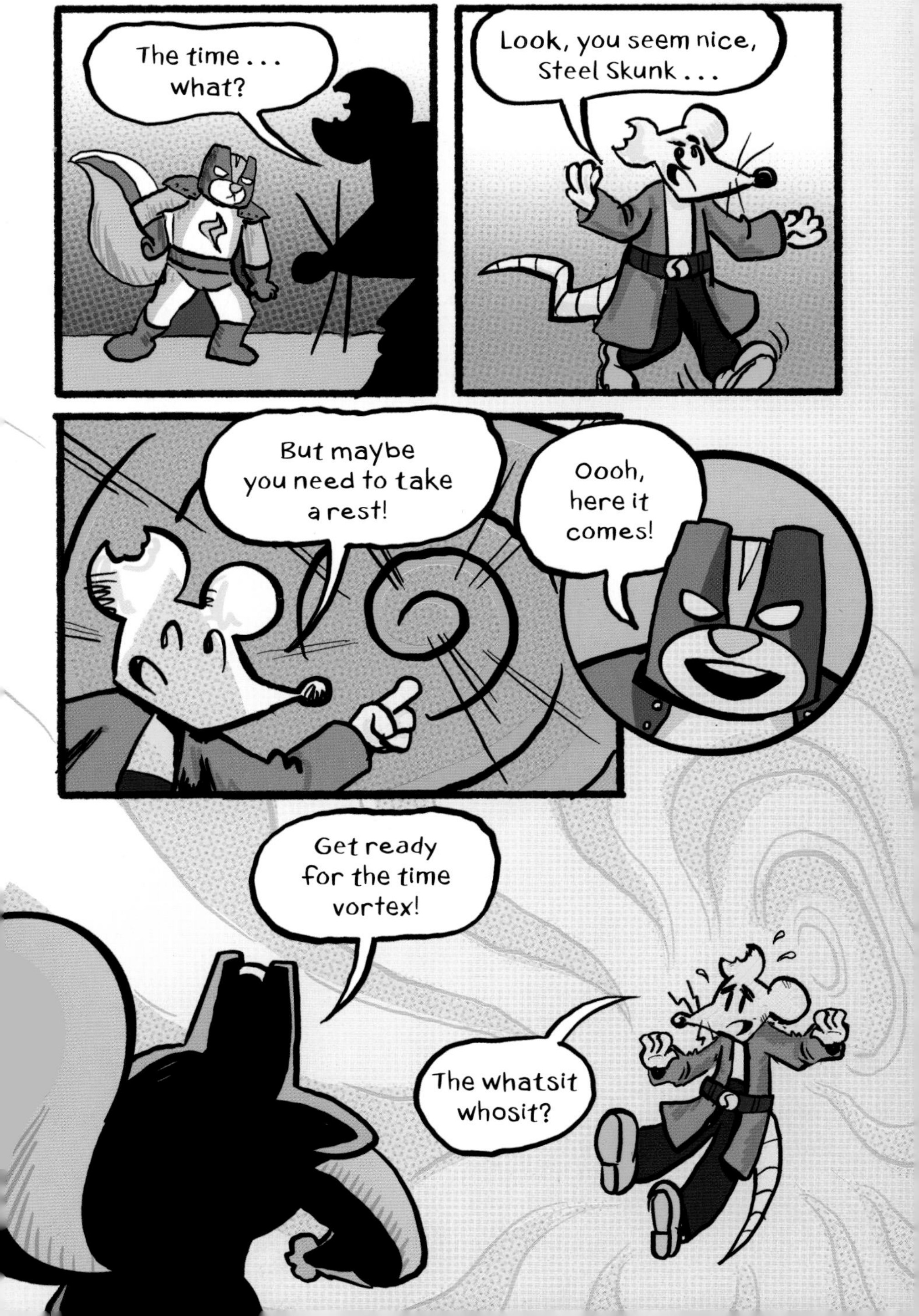
The time . . . what?
Look, you seem nice, Steel Skunk . . .
But maybe you need to take a rest!
Oooh, here it comes!
Get ready for the time vortex!
The whatsit whosit?

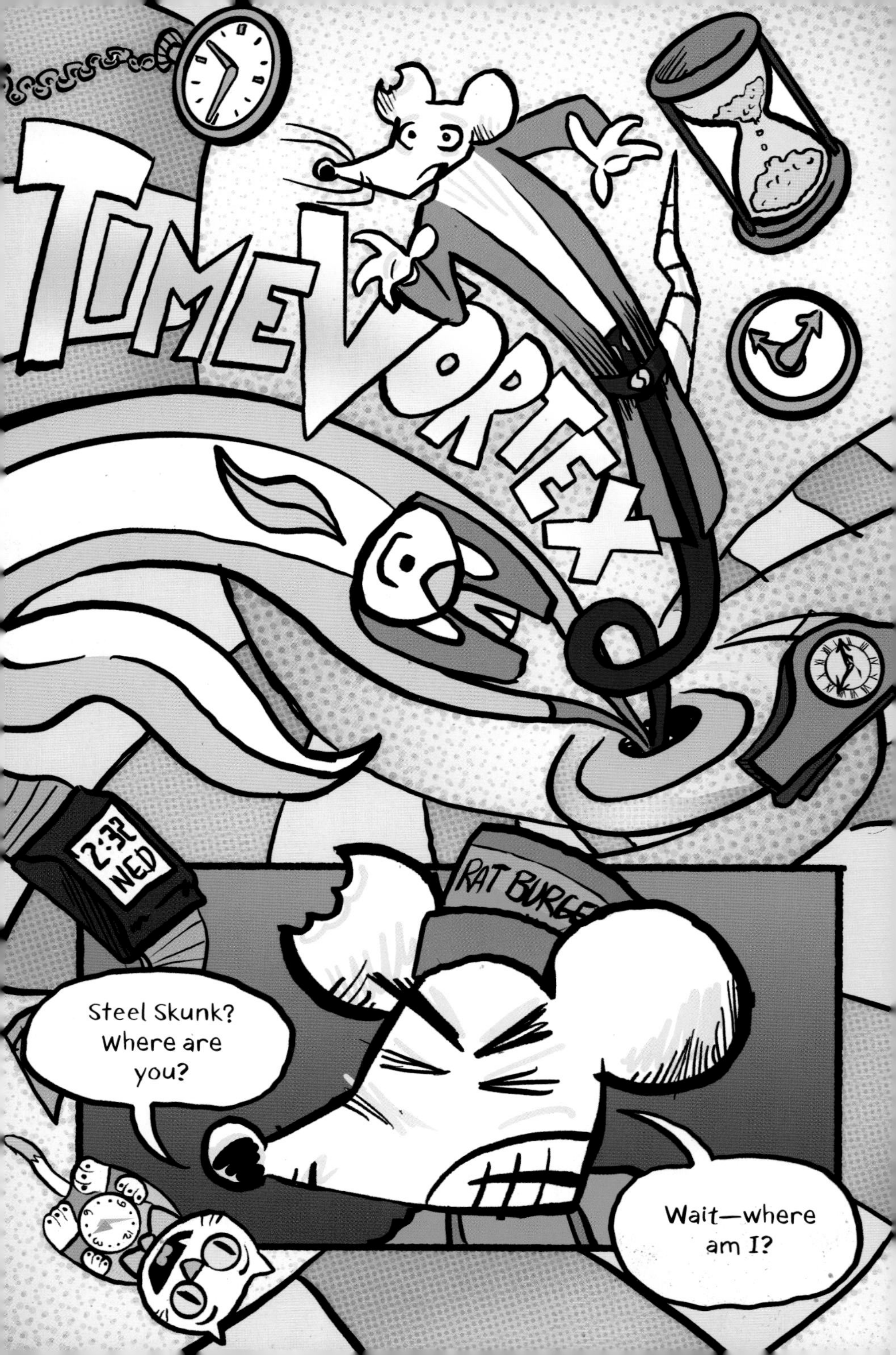
TIME VORTEX
2:32
WED
RAT BURGE
Steel Skunk? Where are you?
Wait—where am I?

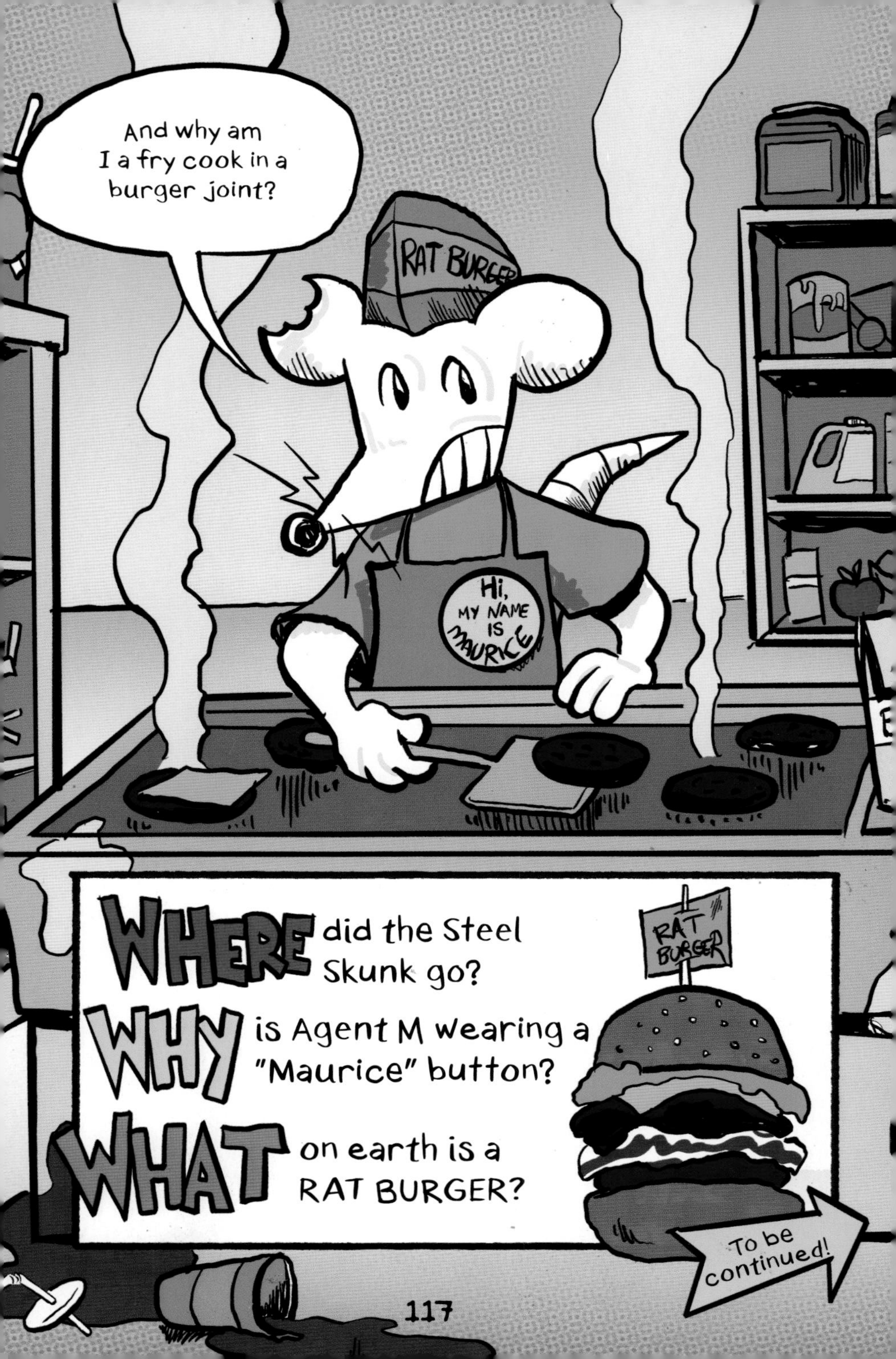
And why am I a fry cook in a burger joint?
RAT BURGER
Hi, MY NAME IS MAURICE
WHERE did the Steel Skunk go?
WHY is Agent M wearing a "Maurice" button?
WHAT on earth is a RAT BURGER?
RAT BURGER
To be continued!

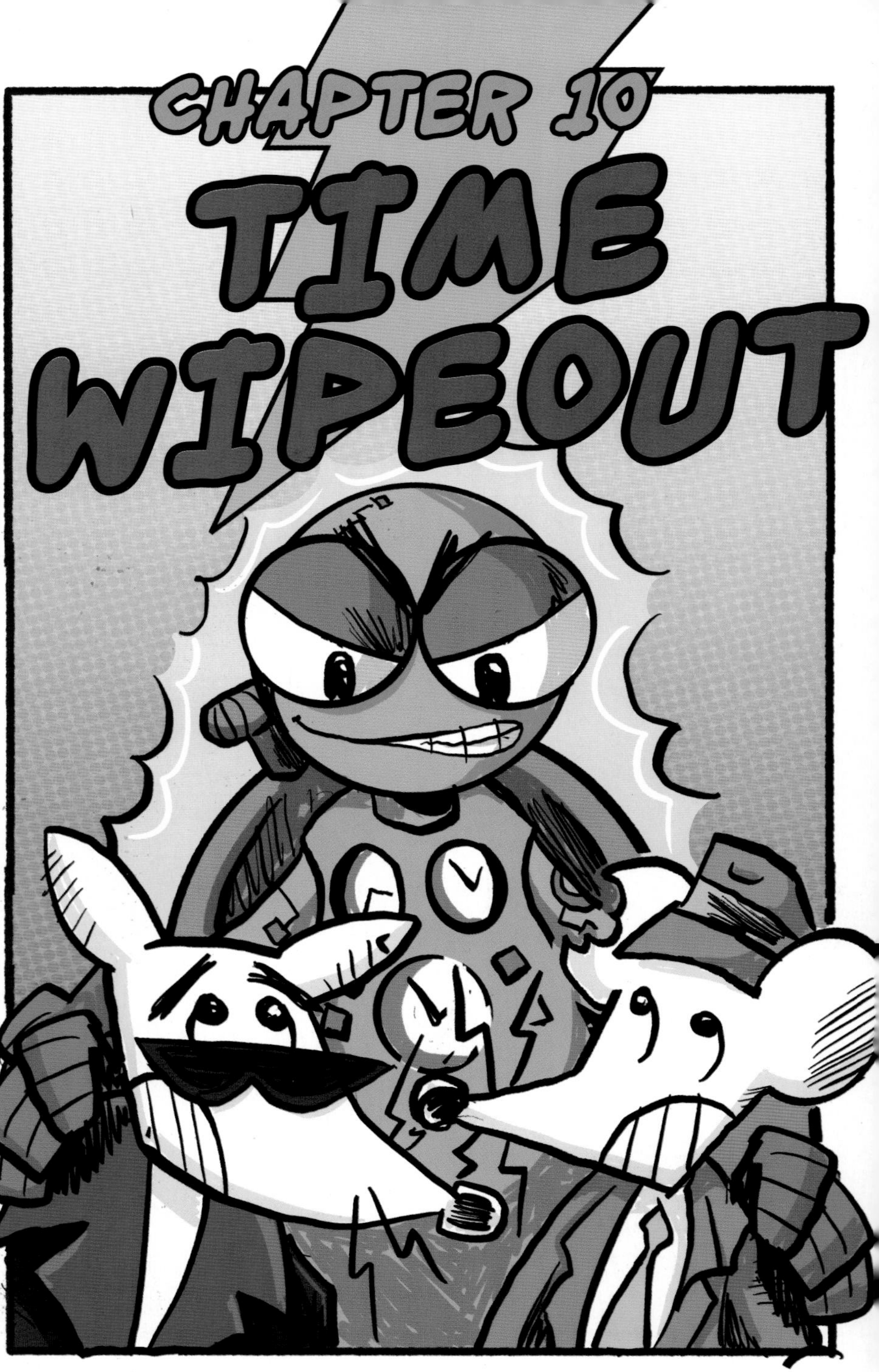
CHAPTER 10
TIME WIPEOUT

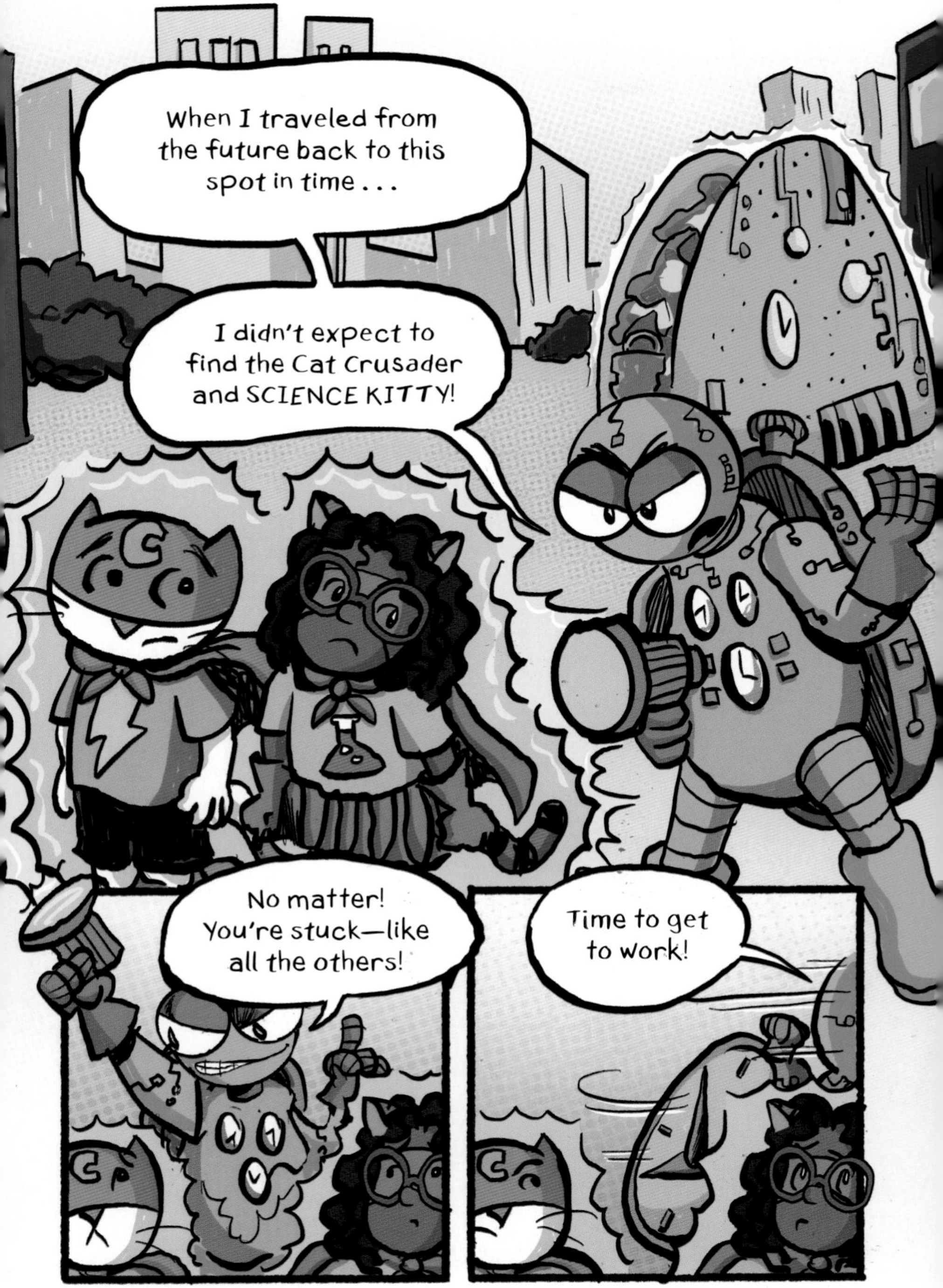
When I traveled from the future back to this spot in time . . .
I didn't expect to find the Cat Crusader and SCIENCE KITTY!
No matter! You're stuck—like all the others!
Time to get to work!

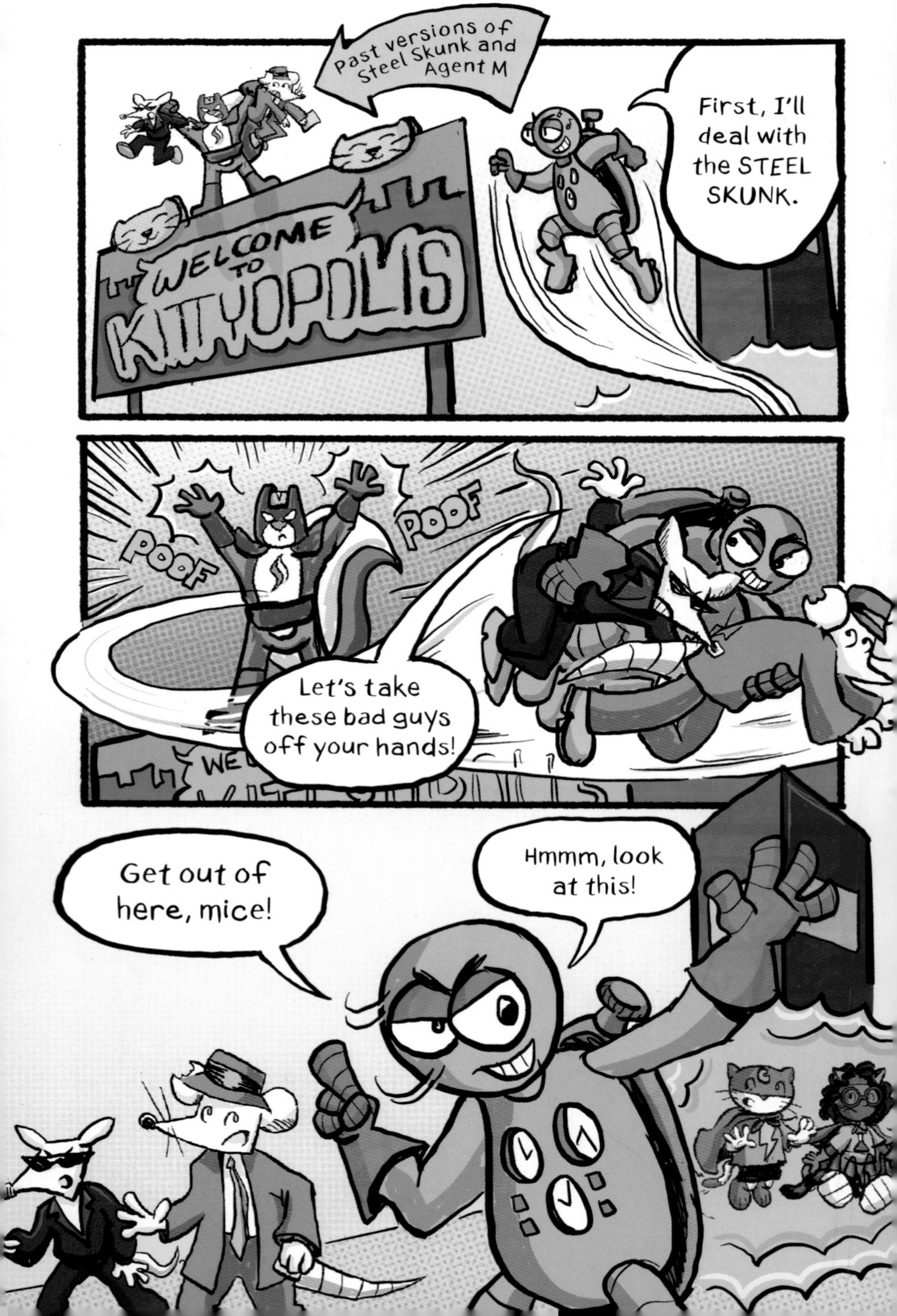
Past versions of Steel Skunk and Agent M
WELCOME TO KITTYOPOLIS
First, I'll deal with the STEEL SKUNK.
POOF
POOF
Let's take these bad guys off your hands!
Get out of here, mice!
Hmmm, look at this!

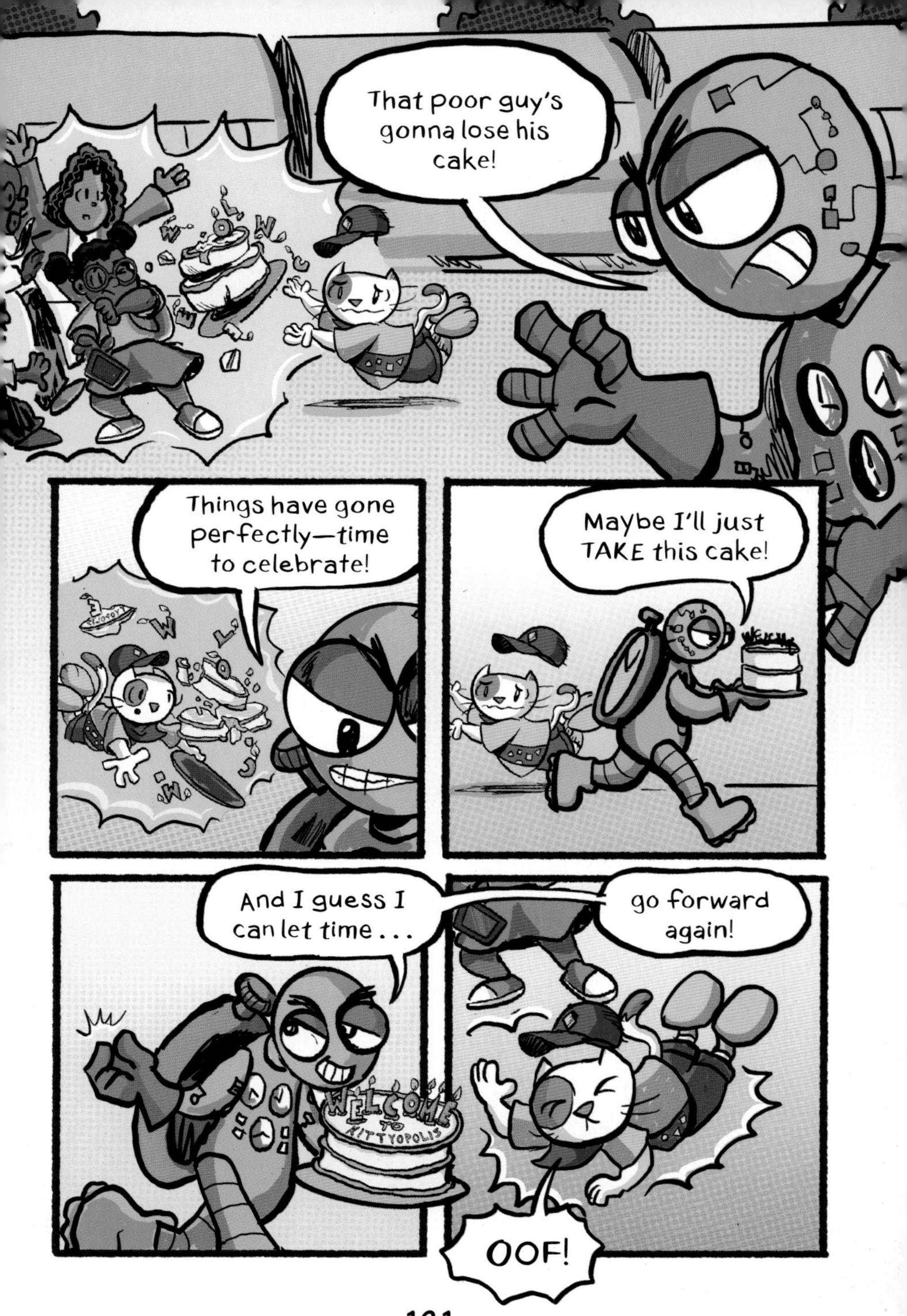
That poor guy's gonna lose his cake!
Things have gone perfectly—time to celebrate!
Maybe I'll just TAKE this cake!
And I guess I can let time . . .
WELCOME TO KITTYOPOLIS
go forward again!
OOF!

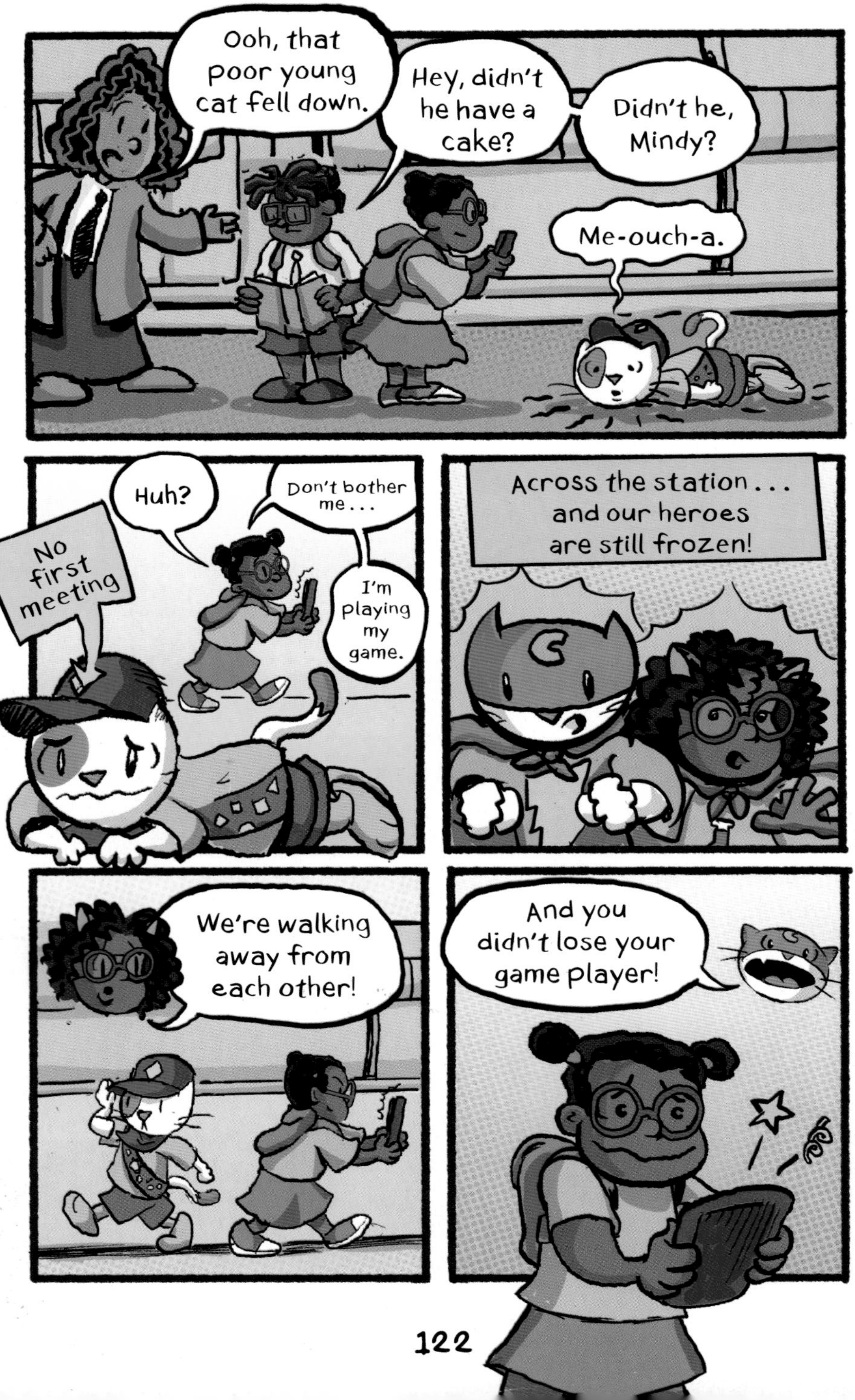
Ooh, that poor young cat fell down.
Hey, didn't he have a cake?
Didn't he, Mindy?
Me-ouch-a.
Huh?
Don't bother me . . .
I'm playing my game.
No first meeting
Across the station . . . and our heroes are still frozen!
We're walking away from each other!
And you didn't lose your game player!

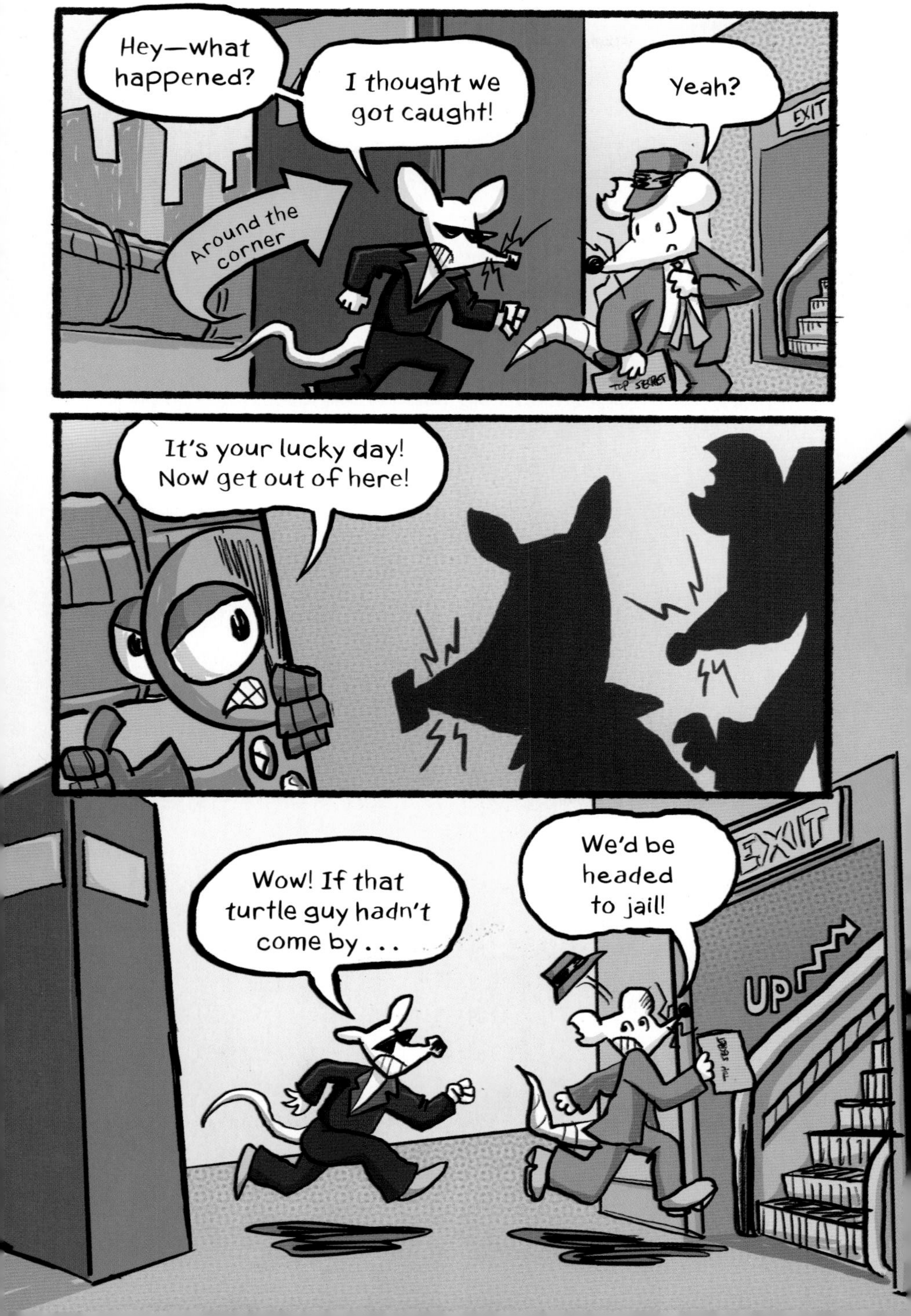
Hey—what happened?
I thought we got caught!
Around the corner
Yeah?
EXIT
TOP SECRET
It's your lucky day! Now get out of here!
Wow! If that turtle guy hadn't come by . . .
We'd be headed to jail!
EXIT
UP
TOP SECRET

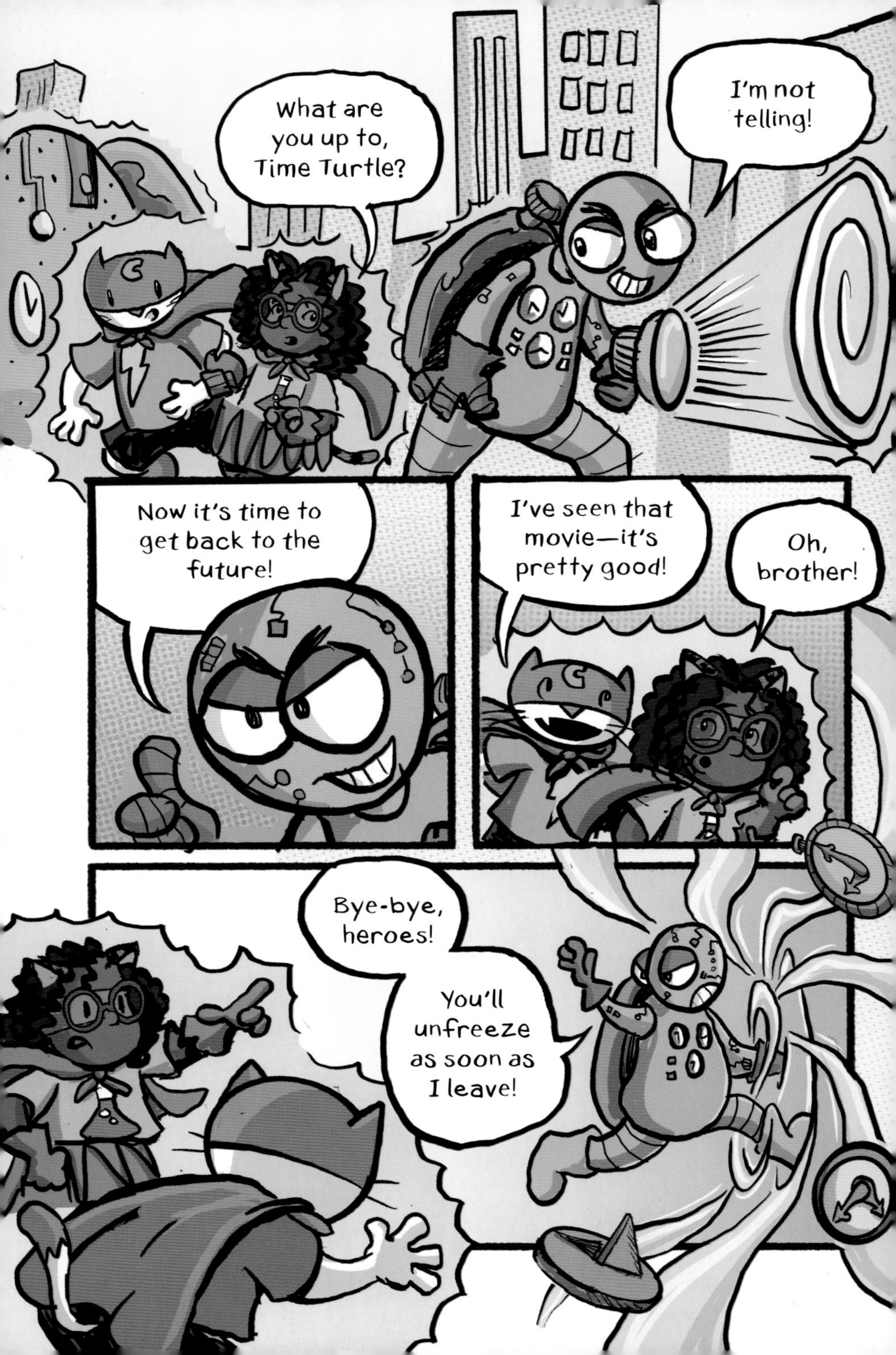
What are you up to, Time Turtle?
I'm not telling!
Now it's time to get back to the future!
I've seen that movie—it's pretty good!
Oh, brother!
Bye-bye, heroes!
You'll unfreeze as soon as I leave!

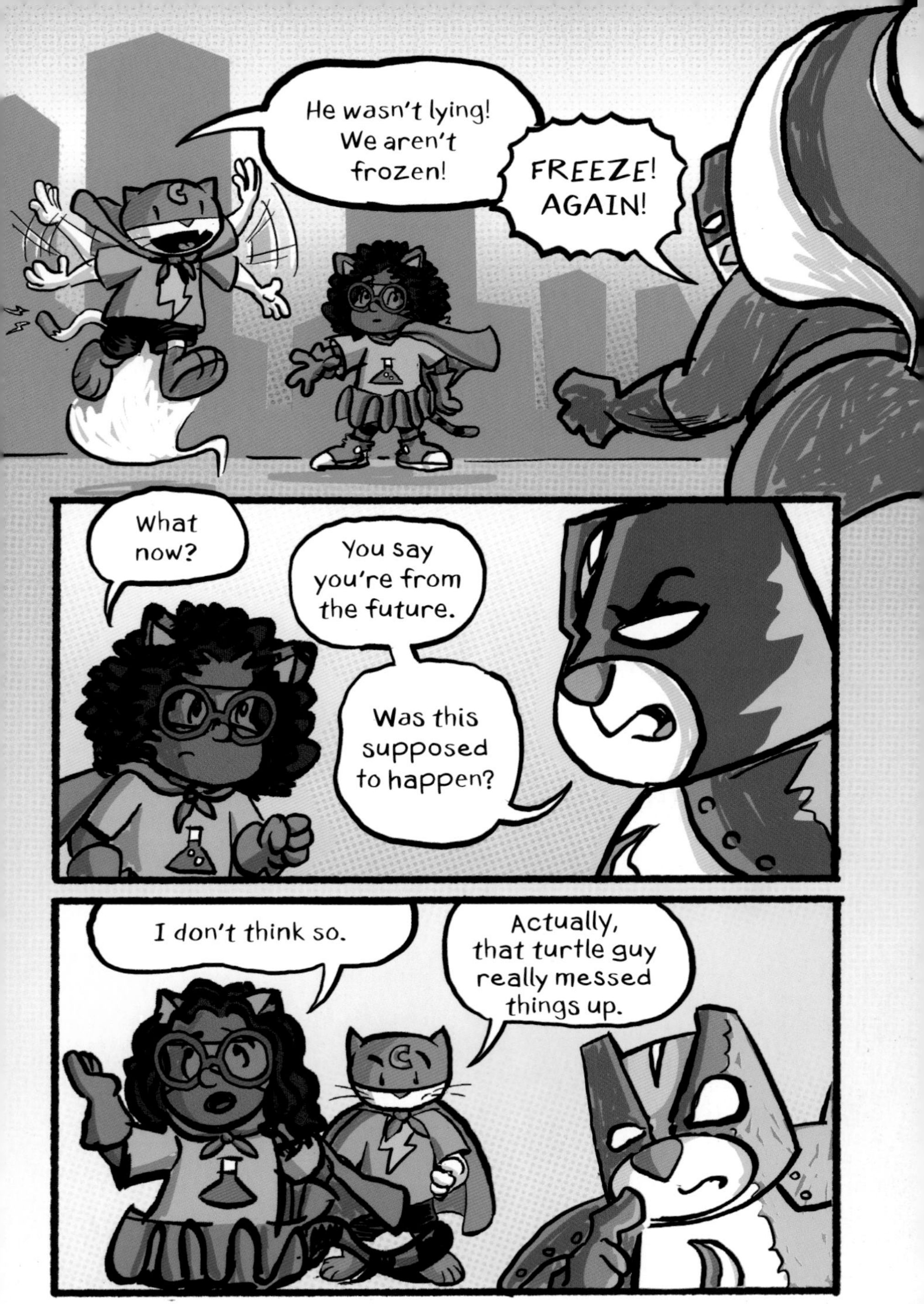
He wasn't lying! We aren't frozen!
FREEZE! AGAIN!
What now?
You say you're from the future.
Was this supposed to happen?
I don't think so.
Actually, that turtle guy really messed things up.

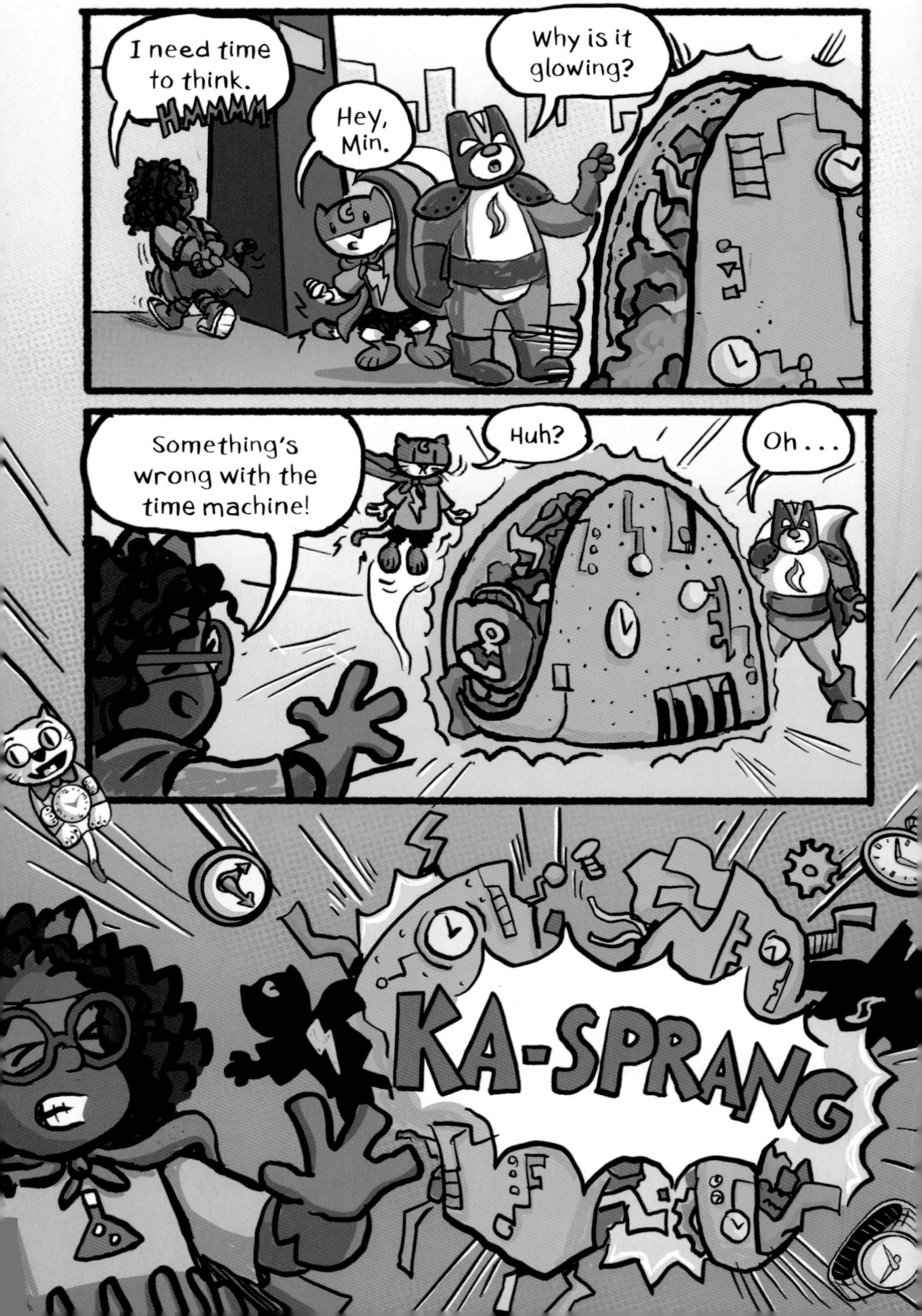
I need time to think.
HMMMM
Hey, Min.
Why is it glowing?
Something's wrong with the time machine!
Huh?
Oh . . .
KA-SPRANG

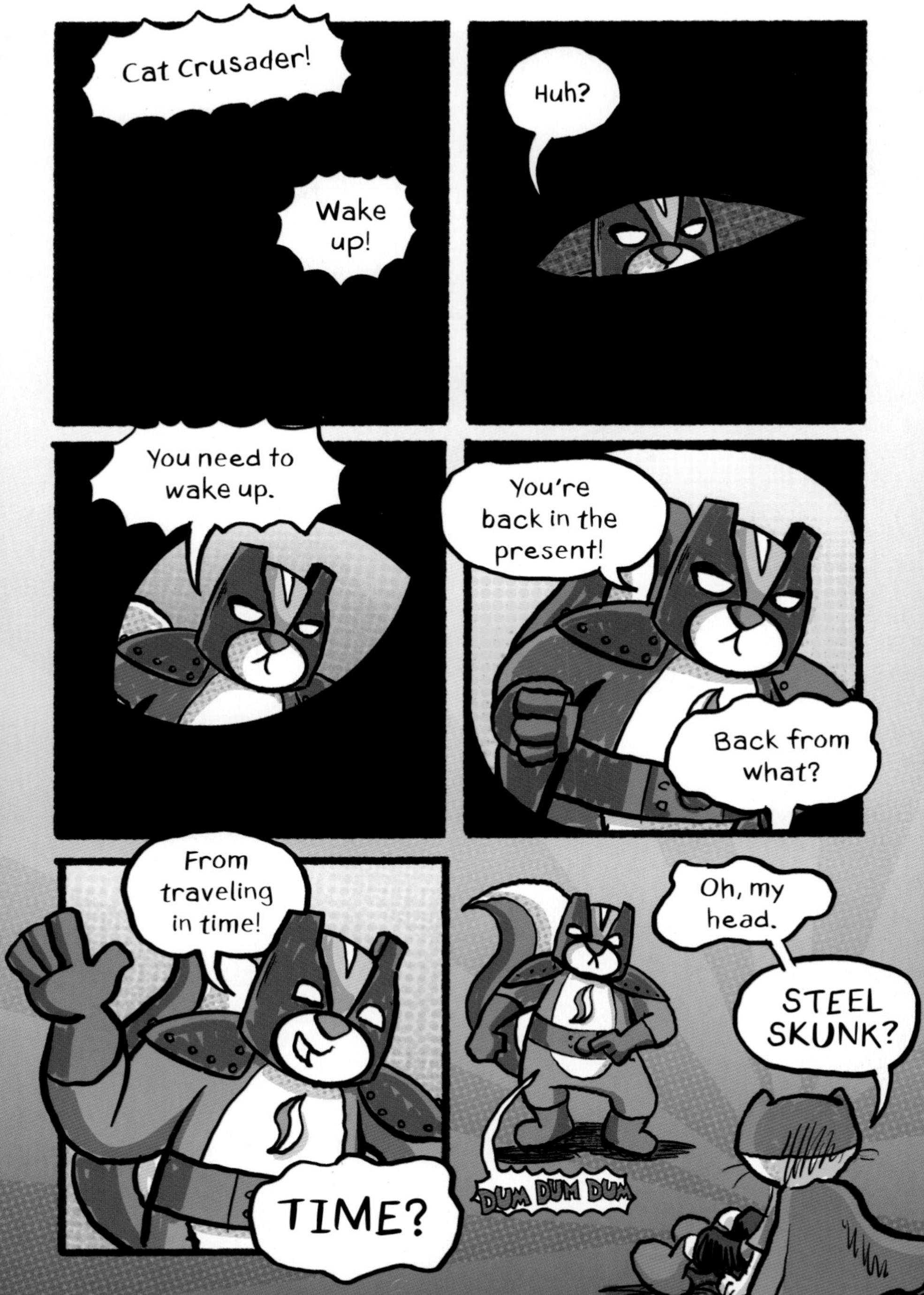
Cat Crusader!
Wake up!
Huh?
You need to wake up.
You're back in the present!
Back from what?
From traveling in time!
TIME?
Oh, my head.
STEEL SKUNK?
DUM DUM DUM

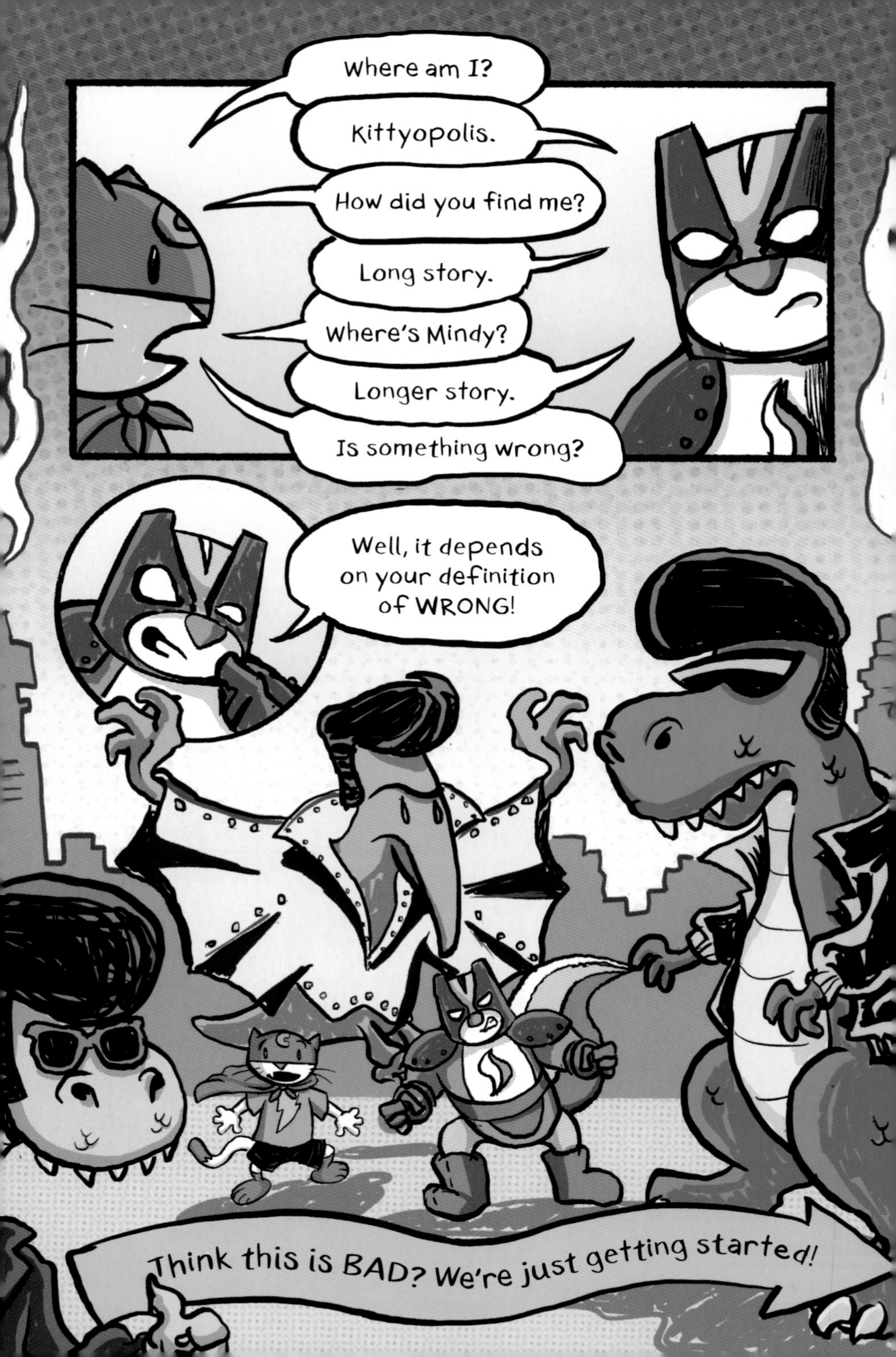
Where am I?
Kittyopolis.
How did you find me?
Long story.
Where's Mindy?
Longer story.
Is something wrong?
Well, it depends on your definition of WRONG!
Think this is BAD? We're just getting started!

CHAPTER 11

DINOSAURS ON MOTORCYCLES!

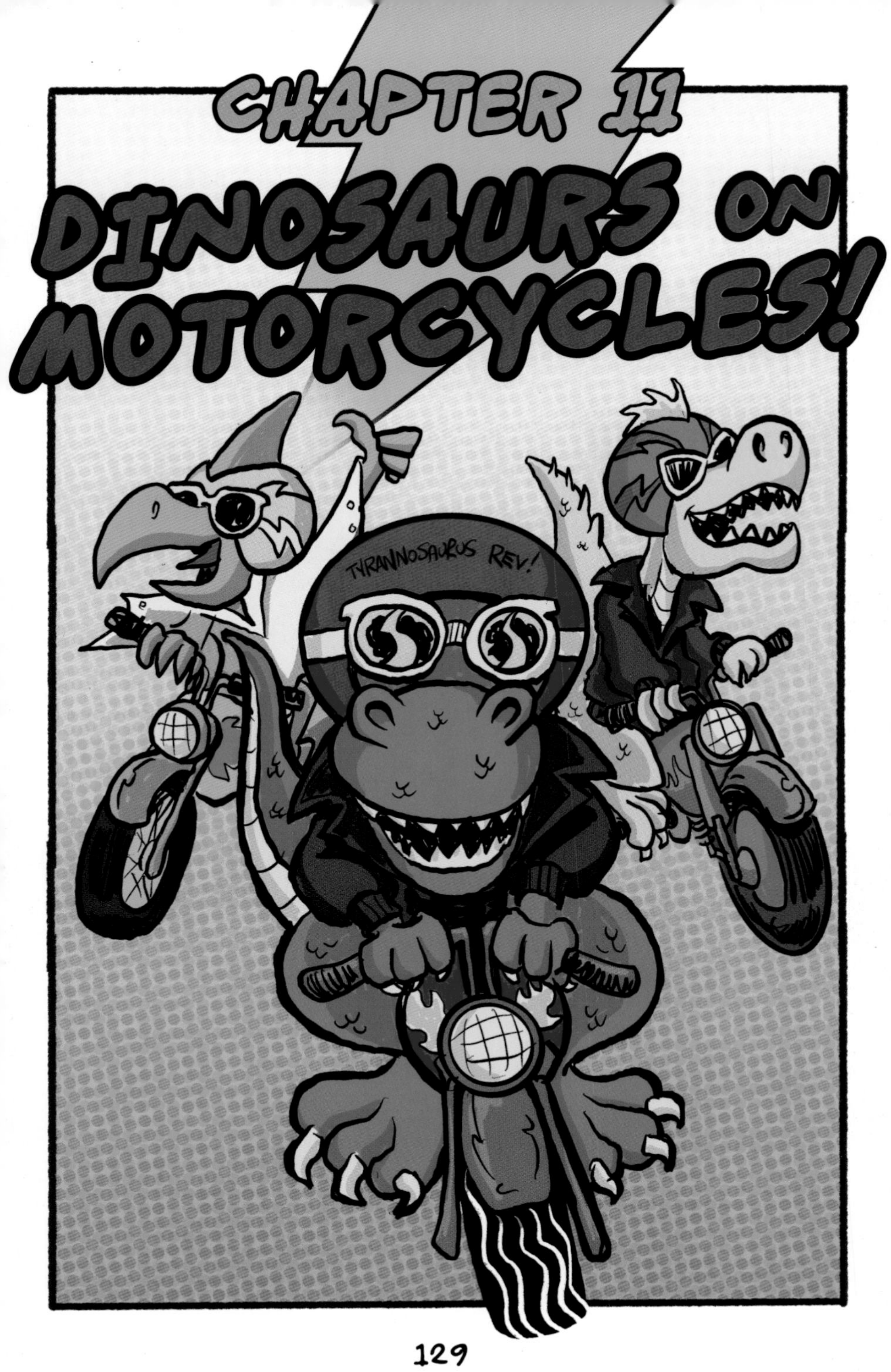
TYRANNOSAURUS REV!

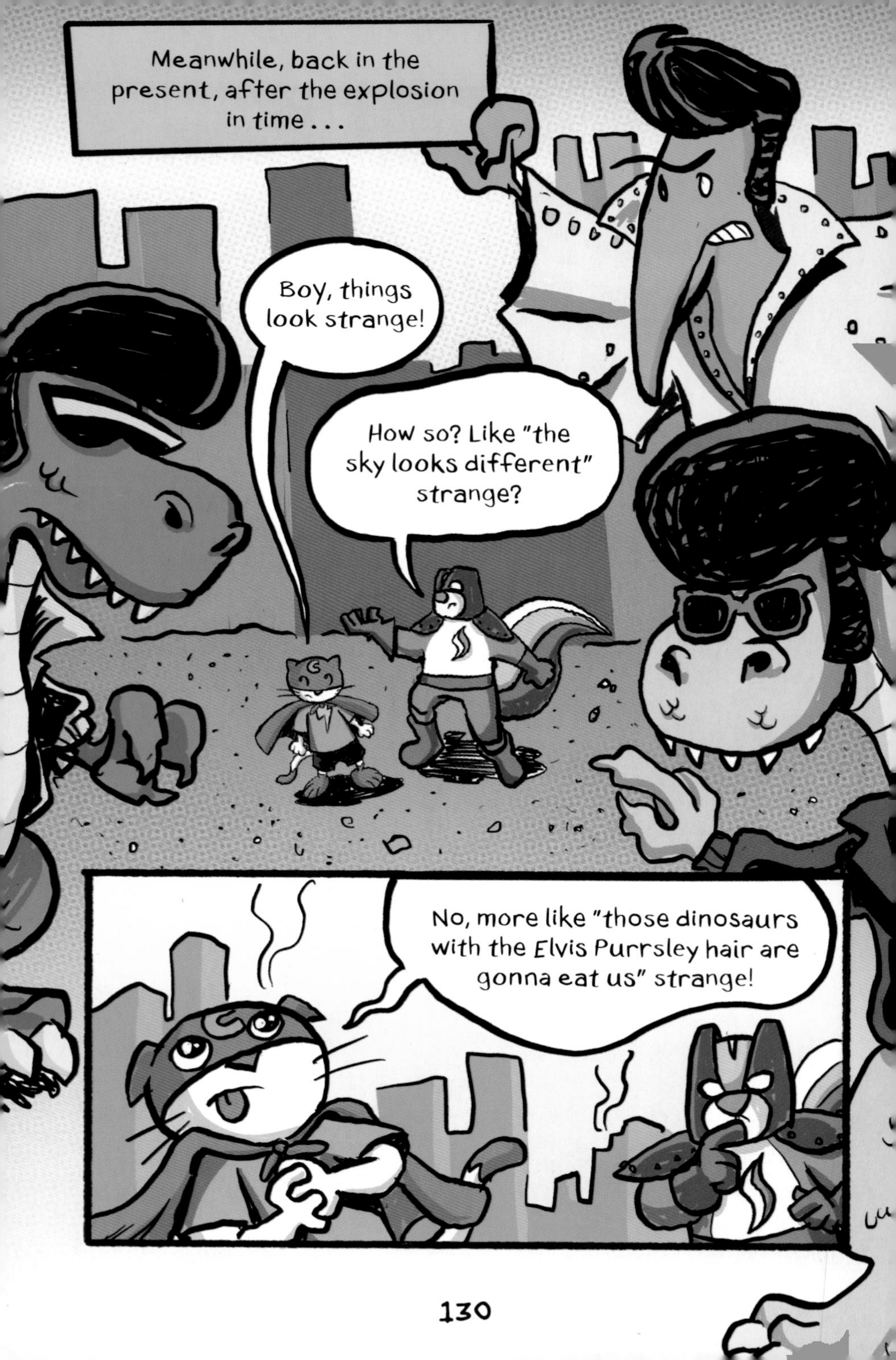
Meanwhile, back in the present, after the explosion in time . . .
Boy, things look strange!
How so? Like "the sky looks different" strange?
No, more like "those dinosaurs with the Elvis Purrsley hair are gonna eat us" strange!

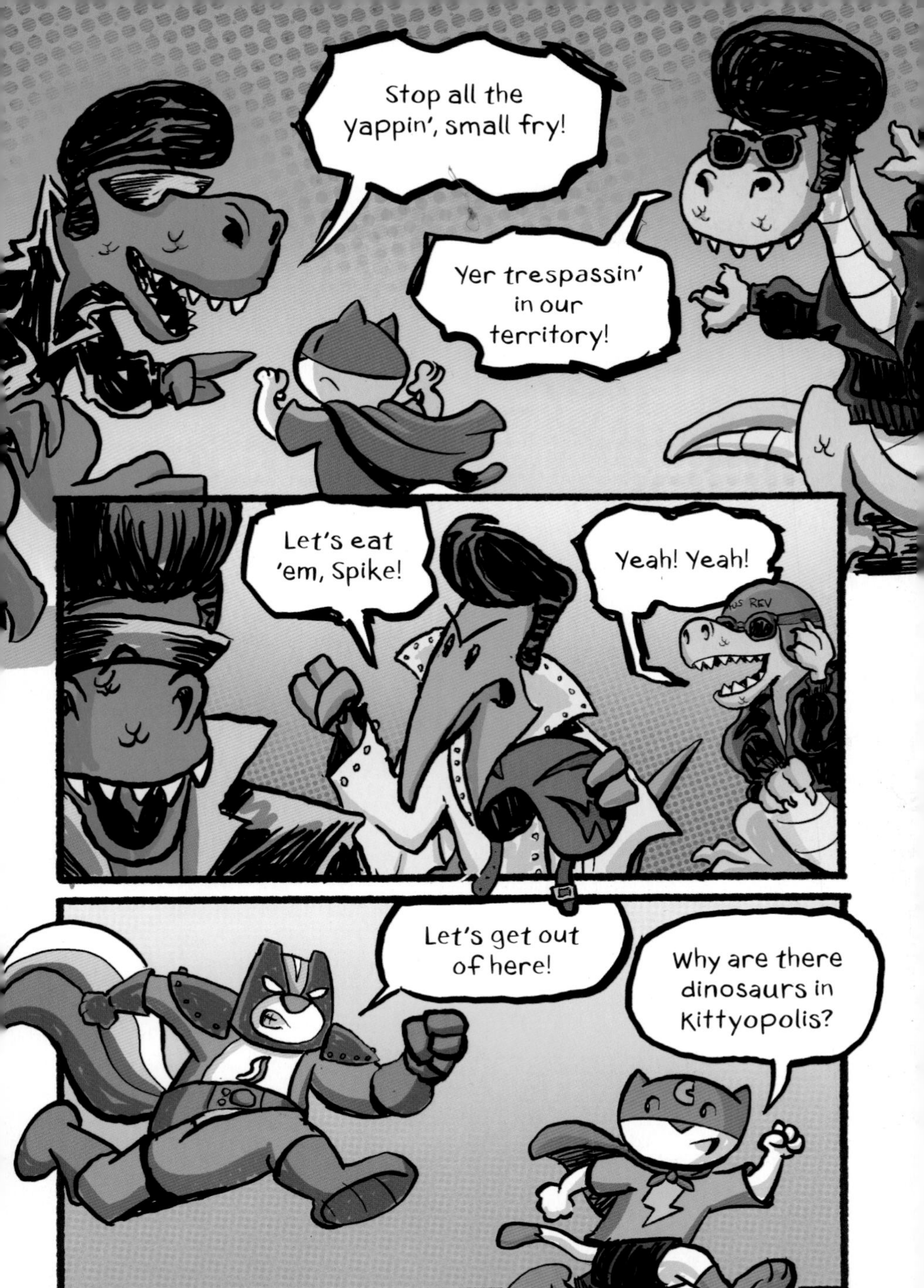
Stop all the yappin', small fry!
Yer trespassin' in our territory!
Let's eat 'em, Spike!
Yeah! Yeah!
Let's get out of here!
Why are there dinosaurs in Kittyopolis?

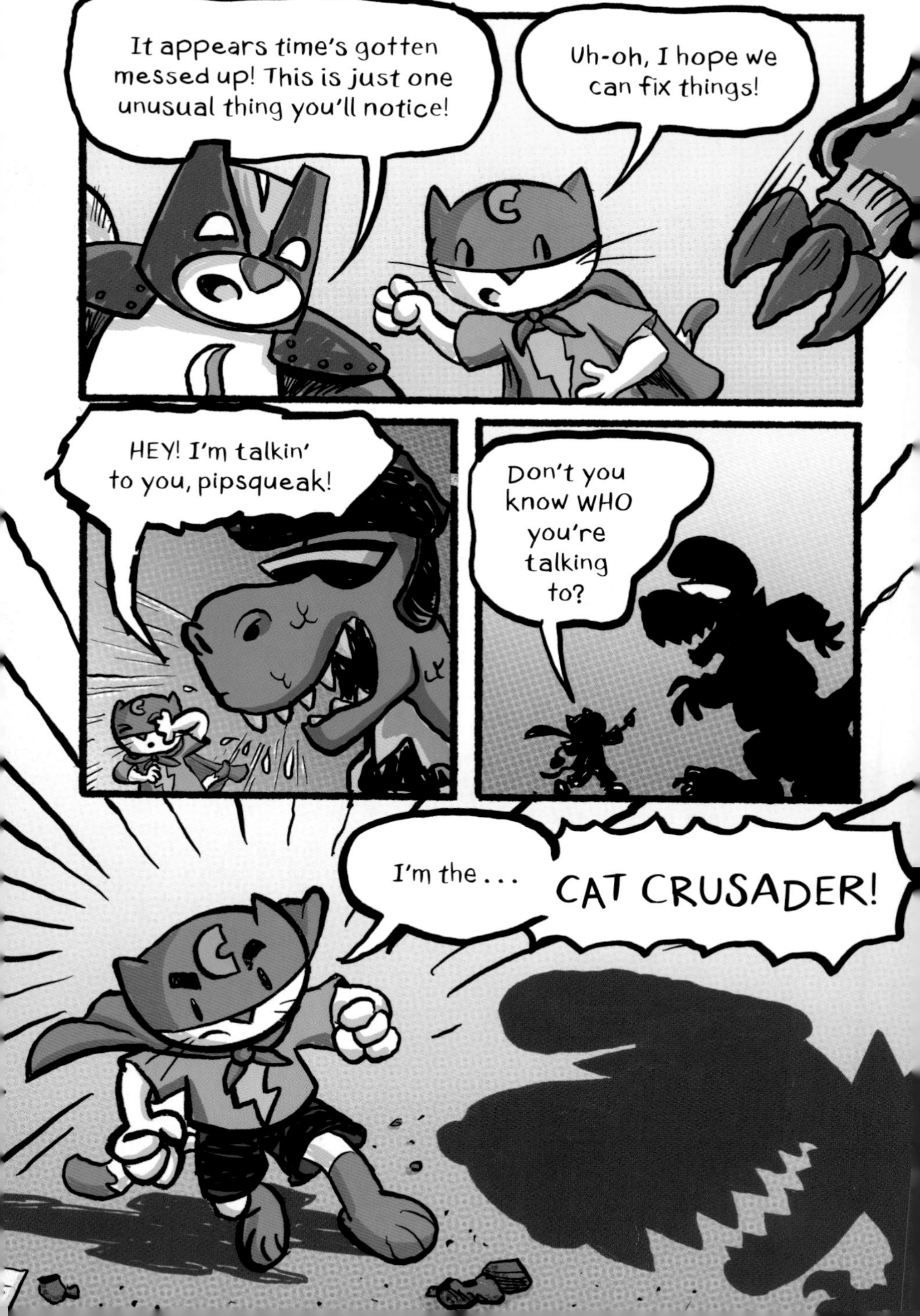
It appears time's gotten messed up! This is just one unusual thing you'll notice!
Uh-oh, I hope we can fix things!
HEY! I'm talkin' to you, pipsqueak!
Don't you know WHO you're talking to?
I'm the . . . CAT CRUSADER!

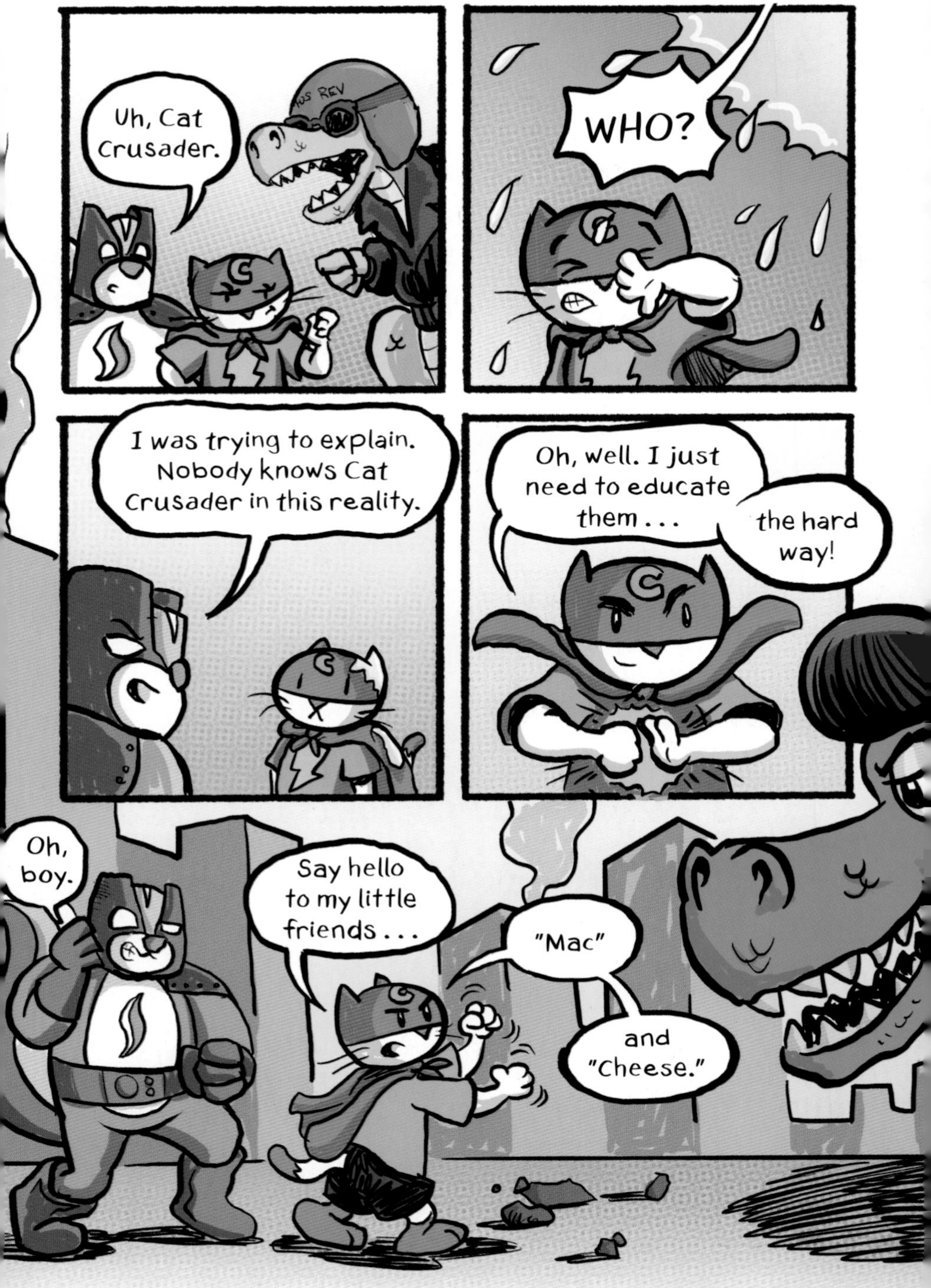
Uh, Cat Crusader.
WHO?
I was trying to explain. Nobody knows Cat Crusader in this reality.
Oh, well. I just need to educate them . . .
the hard way!
Oh, boy.
Say hello to my little friends . . .
"Mac"
and "Cheese."

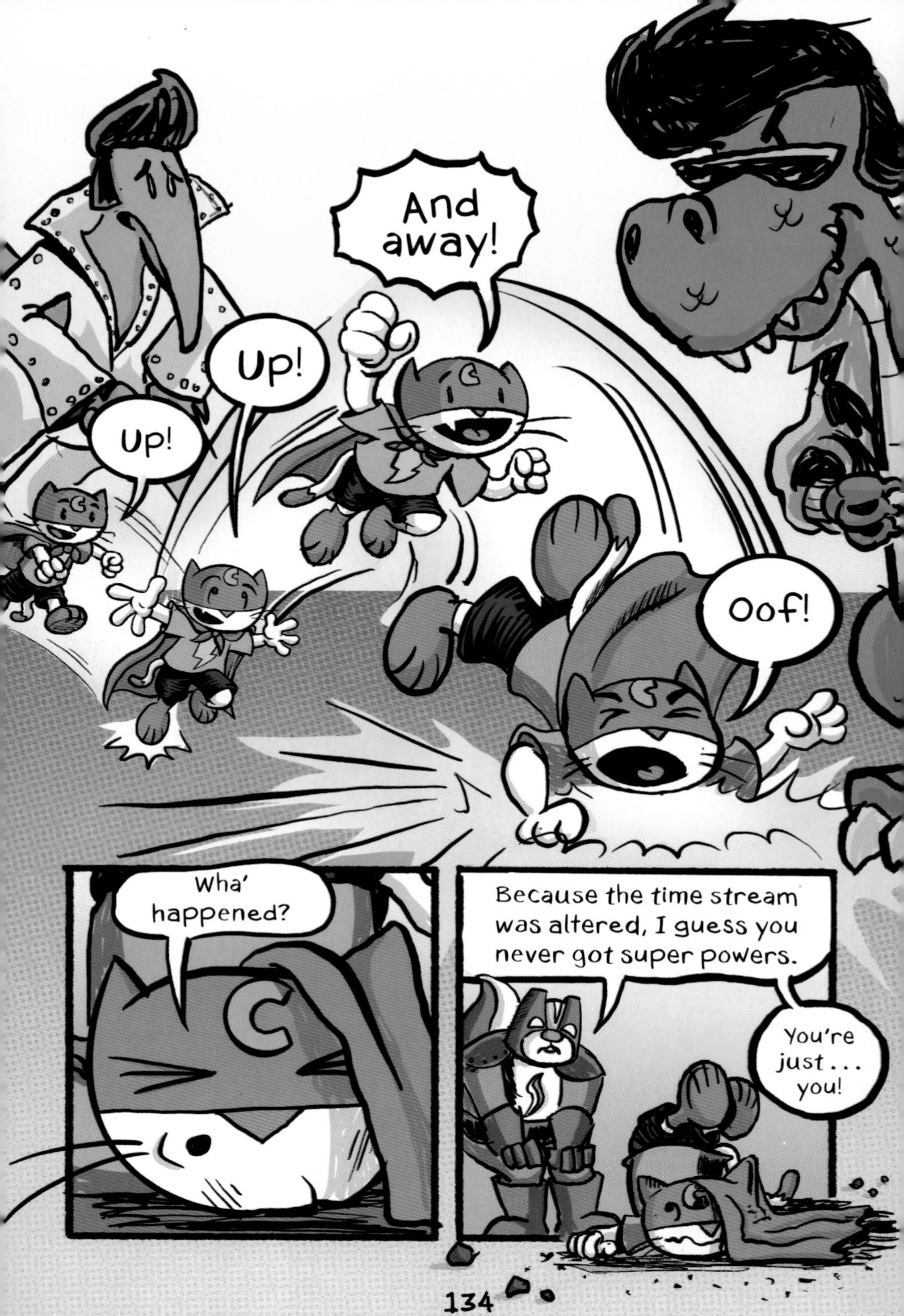
Up!
Up!
And away!
Oof!
Wha' happened?
Because the time stream was altered, I guess you never got super powers.
You're just . . . you!

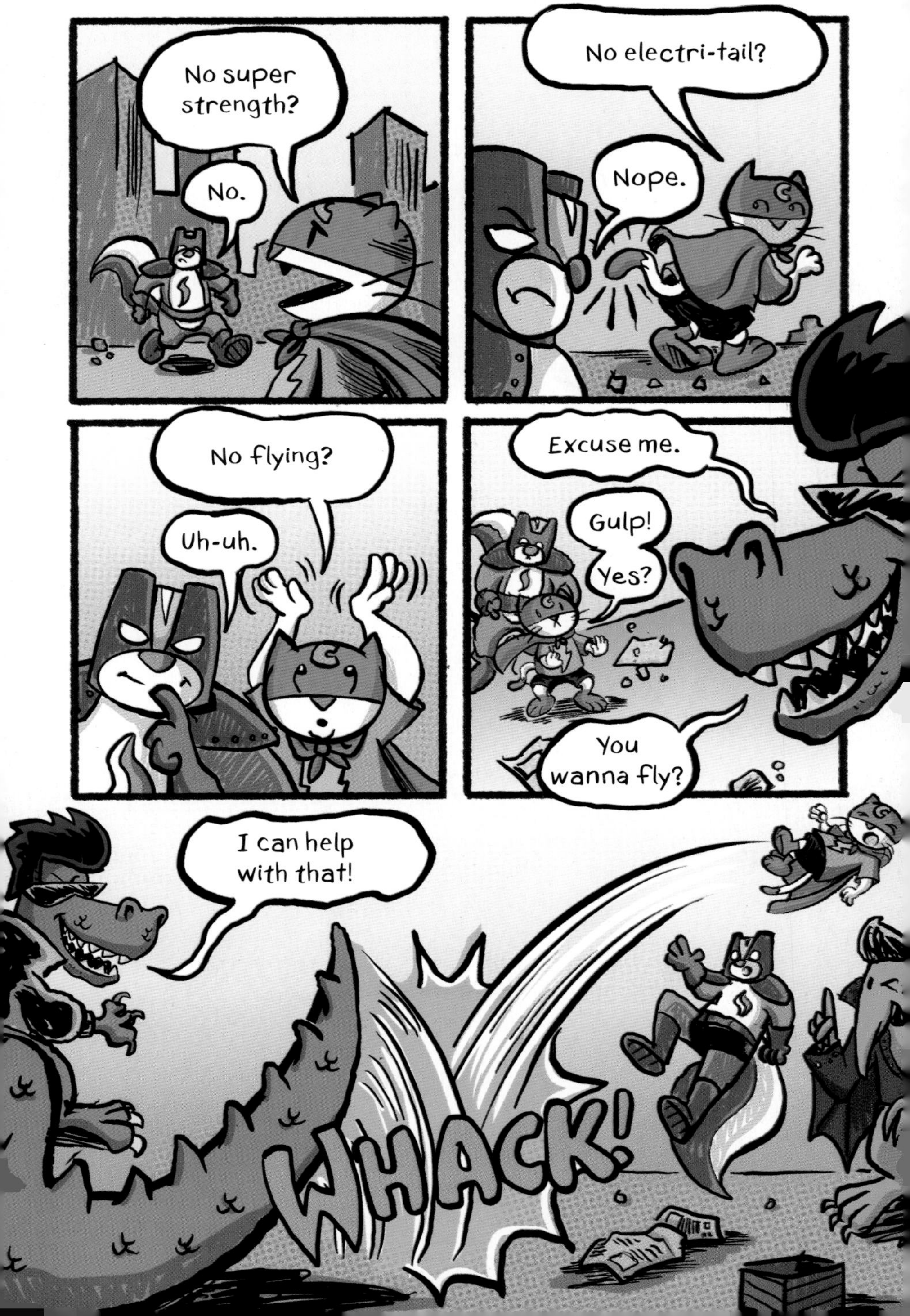
No super strength?
No.
No electri-tail?
Nope.
No flying?
Uh-uh.
Excuse me.
Gulp!
Yes?
You wanna fly?
I can help with that!
WHACK!

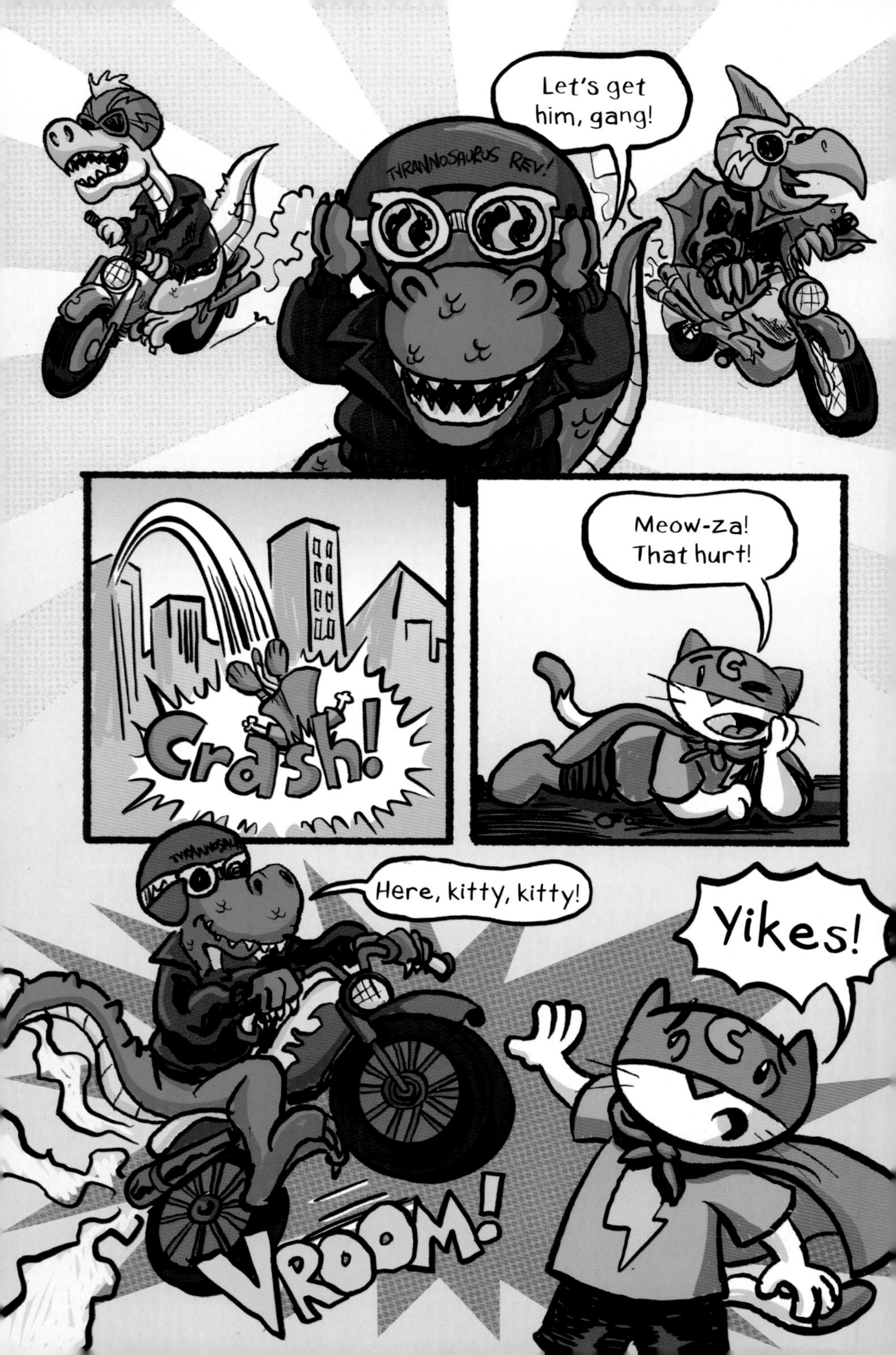
Let's get him, gang!
TYRANNOSAURUS REV!
Crash!
Meow-za! That hurt!
TYRANNOSAURUS
Here, kitty, kitty!
Yikes!
VROOM!

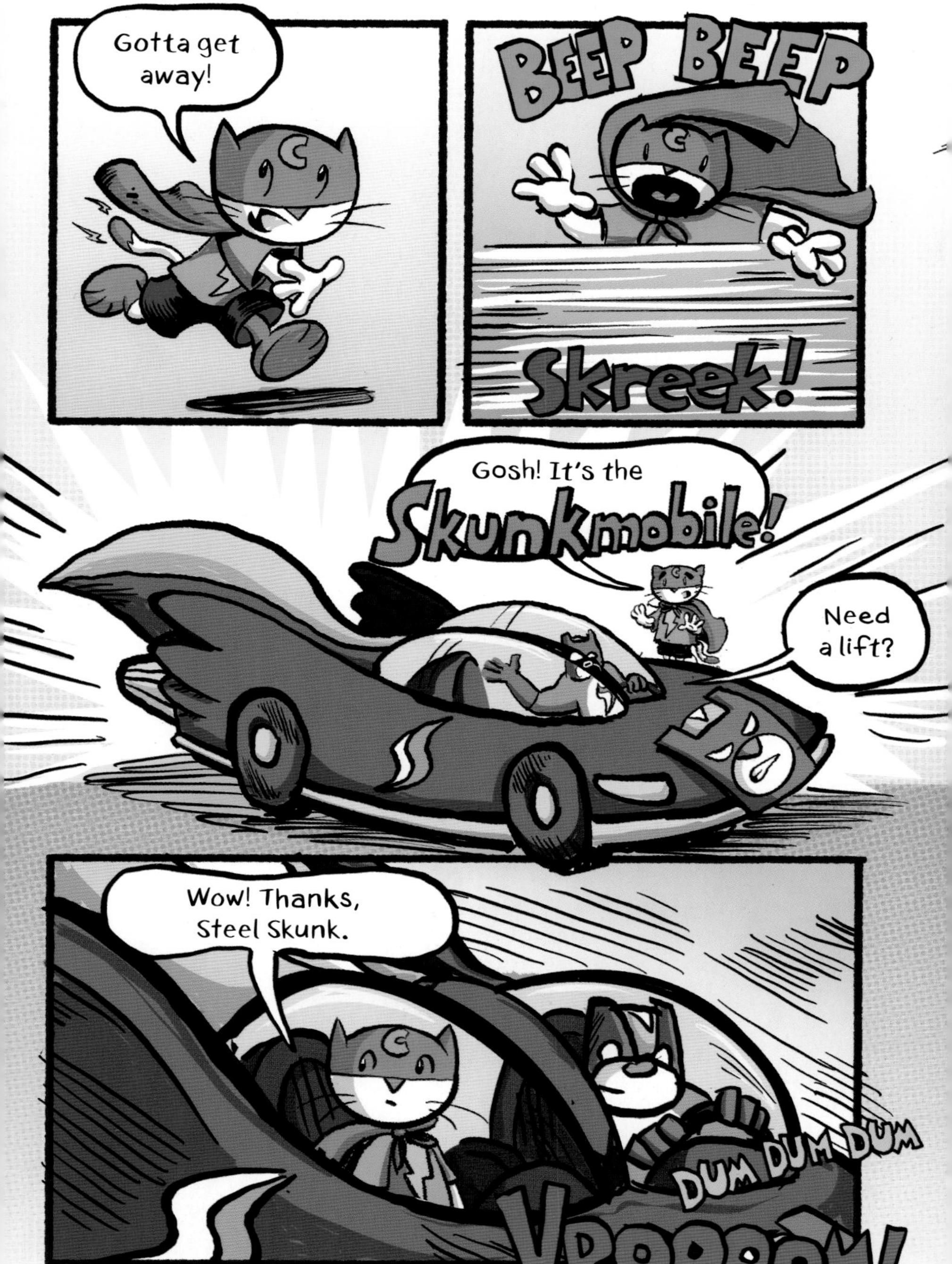
Gotta get away!
BEEP BEEP
Skreek!
Gosh! It's the Skunkmobile!
Need a lift?
Wow! Thanks, Steel Skunk.
DUM DUM DUM
VROOOOOM!

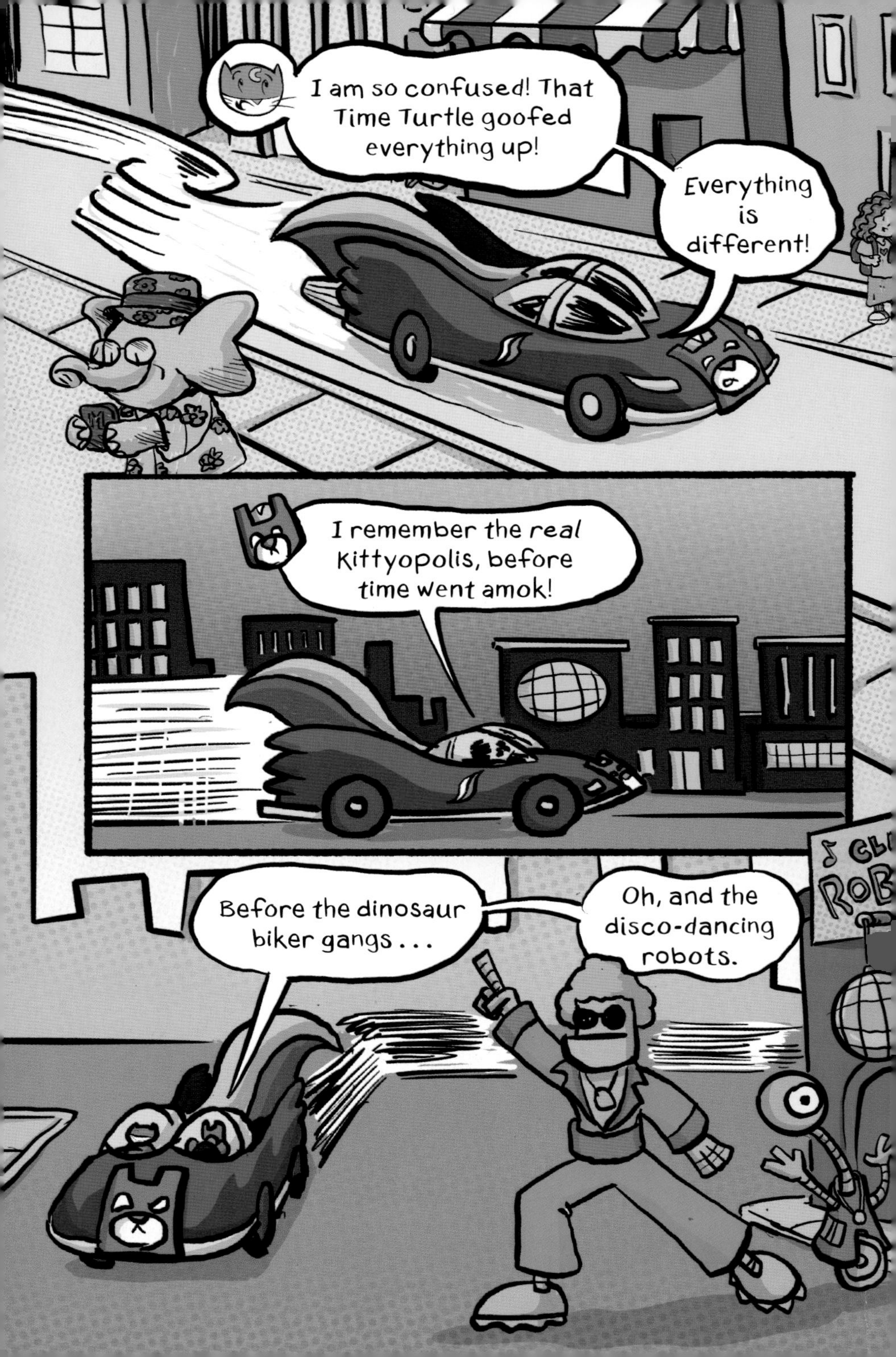
I am so confused! That Time Turtle goofed everything up!
Everything is different!
I remember the *real* Kittyopolis, before time went amok!
Before the dinosaur biker gangs . . .
Oh, and the disco-dancing robots.

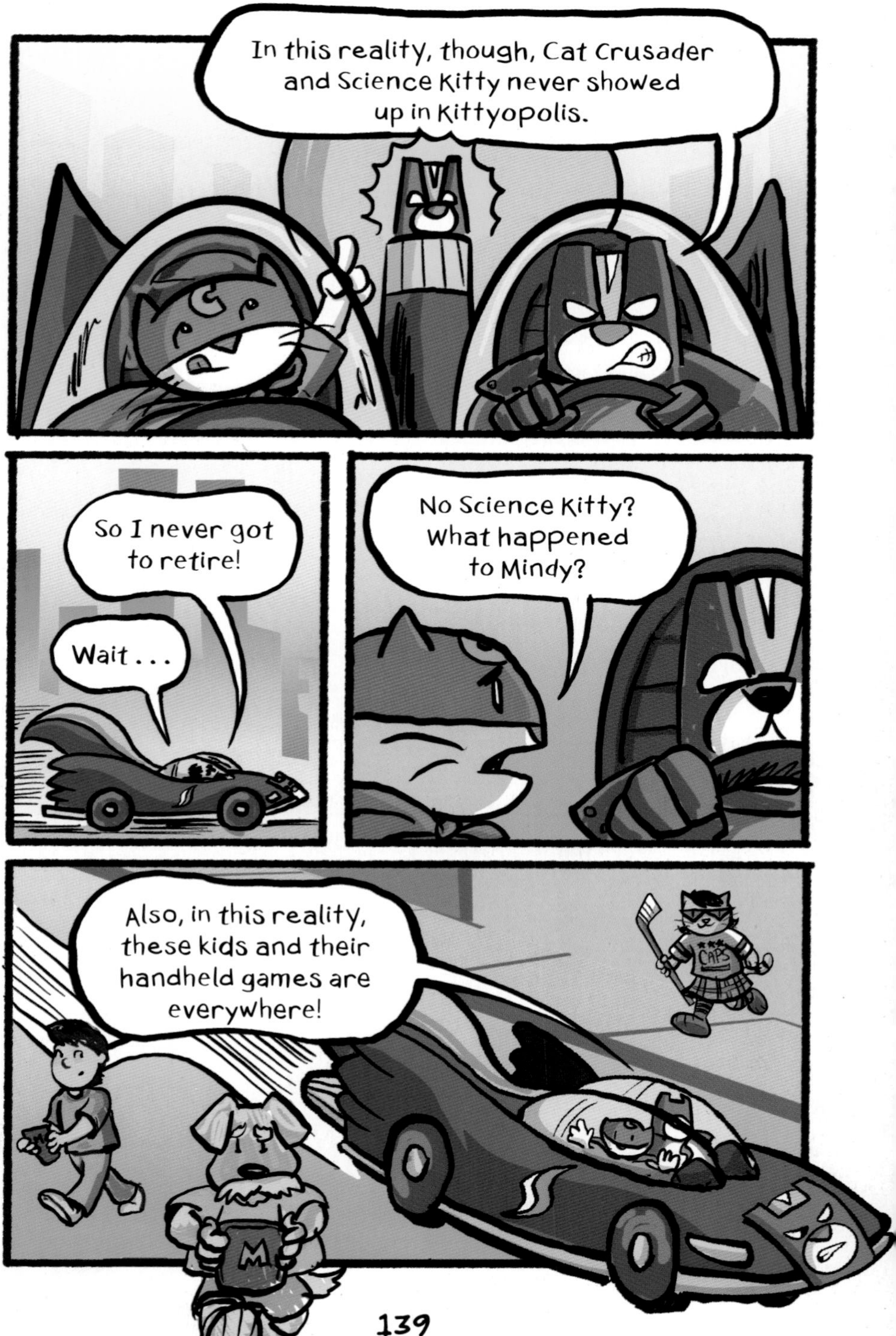

In this reality, though, Cat Crusader and Science Kitty never showed up in Kittyopolis.
So I never got to retire!
Wait . . .
No Science Kitty? What happened to Mindy?
Also, in this reality, these kids and their handheld games are everywhere!
CAPS
M

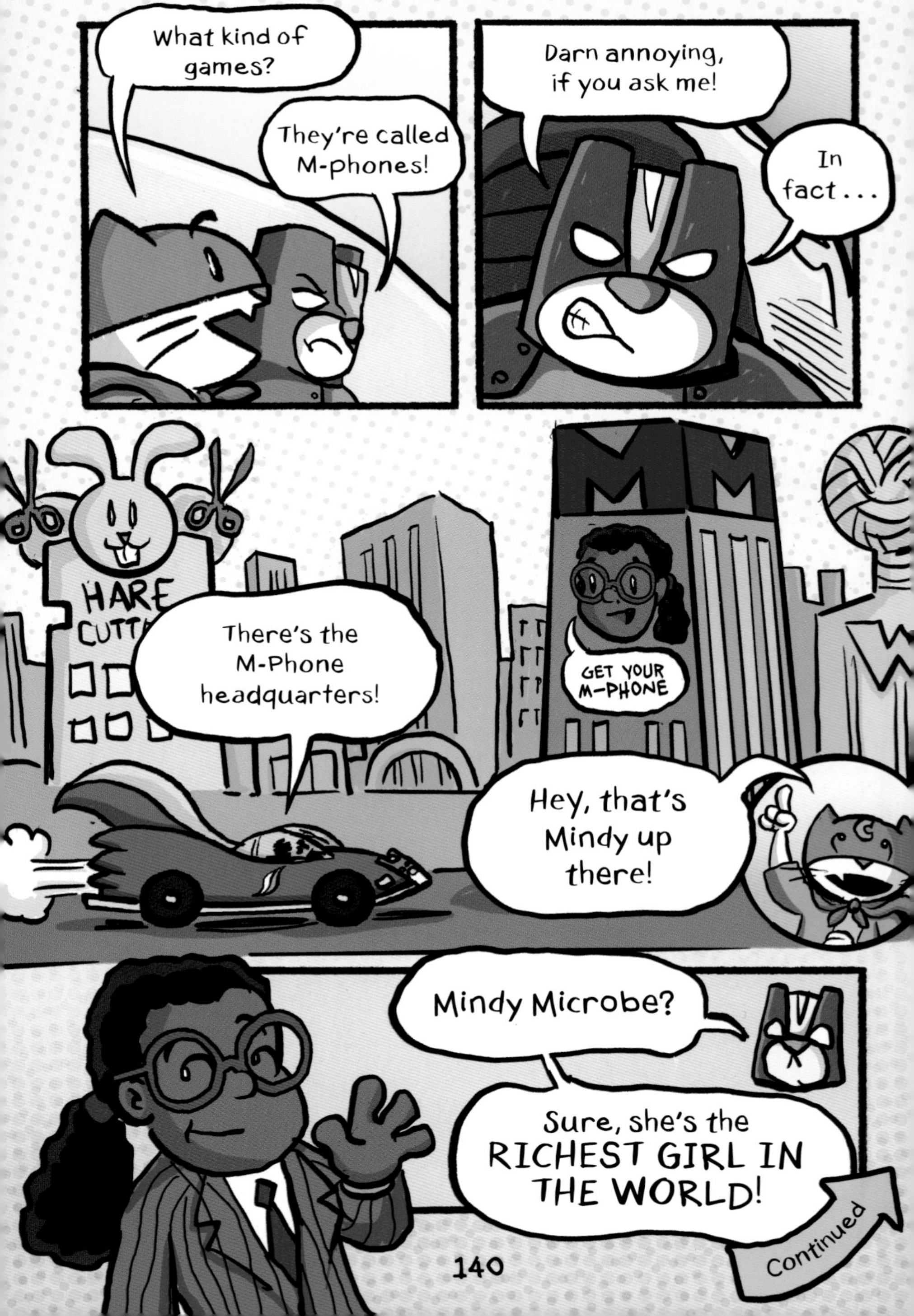
What kind of games?
They're called M-phones!
Darn annoying, if you ask me!
In fact . . .
HARE CUTT
There's the M-Phone headquarters!
GET YOUR M-PHONE
Hey, that's Mindy up there!
Mindy Microbe?
Sure, she's the RICHEST GIRL IN THE WORLD!
Continued

CHAPTER 12

MINDY THE MOGUL*

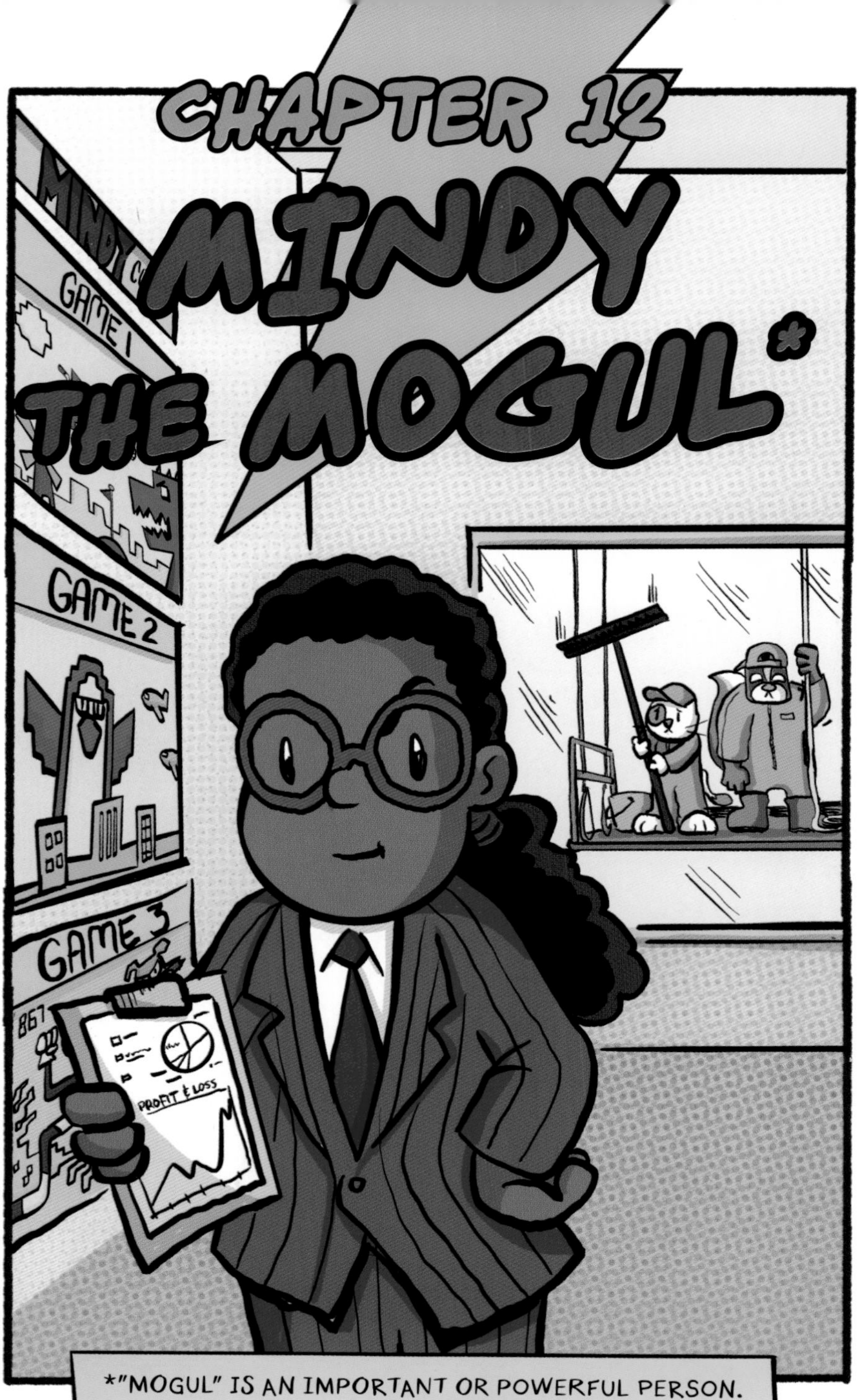
MINDY
GAME 1
GAME 2
GAME 3
867
PROFIT & LOSS

*"MOGUL" IS AN IMPORTANT OR POWERFUL PERSON.

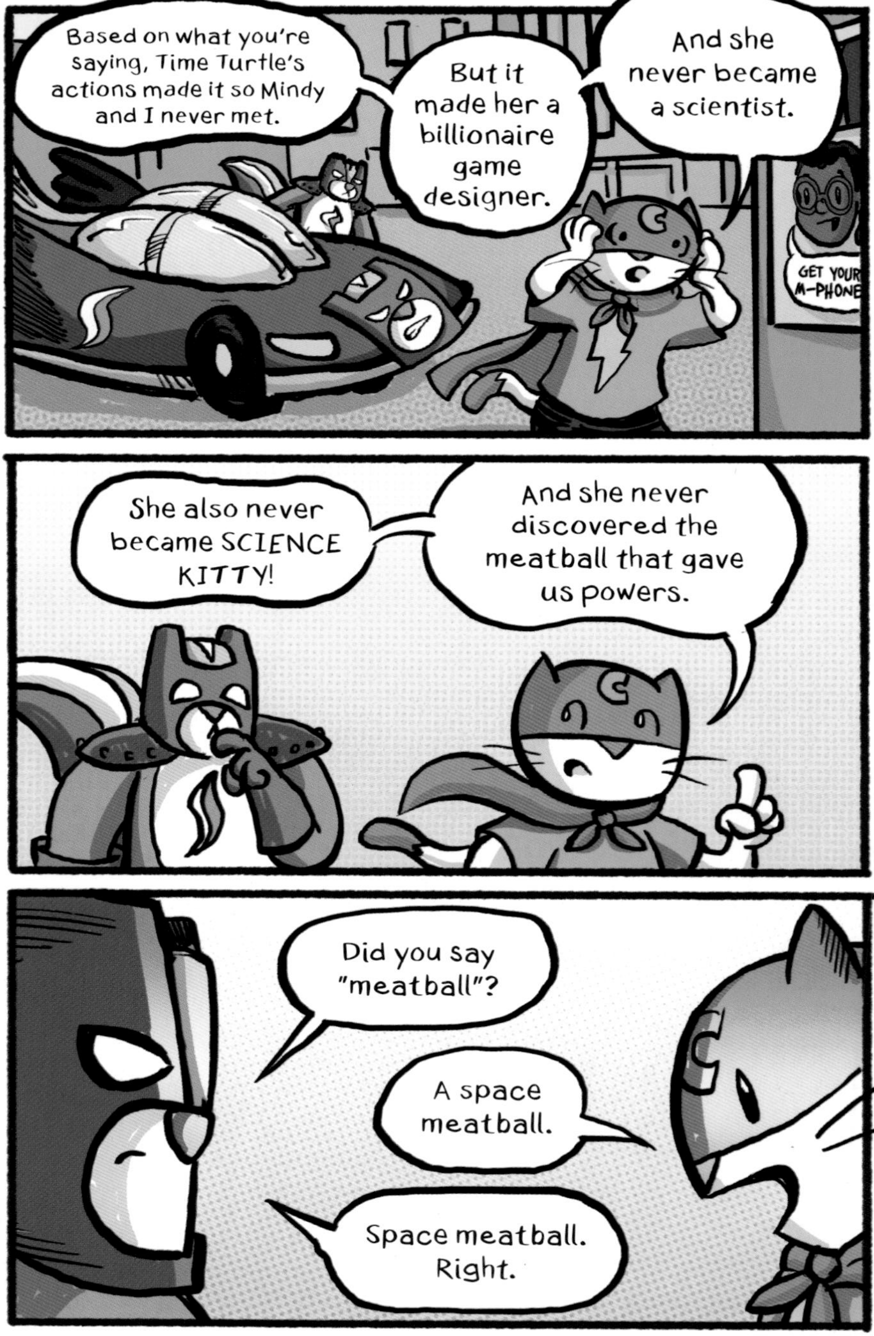
Based on what you're saying, Time Turtle's actions made it so Mindy and I never met.
But it made her a billionaire game designer.
And she never became a scientist.
GET YOUR M-PHONE
She also never became SCIENCE KITTY!
And she never discovered the meatball that gave us powers.
Did you say "meatball"?
A space meatball.
Space meatball. Right.

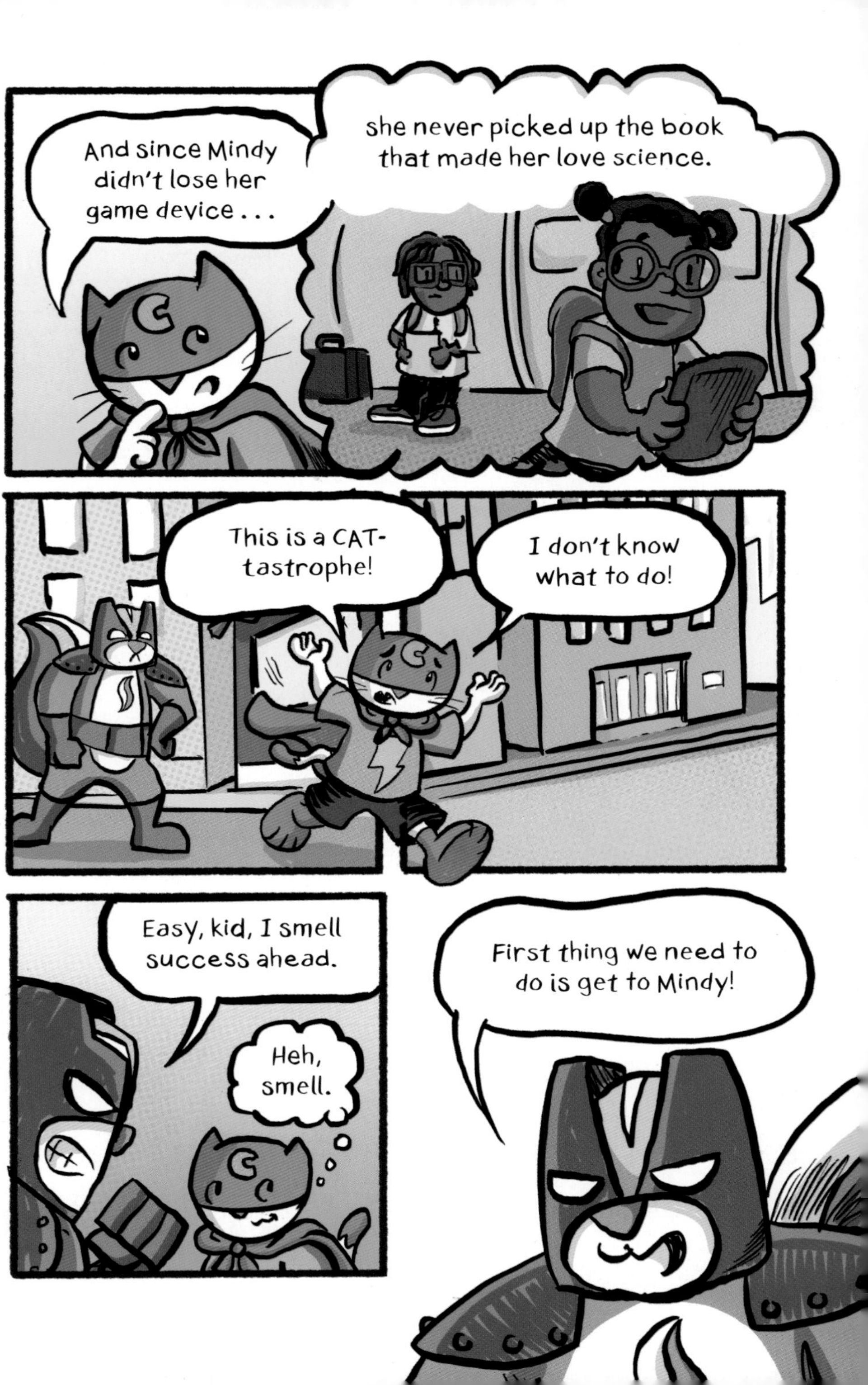
And since Mindy didn't lose her game device . . .
she never picked up the book that made her love science.
This is a CAT-tastrophe!
I don't know what to do!
Easy, kid, I smell success ahead.
Heh, smell.
First thing we need to do is get to Mindy!

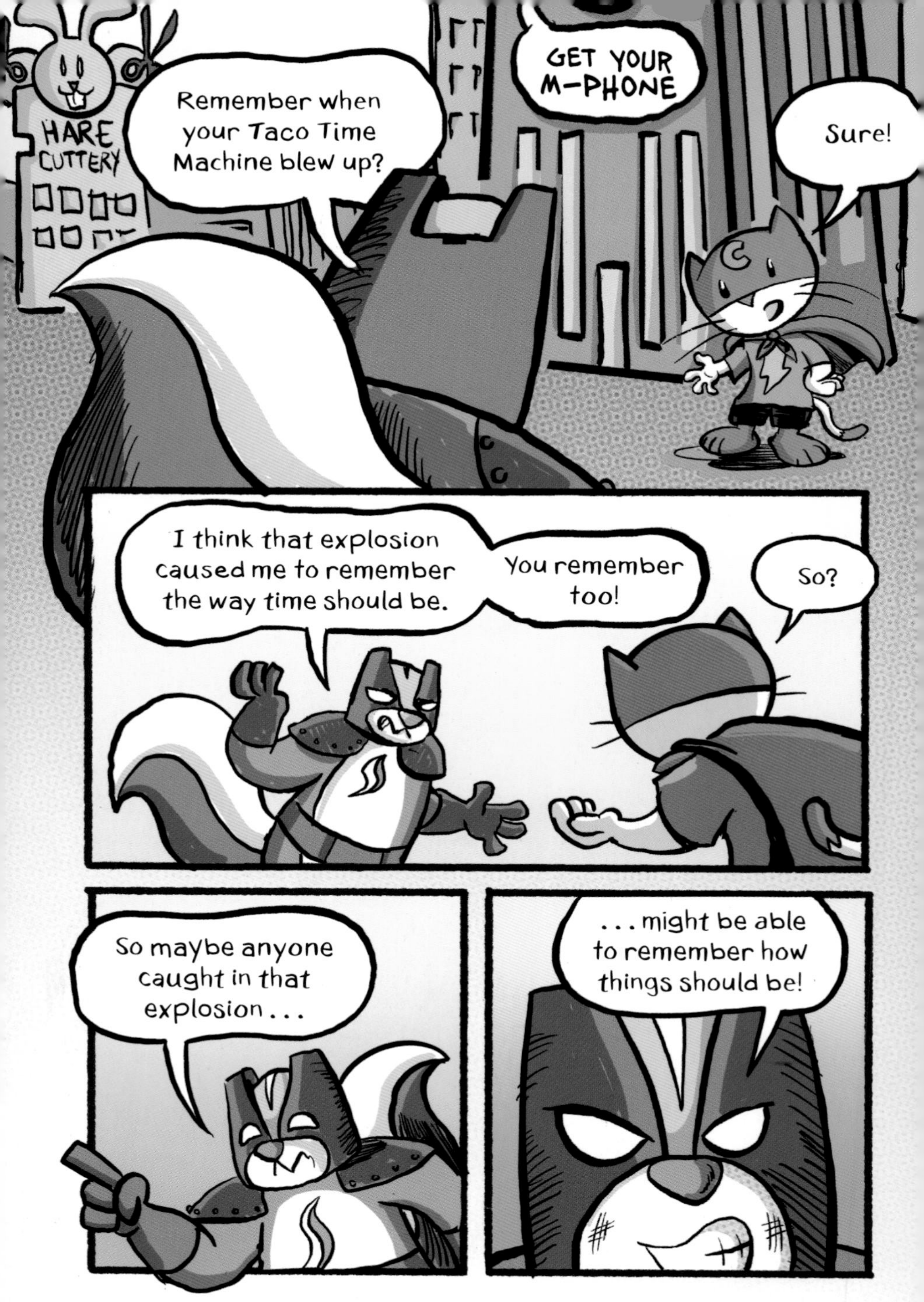
HARE
CUTTERY
Remember when your Taco Time Machine blew up?
GET YOUR M-PHONE
Sure!
I think that explosion caused me to remember the way time should be.
You remember too!
So?
So maybe anyone caught in that explosion . . .
. . . might be able to remember how things should be!

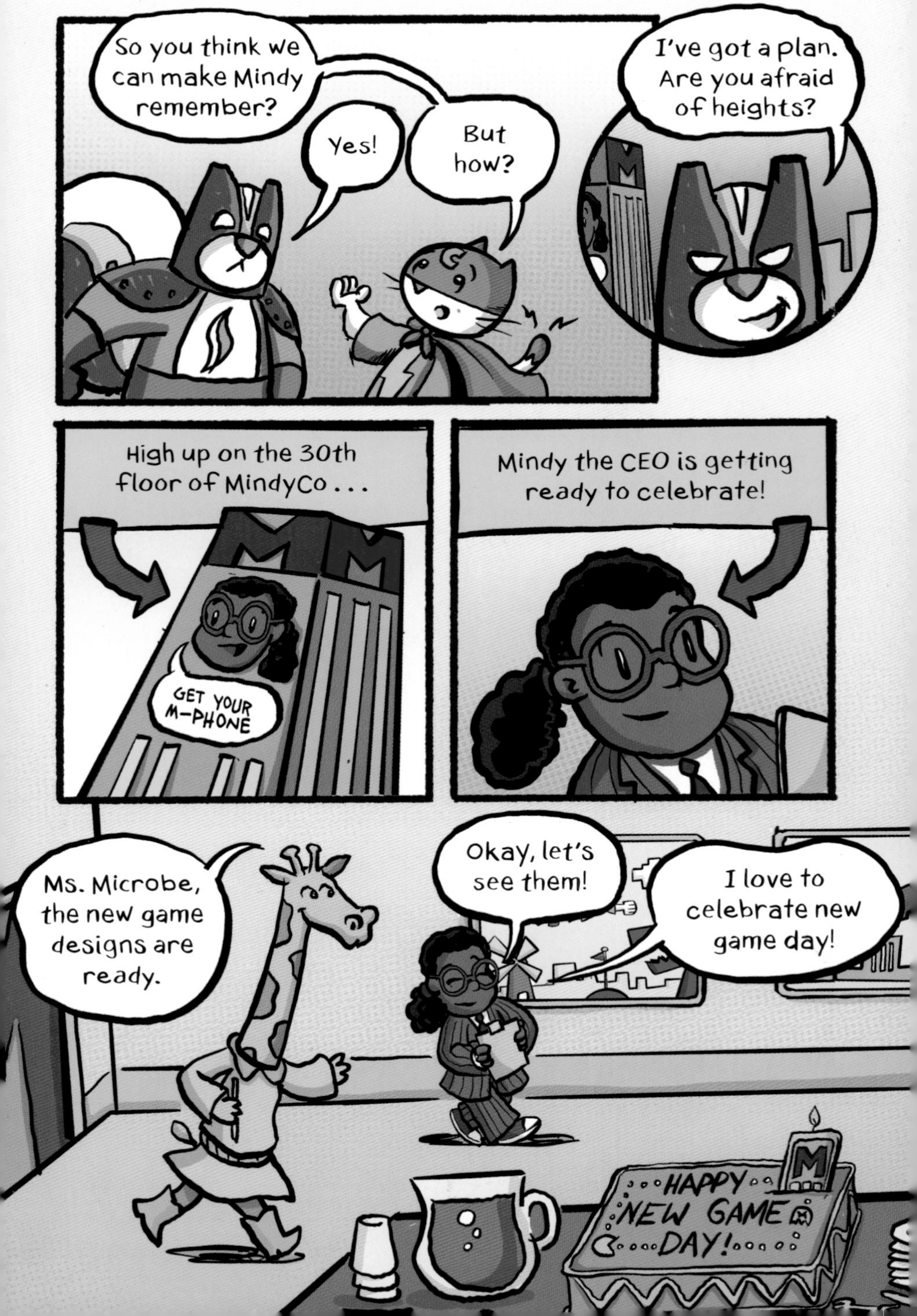

So you think we can make Mindy remember?
Yes!
But how?
I've got a plan. Are you afraid of heights?
High up on the 30th floor of MindyCo . . .
GET YOUR M-PHONE
Mindy the CEO is getting ready to celebrate!
Ms. Microbe, the new game designs are ready.
Okay, let's see them!
I love to celebrate new game day!
HAPPY NEW GAME DAY!

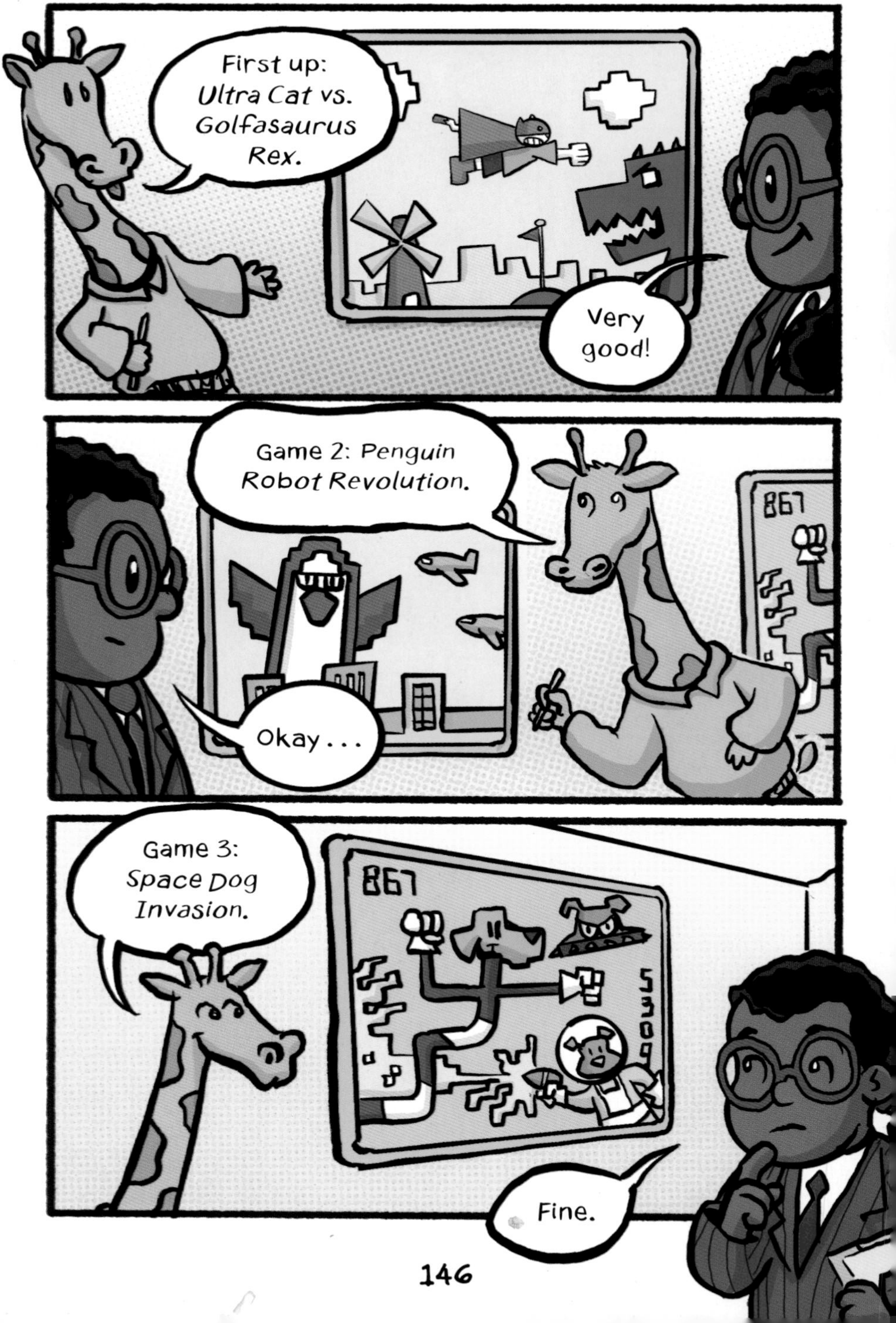
First up: Ultra Cat vs. Golfasaurus Rex.
Very good!
Game 2: Penguin Robot Revolution.
Okay . . .
Game 3: Space Dog Invasion.
Fine.

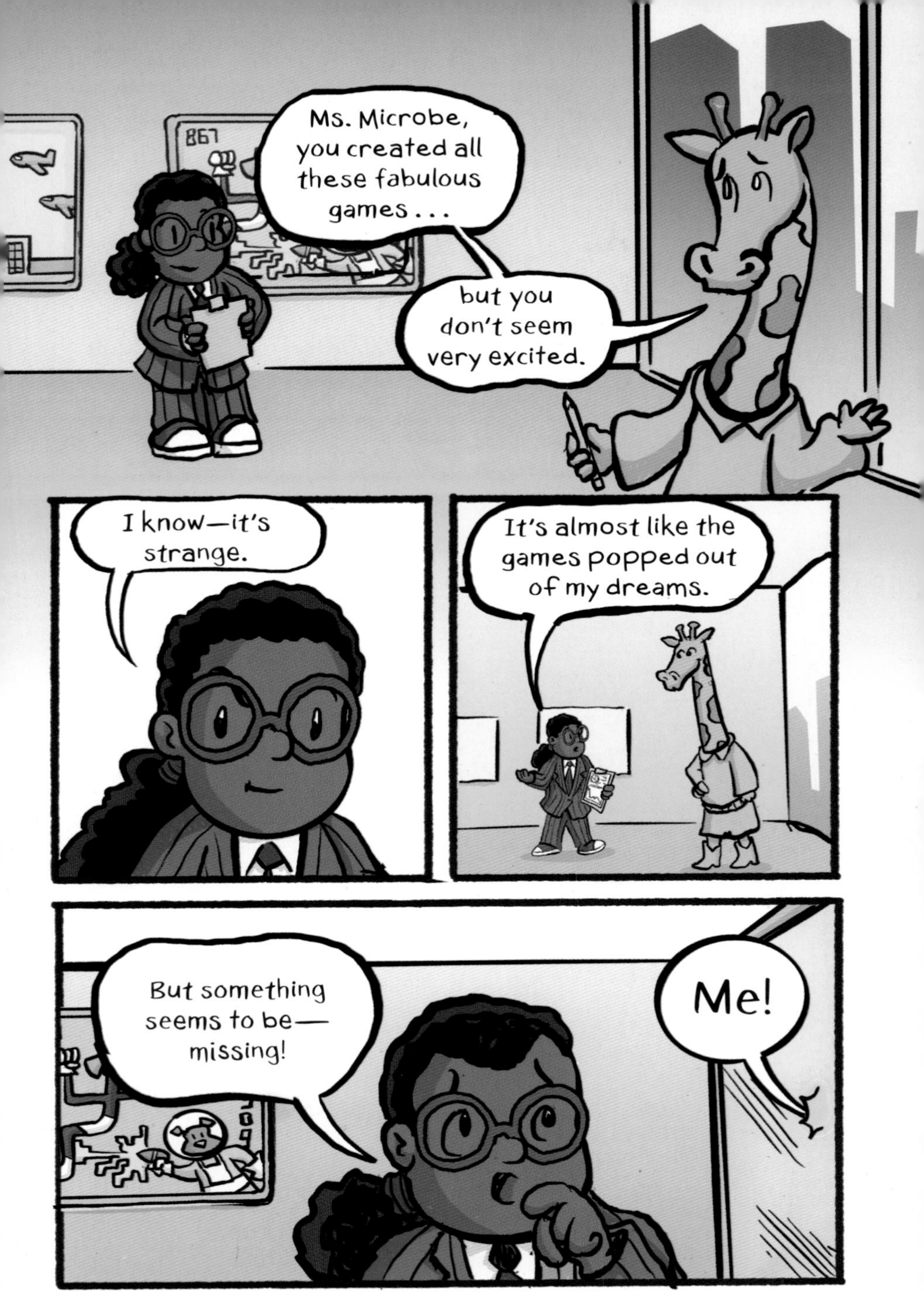
Ms. Microbe, you created all these fabulous games . . .
but you don't seem very excited.
I know—it's strange.
It's almost like the games popped out of my dreams.
But something seems to be— missing!
Me!

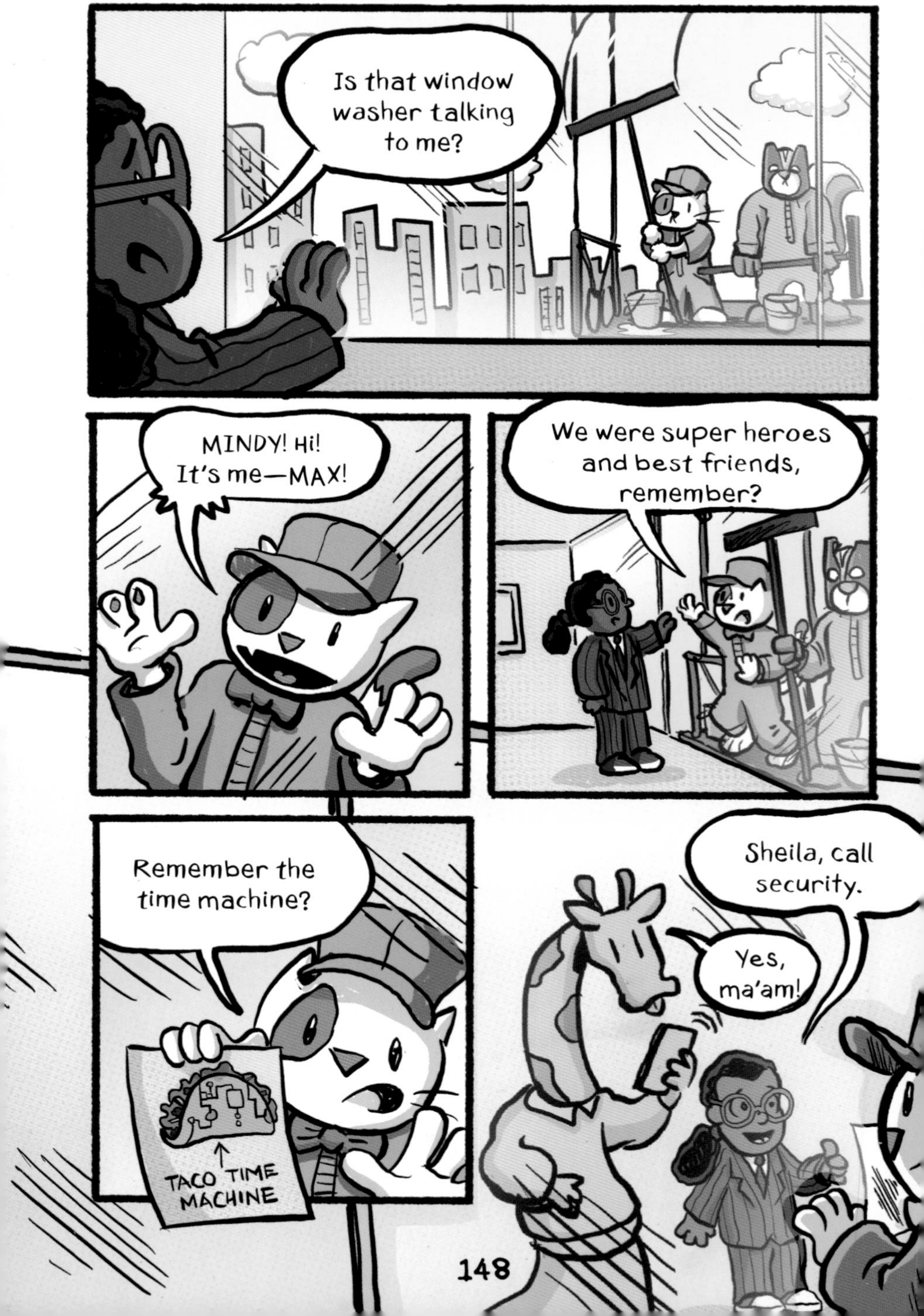
Is that window washer talking to me?
MINDY! Hi! It's me—MAX!
We were super heroes and best friends, remember?
Remember the time machine?
TACO TIME MACHINE
Sheila, call security.
Yes, ma'am!

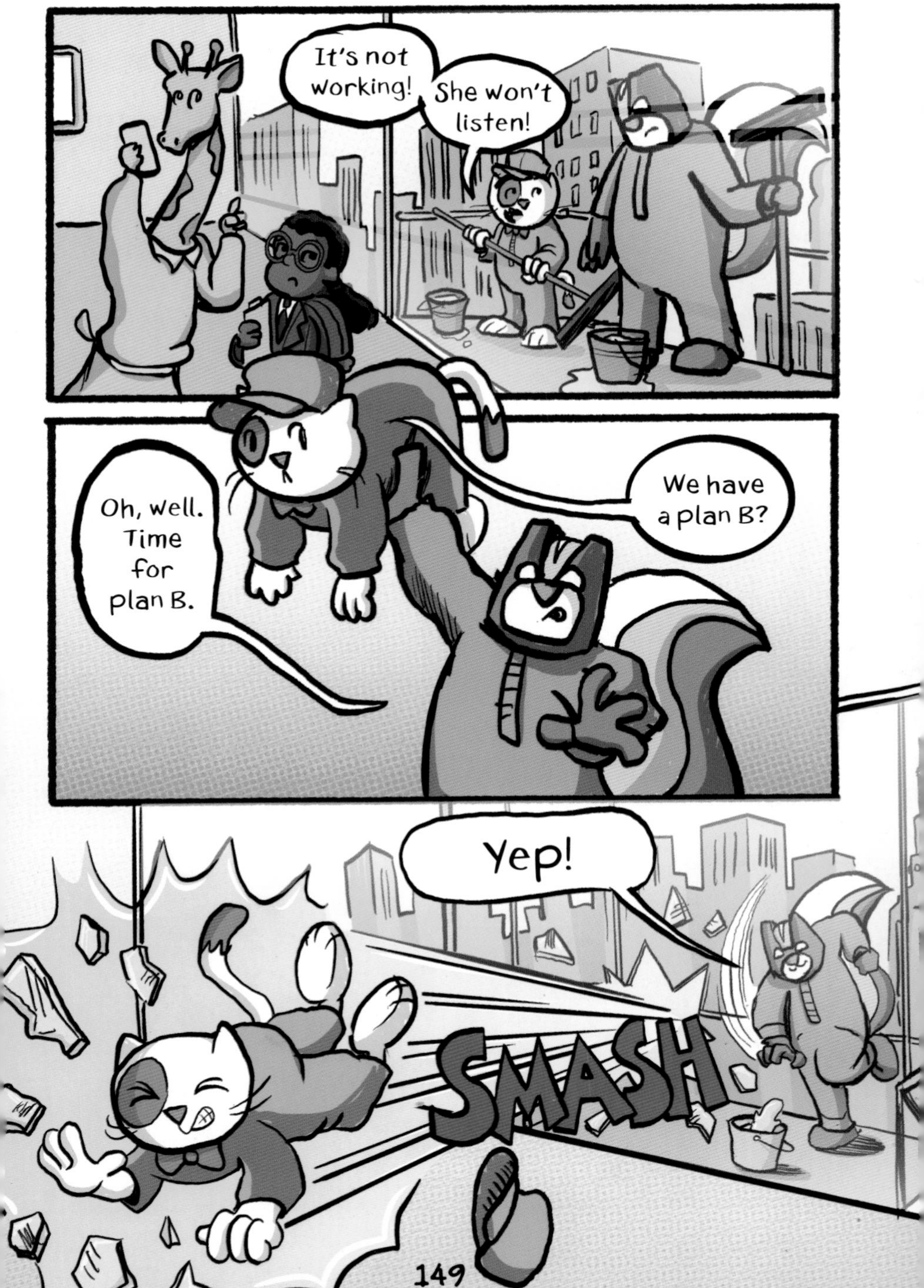
It's not working!
She won't listen!
Oh, well. Time for plan B.
We have a plan B?
Yep!
SMASH

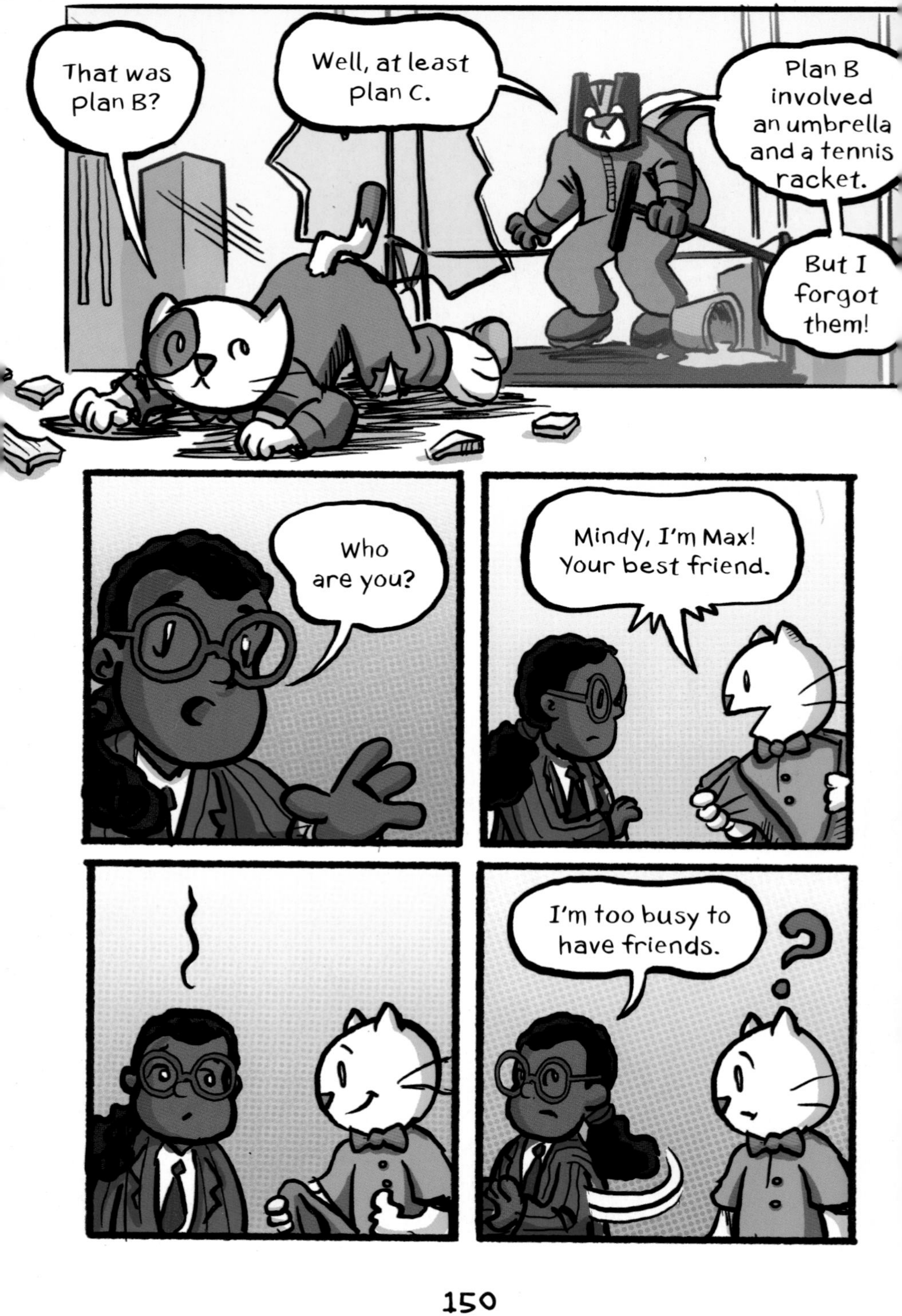
That was plan B?
Well, at least plan C.
Plan B involved an umbrella and a tennis racket.
But I forgot them!
Who are you?
Mindy, I'm Max! Your best friend.
I'm too busy to have friends.

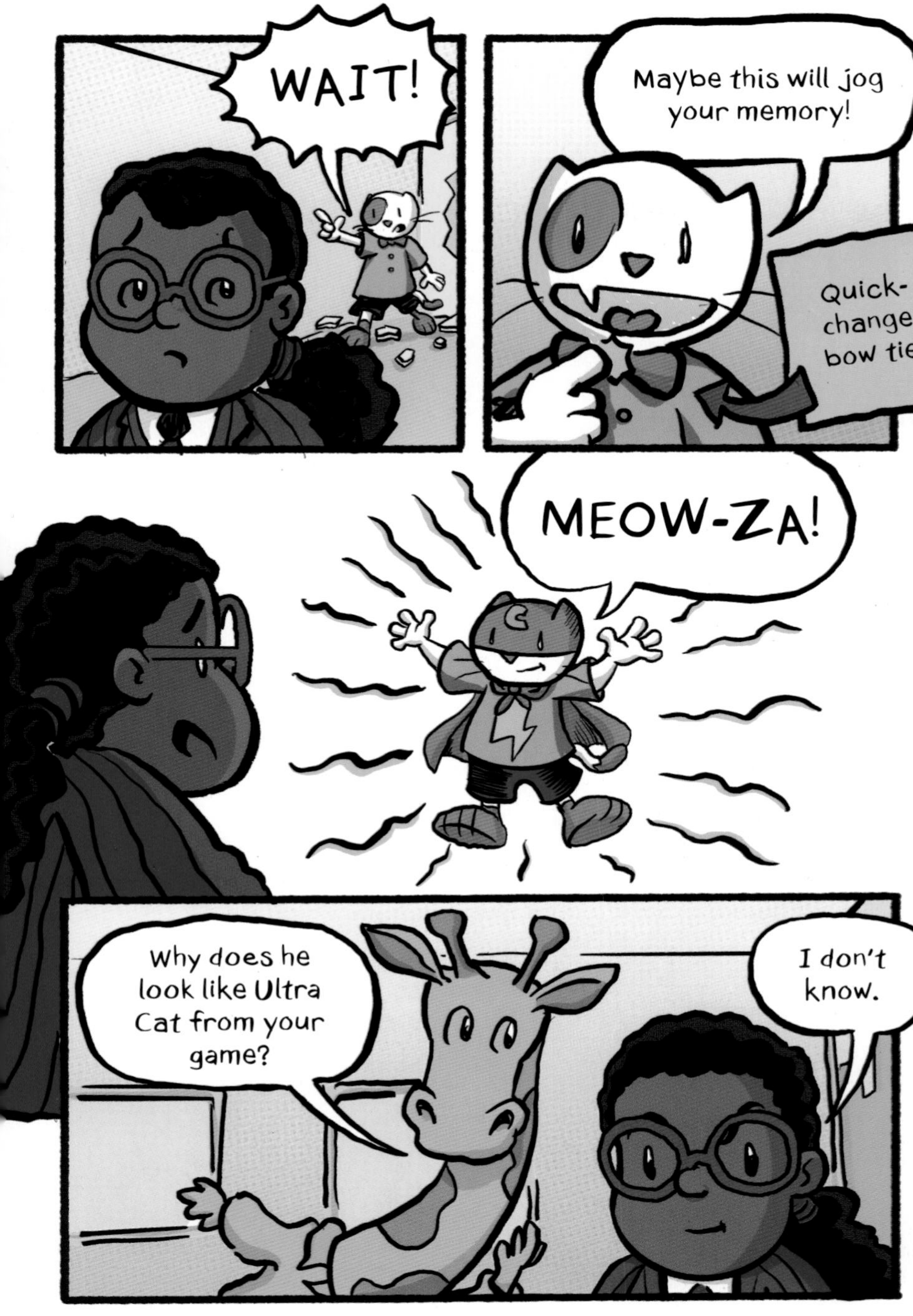
WAIT!
Maybe this will jog your memory!
Quick-change bow tie
MEOW-ZA!
Why does he look like Ultra Cat from your game?
I don't know.

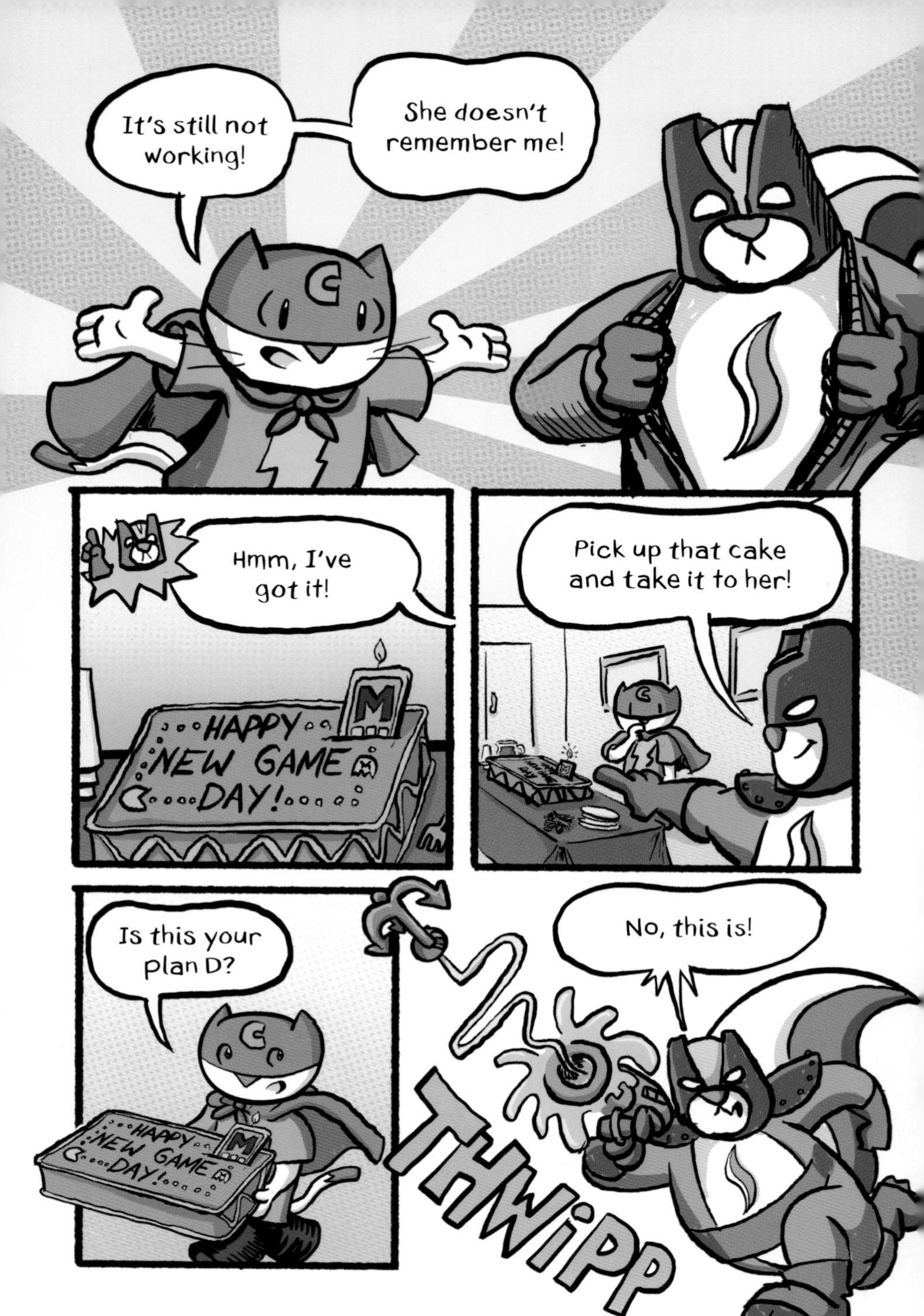
It's still not working!
She doesn't remember me!
Hmm, I've got it!
HAPPY NEW GAME DAY!
Pick up that cake and take it to her!
Is this your plan D?
HAPPY NEW GAME DAY!
No, this is!
THWiPP

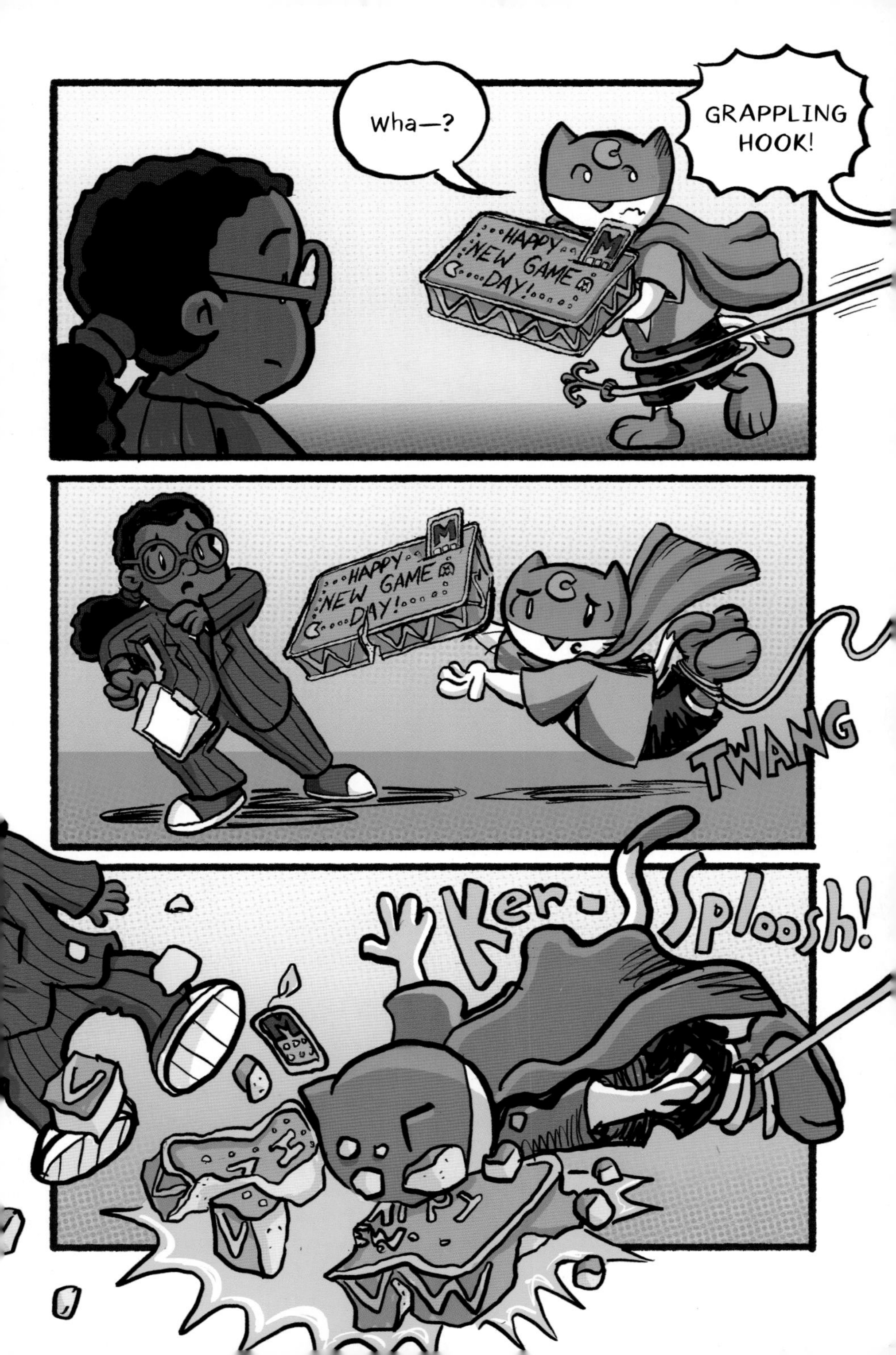
Wha—?
GRAPPLING HOOK!
HAPPY NEW GAME DAY!
HAPPY NEW GAME DAY!
TWANG
Ker-Sploosh!

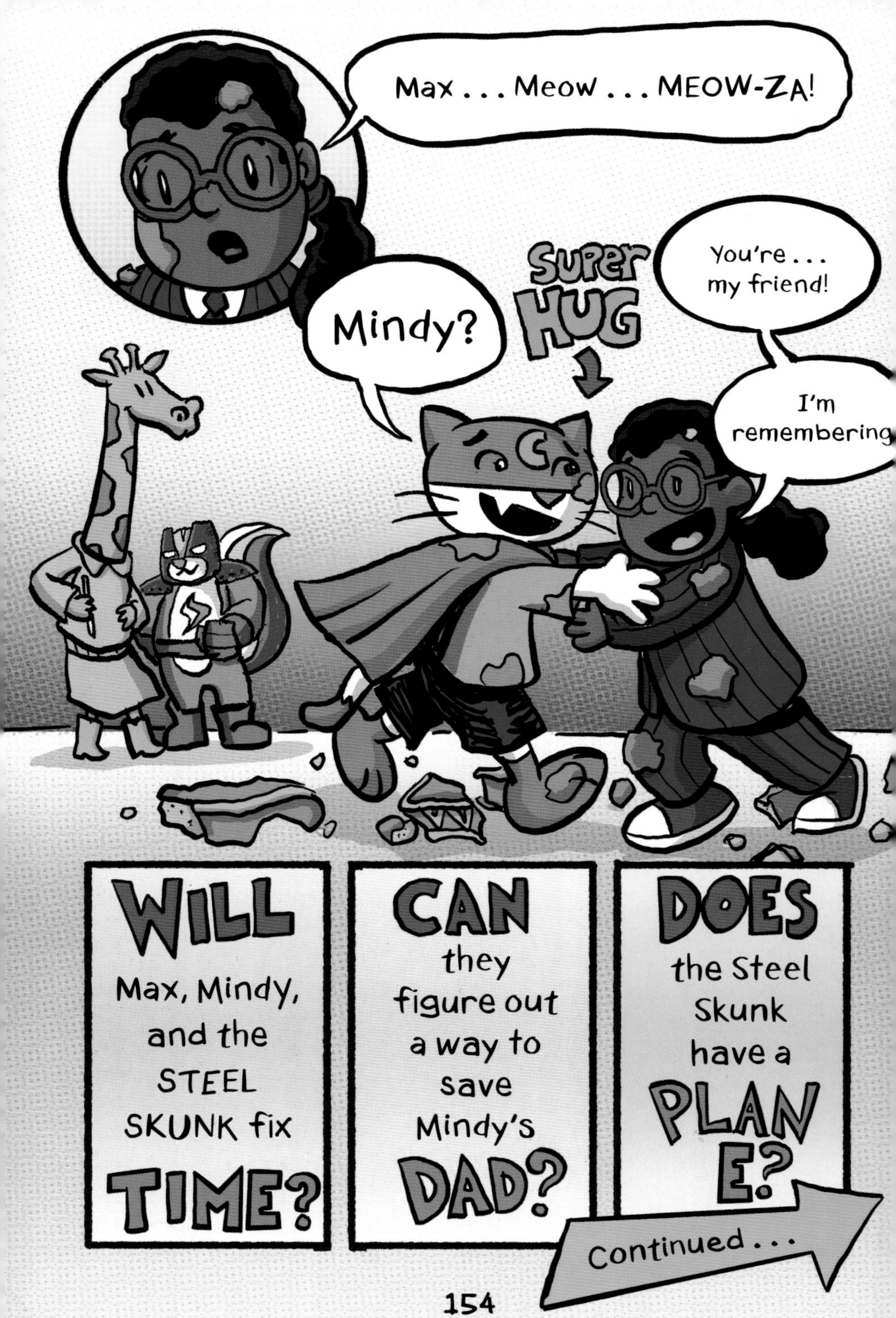
Max . . . Meow . . . MEOW-ZA!
Mindy?
SUPER HUG
You're . . . my friend!
I'm remembering
WILL Max, Mindy, and the STEEL SKUNK fix TIME?
CAN they figure out a way to save Mindy's DAD?
DOES the Steel Skunk have a PLAN E?
Continued . . .

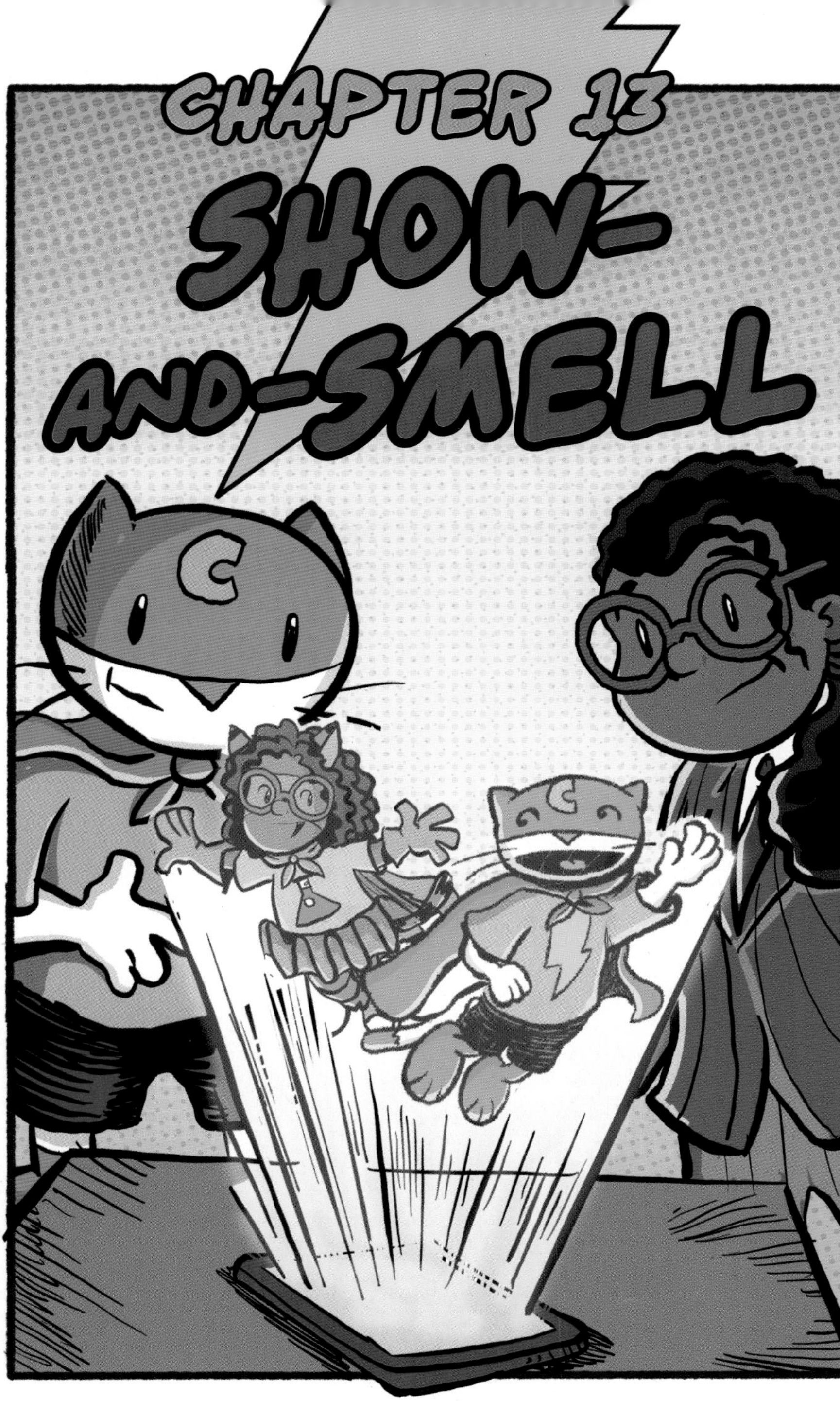
CHAPTER 13
SHOW-AND-SMELL

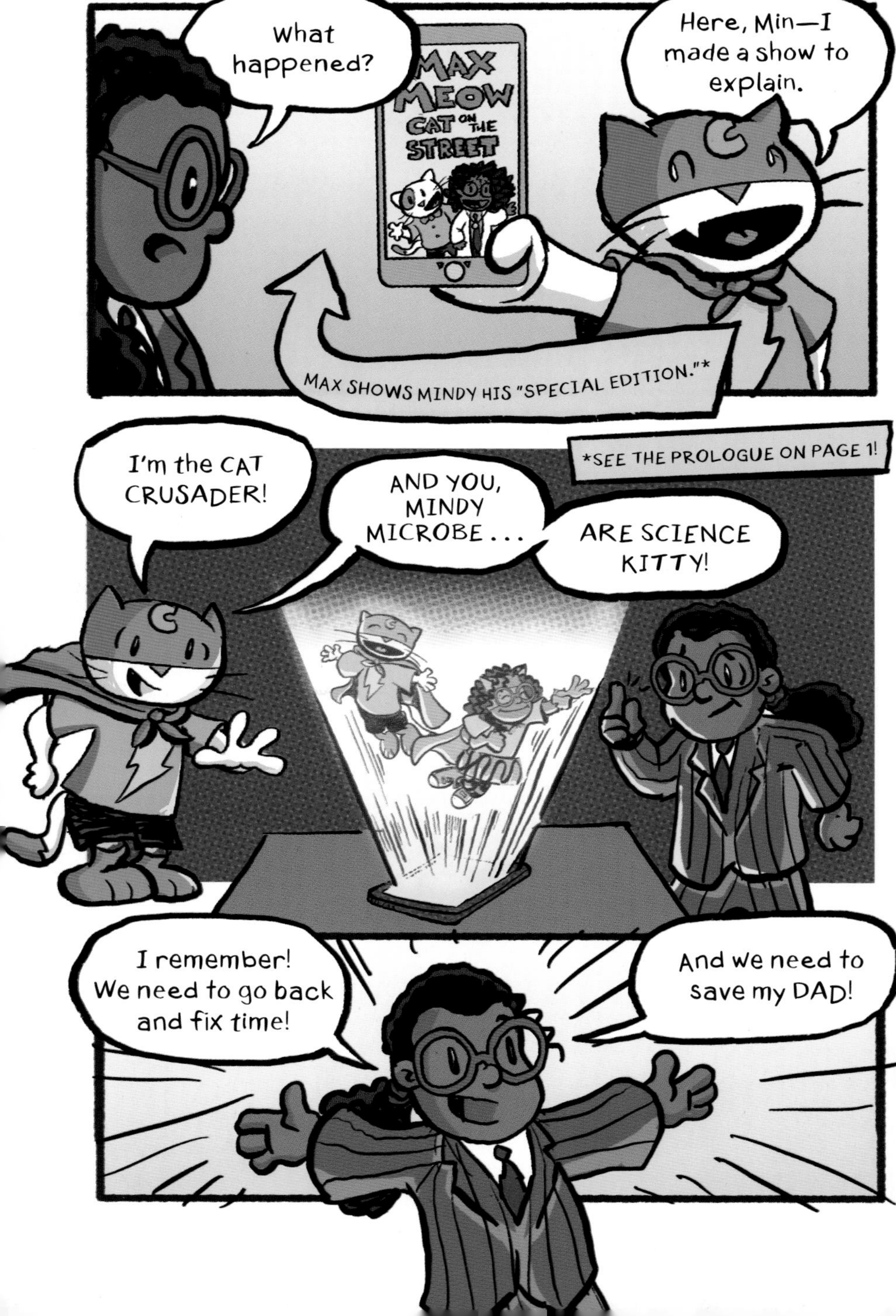
What happened?
MAX MEOW CAT ON THE STREET
Here, Min—I made a show to explain.
MAX SHOWS MINDY HIS "SPECIAL EDITION."*
*SEE THE PROLOGUE ON PAGE 1!
I'm the CAT CRUSADER!
AND YOU, MINDY MICROBE . . .
ARE SCIENCE KITTY!
I remember! We need to go back and fix time!
And we need to save my DAD!

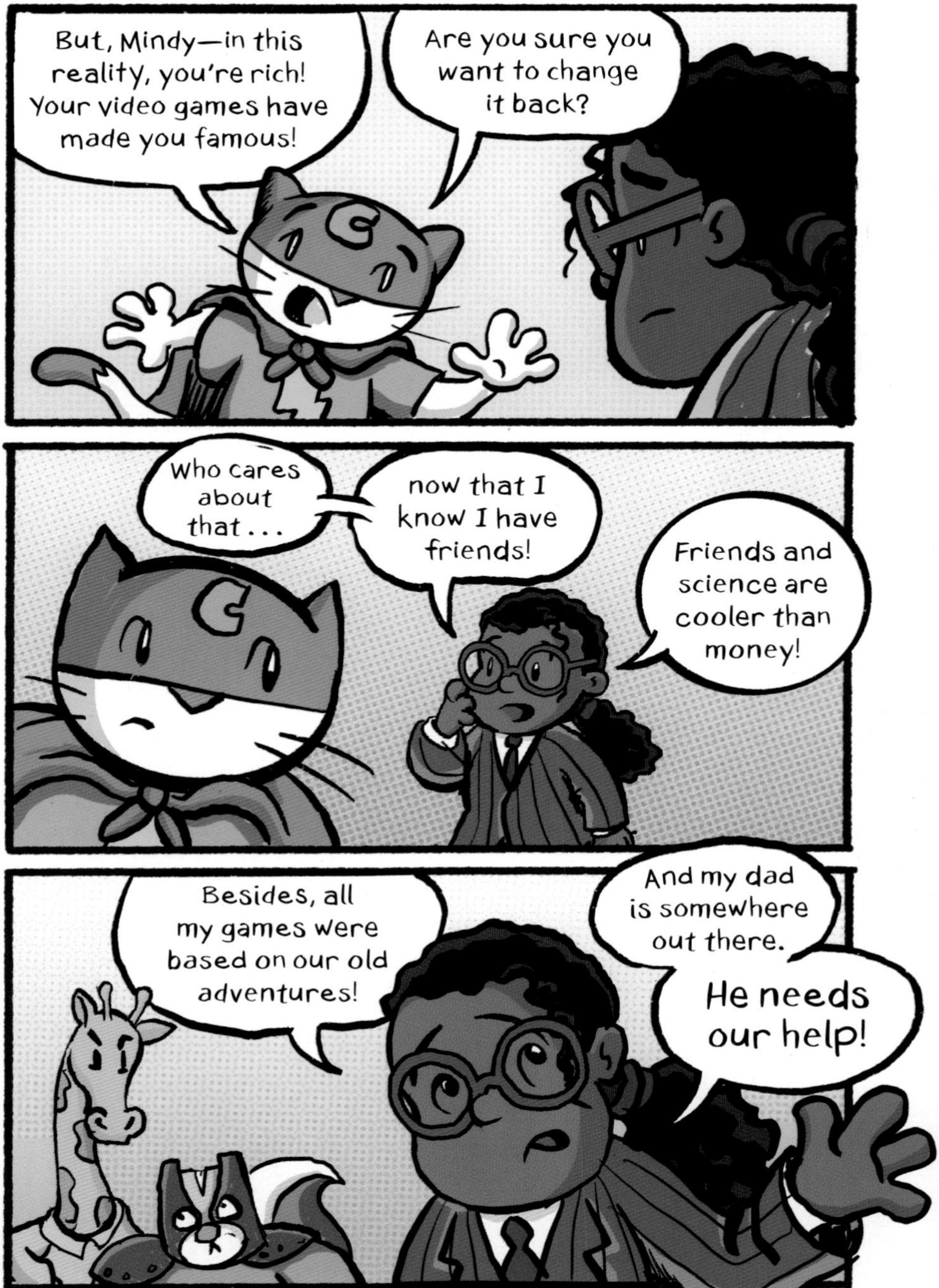
But, Mindy—in this reality, you're rich! Your video games have made you famous!
Are you sure you want to change it back?
Who cares about that . . .
now that I know I have friends!
Friends and science are cooler than money!
Besides, all my games were based on our old adventures!
And my dad is somewhere out there.
He needs our help!

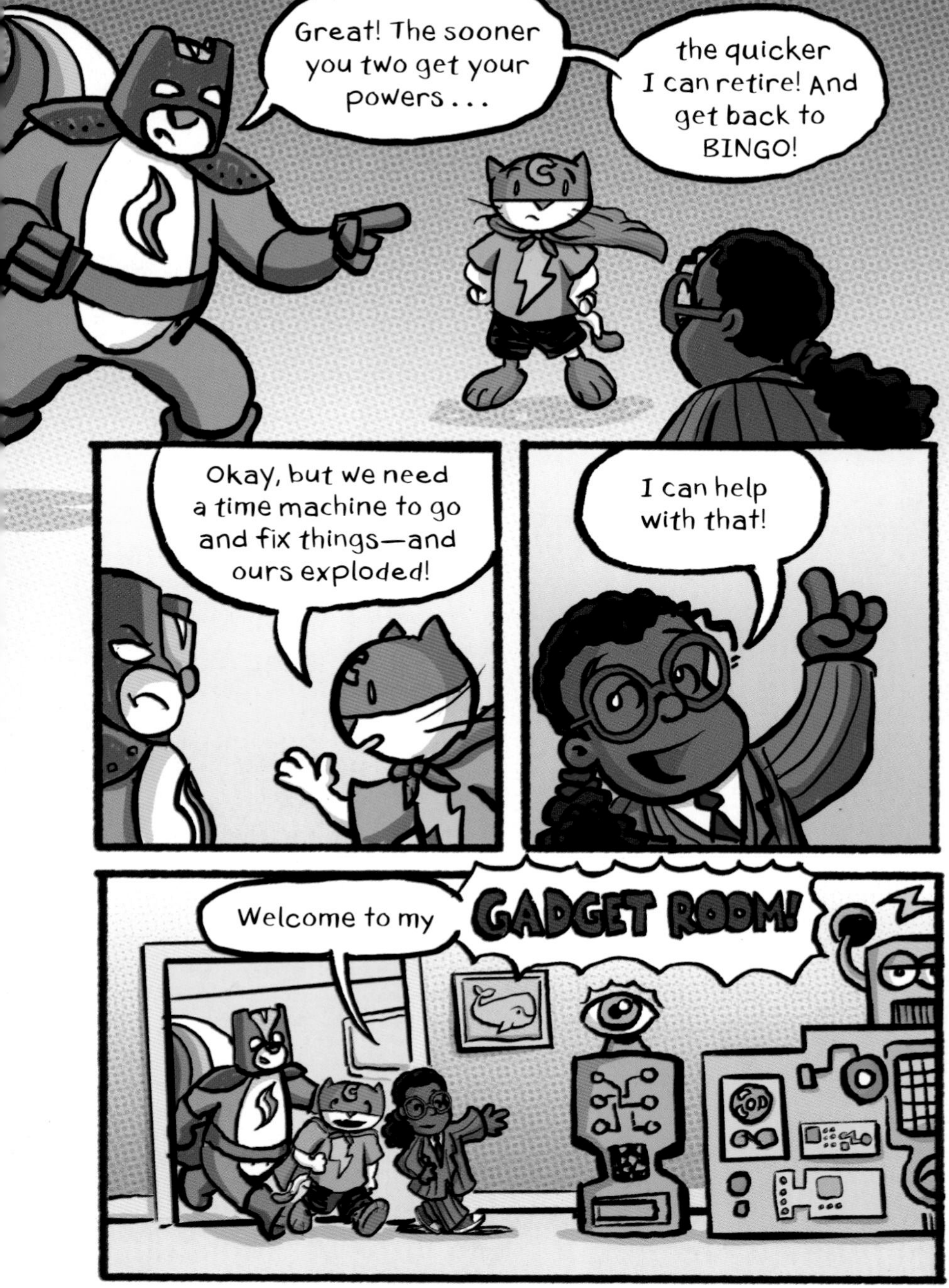
Great! The sooner you two get your powers . . .
the quicker I can retire! And get back to BINGO!
Okay, but we need a time machine to go and fix things—and ours exploded!
I can help with that!
Welcome to my
GADGET ROOM!

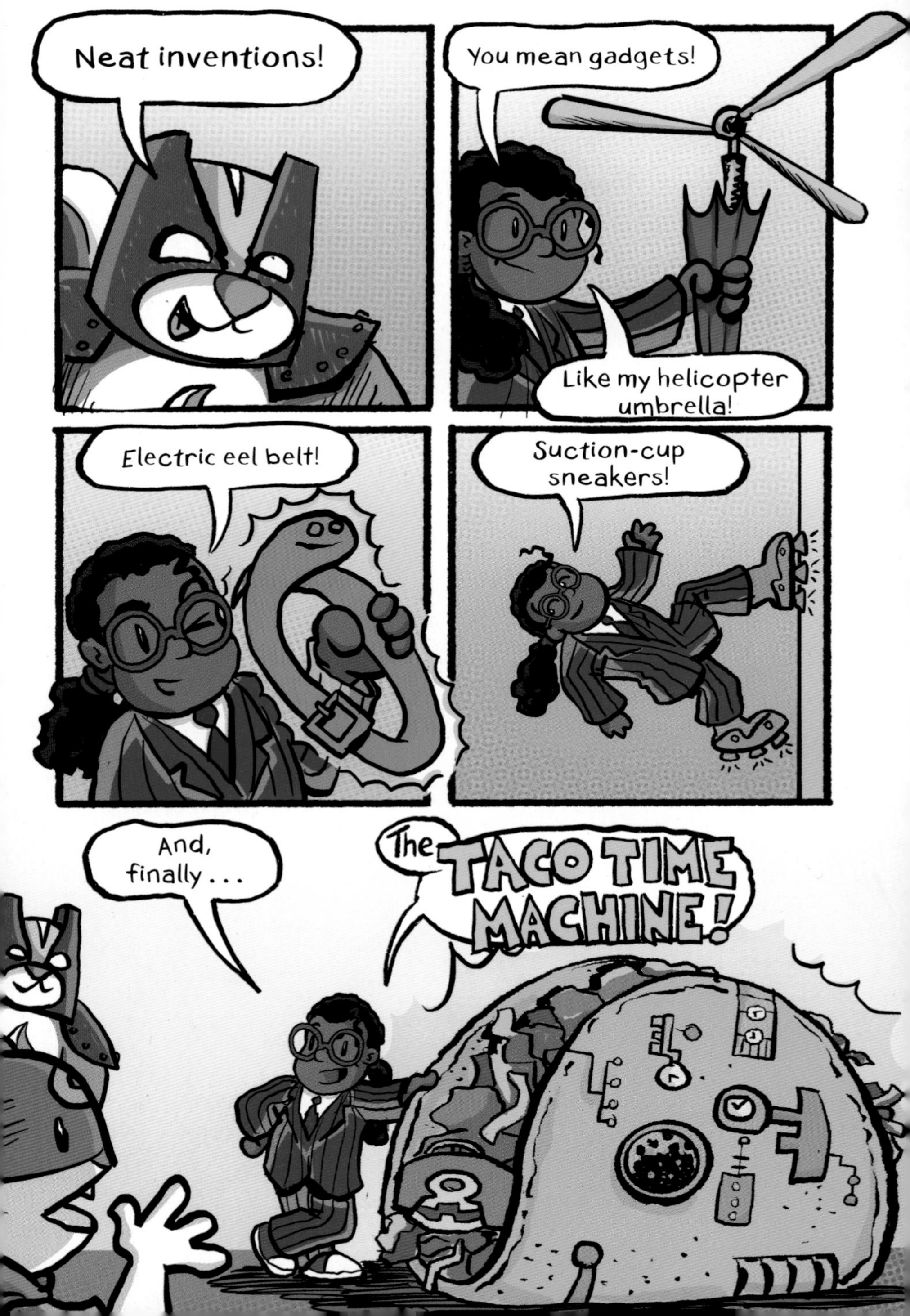
Neat inventions!
You mean gadgets!
Like my helicopter umbrella!
Electric eel belt!
Suction-cup sneakers!
And, finally . . .
The TACO TIME MACHINE!

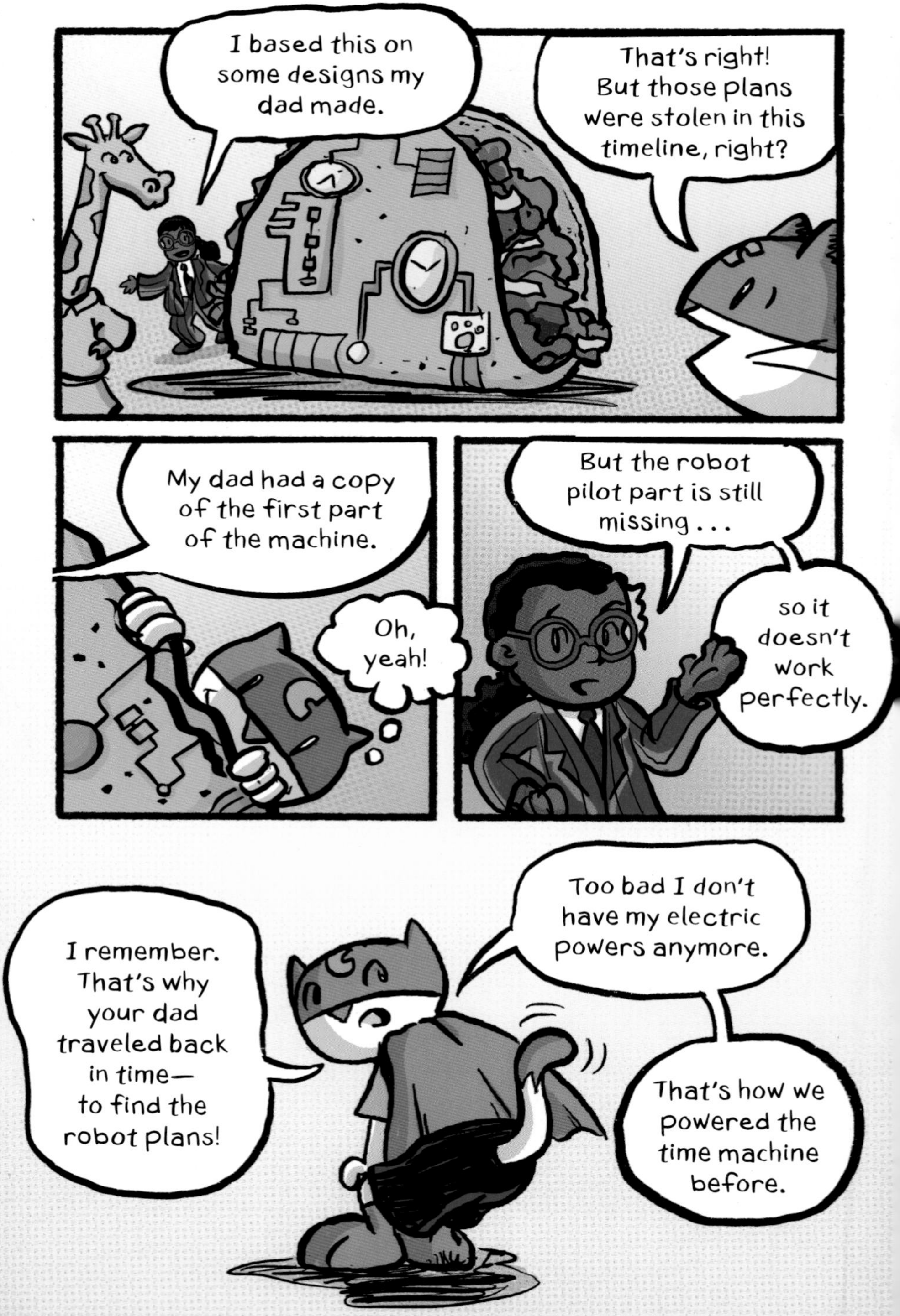
I based this on some designs my dad made.
That's right! But those plans were stolen in this timeline, right?
My dad had a copy of the first part of the machine.
Oh, yeah!
But the robot pilot part is still missing . . .
so it doesn't work perfectly.
I remember. That's why your dad traveled back in time— to find the robot plans!
Too bad I don't have my electric powers anymore.
That's how we powered the time machine before.

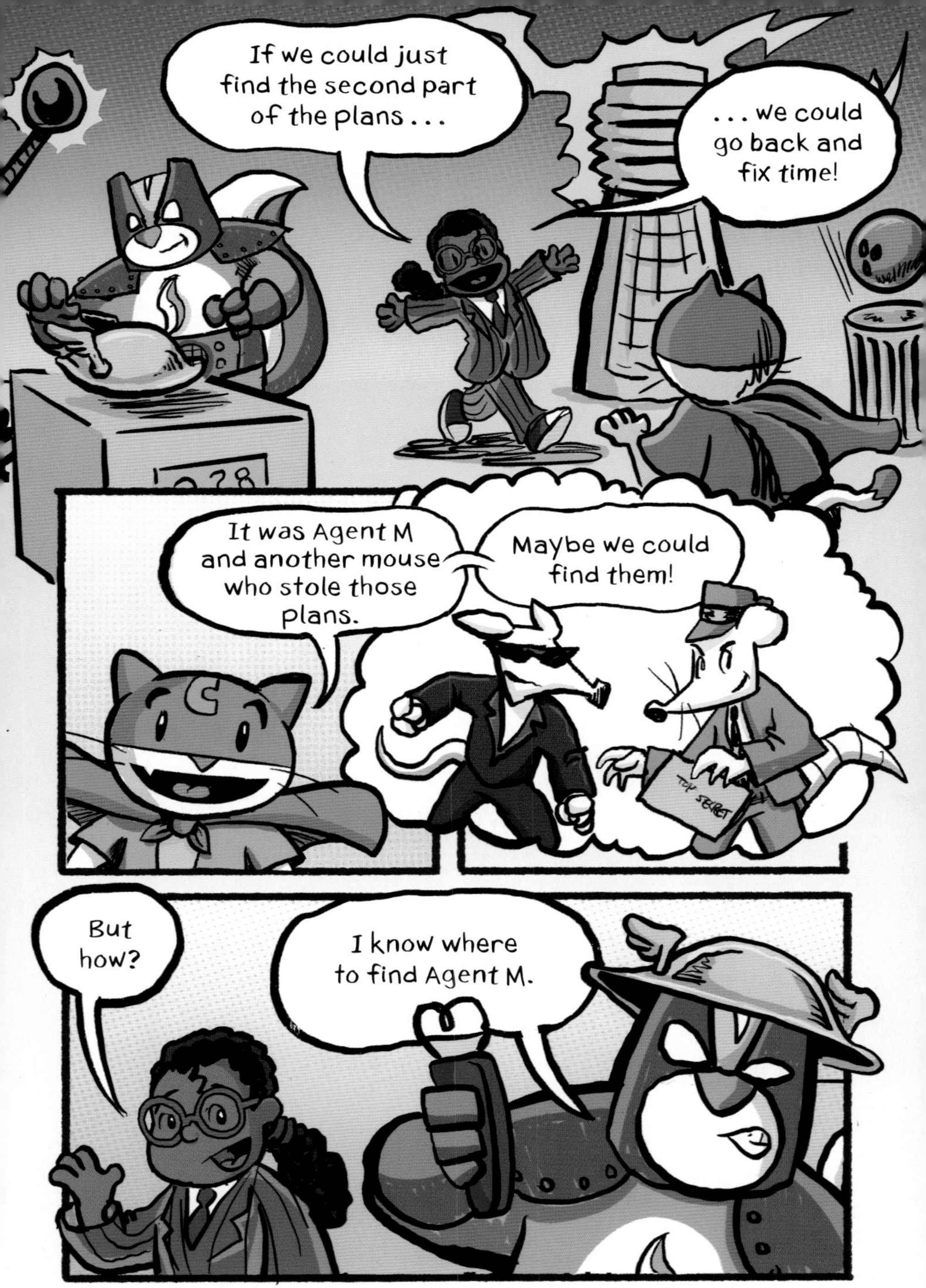
If we could just find the second part of the plans . . .
. . . we could go back and fix time!
It was Agent M and another mouse who stole those plans.
Maybe we could find them!
TOP SECRET
But how?
I know where to find Agent M.

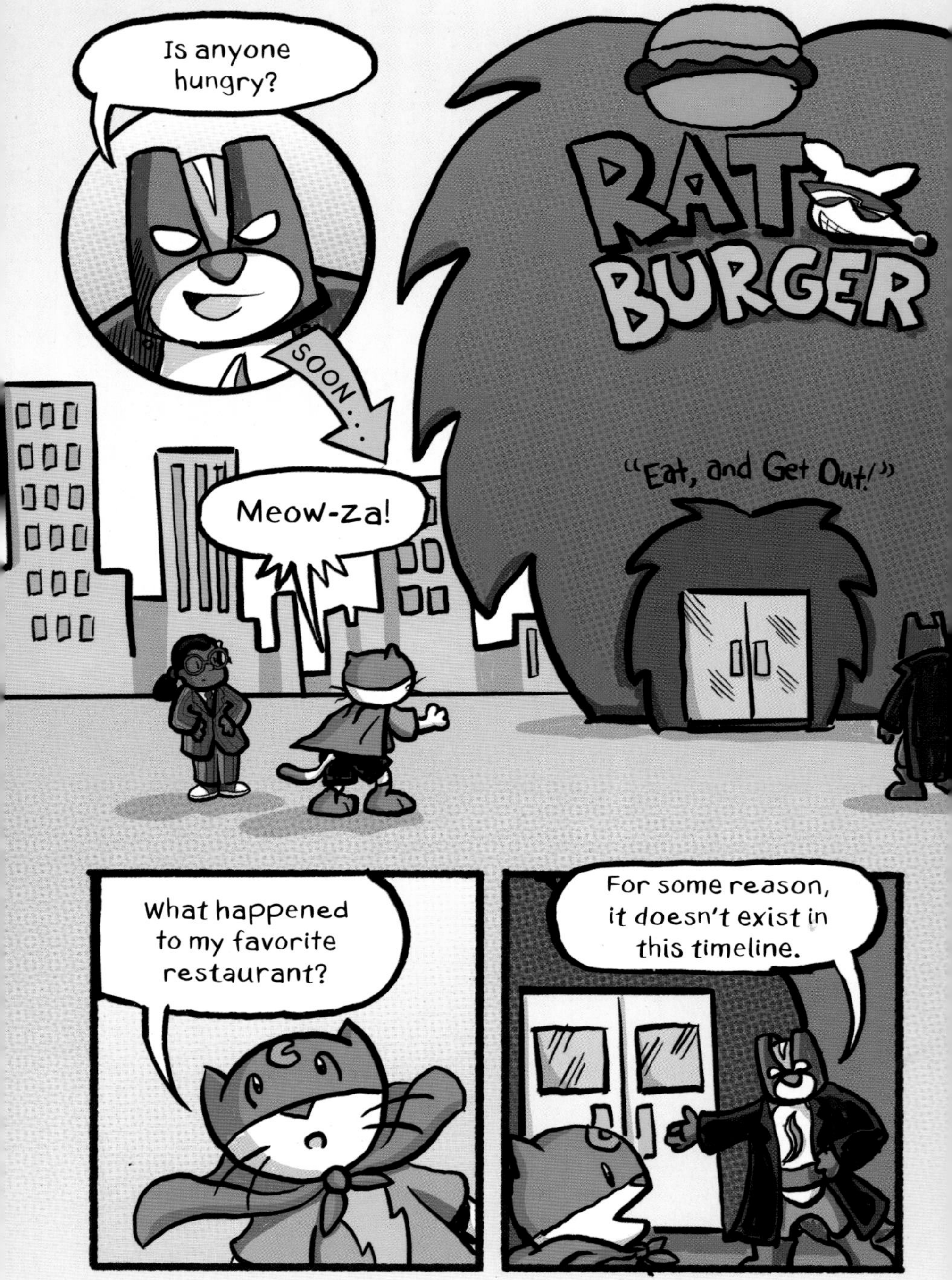
Is anyone hungry?
SOON...
RAT BURGER
"Eat, and Get Out!"
Meow-za!
What happened to my favorite restaurant?
For some reason, it doesn't exist in this timeline.

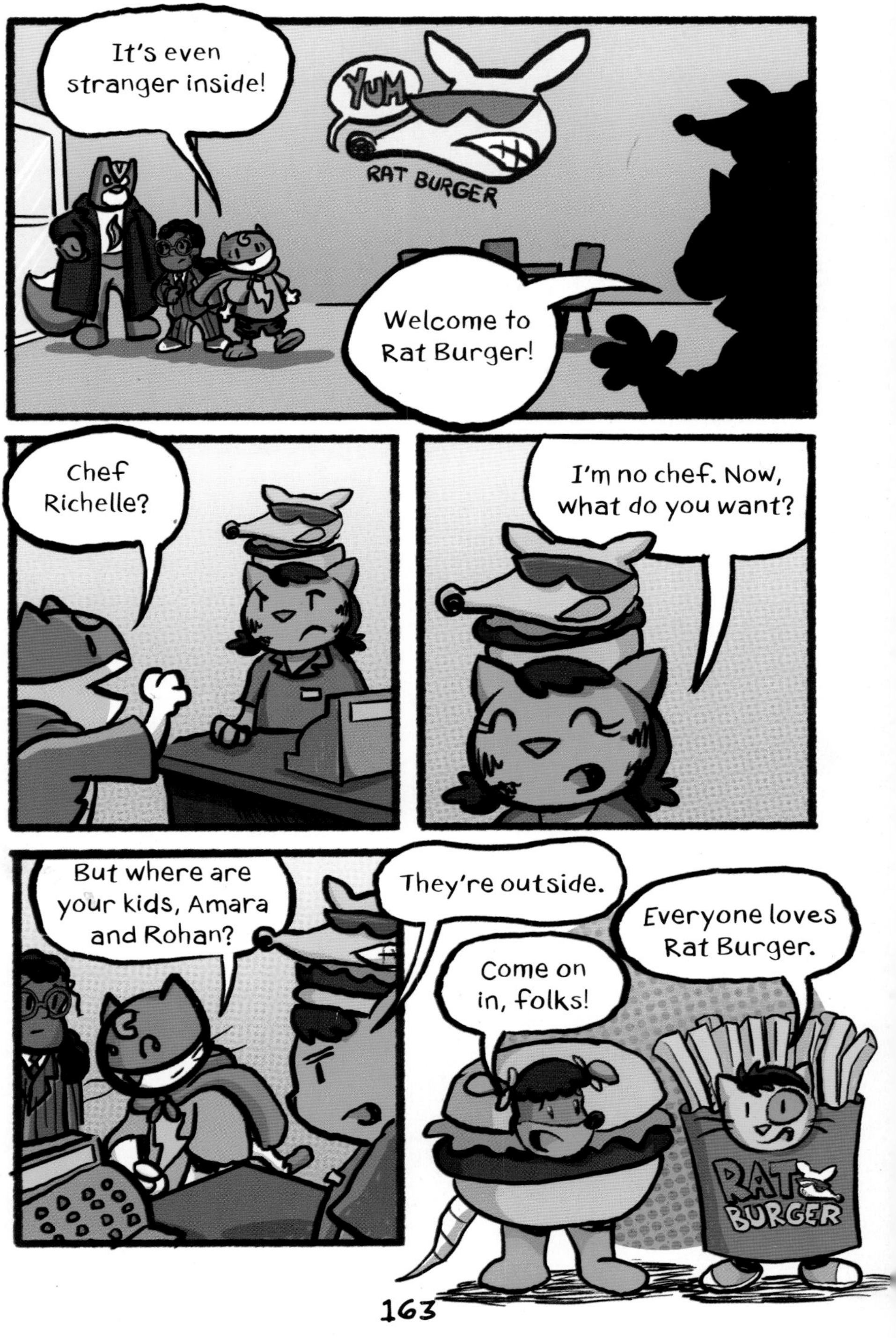
It's even
stranger inside!
YUM
RAT BURGER
Welcome to
Rat Burger!
Chef
Richelle?
I'm no chef. Now,
what do you want?
But where are
your kids, Amara
and Rohan?
They're outside.
Everyone loves
Rat Burger.
Come on
in, folks!
RAT
BURGER

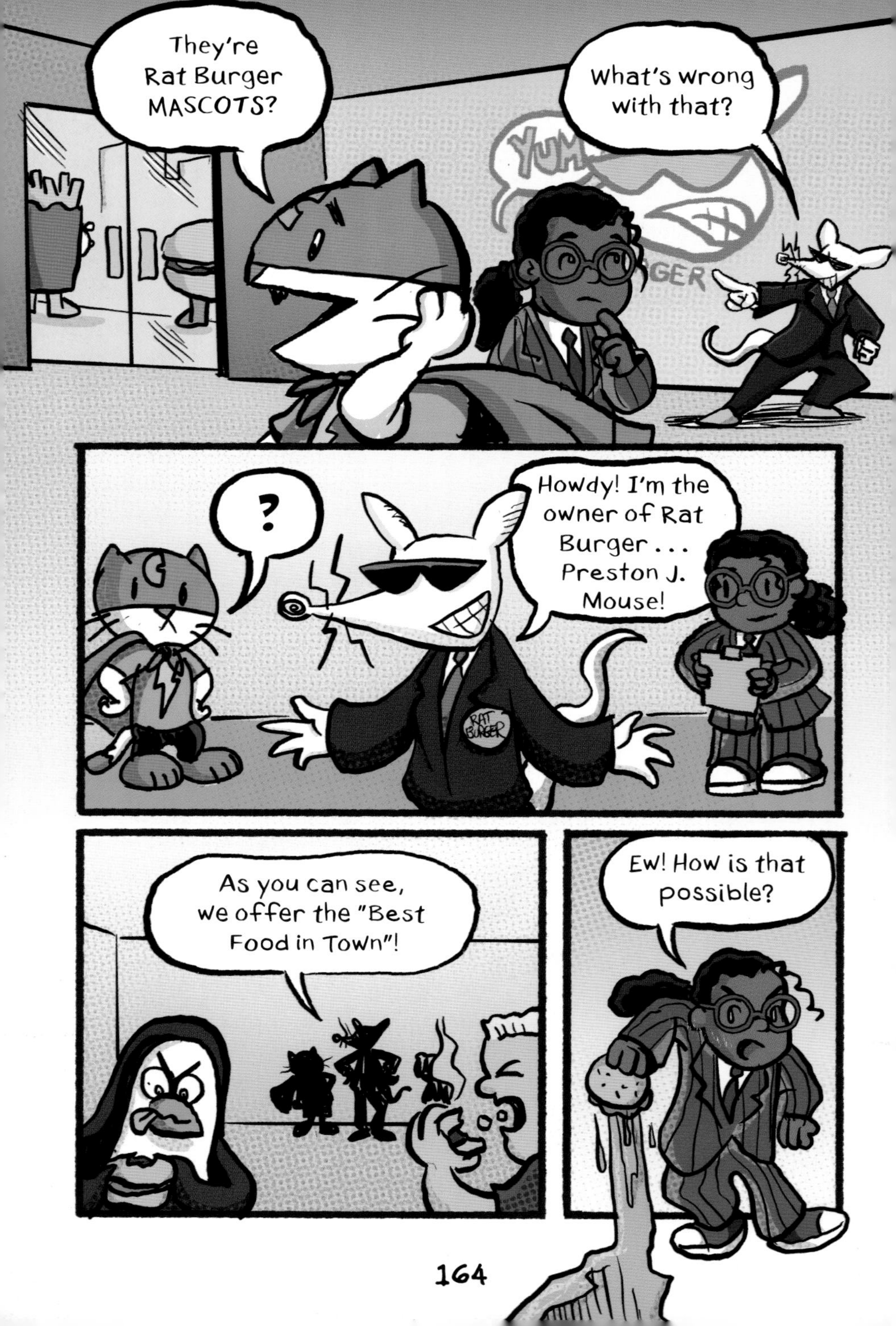
They're Rat Burger MASCOTS?
What's wrong with that?
YUM
GER
?
Howdy! I'm the owner of Rat Burger . . . Preston J. Mouse!
RAT BURGER
As you can see, we offer the "Best Food in Town"!
Ew! How is that possible?

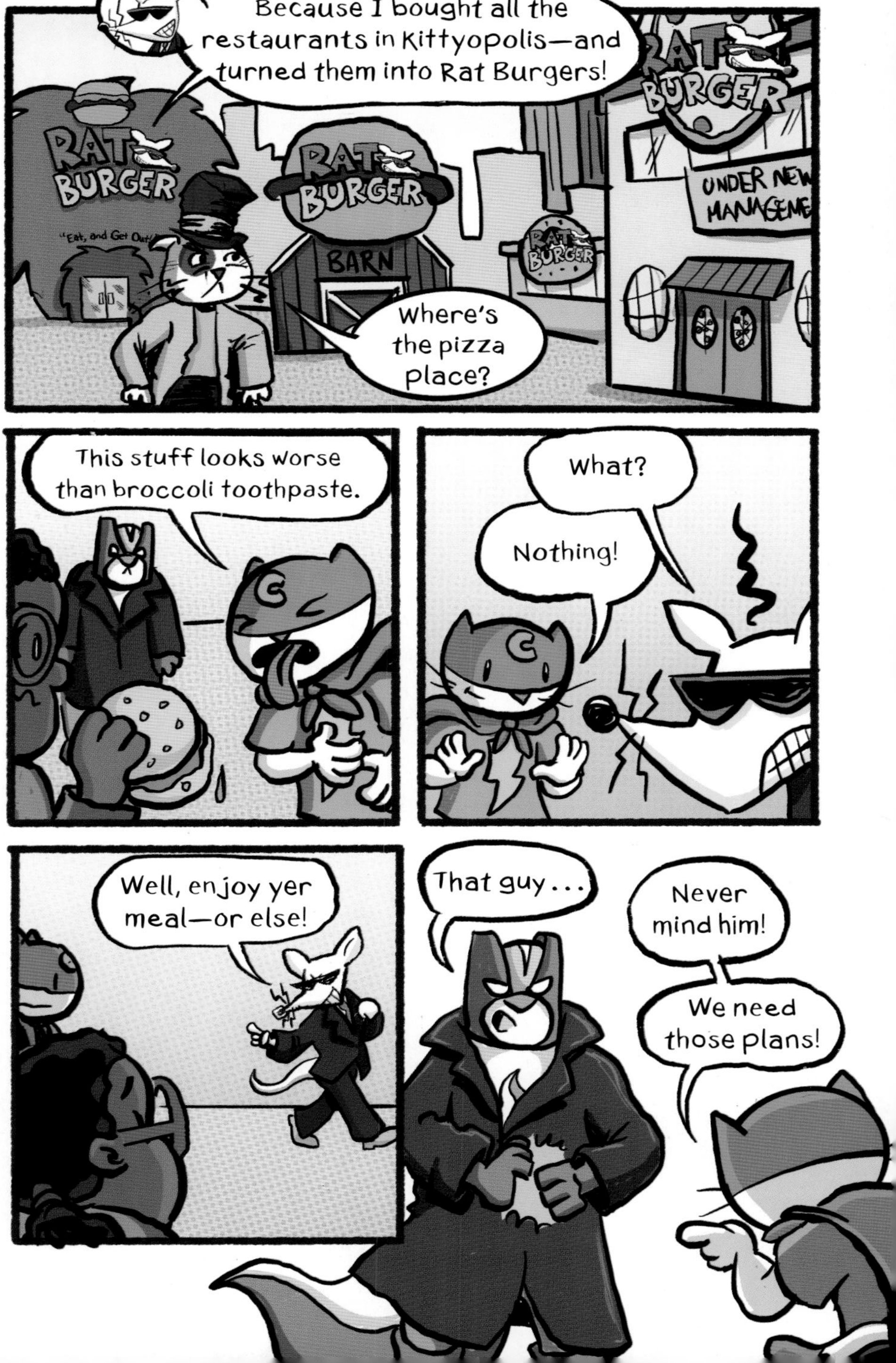

Because I bought all the restaurants in Kittyopolis—and turned them into Rat Burgers!
RAT BURGER
"Eat, and Get Out!"
RAT BURGER
BARN
RAT BURGER
RAT BURGER
UNDER NEW MANAGEME
Where's the pizza place?
This stuff looks worse than broccoli toothpaste.
What?
Nothing!
Well, enjoy yer meal—or else!
That guy . . .
Never mind him!
We need those plans!

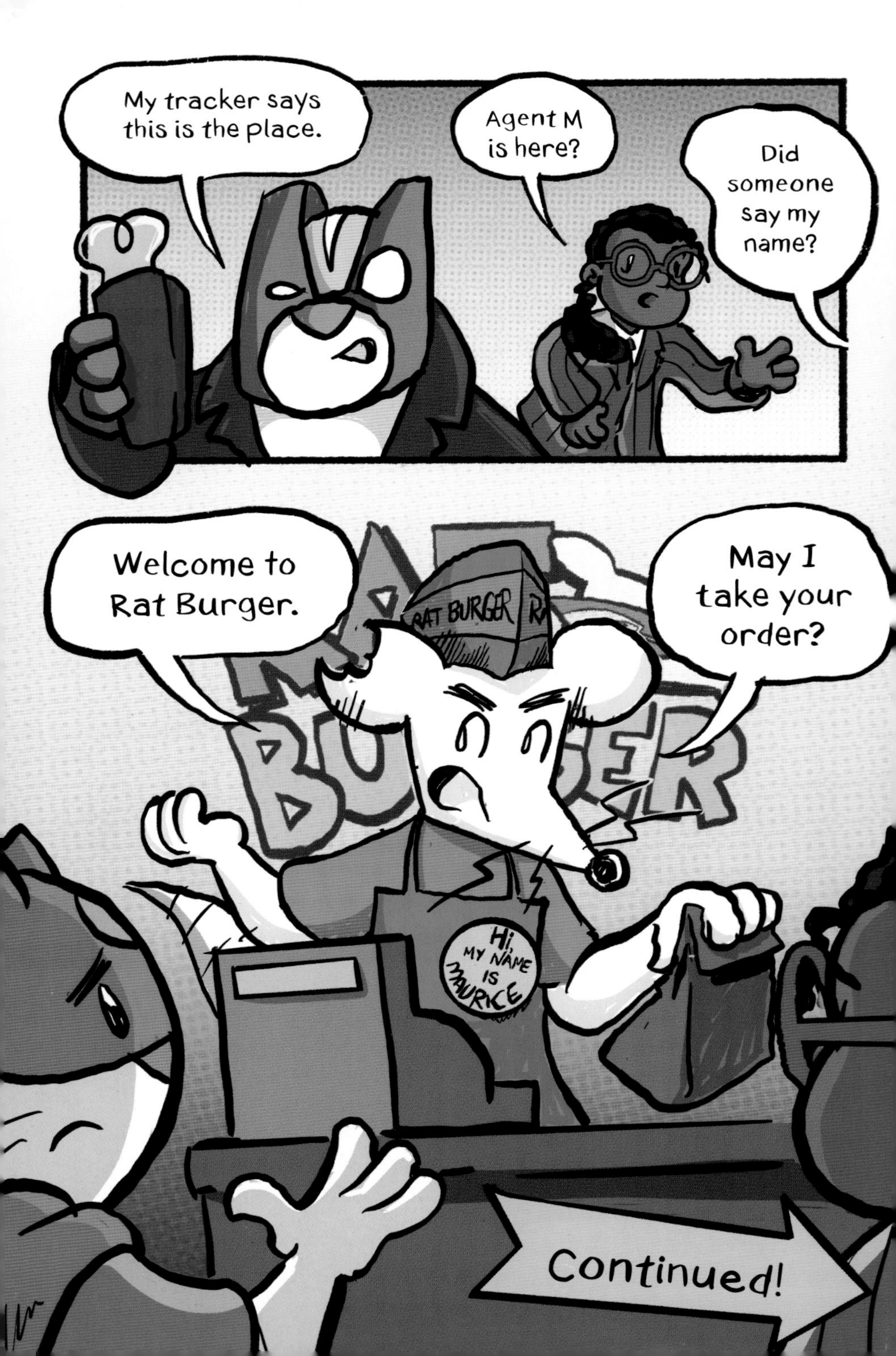
My tracker says this is the place.
Agent M is here?
Did someone say my name?
Welcome to Rat Burger.
RAT BURGER
BURGER
May I take your order?
Hi, MY NAME IS MAURICE
Continued!

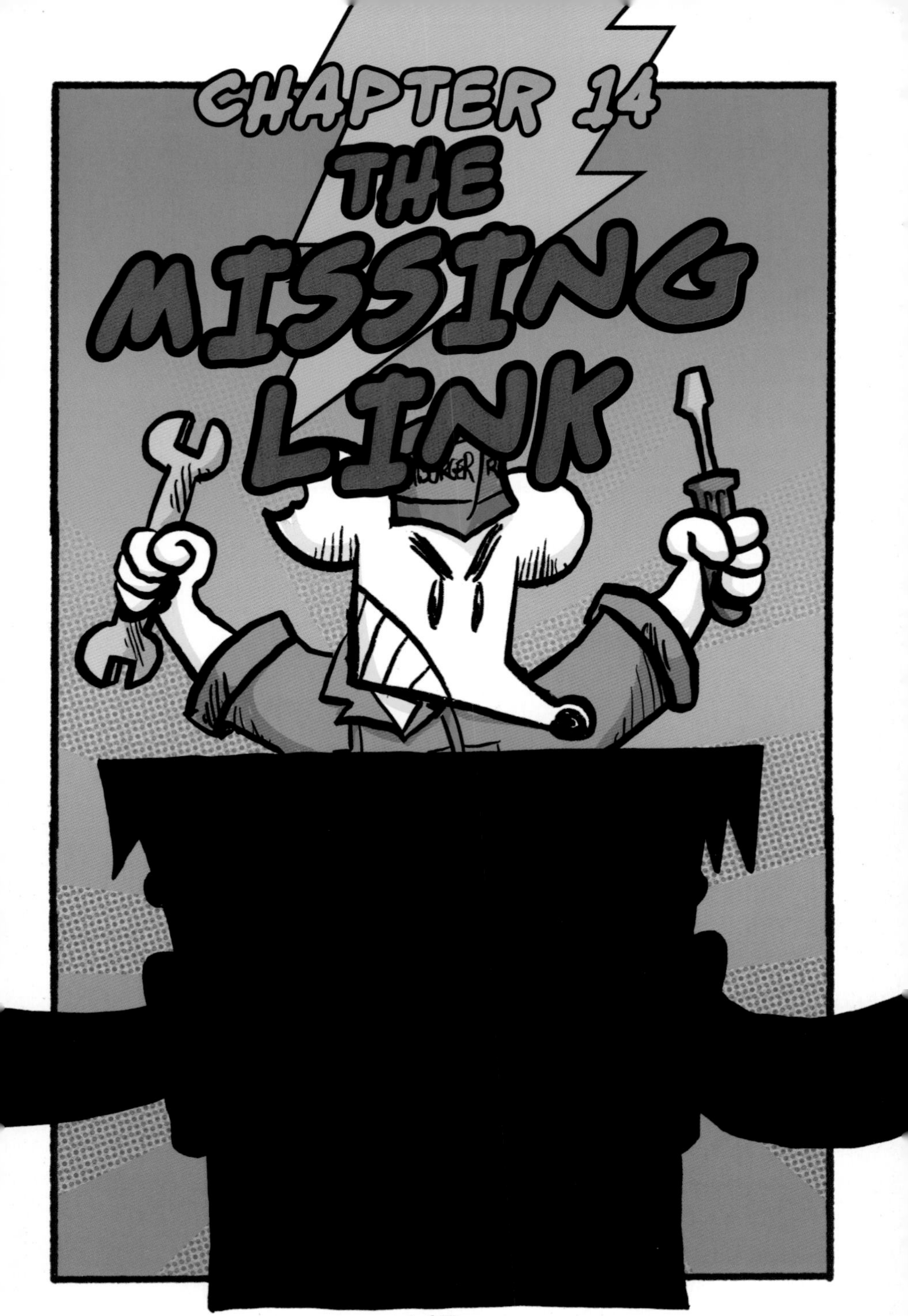
CHAPTER 14
THE
MISSING
LINK

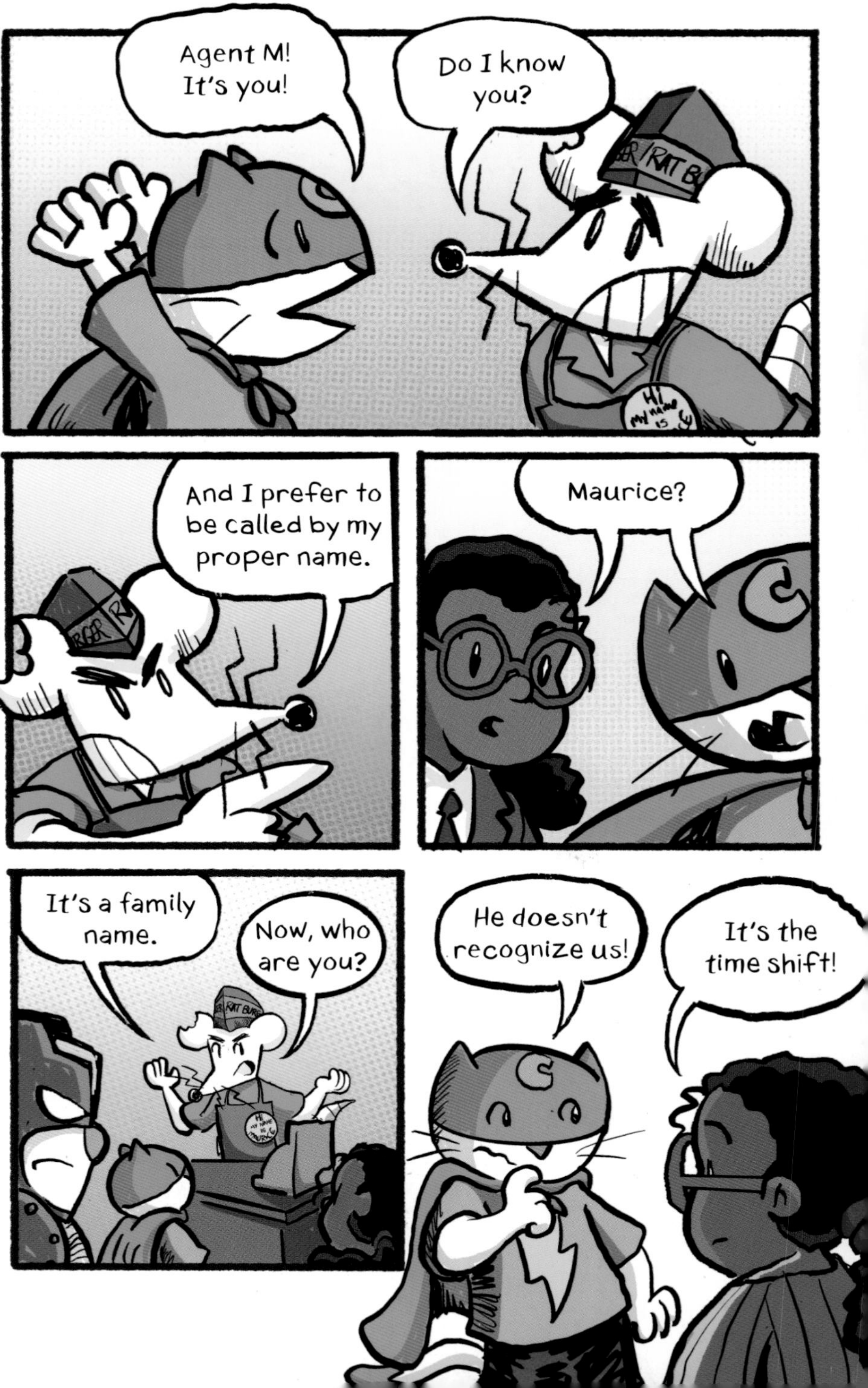
Agent M! It's you!
Do I know you?
RAT BU
And I prefer to be called by my proper name.
Maurice?
It's a family name.
Now, who are you?
RAT BURG
He doesn't recognize us!
It's the time shift!

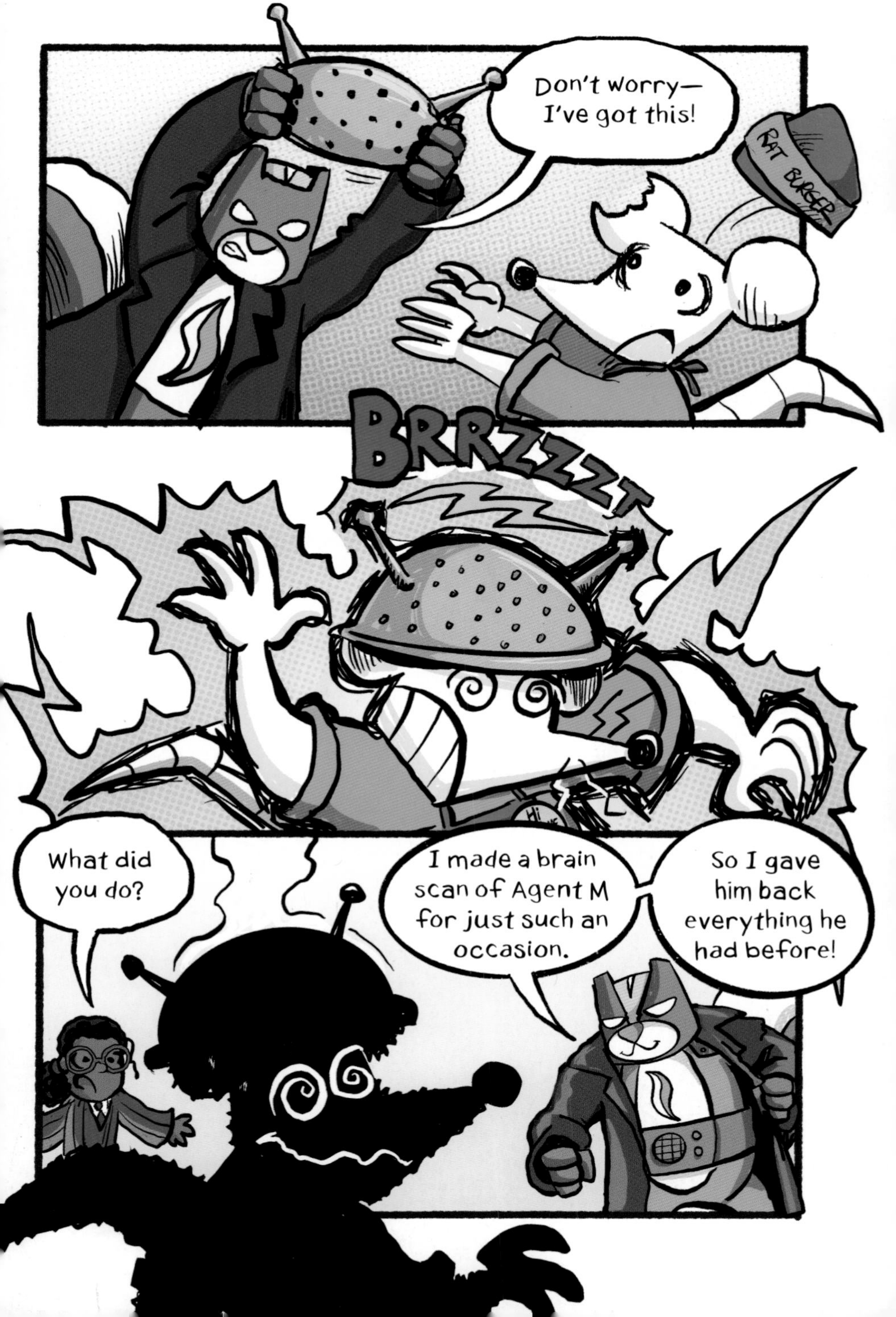
Don't worry—
I've got this!
RAT BURGER
BRRZZZZT
What did you do?
I made a brain scan of Agent M for just such an occasion.
So I gave him back everything he had before!

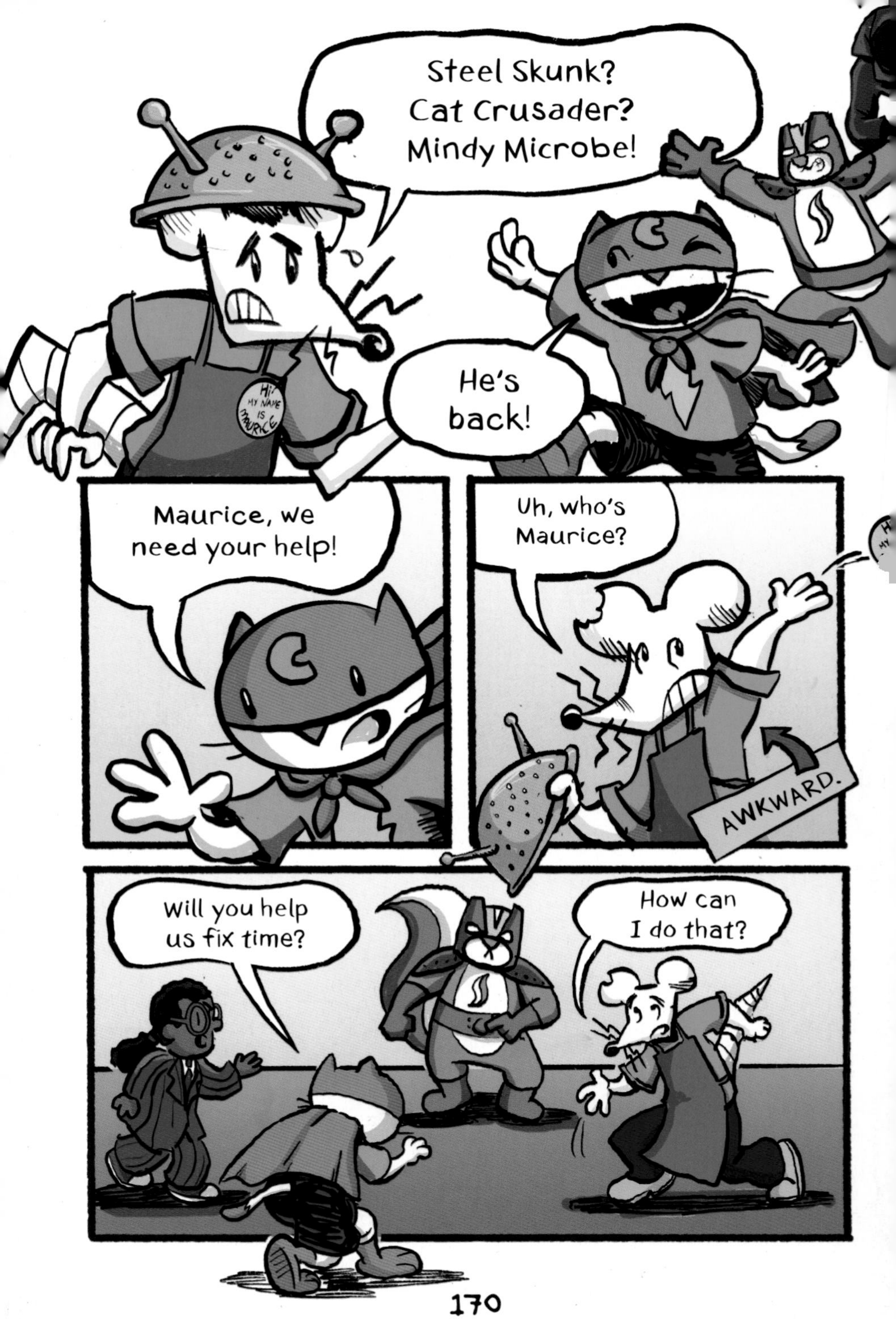
Steel Skunk?
Cat Crusader?
Mindy Microbe!
Hi! MY NAME IS MAURICE
He's back!
Maurice, we need your help!
Uh, who's Maurice?
AWKWARD.
Will you help us fix time?
How can I do that?

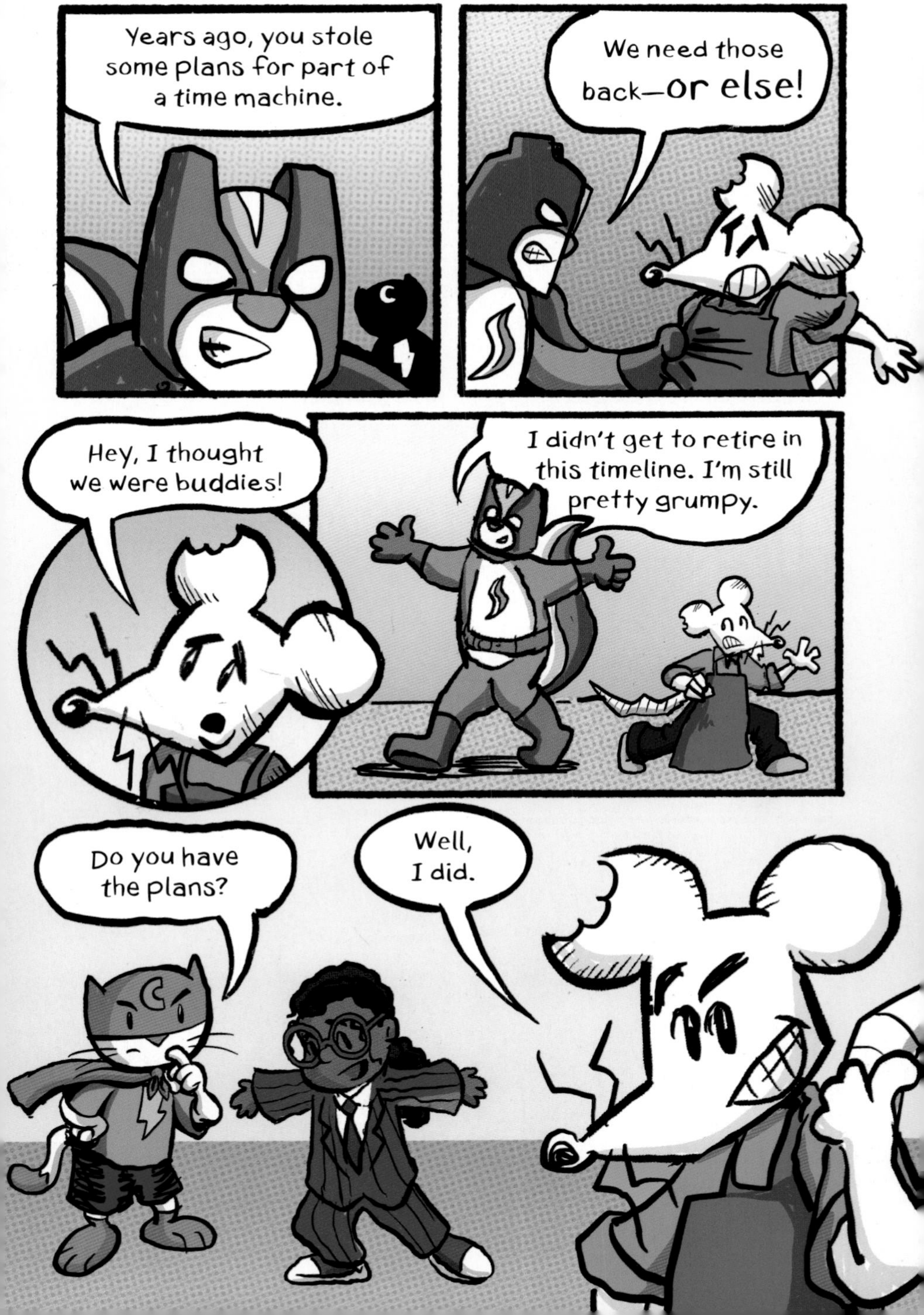
Years ago, you stole some plans for part of a time machine.
We need those back—or else!
Hey, I thought we were buddies!
I didn't get to retire in this timeline. I'm still pretty grumpy.
Do you have the plans?
Well, I did.

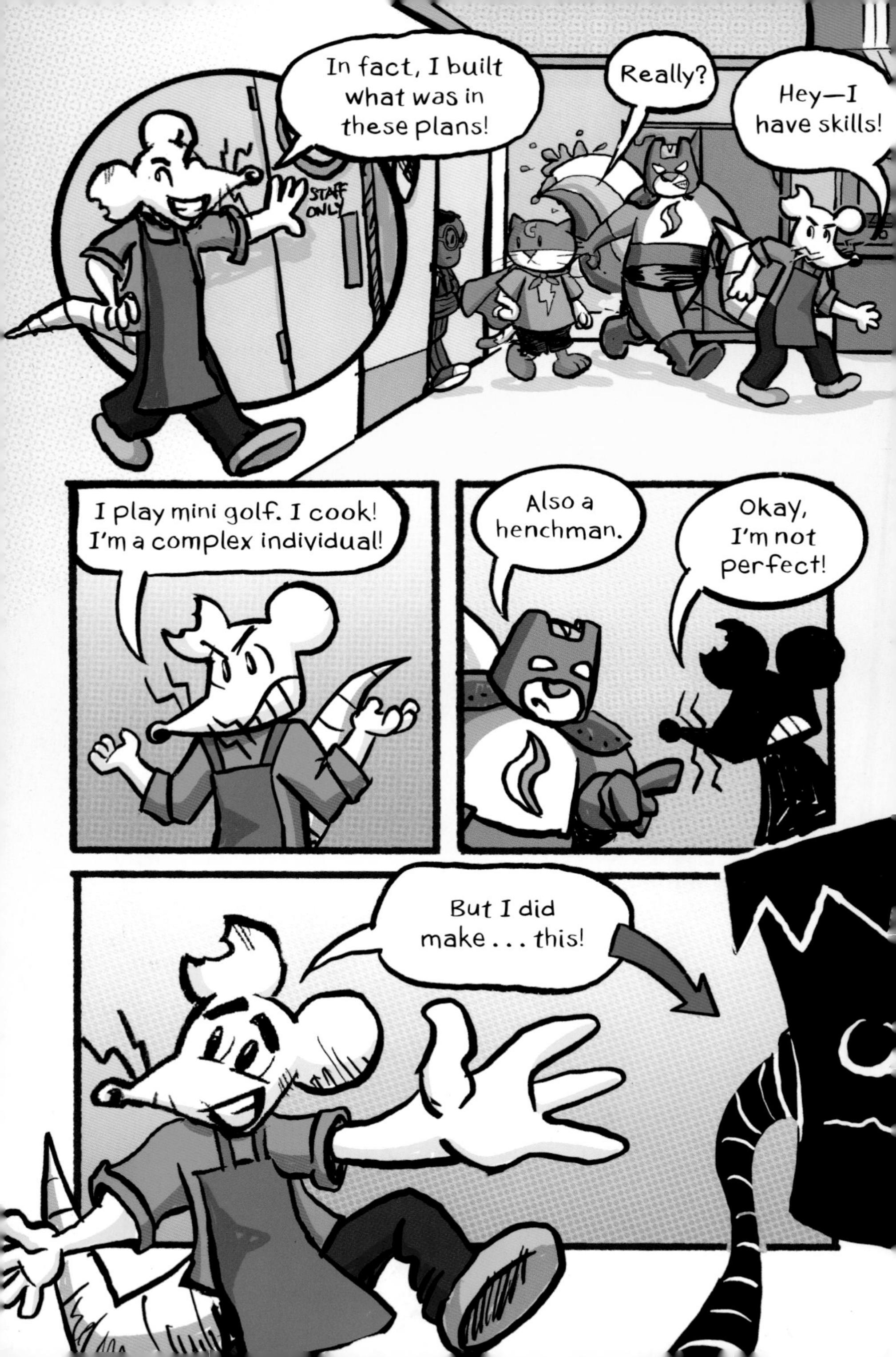
In fact, I built what was in these plans!
STAFF ONLY
Really?
Hey—I have skills!
I play mini golf. I cook! I'm a complex individual!
Also a henchman.
Okay, I'm not perfect!
But I did make . . . this!

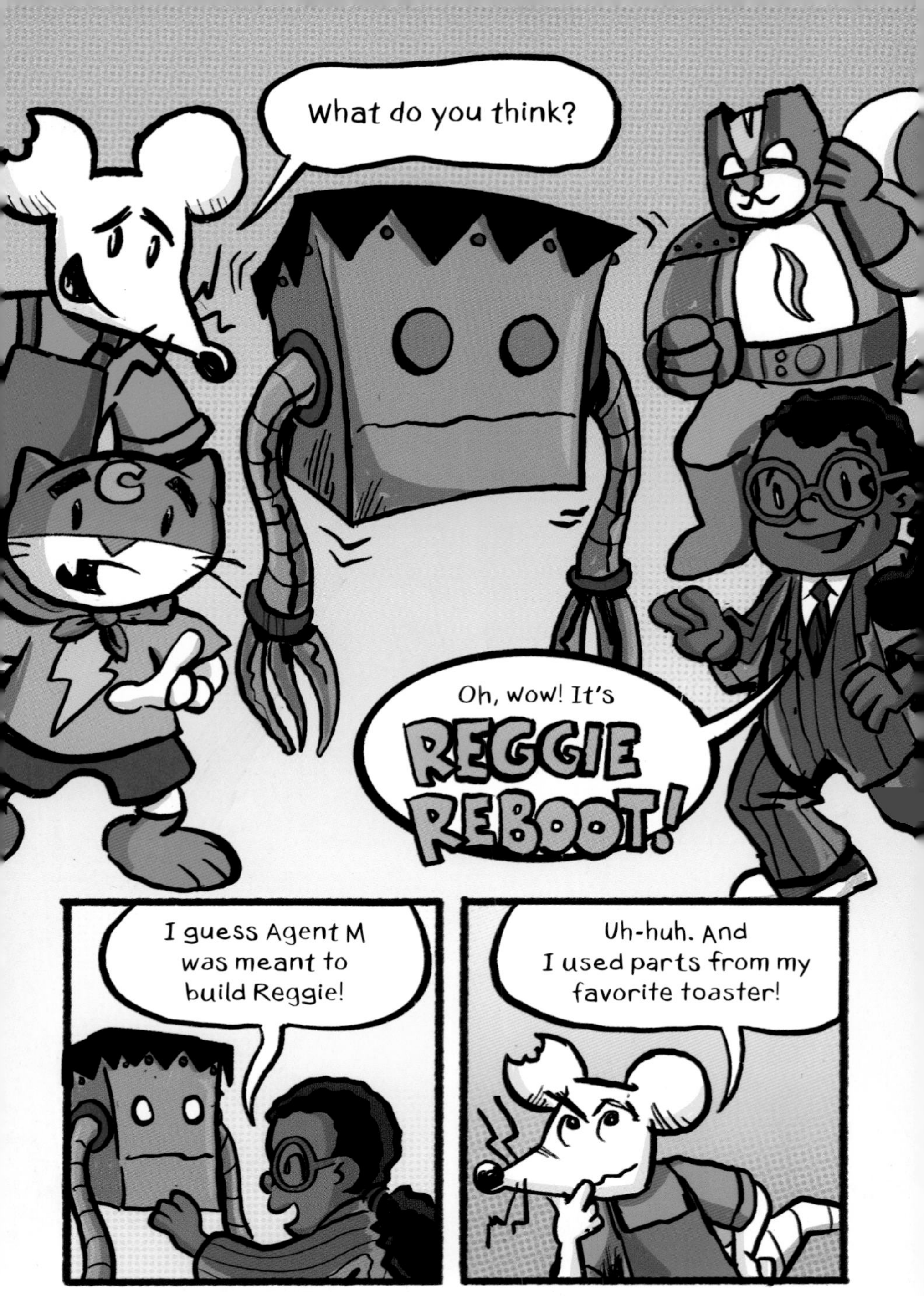
What do you think?
Oh, wow! It's REGGIE REBOOT!
I guess Agent M was meant to build Reggie!
Uh-huh. And I used parts from my favorite toaster!

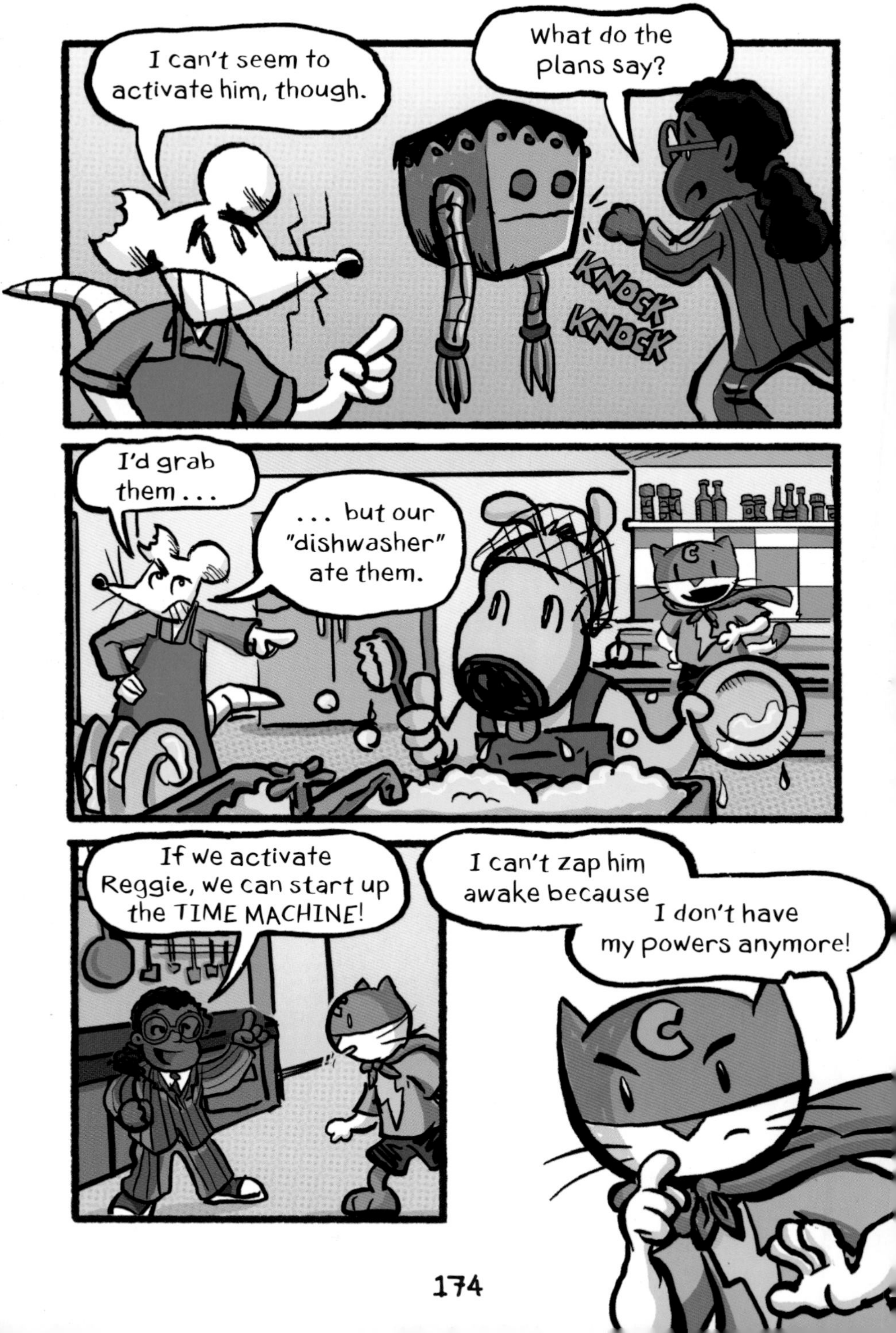
I can't seem to activate him, though.
What do the plans say?
KNOCK KNOCK
I'd grab them . . .
. . . but our "dishwasher" ate them.
If we activate Reggie, we can start up the TIME MACHINE!
I can't zap him awake because
I don't have my powers anymore!

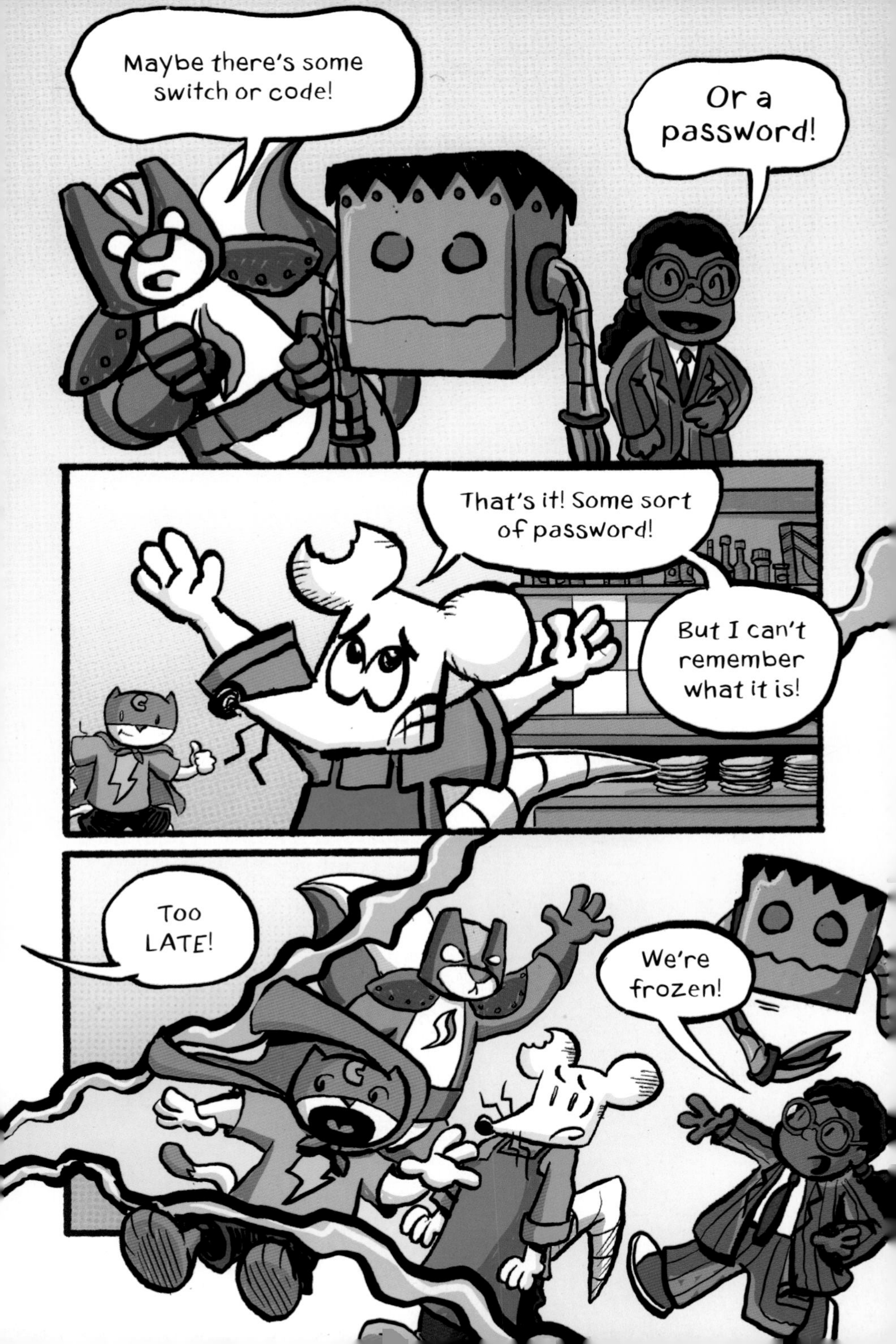
Maybe there's some switch or code!
Or a password!
That's it! Some sort of password!
But I can't remember what it is!
Too LATE!
We're frozen!

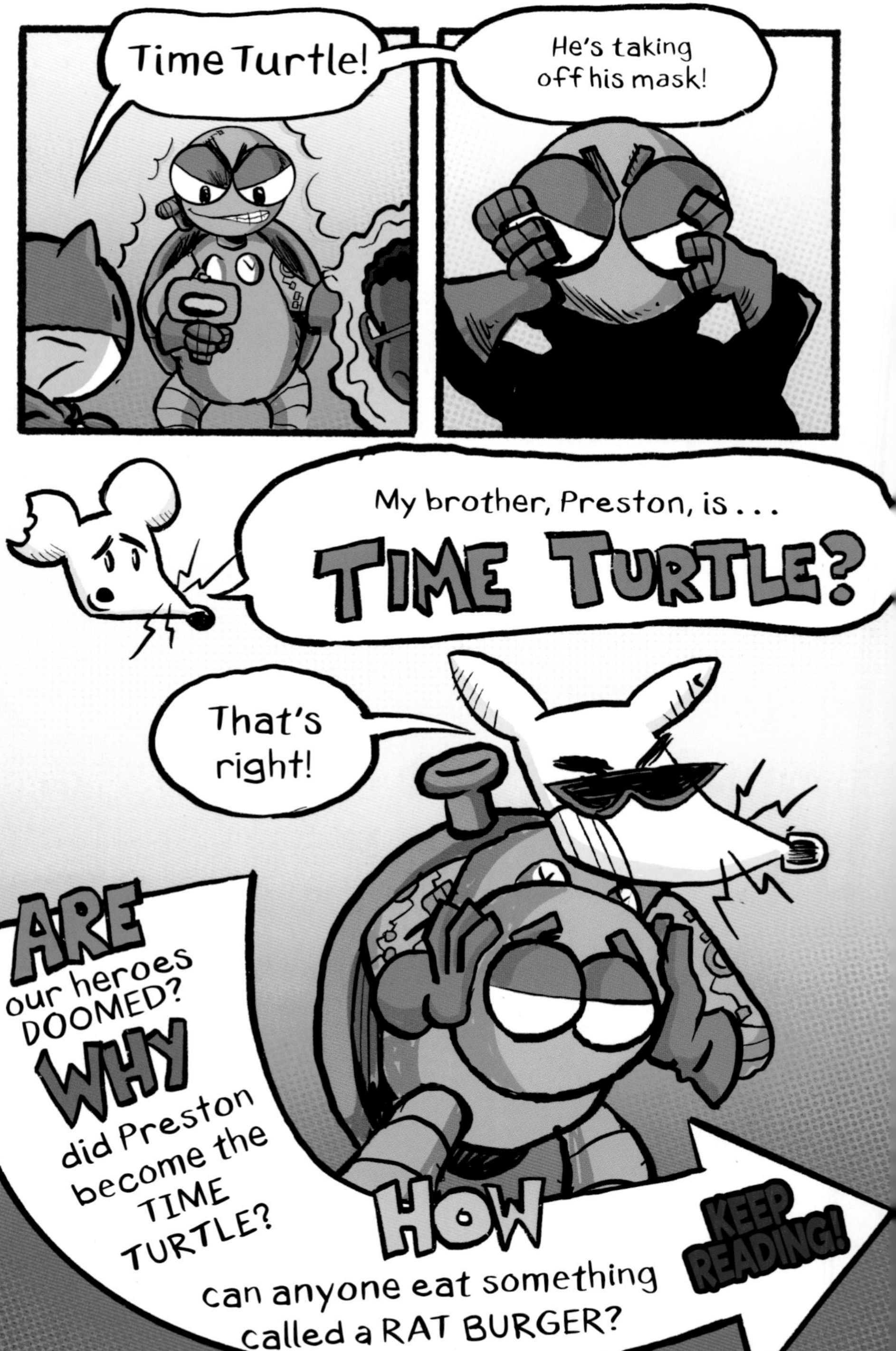
Time Turtle!
He's taking off his mask!
My brother, Preston, is . . .
TIME TURTLE?
That's right!
ARE our heroes DOOMED?
WHY did Preston become the TIME TURTLE?
HOW can anyone eat something called a RAT BURGER?
KEEP READING!

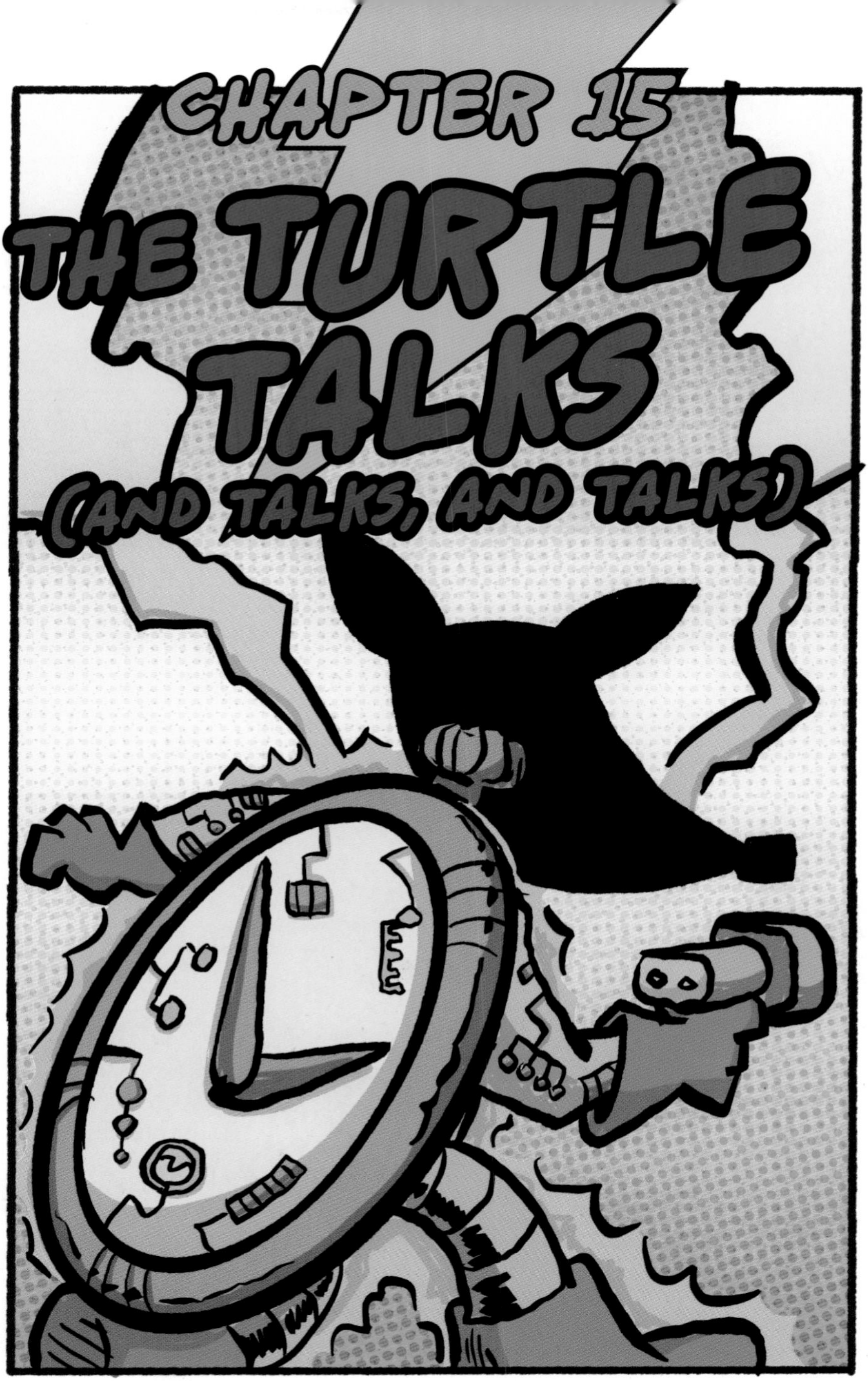
CHAPTER 15
THE TURTLE TALKS
(AND TALKS, AND TALKS)

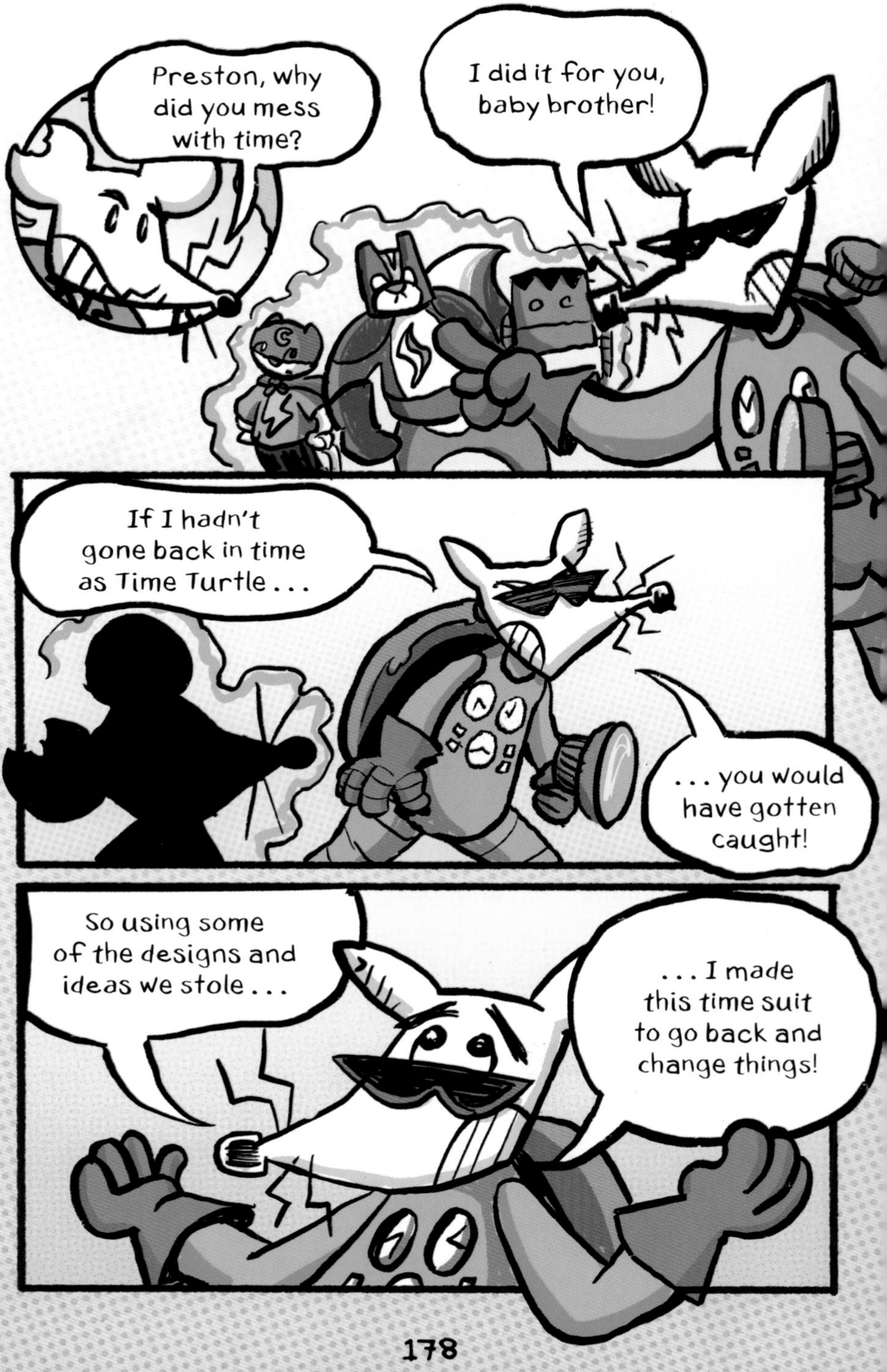
Preston, why did you mess with time?
I did it for you, baby brother!
If I hadn't gone back in time as Time Turtle . . .
. . . you would have gotten caught!
So using some of the designs and ideas we stole . . .
. . . I made this time suit to go back and change things!

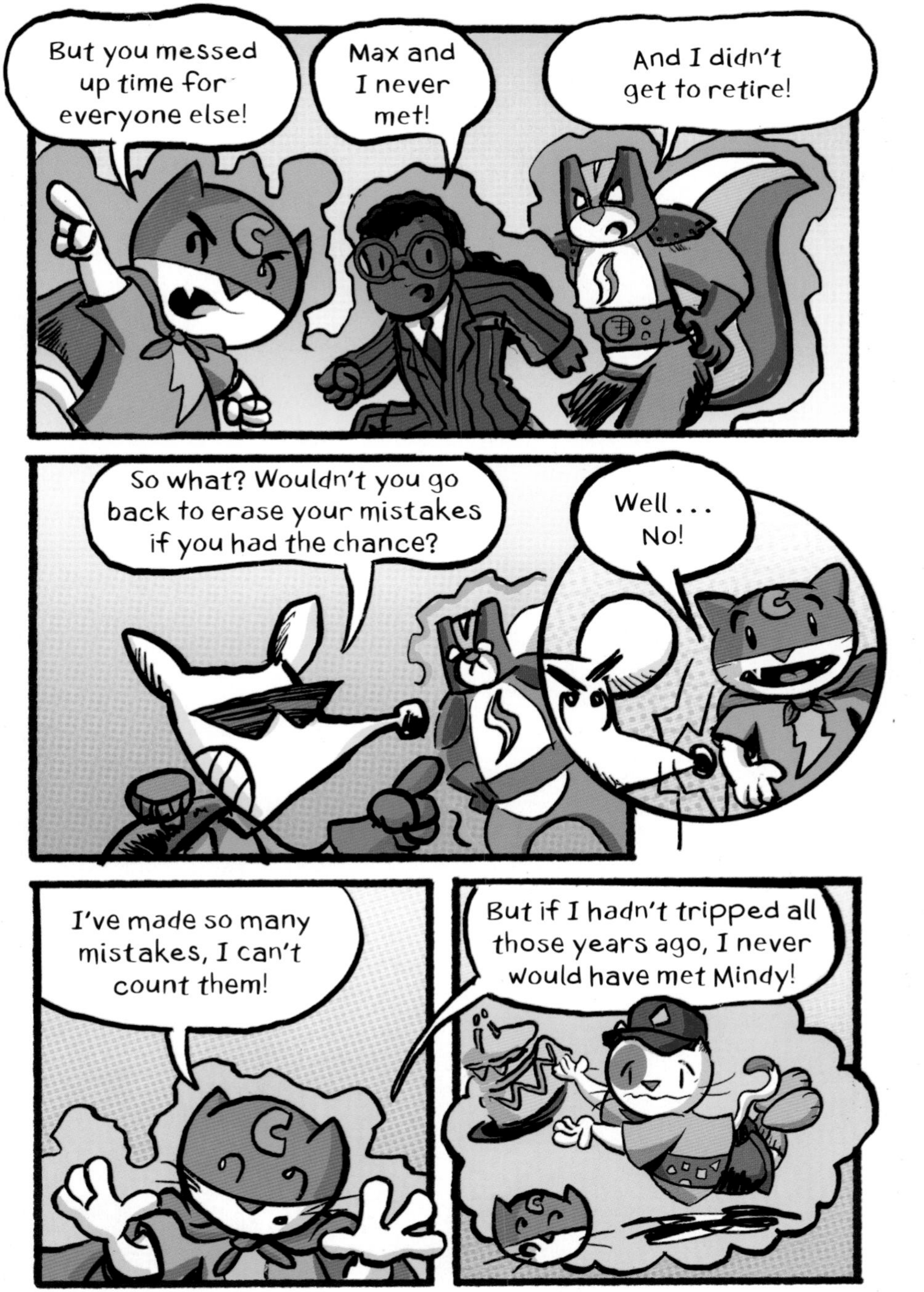
But you messed up time for everyone else!
Max and I never met!
And I didn't get to retire!
So what? Wouldn't you go back to erase your mistakes if you had the chance?
Well . . . No!
I've made so many mistakes, I can't count them!
But if I hadn't tripped all those years ago, I never would have met Mindy!

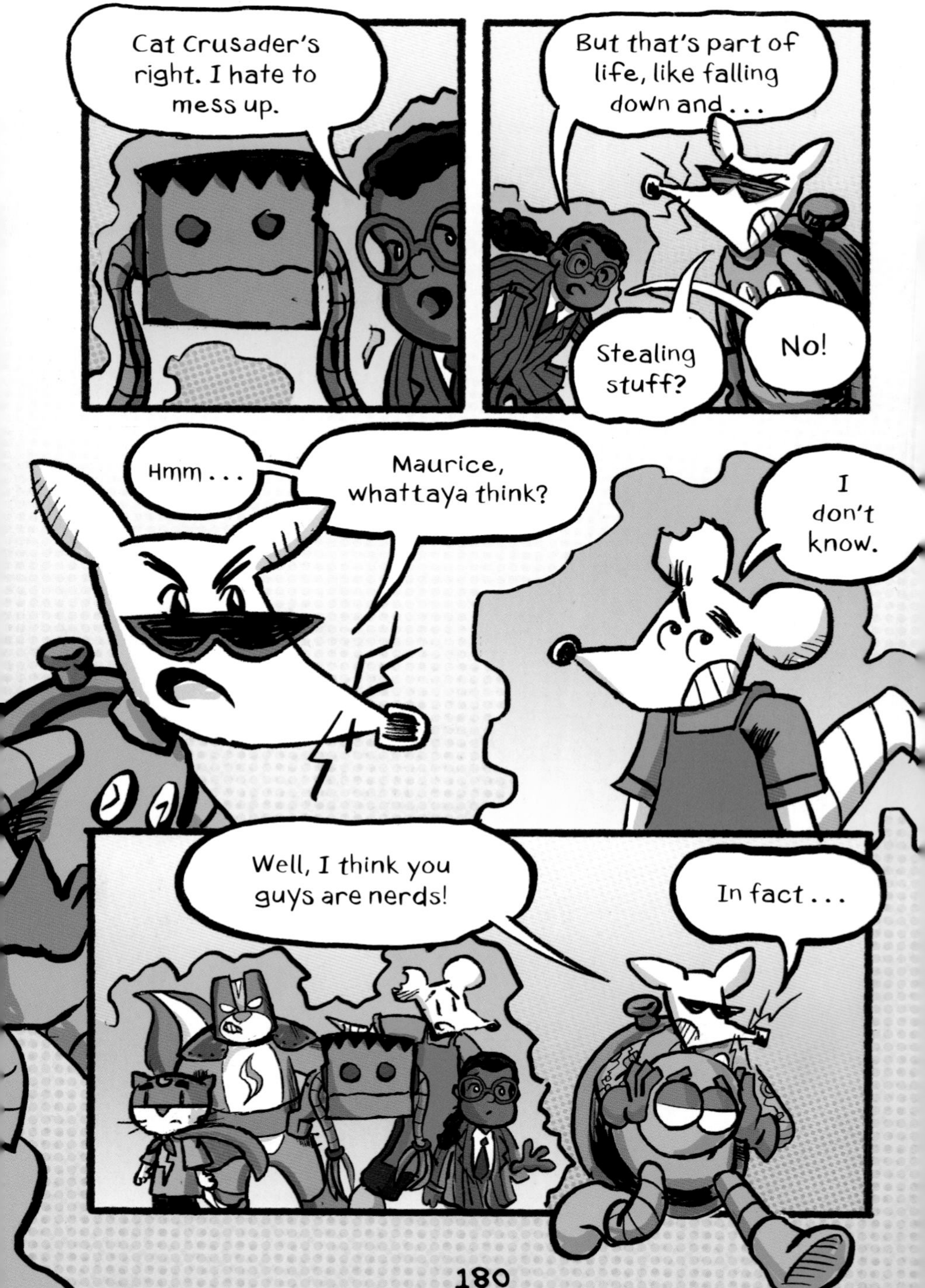
Cat Crusader's right. I hate to mess up.
But that's part of life, like falling down and . . .
Stealing stuff?
No!
Hmm . . .
Maurice, whattaya think?
I don't know.
Well, I think you guys are nerds!
In fact . . .

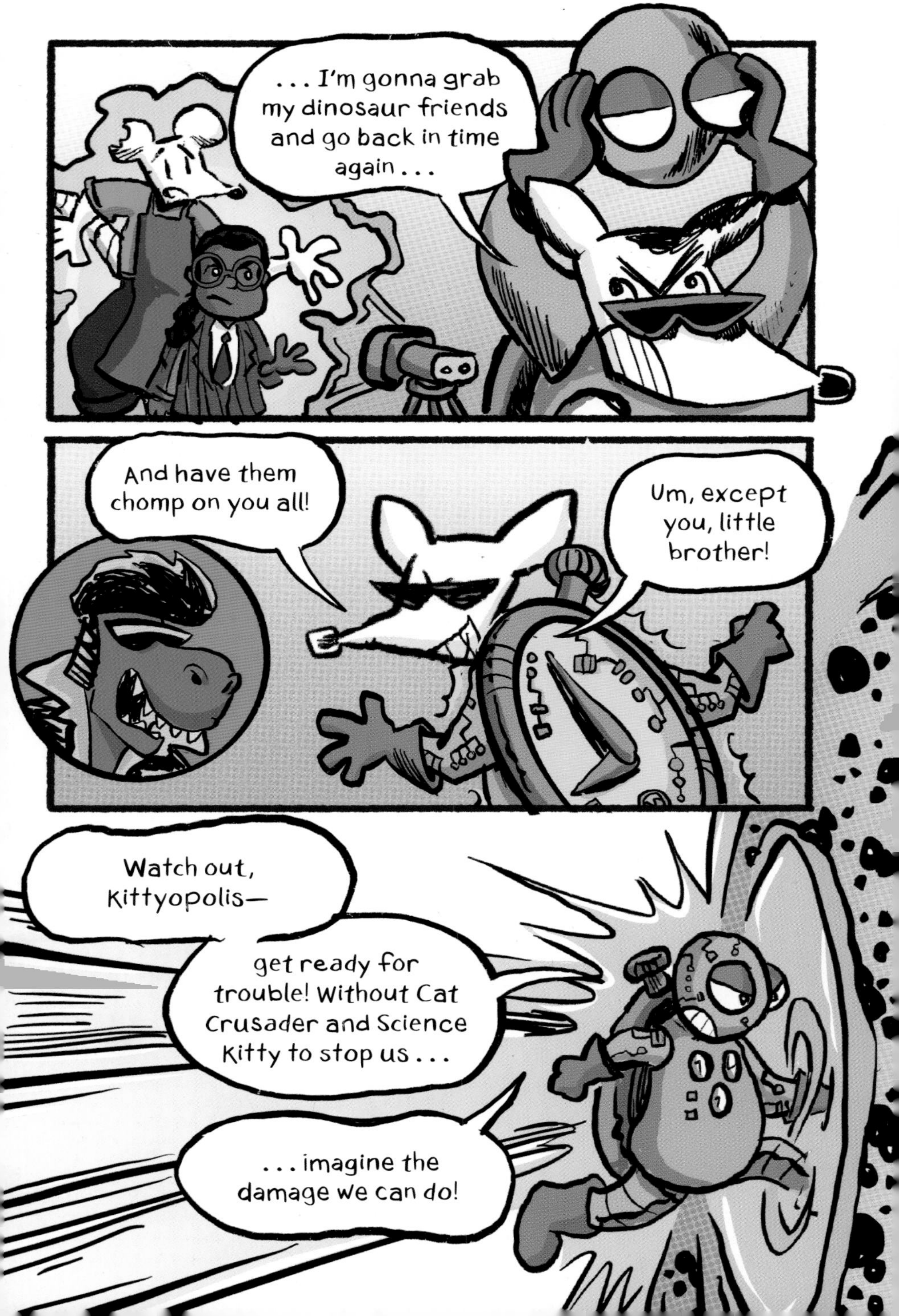
. . . I'm gonna grab my dinosaur friends and go back in time again . . .
And have them chomp on you all!
Um, except you, little brother!
Watch out, Kittyopolis—
get ready for trouble! Without Cat Crusader and Science Kitty to stop us . . .
. . . imagine the damage we can do!

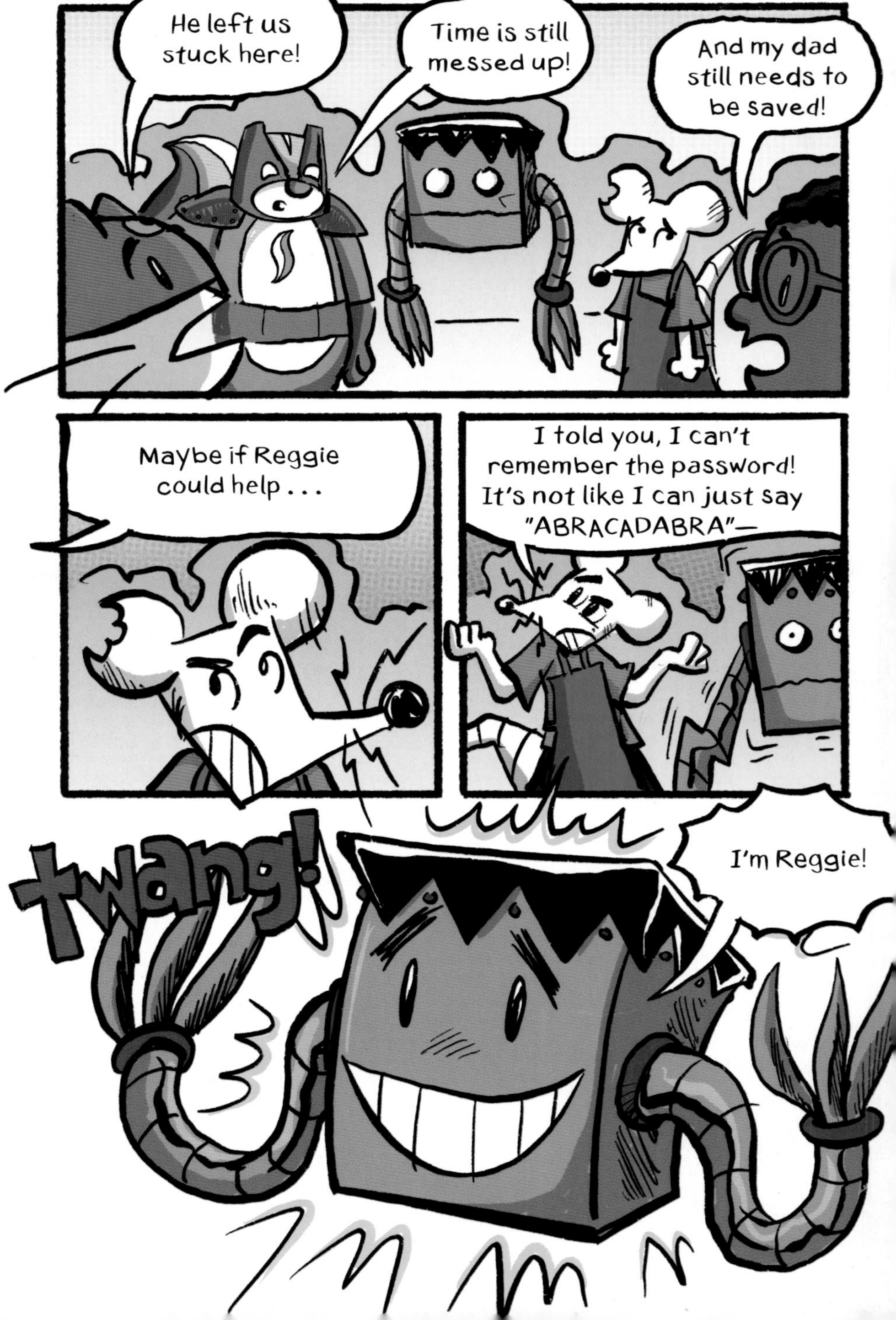
He left us stuck here!
Time is still messed up!
And my dad still needs to be saved!
Maybe if Reggie could help . . .
I told you, I can't remember the password! It's not like I can just say "ABRACADABRA"—
twang!
I'm Reggie!

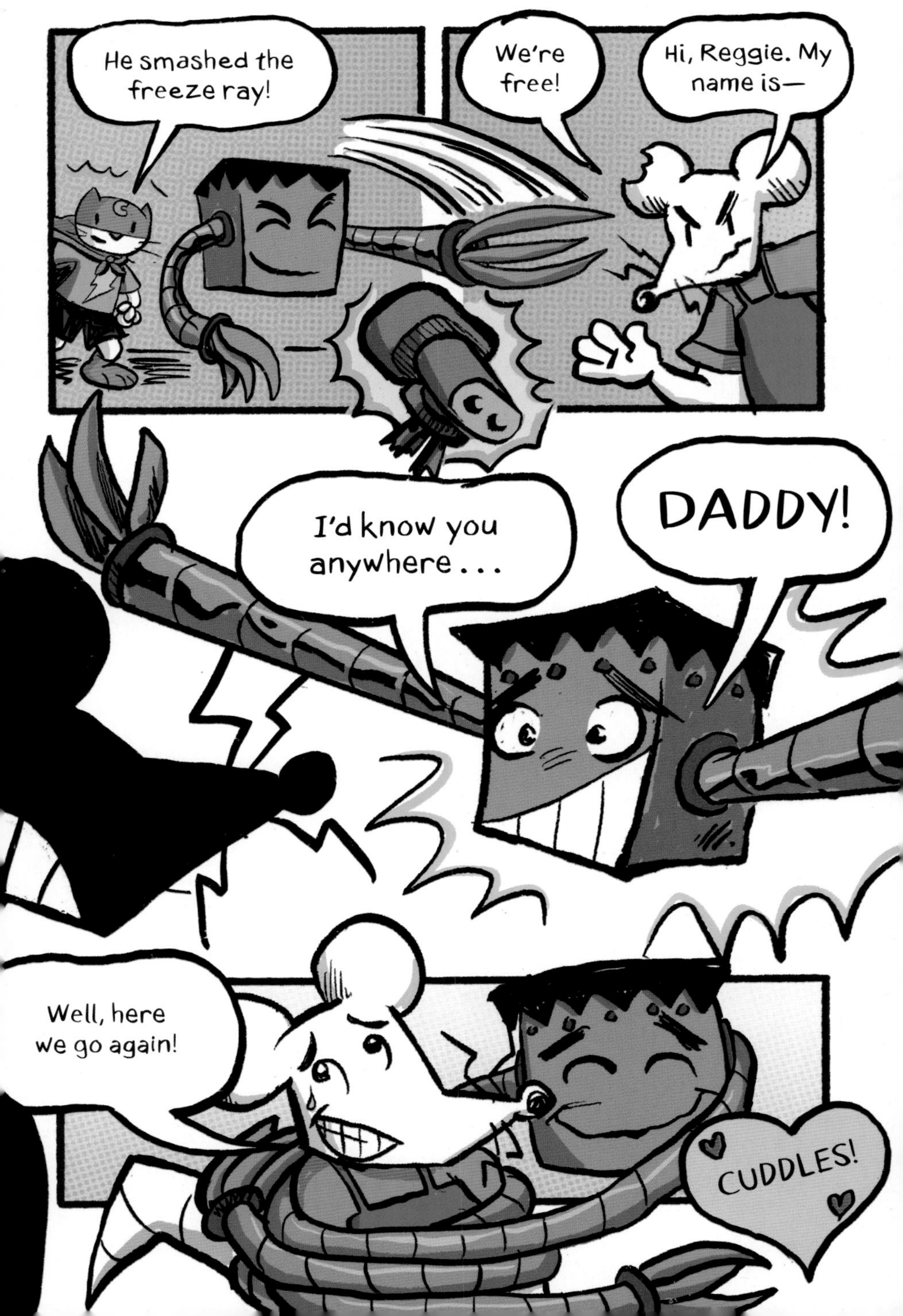
He smashed the freeze ray!
We're free!
Hi, Reggie. My name is—
I'd know you anywhere . . .
DADDY!
Well, here we go again!
CUDDLES!

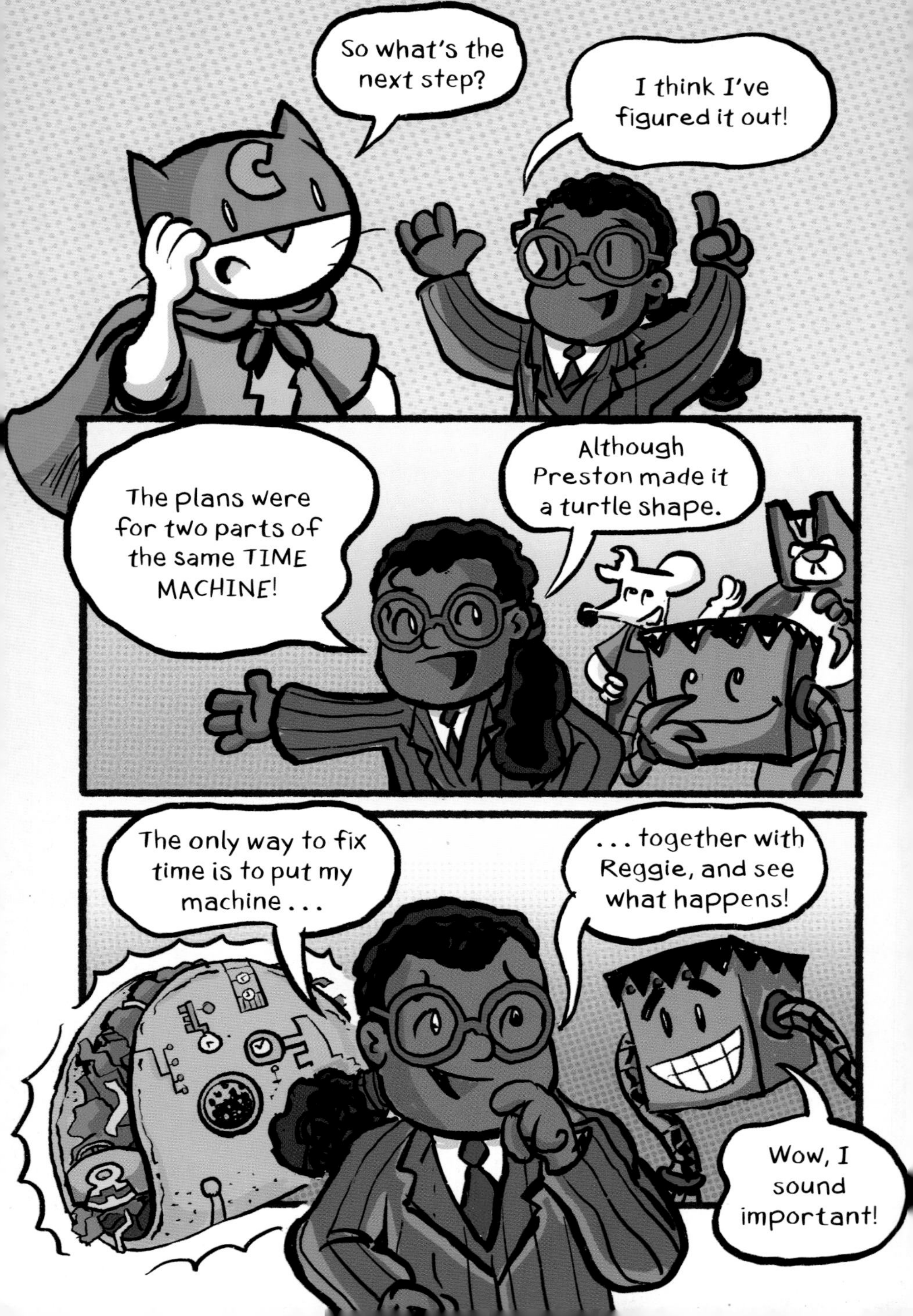

So what's the next step?
I think I've figured it out!
The plans were for two parts of the same TIME MACHINE!
Although Preston made it a turtle shape.
The only way to fix time is to put my machine . . .
. . . together with Reggie, and see what happens!
Wow, I sound important!

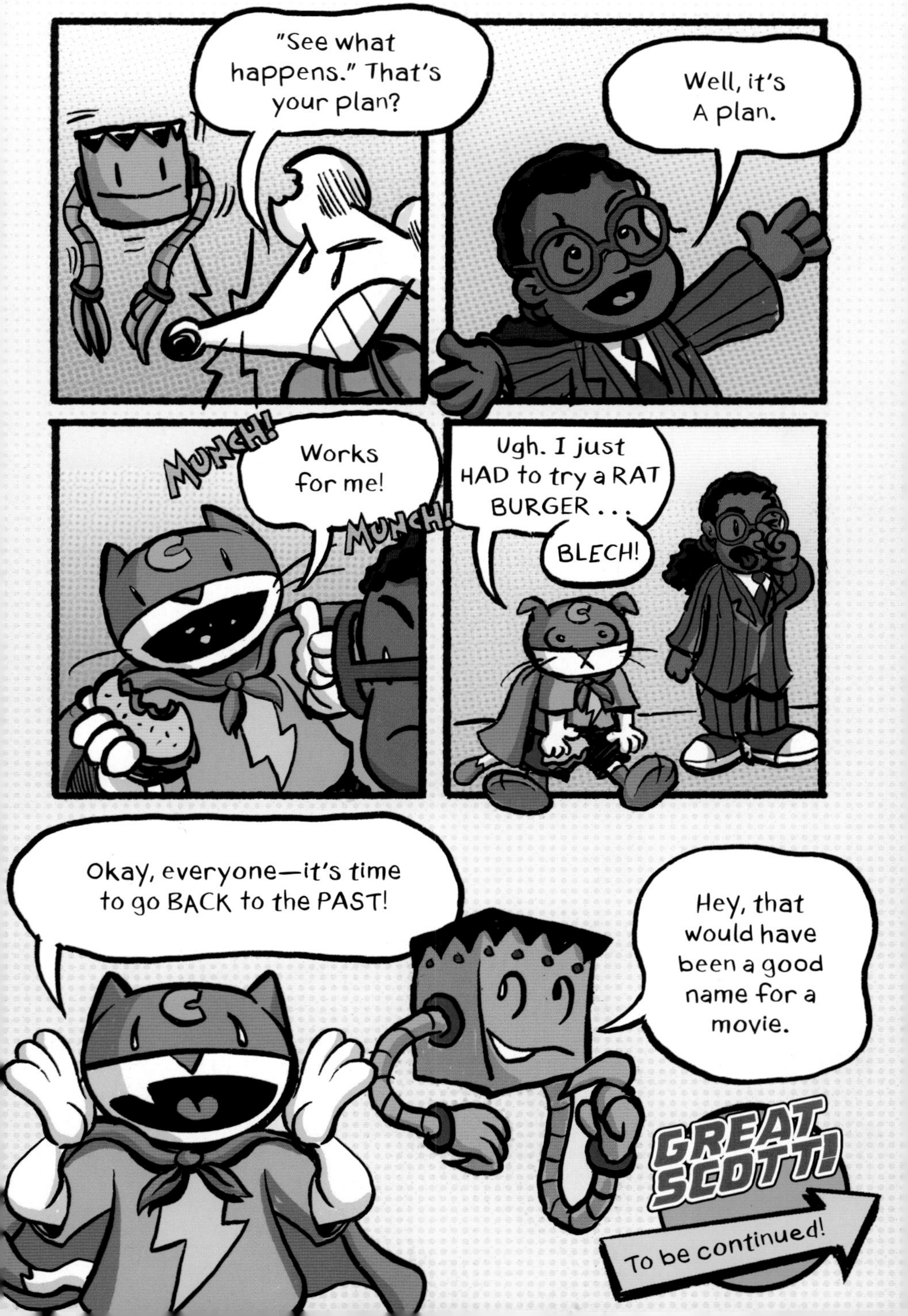
"See what happens." That's your plan?
Well, it's A plan.
MUNCH!
Works for me!
MUNCH!
Ugh. I just HAD to try a RAT BURGER . . .
BLECH!
Okay, everyone—it's time to go BACK to the PAST!
Hey, that would have been a good name for a movie.
GREAT SCOTT!
To be continued!

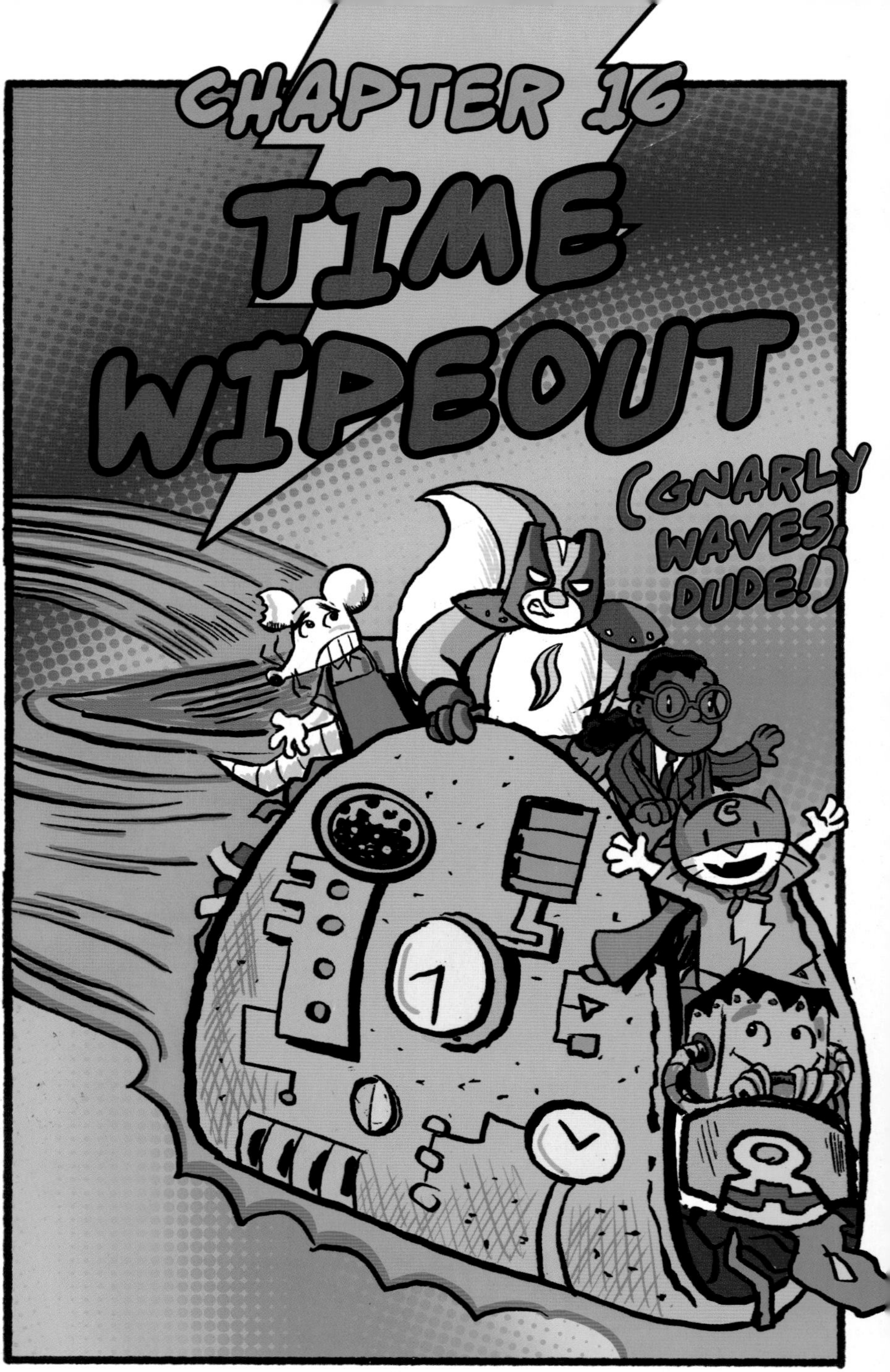
CHAPTER 16
TIME WIPEOUT
(GNARLY WAVES, DUDE!)

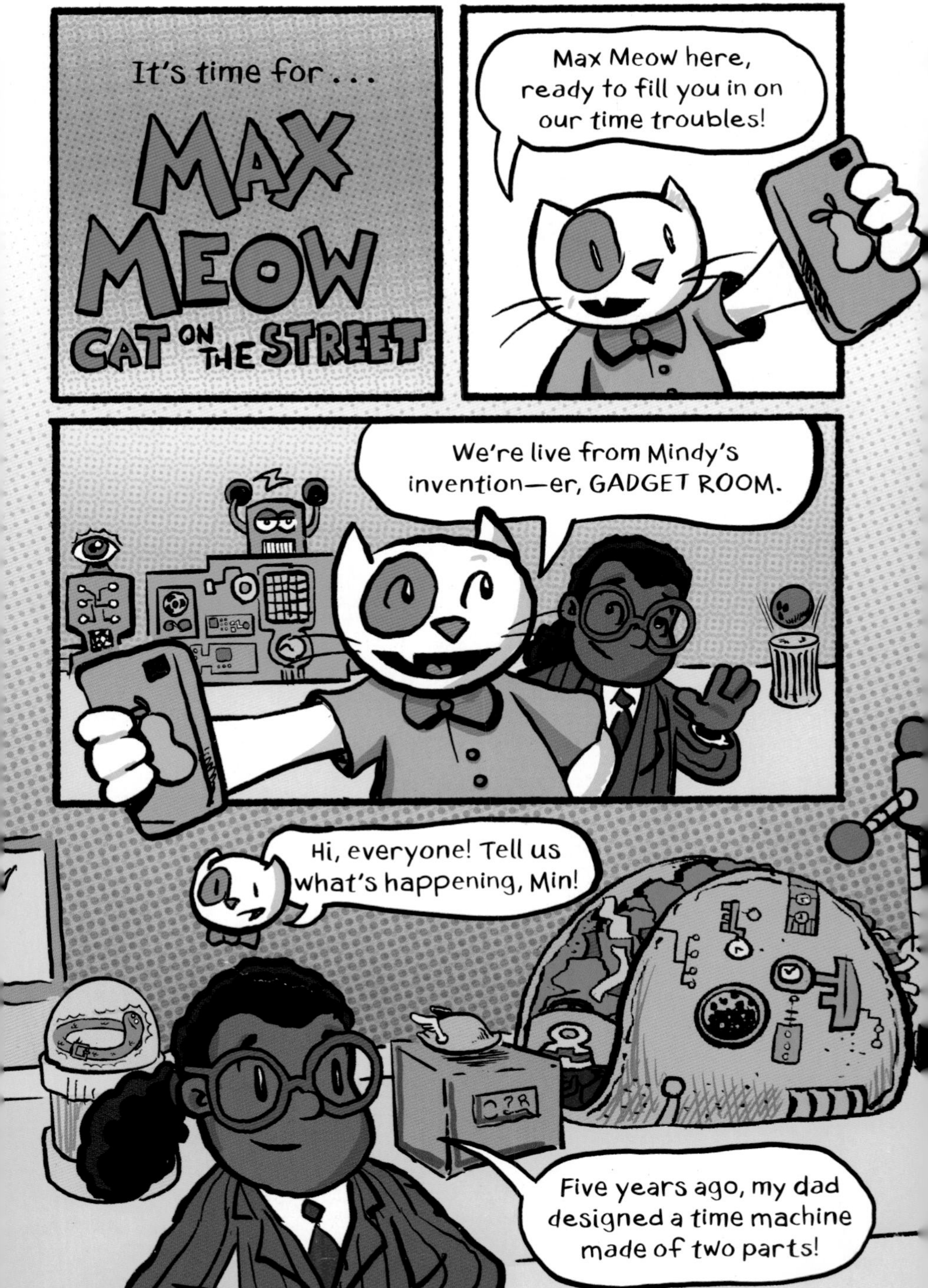
It's time for . . .
MAX MEOW
CAT ON THE STREET
Max Meow here, ready to fill you in on our time troubles!
We're live from Mindy's invention—er, GADGET ROOM.
Hi, everyone! Tell us what's happening, Min!
Five years ago, my dad designed a time machine made of two parts!

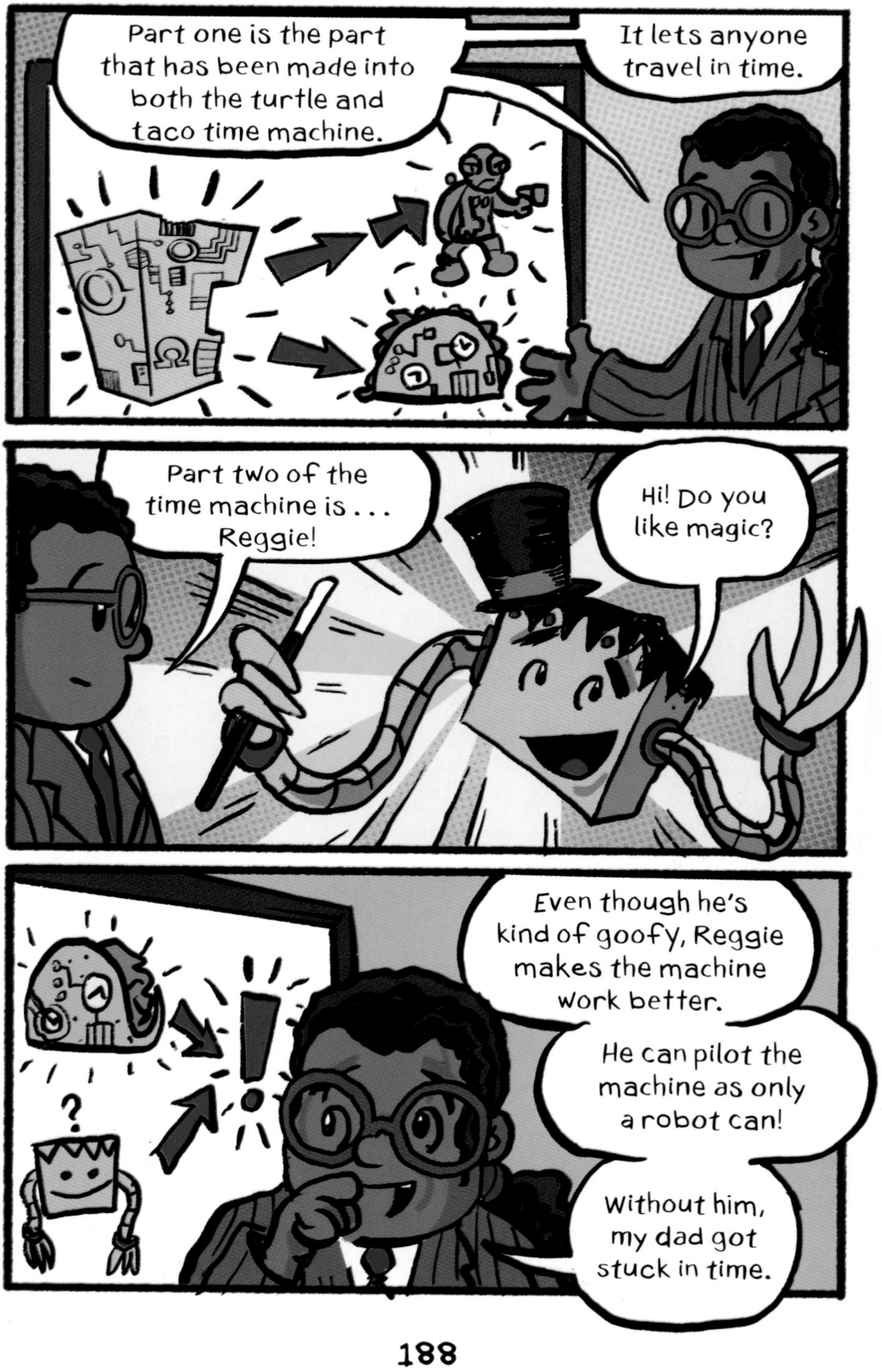
Part one is the part that has been made into both the turtle and taco time machine.
It lets anyone travel in time.
Part two of the time machine is . . . Reggie!
Hi! Do you like magic?
Even though he's kind of goofy, Reggie makes the machine work better.
He can pilot the machine as only a robot can!
Without him, my dad got stuck in time.

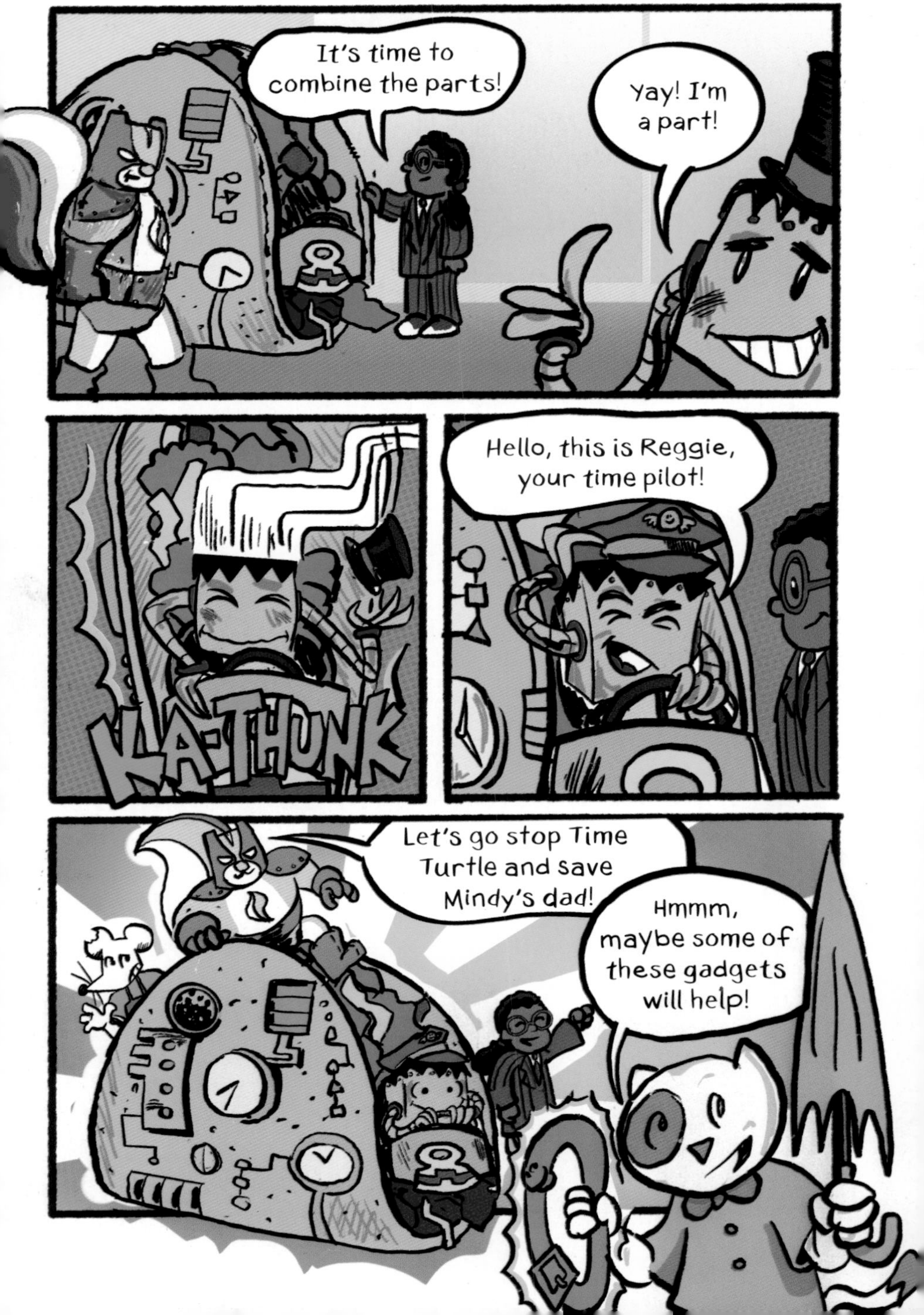
It's time to
combine the parts!
Yay! I'm
a part!
KA-THUNK
Hello, this is Reggie,
your time pilot!
Let's go stop Time
Turtle and save
Mindy's dad!
Hmmm,
maybe some of
these gadgets
will help!

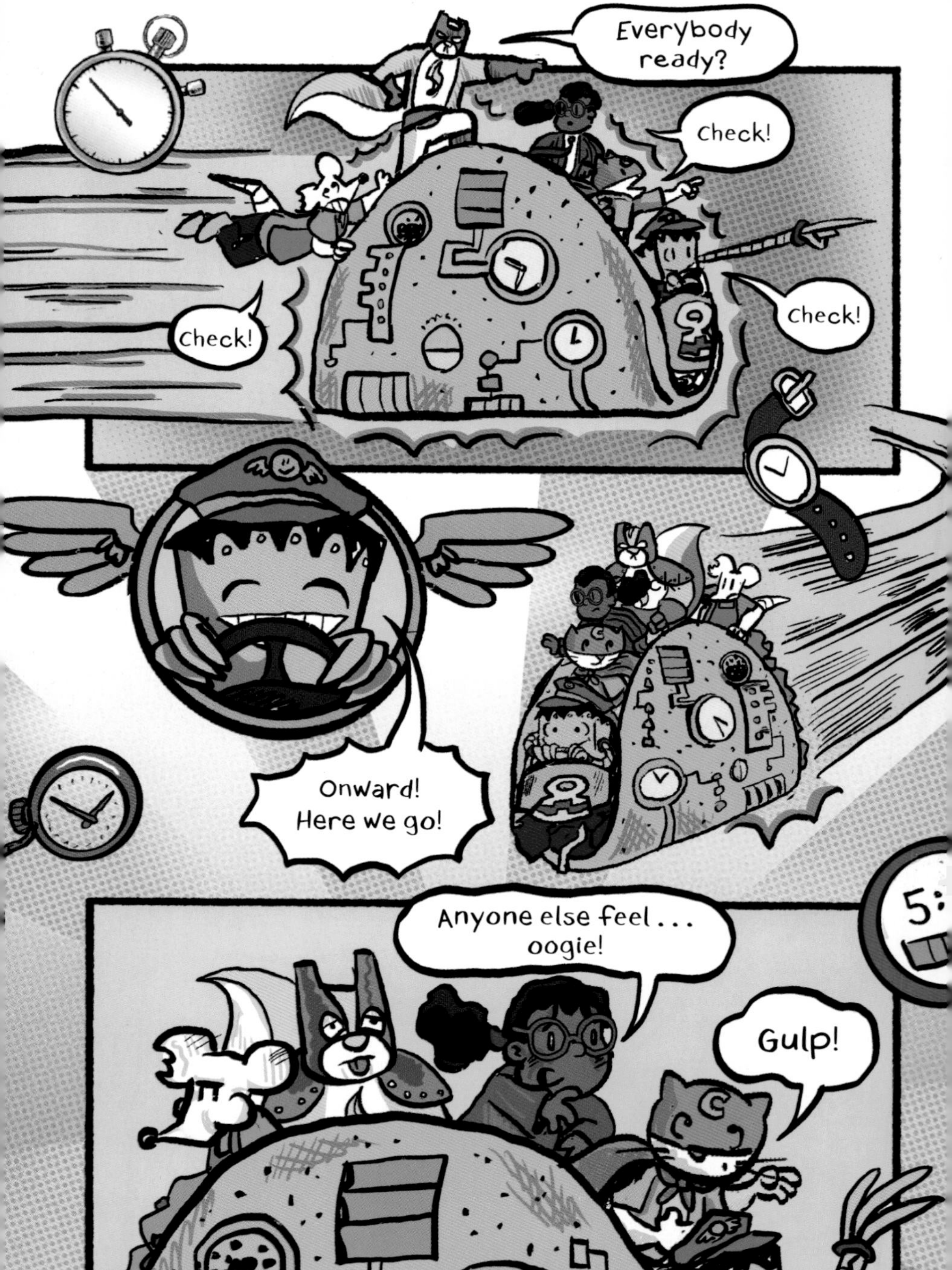
Everybody ready?
Check!
Check!
Check!
Onward! Here we go!
Anyone else feel . . . oogie!
Gulp!

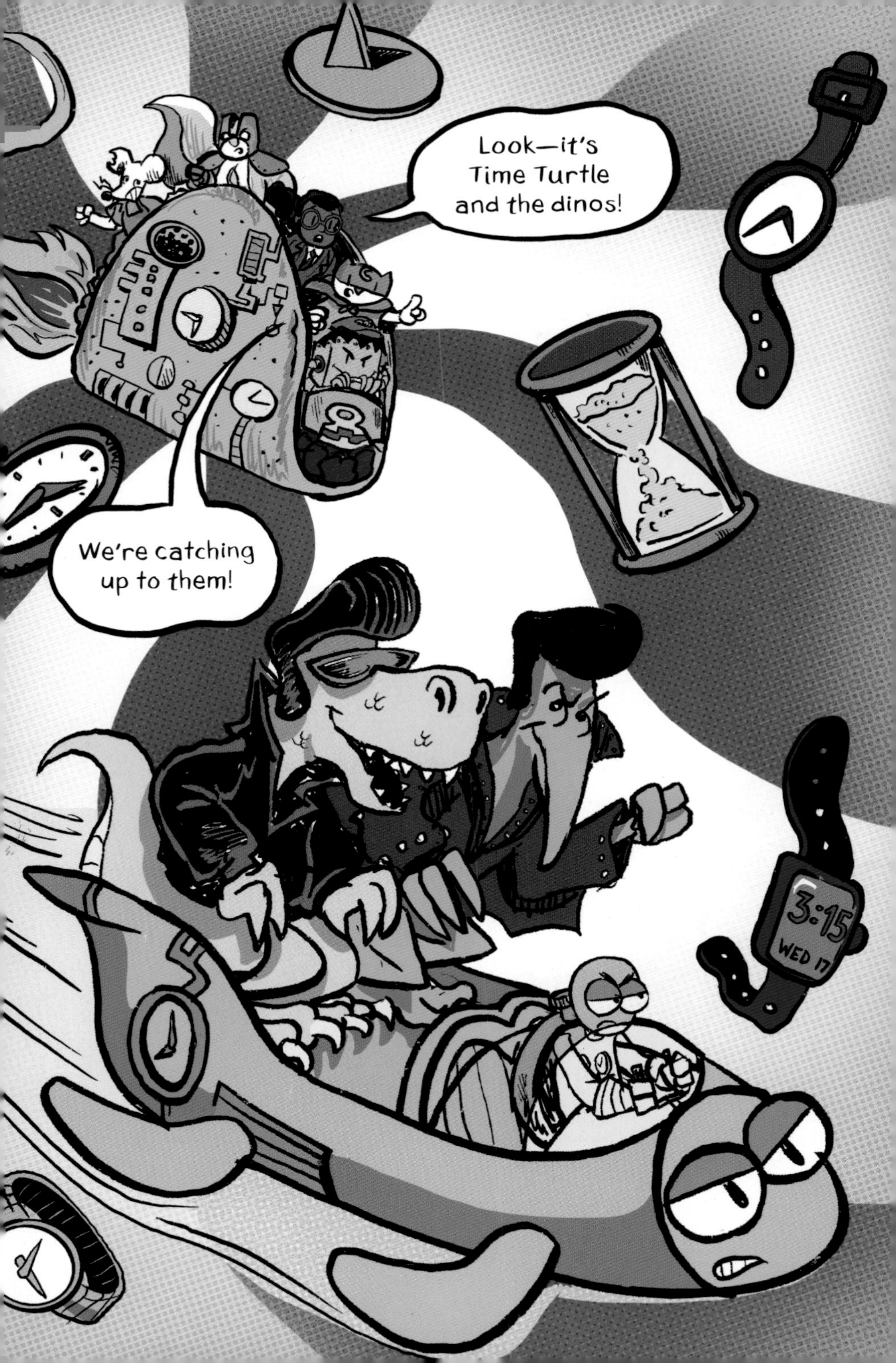
Look—it's Time Turtle and the dinos!
We're catching up to them!
3:15
WED 17

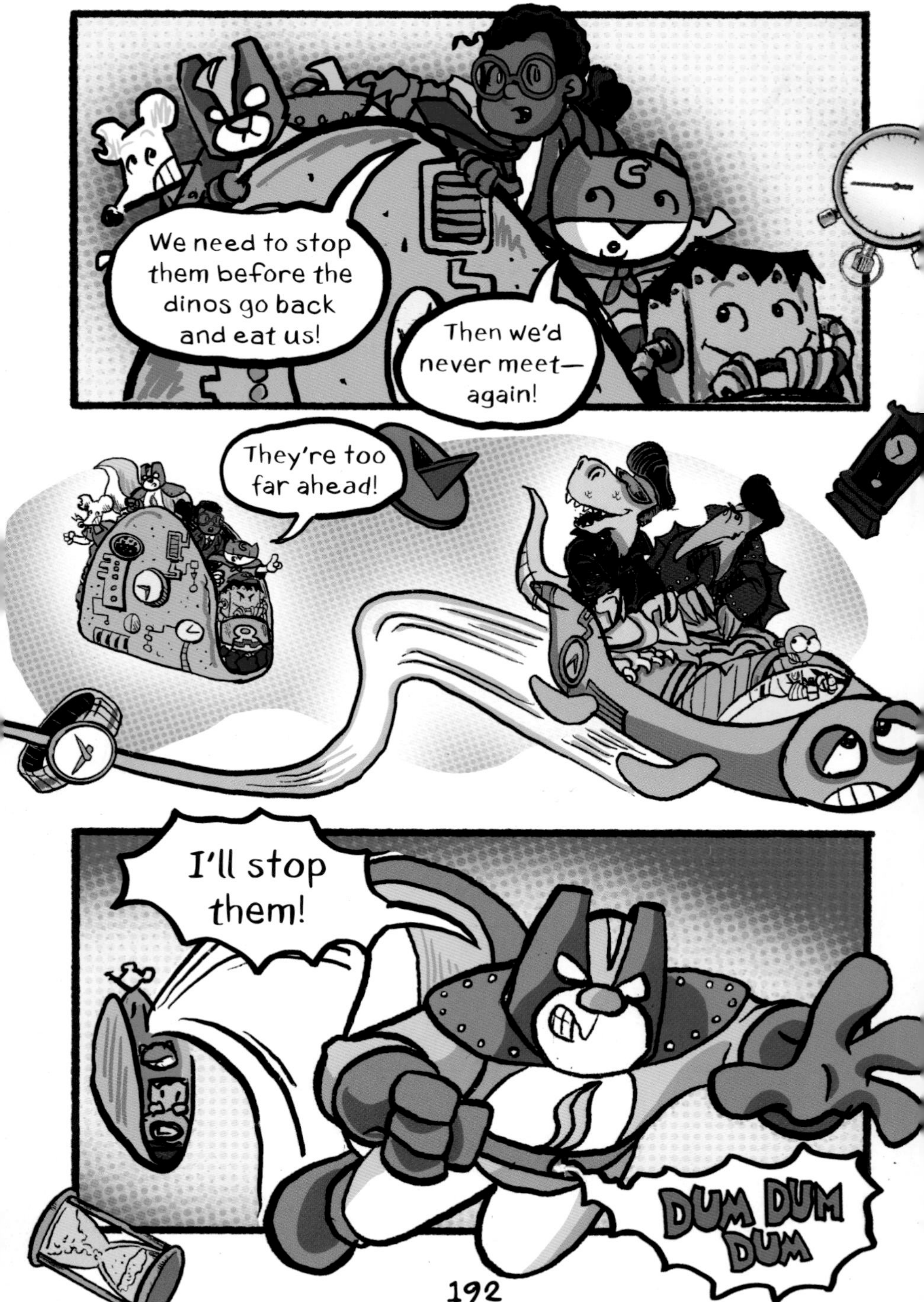

We need to stop them before the dinos go back and eat us!
Then we'd never meet—again!
They're too far ahead!
I'll stop them!
DUM DUM DUM

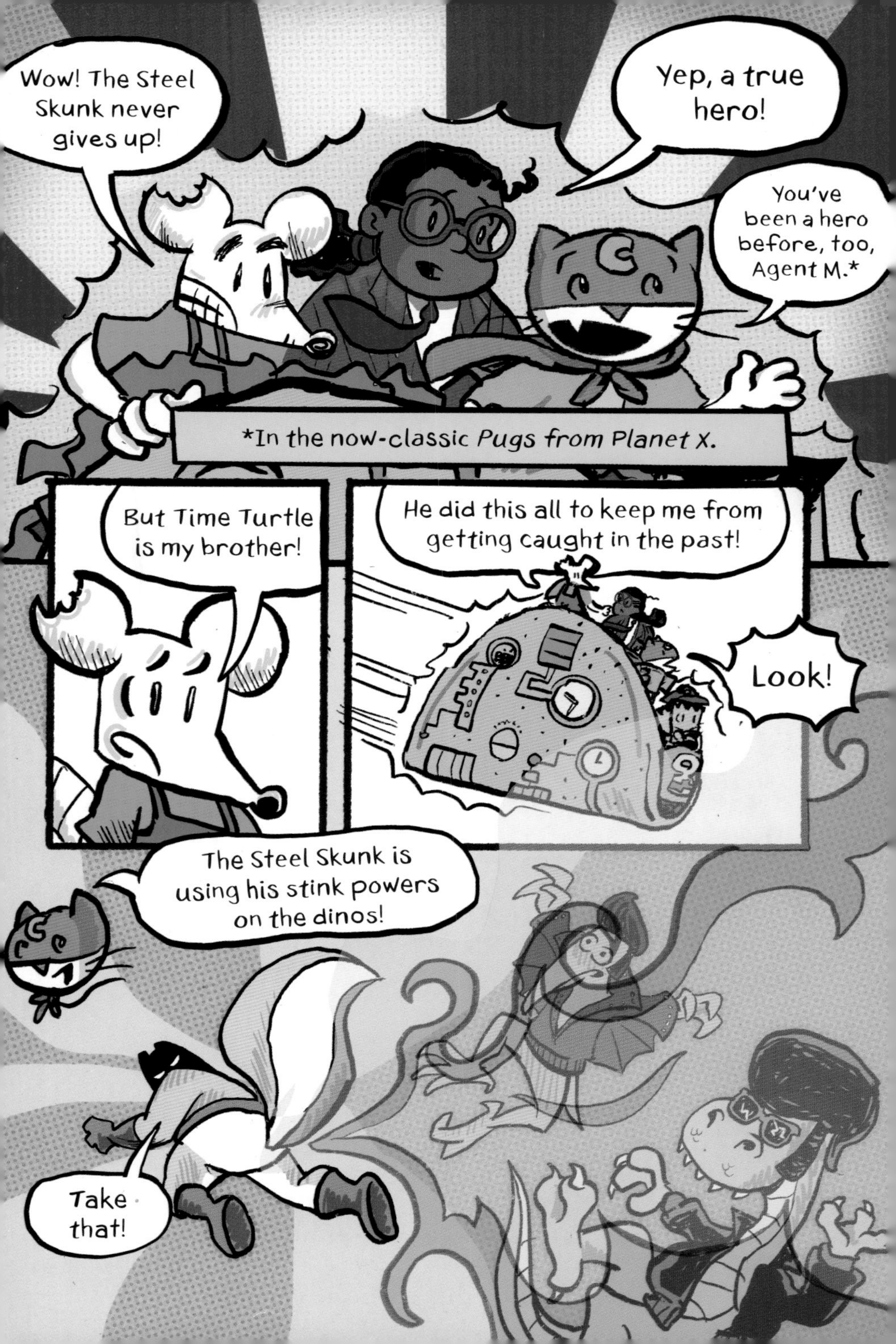
Wow! The Steel Skunk never gives up!
Yep, a true hero!
You've been a hero before, too, Agent M.*
*In the now-classic *Pugs from Planet X*.
But Time Turtle is my brother!
He did this all to keep me from getting caught in the past!
Look!
The Steel Skunk is using his stink powers on the dinos!
Take that!

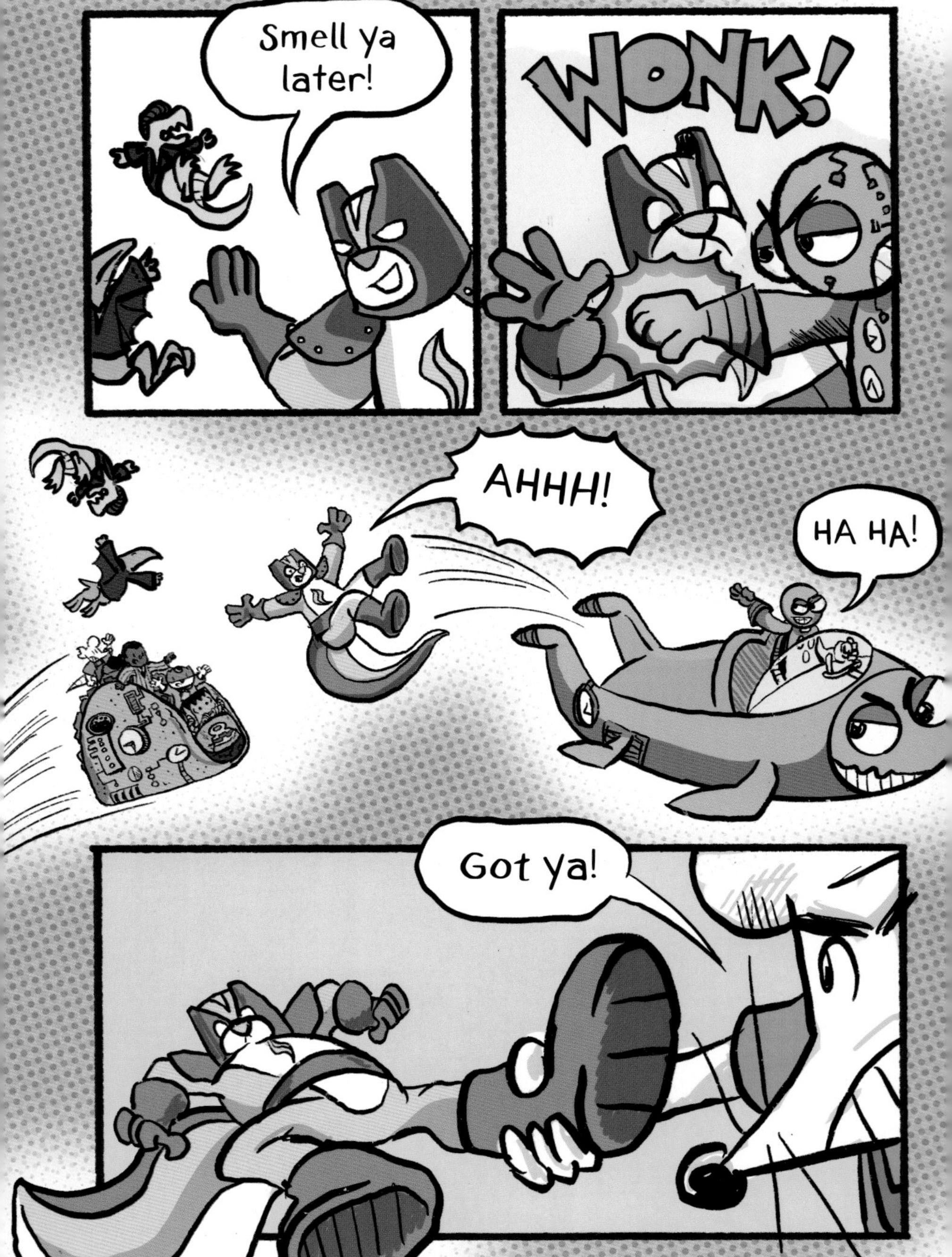

Smell ya later!
WONK!
AHHH!
HA HA!
Got ya!

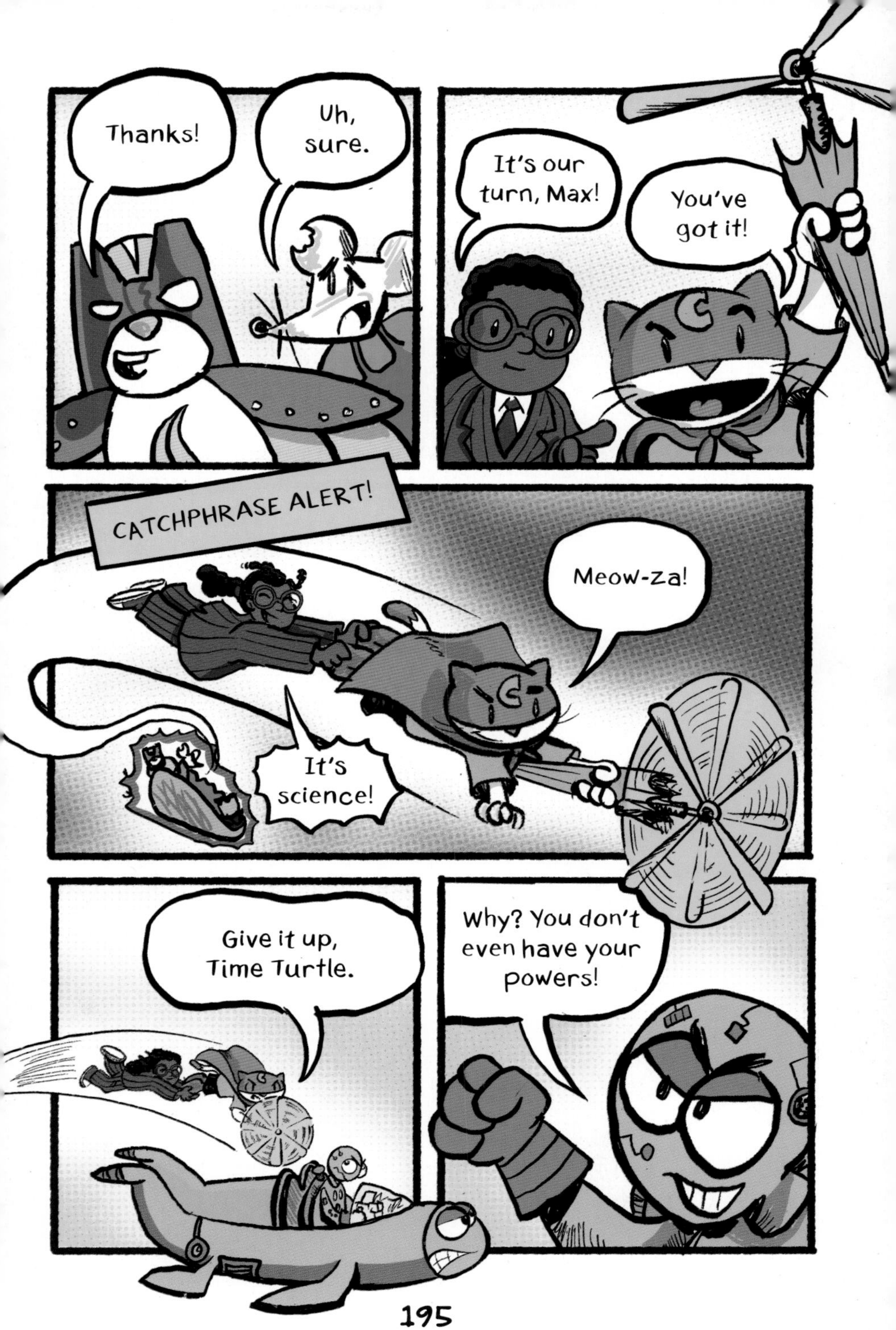
Thanks!
Uh, sure.
It's our turn, Max!
You've got it!
CATCHPHRASE ALERT!
Meow-za!
It's science!
Give it up, Time Turtle.
Why? You don't even have your powers!

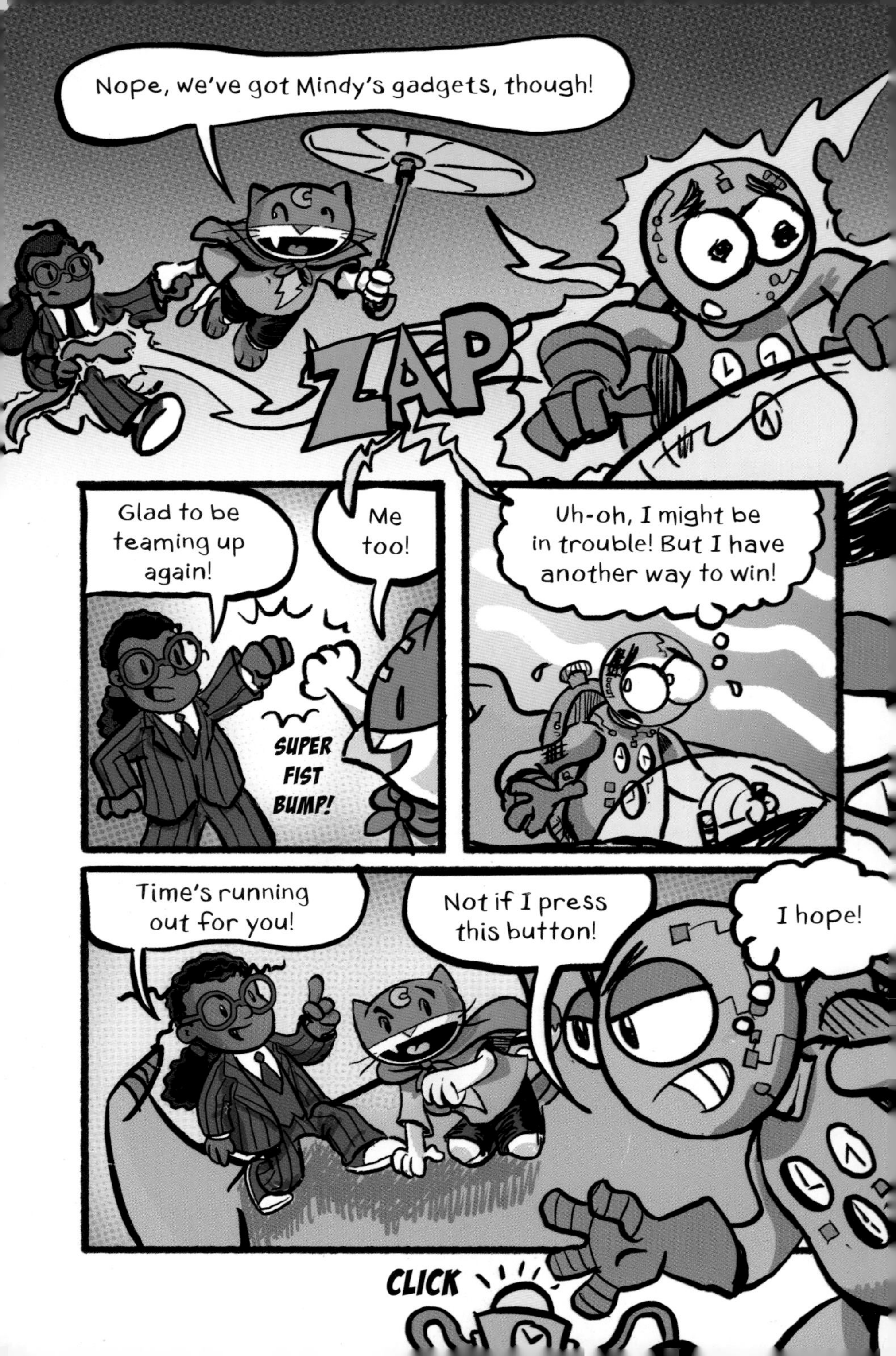

Nope, we've got Mindy's gadgets, though!
ZAP
Glad to be teaming up again!
Me too!
SUPER FIST BUMP!
Uh-oh, I might be in trouble! But I have another way to win!
Time's running out for you!
Not if I press this button!
I hope!
CLICK

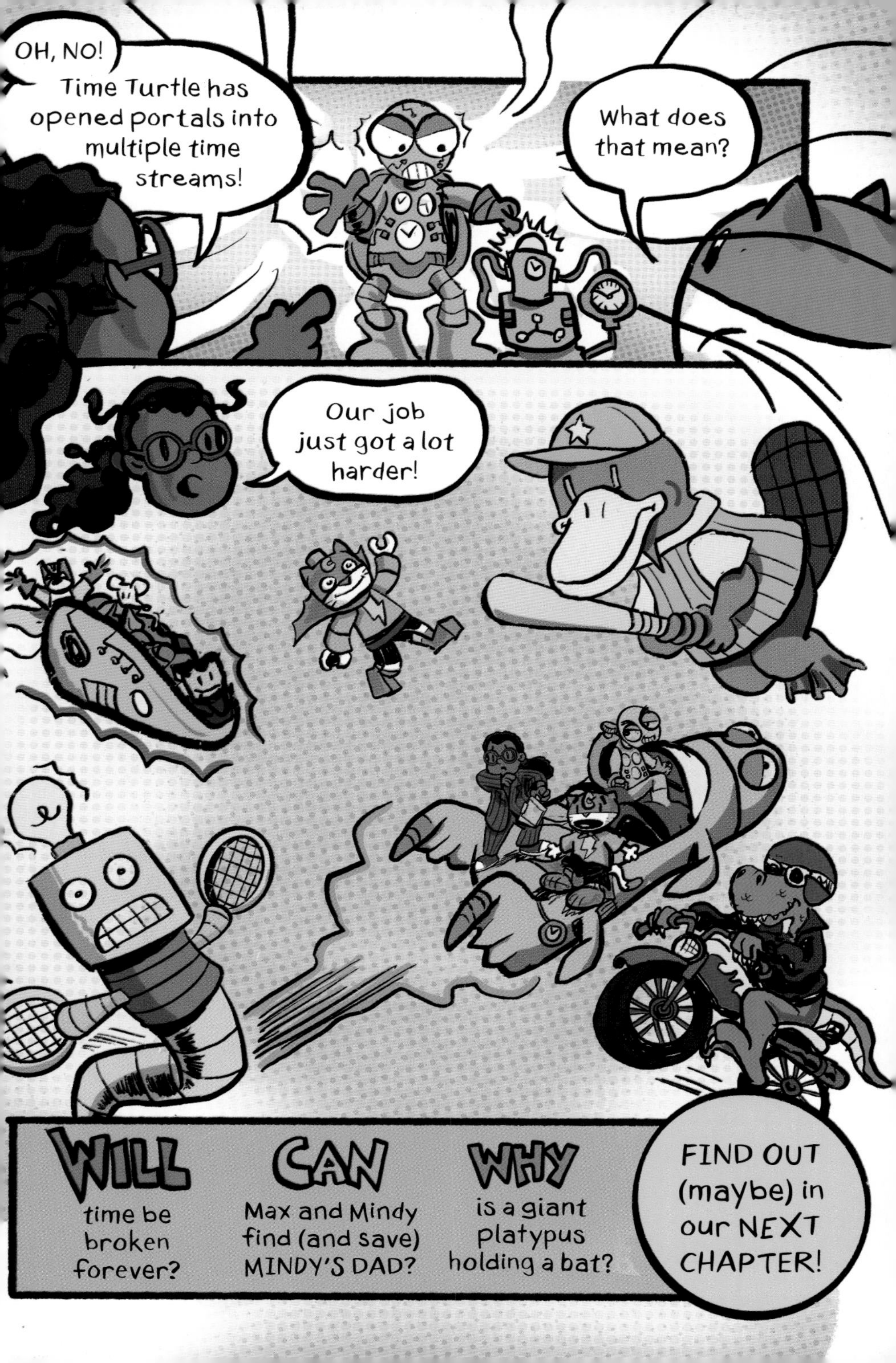
OH, NO!
Time Turtle has opened portals into multiple time streams!
What does that mean?
Our job just got a lot harder!
WILL
time be broken forever?
CAN
Max and Mindy find (and save) MINDY'S DAD?
WHY
is a giant platypus holding a bat?
FIND OUT (maybe) in our NEXT CHAPTER!

CHAPTER 17
TOO MANY LINCOLNS

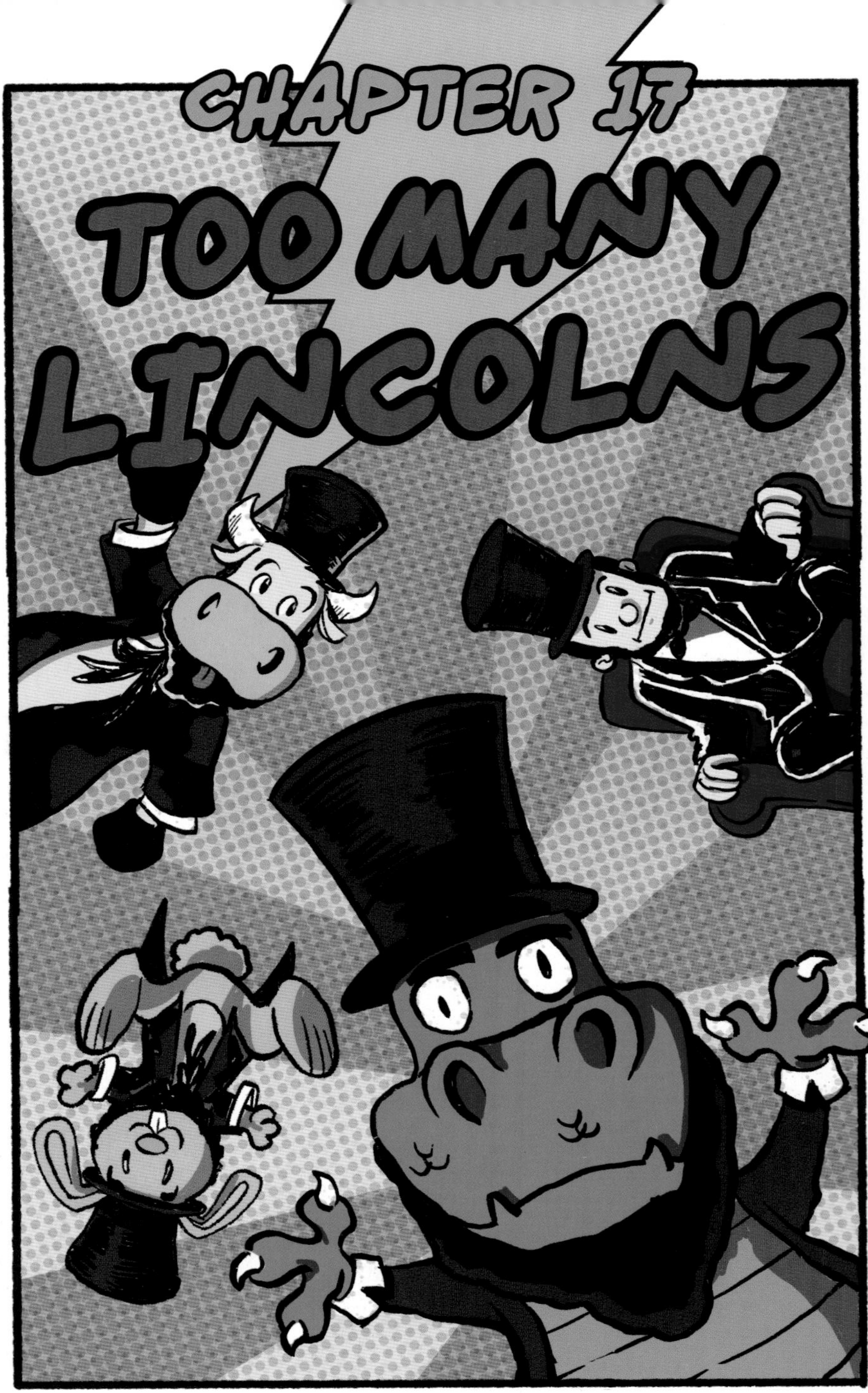

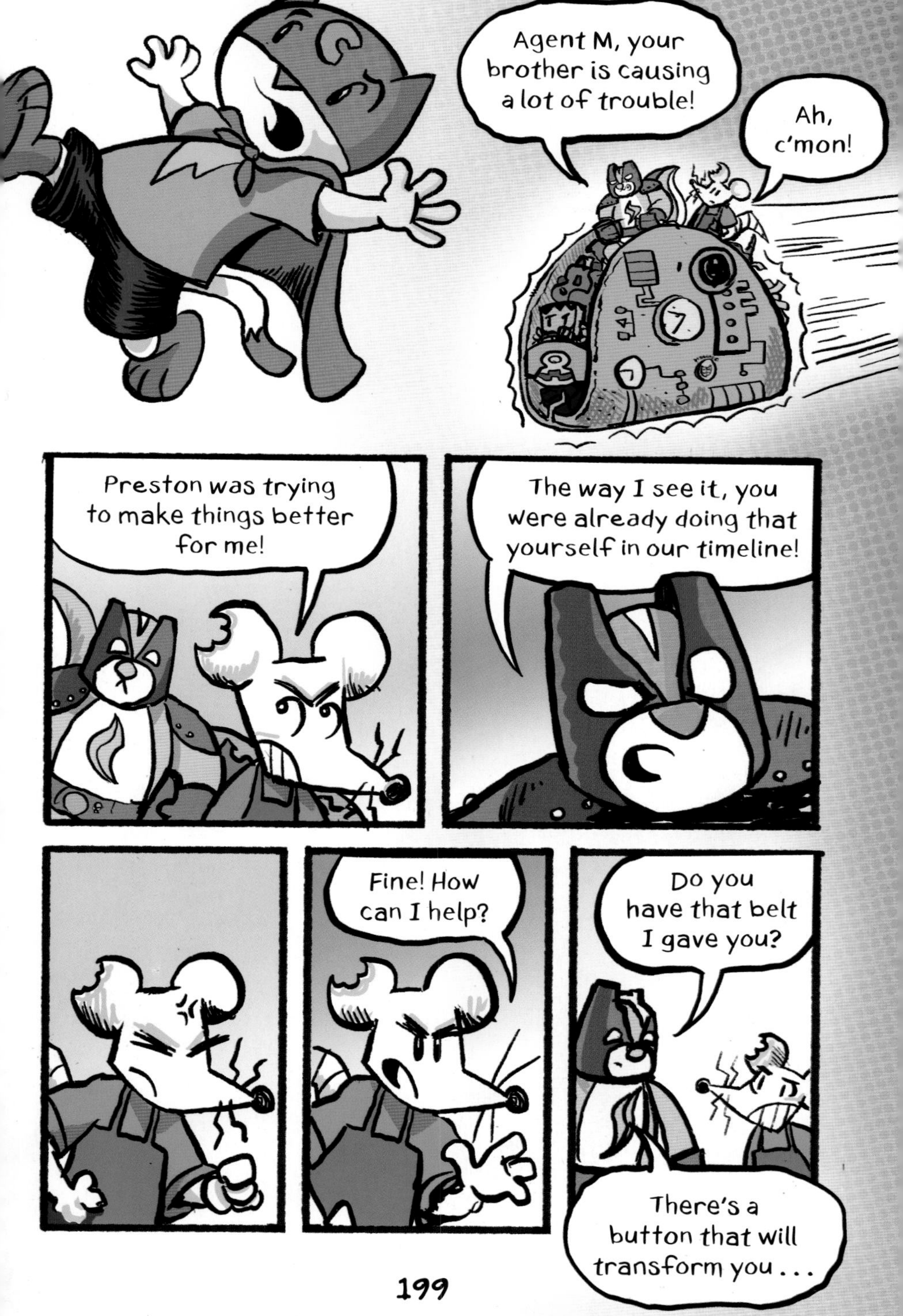
Agent M, your brother is causing a lot of trouble!
Ah, c'mon!
Preston was trying to make things better for me!
The way I see it, you were already doing that yourself in our timeline!
Fine! How can I help?
Do you have that belt I gave you?
There's a button that will transform you . . .

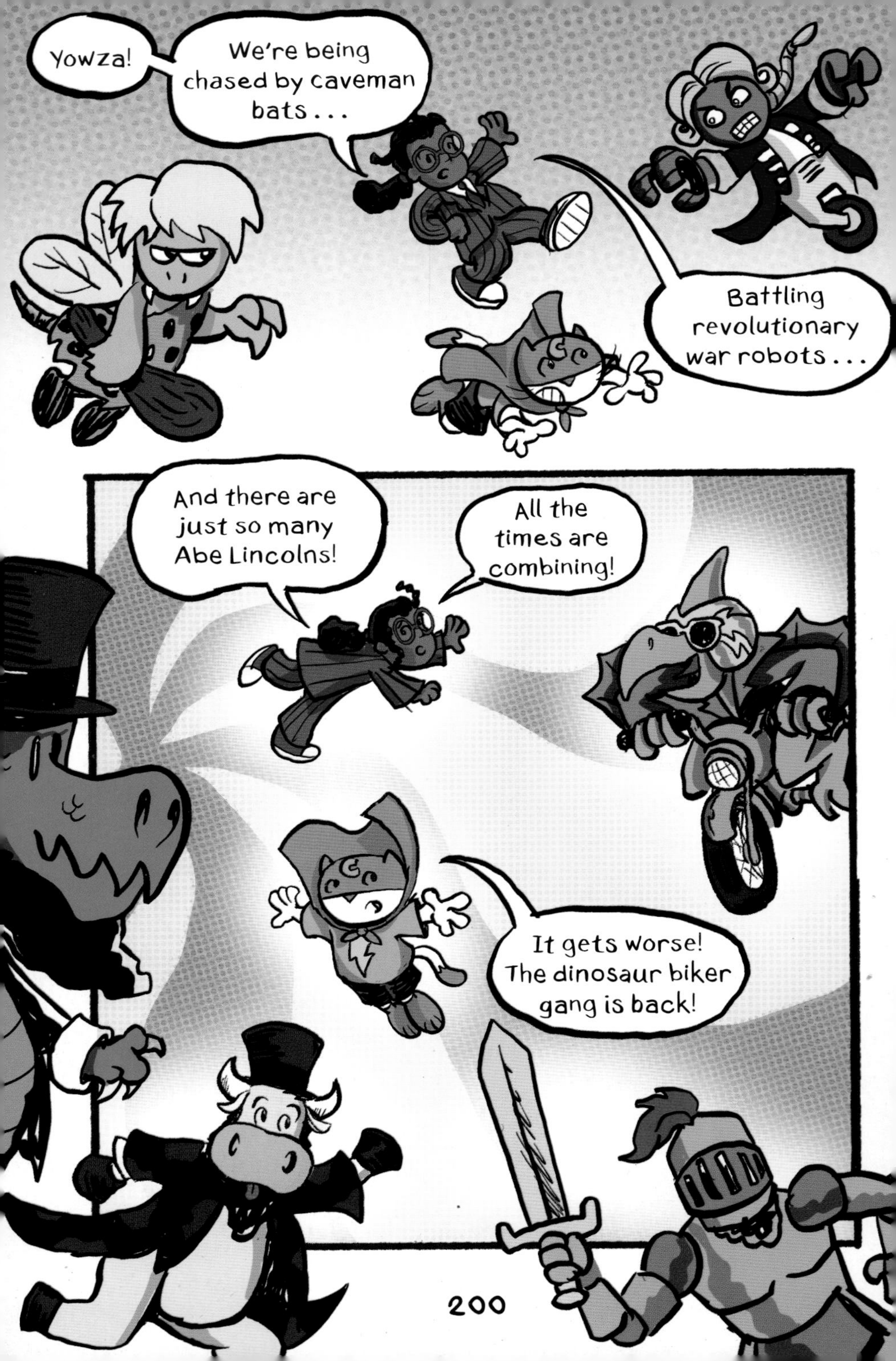
Yowza!
We're being chased by caveman bats . . .
Battling revolutionary war robots . . .
And there are just so many Abe Lincolns!
All the times are combining!
It gets worse! The dinosaur biker gang is back!

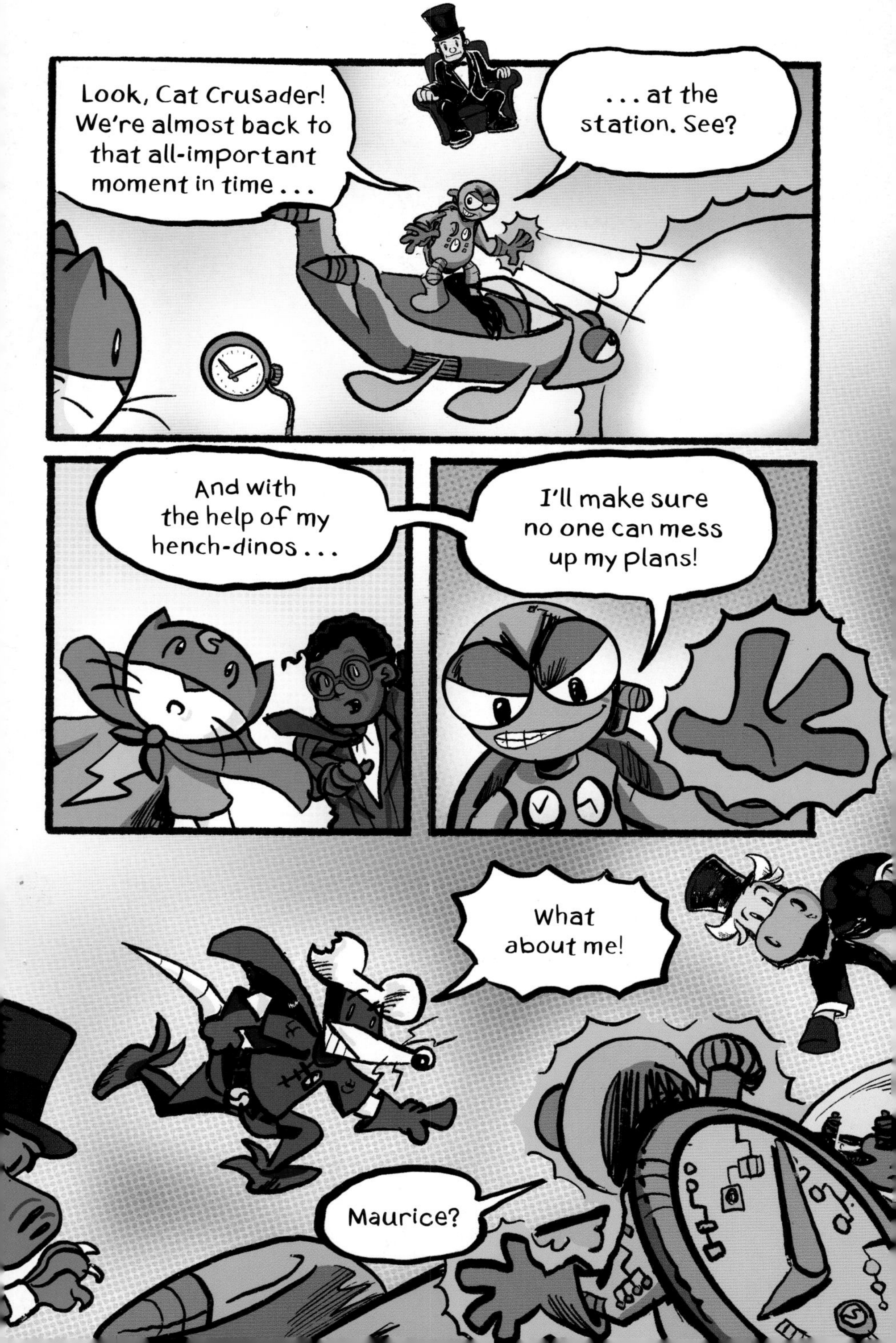
Look, Cat Crusader! We're almost back to that all-important moment in time . . .
. . . at the station. See?
And with the help of my hench-dinos . . .
I'll make sure no one can mess up my plans!
What about me!
Maurice?

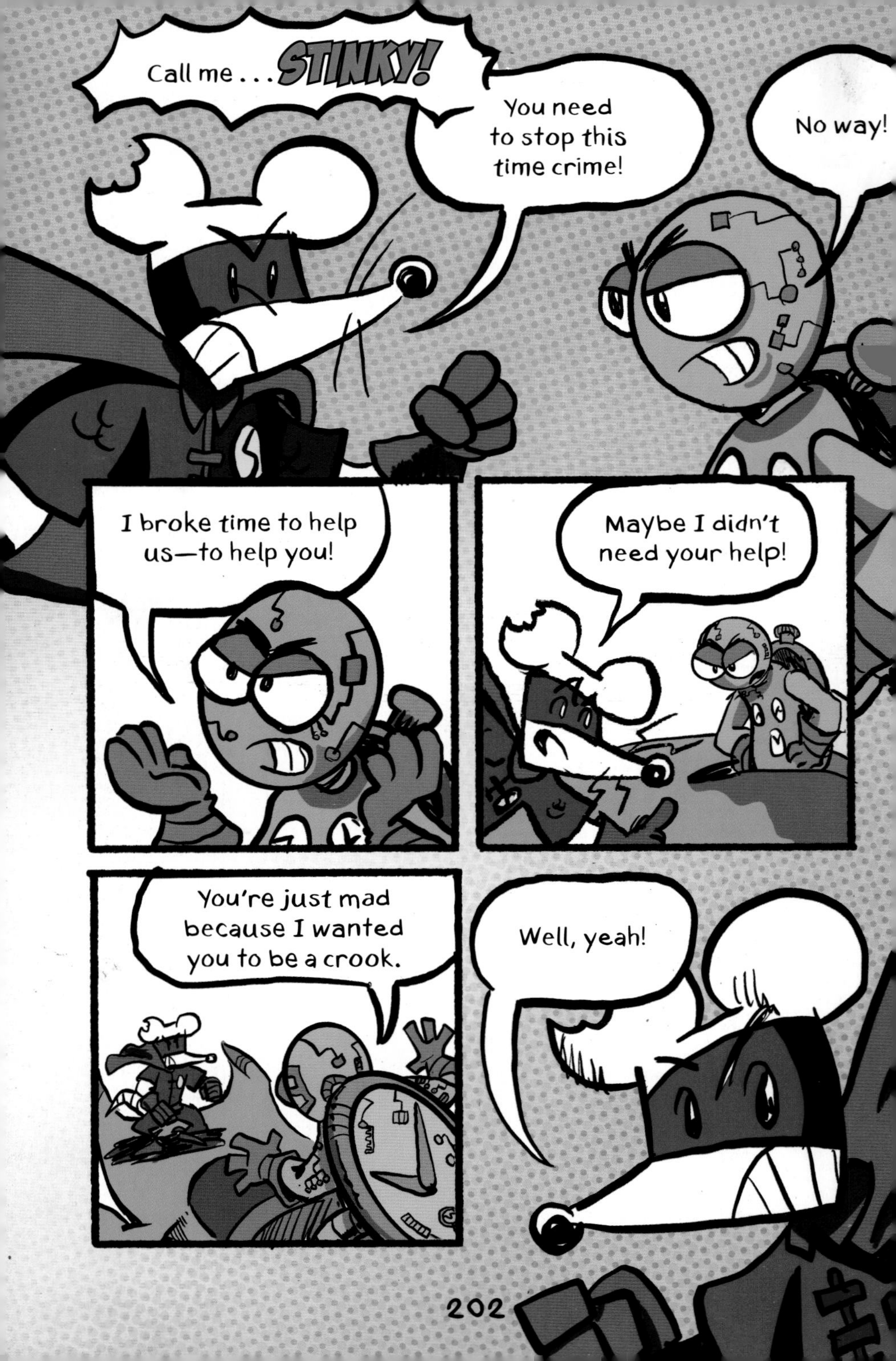
Call me . . . STINKY!
You need to stop this time crime!
No way!
I broke time to help us—to help you!
Maybe I didn't need your help!
You're just mad because I wanted you to be a crook.
Well, yeah!

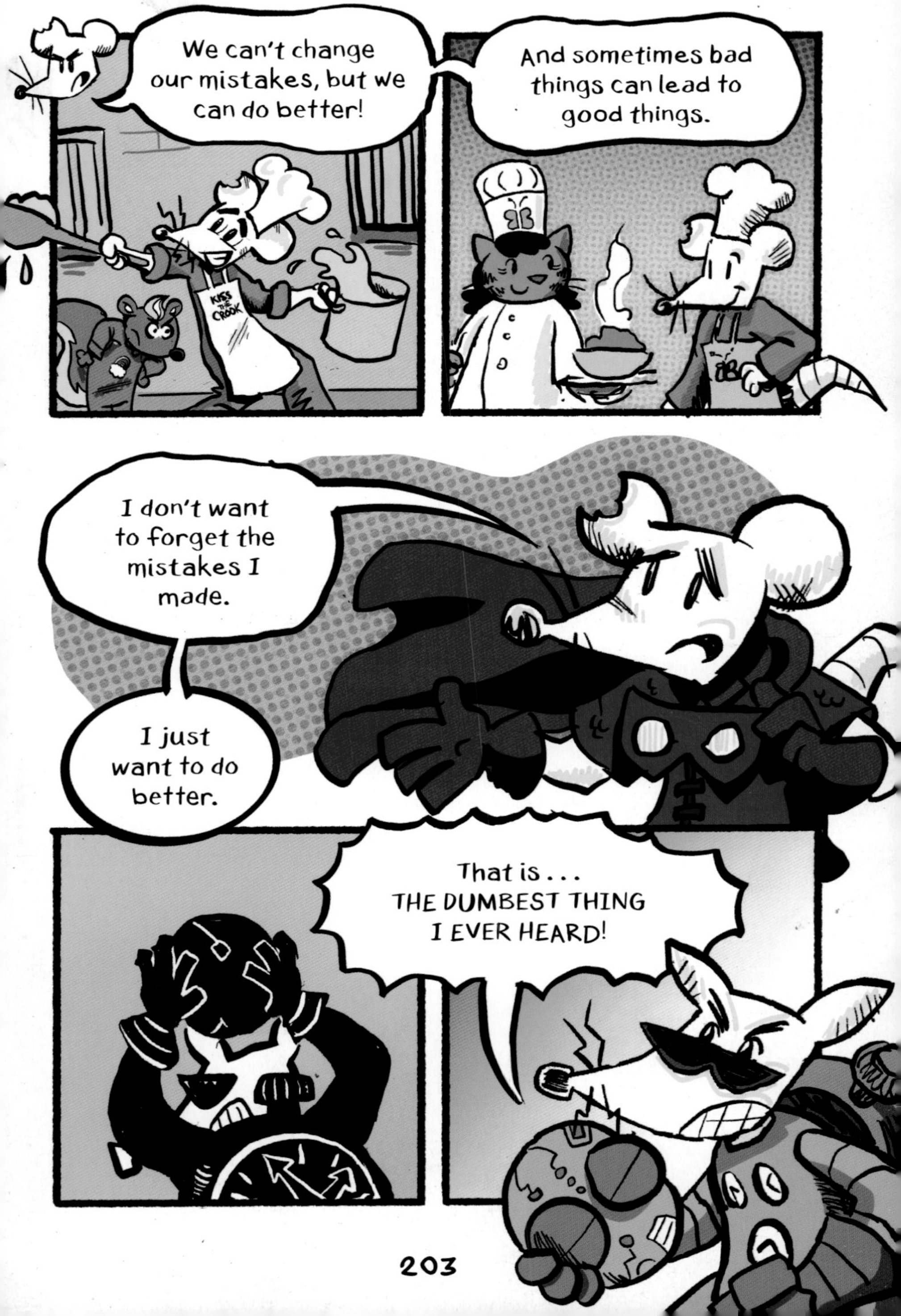
We can't change our mistakes, but we can do better!
KISS THE CROOK
And sometimes bad things can lead to good things.
I don't want to forget the mistakes I made.
I just want to do better.
That is . . . THE DUMBEST THING I EVER HEARD!

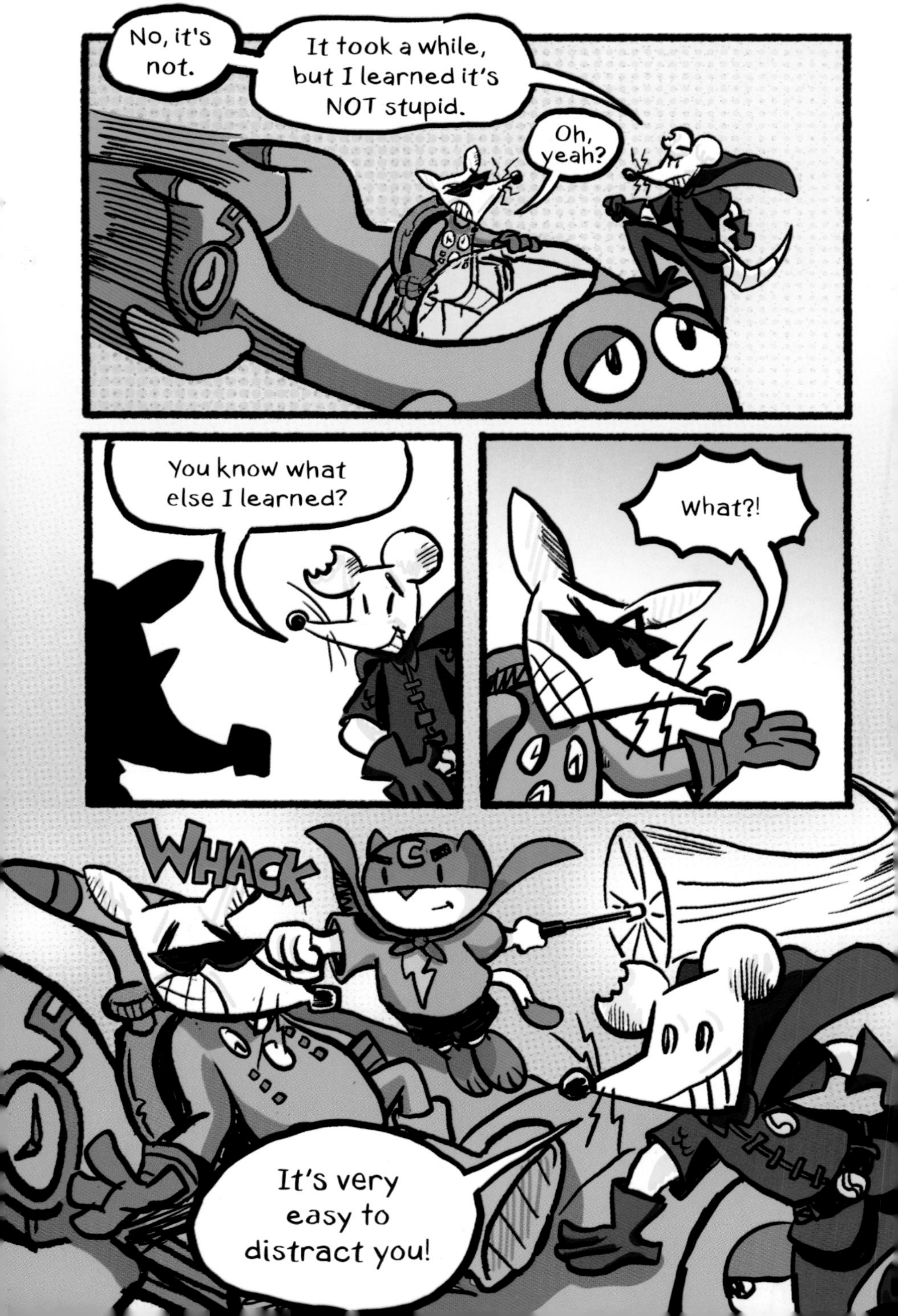
No, it's not.
It took a while, but I learned it's NOT stupid.
Oh, yeah?
You know what else I learned?
What?!
WHACK
It's very easy to distract you!

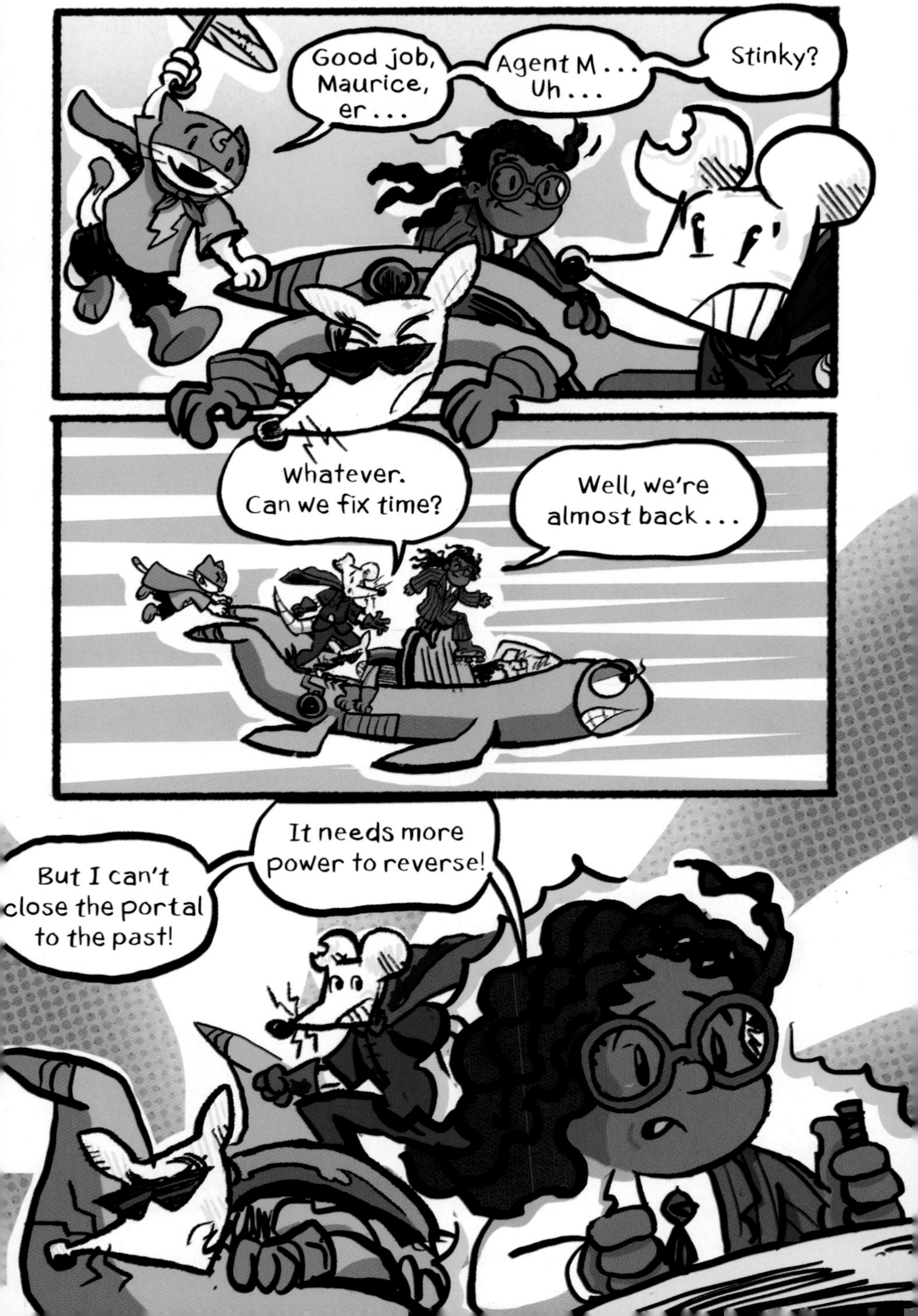
Good job, Maurice, er . . .
Agent M . . . Uh . . .
Stinky?
Whatever. Can we fix time?
Well, we're almost back . . .
But I can't close the portal to the past!
It needs more power to reverse!

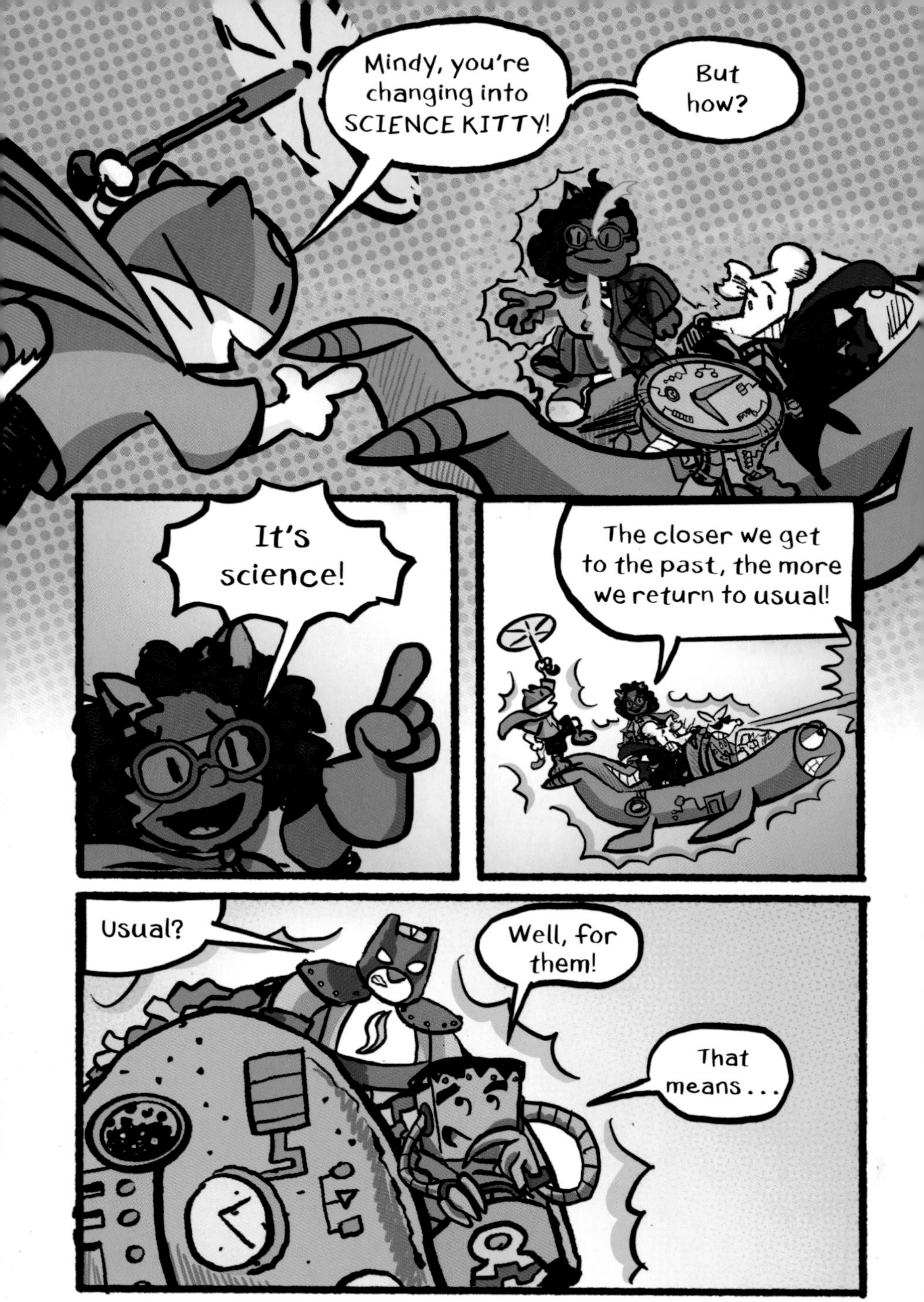
Mindy, you're changing into SCIENCE KITTY!
But how?
It's science!
The closer we get to the past, the more we return to usual!
Usual?
Well, for them!
That means . . .

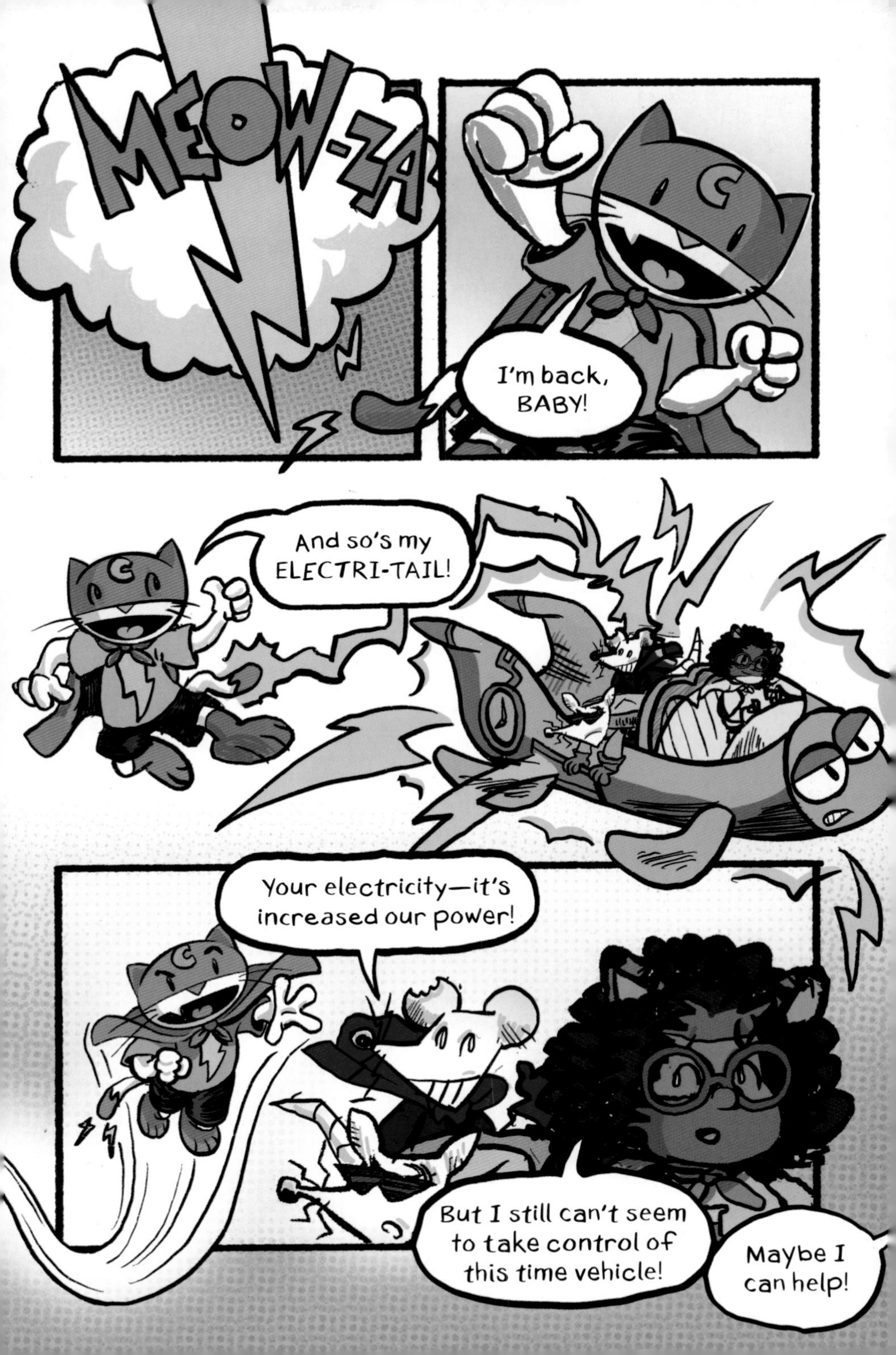
MEOW-ZA
I'm back, BABY!
And so's my ELECTRI-TAIL!
Your electricity—it's increased our power!
But I still can't seem to take control of this time vehicle!
Maybe I can help!

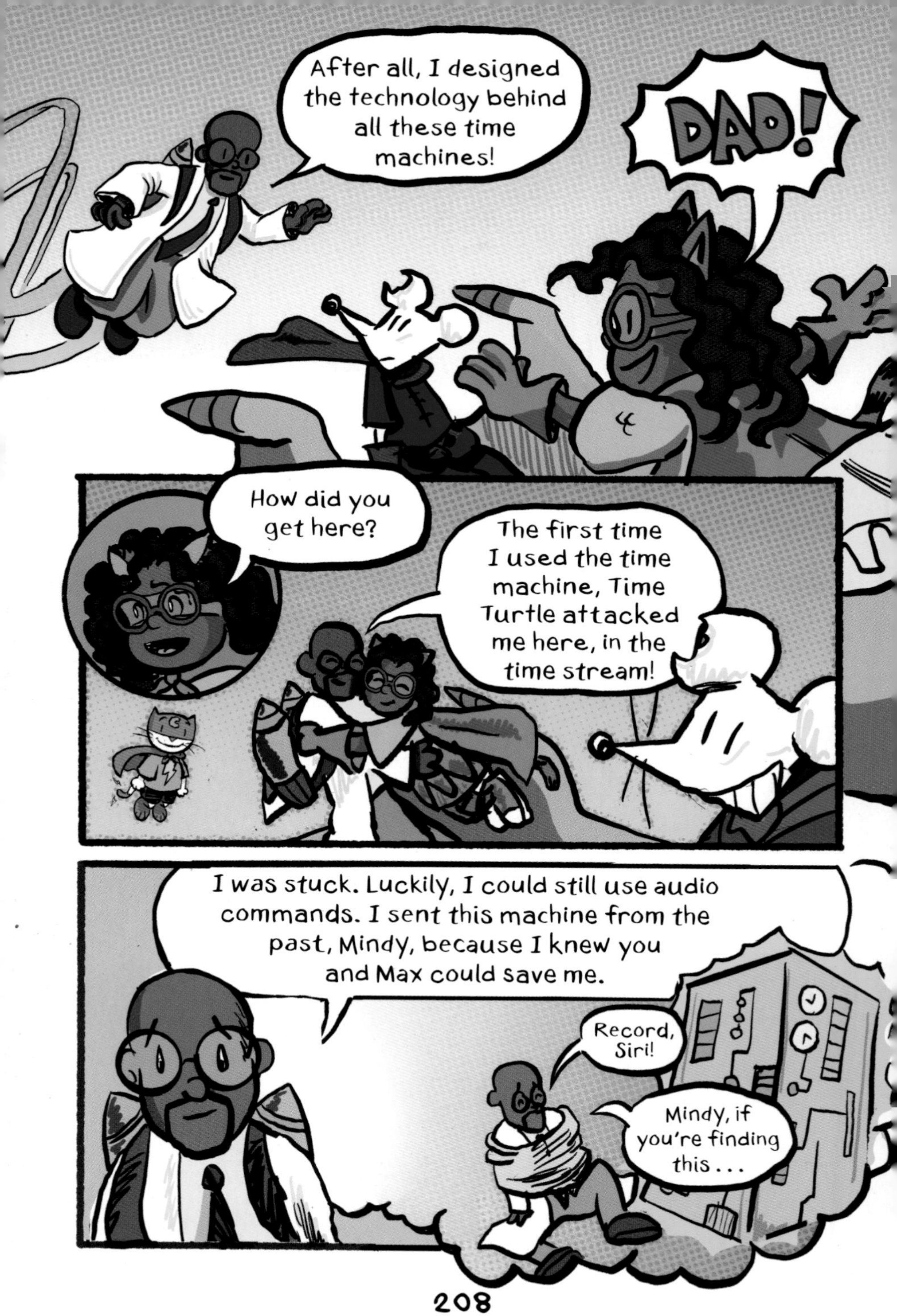
After all, I designed the technology behind all these time machines!
DAD!
How did you get here?
The first time I used the time machine, Time Turtle attacked me here, in the time stream!
I was stuck. Luckily, I could still use audio commands. I sent this machine from the past, Mindy, because I knew you and Max could save me.
Record, Siri!
Mindy, if you're finding this . . .

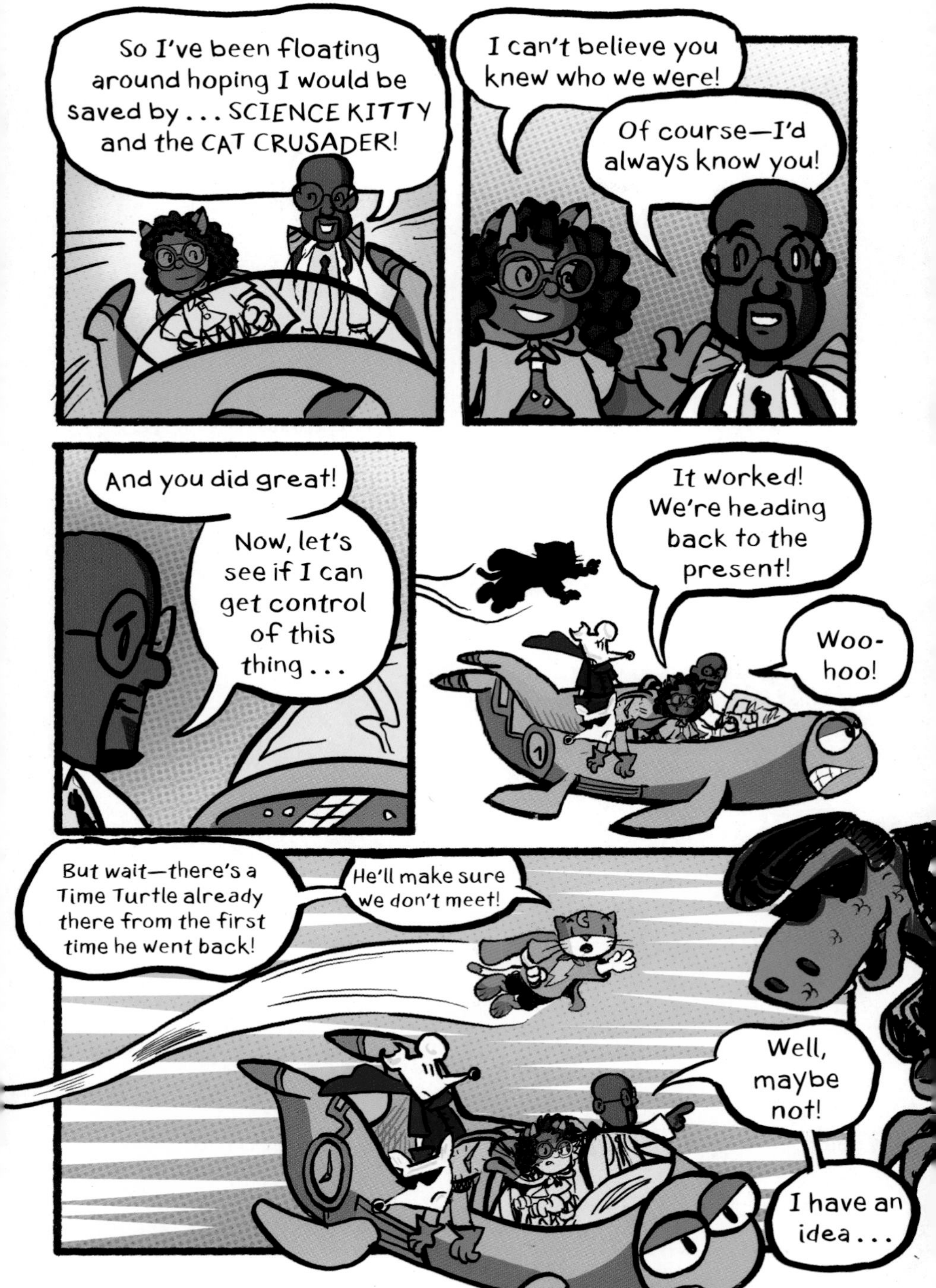
So I've been floating around hoping I would be saved by . . . SCIENCE KITTY and the CAT CRUSADER!
I can't believe you knew who we were!
Of course—I'd always know you!
And you did great!
Now, let's see if I can get control of this thing . . .
It worked! We're heading back to the present!
Woo-hoo!
But wait—there's a Time Turtle already there from the first time he went back!
He'll make sure we don't meet!
Well, maybe not!
I have an idea . . .

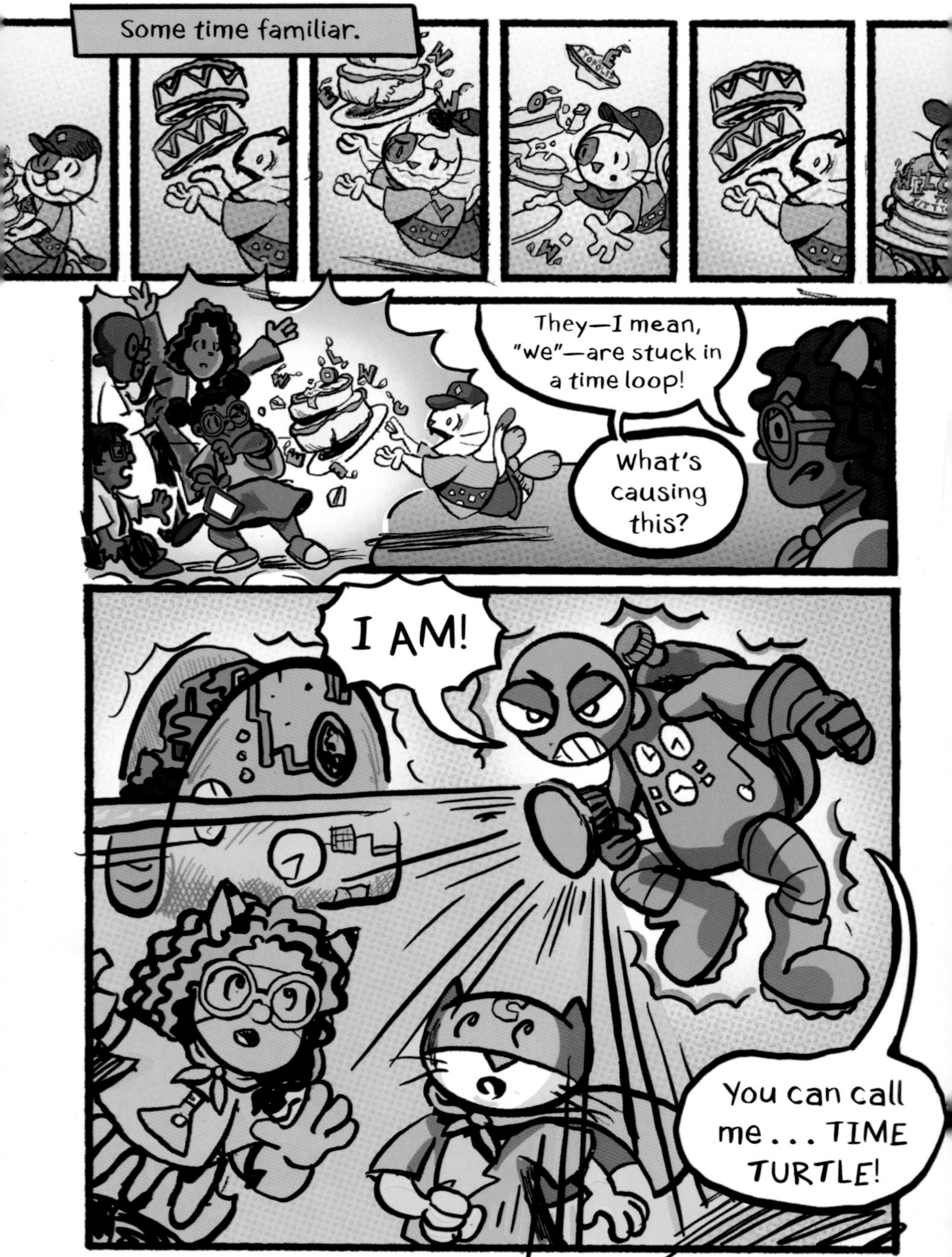
Some time familiar.
They—I mean, "we"—are stuck in a time loop!
What's causing this?
I AM!
You can call me . . . TIME TURTLE!

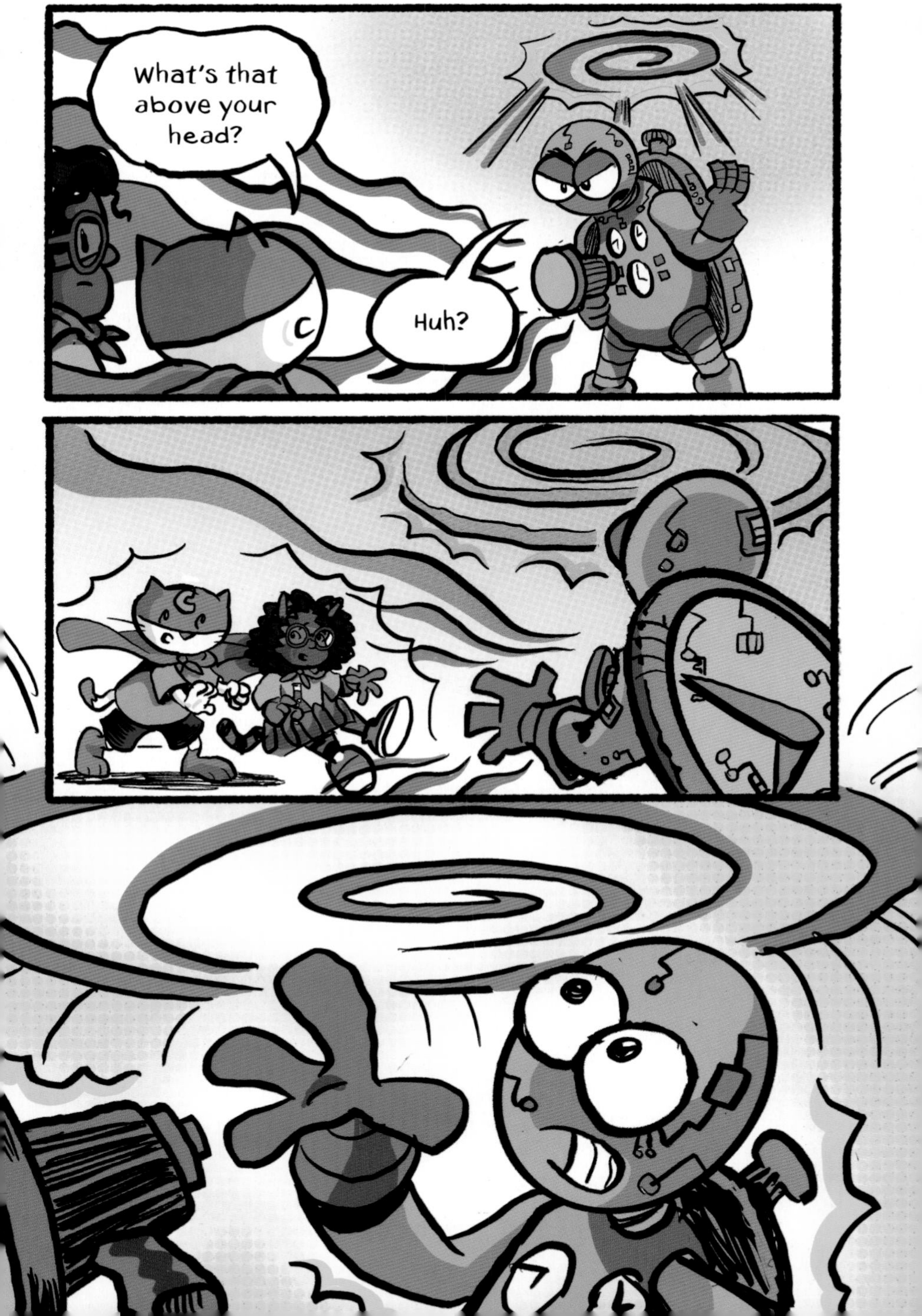

What's that above your head?
Huh?

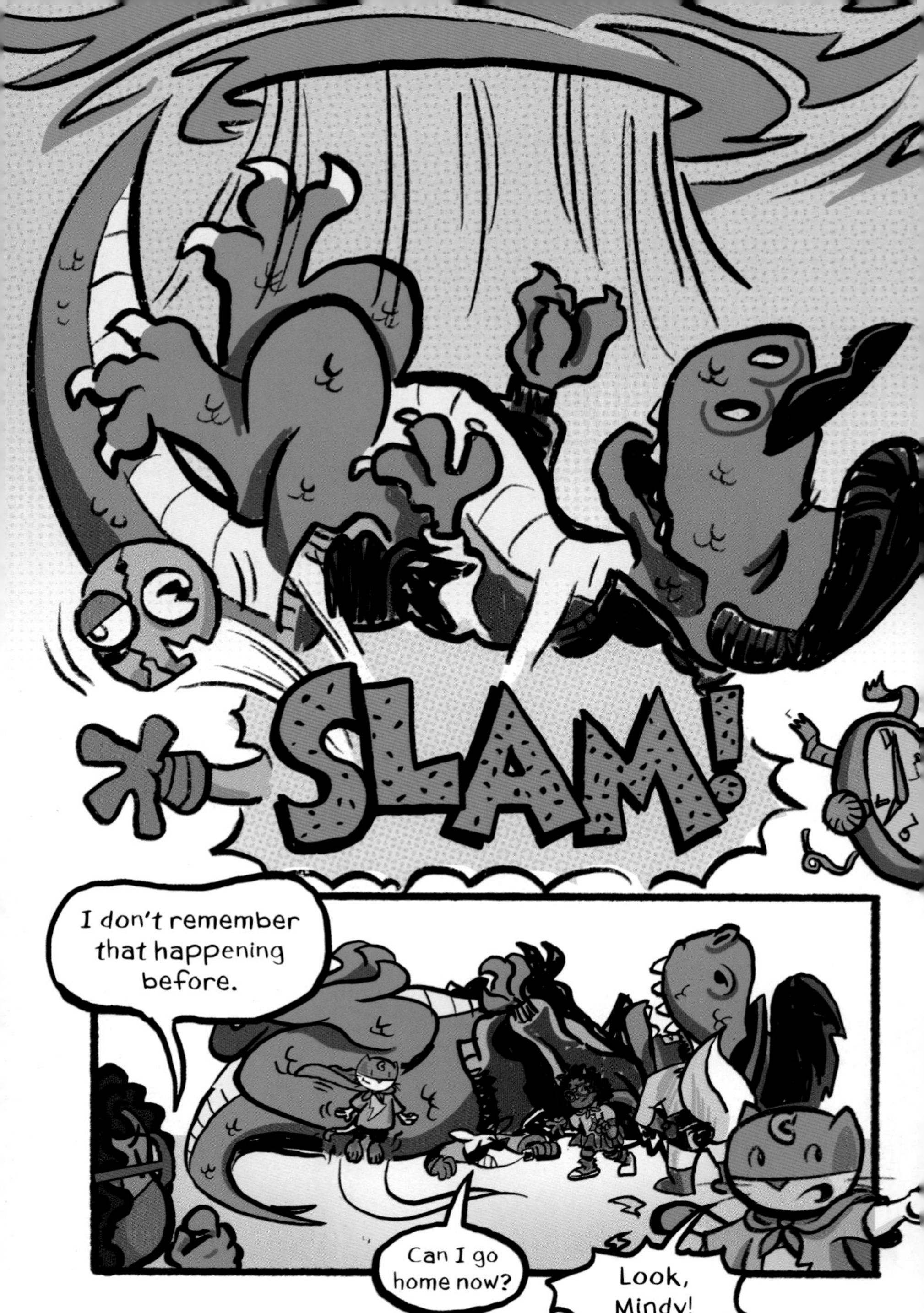
SLAM!
I don't remember that happening before.
Can I go home now?
Look, Mindy!

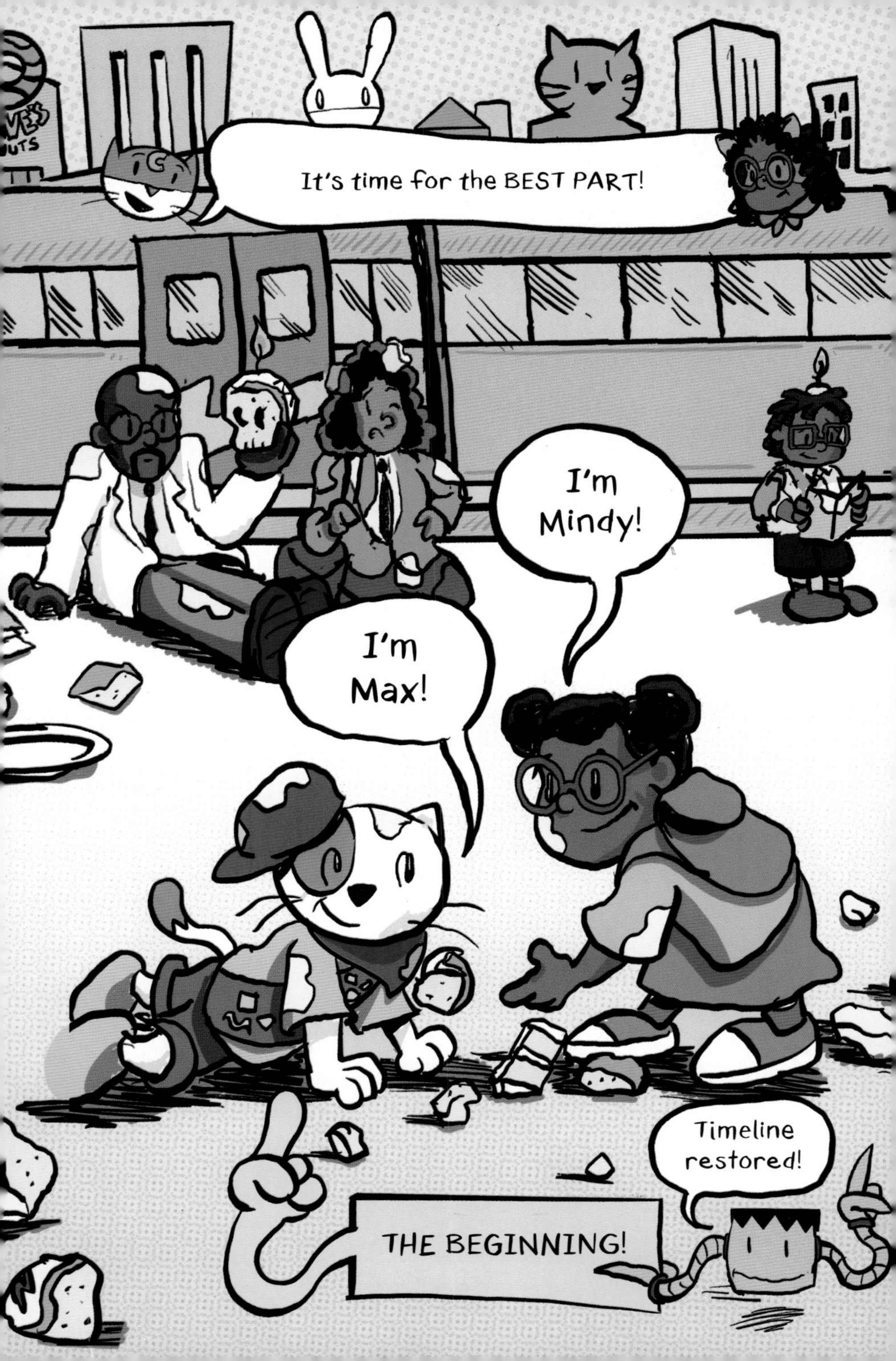
It's time for the BEST PART!
I'm Mindy!
I'm Max!
Timeline restored!
THE BEGINNING!

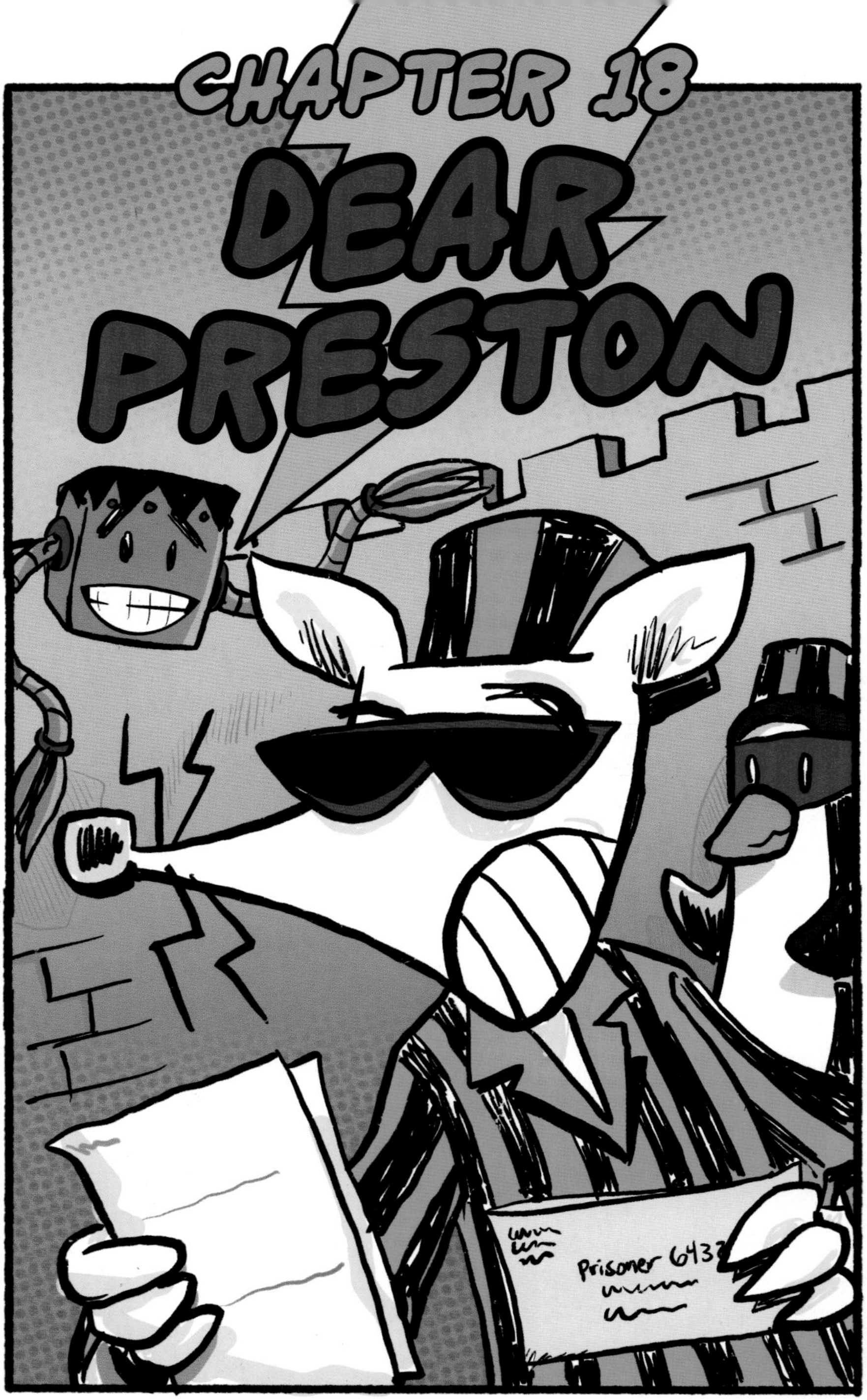
CHAPTER 18
DEAR PRESTON
Prisoner 643

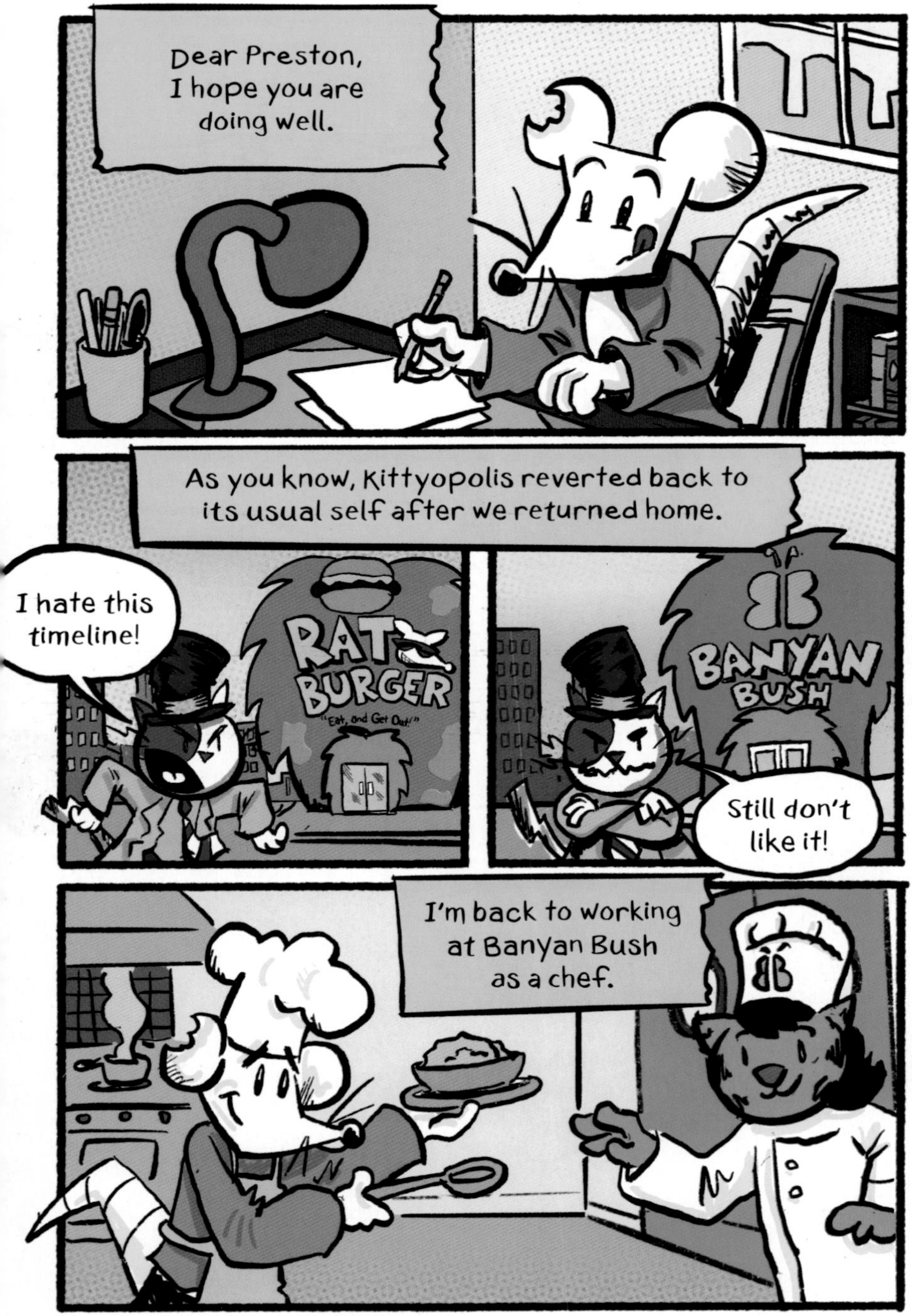
Dear Preston,
I hope you are doing well.
As you know, Kittyopolis reverted back to its usual self after we returned home.
I hate this timeline!
RAT BURGER
"Eat, and Get Out!"
BANYAN BUSH
Still don't like it!
I'm back to working at Banyan Bush as a chef.

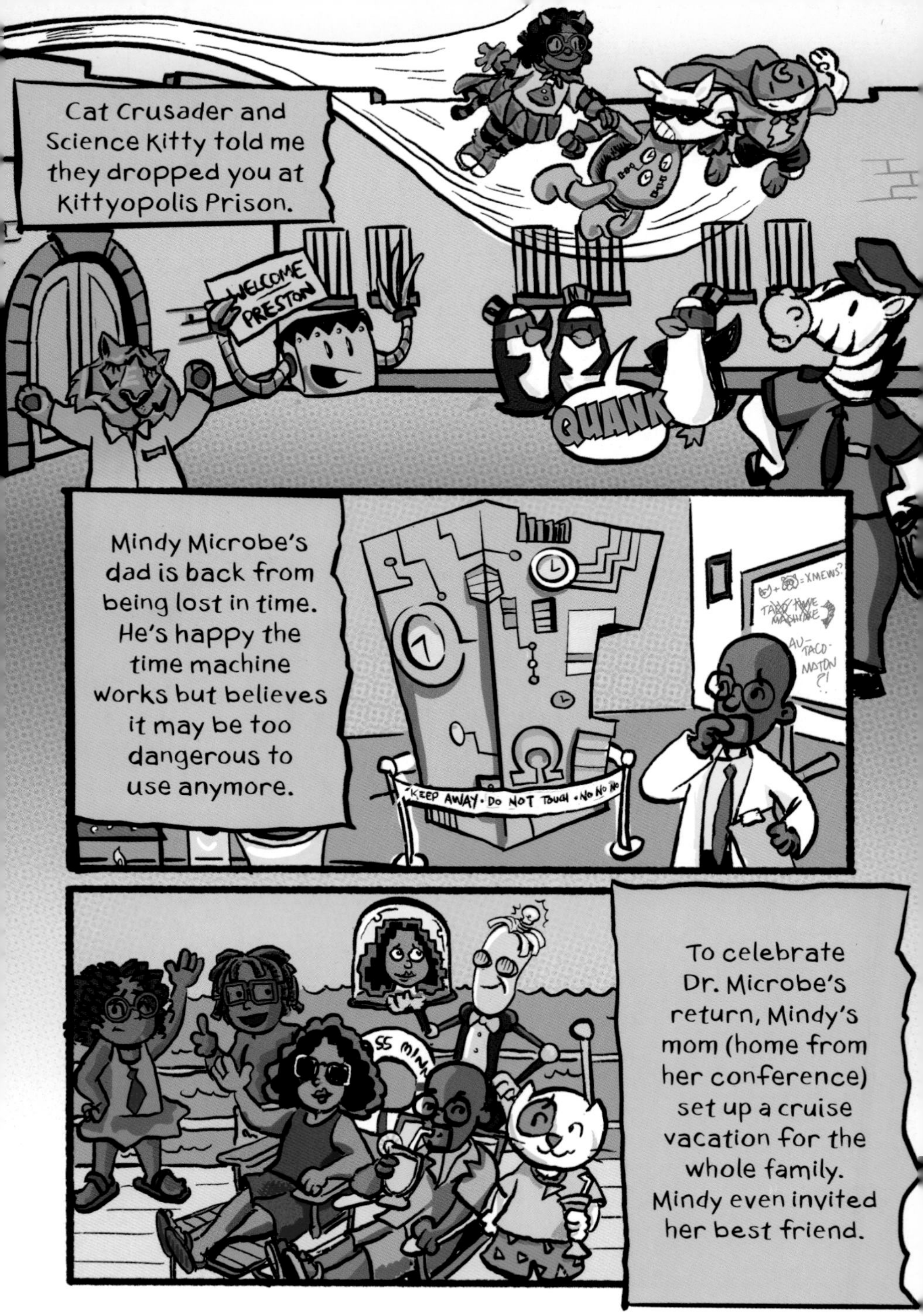
Cat Crusader and Science Kitty told me they dropped you at Kittyopolis Prison.
WELCOME PRESTON
QUANK
Mindy Microbe's dad is back from being lost in time. He's happy the time machine works but believes it may be too dangerous to use anymore.
KEEP AWAY • DO NOT TOUCH • NO NO NO
To celebrate Dr. Microbe's return, Mindy's mom (home from her conference) set up a cruise vacation for the whole family. Mindy even invited her best friend.

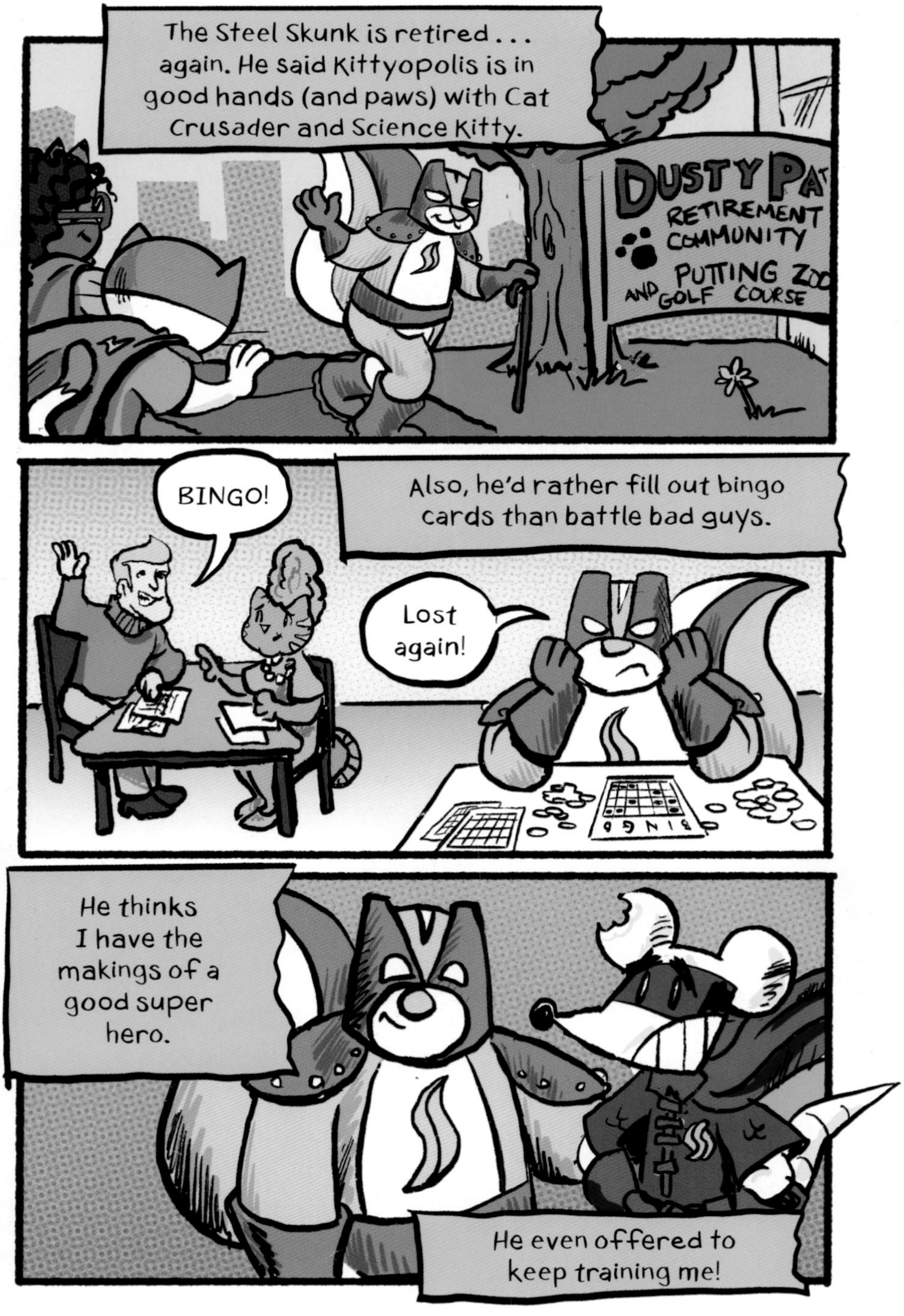
The Steel Skunk is retired . . . again. He said Kittyopolis is in good hands (and paws) with Cat Crusader and Science Kitty.
RETIREMENT COMMUNITY
AND GOLF COURSE
BINGO!
Also, he'd rather fill out bingo cards than battle bad guys.
Lost again!
He thinks I have the makings of a good super hero.
He even offered to keep training me!

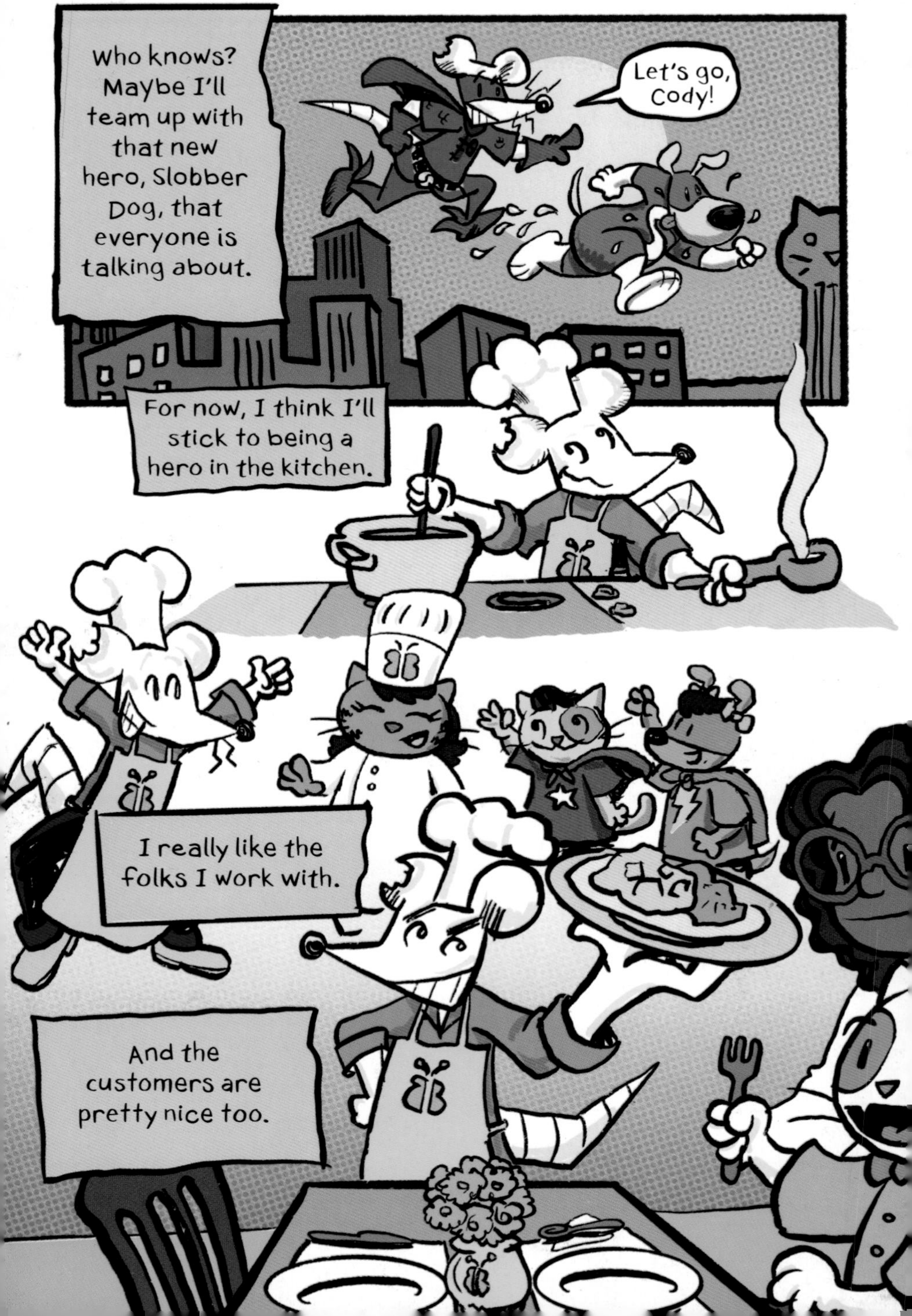
Who knows? Maybe I'll team up with that new hero, Slobber Dog, that everyone is talking about.
Let's go, Cody!
For now, I think I'll stick to being a hero in the kitchen.
I really like the folks I work with.
And the customers are pretty nice too.

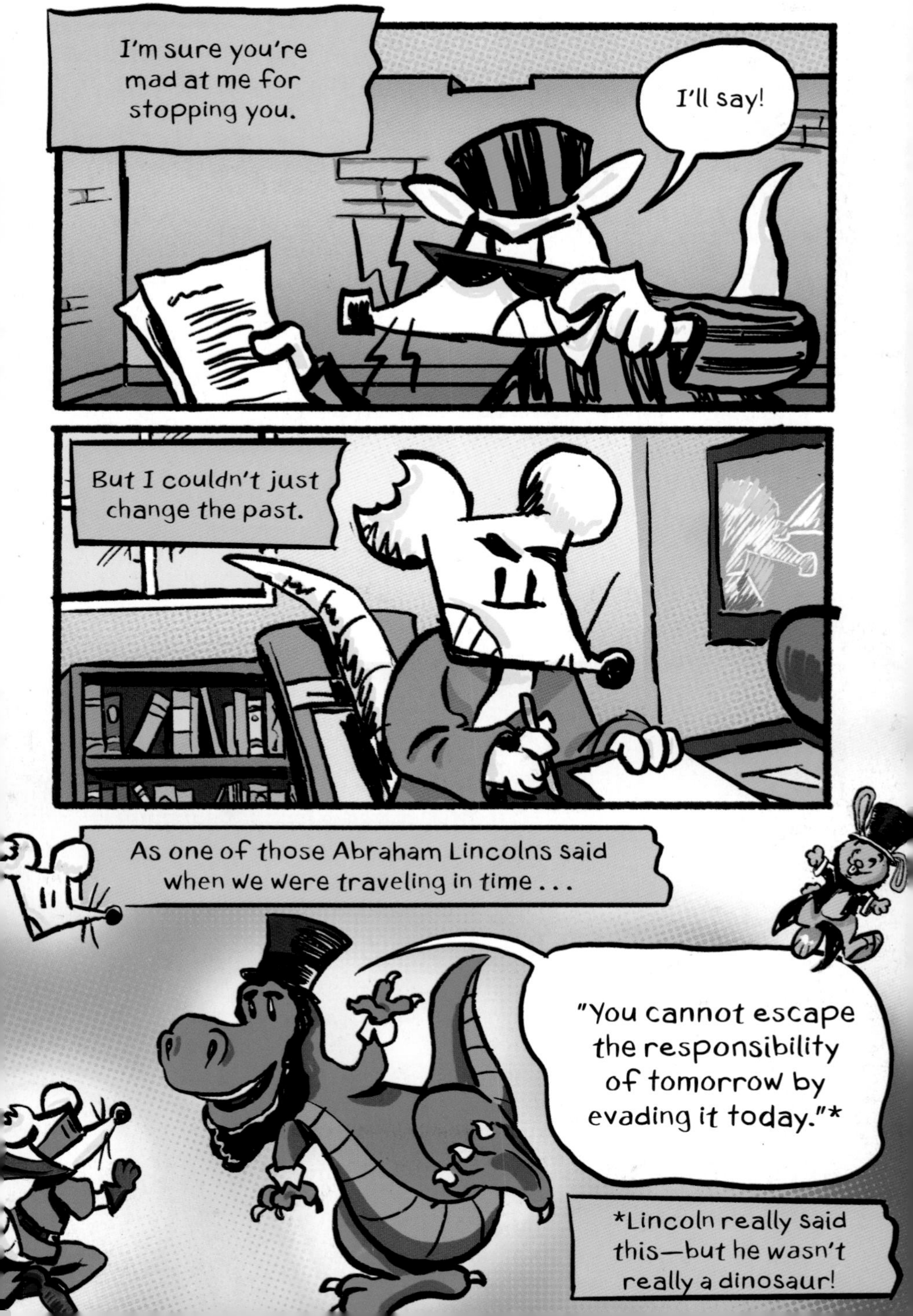
I'm sure you're mad at me for stopping you.
I'll say!
But I couldn't just change the past.
As one of those Abraham Lincolns said when we were traveling in time . . .
"You cannot escape the responsibility of tomorrow by evading it today."*
*Lincoln really said this—but he wasn't really a dinosaur!

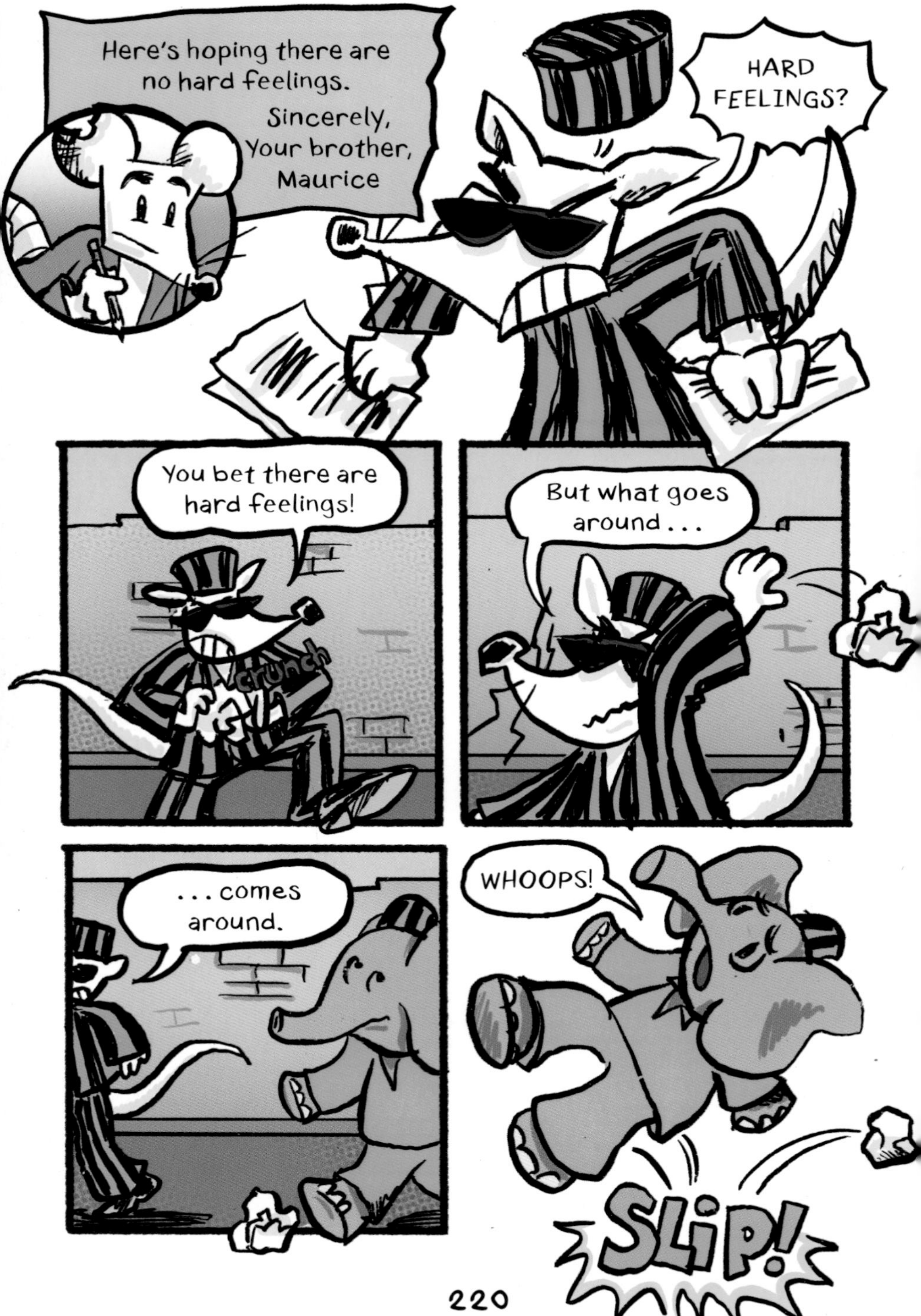
Here's hoping there are no hard feelings.
Sincerely, Your brother, Maurice
HARD FEELINGS?
You bet there are hard feelings!
crunch
But what goes around . . .
. . . comes around.
WHOOPS!
SLIP!

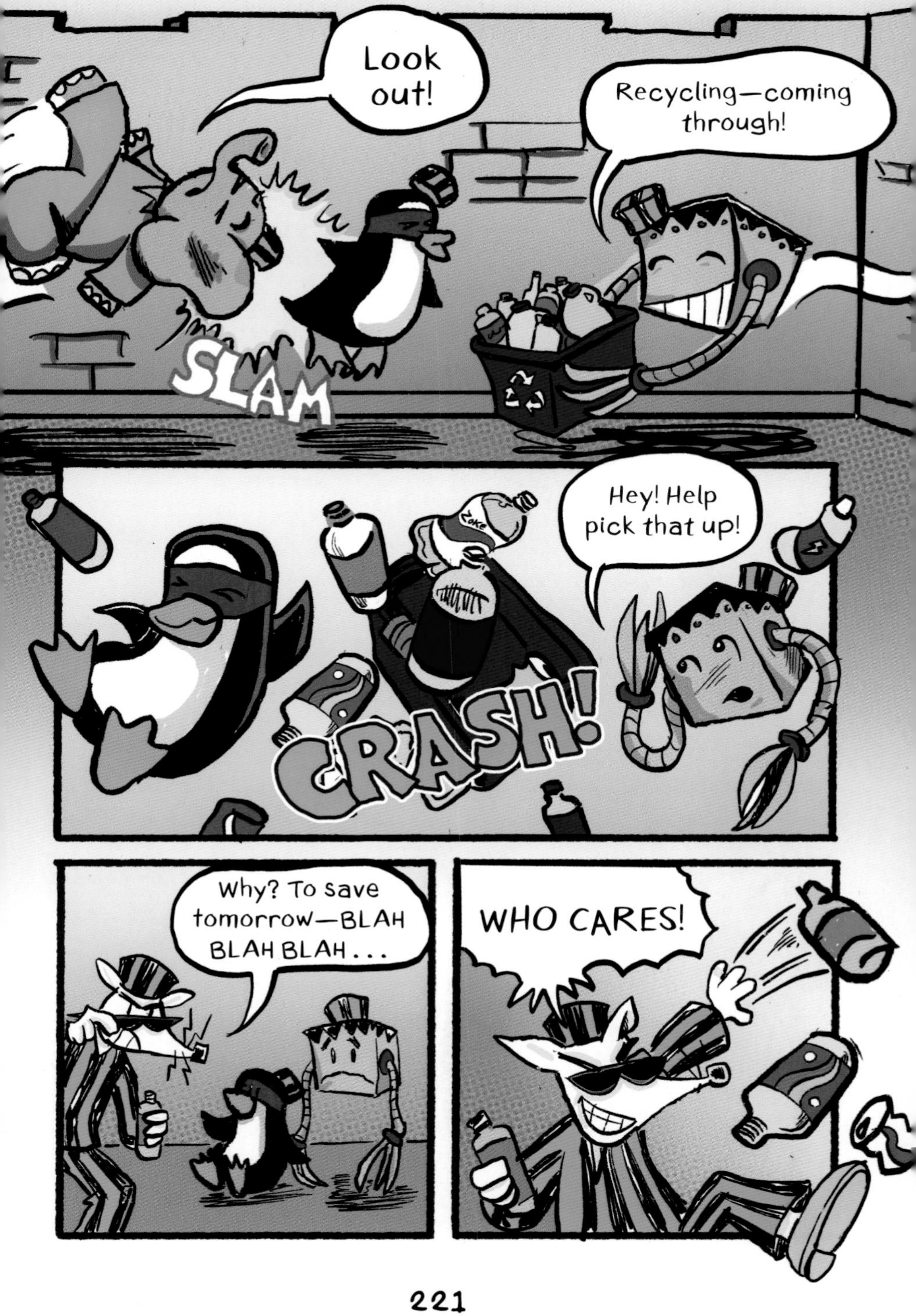

Look out!
Recycling—coming through!
SLAM
Hey! Help pick that up!
ZOKE
CRASH!
Why? To save tomorrow—BLAH BLAH BLAH . . .
WHO CARES!

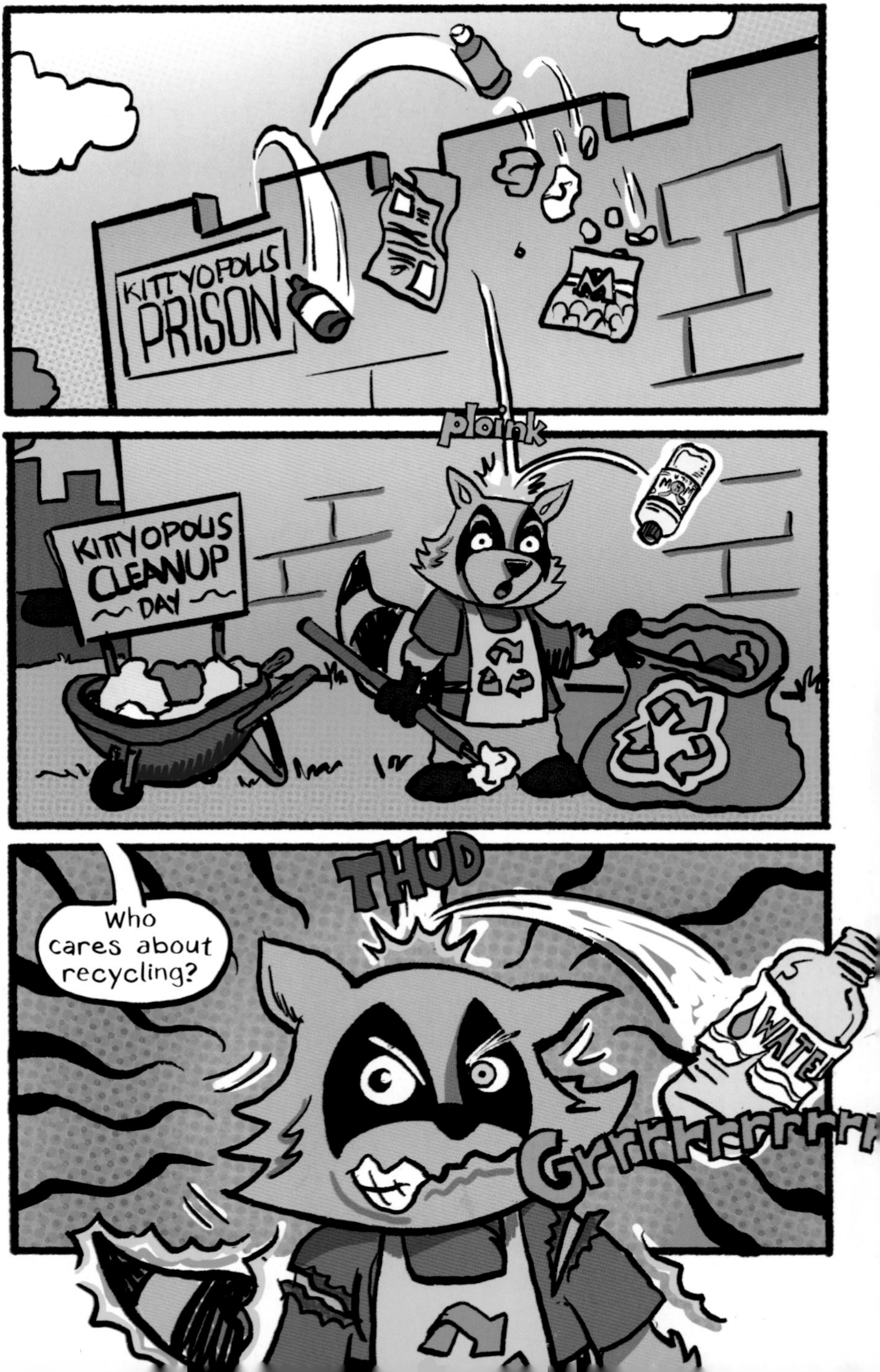
KITTYOPOLIS PRISON
ploink
KITTYOPOLIS CLEANUP DAY
THUD
Who cares about recycling?
Grrrrrrrrrr

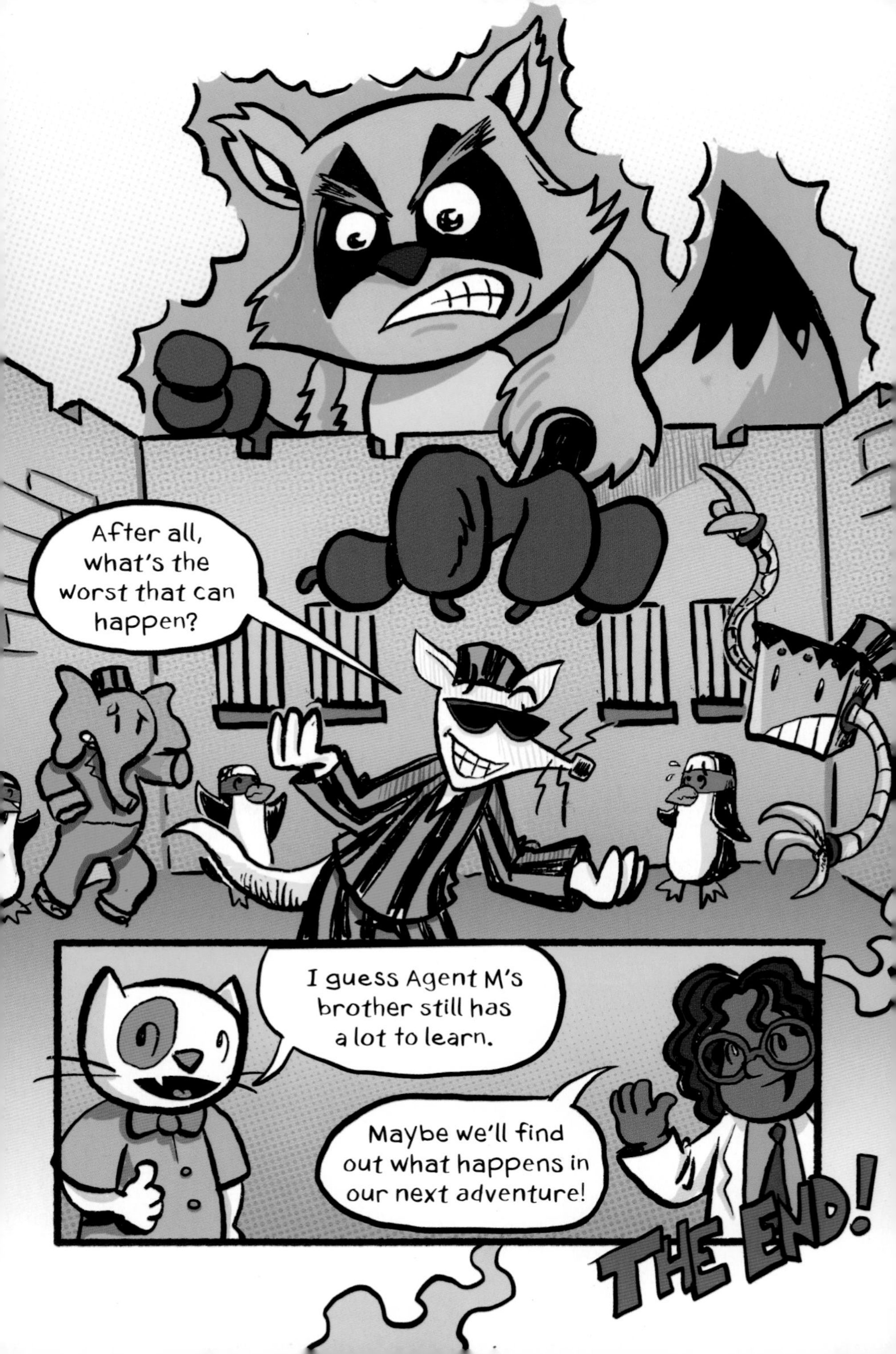
After all, what's the worst that can happen?
I guess Agent M's brother still has a lot to learn.
Maybe we'll find out what happens in our next adventure!
THE END!

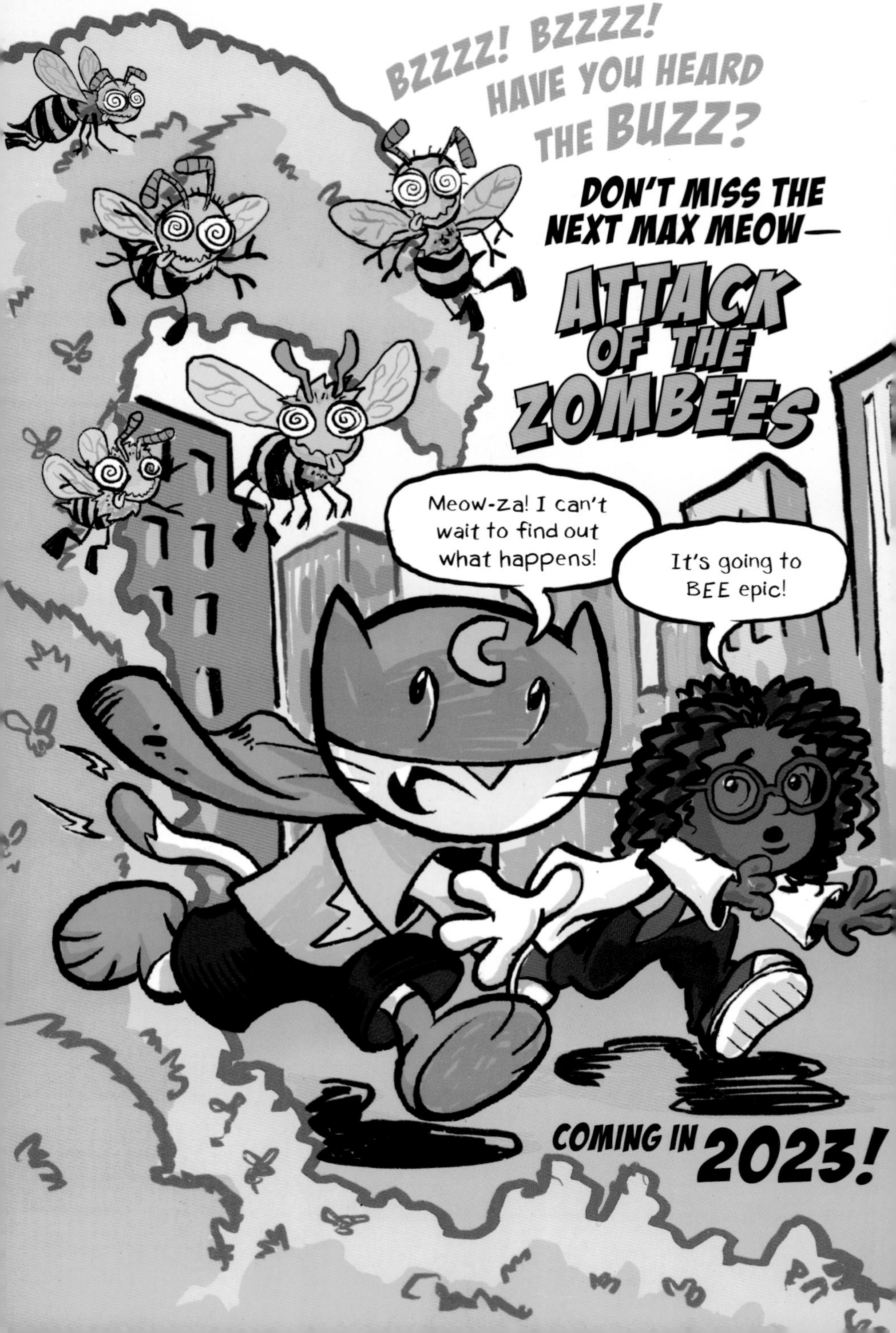
BZZZZ! BZZZZ!
HAVE YOU HEARD
THE BUZZ?
DON'T MISS THE
NEXT MAX MEOW—
ATTACK
OF THE
ZOMBEES
Meow-za! I can't wait to find out what happens!
It's going to BEE epic!
COMING IN 2023!

THE CAT'S OUT OF THE BAG!

DO YOU LIKE CATS?

Of course!

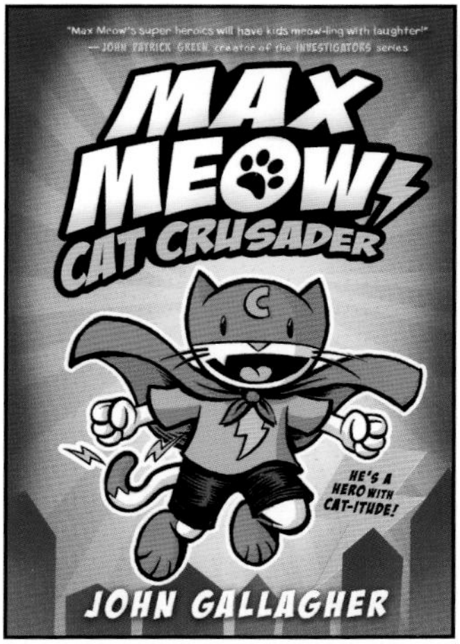
"Max Meow's super heroics will have kids meow-ling with laughter!"
—JOHN PATRICK GREEN, creator of the INVESTIGATORS series
MAX MEOW
CAT CRUSADER
HE'S A HERO WITH CAT-ITUDE!
JOHN GALLAGHER

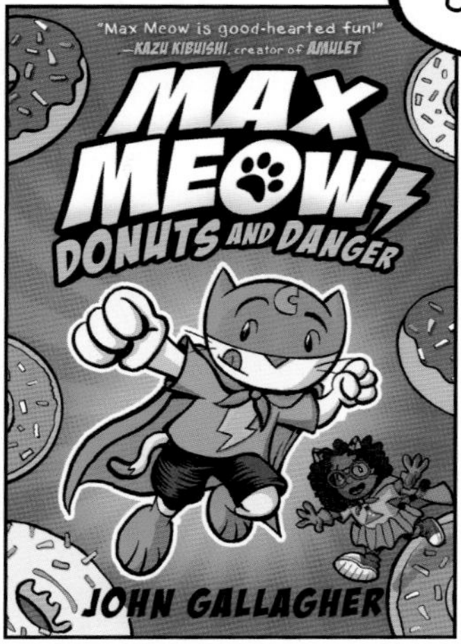
"Max Meow is good-hearted fun!"
—KAZU KIBUISHI, creator of AMULET
MAX MEOW
DONUTS AND DANGER
JOHN GALLAGHER

DO YOU LIKE COMICS?

Who doesn't?

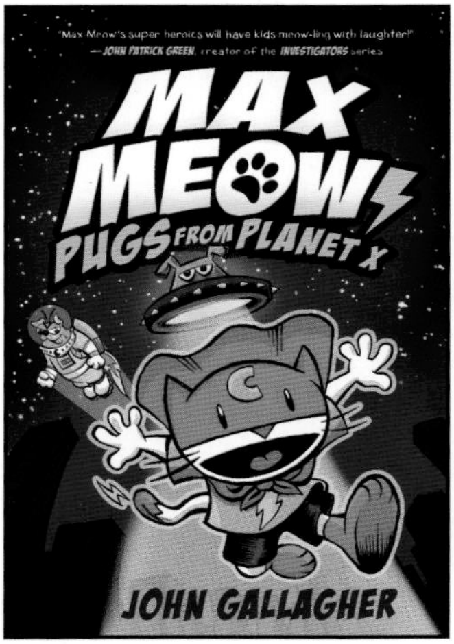
"Max Meow's super heroics will have kids meow-ling with laughter!"
—JOHN PATRICK GREEN, creator of the INVESTIGATORS series
MAX MEOW
PUGS FROM PLANET X
JOHN GALLAGHER

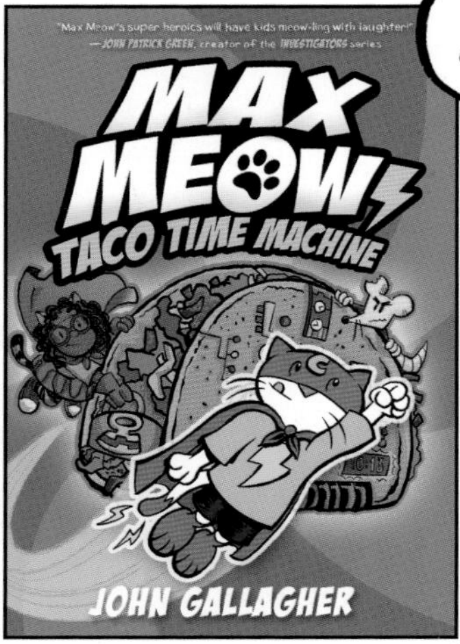
"Max Meow's super heroics will have kids meow-ling with laughter!"
—JOHN PATRICK GREEN, creator of the INVESTIGATORS series
MAX MEOW
TACO TIME MACHINE
JOHN GALLAGHER

THEN MAX MEOW IS FOR YOU!

It's the best!

Max! Is that you?

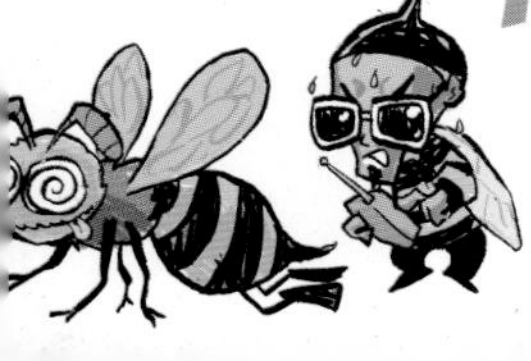

Learn to draw Agent M!

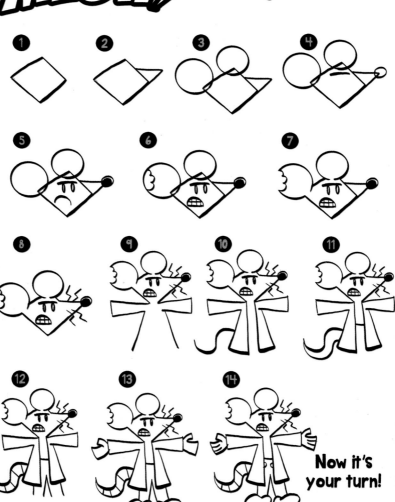

Now it's
your turn!

226

Learn to draw Max Meow!

Now it's your turn!

227

ACKNOWLEDGMENTS

PRODUCTION AND ART ASSISTANT
J. Robert Deans

COLOR AND FLATTING ASSISTANTS
Sydney Cluff
J. Robert Deans
Giovanni Lucca

SPECIAL THANKS

My wife, Beth, and kids, Katie Ryn, Jack, and Will; my mom, Jane Gallagher; my agent, Judith Hansen; my editor, Shana Corey; my art director, April Ward; PR Wiz Kris Kam; Max's early reader, moukies; Max's copyeditor, Melinda Ackell; the Beldons and their pugs (Oscar, Quincy, and Gnocchi); and Rodney Ries, Avalon R., Chase B., Braden Aust, Peter and Patty Christian, Mark and Robin Sullivan, Kazu Kibuishi, Captain Blue Hen's Joe Murray, Jon Cohen of Beyond Comics, the Pinecrest School, Oak View Elementary Comic Class students, Marc and Shelly Nathan, and the *Ranger Rick* magazine team.

And PAW-some thanks to the librarians, teachers, comic shop owners, and booksellers who share the magic of reading and creativity, and the readers for whom this book was made.

JOHN GALLAGHER has loved comics since he was five. He learned to read through comics and went on to read every book in his elementary school library. When he told his mom there was nothing left to read, she said, "Just because a book's over doesn't mean the *stories* end. Why don't *you* tell me what happens next?" And so John began creating comics to continue his favorite stories. John never stopped drawing comics. He's now the art director of the National Wildlife Federation's *Ranger Rick* magazine and the cofounder of Kids Love Comics, an organization that uses comics and graphic novels to promote literacy. He also leads workshops teaching kids how to create their own comics. John lives in Virginia with his wife and their three kids. Visit him at MaxMeow.com and on social media.

@JohnBGallagher @MaxMeowCatCrusader
@johngallagher_cartoonist

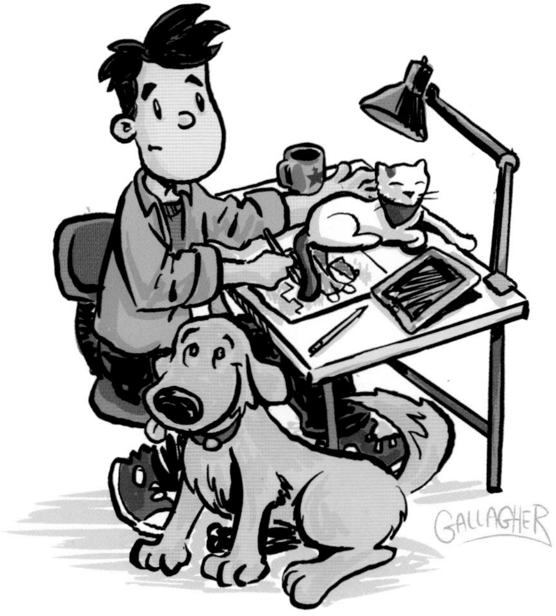
GALLAGHER